JULIET MARILLIER

Daughter of the Forest

Book One of the Sevenwaters Trilogy

HarperCollins*Publishers*

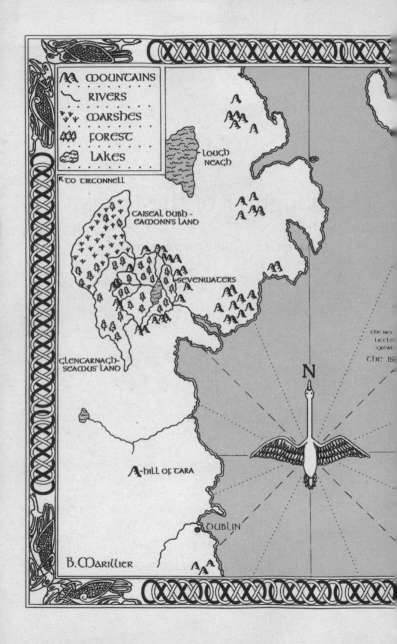

MOUNTAINS
RIVERS
MARSHES
FOREST
LAKES

LOUGH NEAGH

TO TIRCONNELL

CAISEAL DUBH –
EAMONN'S LAND

SEVENWATERS

GLENCARNAGH –
SEAMUS' LAND

THE NET
LITTLE
GREAT
THE IS

N

A – HILL OF TARA

DUBLIN

B. MARILLIER

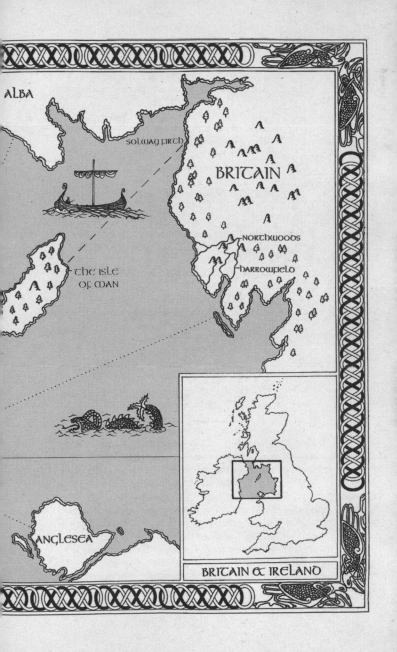

HarperCollins*Publishers*
77–85 Fulham Palace Road,
Hammersmith, London W6 8JB

www.**fire**and**water**.com

This paperback edition 2002
6

Previously published in paperback by *Voyager* 2001
First published in Great Britain by *Voyager* 2000

ISBN 0 00 648398 4

Set in Palatino

Printed in Great Britain by
Clays Ltd, St Ives plc

Author's note

The framework for *Daughter of the Forest* is a Germanic tale, *The Six Swans*, from the collection of the Grimm brothers. Beneath the classic fairytale elements (a wicked stepmother, a transformation, a trial by silence) is a story of courage born from loss, and lives forever altered. With its swan imagery and its remote forest setting, the Germanic story settles easily into the Irish landscape and may indeed even owe something to the Celtic tradition, a major influence on European folktales from the thirteenth century onwards. The Children of Lir, the tale of Aengus Og and his swan-bride, these are Irish myths in which child turns to swan and swan to beautiful maiden, in the space of an eye blink.

In my story I sought the human dilemmas at the heart of the fairytale, for such tales have at their core the most wondrous and the harshest of human experience, the best and worst of human behaviour. Honour, trust, courage, true love. Treachery, betrayal, cowardice and hatred. They amuse, shock and reassure us. They make us laugh and they make us cry. Their innate truths touch a chord deep within us and they show how subtle are the margins between the tangible world and that which is ever present, but forever Other. Most importantly, they awaken in us a sense of wonder, a recognition of the mysterious patterns of being – the spiral dance of birth, death, rebirth.

The reader may appreciate some assistance with the Old Irish Gaelic names and terms that are used in this story. An approximate pronunciation for some of these is given here, with the accented syllable underlined:

Diarmid	Dear-mid
Eamonn	Ay-mon
Eilis	Eye-lish
Padriac	Pad-ric
Seamus	Shay-mus
Sorcha	Sor-ra

The passing of the year is marked for Sorcha and her brothers by the eight festivals of the Druidic calendar. Christian feast days sometimes came to be celebrated on the same day, probably for purely practical reasons, for example Lugnasad (Lammas) and Imbolc (Candlemas). There are four major festivals, sometimes called the fire festivals, as well as the solstices and equinoxes:

Samhain	Sow-an	1 November
Meán Geimhridh (winter solstice)	Myawn gev-ree	21 December
Imbolc	Imulc	1 February
Meán Earraigh (spring equinox)	Myawn ah-ree	21 March
Beltaine	Bal-te-na	1 May
Meán Samhraidh (summer solstice)	Myawn sour-ee	21 June
Lugnasad	Loonasa	1 August
Meán Fómhair (autumn equinox)	Myawn foh-wer	21 September

Some other terms used:

túath   a tribal community in early Christian Ireland, ruled by a king or lord. Seven-waters is unusual in that Lord Colum has few male relatives apart from his sons, and therefore rules without the backup of a strong extended family/kinship group. There is only one major fortress within his túath. It was more usual for a túath to contain several ring-forts controlled by the king's kinsmen or nobles who paid for the privilege in cattle and in military or social service.

brithem — in old Irish Brehon law, a maker of judgements

finn-ghaill — literally, fair foreigners – the Vikings (as opposed to dubh-ghaill, dark foreigners – the Danes)

Ogham — secret alphabet of the druids, with 25 letters, each of which also indicates a particular plant, tree or element. Ogham signs might be carved on a tree trunk or a stone, or indicated by gestures the druids had no other written language. They were used symbolically rather than for speech or writing as such.

To the strong women of my family:
Dorothy, Jennifer, Elly and Bronya

CHAPTER ONE

Three children lay on the rocks at the water's edge. A dark-haired little girl. Two boys, slightly older. This image is caught forever in my memory, like some fragile creature preserved in amber. Myself, my brothers. I remember the way the water rippled as I trailed my fingers across the shining surface.

'Don't lean over so far, Sorcha,' said Padriac. 'You might fall in.' He was a year older than me and made the most of what little authority that gave him. You could understand it, I suppose. After all, there were six brothers altogether, and five of them were older than he was.

I ignored him, reaching down into the mysterious depths.

'She might fall in, mightn't she, Finbar?'

A long silence. As it stretched out, we both looked at Finbar, who lay on his back, full length on the

1

warm rock. Not sleeping; his eyes reflected the open grey of the autumnal sky. His hair spread out on the rock in a wild black tangle. There was a hole in the sleeve of his jacket.

'The swans are coming,' said Finbar at last. He sat up slowly to rest his chin on raised knees. 'They're coming tonight.'

Behind him, a breeze stirred the branches of oak and elm, ash and elder, and scattered a drift of leaves, gold and bronze and brown. The lake lay in a circle of tree-clothed hills, sheltered as if in a great chalice.

'How can you know that?' queried Padriac. 'How can you be so sure? It could be tomorrow, or the day after. Or they could go to some other place. You're always so sure.'

I don't remember Finbar answering, but later that day, as dusk was falling, he took me back to the lake shore. In the half light over the water, we saw the swans come home. The last low traces of sun caught a white movement in the darkening sky. Then they were near enough for us to see the pattern of their flight, the orderly formation descending through the cool air as the light faded. The rush of wings, the vibration of the air. The final glide to the water, the silvery flashing as it parted to receive them. As they landed, the sound was like my name, over and over: *Sorcha, Sorcha*. My hand crept into Finbar's; we stood immobile until it was dark, and then my brother took me home.

If you are lucky enough to grow up the way I did, you have plenty of good things to remember. And some that are not so good. One spring, looking for the tiny green frogs that appeared as soon as the first warmth was in the air, my brothers and I splashed knee deep in the stream, making enough noise

2

between us to frighten any creature away. Three of my six brothers were there, Conor whistling some old tune; Cormack, who was his twin, creeping up behind to slip a handful of bog weed down his neck. The two of them rolling on the bank, wrestling and laughing. And Finbar. Finbar was further up the stream, quiet by a rock pool. He would not turn stones to seek frogs; waiting, he would charm them out by his silence.

I had a fistful of wildflowers, violets, meadow-sweet and the little pink ones we called cuckoo flowers. Down near the water's edge was a new one with pretty star-shaped blooms of a delicate pale green, and leaves like grey feathers. I clambered nearer and reached out to pick one.

'Sorcha! Don't touch that!' Finbar snapped.

Startled, I looked up. Finbar never gave me orders. If it had been Liam, now, who was the eldest, or Diarmid, who was the next one, I might have expected it. Finbar was hurrying back towards me, frogs abandoned. But why should I take notice of him? He wasn't so very much older, and it was only a flower. I heard him saying, 'Sorcha, don't –' as my small fingers plucked one of the soft-looking stems.

The pain in my hand was like fire – a white-hot agony that made me screw up my face and howl as I blundered along the path, my flowers dropped heed-less underfoot. Finbar stopped me none too gently, his hands on my shoulders arresting my wild progress.

'Starwort,' he said, taking a good look at my hand, which was swelling and turning an alarming shade of red. By this time my shrieks had brought the twins running. Cormack held onto me, since he was strong, and I was bawling and thrashing about with the pain.

Conor tore off a strip from his grubby shirt. Finbar had found a pair of pointed twigs, and he began to pull out, delicately, one by one the tiny needle-like spines the starwort plant had embedded in my soft flesh. I remember the pressure of Cormack's hands on my arms as I gulped for air between sobs, and I can still hear Conor talking, talking in a quiet voice as Finbar's long deft fingers went steadily about their task.

'. . . and her name was Deirdre, Lady of the Forest, but nobody ever saw her, save late at night, if you went out along the paths under the birch trees, you might catch a glimpse of her tall figure in a cloak of midnight blue, and her long hair, wild and dark, floating out behind her, and her little crown of stars . . .'

When it was done, they bound up my hand with Conor's makeshift bandage and some crushed marigold petals, and by morning it was better. And never a word they said to my oldest brothers, when they came home, about what a foolish girl I'd been.

From then on I knew what starwort was, and I began to teach myself about other plants that could hurt or heal. A child that grows up half-wild in the forest learns the secrets that grow there simply through common sense. Mushroom and toadstool. Lichen, moss and creeper. Leaf, flower, root and bark. Throughout the endless reaches of the forest, great oak, strong ash and gentle birch sheltered a myriad of growing things. I learned where to find them, when to cut them, how to use them in salve, ointment or infusion. But I was not content with that. I spoke with the old women of the cottages till they tired of me, and I studied what manuscripts I could find, and tried things out for myself. There was always more to learn; and there was no shortage of work to be done.

When was the beginning? When my father met my mother, and lost his heart, and chose to wed for love? Or was it when I was born? I should have been the seventh son of a seventh son, but the goddess was playing tricks, and I was a girl. And after she gave birth to me, my mother died.

It could not be said that my father gave way to his grief. He was too strong for that, but when he lost her, some light in him went out. It was all councils and power games, and dealing behind closed doors. That was all he saw, and all he cared about. So my brothers grew up running wild in the forest around the keep of Sevenwaters. Maybe I wasn't the seventh son of the old tales, the one who'd have magical powers and the luck of the Fair Folk, but I tagged along with the boys anyway, and they loved me and raised me as well as a bunch of boys could.

Our home was named for the seven streams that flowed down the hillsides into the great, tree-circled lake. It was a remote, quiet, strange place, well guarded by silent men who slipped through the woodlands clothed in grey, and who kept their weapons sharp. My father took no chances. My father was Lord Colum of Sevenwaters, and his túath was the most secure, and the most secret, this side of Tara. All respected him. Many feared him. Outside the forest, nowhere was really safe. Chieftain warred against chieftain, king against king. And there were the raiders from across the water. Christian houses of scholarship and contemplation were ransacked, their peaceful dwellers killed or put to flight. Sometimes, in desperation, the holy brothers took up arms themselves. The old faith went underground. The Norsemen made their claim on our shores, and at Dublin they set up a ship-camp and began to winter over, so that no time of year was safe. Even I had seen their work, for there was a ruin at Killevy, where raiders had killed the holy women and destroyed their sanctuary. I only went there once. There was a shadow over that place. Walking amongst the tumbled stones, you could still hear the echo of their screaming.

But my father was different. Lord Colum's authority was absolute. Within the ring of hills, blanketed by ancient forest, his borders were as close to secure as any man's might be in these troubled times. To those who did not respect it, who did not understand it, the forest was impenetrable. A man, or a troop of men, who did not know the way would become hopelessly lost there, prey to the sudden mists, the branching, deceptive paths, and to other, older things, things a Viking or a Briton could not hope to understand. The forest protected us. Our lands were safe from marauders, whether it be raiders from across the sea or neighbours intent on adding a few acres of grazing land or some fine cattle to their holdings. They held Sevenwaters in fear, and gave us a wide berth.

But Father had little time for talk of the Norsemen or the Picts, for we had our own war. Our war was with the Britons. In particular it was with one family of Britons, known as Northwoods. This feud went back a long way. I did not concern myself with it greatly. I was a girl, after all, and anyway I had better things to do with my time. Besides, I had never seen a Briton, or a Norseman, or a Pict. They were less real to me than creatures from an old tale, dragons or giants.

Father was away for much of the time, building alliances with neighbours, checking his outposts and guard towers, recruiting men. I preferred those times, when we could spend our days as we wished, exploring the forest, climbing the tall oaks, conducting expeditions over the lake, staying out all night if we wanted to. I learned where to find blackberries and hazelnuts and crabapples. I learned how to start a fire even if the wood was damp, and bake marrows or onions in the coals. I could make a shelter out of bracken, and steer a raft in a straight course.

I loved to be out of doors and feel the wind on my face. Still, I continued to teach myself the healer's art, for my heart told me this would be my true work. All of us could read, though Conor was by far the most skilful, and there were old manuscripts and scrolls tucked away on an upper floor of the stone fortress that was our home. These I devoured in my thirst for knowledge and thought it nothing unusual, for this was the only world I had known. I did not know that other girls of twelve were learning to do fine embroidery, and to plait one another's hair into intricate coronets, and to dance and sing. I did not understand that few could read, and that the books and scrolls that filled our quiet upstairs room were priceless treasure in a time of destruction and pillage. Nestled safe amongst its guardian trees, hidden from the world by forces older than time, our home was indeed a place apart.

When my father was there, things were different. Not that he took much interest in us; his visits were short, and taken up with councils and meetings. But he would watch the boys practising with sword or staff or throwing axe as they galloped and wheeled on horseback. You could never tell what Father was thinking, for his eyes gave nothing away. He was a man of solid build and stern appearance, and everything about him spoke of discipline. He dressed plainly; still, there was something about him that told you, instantly, that he was a leader. He wore his brown hair tied tightly back. Everywhere he went, from hall to courtyard, from sleeping quarters to stables, his two great wolfhounds padded silently behind him. That, I suppose, was his one indulgence. But even they had their purpose.

Each time he came home, he went through the motions of greeting us all and checking our progress, as if we were some crop that might eventually be fit for harvest. We hated this ritual parade of family identity, though it became easier for the boys once they reached young manhood and Father began to see them as of some use to him. We would be called into the great hall, after we'd been quickly tidied up by whatever servant currently had the thankless task of overseeing us. Father would be seated in his great oak chair, his men around him at a respectful distance, the dogs at his feet, relaxed but watchful.

He would call the boys forward one by one, greeting them kindly enough, starting with Liam and working gradually downwards. He would question each of them briefly on his progress and activities since last time. This could take a while; after all, there were six of them, and me as well. Knowing nothing of any other form of parental guidance, I accepted this as the way things were done. If my brothers remembered a time when things were different, they didn't talk about it.

The boys grew up quickly. By the time Liam was twelve, he was undergoing an intensive training in the arts of war, and spending less and less time with the rest of us in our joyous, undisciplined world. Not long after, Diarmid's particular skill with the spear earned him a place beside his brother, and all too soon both were riding out with Father's band of warriors.

Cormack could scarcely wait for the day when he would be old enough to join seriously in these pursuits; the training all the boys received from our father's master at arms was not enough to satisfy his thirst to excel. Padriac, who was the youngest of the boys, had a talent with animals, and a gift for fixing things. He, too, learned to ride and to wield a sword, but more often than not you'd find him helping to deliver a calf or tending a prize bull gored by a rival.

The rest of us were different. Conor was Cormack's twin, but he could scarce have been less like in temperament. Conor had always loved learning, and when he was quite little he had struck up a bargain with a Christian hermit who lived in a hillside cave above the southern lakeshore. My brother would bring Father Brien fresh fish and herbs from the garden, with maybe a loaf or two scrounged from the kitchens, and in return he was taught to read. I remember those times very clearly. There would be Conor, seated on a bench beside the hermit, deep in debate on some fine point of language or philosophy, and there in a corner would be Finbar and myself, cross-legged on the earthen floor, quiet as fieldmice. The three of us soaked up knowledge like little sponges, believing in our isolation that this was quite usual. We learned, for instance, the tongue of the Britons, a harsh, clipped sort of speech with no music in it. As we learned the language of our enemies, we were told their history.

They had once been a people much like us, fierce, proud, rich in song and story, but their land was open and vulnerable, and had been overrun time after time, until their blood became mixed with that of Roman, and of Saxon, and when at last some semblance of peace had come about, the old race of that land was gone, and in its place a new people dwelt across the water. The holy father told us that much.

Everyone had a story about the Britons. Recognisable by their light-coloured hair, and their tall stature, and their lack of any decency whatever, they had begun the feud by laying hold of something so untouchable, so deeply sacred to our people, that the theft of it was like the heart had been torn out of us. That was the cause of our war. Little Island, Greater Island and the Needle. Places of high mystery. Places of immense secrecy; the heart of the old faith. No Briton should ever have set foot on the Islands. Nothing would be right until we drove them out. That was the way everybody told it.

It was plain that Conor was not destined for a warrior. My father, rich in sons, grudgingly accepted this. He could see, perhaps, that a scholar in the family might be of some use. There was always record keeping and accounts to be done and maps to be crafted, and my father's own scribe was getting on in years. Conor, therefore, found his place in the household and settled into it with content. His days were full, but he always had time for Finbar and me, and the three of us became close, linked by our thirst for knowledge and a deep, unspoken understanding.

As for Padriac, he could turn his hand to anything, but his great love was to examine things and find out how they worked; he would ask questions till it drove you crazy. Padriac was the only one that could break through Father's guard; sometimes you'd catch the ghost of a smile on Colum's dour features when he looked at his youngest son. He didn't smile at me. Or at Finbar. Finbar said that was because we

10

reminded Father of our mother, who had died. We were the two who inherited her curling, wild hair. I had her green eyes, and Finbar her gift of stillness. Besides, by being born, I had killed her. No wonder Father found it hard to look at me. But when he spoke to Finbar his eyes were like winter. There was one time in particular. It was not long before *she* came, and our lives changed forever. Finbar was fifteen; not yet a man, but most certainly no longer a child.

Father had summoned us, and we were all assembled in the great hall. Finbar stood before Lord Colum's chair, back straight as a spear, waiting for the ritual inquisition. Liam and Diarmid were young men now, and so were spared this ordeal. But they were present on the sidelines, knowing that this reassured the rest of us.

'Finbar. I have spoken to your instructors.'

Silence. Finbar's wide grey eyes appeared to look straight through Father's.

'I'm told your skills are developing well. This pleases me.' Despite these words of praise, Father's gaze was chill, his tone remote. Liam glanced at Diarmid and Diarmid grimaced back, as if to say, *here it comes*.

'Your attitude, however, apparently leaves a great deal to be desired. I'm told that you have achieved these results without applying a great deal of effort or interest, and in particular, that you frequently absent yourself from training with no reason.'

Another pause. At this point it would most certainly have been a good idea to say something, just to avoid trouble; 'yes, Father' would have been enough. Finbar's utter stillness was an insult in itself.

'What's your explanation, boy? And none of your insolent looks, I want an answer!'

Father leaned forward, his face close to Finbar's, and the expression on his face made me shiver and move nearer to Conor. It was a look to terrify a grown man. 'You are of an age now to join your brothers at my side, at least while I remain here; and before long, in the field. But there's no place for dumb insolence on a campaign. A man must learn to obey without question. Well, speak up! How do you account for this behaviour?'

But Finbar wasn't going to answer. *If I have nothing to say to you, I will not speak.* I knew the words were in his mind. I clutched Conor's hand. We had seen Father's anger before. It would be foolish to invite it.

'Father.' Liam stepped forward diplomatically. 'Perhaps –'

'Enough!' Father commanded. 'Your brother does not require you to speak for him. He has a tongue, and a mind of his own – let him use both.'

Finbar seemed perfectly composed. Outwardly, he looked quite calm. It was only I, who shared every breath he took, knew his every moment of pain or joy as if it were my own, that felt the tension in him and understood the courage it took for him to speak.

'I will give you an answer,' he said. His tone was quiet. 'To learn to handle a horse, and to use sword and bow, that is worthy enough. I would use these skills to defend myself, or my sister, or to aid my brothers in time of peril. But you must spare me your campaigning. I will have none of it.'

My father was incredulous – too taken aback to be angry, yet, but his eyes became glacial. Whatever he had expected, it was not a confrontation of this kind. Liam opened his mouth to speak again, but Father silenced him with a savage look.

'Tell us more,' he invited politely, like a predator

encouraging its meal into a honeyed trap. 'Can you be so little aware of the threat to our lands, to the very fabric of our life here? You have been instructed on all these matters; you have seen my men return bloodied from battle, have seen the havoc these Britons wreak on lives and land. Your own brothers think it honourable work to fight alongside their father so the rest of you can enjoy peace and prosperity. They risk their lives to win back our precious Islands, torn from our people by this rabble, long years since. Have you so little faith in their judgement? Where have you learned this ill-conceived rubbish? *Campaigning*?'

'From the evidence of my own eyes,' said Finbar simply. 'While you spend season after season pursuing this perceived enemy across land and sea, your villagers grow sick and die, and there is no master to turn to for help. The unscrupulous exploit the weak. Crops are ill tended, herd and flock neglected. The forest guards us. That is just as well, for you would otherwise have lost home and people to the Finnghaill long since.'

Father drew a deep breath. His men took a pace back. 'Please go on,' he said in a voice like death. 'You are an expert on the subject of the Norsemen, I see.'

'Perhaps –' Liam said.

'Silence!' It was a roar this time, stopping Liam almost before he got a word out. 'This matter is between your brother and me. Out with it, boy! What other aspects of my stewardship have you found fault with, in your great wisdom? Don't stint, since you are so outspoken!'

'Is that not enough?'

I detected, at last, a touch of unsteadiness in Finbar's voice. He was after all still just a boy.

'You value the pursuit of a distant enemy before

keeping your own house in order. You speak of the Britons as if they were monsters. But are they not men like us?'

'You can hardly dignify such a people with the title of men,' said our father, stung to direct response at last. His voice was harsh with building anger. 'They come with evil thoughts and barbarian ways to take what is rightfully ours. Would you see your sister subject to their savagery? Your home overrun by their filth? Your argument shows your ignorance of the facts, and the sorry gaps in your education. What price your fine philosophy when you stand with a naked sword in your hand, and your enemy before you poised to strike? Wake up, boy. There is a real world out there, and the Britons stand in it with the blood of our kinsmen on their hands. It is my duty, and yours, to seek vengeance, and to reclaim what is rightly ours.'

Finbar's steady gaze had never left Father's face.

'I am not ignorant of these matters,' he said, still quietly. 'Pict and Viking, both have troubled our shores. They have left their mark on our spirits, though they could not destroy us. I acknowledge that. But the Britons, too, suffered the loss of lands and lives from these raids. We do not fully understand their purpose, in taking our Islands, in maintaining this feud. We would be better, perhaps, to unite with them against our common enemies. But no: your strategy, like theirs, is to kill and maim without seeking for answers. In time, you will lose your sons as you lost your brothers, in blind pursuit of an ill-defined goal. To win this war, you must talk to your foe. Learn to understand him. If you shut him out, he will always outwit you. There is death and suffering and a long time of regret in your future, if

14

you follow this path. Many will go with you, but I will not be amongst them.'

His words were strange; his tone chilled me. I knew he spoke the truth.

'I will hear no more of this!' thundered Father, rising to his feet. 'You speak like a fool, of matters you cannot comprehend. I shudder to think a son of mine could be so ill-informed, and so presumptuous. Liam!'

'Yes, Father?'

'I want this brother of yours equipped to ride with us when next we travel north. See to it. He expresses a wish to understand the enemy. Perhaps he will do so when he witnesses the shedding of blood at first hand.'

'Yes, Father.' Liam's expression and tone were well-schooled to neutrality. His glance at Finbar, though, was sympathetic. He simply made sure Father wasn't looking.

'And now, where is my daughter?'

Stepping forward reluctantly, I passed Finbar and brushed his hand with mine. His eyes were fierce in a face bleached of colour. I stood before Father, torn with feelings I hardly understood. Wasn't a father meant to love his children? Didn't he know how much courage it had taken, for Finbar to speak out this way? Finbar saw things in a way the rest of us never could. Father should have known that, for people said our mother had possessed the same gift. If he'd bothered to take the time, he would have known. Finbar could see ahead, and offer warnings that were ignored at your own peril. It was a rare skill, dangerous and burdensome. Some called it the Sight.

'Come forward, Sorcha.'

I was angry with Father. And yet, I wanted him to recognise me. I wanted his praise. Despite everything, I could not shut off the wish deep inside me. My brothers loved me. Why couldn't Father? That was what I was thinking as I looked up at him. From his viewpoint I must have been a pathetic little figure, skinny and untidy, my curls falling over my eyes in disarray.

'Where are your shoes, child?' asked Father wearily. He was getting restless.

'I need no shoes, Father,' I said, hardly thinking. 'My feet are tough, look,' and I raised one narrow, grubby foot to show him. 'No need for some creature to die so I can be shod.' This argument had been used on my brothers till they tired of it and let me run barefoot if it suited me.

'Which servant has charge of this child?' snapped Father testily. 'She is no longer of an age to be let loose like some – some tinker's urchin. How old are you, Sorcha – nine, ten?'

How could he not know? Didn't my birth coincide with his loss of all he held most dear in the world? For my mother had died on midwinter day, when I was not yet a day old, and folk said it was lucky for me Fat Janis, our kitchen woman, had a babe at the breast and milk enough for two, or I'd likely have died as well. It was a measure of Father's success in closing off that former life, perhaps, that he no longer counted every lonely night, every empty day, since she died.

'I'll be thirteen on midwinter eve, Father,' I said, standing up as tall as I could. Perhaps if he thought me grown-up enough, he would start to talk to me properly, the way he did to Liam and Diarmid. Or to look at me with that hint of a smile he sometimes turned on Padriac, who was closest to me in age. For an instant, his dark, deepset eyes met mine, and I stared back with a wide green gaze that, had I but known it, was the image of my mother's.

'Enough,' he said abruptly, and his tone was dismissive. 'Get these children out of here, there's work to be done.'

Turning his back on us, he was quickly engrossed in some great map they were rolling out on the oak table. Only Liam and Diarmid could expect to stay; they were men now, and privy to my father's strategies. For the rest of us, it was over. I stepped back out of the light.

Why do I remember this so well? Perhaps his displeasure with what we were becoming made Father take the choice he did, and so bring about a series of events more terrible than any of us could have imagined. Certainly, he used our wellbeing as one of his excuses for bringing her to Sevenwaters. That there was no logic in this was beside the point – he must have known in his heart that Finbar and I were made of strong stuff, already shaped in mind and spirit, if not quite grown, and that expecting us to bend to another will was like trying to alter the course of the tide, or to stop the forest from growing. But he was influenced by forces he was unable to understand. My mother would have recognised them. I often wondered, later, how much she knew of our future. The Sight does not always show what a person wants to see, but I think she must have known, as she bade us farewell, what a strange and crooked path her children's feet would follow.

As soon as Father dismissed us from the hall, Finbar was gone, a shadow disappearing up the stone steps to the tower. As I turned to follow, Liam winked at me. Fledgling warrior he might be, but he was my brother. And I got a grin from Diarmid, but he wiped his face clean of all expressions but respect as he turned back towards Father.

Padriac would be away off outdoors; he had an injured owl in the stables that he was nursing back to health. It was amazing, he said, how much this task had taught him about the principles of flight. Conor was working with my father's scribe, helping with some calculations; we wouldn't be seeing much of him for a while. Cormack would be off to practise with the sword or the staff. I was alone when I padded up the stone steps on my bare feet and into the tower room. From here you could climb up further, onto a stretch of slate roof with a low battlement around it, probably not sufficient to arrest a good fall, but that never stopped us from going up there. It was a place for stories, for secrets; for being alone together in silence.

He was, as I'd expected, sitting on the most precarious slope of the roof, knees drawn up, arms around them, his expression unreadable as he gazed out over the stone-walled pastures, the barns and byres and cottages, to the smoke grey and soft green and misty blue of the forest. Not so far away the waters of the lake glinted silver. The breeze was quite chill, catching at my skirts as I came up the slates and settled myself down next to him. Finbar was utterly still. I did not need to look at him to read his mood, for I was tuned to this brother's mind like the bow to the string.

We were quiet for a long time, as the wind tangled our hair, and a flock of gulls passed overhead, calling amongst themselves. Voices drifted up from time to time, and metal clashed on metal: Father's men at combat in the yard, and Cormack was amongst them. Father would be pleased with him.

Slowly Finbar came back from the far reaches of the mind. His long fingers moved to wind themselves around a strand of his hair.

'What do you know of the lands beyond the water, Sorcha?' he asked quite calmly.

'Not much,' I said, puzzled. 'Liam says the maps don't show everything; there are places even he knows little about. Father says the Britons are to be feared.'

'He fears what he does not understand,' said Finbar. 'What about Father Brien and his kind? They came out of the east, by sea, and showed great courage in doing so. In time they were accepted here, and gave us much. Father does not seek to know his foes, or to make sense of what they want. He sees only the threat, the insult, and so he spends his whole life pursuing them, killing and maiming without question. And for what?'

I thought about this for a while.

'But you don't know them either,' I ventured, logically enough. 'And it's not just Father that thinks they're a danger. Liam said if the campaigns didn't go right up to the north, and to the very shore of the eastern sea, we'd be overrun one day and lose everything we have. Maybe not just the Islands, but Sevenwaters as well. Then the old ways would be gone forever. That's what he says.'

'In a way that's true,' said Finbar, surprising me. 'But there are two sides to every fight. It starts from something small, a chance remark, a gesture made lightly. It grows from there. Both sides can be unjust. Both can be cruel.'

'How do you know?'

Finbar did not reply. His mind was closely shuttered from mine; not for now the meeting of thoughts, the silent exchange of images that passed so often between us, far easier than speech. I thought for a while, but I could think of nothing to say. Finbar chewed the end of his hair, which he wore tied at the nape of the neck, and long. His dark curls, like mine, had a will of their own.

'I think our mother left us something,' he said eventually. 'She left a small part of herself in each of us. It's just as well for them, for Liam and Diarmid, that they have that. It stops them from growing like him.'

I knew what he meant, without fully understanding his words.

'Liam's a leader,' Finbar went on, 'like Father, but not quite like. Liam has balance. He knows how to weigh up a problem evenly. Men would die for him. One day they probably will. Diarmid's different. People would follow him to the ends of the earth, just for the fun of it.'

I thought about this; pictured Liam standing up for me against Father, Diarmid teaching me how to catch frogs, and to let them go.

'Cormack's a warrior,' I ventured. 'But generous. Kind.' There was the dog, after all. One of the wolfhounds had had a misalliance, and given birth to cross-bred pups; Father would have had them all drowned, but Cormack rescued one and kept her, a skinny brindled thing he called Linn. His kindness was rewarded by the deep, unquestioning devotion only a faithful dog can give. 'And then there's Padriac.'

Finbar leaned back against the slates and closed his eyes.

'Padriac will go far,' he said. 'He'll go farther than any of us.'

'Conor's different,' I observed, but I was unable to put that difference into words. There was something elusive about it.

'Conor's a scholar,' said Finbar. 'We all love stories, but he treasures learning. Mother had some wonderful old tales, and riddles, and strange notions that she'd laugh over, so you never knew if she was serious or not. Conor got his love of ideas from her. Conor is – he is himself.'

'How can you remember all this?' I said, not sure if he was making it up for my benefit. 'You were only three years old when she died. A baby.'

'I remember,' said Finbar, and turned his head away. I wanted him to go on, for I was fascinated by talk of our mother, whom I had never known. But he had fallen silent again. It was getting late in the day; long tree shadows stretched their points across the grass far below us.

The silence drew out again, so long I thought he might be asleep. I wriggled my toes; it was getting cold. Maybe I did need shoes.

'What about you, Finbar?' I hardly needed to ask. He was different. He was different from all of us. 'What did she give you?'

He turned and smiled at me, the curve of his wide mouth transforming his face completely.

'Faith in myself,' he said simply. 'To do what's right, and not falter, no matter how hard it gets.'

'It was hard enough today,' I said, thinking of Father's cold eyes, and the way they'd made Finbar look.

It will be much harder in time. I could not tell if this thought came from my own mind, or my brother's. It sent a chill up my spine.

Then he said aloud, 'I want you to remember,

Sorcha. Remember that I'll always be there for you, no matter what happens. It's important. Now come on, it's time we went back down.'

When I remember the years of our growing up, the most important thing is the tree. We went there often, the seven of us, southward through the forest above the lake shore. When I was a baby, Liam or Diarmid would carry me on his back; once I could walk, two brothers would take my hands and hurry me along, sometimes swinging me between them with a one, two, three, as the others ran on ahead towards the lake. When we came closer, we all became quiet. The bank where the birch tree grew was a place of deep magic, and our voices were hushed as we gathered on the sward around it.

We all accepted that this land was a gate to that other world, the realm of spirits and dreams and the Fair Folk, without any question. The place we grew up in was so full of magic that it was almost a part of everyday life – not to say you'd meet one of them every time you went out to pick berries, or draw water from your well, but everyone we knew had a friend of a friend who'd strayed too far into the forest, and disappeared; or ventured inside a ring of mushrooms, and gone away for a while, and come back subtly changed. Strange things could happen in those places. Gone for maybe fifty years you could be, and come back still a young girl; or away for no more than an instant by mortal reckoning, and return wrinkled and bent with age. These tales fascinated us, but failed to make us careful. If it was going to happen to you, it would happen, whether you liked it or not.

The birch tree, though, was a different matter. It held her spirit, our mother's, having been planted by the boys on the day of her death, at her own request. Once she had told them what to do, Liam and Diarmid, six and five years old, took their spades down to the place she had described, dug out the soft turf and planted the seed there on the flat grassy bank above the lake. With small, grubby hands the younger ones helped level the soil and carried water. Later, when they were allowed to take me out of the house, we all went there together. That was the first time for me; and after that, twice a year at midsummer and midwinter we'd gather there.

Grazing animals might have taken this little tree, or the cold autumn winds snapped its slender stem, but it was charmed; and within a few years it began to shoot up, graceful both in its bare winter austerity and in its silvery, rustling summer beauty. I can see the place now, clear in my mind, and the seven of us seated cross-legged on the turf around the birch tree, not touching, but as surely linked as if our hands were tightly clasped. We were older then, but children still. I would have been five, perhaps, Finbar eight. Liam had waited until we were big enough to understand, before telling us this story.

. . . now there was something frightening about the room. It smelled different, strange. Our new little sister had been taken away, and there was blood, and people with frightened faces running in and out. Mother's face was so pale as she lay there with her dark hair spread around her. But she gave us the seed, and she said to us, to Diarmid and me, 'I want you to take this, and plant it by the lake, and in the moment of my passing the seed will start to grow with new life. And then, my sons, I will always be there with you, and when you are in that place you will know that you are part of the one great magic that binds us all together. Our strength comes from that magic, from the earth and the sky, from the fire and the water. Fly high, swim deep, give back to the earth what she gives you . . .'

She grew tired, she was losing her life blood, but she had a smile for the two of us and we tried to smile back through our tears, hardly understanding what she told us, but knowing it was important. 'Diarmid,' she said, 'look after your little brothers. Share your laughter with them.' Her voice grew fainter. 'Liam, son. I fear it will be hard for you, for a while. You'll be their leader, and their guide, and you are young to carry such a burden.'

'I can do it,' I said, choking back my tears. People were moving about the room, a physician muttering to himself and shaking his head, women taking away the bloody cloths and bringing fresh ones, and now somebody tried to make us leave. But Mother said no, not yet, and she made them all go out, just for a little. Then she gathered us around her bed, to say good-bye. Father was outside. He kept his grief to himself, even then.

So she spoke softly to each of us, her voice growing quieter all the while. The twins were on either side of her, leaning in, each the mirror image of the other, eyes grey as the winter sky, hair deep brown and glossy as a ripe chestnut.

'Conor, dear heart,' she said. 'Do you remember the verse about the deer, and the eagle?' Conor nodded, his small features very serious. 'Tell me then,' she whispered.

'My feet will tread soft as a deer in the forest,' said Conor, frowning with concentration. 'My mind will be clear as water from the sacred well. My heart will be strong as a great oak. My spirit will spread on eagle's wings, and fly forth. This is the way of truth.'

'Good,' she said. 'Remember, and teach it to your sister, when she is older. Can you do that?'

Another solemn nod.

'It's not fair!' Cormack burst out, angry tears overwhelming him. He put his arms around her neck and held on tight. 'You can't die! I don't want you to die!'

She stroked his hair, and soothed him with gentle words, and Conor moved around to take his twin's hand in his own, and Cormack grew quiet. Then Diarmid held Padriac up so Mother's arm could encircle the two of them for a moment. Finbar, standing next to her pillow, was so still you could have missed him entirely, watching silently as she let her sons go, one by one. She turned to him last of us boys, and she didn't say anything this time, but motioned to him to take the carved piece of stone she wore around her neck, and to put it on his own. He wasn't much more than an infant – the cord came down below his waist. He closed a small fist around the amulet. With him she had no need for words.

'My daughter,' she whispered at last. 'Where's my Sorcha?' I went out and asked, and Fat Janis came in and put the newborn baby in our mother's arms, by now almost too weak to curl around the little bundle of woollen wrappings. Finbar moved closer, his small hands helping to support the fragile burden. 'My daughter will be strong,' Mother said. 'The magic is powerful in her, and so in all of you. Be true to yourselves, and to each other, my children.' She lay back then, eyes closed, and we went softly out, and so we

25

did not witness the moment of her passing. We put the seed in the ground and the tree took form within it and began to grow. She is gone, but the tree lives, and through this she gives us her strength, which is the strength of all living things.

My father had allies as well as enemies. The whole of the northern land was patchworked with túaths like his, some larger, most a great deal smaller, each held by its lord in an uneasy truce with a few neighbours. Far south at Tara dwelt the High King and his consort, but in the isolation of Sevenwaters we were not touched by their authority, nor they, it seemed, by our local feuds. Alliances were made at the council table, reinforced by marriages, broken frequently by disputes over cattle or borders. There were forays and campaigns enough, but not against our neighbours, who held my father in considerable respect. So there was a loose agreement between them to unite against Briton, Pict and Norseman alike, since all threatened our shores with their strange tongues and barbarian ways. But especially against the Britons, who had done the unthinkable and got away with it.

I could hardly be unaware that prisoners were sometimes taken, but they were closely housed and guarded with grim efficiency, and none of my brothers would talk about it. Not even Finbar. This was odd, for mostly he kept his mind open to me, and my own thoughts were never shut away from him. I knew his fears and his joys; I felt with him the sunlit spaces and the dark mystic depths of our forest, the heartbeat of the goddess in its dappled paths and spring freshness. But there was, even then, one part of himself that he kept hidden. Perhaps, even so early,

26

he was trying to protect me. So, the prisoners were a mystery to me. Ours was a household of tall armoured figures, curt exchanges, hasty arrivals and departures. Even when my father was away, as for the best part of the year he was, he left a strong garrison behind, with his master at arms, Donal, in iron-fisted control.

That was one side of the household; the other, the more domestic, was secondary. What servants we had went about their tasks efficiently enough, and the folk of the settlement did their share, for there were stone walls to be maintained, and thatching to be done, and the work of mill and dairy. The herds must be driven to high ground in summer, to take advantage of what grazing there was, pig-boys must do their best to track their wayward charges in the woods, and the women had spinning and weaving to do. Our steward took sick with an ague, and died; and after that Conor took charge of the purse, and the accounts, while Father was away. Subtly he began to assume authority in the household; even at sixteen he had a shrewd sobriety that belied his years and appeared to inspire trust even in the hardbitten soldiers. It became plain to all that Conor was no mere scribe. In Father's absence, small changes occurred unobtrusively: an orderly provision of dry turf to the cottagers in good time for winter, a stillroom set up for my use, with a woman to help me and take draughts and potions to the sick. When the little folk got to Madge Smallfoot's husband, and he drowned himself in a long drop from rocks into the lake (which is how Smallfoot's Leap got its name) it was Conor who made arrangements for Madge to come and work for us, rolling pastry and plucking chickens in our kitchens. These things were little enough, maybe, but a start.

27

Finbar did not go on the autumn campaign that year. Despite Father's orders, it was Liam and Diarmid and, to his delight, young Cormack who departed abruptly one bright crisp morning. The call to arms was early, and unexpected. Unusually, we were entertaining guests: our nearest neighbour, Seamus Redbeard of Glencarnagh, and several of his household. Seamus was one of the trusted ones, my father's closest ally. But even he had not entered the forest without an escort of my father's men, who met him on his own border and saw him safe to the keep of Sevenwaters.

Seamus had brought his daughter, who was fifteen years old and had a mane of hair the same startling hue as her father's. Her locks may have been fiery, but Eilis was a quiet girl, plump and rosy-cheeked; in fact, I found her rather boring compared with my brothers. Our guests had been with us for ten days or so, and because Eilis never wanted to climb trees, or swim in the lake, or even help me with brewing and preserving, I soon tired of her company and left her to her own devices. I was amazed that the boys took so much interest in her, for her conversation, when she spoke at all, ran mostly to the immediate and superficial. This could surely be of little interest to them. Yet in turn Liam, Diarmid and Cormack could be seen patiently escorting her around the keep and the gardens, bending with apparent fascination to catch every word she said, taking her hand to help her down steps I could have traversed with a few neatly executed jumps.

It was odd, and grew odder – though the strangest thing was that it took me so long to realise what was happening. After the first few days, she showed her allegiance, attaching herself firmly to Liam. He, whom I would have thought the busiest, always seemed to have time for Eilis. I detected something new in his face, now grown to the long-boned hardness of manhood. It was a warning to his brothers to keep off; and they heeded it. Eilis went walking in the woods with Liam, when she would not go with me. Eilis, most demure at table, could sense when Liam's dark eyes were fixed on her from across the noisy hall; she looked up shyly, met his gaze for an instant, and blushed becomingly, before her long lashes shielded the blue eyes again. Still I was ignorant, until the night my father rapped the board for silence.

'My friends! My good neighbours!'

There was a hush amongst the assembled guests; goblets paused half way to waiting lips, and I sensed an air of expectancy, as if everyone knew what Father was going to say, except me.

'It is good, in these times of trouble, to make merry together, to drink and laugh and share the fruits of our pastures. Soon enough, at full moon, we must venture forward again, this time perhaps to make our shores safe once and for all.'

A few whistles and shouts of acclaim here, but they were clearly waiting for something more. 'Meanwhile, you are welcome in my hall. It is a long time since such a feast was held here.'

He was grim for a moment. Seamus Redbeard leaned forward, his face flushed.

'Sure and you're a fine host, Colum, and let none tell you different,' he pronounced, his speech suffering a bit from the quality of our ale. Eilis was blushing and looking down at her plate again. Out of the corner of my eye, I caught Cormack feeding slivers of meat to his dog, Linn, who had squeezed her long-limbed body under the table. He'd hold a morsel of beef or chicken very casually between thumb and forefinger, and an instant later the great whiskery muzzle would appear, and disappear, and Cormack would rest his empty hand on the table's edge, his eyes fixed carefully elsewhere and his dimples showing just a little.

'And so I charge you, drink to the happy pair! May their union be long and fruitful, and a sign of friendship and peace between neighbours.'

I'd missed something; Liam was standing, rather pale but unable to keep a smile off his usually serious face, and then he was taking Eilis' hand, and I finally saw the way they looked at each other and knew it for what it was.

'Married? Liam?' I said to nobody in particular. 'To *her*?' but they were all laughing and cheering, and even my father looked almost contented. I saw the old hermit, Father Brien, speaking quietly to Liam and Eilis amidst the crowd. Clutching my hurt to myself, I slipped out of the hall, right away from the torches and candles and noise, to the stillroom which was my own place. But not to work; I sat in the deep window embrasure with a single stub of candle to keep me company, and stared out into the darkened kitchen garden. There was a sliver of moon, and a few stars in the black; slowly the garden's familiar faces showed themselves to me, though I knew them so well I could have seen them in pitch darkness: soft blue-green wormwood, that warded off insects; the yellow tips of rioting tansy, dainty grey lavender with its brilliant spikes of purple and blue, the rough stone walls blanketed in a soft drift of green where an ancient creeper flourished. There were many more; and behind me on shelves, their oils and essences gleaming in bottle, jar or crucible, for cure or palliative; their dried leaves and blooms hanging above me in orderly bundles. A delicate healing smell hung in the quiet air. I took a few deep breaths. It was very cold; the old cloak I'd left on a hook behind the door here was some help, but the chill went straight to your bones. The best of summer was over.

I must have sat there for quite some time, cold even amidst the comfort of my own things. It was the end of something, and I didn't want it to end. But there was nothing to be done about it. It was impossible not to cry. Tears flooded silently down my cheeks and I made no effort to wipe them away. After a while, footsteps sounded on the flagstones outside and there was a gentle tap at the door. Of course, one of them would come. So close were we, the seven of us, that no childhood injury went unnoticed, no slight, real or imagined, went unaddressed, no hurt was endured without comfort.

'Sorcha? Can I come in?'

I'd thought it would be Conor; but it was my second brother, Diarmid, who ducked under the lintel and entered, disposing his long frame on a bench near my window. The flickering candle flame showed me his face in extremes of shadow and light; lean, straight-nosed, a younger version of Liam's, save for the fuller mouth so ready to break into a wicked grin. But for now, he was serious.

'You should come back,' he said in a tone that told me he didn't care, himself, about the niceties. 'Your absence was noted.'

I swallowed, and rubbed a corner of the old cloak over my wet cheeks. It seemed to be anger I was feeling now more than sorrow.

'Why do things have to change?' I said crossly. 'Why can't we go on the way we are? Liam was quite happy before – he doesn't need *her*!'

To his credit, Diarmid didn't laugh at me. He stretched his legs out across the floor, apparently thinking deeply.

'Liam's a man now,' he said after a while. 'Men do marry, Sorcha. He'll have responsibilities here – a wife can share that with him.'

'He's got us,' I said fiercely. Diarmid did smile then, showing a set of dimples that rivalled Cormack's for charm. It made me wonder why Eilis hadn't chosen him instead of the serious Liam.

'Listen to me, Sorcha. No matter where we are, or what we do, the seven of us will never be truly separate. We'll always be the same for one another. But we are growing up; and grown up people do marry, and move away, and let other people into their lives. Even you will do that one day.'

'Me!' I was aghast.

'You must know that.' He moved closer and took my hand, and I noticed that his were large and rough, a man's hands. He was seventeen now. 'Father already plans a marriage for you, in a few years' time, and doubtless then you will go away to live with your husband's family. We will not all remain here.'

'Go away? I would never go away from Sevenwaters! This is home! I would die before I'd move away!'

Tears sprang to my eyes again. I knew I was being foolish; I was not so ignorant as to have no understanding of marriages and alliances and what was expected. It was just that the sudden blow of Liam's betrothal had shocked me; my world was changing, and I was not ready for it.

'Things do change, Sorcha,' said Diarmid sombrely. 'And not always as we want. Not all of us would have wished Eilis to be for Liam; but that's the way it is, and we must accept it.'

'Why does he want to marry *her*, anyway?' I demanded childishly. 'She's so boring!'

'Liam's a man,' said Diarmid sternly, obviously putting aside his own regrets. 'And she's a woman. Their marriage was arranged a while back. They're fortunate that they want each other, since they are pledged regardless. She will be a good wife to him.'

'I'll never have an arranged marriage,' I said vehemently. 'Never. How could you spend your whole life with someone you hated, or someone you couldn't talk to? I'd rather not marry at all.'

'And be an old wise woman among her possets and simples?' grinned my brother. 'Well, you're ugly enough for the job. In fact, I think I can see your wrinkles growing already, granny!'

I punched him in the arm but found myself grinning back. He gave me a quick hug, hard enough to stop me lapsing into tears again.

'Come on,' he said. 'Wash your face, comb your hair, and let's brave the party for a bit more. Liam will be worried if you stay away all night. He needs your approval, so you'd better put a good face on it.'

I did not dance at the betrothal, but I moved amongst the folk there, and kissed Eilis' rosy cheek and told Liam I was glad for him. My red eyes must have betrayed my true feelings, but in the smoke and torchlight, after somewhat more ale than he was accustomed to take, Liam didn't seem to notice. The others were watching me; Diarmid kindly, bringing me some mead, making sure I was not alone too long; Conor a little severe, as if he understood my selfish thoughts all too well. Padriac and Cormack were making the most of this rare visit by a household of women, and dancing with the prettiest of Eilis' ladies; by the amount of giggling and winking that was going on, my brothers' youth was no impediment to their popularity. Finbar was deep in debate with a grizzled old warrior, one of Redbeard's household.

My father had relaxed; it was a long time since I had seen him so. Opening his house to guests had been a trial, but a necessary one, in the interest of a strategic alliance with his neighbour. Father had observed my return, and when I made myself useful chatting to Eilis' elderly chaperone, he even acknowledged me with a nod of approval. Clearly, I thought bitterly, a daughter like Eilis was just what he wanted – biddable, soft, a sweet thing with no mind of her own. Well, I could play the part tonight, for Liam's sake, but he'd better not think I was going to keep it up.

The night wore on; mead and ale flowed, platters of food came and went. The best was on offer: roast pig, soft wheaten bread, spiced fruit and a mellow cheese made from ewes' milk. There was more music and dancing – the musicians had come from Seamus' household, and made up in vigour what they lacked in subtlety. The fellow on the bodhran had arms like a blacksmith's, and the piper a taste for the mead. Such was the noise of stamping feet, of whistling and cheering, that it was some minutes before the commotion at the great door, the clash of metal and the shouting came to the notice of our guests. Slowly the sound of revelry died down, and the crowd parted to admit a small band of my father's men, still in their field armour and carrying naked swords. They came up to my father's chair, and between them they dragged a captive whose face I could not see, but whose hair, gripped from behind by a large mailed fist, caught the torchlight and shone like ripples of bright gold.

'My lord Colum!' the captain boomed out. 'I regret this disturbance to your festivities.'

'Indeed,' responded my father in his iciest tones. 'Your business must be pressing indeed, to warrant such an intrusion. What is your purpose? I have guests here.'

He was displeased at the interruption; but at the same time his hand had moved to his sword belt. The lord Colum knew his men well; not for nothing would they risk his anger in such a way. There was an instant alertness about him that bespoke a professional. Beside him, Seamus Redbeard was slumped in his chair, smiling beatifically at nothing in particular. He might have indulged himself too generously tonight, but his host was cold sober.

'A captive, my lord, as you see. We found him on the northern rim of the lake, alone; but there must surely be more of his kind close by. This is no hired man, Lord Colum.'

There was a violent movement, and the soldier's voice was cut short as his prisoner jerked at the restraints that held him. People jostled for a better look, but all I could see through the press of bodies was the bright burnished gold of his hair, and the big fist of the man that gripped it, and the way the prisoner held himself tall, as if he were the only person in the world that mattered.

I ducked under a few arms and pushed past a group of whispering girls, and clambered up onto the wide stone bench that skirted the great hall. Then another precarious step onto the rim of a pillar, and I gained myself an unimpeded view straight over the heads of the muttering, craning crowd. The first thing

I saw was Finbar, perched in the identical spot on the other side. His look passed right over me and settled on the prisoner.

The captive's face was badly bruised; his nose had been bleeding and the shining curls were on closer inspection tangled with sweat and blood over his brow. Beneath them, his eyes burned like coals as they fixed on my father. He was young, and hurt, and desperate with hatred. He was the first Briton I had ever seen.

'Who are you, and what is your purpose here?' demanded my father. 'Speak now, for silence will bring you no good, that I promise. We have no welcome but death for your kind, for we know of but one intention you can have in our lands. Who sent you here?'

The young man drew himself up, jerking contemptuously on the ropes that tied his hands tight behind his back. He spat with stunning accuracy at Father's feet. Instantly, one captor tightened the rope, twisting his arms harder, and the other used the full force of a gauntleted fist across the prisoner's face, leaving a red weal on mouth and cheek. Resentment and fury blazed from the young man's eyes, but he set his lips grimly and remained silent. Father rose to his feet.

'This exhibition is no sight for ladies, and has no place in this hall of celebration,' he said. 'It is, perhaps, time to retire.' He swept a dismissing glance around the hall, managing somehow to thank and farewell his guests in an instant. 'Men, hold yourselves in readiness for an early departure. It seems our venture can no longer wait for full moon. Meanwhile, we shall see what this unwelcome visitor has to tell us; let my captains come to me, and all others depart. My guests, I regret this untimely end to our feast.'

The household, in an instant, snapped back into campaign mode. Servants appeared; flasks, goblets and platters disappeared. Eilis and her ladies made a swift departure to their quarters, with Seamus not long after, and soon there were left just Father and a handful of his most trusted men. Somewhere in the midst of it all, the captive was dragged out, still silent in his blazing rage. If instructions were given to his guards, I missed them.

And in the darkened hall, Finbar and myself, one on each side, blending into the shadows as both of us knew well how to do. I could not explain why I stayed, but the pattern was already forming that would shape our destinies, had I but known it.

'. . . already here, so close; this means they have intelligence enough of our positions to pose a real threat to . . .'

'. . . eradicate them, but quickly, before the information . . .'

'It's imperative that he talks.' This was Father, his voice authoritative. 'Tell them that. And it must be tonight, for speed is essential in this exercise. We move out at dawn. Tell your men to sleep while they can, then check all for readiness.' He turned to one of the older men. 'You will supervise the interrogation. And make sure he's kept alive. Such a captive could prove valuable as a hostage, after he's served his purpose. Clearly this is no ordinary foot soldier. He may even be kin to Northwoods. Tell them to tread carefully.'

The man nodded assent and left the hall, and the others returned to their planning. I felt a little sorry for Liam – only just engaged, and he was off campaigning already. Maybe life was like that if you were a man, but it did seem rather unfair.

'Sorcha!' A whisper behind me almost made me cry out and reveal my hiding place. Finbar tugged at my sleeve, drawing me silently outside into the courtyard.

'Don't creep up on me like that!' I hissed. His fingers on my lips silenced me quickly, and not until we were around the corner and he had checked carefully that nobody was within earshot did he speak.

'I need you to help me,' he whispered. 'I didn't want to ask you, but I can't do this alone.'

'Do what?' My interest was caught immediately, even though I hadn't the faintest idea what he was talking about.

'We can't do much now,' he said, 'but we might get him away by morning, if you can give me what I need.'

'What?' I said. 'What do you mean?'

'Poison,' said Finbar. He was leading me quickly through the archway to the gardens. Both of us had the ability to move fast and silently over any sort of terrain. It came of growing up half wild. We had, in fact, a variety of unusual skills.

Once we were in the stillroom, and both outer and inner doors bolted, I made Finbar sit down and explain. He didn't want to; his face had that stubborn expression it sometimes took on when the truth was painful or hurtful, but had to be told. One thing neither of us ever learned was the skill of lying.

'You'll have to explain,' I said. 'You can't just say poison and then stop. Anyway, I can tell what you're thinking. I'm twelve and a half now, Finbar; I'm old enough to be trusted.'

'I do trust you, Sorcha. It's not that. It's just that if you help me now, you'll be at risk, and besides, it's . . .' He was twisting the end of his hair with his fingers again. He shut his words off, but I was tuned to his thoughts, and for a moment he forgot to shield them. In the darkness of the quiet room I caught a terrifying glimpse of a glowing brazier, and mangled, burning flesh, and I heard a man screaming. I wrenched myself back, shaking. Our eyes met in the horror of our shared vision.

'What sort of poison?' I asked unsteadily, my hands fumbling for tinder to light a candle.

'Not to kill. A draught strong enough to send a man to sleep for the morning. Enough of it to doctor four men; and tasting fair, so they will take it in a tankard of ale and not know different. And I need it before sunrise, Sorcha. They take their breakfast early, and the guard changes before mid-morning. It's little enough time. You know how to make such a potion?'

In the dark, I nodded reluctantly. We two need not see each other, save in the mind's eye, to reach an understanding.

'You're going to have to tell me,' I said slowly. 'Tell me what this is for. It's him, isn't it? That prisoner?'

The candle flared and I shielded it with my hand. It was very late now, well past midnight, but outside there were subdued sounds of activity, horses being moved, weapons sharpened, stores loaded; they were preparing already for a dawn departure.

'You saw him,' said Finbar with quiet intensity. 'He's only a boy.'

'He was older than you,' I couldn't resist pointing out. 'Sixteen at least, I thought.'

'Old enough to die for a cause,' said my brother, and I could feel how tight stretched he was, how his determination to make things right drove him. If Finbar could have changed the world by sheer effort of will, he would have done it.

'What do you want me to do? Put this Briton to sleep?' By the dim light of the candle I was scanning my shelves; the packet I wanted was well concealed.

'He held his tongue. And will continue to do so, if I read him right. That will cost him dearly. Briton or no, he deserves his chance at freedom,' said Finbar soberly. 'Your draught can buy that for him. There's no way to save him the pain; we're too late for that.'

'What pain?' Maybe I knew the answer to my own question, but my mind refused to put together the clues I'd been given, refused to accept the unacceptable.

'The draught is for his guards.' Finbar spoke reluctantly. Plainly, he wished me to know as little as possible. 'Just make it up; I'll do the rest.'

My hands found the packet almost automatically: nightshade, used in moderation and well mixed with certain other herbs, would produce a sound slumber with few ill effects. The trick lay in getting the dose just right; too much, and your victim would never wake. I stood still, the dried berries on the stone slab before me.

'What's the matter?' asked Finbar. 'Why are you still holding back? Sorcha, I need to know you will do this. And I must go. There are other matters to attend to.'

He was already on his feet, eager to leave, his mind starting to map out the next part of his strategy.

'What will they do to him, Finbar?' Surely not – surely not what I had seen, in that flash of vision that had sickened me so.

'You heard Father. He said, keep him alive. Let me worry about it, Sorcha. Just make up the draught. Please.'

'But how could Father –'

'It becomes easy,' Finbar said. 'It's in the training;

the ability to see your enemy as something other than a real man. He is a lesser breed, defined by his beliefs – you learn to do with him what you will, and bend him to your purpose.' He sensed my horror. 'It's all right, Sorcha,' he said. 'We can save this one, you and I. Just do as I ask, and leave the rest to me.'

'What are you going to do? And what if Father finds out?'

'Too many questions! We don't have much time left – can't you just do it?'

I turned to face him, arms folded around myself. Truth to tell, I was shivering, and not just from cold.

'I know you don't lie, Finbar. I have no choice but to believe what you've told me. But I've never poisoned anyone before. I'm a healer.'

I looked up at his silent face, the wide, mobile mouth, the clear grey eyes which always seemed intent on a future path that held no uncertainty whatever.

'It happens,' he said quietly. 'It's part of war. Sometimes they talk. Sometimes they keep silent. Often they die. Just occasionally they escape.'

'You'd better go and get on with it, then,' I said in a voice that sounded like somebody else's. My hands sought a sharp knife and began automatically to slice and chop the ingredients of my sleeping draught. Henbane. Witch's bonnet. The small blue fungi some call devil spawn. Nightshade, not too much. 'Go on, Finbar.'

'Thanks.' There was a flash of that smile, the generous smile that lit up his whole face. 'We make a good team. A foolproof team. How can we fail?'

He hugged me for a moment, just long enough for me to feel the tension of his body, the rapid beat of his heart. Then he was gone, slipping away into the shadows as silent as a cat.

It was a long night. Awareness that the slightest error could make me a murderer kept me alert, and before daybreak the sleeping draught was ready, corked safely in a small stone bottle convenient to conceal in the palm of the hand, and the stillroom was immaculately clean, every trace of my activity gone. Finbar came for me as the sound of jingling harnesses and hurrying, booted feet increased out of doors.

'I think you'd better do this part as well,' he whispered. 'They'll be less likely to notice you.' I remembered, vaguely, that he was supposed to be joining the campaign this time – had not Father decreed that it would be so? Then I was too busy to think, slipping silently to the kitchens on my brother's whispered instructions, edging behind and between servants and men at arms who were snatching a last bite to eat, preparing ration packs, filling wine and water bottles. Fat Janis, Finbar had said, go to where Fat Janis has her iron pot on the stove. If they've been working at night, she'll take them mulled ale first thing in the morning. Her special brew. They say it has some interesting side effects. She carries it over to them herself; and maybe gets favours in return. What sort of favours? I'd asked him. Never mind, said Finbar. Just make sure she doesn't see you.

There were a couple of things I was good at. One was potions and poisons, and another was being quiet and staying unseen when it suited me. It was no trouble adding the draught to the mulled ale; Janis turned her back for an instant, laughing at some wisecrack by the tallest man at arms as he crammed a last piece of sausage in his mouth and made for the door, buckling his sword belt as he went. I was finished and gone before she turned back, and she never saw me. Easy, I thought as I slipped towards the door. Must have been fifteen people there, and not one of them spotted me. I was nearly outside when something made me look back. Straight across the kitchen, meeting my startled eyes full on, was my brother Conor. He stood in the far corner of the room, half in shadow, a list of some sort in one hand and a quill poised in the other. His assistant, back turned, was packing stores into a saddle bag. I was frozen in shock: from where he stood, my brother must have seen everything. How could I not have noticed him before? Paralysed between the instinct to bolt for cover, and the anticipated call to account for myself, I hesitated on the threshold. And Conor dropped his gaze to his writing and continued his list as if I had been invisible. I was too relieved to worry about a possible explanation, and fled like a startled rabbit, trembling with nerves. Finbar was nowhere to be seen. I made for the safest bolt-hole I could think of, the ancient stable building where my youngest brother, Padriac, kept his menagerie of waifs and strays. There I found a warm corner amongst the well seasoned straw, and the elderly donkey who had prior claim shifted grudgingly, making room for me against her broad back. Hungry, cold, confused and exhausted, I found escape, for the time being, in sleep.

CHAPTER TWO

Our story cannot be told without some mention of Father Brien. I said he was a hermit, and that he would exchange a little learning for a loaf or a bag of apples. That was true; but there was a lot more to Father Brien than met the eye. It was said he'd once been a fighting man, and had more than a few Viking skulls to his credit; it was said that he'd come from over the water, all the way from Armorica, to put his skills with pen and ink to work in the Christian house of prayer at Kells; but he'd been living alone a long time, and he was old, fifty at least, a small, spare, grey-haired man whose face had the calm acceptance of one whose spirit has remained whole through a lifetime of trials.

A trip to Father Brien's was an adventure in itself. He lived up on the hillside south of the lake, and we took our time getting there, because that was part of the fun. There was the bit where you crossed the stream on a rope, swinging wildly between the great oaks. Cormack fell in once; fortunately, it was summer. There was the part where you had to scramble up a rock chimney, which took its toll on knees and elbows, not to speak of the holes it made in your clothing. There were elaborate games of hide and seek. In fact, you could get there in half the time on a cart track, but our way was better. Sometimes Father Brien was from home, his hearth cold, his floor swept bare and clean. According to Finbar, who somehow knew these things, the holy father would climb right to the top of Ogma's Peak, a fair way for an old man, and stand there still as a stone, looking out eastwards to the sea and beyond it, towards the land of the Britons; or away to the Islands. You could not see the Islands from this vantage point; but ask any man or woman where they were, and you would see their finger point with complete confidence to the east, and a little south. It was as if they had a map imprinted on their spirit, that neither time nor distance could erase.

When the hermit was at home, he was happy to talk to us in his quiet, measured way, and he bartered learning for the necessities of life. He knew many different tongues; his knowledge of herb lore was sound, too, and he could set bones with skill. From him I got many of the rudiments of my craft, but my obsession with the healing properties of plants drove me further, and I surpassed him soon enough in this.

There were times when we helped each other in tending to the sick; he had the strength to wrench a joint back into place, or strap a broken limb; I had the skill to brew a draught or prepare a lotion just right for its purpose. Between us we helped many, and people grew used to me, still a child, peering into their eyes or down their throats, and prescribing

45

some nostrum. My remedies worked, and that was all people really cared about.

There'd been some that were hard to help. When the Fair Folk got to you, there wasn't much hope. There was a girl once, who'd lost her lover to the queen under the hill. Out courting in the forest at night, silly things, and strayed into a toadstool ring while their thoughts were elsewhere. The queen took him, but not her. All she saw was the red plume of his cap disappearing into a crack in the rocks, and their high voices laughing. When the girl got to us, her mind was half gone, and neither Father Brien's prayers nor my sleeping draughts gave her much peace. He did his best, treating spellbound lover and mazed wanderer with the same commitment as he gave the cuts and burns of farmer and blacksmith. His hands were strong, his voice gentle, his manner entirely practical. He listened much and said little.

He made no attempt to impose his religion on us, though there was plenty of opportunity. He understood that our household followed the old ways, even if the observance of them had slipped somewhat since the death of our mother. From time to time I heard him discussing with Conor the ways in which the two faiths differed, and what common ground they might have, for he shared Conor's love of debate. Sometimes I wondered if Father Brien's tolerant views had been the cause of his departure from the house of prayer at Kells, for it was said that in other parts of Erin the spread of the Christian faith had been hastened with sword and fire, and that now the old beliefs were little more than a memory. Certainly, Father Brien never sought to convert us, but he did like to say a few prayers before each campaign departure, for whatever he thought of my father's purpose, there could be no harm in sending the men on their way with a blessing.

The clank of metal awoke me. I got groggily to my feet, picking straw out of my hair. The donkey had her nose deep in the feed trough.

'You missed everything,' observed Padriac, busily forking fresh straw into the stall. 'Finbar's going to be in trouble again. Nowhere to be found, this morning. Father was highly displeased. Took Cormack instead. You should have seen the grin on his face. Cormack, that is, not Father. I'll eat my hat if I ever see *him* crack a smile. Anyway, off they went, after the old man said his paternosters and his amens, and now we can get back to normal. Until next time. I wouldn't want to be Finbar, when Father catches up with him.'

He put his fork away and moved to check on the owl, tethered on a perch in a dark corner of the barn. Her wing was close to mending and he hoped to release her into the wild soon. I admired his persistence and patience, even as I averted my eyes from the live mice he had ready for her meal.

Finbar had disappeared. But it was not unusual for him to go off into the forest, or down to the lake, and nobody commented on his absence. I had no idea where he had gone, and did not raise the subject for fear of drawing attention to myself, or to him and our nocturnal activities. I was worried, too, about my poison, and it was with some relief that I saw the four guards emerge, that first afternoon, to sit in the courtyard clutching their heads, yawning widely and generally looking sorry for themselves. By supper time the word had got around that the prisoner had escaped, slipped away somehow between Colum's departure and the change of guards, and there were many and varied theories as to how such an unthinkable thing could have happened. A man was despatched after Lord Colum, to give him the bad news.

'The Briton won't get far,' said Donal sourly. 'Not in the state he was in. Not in this forest. Hardly worth going after him.'

On the second day, Eilis and her retinue left for home, with their own six men and two of ours as escort. The weather was turning; gusts of cool wind whipped the skirts of the ladies and the cloaks of their men at arms, and scudding clouds raced across the sun. Conor, as the eldest son still home and therefore de facto master of the house, bid Eilis a formal farewell and invited her to return when things settled down. Eilis thanked him prettily for the hospitality, though in my eyes it had been somewhat lacking. I wondered how long she'd have to wait to see Liam again, and whether she minded very much. Then I forgot her, for Finbar appeared at supper the next night, as if he'd never been away. Padriac, absorbed in his own pursuits, had hardly noticed his brother's absence; Conor made no comment. I stared at Finbar across the table, but his thoughts were concealed from me and his eyes were intent on his plate. His hands breaking bread, lifting a goblet, were steady and controlled. I waited restlessly until the meal was over, and Conor stood, signalling permission to leave. I followed Finbar outside, slipping behind him like a smaller shadow, and confronted him in the long walk under the willows.

'What happened? Where were you?'

'Where do you think?'

'Taking that boy somewhere, that's what I think. But where?'

He was quiet for a bit, probably working out how little he could get away with telling me.

'Somewhere safe. It's best if you don't know.'

'What do you mean?'

'Think about it, Sorcha. Even you have put yourself at risk now. If Father, or Liam, found out what we've done, they would be ... well, angry is an understatement.'

'All we did was save someone from being hurt,' I said, knowing there was far more to it than that.

'They would see it as a betrayal. Stabbing your own kin in the back. Setting free a spy. To them it's all black and white, Sorcha.'

'Whose side are you on anyway?'

'There are no sides, not really. It's more a case of where you come from. Don't the Britons come here to seize our lands, learn our secrets, destroy our way of life? To help them is to go against kinship and brotherhood and all that's sacred. That's the way most people see it. Maybe it's the way we should see it.'

After a long time I said, 'But life is sacred, isn't it?'

Finbar chuckled. 'You should have been a brithem, Sorcha. You always find the argument I can't answer.'

I raised my brows at him. I, with my bare feet and straggly hair, a maker of judgements? I found it hard enough to tell the difference between right and wrong sometimes.

We both fell silent. Finbar leaned back against a tree, resting his head against the rough bark, his eyes closed. His dark figure blended into the shadows as if he were part of them.

'So why did you do it?' I asked after a while. He took some time to answer. It was getting cold, and an evening dampness was in the air. I shivered.

'Here,' said Finbar, opening his eyes and putting

49

his old jacket around my shoulders. He was still wearing the same shirt he'd had on that night. Was it really only three days ago?

'It's as if everything is part of a pattern,' he said eventually. 'Almost as if I'd had no choice, as if it was all set out for me, on a sort of map of my life. I think Mother saw what was ahead for all of us, maybe not exactly, but she had an idea of where we were going.' He touched the amulet that hung always around his neck. 'And yet, as well as that, it's all about choices. Wouldn't it be easier for me to be one of the boys, to earn Father's love with my sword and bow – I could do it – take my place at his side and defend our lands and our honour? It would be good to have recognition, and fellowship, and some kind of pride. But I choose this path instead. Or it is chosen for me.'

'So where's the boy then? Did he get away?'

As I have said, Finbar and I had two ways of talking. One was with words, like everyone else. The second was for us alone; it was a silent skill, the transfer of image or thought or feeling straight from one mind to the other. He used it now, showing me Father Brien's cart, loaded with bundles and boxes, making its slow way along the rutted track to the hermit's cave. I felt wincing pain at each jolt of the cart, though Father Brien held the old horse to a stately walk. A wheel rim got stuck; the good Father's young helper jumped down to lever it back onto the track. There was a spring in this young man's step that revealed him as my brother even while the hood concealed his face, for Finbar always walked thus, with a bouncing stride and his toes out. Then an image of the two of them, outside the cave, lifting one long bundle with special care from the cart. A gleam of gold amidst the stained wrappings. That was all; the shutters closed.

'He was in no state to go any further,' said Finbar flatly. 'But he's in good hands. That's all you need to know – no,' as I made to interrupt, 'I won't have you involved any more. I've put enough people at risk already. It's finished, for you at least.'

And that, indeed, was all I could get out of him that night. He was becoming alarmingly adept at closing his mind to me, and neither by pleading nor by trying to read him at an unguarded moment could I learn any more. However, his prediction proved to be entirely wrong.

There followed a quieter time. With Father and the older boys away, we fell back into our old routine, although the guard had increased around the keep and the enclosure. Conor controlled the household affairs with calm competence, arbitrating when two cottagers came to blows over an errant flock of geese, overseeing the autumn brewing and baking, the culling of yearling calves, the salting of meat for winter. For Finbar, Padriac and me it was a good time. Donal still put the boys through their paces with sword and bow, and they still spent time with Conor, following more learned pursuits. I usually slipped into these lessons, thinking a little scholarship would do me no harm, and that I might pick up something interesting. Each of us could read and write thanks to Father Brien's kindness and patience. It was not until much later that I realised how unusual this was, for most households were lucky if they had a scribe who knew sufficient of basic letters to set down a simple inventory. For more complex tasks, such as drawing up contracts between neighbours, one must seek out a monk, or a druid, according to one's own persuasion.

Druids were hard to find, and harder still to pin down. We owed a great deal to Father Brien's openness of mind. We knew the runes, and we could reckon, and make a map, and had a fine repertoire of tales both old and new. In addition, we could sing, and play the whistle, and some of us the small harp. We'd had a bard once, that wintered over; that was a while ago, but he taught us the rudiments, and we had an instrument that had been Mother's, a fine little harp with carvings of birds on it. Padriac, with his genius for finding out and fixing, replaced the broken pegs and restrung it, and we played it in an upper room, where Father couldn't hear us. Without asking, we knew this reminder of her would be unwelcome.

Padriac's owl got better, and was eager to be gone. Padriac had waited until the wing was quite mended, and then one day at dusk we went out into the forest to set her free. There was a grin of pure delight on my brother's face as he released her from his glove for the last time and watched her spread wide those great grey-white wings and spiral up, up, into the tree tops. I did not tell him I had seen the tears in his eyes.

Finbar was quiet. I felt he had plans, but he chose not to share them with me. Instead, between his bouts of archery and horsemanship, his scribing and reckoning, he went for long solitary walks, or could be found sitting in his favourite tree, or up on the roof deep in impenetrable thought. I left him alone; when he wanted to talk, I'd be there. I busied myself with the gathering of berries and leaves, the distillery and decoction, the drying and crushing and storing away, in preparation for winter's ills.

I have spoken of the keep where my family lived, a stark stone tower set deep in the forest, its walls pierced here and there by narrow window slits. Its courtyard, its hedges, its kitchen garden did little to soften the grim profile. But there was more to Sevenwaters than this. Without our walled fields, our thatched barns to house herd and flock over winter, our gardens with their rows of carrots, parsnips and beans, our mill and our strawrope granaries, we could not have survived in such isolation. So, while we felled as few trees as we could, and then only with the deepest respect, the forest had been cleared behind the keep and for some distance to the north, to make room for farm and small settlement. There was no need for ditch or wall here, to keep out marauders. There was no need for escape tunnel or secret chamber, although we did make use of caves to store our butter and cheese against the winter, when the cows would not give milk. Here and there, at other points in the vast expanse of forest, several small settlements existed, all within my Father's túath. They paid tribute, and received protection. All were people of Sevenwaters, whose fathers and grandfathers had dwelt there before them. They might venture out beyond the boundaries sometimes, to a market perhaps or to ride with my father's campaigns, when the services of a good smith or farrier were required. That was all right, for they were forest folk and knew the way. But no stranger ever came in without an escort and a blindfold. Those foolish enough to try, simply disappeared. The forest protected her own better than any fortress wall.

The folk of our own settlement, those that worked Lord Colum's home farm and tended his beasts, had their small dwellings on the edge of the open ground, where a stream splashed down to turn the mill wheel. Every day I would make my way along the track to these cottages to tend to the sick. The crossbred wolfhound, Linn, was my constant companion, for on Cormack's departure she had attached herself to me, padding along quietly behind me wherever I went. At any possible threat, a voice raised in anger, a pig crossing the track in search of acorns, she would place herself on an instant between me and the danger, growling fiercely. Autumn was advancing fast, and the weather had turned bleak. Rain ran down the thatch, turning the path into a quagmire. Conor had overseen some repairs on the most ancient of the cottages, a precarious structure of wattle and clay, and Old Tom, who lived there with his tribe of children and grandchildren, had come out to wring my hand with gratitude when I passed by earlier.

'Sure and the hand of the goddess herself rests on your brother,' he half-sobbed, 'and on you too, girl. One of the wise ones, like his father might have been, that's young Conor. Not a drip in the place, and the peat all cut and dried for hard times.'

'What do you mean?' I asked, intrigued. 'Wise ones? What wise ones?'

But he was already shuffling back inside, eager no doubt to warm his stiff joints by the little turf fire whose smoke curled up through the chimney opening.

I called on a young woman recently delivered, with much difficulty, of twin daughters. I had assisted the village women through the long night of this birth, and was keeping a close eye on the mother, making sure she took the herbal teas I had provided to tighten the womb and bring in the milk. I chose a bad time to make my departure, for the clouds opened as I was half way home, drenching me to the skin and quickly coating my feet in liquid mud. I struggled on; the rumble of thunder deafened me to the squeak of cart wheels approaching, and suddenly there was Father

Brien alongside me, an old sack over his head and shoulders. The horse stood stolid in the rain, ears back.

'Jump on,' shouted the Father over the din of the storm, and stretched out a hand to haul me up onto the seat beside him.

'Thanks,' I managed. There wasn't much point in talking against the roaring of the elements, so I sat quietly and pulled my cloak closer about me. There was a place where the track passed briefly into a grove of old pines, whose lower branches had been trimmed away. Once we reached this semi-shelter, Father Brien slowed the horse right down; the needled canopy filtered the worst of the rain off us, and the noise faded to a dull, distant rumbling.

'I need your help, Sorcha,' said Father Brien, relaxing his hold on the reins and letting the old horse lower his head to search for something to graze on.

I looked at him, taken aback. 'You came down here to find me?'

'Indeed, and must travel home today. I would not venture out in such weather without a good reason. I have a patient who is beyond my power to heal; God knows I have tried, and made some ground. But he needs something now which I cannot give him.'

'You want me to help? To make an infusion, a decoction?'

Father Brien sighed, looking down at his hands.

'I wish it were so simple,' he said. 'Brews and potions I have tried, some with good effect. I have employed many elements you have taught me, and some of my own. I have prayed, and talked, and counselled. I can do no more, and he is slipping away from me.'

I did not need to ask who this patient was.

'I'll help, of course. But I don't know if I'll be

55

much use. My skills are mainly with medicines. You make it sound as if something more is needed?'

There was no way I was going to ask him directly what was wrong with the boy; this was dangerous ground. I had no idea how much he knew, or what I was supposed to tell him.

'You will see for yourself,' he said, picking up the reins. 'In any event, we must go straight back, once you collect your things. I've given him a sleeping draught, and that will keep him quiet for most of today, but we must be there when he wakes, or he may do himself ill.'

'I'm not sure Conor will let me go,' I said.

'Why don't we ask him now?' said Father Brien.

We found Conor alone, writing. There was no mention of Britons, nor of escaped prisoners; Father Brien explained simply that he needed to consult me about a patient, and Conor showed a remarkable lack of curiosity as to the details. He seemed almost to have expected the request, and agreed on the condition that it was only for a few days, and that I would come home as soon as he sent Finbar to collect me. I left the two of them talking, and went to pack a small bundle, wondering as I scanned the stillroom shelves what we might be dealing with: burns, bruises, fever, shock? Father Brien had not been very specific. I took some clothing for myself and small necessities, enough for a few days. I left my wet cloak steaming gently before the kitchen fires. I took a larger one belonging to one of the boys. Regretfully, I was forced to admit that the onset of autumn required me to go shod outdoors, and I thrust my cold feet into a pair of boots which were somewhat too big for them. It was handy being the youngest, and smallest.

'A few days only, mind,' Conor was saying as I

made my way back to the cart. 'I'll send Finbar up for her. And take care on the road; it'll be slick going up that last hill.'

Father Brien was already seated, and despite the brevity of the stop, there was a basket from our kitchens, with bread and cheese and vegetables, tucked in behind him. He gave my brother a grave nod. Conor lifted me up, none too gently, and we were away before I could say a word.

The rain slowly abated to a drizzle. We made our way under bare-branched willows, between the first outcrops of rock, beside the bleakly grey waters of the lake, where not a bird could be seen.

'You know who this boy is, I take it?' said Father Brien casually, never taking his eyes off the track ahead.

'I know what he is,' I corrected cautiously. 'Not who. I have an idea of what happened to him. What I don't know is what I'm supposed to do for him. You'd better tell me that before we get there, if I'm to be of some use.'

He glanced at me sideways, apparently amused.

'Fair enough,' he said. 'The boy had some injuries. Serious injuries. He'd likely have died, if your brother hadn't got him away.'

'With a bit of help from me,' I said, somewhat miffed that my part in the rescue was forgotten already.

'Yes, I heard about that,' said the learned Father. 'Took a bit of a risk, didn't you?'

'I know my dosages,' I said.

'You do, better than most of us, Sorcha. But as I said, this patient has been dosed, and anointed, and prayed over. He was – he had a number of hurts, and these I have attended to as well as I could. Although he will never be quite as he was, his body is healing well enough. His mind is another matter.'

'You mean – he went crazy because of what they did to him? Like that man that used to work in the mill, Fergal his name was – he turned very odd after the little people had him overnight. Is that what you mean?' I remembered the miller, slack-mouthed, trembling, crouched by the hearth covered in dirt.

Father Brien sighed. 'Crazy – no, not quite. This one is of stronger fabric than the Fergals of this world. He may be young, but he is a warrior; it's in his nature to fight back. He resisted his tormentors all through that long night, and I don't doubt that not one word escaped his lips. He's been very sick. He had a raging fever, and some of his injuries might have killed a weaker man outright. He fought death hard, and for a while I thought he had won. But his next battle is the hardest; the battle against himself. He is, after all, not much more than a boy, and the strongest of men suffers damage when his own kind turns against him in evil. The lad will not admit that he is hurt and frightened; instead, he turns his anguish inwards and torments himself.'

I tried to get my mind around this.

'You mean he wants to die?'

'I don't think he knows what he wants. What he needs is peace of mind, a space of time without hate, to put body and spirit together again. I thought to send him to the brothers in the west; but he is too weak to be moved, and cannot yet be trusted in other hands.'

There was quiet for a time, save for the gentle thudding of hooves and a sigh of wind amongst the rocks. We were getting closer now. The track grew narrow and steep, and the trees closed in. Up here there were great oaks, their upper reaches bare of leaves, but shawled with goldenwood, and the depths of the forest were dark with ancient growth. The old horse knew his way, and ambled steadily on.

'Father, if you couldn't heal this boy, I'm sure I can't. As my brothers keep telling me, I'm only a child. Maybe I can fix a wheezy chest, or a case of nettle rash, but this – I hardly know where to start.'

The cart jolted over a stone, and Father Brien's hand shot out to steady me.

'Nonetheless,' he said in his measured way, 'if you cannot, none here can. Conor was sure you were the one to help me. I believe you will know what to do, when you see him. I also believe he will not fear you as he does me. And fear is a great barrier to healing.'

'Conor was sure?' I said, taken aback. 'Conor knew about the boy? But –'

'You need not trouble yourself about Conor,' said Father Brien. 'He will not betray your secret.'

We turned under a rock wall and he drew the horse to an abrupt halt. He swung himself down and reached to help me.

'I hope, while you are here, that we can talk of a number of things. But let us tend to this boy, first of all. And you can decide for yourself what you can do, and what you cannot.'

The air inside the cave was heavy with the smell of curative herbs. My nose told me he'd been burning a mixture to keep the boy longer in the peace of an oblivious sleep; calamint for protection and courage, thyme to keep night terrors away. Also, harder to detect, the spores of a plant we called wolf's claw, and I wondered how he'd known about that one, the use of which was extremely dangerous. A person could not be left under its influence for too long. Wake the sleeper must, and confront his fears, or risk being lost in the dark places of the mind forever.

The outer cave was cool and dry, with openings high in the rock walls. This was Father Brien's healing place. There were many shelves, crowded with dried herbs and spices, bowls and jars and neat piles of folded cloth. A pair of huge oak planks, supported by great stones, served as a working table. An inner chamber opened off this orderly space, and here there was a straw pallet on which lay his charge, rolled deep in a blanket and curled up on himself in protection. Father Brien himself ate and slept in the tiny stone cottage, little more than a cell, nestled under rowan trees not far from the cave mouth. He looked as if he hadn't had much sleep recently; his eyes were deeply shadowed.

'The burns are healing well,' said Father Brien softly. 'He had some internal injuries; with those I did what I could. They'll mend well enough in time. The fever was bad, but I brought it down with sponging and white oak infusions. At the height of it, he spoke much, and revealed more of himself than he would have perhaps wished. But he understands where he is now, and keeps his mouth shut most of the time, even when I speak to him in his own tongue. He does not take kindly to my prayers, or to my good advice. And twice I have stopped him from seeking some instrument to destroy himself, or me. He is still very weak, but not so weak that he could not do some harm, given the opportunity.' He stifled a huge yawn. 'You may like to rest until he wakes; then we shall see.'

I scrutinised the hermit's serene face, now pallid with tiredness.

'He won't wake for a while yet,' I said, glancing at the cocooned figure. 'Let me sit here with him, and you go and get some sleep.'

'You should not be alone with him,' he said. 'He's

unpredictable, and though I need your help, I'm under strict orders not to put you at any risk, Sorcha.'

'Nonsense,' I replied, settling down on the three-legged stool at the rear of the chamber. 'There's your little bell there; and I have a loud voice. Besides, haven't I six brothers to keep in line? Be off with you; a short sleep at least, or you'll be precious little use to anyone.'

Father Brien smiled ruefully, for indeed he was near dropping from exhaustion. 'Very well,' he said, 'but make sure you call me immediately he wakes. Those brothers of yours were very firm.'

He'd said I would know what to do, when I saw the boy. Well, there he was, and a sorry sight to be sure, curled up like a chastised dog, sleeping the dead sleep of one punished almost beyond endurance. His lids were heavy, and there wasn't a lot of spring left in the sunny curls. I tried to imagine him waking; maybe staring at me with the vacant eyes of an idiot, or the mad ones of a wild creature cornered; but all that came into my mind was one of the old stories, and the picture of the hero, Culhan the Venturer, stepping through the woods silent as a deer. I leaned my back against the rock wall and rehearsed his tale quietly to myself. This was a story often told, one of those tales which have a tendency to grow and change from one telling to the next. Culhan had a lot of adventures; he endured many trials to win his lady and regain his honour. It took a while to tell them all out loud, and the boy slept on.

I got up to the part where Culhan must cross the bridge of spears to reach the magical island where his love is imprisoned. While he has faith in his ability, his feet can tread the needle-sharp span of the bridge without harm. But let any seed of doubt take root in his heart, and the spears will slice his feet in two.

'So Culhan took a step, and another. His eyes were like a blue fire, and he fixed them on the distant shore. Before him, the bridge rose in a single, glittering span, and the rays of the sun, catching the spear-points, dazzled his sight.'

I was drowsy myself, with the fumes from Father Brien's tiny brazier; in its lidded compartment, the small supply of soporific herbs must be nearly gone, and the air was starting to clear.

'From her high window, the lady Edan watched the step of his bare feet as they moved with sure and steady grace over the bridge. Then the sun was blotted out as a huge bird of prey swooped down towards the hero.'

I was not so absorbed in my story as to miss the faintest of movements from the pallet beside me. His eyes were firmly closed, but he was awake. I went on, conscious only then in what tongue I had been speaking.

'Shrieking with rage, the enchanter Brieden in birdlike form, struck out at Culhan again and again with talons of iron, with cruel beak and venomous will. For but an instant, the hero faltered, and three drops of bright blood fell from his foot into the swirling waters of the lake. Instantly they changed into the form of three red fishes, that darted away amongst the reeds. The bird gave a harsh cry of triumph. But Culhan drew a deep breath and, never looking down, moved on across the span; and the great bird, shrieking with despair, plunged into the water itself. What became of the enchanter Brieden nobody knows; but in that lake it is rumoured a huge fish lives, of unspeakably foul appearance and exceptional strength. So Culhan came across the bridge of spears, and took back the lady Edan. But ever after, his right foot bore the scar, deep along the length of it, of his moment of doubt. And in his children, and his children's children, this mark can still be found.'

The tale was finished, until its next telling. I got up for the pitcher of water from the table, and saw him watching me from slitted eyes, deep blue and hostile. There was still the faintest shadow of the defiant fury he'd shown in my father's hall, but his skin was pallid and his eyes sunken. I didn't like the look of him much at all.

'Drink,' I said in his own tongue, kneeling down beside the pallet and holding out the cup I'd filled. It was plain water this time; he would just have to live with the consequences, for I knew the signs of one who had been too long under the drugging influence of certain herbs, and I must at least taper off the dosage. He stared at me, silent.

'Drink it,' I repeated. 'You've been asleep a long time; your body needs this. It's just water.'

I took a sip myself, to reassure him. He must be intensely thirsty, there was no doubt of it, after the best part of a day's sleep with the brazier burning; but his only movement was to edge a little away from me, never taking his eyes off my face. I held the cup out towards his lips, my hand brushing his arm as I did so. He started violently, clutching the blanket tightly around him and pressing back hard against the wall, as far away from me as he could get. I could smell the fear and feel the fine vibration that ran through every part of his body. It was like the trembling of a high-bred horse that has been mistreated.

My hand was still steady; I hadn't spilt a drop, though my heart was pounding. I put the cup down by the bed and retreated to my stool.

'Well then, drink it when you're ready,' I said,

settling down and folding my hands in my lap. 'Did you ever hear the story of the cup of Isha now? It was a strange one indeed, for when Bryn found it, after he bested the three-headed giant and entered the castle of fire, it spoke to him as he reached out to take it, dazzled by the emeralds and silver ornaments on it. *He who is pure of heart may drink from me*, it said in a voice that was small but terrible. And Bryn was afraid then to take it, but the voice fell silent, and he took the cup and hid it deep in his cloak.'

I watched him carefully as I spoke; he was still hunched, half-sitting, against the far wall, hugging the blanket around him.

'It wasn't until much later that Bryn came to a little stream and, remembering the cup, took it out to get himself a drink. But strangely, when he drew the goblet from his cloak, it was already full with clear water. He set it on the ground, wondering much, and before he could stop it, his horse bent down its neck and took a long drink. Stranger still, no matter how deep the beast drank, the cup of Isha remained full to the brim. There seemed to be no ill effect on the horse; still, Bryn himself did not use the cup, but dipped his hands into the stream and quenched his thirst that way. For, he reasoned, a dumb animal must be pure of heart, for it knows no different, but plainly this cup is deeply enchanted and must be meant for the greatest man on earth, and I am but a lowly traveller. How could I be worthy enough to drink from such a magical vessel?'

The boy moved one hand; his fingers made a weak semblance of the sign used to ward off evil. I'd seen it sometimes, when travellers passed through, but never before directed at myself.

'I'm no sorceress,' I said. 'I'm a healer; and I'm here to help you get better. That might be hard for you to believe, but it's the truth. I don't lie. There's no reason to be afraid of me, or of Father Brien. We mean you no harm.'

The boy coughed, and tried to moisten his lips with a parched tongue.

'Playing games,' he managed, and the bitterness of his slurred speech was shocking. 'Cat and mouse. Why not just finish me off?'

He had to force the words out, and I could hardly understand him. Still, the fact that he spoke at all was something.

'Does it take so long to learn I won't talk? *Just finish it, damn you.*'

This seemed to exhaust him, and he lay back on the bed, staring up at nothing, the blanket still clutched around him. I chose my words carefully.

'It's men that play games,' I said, 'and men that did this to you. But I'm not asking you to tell any secrets, or do anything but get well. This is no cup of Isha; drink from it and you get only what your body needs. Anyway, it was one of my brothers that rescued you, and I helped him. Why would I want to harm you, after that?'

He turned his head slightly then, and his look was dismissive.

'One of your brothers,' he said. 'How many of them do you have?'

'Six.'

'Six,' he echoed scornfully. 'Six killers. Six demons from hell. But how could you understand? You're a girl.'

His tone held both venom and fear. I wondered how Father Brien had managed thus far; perhaps the herbs had kept the boy cooperative and docile, so that what he needed could be done without dispute.

'My brother risked a great deal to help you,' I said, 'and so did I.' *But you were tortured in my house, by my people.* 'My brother always does what is right. He never betrays a secret. And I may seem a child to you, but I do know what I'm doing – that's why I was sent for. I don't know what they plan for you, but you will certainly be helped to reach a place of refuge, and then to return home.'

He gave a harsh bark of laughter, so sudden it startled me.

'Home!' he retorted bitterly. 'I think not.' He had relaxed his grip on the blanket, and twisted his fingers together. 'There's no place for me there, or anywhere. Why should you bother with me? Go back to your dolls and your embroidery. Sending you here was foolish. What do you think it would take for me to kill you? A quick grab at the hair, a little twist of the neck . . . I could do it. What was he thinking of, this brother?'

He flexed his fingers.

'Good,' I said approvingly, trying to keep my voice steady. 'At least you're starting to think, and look around you. Maybe my brother was wrong, and Father Brien; expecting a warrior such as yourself to repay a debt in kind. Maybe they thought there was a code of honour amongst your people, as with ours.'

'Honour? Huh!' He looked directly at me, and I could see that his face might be handsome in the way of the Britons, were it not for the marks of pain and exhaustion. The nose was long and straight, the planes of the face well chiselled and strong. 'You know nothing, girl. Tell your brother to take you through a village after he and his men have finished with it. Let him show you what's left. Ask him if he's ever spitted a pregnant woman like a sucking pig.

Remind him of your people's habit of slicing the limbs off their victims while they scream for a quick end.' His voice rose. 'Question him on the creative uses of hot iron. Then talk to me about codes of honour.'

He broke off, and began to cough, and I went over to him without thinking and held up the cup of water to his lips. Between the paroxysm of coughing, and trying to breathe, and the trembling of my hand, most of the water went over the bed, but he did swallow a couple of drops despite himself. He drew breath finally, wheezing painfully, and looked at me over the rim of the cup, seeing me for the first time.

'Damn you,' he said quietly, and he took the cup out of my hand and drank the little that was left. 'Damn you all.'

Father Brien chose this moment to appear at the doorway, took one look at my face and ordered me outside. Sitting under the rowans, listening to the small sounds of bird and insect about their daily business, I wept for my father, and for my brothers, and for myself.

Father Brien stayed inside a long while. After a time, my tears subsided to a faint hiccup or two, and I blew my nose and tried to get past the hurt of what the boy had said, and concentrate on why I was there. But it was hard; I had to argue with myself every step of the way.

Finbar is good. I know him as I know myself.

Why didn't he speak up, then? Why wait until the damage was done, to perform a rescue? And what about the others? They did nothing.

Liam is my big brother. Our guide and protector. Our mother gave him that task. He would not do evil things.

Liam is a killer like his father. So is the smiling

Diarmid. He turns a sunny face to you, but truly he seeks to be just like them both.

What about Conor, then? He does not go to war. He is just. He is a thinker.

He, too, could speak out, and does not.

But he helped us. At least I think he did; he knew about the boy, and he never stopped me.

Conor is a skilful player of games.

Cormack knows nothing of war yet; to him it's all fun and sport, a challenge. He would not condone torture.

He'll learn soon enough. He hungers for the taste of blood.

And what about Padriac? Surely he is quite innocent of all this, absorbed in his creatures and his experiments?

True enough. But for how long? And what of yourself, Sorcha? For you are no longer innocent.

So I warred with myself, and could not ignore that other voice. Still it was agony to believe: could the brothers that had tended my bruised knees and taken me along, with reasonable patience, on so many childhood adventures really be the cruel and unscrupulous savages the boy had depicted? And if so, where did that leave me, and Finbar? I was not so naive, even at twelve, as to believe only one side in this conflict was capable of torture and hurt. Had we saved the true enemy? Was nobody to be trusted?

Father Brien took his time. I stayed where I was while the conflict within me slowly abated, and my mind was taken over by a stillness that emanated from the old trees themselves, and from the ground which nourished them. This was a familiar feeling, for there were many places in the great forest where you could drink in its energy, become one with its ancient heart. When you were in trouble, you could find your way in these places. I knew them, and Finbar knew them; of the others I am not so sure, for often when the two of us sat quiet in the fork of a great oak or lay on the rocks looking into the water, they were running, or climbing, or swimming in the lake. Even so, I was learning how little I knew my own brothers.

The rain had stopped completely, and in the shelter of the grove the air was damp and fresh. Birds came out of hiding; their song fluted overhead, passing and passing, very high. At such still moments, voices had spoken to me many times, and I had taken these to be the forest spirits or the souls of the trees themselves. Sometimes I felt it was my mother's voice that spoke. Today, the trees were quiet, and I was in some distant place of the mind when a slight movement on the other side of the clearing startled me out of my trance.

There was not the least doubt in my mind that the woman who stood there was not of our world; she was exceptionally tall and slender, her face milk-white, her black hair down to her knees, and her cloak the deep blue of the western sky between dusk and dark. I stood up slowly.

'Sorcha,' she said, and her voice was like a terrible music. 'You have a long journey before you. There will be no time for weeping.'

It seemed crucially important to ask the right questions, while I had the chance. Awe made me tongue-tied, but I forced the words out.

'Are my brothers evil, as this boy tells me? Are we all cursed?'

She laughed, a soft sound but with a strength in it beyond anything human.

'No man is truly evil,' she said. 'You will discover

this for yourself. And most of them will lie, at least some of the time, or tell the half-truths that suit them. Bear this in mind, Sorcha the healer.'

'You say a long journey. What must I do first?'

'A longer journey than you can possibly imagine. You are already on the path set out for you, and the boy, Simon, is one of its milestones. Tonight, cut golden-wood. This herb you may use, to quieten his mind.'

'What else?'

'You will find the way, daughter of the forest. Through grief and pain, through many trials, through betrayal and loss, your feet will walk a straight path.'

She began to fade before my eyes, the deep blue of her cloak merging with the darkness of the foliage behind her.

'Wait –' I started forwards across the clearing.

'Sorcha?' It was Father Brien's voice, calling me from within the cave. And she was instantly gone, as if there had been nothing there but afternoon shadows shifting in the breeze. Father Brien emerged from the cave mouth, drying his hands on a cloth.

'I see we have a visitor,' he said mildly. I glanced at him sharply, then away into the shadows. Emerging cautiously into the clearing, as if uncertain of her welcome, was the dog, Linn. It seemed she had trailed me all the way up here. I spoke kindly to her and she ran to me in frenzied response, her whole body wagging in belated recognition and the urgent need of affection.

'Come inside,' said Father Brien. 'Bring the hound, she can do no harm. We need to talk about this boy, and quickly. The effects of my draught are all but gone, and I hesitate to give him more. But if he cannot be convinced to cooperate, I will be unable to attend to his injuries.' He turned to go inside. 'Are

70

you recovered?' he added gently. 'He knows where to aim his words for most hurt. This is perhaps the only weapon he has left to him.'

'I'm all right,' I said, my head still full of my vision. I put a hand down to touch the dog's rough coat, and the rasp of her tongue on my fingers reassured me that the real world was still there, as well as the other. 'I'm fine.'

The boy sat hunched on the pallet, his back to us. For all his defiant words and angry looks, the set of his shoulders reminded me of a small creature chastised too hard, who retreats into himself in bewilderment at a world turned wrong.

'His wounds must be cleaned and dressed,' said Father Brien in our own tongue. 'I've managed quite well while he was half-asleep, despite his fear of my touch. But now . . .'

'He must come off these herbs,' I said, 'if you want any chance of returning him home in his right mind. We should clear the air completely, and he should be taken outside in the warmth of the day, if we can manage it. Can he walk?'

A look crossed Father Brien's placid face briefly; a chilling look that mingled disgust and pity.

'I have not dared to move him, save to tend to his injuries,' he said carefully. 'He is still in great pain, and withdrawing the soporifics too quickly will be hard for him to bear. Without them, sleep will be difficult, for he fears his dreams.'

My vision still bright before my eyes, I felt a strong sense of what must be done, though truth to tell, the Lady had given me little by way of practical instructions. But something within me knew the path.

'Tomorrow,' I said. 'Tomorrow he must be shown the sun, and the open sky. From now on, just the one herb, just goldenwood, and it must be cut at night. I'll do that later. Now what about dressing these wounds?'

I moved towards the pallet. Linn slipped past me and padded trustingly up to the boy on her large hound paws. She knew that he was not Cormack; but he was close enough. She sidled forward and thrust her cold nose into his hand.

'Easy, Linn,' I said in the language the boy knew. After the first instinctive clenching of his fist, he let his fingers relax and she licked them enthusiastically. He watched her through narrowed eyes, giving nothing away.

Father Brien had prepared a bowl of warm water with chamomile and mallow root; and soft cloths. There had perhaps been an attempt to start the task while I was outdoors, for the bedding was disarranged and more water had been spilt. He moved towards the bed.

'I said, no.' The boy spoke with finality.

'You must know,' replied Father Brien, unperturbed, 'as a soldier, what happens if such wounds are left untreated; how they attract evil humours, and turn foul, and how fevers then overtake the man so that he sees apparitions and, burning, dies. Would you invite such an end for yourself?' His tone was mild as he washed his hands with care and dried them on the cloth.

'Let her do it.' The boy threw a glance at me without turning his head. 'Let her see what her people have done, and so pay penance for it. I spoke plain truth. My body is witness to that.'

'I think not,' said Father Brien quickly, and for the first time there was an edge to his voice. 'Sorcha is a child; such injuries are not fit for a girl's eyes, and it shames you to suggest this. It is man's work, and I will do it.'

'Touch me again and I'll kill you both.' He meant this all right; and might just have enough strength to try. 'Let the girl do it, or leave me to rot. I can go no lower, surely.'

'I doubt if you could manage to do what you say, however much you might want to,' I said. 'But I'll tend your wounds, on one condition.'

'Condition?' the Briton snapped. 'What condition?'

'I'll do everything that needs doing,' I told him firmly. 'But only if you cooperate. You must listen when I talk to you, and do as I bid, for I have the power to heal you.'

He laughed at me. It was not a pleasant sound.

'Arrogant little witch, aren't you? I'm not sure I wouldn't rather be left to the decay and the fever. Still, the end result might be the same, anyway. What do you think, old man?'

'I don't like it, and neither would your brothers, Sorcha. You should leave this to me.'

'Then why did you bring me here?' I asked simply. And since he had no answer to this, he fell silent.

'Out,' said the boy, knowing a victory when he saw it, and Father Brien went, reluctantly submitting to the inevitable.

'I'll be just outside, Sorcha,' he said in our tongue, of which it seemed the boy had no understanding, 'and this time don't wait so long to call. What you see will distress you, and I can offer no help for that. Treat him as you would a sick animal, and try not to take the guilt for what was done on yourself, child.'

'I'll be all right,' I said, for the spirit of the Forest Lady was still on me and my sense of purpose strong.

I will not dwell on what came next. To strip before me and submit to my ministrations was painful for him, both in body and spirit. To witness his injuries,

73

to comprehend the vile nature of man's imagination, was an experience that burned as deep into my heart as the instruments of torture had into his body. He would never be whole again, or know that heedless joy in his manhood that I had seen in my brothers as they wrestled together for sport, or flirted with a likely lass. That another man could do this to him was unthinkable. As I worked, I told him the rest of the tale of Isha, for that took both our minds beyond the dreadful task; and Linn sat anxiously by the bed, licking delicately at the Briton's tightly clenched fist. Still he cringed from my touch, but having agreed to the bargain, he was stoical under the pain, and only cried out once.

At last, the tale was almost finished, and my work over. My body drenched with sweat and my face wet with tears, I eased the patient into the most comfortable position that could be managed, and spread a fresh blanket over his cleanly wrapped body. In the few moments it took me to fetch the pitcher of water, the dog was up on the bed and stretched out beside him, tail thumping gently. Her expression told me she hoped I would pretend not to notice.

'Well done, Simon,' I said, holding a cup of water for him to sip, and this time he did; he was too exhausted to protest, beyond fear. 'Perhaps you can sleep now – one of us will be here if you need us. Linn!' I snapped my fingers. 'Down!'

'No . . .' His voice was a thread of sound. 'Leave her.' His hand curled into her wiry grey coat.

I moved, thinking to fetch Father Brien. I was too tired to feel hungry, but my work for that day was not over yet.

'No.'

I looked down at him.

'Stay.'

'I'm not a dog, to do your bidding,' I said. 'I must eat, and so should you.'

'The tale,' he said weakly, surprising me. 'Finish the tale. Did Bryn ever drink from the cup, or did he doubt himself forever?'

I sat down again slowly.

'He did,' I said, finding the will to go on from somewhere deep within me, though it was quite an effort. 'It was much, much later, and it crept up on him unnoticed, for after all his adventures, and the ill that befell so many others after they tried to use the cup of Isha, what did he do but put it on a shelf at the back of his cottage, and forget about it. There it sat, with its emeralds and rubies, amongst the old crocks and pewterware, and not a soul noticed it for many a long day. For Bryn stayed in his cottage, beside the enchanted forest with its tangle of thorns, and grew old there; and still he guarded its one entrance, and let none pass, neither man nor beast. There were plenty of young girls that would have wooed him away, if he'd have liked, but he refused them all politely. I'm just a humble man, he'd say, not good enough for the likes of you, fine ladies. And besides, my heart is given.

'Over the years, there were plenty of chances to ride away – to a war with the soldiers, or to make a fortune with travellers, but he'd have none of it. This is my watch, he told them, and here I stay, though I die at my post. And when the three score years were up, and Bryn was an old, old man with a white beard down to his boot tops, the curse was lifted and the wall of thorns dissolved; and out came an old, old lady in a tattered white gown, with a face wrinkled like a prune. But Bryn knew her instantly for his beloved, and fell on his knees before her, giving thanks for her deliverance.

' "I'm thirsty," said the old woman in a cracked voice (but to Bryn it was the most heavenly sound he'd ever heard). "Fetch me a drink, if you please, soldier." And since there was only one cup in his humble house fit for a lady of her standing, the old man fetched the cup of Isha from his dusty kitchen shelves and lo, it was full to the brim with fresh, clear water. With trembling hands he offered it to the lady.

' "You must drink first," she said, and he was powerless to go against her will. So he took a sip, and she took a sip, and the precious stones on the cup glowed bright as stars. When Bryn looked up, there was his sweetheart before him, as young and lovely as the day he'd lost her. And when he looked in the cup of Isha, his reflection showed curls of raven black and a dazzling, sunny smile. "But – but I thought . . ." he could scarce get a word out, for his heart was beating like a great drum. His sweetheart smiled, and took his hand. "You could have drunk from it all along," she said, "for who but a man pure of heart could wait three score years for his beloved?" She put the cup down on a stone beside the road, and then they went into the little cottage together, and got on with the rest of their lives. And the cup of Isha? There it rests amongst the bracken and daisies, waiting for the next traveller to find it.'

The boy was almost asleep, his face nearer to repose than I'd seen it yet, but wary still. He spoke in a whisper.

'If you're not a witch,' he said, 'how did you know my name?'

One of the Fair Folk told me. That was the truth, but I could hardly expect him to believe it. I thought quickly.

As I said before, lying was a skill I never came to grips with, being no better at it than my brother Finbar.

'I will answer that when I see you on your feet and out in the air,' was the best I could manage. 'Now you must rest, while I see what food Father Brien has for us. The dog must be hungry too.'

But when I tried to call Linn to follow me, she lowered her whiskery muzzle onto her paws, and simply looked at me with liquid, doggy eyes. Simon's hand rested on her back, fingers moving against her rough coat. And so I left the two of them, for a while.

There followed the strangest time of my young life, up till then at least, for what came later was not merely strange but almost outside mortal understanding. On that first night I did as the Lady had bid me, going out alone under the great oaks, and climbing up high to where the delicate net of goldenwood hung suspended like a constellation of stars between the massive boughs of the forest giant. I used a small sickle to cut down what I needed. Father Brien was somewhat concerned that I might fall, or cut myself instead of the plant. But I explained to him how this herb is sacred to those of the old faith. Indeed, it is so mystic and powerful that its true name is secret, neither to be spoken aloud nor given written form. We called it goldenwood, or birdlime, or some other name in place of its true title. It is a strange herb, outside the laws of nature, for it does not grow towards the light, as other plants do, but in what direction it will, up, down, to east or west as the fancy takes it. Nor does it root in the ground, but grows from the upper reaches of oak, apple, pine or poplar, twining itself around their limbs, resting in their canopies. It takes no account of the seasons, for it can bear both ripe and green berries, and flowers, and new leaves all at the same time. There are strict rules about cutting it, and I had followed them as well as I could, since it appeared I had been given permission.

Goldenwood could be used in many ways, and I employed most of them in my attempt to help the Briton. Woven in a circle and hung over his pallet, it had some efficacy in keeping his night terrors at bay. I made an infusion, and we all drank that, but sparingly. My cure relied partly on clearing Simon's body of the herbal influences which had been so essential up till now; but this physic, the most powerful of all, he still needed. As I had gathered it under a waxing moon, I had seen an owl fly overhead, dipping and rising in the cold silence of the night sky. Maybe she was the one I knew, now again part of the dark world's fabric.

The few days Conor had sanctioned came, and went, and so did Finbar. He rode up on a sturdy hill pony whose strong back could easily bear us both home. Father Brien was in his cottage, doing some fine work with pen and inks, while Simon and I sat (or lay, in his case) on the grass a little further down the hill. Moving him had been a nightmare, the first time. Every step was agony for him, but he refused to be carried by an old man and a scrawny brat who talked too much, as he put it. So he walked, and put his teeth through his lip keeping silent, and I felt the pain piercing through my own body as I held his arm and walked beside him.

'I hope you know what you're doing, Sorcha,' said Father Brien. He looked anxious, but he was leaving the treatment in my hands. On the other side of Simon, the dog padded steadily along, curbing her usual high spirits, leaning in slightly to help him stay upright. His hand gripped her collar.

'I do,' I said, and Father Brien took my word for it.

So, on the day Finbar came there we were, the three of us, Simon, me and the dog, but she had left our side to sniff around under the trees, tail whipping from side to side as she scented rabbit. We'd talked a lot by then or rather, I'd talked and Simon listened, having little choice in the matter. I asked him nothing, and he gave away nothing; so I relied on the old tales, and snippets of song, and occasionally I talked about my forest and some of the strange things that happened there. He could be rude, and even cruel, and he was both when it suited him. I heard plenty about my people's nature, and what they had done over the years to his own folk; and he was imaginative in his insults to me and to Father Brien. These I could handle well enough; the tales of war were harder for me, which is probably why I talked most of the time – at least that kept him quiet. His mood was changeable; it could snap from exhausted tolerance to fury to terror at a moment's notice, and tending him drained my energy more than any other patient I had encountered. I dressed his wounds twice a day, for he would let Father Brien nowhere near him. This was one task I never got used to.

By then there was a sort of acceptance developing between us. Although he scoffed at the unlikeliness of it all, I knew he liked my tales. The fresh air and the walking, hard though it was for him, had brought a slightly better colour to his face, and the cornflower eyes were not quite so lifeless. I brushed his hair; he made more fuss about the pulling out of knots and tangles than he ever had about the cruel pain of his injuries. I took his general ill temper as a good sign; for anything was better than the blank-eyed despair with which he waited for the endless day to pass, the ashen-faced terror of his night waking.

Then Finbar came. His pony had walked the last part of the dirt track; he left her some distance away and came on by foot. From habit, he moved in total silence, so his appearance was quite sudden, there on the edge of the grove. And Simon was up in a flash, his swift rasping intake of breath the only indicator of what this movement cost him, and then I felt my hair gripped from behind and cold metal at my neck.

'Move one step further and I'll slit her throat,' he said, and Finbar stopped dead, white-faced. There was no sound save for the single note of a distant bird calling to a rival; and Simon's laboured breathing somewhere behind me. Finbar stretched out his hands very slowly, showing them relaxed and empty; and then he lowered himself to the ground, back straight as a young tree, eyes watchful. His freckles stood out against his pallor and his mouth was a thin line. I could hear Father Brien humming to himself within the cottage. The knife eased away from my throat, slightly.

'This is your brother?'

'One of them,' I managed, my voice coming out in a sort of squeak. Simon loosened his grip a little. 'Finbar saved you. He brought you here.'

'Why?' The voice was flat.

'I believe in freedom,' said Finbar with admirable steadiness. 'I've tried to right wrongs where I can. You are not the first I have helped in such a way, though what became of them afterwards I do not know. Will you let my sister go?'

'Why should I believe you? Who in his right mind would send a little girl into his enemy's arms, alone except for a doddering cleric? Who would turn traitor to his own family? What sort of man does that? Maybe you have a troop of warriors, there in the trees, ready to take me and finish what they started.'

Simon's voice was under control, but I could feel the tension in his body, and knew staying upright and holding me must be agony for him. He would not last much longer. I spoke to Finbar directly, without words, mind straight to mind.

Leave this to me. Trust me.

Finbar blinked at me, relaxing his guard for a moment. I read in his thoughts an anger and confusion that I had not seen in him before.

It's not you I don't trust. It's him.

I have never been prone to the weaker characteristics of a woman; in fact, despite my small size and apparent delicacy I am a strong person and able to endure much. I should never have thought myself capable of such a deception, and I risked much in my guess at Simon's probable reaction. But at the time, it was the only thing I could think of. So I gave a slight moan, and buckled at the knees, and it was to Simon's credit that he dropped the knife and managed to catch me before I hit the ground. I kept my eyes firmly shut, listening to Finbar making noises of brotherly concern, and Simon regaining his weapon and warning my brother away. Then Father Brien's voice – alerted by the noise, he was at my side quickly and wiping my face with a damp cloth that smelt of lavender. Opening my eyes cautiously, I met a very wry expression on the good Father's face. He didn't miss much.

I turned my head one way. Finbar sat exactly as before, cross-legged, bolt upright, his expression well-schooled. I turned my head the other way. Simon was very close, his back against a large stone, the knife held loosely between his hands. I felt he had been watching me, but now his eyes were turned away, towards the trees. I did not like the look of his skin, which was showing that sweaty pallor that I'd hoped was gone for good.

All four of us were apparently at a loss as to where to go next. The problem was solved unexpectedly by the wolfhound, Linn, who had tired of her rabbit hunt, and now hurtled towards us out of the forest, ecstatic to see so many friends at once. First she leapt on Finbar, planting her feet on his shoulders and washing his face with some vigour. Then she bolted over to me, careless of my apparently delicate state of health, and planted heavy feet on my stomach in passing. She circled Simon, quivering with anticipation, but careful, still, not to hurt him.

'Well, children,' said Father Brien matter-of-factly, 'I shall fetch a cup of mead, for I believe we all have need of it. Then we shall talk. Try not to harm one another for a few moments, I beg you.'

He rose, and Simon let him go. Clearly, though, I was not yet free to do the same, for as soon as I managed to sit upright I felt his hand around my arm again, and there was still a fierce determination in his grip. Clearly there was some reserve of strength there that even I had not guessed at.

We sat in uneasy silence until Father Brien returned, bearing a jug and some cups, and then Finbar began to speak in our tongue.

'No!' I said sharply, cutting him off. 'Speak so that Simon can understand you. There have been enough secrets already. We may be enemies but we can at least be civil.'

'You think so?' said Finbar, brows raised. 'The Briton here has hardly shown civility.'

'Now,' said Father Brien, giving each of us a cup, 'let us simulate a truce, at least, and attempt to sort this out. I believe Finbar is here on peaceful business, young man; he was to collect his sister and escort her home.'

'As you see, I am unarmed,' said Finbar, his hands open on his knees. A strand of hair fell across his eyes, but he made no attempt to brush it away. It was me he was watching this time. 'I'm here to fetch Sorcha, that's all. I had been thinking of asking after your health, to see maybe if saving you was worth the bother; but I won't trouble myself with that now.'

He has no intention of hurting me. Can't you see that?

Finbar raised his brows at me, disbelieving. Simon was silent, his cup untouched on the grass beside him. I felt his hand burning against my skin, through the thin fabric of my dress. The dog sniffed at the mead.

'Any news from your father, Finbar?' Father Brien asked casually.

'Not yet. It will be some time longer, I think. Your patient will be safe enough until he can travel. It would be good to be able to say the same for my sister. For one who was called here to heal, it seems she has not been treated kindly. I think I have come none too soon.'

Simon's voice was cruel. 'What did you expect? A jubilant welcome? Fawning gratitude? Give me one reason why I should be thankful to be returned to life!'

There was a silence.

'Son,' said Father Brien eventually, 'the future seems dark to you at present, and there is no telling where your way will lead. But there is a light on every path. In time you will find it.'

'Spare me your homespun faith,' said Simon wearily. 'I despise it, and you.'

'You are hardly in a position to throw it back in his

face,' said Finbar mildly. 'He cares for you and your kind because of that very faith. Without it, he might be a killer like my kinsmen. And, perhaps, like yours.'

'Indeed, I was once just such a man. I know the power of a cause, and how it can blind you to reality. Finbar sees this already. Perhaps your mission in life will be to learn it.' Father Brien was reflective.

'What do I care for your missions! I am fit for nothing. As fast as she patches me up, I fall apart, stinking of decay. You would have done better not to meddle, but to leave me where I was. The end would have been quicker.' Simon's voice was still under control, but a convulsive shiver ran through his body. I opened my mouth to speak, but Finbar got in first.

'I'm taking my sister home,' he said. 'I thought to help you, and so did she. But I will not have her hurt or threatened. We have done what we can, and it seems you have no further need for our services.'

Simon laughed derisively. 'Not so fast, big brother,' he said. 'I still have my knife, and I am not quite helpless. The little witch stays with me. You sent her here to heal me; so let her heal me. For she seems to believe the impossible can happen, if we do not.'

'You forget that she is just a child,' said Father Brien.

'Child? Huh!' Simon gave a mirthless chuckle. 'Outwardly, perhaps. But she's like no child I've ever known. What child knows the properties of herbs, and a thousand stories each stranger than the last, and how to . . .' His voice faltered. Finbar glanced at Father Brien, who gazed back at him reflectively. My arm was starting to hurt a lot, where Simon's fingers clutched it.

'It's not up to you to decide,' I said as firmly as I

could. I looked at each of them in turn – Finbar with his ashen face and clear grey eyes, the mild, penetrating gaze of Father Brien. Simon's touch communicated his pain and despair. 'I have a job to do here, and it's not finished. Between you, you've already undone most of my good work this afternoon. Finbar, you must go home, and leave me to my proper task. Believe that I am safe here, and best left alone. I will call you when I am ready.'

He needs me, Finbar.

I won't leave you here. He tried to keep me out of his thoughts, but he could not quite conceal his guilt and confusion. This worried me. Wasn't Finbar the brother who was always so certain, who always knew what to do?

You must leave me. This is my choice.

And so he did, eventually. It was fortunate that Father Brien trusted me and believed in what I was doing, for it was he who persuaded my brother to move back into the cottage and leave me alone awhile with my patient. Simon let them go, silent. It was only after they were out of sight, and the cottage door closed with a thud, that the restraining grip on my arm changed to a clutch for support, and he let out his breath in a long shuddering gasp. Between us, the dog and I got him back into the cave and lying down, and I broke all my rules and made him a draught that would give him a reasonable sleep. Then I sat by him, talking of nothing much, watching him grapple with the pain and fight to keep silent. After a while, the effects of the herbal infusion stole over him and his features began to relax, his eyes clouding. My arm was hurting quite a lot, and I went quietly over to Father Brien's shelves to seek an ointment, perhaps mallow root or elderflower. I found what I wanted in a shallow lidded bowl, and returned to my stool to anoint my bruises. There was a ring of reddened flesh right around my upper arm. Massaging with the salve relieved the pain a little.

Something made me glance up as I placed the lid back on the bowl. Simon was still awake, just, heavy lids not quite masking the startling blue of his eyes. 'You bruise too easily,' he said indistinctly. 'I didn't mean to hurt you.' Then his lids dropped and he was asleep. The dog moved in closer, wedging herself alongside him on the narrow pallet.

There was a short spell, then, for explanations and decisions. I went to the cottage and we stayed there, but with the door open, for as I told the others, Linn would alert me if Simon wakened. Father Brien insisted that both Finbar and I ate and drank, although neither of us had the stomach for it.

It took a while to persuade Finbar to go home. He still believed me to be in danger, and swore that Conor would never agree to my staying. I used his old argument against him: you should not assume a Briton was evil just because of his golden hair, or his height, or his strange manner of speaking. He was a human being with strengths and weaknesses, just like us. Hadn't Finbar said so himself many times, even to our father?

'But he threatened to kill you,' said Finbar, exasperated with me, 'he held a knife at your throat. Does that mean nothing?'

'He's sick,' I said. 'He's scared. And I'm here to help him. Besides, I was told . . .' I broke off.

Finbar's gaze sharpened. 'Told what?'

I could not lie. 'Told that this was something I must do. Just the first step on a long and difficult path. I know I have to do it.'

'Who told you this, Sorcha?' asked Father Brien gently. They were both staring at me intently now. I chose my words with care.

'You remember Conor's old story, the one about Deirdre, Lady of the Forest? I think it was her.'

Father Brien drew his breath in sharply. 'You have seen Them?'

'I think so,' I said, surprised. Whatever reaction I had expected from him, it was not this. 'She told me this was my path, and I must keep to it. I'm sorry, Finbar.'

'This Briton,' said Finbar slowly. 'He is not the first I have met, or spoken with. The others, though, were older men, more hardened, and at the same time simpler. They were glad enough to take their freedom and go. This one plays games, he toys with us and relishes our confusion. If indeed you have received such an instruction, you have no choice but to obey; yet I can hardly believe this boy means you no harm. I am not happy to leave you here, and I think Conor would agree with me.' He twisted a lock of hair between his fingers. The colour had returned to his face, but his mouth was grim.

I stared at him. 'Why should Conor decide?' I asked. 'He may be in charge, for now, but he's only sixteen.'

'Conor is old beyond his years,' said Father Brien in his measured way. 'In that, he resembles the two of you. He too has a path set out for him. You have, perhaps, taken this brother for granted; the quiet one, with his steady reliability, his kindness and fairness, his fund of knowledge. But you know him less well than you think.'

'He does seem to know a lot of odd things,' I said. 'Things that surprise you.'

'Like the Ogham,' said Finbar quietly. 'The signs, and where to find them, and how to read their meaning. What we know of that we learned from Conor.'

'But where did he learn it?' I said. 'Not from any book, I know that much.'

'Conor is expert in a number of matters,' said Father Brien, gazing out of his small window. The late afternoon sun caught the wisps of greying hair that fringed his calm brow, turning them to a flaming aureole. 'Some he learned from me, as the rest of you did. Some he taught himself from the manuscripts gathering dust in your father's library; as did you, Sorcha, with your cures and your herb lore. You will find, as you grow older, that as well as this knowledge Conor has other, more subtle skills; he carries ancient crafts that belong to your line, but which have been largely forgotten in today's world. You see the village people, how they revere him. It is true that in your father's absence Conor is a good steward, and they acknowledge that with due thanks. But their recognition of him goes far deeper.'

I remembered something then. 'The old man in the village, old Tom who used to be the thatcher, he said something – he said that Conor was one of the wise ones, like Father, or like Father should have been. I didn't understand him.'

'The family of Sevenwaters is an ancient one, one of the oldest in this land,' said Father Brien. 'This lake and this forest are places where strange things come to pass, where the unexpected is commonplace. The coming of such as I, and our faith, may have changed things on the surface. But underneath, here and there, the magic runs as deep and as strong as in the days when the Fair Folk came out of the west. The threads of many beliefs can run side by side; from time to time they tangle, and mesh into a stronger rope. You have seen this for yourself, Sorcha; and you, Finbar, feel its power compelling you to action.'

'And Conor?' asked Finbar.

'Your brother has inherited a weighty legacy,' said Brien. 'It chooses whom it will; and so it did not fall to the eldest, or even to the second, but to the one best able to bear it. Your father had the strength, but he let the burden pass him by. Conor will be the leader of the old faith, for these people, and he will do it quietly and with discretion, so that the ancient ways can still prosper and give guidance, hidden deep in the forest.'

'You mean Conor is – you mean he is a druid? How could he learn this from books?' I asked, confused. Had I known my own brother so ill?

Father Brien laughed softly. 'He could not,' he said wryly. 'This lore is never committed to the page; the tree script that he showed you is its only form of writing. He has learned, and learns, from others of his kind. They do not show themselves, not yet, for it has been a struggle for them to hold on. Their numbers are dwindling. Your brother has a long path to travel yet; he has barely begun his journey. Nineteen years, that is the allotted span for the learning of this wisdom. And it goes without saying that talk of this is not to be spread abroad.'

'I wondered, sometimes,' said Finbar. 'One cannot listen, and move through the villages, without learning whom the people trust and why. It explains why he leaves us to follow our own ways.'

'What did you mean,' I said, still thinking hard, 'about our father being the one, and giving it up?' For I could not imagine Father, with his tight, closed expression and his obsession with war, as the conduit

89

for any kind of spiritual message. Surely that was wrong.

'You need to understand,' said Father Brien gently, 'that your father was not always as he is now. As a young man, he was a different creature entirely, handsome and merry, a man who would sing and dance and tell tales with the best of them, as well as beating them all hollow at riding and archery and combats with sword or bare fists. He was, you'd have said, one favoured by heaven with the full range of blessings.'

'So what changed him?' asked Finbar bleakly.

'When his father died, Lord Colum became master of Sevenwaters. There was, as yet, no call on him to be anything more, for there was one far older and wiser that kept the ancient ways alive in these parts. Your father met your mother; and, as it often is with your kin, he loved her instantly and passionately, so that to be without her was like death to him. They were blissfully happy for eight years; and then she died.'

His face had changed; I watched the light play over his calm features, and thought I detected a deep sorrow there, buried somewhere well within.

'Did you know her?' I asked.

Father Brien turned to me, his eyes showing no more than a faint sadness. Perhaps I had imagined what I saw.

'Oh, yes,' he said. 'I had been presented with a choice. They valued my skill with the pen, in the house of Kells, but my ideas caused – unrest. Conform, I was told, or live alone. I had known your father before I took holy orders, a long time ago when I was a fighting man. When I left the chapter house he offered me a place here, an act of some generosity, considering the differences between us. I met your mother. I saw their joy in each other, and how her death took all the light from him.'

'He had us,' said Finbar bitterly. 'Another man might have thought that reason enough to live, and live well.'

'I think you are too harsh,' said Father Brien, but he spoke kindly. 'You know not, yet, the sort of love that strikes like a lightning bolt; that clutches hold of you by the heart, as irrevocably as death; that becomes the lodestar by which you steer the rest of your life. I would not wish such a love on anyone, man or woman, for it can make your life a paradise, or it can destroy you utterly. But it is in the nature of your kin to love this way. When your mother died, it took great strength of will for Colum to endure her loss. He survived; but he paid a high price. He has little left for you, or for anyone.'

'He had a choice, didn't he?' said Finbar slowly. 'He could have turned another way, after she died – taken another path, become the sort of leader you say Conor will be.'

'He could, for the Ancient was near the end of his days, and the wise ones came to Colum, seeking a man of his line to join their number. They must have wanted him very particularly, to make such an approach. Far better to begin the long years of learning as a child, or a very young man. Yet they asked him. But Colum was deep in despair. Had it not been for his duty to his túath, and to his children, he might well have ended his own life. So he refused them.'

'And that's how they came to choose Conor?'

'Not then. Conor was only a child; they waited, first, and watched you growing up, the seven of you. And the old one delayed his passing. They watched Conor as he learned to read and write, as he practised his verses and his tales, as he taught the rest of you the wisdom of trees, and how to look after one another. In time, it became clear that he was the one, and they told him.'

We sat there in silence for a while, taking this in, as the sun's rays slanted lower through the window and the air grew cool with early evening. No sound came from the cave. I hoped Simon's sleep was dreamless.

'You can see,' said Father Brien eventually, 'what drives your father so hard. Holding onto his lands, and winning back the Islands that were lost so long ago, has taken her place as the sole purpose of his existence. By keeping that foremost in his mind, he holds the wolves of memory at bay. When they close in around him, he goes to war again and silences their howling with blood. This path takes a heavy toll on him. He has, however, rendered his lands and those of his neighbours very secure, and earned great respect throughout the north of this country with his campaigning. He has not won the Islands back, not yet; this he plans to do, perhaps, when all his sons are grown.'

'He'll do it without me,' said Finbar. 'I know the Islands to be mysterious beyond understanding, a place of the spirit, and I long to visit the caves of truth. But I would not kill for the privilege. That is faith gone mad.'

'As I said, a cause can blind you to reality,' said Father Brien. 'Men have fought over these Islands since the days of Colum's great-great-grandfather, since the first Briton trod on that soil, not knowing it was the mystic heart of your people's ancient beliefs. So the feud was born, and a great loss of lives and fortunes followed. Why else would the lord Colum, his father's seventh son, be the one to inherit? His brothers were slain, all of them, fighting for the cause. And their father let them go, one by one.'

'But now he sets his own sons on the same path,' added Finbar grimly.

'Perhaps,' Brien replied. 'But your brothers do not share the obsession of Lord Colum, and besides, there is Conor, and yourselves. It may at last be time for this pattern to be broken.'

I was thinking hard. After a while I ventured, 'You're saying Conor will let me stay here, and try to help Simon – that he understands what the Lady told me, about this all being part of some great design set out for us?'

Father Brien smiled. 'If anyone can break away from a set path it is you, child. But you are right about Conor. He knew quite well why you came to stay here. It is a measure of his strength, and his stature, that he can reconcile this knowledge with his administration of your father's business.'

I frowned. 'You almost make it sound as if Conor should one day be head of the family,' I said. 'But what about Liam? He's always been our leader, ever since Mother told him he had to be; and he's the eldest.'

'There are leaders, and leaders. Don't underestimate any of your brothers, Sorcha,' said Father Brien. 'Now eat, the two of you, for today's work is by no means over.'

But we had no appetite, and the bread and cheese were still barely touched when Finbar said his farewells and with some reluctance turned his pony's head in the direction of home. His parting shot to me was not spoken aloud.

I still don't trust your Briton. You'd better give him a message from me. Tell him, if he lays a finger on you again,

*he'll have not just me but the six of us to answer to. Make
sure you tell him that.*

I refused to take this seriously. Finbar, threatening
violence? Hardly.

*I'll tell him no such thing. You're starting to sound just
like your big brothers. Now get going, and leave me to deal
with this. And don't worry about me, Finbar. I'll be fine.*

'Hm,' he said aloud in a very brotherly way.
'Where have I heard that before? Maybe it was just
before you climbed the fence to pat the prize bull; or
perhaps it was the time you were so sure you could
jump across that creek just as well as Padriac could,
even with your short legs? Remember what happened then?'

'Be off with you!' I retorted, giving the pony a
sharp smack on the rump, and he was away. In the
cave, the dog began to bark. It was time to get back to
work.

CHAPTER THREE

S ome broken things you can't mend. Some you have to put together very slowly, piece by fragile piece, waiting until the last bit of work is strong enough before you try the next. It takes a lot of patience.

It was thus with Simon. Finbar's visit had set us back a good deal, and I had first to repair that damage before starting again on the long process of healing. Simon had made a bargain with me, and it seemed he was a man of his word. Therefore, though he was often in the blackest state of mind, with little will for survival in his damaged body, he would always grit his teeth and follow my orders.

Six or seven days went by, and we moved on with painful slowness. Night time was the worst. Because Simon would not tolerate Father Brien's help, it was I who must attend his every need, though the good Father assisted me as subtly as he could by making sure cloths and salves were close at hand, by keeping linen fresh and providing food and drink, as if by magic, whenever I might find myself free to partake of it. Nonetheless, I was tired, with a bone-deep weariness I had never known before. I used the goldenwood as sparingly as I could. With its help, Simon slept for a short span before the nightmares began, and I learned to fall asleep the instant he did, since for me too this was the only time of respite.

There was a pattern of sorts to these nights. Simon would cry out, and I would wake with a start to find him sitting bolt upright, hands over his face, shivering and gasping. He never told me what he saw, but I could imagine. Then I would light a candle, and I would pass him a cloth to wipe the sweat from his body, while the dog retreated to the doorway, whining anxiously. I ran through many songs and stories during those dark times, and my throat became dry and sore with talking. Some of it Simon heard, and some of it ran past him like leaves in the wind. When the fear was at its worst he let me put my arms around him and sing lullabies, and stroke his hair as if he were a frightened child. At length he would fall asleep again, and exhaustion would overwhelm me, sitting by his bed, so that I slept where I was, my head on the pallet, my hand in his. Such spells were brief. He might wake four, five times in one night; the temptation to dose him with something powerful enough to give us all a whole night's rest was strong, but I knew his path to recovery lay in cleansing the body and learning to live with the fear. For the memories would be with him always, in one guise or another.

He wouldn't let Father Brien near him. It was I, only I who must do it all, wake in an instant, soothe and comfort, keep wounds cleaned and dressed, be there to deal with Simon's every need. That was hard, but it was our agreement. Still, at night Father Brien never left us alone. He would sit in the outer chamber, a candle by his side, waiting until the blessing of sleep should come again. His silent presence was reassuring, for I found the demons of night a formidable challenge.

There were times when I hated Simon, though I could not have said why. I suppose I knew that after this, things would never be quite the same for me. And, after all, I was not yet thirteen, and my mind still strayed to how nice it would be to be home, riding ponies with Padriac or planting out crocus bulbs for spring flowering. I had a longing to work in my little garden, so quiet and orderly, full of fresh scents and healthy, growing things.

After eight or nine such nights, Father Brien and I were looking like ghosts, wan and drained. Then there was a day when the sun came out early, and the air was a little warmer, and I made Simon get up and walk outside, further than usual, so that we were high enough to see over the trees and glimpse the silver of the lake water cradled in the deep grey-green shadows of the forest.

'Our home is down there,' I told him, 'quite near the lake shore, but it's hidden by the trees. On this side, the forest goes right down to the water's edge. On our side, there are rocks in the water, and you can lie on them and watch the fish. And there are paths through the forest, each different from the last.'

'It would be easy to get lost.'

'We don't,' I said. 'But it happens, when people don't know the way.' I thought about this for the first time. How was it that we always did know the way?

Simon leaned back against the trunk of a leafless ash tree, shutting his eyes. 'I have a story for you,' he said, surprising me greatly. 'I don't have your skill in telling, but it's simple enough.'

'All right,' I said cautiously, not knowing what to expect.

'There were two brothers,' said Simon, and his voice was flat and expressionless. 'They were like enough in looks, and strength, and intelligence; but the one had a few years' advantage over the other. Funny, what a difference a few years can make. Their father died; and because of those few years, the elder brother inherited the whole estate. And the other? Just a little parcel of land nobody wanted, that's all he got. The elder was loved by all; he had those few years to establish his claim on their hearts, and gain their loyalty, and he did so with never a thought to his brother. And the younger? Somehow although he was just as good, and strong, and talented as his brother, nobody ever seemed to know it.

'The elder was a leader, and his men looked up to him and respected him. He was a man incapable of error, and he commanded total loyalty wherever he went, without effort. The younger? He did his best; but it was never quite good enough.' Simon fell into silence, as if unwilling to go on.

'So what happened?' I asked eventually.

Simon stretched his mouth into what might have passed for a grin, if not for the coldness of his blue eyes. 'The younger got a chance to prove himself. To do something that everyone, even his brother, couldn't fail to recognise. After that, he thought, I will be like him, just as good as him, better even. He took the chance, and failed.'

'And then what?'

'I don't know, little witch. This story doesn't seem to have an ending. How would you finish it?' He lowered himself to the ground cautiously.

I moved over to make room for him on a fallen branch. Linn was in her element, snuffling around in the autumn leaves, darting here and there, running back to check on us from time to time then bounding off after a new scent.

I chose my words with care. 'It has the makings of a learning tale, though they usually have three brothers, not just the two. I think the younger brother would head off into the world to seek his fortune, and leave his big brother behind. On the way he'd meet three people, or creatures – it's usually three.'

'You have an answer for everything,' said Simon bleakly. 'Tell me the rest.'

'Well, you could end the story in a few different ways,' I said, warming to the task. 'Let's say the little brother meets an old woman. He's hungry, and he only has one oat cake, but he gives it to her. She thanks him, and he goes on. Maybe next he sees a rabbit caught in a snare; and he frees it.'

'He'd more likely skin it and have it for his supper,' said Simon. 'Especially after the oat cake.'

'But this rabbit looks at him with such beautiful green eyes,' I said. 'He has to let her go. Lastly he meets a giant. The giant challenges him to a fight with staves. The young man agrees, feeling he has nothing to lose. They fight for a while, and he gets in a few good blows before the giant knocks him out cold. When he comes to, the giant thanks him politely for a decent bout; of all the travellers that have passed that way, he's the first who has dared to stop and give the giant a bit of amusement. After that, the giant comes along with him, as a sort of bodyguard.'

'Convenient,' said Simon. 'What next?'

'There would be a castle, and a lady in it,' I said, gathering a handful of fallen leaves and berries and absently starting to weave them together. 'He'd see her from a way off, maybe riding by in all her finery as he and his giant friend are trudging along the road, and the instant he sees her, he loves her and he wants her for his own. But there's a problem. To win her, he has to accomplish a task.'

'Or maybe three.'

I nodded. 'That's more common. And here's where his good deeds in the past help him. Perhaps he needs to clean out a huge stable before sunrise, and the old woman turns up with a magic broom and does it in a flash. Then maybe fetching some object, a golden ball, from a deep narrow place, the bottom of a long tunnel under the ground. The rabbit could do that. The last would be a feat of strength, and that's where the giant comes in. So our hero wins the lady, and lives happily ever after.'

'What about his brother?'

'Him? Well, you see, by the time the younger brother has finished all his adventures, and won the lady's heart, he's forgotten all about his big brother and how jealous he was. He's got his own life.'

'I don't like this ending,' said Simon. 'Try another.'

I thought for a bit. 'What if he went to war, and came back to find his brother had died, and all the lands were his?'

Simon laughed, and I didn't like the harshness of it. 'How do you think he would feel about that?'

'Confused, I should think. He gets his heart's desire, which is to take his brother's place. But for ever more, he thinks about those years he wasted, envying his brother instead of getting to know him.'

100

'His brother wasn't interested,' said Simon flatly, and I thought I'd come too close to the mark. I concentrated on the wreath I was weaving. Leaves of russet, deepest brown, golden yellow. Some were already fragile, the last trace of summer slipping away from their skeletal bodies. Berries red as blood. He watched me.

'Sorcha,' he said after a while, and it was the first time he'd used my name instead of 'witch' or 'girl' or something worse. 'How can you believe in these tales? Giants, and faeries, and monsters. They are a child's fantasies.'

'Some may be true, and some not,' I said, threading a long pointed leaf under, and through, and around itself. 'Does it matter?'

He got up, and I heard the change in his breathing as he swallowed a gasp of pain; silence meant control.

'Nothing in life is like your stories,' he said. 'You dwell in your own little world here; you can have no idea of what exists outside it. I wish –' he broke off.

'Wish what?' I asked when he did not go on.

'I would almost wish that you should never discover it,' he said with his back turned to me.

'Don't you think I have begun to?' I stood up, the little wreath in one hand. 'I have seen what they did to you. I have listened to you crying for help. And you have told me yourself such stories of cruelty that I must believe them true. You have hardly thought to spare me.'

'You shut that world out, with your tales.'

'Not entirely,' I said as we began the slow walk back. 'Not for you, or for myself. The tales make it a bit easier, that's all. But you will have to talk about it eventually, if you are to heal and return home.'

Father Brien had given him a strong stick of ash,

and he used it to help him walk; he was still painfully hesitant, but he moved along now without my support. Here, the path was thickly covered with fallen leaves, and the tangled network of bare branches let cold light through to touch them with gold and silver. Linn was ecstatic, digging and sniffing here and there. A bird called; another answered.

'Will I ever be able to sleep again?' he asked suddenly, taking me by surprise. My answer was guarded; I had seen those taken by the Fair Folk, how their madness never quite left them by night or day, how the whirl of memories in their heads gave them no peace.

'It might take a long time,' I said gently. 'You have made some progress; but I cannot lie to you. Such damage does not heal easily. You may be your own best helper, if you choose the right path.'

Simon's body was healing. He had been young, and strong, and resilient, and he was winning the fight against the damage and invasions of that night and the evil humours that had followed. After a time he began to walk without the stick, and he exchanged his first few words with Father Brien, almost without noticing. I greeted each small victory with joy. A kind word, an attempt to do something new for himself, a spontaneous smile, each was a priceless gift. Once the healing process took hold, it gathered speed, and I began to believe we might eventually be able to send him back to his own folk.

It was clear, however, that he could not yet leave our care. Late autumn weather was closing in and the nights were longer and colder. And Simon could not yet shake the demons that beset him during the times of darkness. Over and over, his torturers visited and tormented him, and he fought them, or fled from them, or gave himself up to their mercies. One night I got a black eye out of it, when he rose from his bed half-asleep and tried to escape out into the night. Between us, Father Brien and I stopped him, but I caught the full force of his arm across my face. In the morning he would not believe that he had done this. Another time he caught me off guard, waking before I did, suddenly and in terror, but silent for once; and he had the knife in his hand and turned in on himself before I was aware of it. How I moved fast enough I'll never know, but I grabbed his wrist and hung on, and screamed for Father Brien, and the two of us tried to calm him, while he wept and raved and begged us to kill him and let that be an end of it. And slowly, slowly I spoke to him and sang to him until he grew quiet and almost slept, but not quite. He had stopped talking, but his eyes spoke to me, and their message was plain. He understood too well what the future would be for him, and he asked me why I would not end his pain. What right had I to refuse this?

I had told him many tales. But I could not tell him why I believed he must live and grow well and move on. If he scoffed at the tales of Culhan and the old heroes, the sagas of the folk from the west, if he found the stories of the little folk and the tree people odd, though I myself had seen their work with my own eyes, how could I expect him to believe his destiny and mine were somehow linked in what the Forest Lady had told me? He would never believe that I had seen her myself, there in the clearing in her cloak of midnight and the jewels bright in her hair. Simon was of another folk entirely, a practical, earth-bound people who could credit only the evidence of their own eyes. And yet, if ever I met a person who needed to let the magic and the mystery of the old ways flow through his spirit, it was him. I used it to heal him whether he knew it or not, but without his own faith in himself it could go only so far. Until he could be convinced of a reason to live, we could not safely let him go, even if his body was well enough mended, for he would not last even the first night without us.

I tried to talk of this with him, but he shut me out whenever I drew close to his home, or his family, or whatever it was that drove him. At first he was, I think, adhering strictly to his soldier's training, which had held him silent under torture and which was born of the feud between our peoples. I was the enemy; I should know nothing of him that might give me the advantage, or put his kind at risk. However, those nights of torment, which we endured together whether we wished it or not, changed both of us. Towards the end he recognised me, somehow, as part of his world, and at the same time he knew I was neither of the one side nor the other in this long struggle. With my herbs and my stories, I was to Simon some strange, alien kind of being, but slowly he began to trust me just a little, despite himself.

Father Brien was making plans as best he could. Time was passing and still the night terrors persisted. Wet weather had come on, and I could not keep up Simon's walks; he was restless now, confined to the cave even by daytime, and he vented his frustrations on me by arguing every point. Why must he eat and drink when I told him – what was the use? And, frequently, why did I not go home and play with my dolls, instead of experimenting on him? Why should I bother mending his outdoor clothes, when he would never be fit to do other than lie around being tormented by a crazy girl and a pious old fool? After a while he was driving both of us mad, but at least Father Brien had the luxury of retreating to the cottage to write or meditate. I had made a promise to Simon and I was stuck with him.

I was trying to sew, and kept my eyes on my work as Simon paced around me.

'What are you doing anyway?' he demanded, looking more closely at the over-tunic I had in my hands. 'What is that?'

I showed him. 'You will hardly notice it,' I said. 'But it will help to protect you. The rowan tree is one of the most sacred; such a cross is sewn into all my brothers' garments, when they go to war.' The red thread with which I had bound the tiny rowan cross showed like a drop of blood against the cream wool of the lining. I bit off the thread and folded the tunic, and it was like any other garment.

'I'm not going to war,' said Simon. 'I'm hardly fit for it any more. And maybe wasn't then,' he added in a lower voice, turning away from me.

I placed needles and thread carefully back in their box. 'What do you mean?' I asked.

'I – nothing,' he said, sitting on the edge of the bed, and looking at the floor. I sat still, waiting. After a while he looked up, and his face was white.

'The problem is,' he said with difficulty, 'the problem is not knowing. Not knowing if I – if I was strong enough.'

'Strong enough for what?' But I could guess.

'The problem is – *I can't remember*. Not all of it.' He was shivering now as the memories came flooding back, not in the unthinking visitations of night but by full, waking daylight. 'Not all of it. I'm pretty sure I held out. I held out a long time, I know it, because they were angry, they were so angry –'

'It's all right, Simon,' I said, moving over quickly to kneel beside him and take both his hands. 'You can tell me.' He clutched my hands painfully, like a lifeline.

'But at the end, when they – when they –' he closed his eyes, his face contorted with remembered pain. 'Then I – I don't know if I – I might have –' He seemed unable to complete this thought, as if finding the words was beyond his endurance.

'You think you may have told them something you shouldn't have, something secret?'

He nodded miserably. 'I told you he failed. Betrayed his trust, gave up his own men to the enemy. How could he go back, after that?' He wrenched his hands out of my grasp. 'Who would befriend him, after such a deed? He'd better have died.'

'You don't know for sure,' I said carefully. 'I believe you – he –'

'His brother,' said Simon. 'You remember the story? His brother waits for the troop to come back, but they do not. He waits for a little longer, and then he sends out a scout to look for them. It's a long way, across the water. He finds the place where they were camped. But they are all dead; limbs hacked, sightless eyes open for the crows to feed on. Betrayed by one of their own. After that, his brother curses him, that he should never return home to those he has failed so utterly. But to the younger brother, this is nothing new. He was never wanted; he might have known the pattern of his life could never change. His brother is the hero of every tale; but he is doomed to failure.'

'Nonsense!' I retorted, and I was so angry with him I grabbed hold of his shoulders and gave him a good shake. 'The end of the story is of *your* making, nobody else's. You can do with it as you choose.

106

There are as many paths open to your hero as branches on a great tree. They are wonderful, and terrible, and plain and twisted. They touch and part and intermingle, and you can follow them whatever way you will. Look at me, Simon.'

He blinked at me once, twice; the candlelight showed his eyes a soft blue, morning sky colour. And cold with self-loathing.

'I believe in you,' I said quietly. 'You are a brave man, and a true one; and I know in my heart that you kept your secrets that night. I trust you better than you trust yourself. You could have hurt me many times, and Father Brien as well, but you did not. There is a future for you. Don't throw my gift of healing back in my face, Simon. We have come this far; let us go on.'

He sat there for a long time in silence; so long that I had time to tidy up, and fetch water, and ready the cloths and salves for the dressing of his wounds. Finally he spoke.

'You make it hard to say no.'

'You made a promise,' I said. 'Remember? You cannot say no.'

'How long must I do your bidding?' he asked, half joking. 'Years?'

'Well,' I said, 'I've been keeping my big brothers in line since I was pretty small. You just might have to get used to it. Until you are well, at least.' And we began, again, the cruel task of washing, and salving, and bandaging.

As it grew dark outside I told the tale of a warrior queen who had men after her like flies, but she never kept one for long; and Simon, who had heard it several times before, offered a dry commentary on the more unsavoury parts of the action. And eventually the job was over, the linen cleared away, and Father Brien came with soup and elderflower wine. There was a sort of peace around the three of us that night as we sat quietly by the fire with our simple meal; and later, Simon fell asleep like a child, cheek pillowed on one hand.

'I'll have to leave you for the day tomorrow,' said Father Brien. 'I need to call at the village to the west, for one of my brothers will be there awaiting papers from me; and we need supplies. I won't ask if you can manage without me, for you have done so all along. But I will make sure to be back by nightfall. I will not have you left alone after dark.'

'He is doing well,' I said. 'Another moon or two, and he may be ready to go on – but where?'

'I'll set that in train tomorrow,' said Father Brien. 'The brothers in the west will take him, I think. He can stay there a while, and when he is ready they will conduct him safely to his home, wherever that is.'

'How?'

'It can be arranged. But you are right; he cannot go while he is a risk to himself. And he cannot ride; by the time you suggest, he may perhaps be able to withstand the jolting of a cart. I will know more tomorrow night.'

True to his word, he was off at dawn the next day, taking advantage of a lull in the persistent rain. Simon and I had slept better, for he had woken only twice, and there was a little more colour in his cheeks. We watched from the doorway as the cart trundled away under the trees.

The morning was peaceful. There was a fine drizzle, on and off, and in between low slanting sunlight, as if the day could not make up its mind to be foul or fair. I tied back my hair and got to work preparing salves from dried lavender. I measured oil and beeswax; Simon watched me. Later, we shared some green apples and a rather hard bannock. Our supplies were indeed in need of replenishment. I wondered if there might be enough flour left for me to bake a few rolls.

Linn heard it before we did. Her ears pricked, she growled deep in her throat. I stared at her; there was no sound from outside. Then, an instant later, the silent message flashed into my mind with an urgent clarity.

Hide him, Sorcha. Now, quickly.

No time to question. I grabbed Simon by the arm.

'Someone's coming,' I said, 'get over to the cottage, quickly. Go in and bar the door.'

'But –'

'Don't argue. Do as I say. And keep out of sight! Do it, Simon!'

He stared at me for a moment; my face must have been white, for Finbar's message had the ring of extreme urgency. Linn barked once, twice, then she was out the door and down the track, tail streaming like a banner behind her.

'Hurry!' I half-dragged the unwilling Simon across the clearing to the cottage and shoved him inside. And now we could both hear it – the drum of hoofbeats, more than one horseman approaching fast up the track. 'Stay out of sight! You'll be safe here until they've gone.'

'But what about –'

'Shut the door! Quickly!' Hoping he would have the sense to obey me, I left him and ran back to the cave, my feet squelching across the two sets of prints in the mud.

I threw myself inside, heart pounding, and only just in time, for there were voices, and the hoofbeats and barking mingled, and three men rode into the clearing: Finbar first, his face tight with anxiety, and two soldiers in field armour, with swords at their sides – my brother Liam, tall and grim; and Cormack, looking impressively grown up.

The dog was beside herself, and as Cormack slid down from his horse her barking reached a pitch of ecstasy. She jumped up, planting her forefeet on his chest, and licked his face with little sounds of delight. Cormack grinned, scratching her behind the ears. But the faces of the others bore no trace of good humour.

Finbar's eyes were questioning as he approached the cave entrance where I stood. *Where is he?* But there was no time to respond.

'Come in,' I said hospitably. 'Father Brien is away to the village; the cottage is locked up. I'm surprised to see you all – is Father then returned so soon?' I was quite pleased with this speech – unfortunately my hands were shaking with nerves, and I thrust them into the pockets of my apron.

'We have news, Sorcha,' said Liam, stooping to come in, and removing his wet cloak at the same time. Over the field armour he still wore his battle tunic, with the symbol of Sevenwaters on the breast. Two torcs interlocked; the outer world, and the inner. This world and the Otherworld. For in the life of the lake and the forest the two were inextricably entwined. 'You must come home with us straight away,' he went on. 'There are changes afoot, and Father requires your presence. He was displeased to learn that you had stayed here so long, whatever the need of your skills in herbalism.'

'Father?' I asked sceptically. 'I'm surprised he

showed the least interest in my whereabouts. Hasn't he better things to occupy his attention?'

Cormack was talking to the dog, getting her to calm down, bringing her inside. Her whole body wriggled and she gave small whines of excitement, as if she could barely contain herself.

'He made no objection to your spending some time learning from Father Brien,' said Finbar pointedly, 'or sharing your skills with him. He has your marriage prospects in mind, maybe – it is a useful craft for a woman. But now –' he broke off, and I detected a note of deep unease in his voice.

'Now what?' There was something none of them was telling me.

Liam picked up a beeswax candle from the table, rolling it between his fingers. Cormack sat down on the edge of the bed, and the dog jumped up beside him, sniffing at the bedding. I watched her; she had her eyes on the doorway, expectant. Was there anything here that might give us away – a pair of boots, a bloodstained bandage? There had been so little time. I looked up at Finbar; something more than the risk that Simon would be found was troubling him.

'Father has returned,' said Liam heavily, 'and with an intended bride. She comes from northern parts, and he will wed her a few days hence. It was sudden, and unexpected. He wants all his children there for the wedding feast.'

'A bride?' After what Father Brien had told us, this seemed nigh-on impossible.

'It's true,' said Cormack. 'Who'd have thought he had it in him? What's more, she's young, beautiful and charming with it. New lease of life for the old man. You should see Diarmid. Follows her around all day making calf's-eyes.'

111

Liam frowned at him. 'It is not so simple,' he said. 'We know next to nothing about this woman, the lady Oonagh is her name, save that he met her when we were quartered with Lord Eamonn of the Marshes, and she was a guest in that house. Of her own folk she has said little, I believe – or he has chosen not to share it with us.'

'I can't believe that he would marry again,' I said, relief that they had not come for Simon mixed with shocked incredulity, 'he is so – so –'

'Impervious?' said Finbar. 'Not to her. She is – different; as glittering and dangerous as some exotic snake. You will know when you see her, why he has done this.'

'Conor doesn't like her,' said Cormack.

Liam stood up. 'We must return, Sorcha,' he said. 'I'm sorry Father Brien was from home, for I had hoped to speak with him in private of these matters. No doubt Father will send for him again, to perform the ceremony. Meanwhile the house is in uproar, and you are needed. Fetch your things now; you can ride down behind me.'

Leave now, straight away? Leave Simon alone, without even saying goodbye, without telling him what was happening? I sent a desperate message to Finbar. *I can't leave now, not like this, he's not ready yet, at least let me –*

'You go on ahead, Liam,' said Finbar. 'I'll help Sorcha pack up, and she can come with me.'

'Are you sure?' Liam was keen to go, already donning his cloak. 'Don't be too long, then. There is much to be done. Come on, Cormack, that foolish hound of yours will doubtless be glad to be away home.'

But she was not. The two of them swung up into the saddle, and at first she circled Cormack's horse, all enthusiasm. But when they rode off down the track, the finality of it struck her suddenly and she paused, then padded back up towards us. She looked around her, sniffing, hesitating. The rain began to come down heavily.

'Linn! Come!' Cormack called her, his horse held in check just where the path entered the forest. 'Come!'

She turned and walked slowly towards him; stopped and looked back again.

'Go on, Linn,' I said, fighting back tears for her, for me, for Simon. 'Go home!'

Cormack whistled, and this time she went to him, but the keenness was gone from her step. They disappeared under the trees.

'Be quick,' said Finbar. 'Where are your things? I'll pack, you talk to him, then we're going.' I did not ask him when I would be able to come back; there was a dreadful finality about all of it. Silently I indicated my bundle, my cloak, my small pots and jars; then I fled back through the rain to the cottage door; but it was barred from inside. True to his word, he had done as I asked.

'Simon!' I yelled over the roar of the downpour. 'It's me, let me in!'

There must have been enough urgency in my voice to conquer his distrust, for the bolts were drawn and the door opened quickly. He had the knife in his hand, but he made no move to touch me, instead retreating to the far end of the room as I stumbled in and slammed the door behind me.

There was no way to do this kindly.

'I have to go, now, straight away. I'm sorry, I didn't mean it to be this way. But my brothers are waiting.'

He stared at me blankly.

'It's too soon, I know, but I have no choice. Father

113

Brien will be back tonight, he will look after you as well as I could –' I was babbling, my distress obvious. Simon put the knife down on the table. His voice was a mere shadow of a sound.

'You promised,' he said.

I could not look at him.

'There is no choice,' I said again, and this time tears began to spill, and I brushed them angrily away. This was helping neither of us. But I could see the long nights ahead for him, and I dared not look up to see the emptiness returning to his eyes.

There was silence, and he did not move, and after a while Finbar called from outside, 'Sorcha! Are you ready?'

Simon's hand grabbed for the knife, and quick as a flash mine shot out and caught him by the wrist.

'I cannot keep my promise,' I said shakily, 'but I hold you to yours. Hold on for today; then let Father Brien help you. Finish the story the way I would have you do it. You owe me this, if no more. I trust you, Simon. Don't fail me.'

I released his wrist and he took up the knife, raising it close to my face so that I was forced to look up. The cornflower-blue eyes gazed straight into mine, and there was a wildness in them that told me his nightmare was right there in front of him. His face was chalk white.

'Don't leave me,' he whispered like a small child afraid of the dark.

'I must.' It was the hardest thing I had ever said.

'Sorcha!' Finbar called again.

There was a quick movement of the blade, and Simon held a long, curling strand of my hair in his fingers. With the other hand he offered me the knife, hilt first.

114

'Here,' he said. Then he turned his back on me, waiting. And I opened the door and went out into the rain.

The lady Oonagh. I felt her presence before ever I saw her. I sensed it in Finbar's silence as we rode home under a thunderous sky. I knew it from the cold wind that whipped tree branches into prostrate surrender as we passed, from the churning turbulence of the lake waters, from the scream of a gull harried on its flight by needles of frozen sleet. I felt it in the heaviness of my own heart, every step of the way. She was there and her hand was on all of us. I knew there was danger. But this foreknowledge did nothing to prepare me.

Finbar deposited me in the courtyard and took himself off to the stables to tend to the horse, for this was a task the boys always did themselves. It was good to be home at last. I longed to slip away quietly to my own quarters, or to the kitchen – some hot water, a fire and dry clothes were all I really wanted right then, and time on my own. But the doors were flung open and in an instant there I was in the great hall, my cloak dripping onto the floor and my boots leaving a trail of mud prints, and though my father was there, all I could see was her, the bride, the lady Oonagh.

She was fair. Cormack had been right. Her hair was a curtain of dark fire, and her skin the white of new milk. It was the eyes that gave her away. When she glanced at my father, all merry sweetness, they were innocent and loving. But gaze right into their mulberry depths, as I did, and you would quail at what you saw there. Their message to me was plain: I am here now. There can be no place for you.

Her voice tinkled like bells. 'Your daughter, Colum? Oh, how sweet! And what is your name, my dear?' I stared at her mutely as the steam began to rise from my clothing.

'Sorcha, you are not fit to be seen!' said Father curtly, and in fact he was right. 'You shame me, appearing before your mother in such a state of dishevelment. Be off, tidy yourself, and then return here. You do me no credit.'

I looked at him. Mother?

The lady Oonagh broke the awkward silence with a peal of laughter. 'Oh, nonsense, Colum, you are too hard on the child! See, you have hurt her feelings! Come, my dear, let us take off this wet cloak, and you must warm yourself by the fire. Where on earth have you been? Colum, I cannot believe you let her go off by herself like this – she could catch her death of cold. That's better, little one – why, you're shivering. Later we'll have a talk, just you and me – I have brought some pretty things with me, and it will be such fun picking out something lovely for you to wear at the wedding feast. Green, I think. I fear your wardrobe has been sadly neglected.' She ran an appraising eye over my homespun gown, my well-worn overtunic which bore many old stains: tincture of elderberry, rosemary oil. And blood.

I opened my mouth to speak, but the words refused to form themselves, and instead I felt a great weariness overwhelm me. My mouth stretched into a huge yawn and my legs turned to jelly under me.

'Sorcha!' Father reprimanded. 'This is too much! Can you not –' But she overruled him again, all solicitude.

'My poor girl, what have you been up to?' Her arm around me was an icy fetter. 'Come now, you must rest – time enough for talk later. Your brother can see you to your room, for you are dead on your feet – Diarmid, my dear?'

And it was only then I realised my second brother had been there all the time, in the shadows behind the lady Oonagh's chair. He came forward, eager to assist, his dimples showing as he gave her a sidelong look, then took my arm to escort me away. She glanced at him under her lashes.

Diarmid babbled on at me all the way to my bed-chamber. How wonderful she was, how vibrant and youthful, how amazing it was that such a beauteous creature had agreed to marry Father who was, after all, getting on in years and not so virile any more.

'Perhaps wealth and power had something to do with it.' I ventured to interrupt the flow of my brother's words.

'Now, now, Sorcha,' Diarmid chided me as we made our way up the broad stone steps. 'Do I detect a note of jealousy here? You weren't happy about Liam's betrothal, I recall. Perhaps you prefer to be the only lady of the house, is that it?'

I turned on him angrily. 'Do you know me so little? At least Eilis is – is harmless. This woman is dangerous; I don't know why she is here, but she will destroy our family if we let her. You are beguiled by her, as Father is. You don't see her – you see some sort of – of ideal, a phantom.'

Diarmid laughed at me. 'What would you know? You're only a child. And besides, you have barely met her. She's a wonderful woman, little sister. Perhaps now she is here, you can learn to grow up a lady.'

I stared at him, deeply wounded by his words. Already the pattern of our existence was beginning to break up around me. We had teased one another end-lessly, had joked and quarrelled as brothers and

117

sisters do. But we had never been cruel to one another. The fact that he couldn't see it just made it worse. And I could not talk to him, for he no longer heard me. We reached my room, and Diarmid was quickly gone, all eagerness to attend again on his new-found goddess.

I dismissed the serving woman who was hovering, and undressed myself. A fire had been lit, and I sat before it with a blanket around me and stared into the flames. Despite my exhaustion, sleep was slow to come, for my mind was crowded with thoughts and images. Perhaps I was being foolish, maybe she was just a well meaning gentlewoman who had fallen for our father's so-called charms. But something felt wrong. I thought of what Cormack had said. *Conor doesn't like her.* I had seen the message in the lady Oonagh's eyes, for all her honeyed words to me. There was something deeply unsettling about Diarmid's fawning admiration, and my father's readiness to be overruled by his lady. And the way servants were scurrying about nervously, as if afraid of taking a wrong step.

And what of Simon? It was still afternoon; he would be waiting alone for Father Brien's return. No teller of tales to fill his silent day, to blot out his visions. No friend to banter with, not even the loyal dog, unquestioning companion in the darkest times. I imagined him watching as the sun moved overhead and down below the trees, waiting for the sound of cartwheels up the track. At least he would not be alone after nightfall.

Finally I lay down and slept. The fire burned away to embers, but my candle flickered on, so that when I woke suddenly some time later, the room was alive with shadows. For a few moments I was back in the cave, and I jumped up wide-eyed, ready to confront the nightmare. But this time there was no screaming; the stone walls were heavily silent, the unicorn and owl on my single tapestry moved slightly in the draught. I lay down again, but Simon was in my thoughts, perhaps even then wrestling with his demons, and I told an old story, silently in my head, until I fell asleep once more.

It was to be many nights before I broke this pattern: the abrupt waking, the pounding heart, the slow realisation of where I was and the overwhelming sense that I had abandoned him. I never slept more than a brief span without waking, and my tiredness added to my confusion and distress by day. For Liam had been right. Changes were afoot, whether we wished them or not.

I disliked most the change in Diarmid, who had fallen well and truly under the lady Oonagh's spell. He would hear no ill of her, and danced attendance on her all day long, or at least, as long as she would let him. It was impossible to carry on a sensible conversation with him. He was, I said to Finbar, like one mazed by the little folk. 'No,' said Finbar, 'not that; but close enough. This is more like the enchantment that comes over a man when he sees the queen under the hill, and yearns for her, though he can never have her without she wills it. She can keep a man dangling this way for a long time, till his face loses its youth and his step its quickness.'

'I have heard such tales,' I said. 'She would spit him out like a piece of apple skin, the moment he lost his flavour.'

Cormack and Padriac avoided problems by keeping out of her way. When asked after, one would be always out riding, or at target practice, and the other busy in the barn or out in the fields somewhere. Finbar gave no excuses for his absence. He simply wasn't there. Lady Oonagh did have a tendency to summon us whenever it suited her, and though her manner was unfailingly cordial and sweet, it was made quite clear that disobedience was frowned upon. Father enforced this rule for her, as indeed he seemed to follow her every bidding. With him, though, she trod more carefully than with hapless, smiling Diarmid. Whatever he was, Lord Colum was not a weak man, and after all, they were not married yet.

There were but a few days left until the wedding. Seamus Redbeard and his daughter were coming; I overheard Liam changing the sleeping arrangements to place Eilis and her waiting woman as far as possible from the lady Oonagh's chamber. Instead of looking pleased that he'd be seeing his betrothed again so soon, my eldest brother was grim and silent. He made several attempts to speak to Father in private, but Oonagh with her tinkling laugh dismissed them, and Father declared gruffly that anything Liam had to say could be said before my lady, for there were no secrets between them.

I wanted to talk to Conor, but he was busy. Much of the ordering of preparations fell to him, and he had little time to spare between the supervision of the kitchen, the airing of linen, the last minute sprucing up of stables and yard. I caught up with him briefly the second evening between supper and bedtime, in a dim corner of the great stairs. It was a good vantage point without much echo, and for once there was nobody else around. I looked at my brother afresh, imagining him in a druid's white robes, his glossy brown hair plaited and tied with coloured cord in the fashion of the wise ones. He had a serenity of gaze, a far-seeing look that you never saw on his twin's face, for Cormack was a man of action who lived for the moment.

'I'm sending for Father Brien, Sorcha,' he said gravely. 'Do you think he will come?'

I nodded. 'If it's just for the day, for the wedding ceremony, then he will come. Who are you sending?'

He looked at me, reading the unspoken question in my eyes. 'I suppose it will have to be Finbar, if I can find him. There is certainly no possibility of your going back, Sorcha. She is watching you closely. You must take great care.'

'You feel it too then?' I was suddenly cold, looking up into my brother's pale face.

He was calm as always, but his unease was palpable. He nodded.

'She watches those of us who are the greatest threat, and she reads us accurately. Diarmid and Cormack are nothing to her, poor innocents, and she sees no threat in Padriac, young as he is. But you, and Finbar, and myself – we have enough strength, perhaps, to resist her if we stand together. That makes her uncomfortable.'

'Liam?'

Conor sighed. 'She tried her charms on him too, make no doubt of it. She discovered soon enough that he was cut from different cloth. Liam fights her in his own way. If he could gain Father's ear, he might speak a word of warning and be heeded. But he, too, has his weak point. I do not like the way this is heading, Sorcha. I wish you had been able to stay away.'

'So do I,' I said, thinking of the work I had abandoned. Still, at least Father Brien would be coming, and could give me news.

'Sorcha.'

I looked up at Conor again. He must have been struggling with himself – not sure how much to tell me, lest he should frighten me.

'What?'

'You must be very watchful,' he said slowly. 'They will wed, I have no doubt of it. Whether or not we speak to Father alone before that day, the result can hardly be different now. What could we say? Lady Oonagh sets not a foot wrong; our fears are based on fantasy, he would tell us, on the wish to resist change, on ignorance. For once she has hold of you, you no longer see her true self. She clothes herself in a mist of glamour; the weak and the vulnerable have no chance.'

'And after they are married?'

Conor's lips became a thin line. 'Perhaps then we will see something of the truth. Believe me, if I could send you away before then, I would do so. But Father is still head of this household, and such a request, so close to his wedding day, would seem passing strange. I will look out for you as best I can, and so will Liam; but you must be careful. As for Finbar . . .'

'Who is she, Conor? What is she?' In my new-found knowledge of Conor, I thought he could answer my question if anyone could.

'I can't say. Nor can I be sure of her reasons for doing this. We have no choice but to wait, hard as that may be. There may be some pattern to this so large, so complex that only time will make it clear. But it is too late to prevent the marriage. Now off you go, little owl – you look as if some sleep would do you good. How was he?'

I knew what he was talking about, despite the sudden change of tack.

'He was mending well enough, until I was forced to leave. Could even that have been part of her plan?'

'She could hardly have known of it. Best not to add that to your worries. It sounds as if you have done some good; perhaps now he can heal himself, with Father Brien's help. And there are others who can guide him to safety. Maybe it's time to let go, and tend to yourself. Go on, off to bed with you.'

The next day there was a bit of sun, weakly filtering between the ever-present clouds, and I set to work in my garden, determined to make up to it for the way I had neglected it. I tied my hair up with a strip of cloth, put on an old sacking apron and armed myself with knife and spade. Overgrown lavender and sprawling wormwood got a good trimming; weeds were rooted out and paths swept clear. As I worked steadily on, my mind slowly began to lose the confusion of fears and worries that plagued it, and the task in hand became all that mattered.

At length it was tolerably tidy, and I fetched the assortment of bulbs I'd lifted last season to dry out for re-planting. Daffodils in the biggest basket; then crocuses, iris, lilies of five different kinds. Some, too, that would grow as well in the wild reaches of the forest as in my sheltered beds: pigs-ears, faery chimes, and the slender pale bulbs of mind's-ease. Throw a handful of its leaves on your camp fire at night, and you would sleep so well you would never awaken.

Padriac had fashioned me a little tool of birch wood, for making the planting holes. As I moved around the garden, digging, setting each bulb in its place with care, smoothing the rich soil back over them, tucking them in for the winter, I recalled Conor's words to us on the day Padriac had offered

123

to make this for me. Don't cut the live wood, he'd said. Find a limb that wind or lightning has taken from the tree, or a birch that has fallen in a great storm. Cut your wood from that if you can. If you must cut new wood, be sure to give due warning. The forest's gifts should not be taken without a by-your-leave. All of us knew this lesson. There would be a quick word, and whether it was to the tree herself or to some spirit that dwelt within, probably made no difference. And sometimes, a small gift was left – nothing of great cost, but always something of signif-icance to the giver – a favourite stone, a special feather, a shining bead of glass. The forest was always generous in her favours to the seven of us, and we never forgot it.

It made sense, now, that Conor had been the one to teach us this lesson.

I had almost finished; I knelt to plant the last few crocuses amongst mossy rocks which would shelter them, later, from the chilly breezes of spring. Crocuses are early risers. The door from the stillroom swung open with a creak.

'My lady?' It was a very young maidservant, ner-vous and ill at ease. 'The lady Oonagh wants you, please. Straight away, she said.' She bobbed an apol-ogy for a curtsy, and fled.

I had been almost happy. Now, as I knelt there with my hands covered in soil and my hair tumbling down, my heart grew cold again, even in the centre of my own quiet place. I could not shut her out, not even here.

I walked back between the lavender beds. They had bloomed well this year, and remnant flower spikes still released a memory of summer into the air as I brushed past them. Inside, I scrubbed my hands, but the nails were still black. I tidied my hair as best I could and hung the apron on a peg. Well, that would have to do. There were limits to the amount of trouble I would take for the lady Oonagh.

She'd been given the best chamber, one whose narrow windows gave a view of the lake and caught the afternoon sun. She was waiting for me, standing demure by the bed, with rolls of cloth and laces and ribbons strewn around her. Her auburn hair outshone the brightest of these adornments, trapping the light in its dark tendrils. She was alone.

'Sorcha, my dear! What took you so long?' It was a gentle enough reprimand. I advanced cautiously across the stone floor.

'I was working in my garden, my lady,' I said. 'I did not expect to be called.'

'Hmm,' she said, and her gaze travelled over me from tousled head to muddy feet. 'And you nearly thirteen years old. It comes of growing up in a houseful of boys, I suppose. But we're going to change all that, my dear. How disappointed your mother would have been, to see you so wild, and on the very threshold of womanhood. It's as well she is not here to see how your upbringing has been neglected.'

I was deeply affronted. 'She would not have been disappointed!' I said angrily. 'Our mother loved us, she trusted us. She told my brothers to look after me, and they have. Maybe I'm not your idea of a lady, but –'

She interrupted me with her cascade of laughter, and her arm around my shoulders. I tensed under her touch.

'Oh, my dear,' she purred, 'you're so *young*. Of course you defend your brothers; and I expect they did the best job they could. But they're only boys, after all, and there's nothing like a woman's touch,

125

don't you agree? And it's never too late to start. We have a year or two, before we must think of a betrothal for you; time enough. Your father wants a good match for you, Sorcha. We must polish your manners, and your appearance, before then.'

I pulled away from her. 'Why should I be polished and improved like goods for sale? I might not even want to marry! And besides, I have many skills, I can read and write and play the flute and harp. Why should I change to please some man? If he doesn't like me the way I am, then he can get some other girl for his wife.'

She laughed again, but there was an edge to it, and a sharpness in her glance.

'Not afraid to speak your mind, are you? A trait you share with certain of your brothers, I notice. Well, we shall talk more of this later. I hope you will learn to trust me, Sorcha.'

I was silent.

Oonagh went over to the bed, where a profusion of cloth was tumbled. She lifted a corner of gauzy green stuff.

'I thought, this one, for the wedding. There's an excellent seamstress in the village, I hear, who'll make it up for you in a day. Come here, my dear.'

I was powerless to refuse. She placed me before a mirror I had never seen before. Its still surface was circled with twining creatures. Their red jewel eyes were on me as I looked at my reflection. Small, skinny, pale. Untidy mop of dark curls, roughly tied back. Neat nose, wide mouth, defiant green eyes. My version of the family face had not the far-seeing serenity of Conor's or the pale intensity of Finbar's. It was softer than Liam's and more fine-boned than Padriac's. The dimples that made Cormack's and

Diarmid's smiles so charming were lacking from my thin cheeks. Nonetheless, I saw my brothers' images as I gazed on my own.

The lady Oonagh had taken up a bone hairbrush, and as I stood there she undid the crude tie that kept my curls off my face, and began to brush out the tangles. I clenched my fists and remained still. Something in the steady motion of the brush, and the way her eyes watched me in the polished bronze of the mirror, sent a chill deep through me. A tiny voice was alive inside me, a little warmth; I focused on the words. *You will find a way, daughter of the forest. Your feet will walk a straight path.*

'You have pretty hair,' she said. The brush moved rhythmically. 'Unkempt, but pretty. You should let me cut it for you. Just a little tidy up – it will sit better under a veil that way. Oh! What has happened here?' Her predatory fingers fluffed the short ends over my brow, where Simon's knife had shorn away a curl.

'I –' I was manufacturing an excuse in my head when my eyes met hers in the mirror. Her face was cold, so cold she seemed not quite human. The brush fell to the ground; her fingers still twined in my hair, and it was as if she could see into me, could read my thoughts, knew exactly what I had been doing. I shrank away from her.

It was only a moment. Then she smiled, and her eyes changed again. But I had seen, and she had seen. We recognised that we were enemies. Whatever she was, whatever she wanted, my heart quailed at it. And yet I believe she was taken aback by the strength she saw in me.

'I'll show you how we'll dress your hair for the wedding,' she said as if nothing had happened. 'Plaited at the sides, and drawn up at the back –'

'No,' I said, backing away, wrenching my hair from her grasp. 'That is, no thank you. I'll dress it myself, or Eilis will. And I will find something to wear –' I glanced longingly at the door.

'I am your mother now, Sorcha,' Oonagh said with a chilling finality. 'Your father expects you to obey me. Your upbringing is in my charge from now on, and you will learn to do as you are told. So, you will wear the green. The woman will come tomorrow to fit your gown. Meantime, try to keep yourself clean. There are servants here to dig up carrots and turn the dungheap – henceforth your time will be better spent.'

I fled; but knew I could not escape her will. I would wear green for the wedding, like it or no, and I would stand by with my brothers and watch the lord Colum wed a – what was she? A witch woman? A sorceress like the ones in the old tales, with a fair face and an evil heart? There was a power about her, that was certain, but she was never one of Them. The Lady of the Forest, whom I believed I had seen in her cloak of blue, inspired more awe – but she was benign, though terrible. I thought Oonagh was of another kind, at once less powerful but more dangerous.

I stood in front of the mirror in my green gown, as she plaited ribbons into my hair and grilled me about my brothers. Again the strange creatures fixed their ruby eyes on me and I answered despite myself.

'Six brothers,' she murmured. 'What a lucky girl you are, growing up in a houseful of fine men! No wonder you are unlike other girls of your age. The little Eilis, for instance. Sweet girl. Fine head of hair. She'll breed well, and lose her bloom soon enough.'

She dismissed poor Eilis with a flick of the fingers as she knotted the green ribbon and twisted the end tight. 'Your brother could have done better. Much better. Serious boy, isn't he? So intense.'

'He loves her!' I blurted out unwisely, rushing to Liam's defence without thinking. I may once have resented his love for Eilis, but I would not stand by and listen to this woman criticising my brother's choice. 'How can you do better than wed for love?'

This sally was greeted with cascades of laughter; even the dour maidservant smiled at my naivety.

'How indeed?' said Oonagh lightly, fitting a short veil over my plaited and woven hair. The figure in the mirror was unrecognisable, a pale, distant girl with shadowy eyes, her elegant dress at odds with her haunted expression. 'Oh, that looks much better, Sorcha. See how it softens the line of the cheek? I may yet be proud of you, my dear. Now tell me, it seems twins run in the family – and yet I have never seen a pair more different in character than young Cormack and Conor. Like peas in a pod, physically, of course. You are all alike, with your long faces and wide eyes. Cormack is a charming boy, and your father tells me he is shaping up to be a promising fighter. His twin is very – reserved. In some ways, almost like an old man.'

I made no comment. The maidservant was rolling up ribbons, her lips thin. Behind me, the seamstress from the village still worked on the fall of the skirt. It was a graceful gown; some other girl might have worn it with pride.

'Conor disapproves of me, I think,' said Oonagh. 'He seems to throw himself into the affairs of the household with a single-mindedness unusual in one so young. Do you think perhaps he is jealous that his twin shines so? Does he really wish to be a warrior and excel in his father's eyes?'

I stared at her. She saw so much, and yet so little. 'Conor? Hardly. He follows a path of his own choice, always.'

'And what is that path, Sorcha? Does a virile young man really wish for a life as a scribe, as a manager of his father's household? A glorified steward? What boy wouldn't rather ride and fight, and live his life to the full?'

Her eyes met mine in the mirror; and the bronze creatures gained power from her gaze, and fixed their baleful glare on me. I was unable to stay silent.

'There is an inner life,' I whispered. 'What you see is Conor's surface, a tiny part of what is there. You'll never know Conor if you only look at what he does. You need to find out what he is.'

There was a short silence, broken only by the rustle of Oonagh's gown as she moved about behind me.

'Interesting. You're an odd girl, Sorcha. Sometimes you seem such a child, and then you'll come out with something that makes you sound like an old crone.'

'I – can I go now? Is this done?' I was suddenly wretched. What else would she make me say? Why could I not control my tongue before her? Her last words had reminded me of Simon, and I could not allow her to tap into my thoughts of him, for if she learnt the truth she would not hesitate to tell Father, and then it would not just be Simon, but Finbar, and I, and Conor as well that would be at risk.

It seemed the fitting was over. The seamstress began to undo the pins, one by one. There were a lot of pins.

'I've seen very little of your youngest brother,' said Oonagh, smiling. She had retreated to perch on the end of the bed, swinging one foot slightly. In her white dress with her hair falling about her shoulders, she seemed about sixteen years old. Until you looked into her eyes. 'Always away off doing things, is Padriac. You'd almost think he was trying to avoid me. What is it keeps him away from crack of dawn till after supper time?'

This seemed safe enough.

'He loves creatures, and mending things,' I said. The seamstress eased the bodice down. It was cold in the chamber, despite the fire. 'He keeps them in the old barn. If there's ever a bird whose wing is broken, or a hound suffers an injury, Padriac will fix it. And he can build just about anything.'

'Mm,' she said. 'So, another one who will not grow up a warrior.' Her tone was cool.

'My brothers are all adept with sword and bow,' I said defensively. 'They may not all choose Father's path, but they are not lacking in the skills of war.'

'Even Finbar?'

The eyes of the creatures glowed. I stared back at them and, gathering up every scrap of will, kept my mouth firmly shut. She was behind me again, suddenly, and the hairbrush was in her hand. She waited as the maidservant began, grimly, to unfasten the network of green ribbons that tamed my hair.

'You are reluctant to speak. But how can I be a good mother to these boys, if I do not know them?' She sighed expressively, her face sweetly rueful. 'I'm afraid Colum has favoured some of his sons and neglected others. I detect a very frosty atmosphere where young Finbar is concerned. What can he have done, to earn such censure? Is it simply a reluctance to participate in warlike pursuits? Or has he never really forgiven his mother for dying and leaving him alone?'

'That's not fair!' I stood up and whirled around to face her, wrenching my hair from the servant's grasp. I was oblivious to the pain. 'Mother didn't choose to die! Of course he misses her – we all do, nothing can ever fill the space she left. But we're not alone, we never have been, we've got each other. Can't you understand that? We are friends, and family, and part of each other, like leaves on the same branch, or pools in the same stream. The same life flows in us all. Talking of jealousy is just silly.'

'Sit down, dear.' Oonagh's voice was quite calm; she did not react to my outburst. 'You spring to your brother's defence – that is natural, as you have had no other companionship, all these years. What grounds have you for comparison, so narrow is your little world? Not surprising, then, that you cannot see his limitations.'

I managed to escape, finally, but there was no way of blotting out her words, and I wondered again what it was she wanted from me, from us. I felt a strong desire to have all my brothers with me, to touch them and talk with them, to feel their strength and comforting sameness. So I looked for them; but Cormack was engaged in a bout with staves, grinning fiercely as he challenged Donal to find a way past his whirling weapon and fancy footwork. And Padriac was fully occupied with some contraption he was building. A raven perched on a rail above him, turning her head this way and that as his fingers went about their delicate task. 'What is it?' I asked my youngest brother, eyeing the intricate folding framework of fine wooden slats and stretched linen.

'Not quite a wing, not quite a sail,' muttered Padriac as his deft fingers fastened another tiny joint. 'With this, a small boat will travel very fast over the water; even in the lightest of winds. See how the panels turn, when I tighten this thread?' Indeed, it was ingenious; and I told him so. I patted the old donkey, and peered into the stalls, where a litter of brindled kittens nestled in a corner of the warm straw. The raven followed me, still limping a little from her injury (attacked by other birds, Padriac thought, but she was mending well). She gave the kittens a wide berth.

There was a long walk, straight between willows, and hedged by a late-flowering plant whose childhood name was angel-eyes, because its round blue blossoms seemed to echo the colour of a spring sky. It was alive with blooms, but the heavens today were leaden; no angels would smile on this wedding. Down by the lake, Liam walked with Eilis. He held his cloak around her shoulders with his arm, careless as to who might be watching, and his head was bent as he spoke to her solemnly. Eilis had her face turned up to his, and she looked at him as if to shut out the rest of the world. For a moment, I felt a dark foreboding, a shadow over the two of them that spread its chill towards me. Then they were gone under the trees, and I went on towards the house.

There was much activity around the kitchen, with carts coming to and fro, and barrels of ale and sides of meat being hefted on shoulders and stowed away. Smells of baking and roasting drifted in the cold air, and horses stamped and snorted. Linn greeted me at the door, snuffling her wet nose into my hand, but she did not go in. It was then that I noticed, among the carts drawn up on the stones, a familiar vehicle of plain, serviceable kind, in whose shafts an old horse waited patiently for his turn to be unbridled and led away to warm stable and rest. And this was odd.

Why would Father Brien be here now, with still a night to go before the wedding? I had been sure he would come down early in the morning and travel back before nightfall, for how could he leave Simon alone after dark?

I went in, but none of my brothers was there, and Fat Janis chased me straight out again, saying she had quite enough to worry about, what with all the fancy baking and the men coming in and helping themselves, without young 'uns underfoot. As she propelled me through the door, she slipped a warm honeycake into my hand with a wink.

I found them eventually back where I'd started, in my own herb garden. It was probably the most private place there was, with its high stone walls and its single door into the stillroom; barring the roof top, that is, but only Finbar and I went up there. Father Brien was on the mossy stone seat, and Conor was leaning next to him, speaking earnestly, while Finbar sat cross-legged on the grass. As I creaked the stillroom door open wider, they fell silent and all three turned their heads in unison to look at me. It was as if they had been waiting for me, and there was clearly something very wrong. 'What is it?' I said, 'what's the matter?' My two brothers looked at Father Brien, and he sighed and got up, taking my hands when I ran up to him.

'You won't be happy with this news, Sorcha,' he said gravely. 'I wish I had better for you.'

'What?' I demanded, not allowing myself to think.

'Your patient is gone,' Father Brien said bluntly. 'The day I was away, I made haste to return by sundown, as we planned. When I reached home, the place was in darkness. At first I feared the worst for the two of you; but I could see your belongings were

134

taken, and no apparent harm done, and the dog had neither remained nor, it seemed, come to any ill. I knew Linn would not have let you be taken without blood being shed. It was plain the horses whose hooves had marked the ground belonged to your brothers.'

'But Simon – I left him safe – he said he would wait for you –'

'There was no sign of him, child,' said Father Brien gently. 'His outer garments were gone, and his ashen staff; though it seemed he took neither food nor water, nor a cloak against the cold, and he left his boots behind. I can hazard a guess at his intentions.'

For he cared not if he lived or died. But he had promised me.

'Didn't you even look for him? Why didn't you send for us?' I was beset with visions of Simon alone in the forest at night, surrounded by his personal demons, slowly weakening with pain and cold. Perhaps already he lay still and silent under the great oaks, with the mosses creeping over his lifeless body.

'Hush, daughter. Of course I searched; but he is a warrior, and though hampered by his injuries, knows how to disappear when he will. And how could I send for you or your brothers? I thought it most likely that he had been taken prisoner again, and brought back here by whoever came to fetch you. I have learnt from Finbar that this nearly did happen.'

'Indeed,' said Finbar. 'Maybe, when he saw how easily he could be taken again, he chose this way, Sorcha. There is a breed of man that would rather die than be captive. And he was as pig-headed a fellow as I ever saw.'

'But he promised,' I said rather childishly, choking back tears. 'How could he come so far, and then throw it all away?' I could not forget that I had broken my own promise. Now I knew how it felt.

Conor put a comforting arm around me. 'What exactly did he promise you, little owl?'

I hiccupped. 'To live, if he could.'

'You cannot know if he has broken this promise or not,' Conor said. 'Probably you will never know. Hard though it is, you must put this behind you, for there is no way you can help your Briton now. Rest easy that you did for him all you could, and think of tomorrow, for we all have other tests and trials ahead of us.'

'Your brother speaks the truth,' said Father Brien. 'We have no choice but to move on. There is a marriage to perform; it gives me no great pleasure to do so, but I am bidden by your father and have no grounds to refuse him. Will he speak with me alone, do you think?'

'You can try,' said Conor. 'The last thing he wants just now is good advice, but coming from you it may be less unwelcome. Both Liam and myself have sought to speak with him privately, and have been refused.'

'What's the point?' put in Finbar. 'He's doomed. You may as well seek to turn back the great tides of the west, or halt the stars in their dance, as step in his way on this. The lady Oonagh has him in her thrall, body and soul. I never thought to see him weakened so; and yet, strangely, I am not surprised. For nigh on thirteen years he has purged himself of any human feeling, has shut out any warmth of spirit. No wonder, then, that he was easy prey for such as her.' His tone was bitter.

'You judge him too harshly,' said Father Brien, scrutinizing my brother's face. 'His decision is unwise, certainly, but he has made it with good intentions. For surely he sees his new bride as a guide and mentor for his younger children, someone to harness their unbridled ways and bring a little warmth to their lives. He is not unaware of his shortcomings as a father. If he cannot reach out to you himself, perhaps he believes that she can.'

Finbar laughed. 'It's clear you have not yet met the lady Oonagh, Father.'

'I have learnt of her, from Conor and from your oldest brother, who greeted me on my arrival. I know what you face here, believe me, and I pray for you all. It is a tragedy, indeed, that your father is blind to her true character. I merely seek to prevent you from judging him too hastily. Again.'

'So you will at least speak with him?'

'I'll try.' Father Brien got up slowly. 'Perhaps we may find him alone now. Conor, will you accompany me? Oh, and by the way –' he fumbled in a deep pocket of his robe, taking something out. 'Your friend did not vanish entirely without token, Sorcha. He left this behind where I would surely find it. I can only deduce it was meant for you. Its meaning is not clear to me.'

He placed the small object in my hand, and the two of them left quietly. Finbar watched me in silence as I turned it this way and that, trying to read its message. The little block of birch wood was, I thought, from Father Brien's special stock, kept dry for the making of holy beads and other items of a more secret nature. It had been smoothed and shaped until it lay comfortably in a small hand such as mine. The carving was surely not the work of one afternoon; it was precise and intricate, showing a degree of skill that surprised me. I could not make out its meaning.

There was a circle, and within it a little tree. By the shape I thought it was an oak. At its foot, there were two waving lines, a river perhaps? Wordlessly I passed it to Finbar, who studied it in silence.

'Why does a Briton leave such a token?' he said finally. 'Does he seek to place you at risk, should it be found? What could his purpose be? I have no doubt it reveals his identity, in some way unknown to us. You should destroy it.'

I snatched the little token back from him. 'I will not.'

Finbar regarded me levelly. 'Don't get sentimental, Sorcha. This is war, remember – and you and I have broken the rules well and truly. We may have saved this boy's life, and we may not. But don't expect him to thank us for it. Campaigners don't leave tracks behind them unless they want to be found. Or unless there is an ambush ready.'

'I will keep it safe,' I said. 'I can hide it. And I know the risks.'

'I'm not sure you do, Sorcha,' said my brother. 'The lady Oonagh is waiting, just waiting, to find any weak spot. Then, like the wolf at night, she'll move in for the kill. You're not very good at hiding your feelings, or at concealing the truth. She would have no mercy on you; and Father, once she told him, would exact full retribution from us both. And think what would happen to Conor, if his part in this were known. I regret ever telling you the full story. You'd have been better just to help me on that night and never know any more.'

This brotherly remark was hardly worth commenting on. Besides, my mind was on other things.

'He can't survive, can he?' I said bluntly.

'You know his chances better than I do,' said

Finbar, frowning. 'A fit man, in these conditions, with the wherewithal to make a fire and hunt game, might make his way across country and keep out of sight. You'd need to know where you were going.'

'It's just such a waste!' I could not really express how I felt, but Finbar read my thoughts clearly enough – he was always good at getting past any shield I might try to put up.

'Let go of it, Sorcha,' he said. 'Father Brien was right, there's nothing any of us can do. If he's gone, he's gone. I suppose his chances of making his way to safety were never great.'

'So why do it? Why take such a risk?'

'Wouldn't you rather die free?' he said.

I spent some time on my own in the stillroom, mostly just thinking, the slight weight of Simon's carving a constant reminder of my bad news; it was well enough concealed in the small bag I wore at my belt, though a safer hiding place would be needed soon. I made up an elderberry salve, and swept the floor. Later, I went out, deciding that after all I was hungry. Fat Janis' honeycake had not gone very far. Supper was not an attractive prospect, for on this important day the whole family would be expected to put in an appearance. Maybe a miracle would happen, and Father Brien would persuade my father to put off the wedding. Maybe.

Outside my door, crouched in a corner of the draughty passageway, was Linn. I almost missed her, for she was cowering in the shadows, but my ears caught her faint whimper.

'What is it, Linn? What's wrong?' I looked closer, and gasped at the great oozing weal that cut across her face from above one eye to the corner of her mouth. Her teeth gleamed through a gashed, bloody lip.

I coaxed her out; she was shivering and flinched even from my friendly touch, but I kept talking quietly, and stroking her gently, and eventually I got her over to the old stables where Padriac greeted me with the shocked outrage I expected. Muttering about certain people and why they shouldn't be allowed near animals, and what he'd do to them when he found out who they were, my youngest brother neatly cleaned and stitched the wound while I held poor Linn still and talked to her of green fields and bones. Padriac was very efficient, but it still took a long time. After he was finished, the dog heaved a great sigh, drank half a bowl of water and settled down in the straw next to the donkey.

It was dusk now and I reminded Padriac that we'd better clean ourselves up for supper; the lady Oonagh frowned on lateness. As we turned to go, there was Cormack, standing back in the shadows, his face linen-white.

'How long have you been there?' I asked, surprised.

'She's well enough,' said Padriac, and there was a strange edge to his voice. 'Why don't you pat your dog, let her know you're here to see her? Why don't you do that, brother?'

There was an awkward silence, and then 'I can't,' said Cormack in a strained voice.

I looked from one of them to the other.

'What's going on?' I asked, bewildered.

'Ask him,' said Padriac furiously. 'Ask him why he won't come in and touch his own dog. The guilt's written on his face, plain to see. This is his handiwork.

Forgive me if I don't stay to chat.' And he was gone, brushing past his elder brother as if he were not there.

'Can this be true?' I said, horrified and incredulous. 'Did you do this, Cormack?' Surely Padriac was wrong. It was Cormack who had saved this dog from drowning, Cormack who had raised her from a small pup, Cormack whose steps she followed with slavish devotion. My brothers might show little mercy to their enemies on the field, but they would never wilfully hurt a creature in their charge.

I stared mutely as Cormack made his way over to the stalls and stood looking down at his damaged hound. He held his arms around himself as if unable to get warm, and when I moved closer I could see that his cheeks were wet.

'You did do it,' I whispered. 'Cormack, how could you? She is a good dog, faithful and true, and sweet-tempered. What possessed you to hurt her?'

He would not look at me. 'I don't know,' he said finally, his voice thick with tears. 'I was in the yard, practising, and she ran up behind me and I – I don't know what got into me, I just let fly with my staff. It was almost as if someone else was doing it.'

I opened my mouth to speak, then thought better of it.

'It wasn't as if she were even in the way, Sorcha. Just – just suddenly, I was angry and I hit her.'

'Speak to her,' I said. 'She forgives you, look.'

Hearing his voice Linn had raised her damaged head from the straw, and her long tail was thumping weakly. The donkey grumbled in its sleep.

'I can't,' said Cormack bleakly. 'How do I know I won't do it again? I'm not fit for any company, man's or beast's.'

'You did a cruel thing,' I said slowly. 'There's no

141

undoing it. You are just lucky that your brother had the skill to mend this damage. But she needs your love, as well, to get better. A dog does not judge you. She loves you, no matter what you do.'

Linn gave a whine.

'Go on,' I said. 'Pat her, talk to her. Then she can sleep easy.'

'But what if –'

'You won't do it again,' I said grimly. 'Trust yourself, Cormack.'

He knelt down, finally, and put out a tentative hand to stroke her neck, never taking his eyes off that ghastly, disfiguring wound. Linn turned her head with some difficulty, and licked his hand. That was how I left them.

I move reluctantly towards a part of our story that is difficult to tell; though not the most difficult. So, we had supper, and Cormack was not there, and neither was Finbar. Father commented on this and was greeted with a wall of silence by his remaining children. Father Brien sat quietly near the foot of the table. He ate sparingly, and excused himself early. Eilis kept glancing nervously at the lady Oonagh, like a frightened animal. Liam held her hand under the table, but his face was like stone. Nobody needed to tell me that Father Brien's talk to Father hadn't changed anything.

Then it was late at night, and most of the household was asleep. As the only girl, I had the luxury of my own chamber for sleeping, and that was where my brothers gathered. We were all there but Diarmid, though Cormack's eyes were red, and he would not sit by his youngest brother. Finbar had appeared from nowhere, like a shadow. We lit seven white candles, and burned juniper berries, and sat there in silence for a while thinking of our mother and trying to share what strength we had. There had been no chance to visit the birch tree together, so we communed with her as best we could. The fire was down to embers, the candles threw a steady light on solemn faces and linked hands.

At such times, we spoke if words came to us, but were content to draw strength from one another's touch, and from our shared thoughts. Not that all of us could communicate mind to mind, as Finbar and I did. That was a skill reserved for few, and how we came by it is a mystery. But still, the seven of us were well tuned to one another, and could feel without words the pain and joy and fear of our siblings. That night, we felt Diarmid's absence like the loss of a limb, for we were united in our sense of impending doom, and our network of protection was incomplete without him. Nobody would hazard a guess at his whereabouts.

Liam shifted slightly, and a candle flickered, sending shadows dancing high on the walls.

'We draw our strength from the great oaks of the forest,' he said quietly. 'As they take their nourishment from the soil, and from the rains that feed the soil, so we find our courage in the pattern of living things around us. They stand through storm and tempest, they grow and renew themselves. Like a grove of young oaks, we remain strong.'

Conor, who was seated on his left, took over.

'The light of these candles is but the reflection of a greater light. It shines from the islands beyond the western sea. It gleams in the dew and on the lake, in the stars of the night sky, in every reflection of the spirit world. This light is always in our hearts, guiding our way. And should any of us lose the light, there will be brother or sister to guide him, for the seven of us are as one.'

It was Cormack's turn next, but he was silent for so long I thought he had decided not to speak. At last he blurted out, 'I did a bad thing today. So bad I should not be here. Tell them, Sorcha. Tell them, Padriac. It has already begun, the shame, the spoiling. I don't think I can do this any more; I'm not fit for it.'

Liam and Conor and Finbar looked at him. Padriac opened his mouth, but I got in first. 'He hurt his dog,' I said. 'Hurt her quite badly, and for nothing. She'll recover, thanks to Padriac's skill. He blames himself; wrongly, I think.'

'How wrongly?' blazed Padriac. 'He did it, he said as much himself.'

'What he said was, it was almost as if someone else was doing it,' I said. 'What if someone else *was* doing it?'

'You mean –'

'I've felt it myself,' I went on miserably. 'Looking into her mirror. She did it somehow, by brushing my hair, with her mind, with her voice. She tried to take away my will, to make me say and do things I didn't want to. And she was very strong. I could not quite keep her out.'

'She was there,' said Cormack slowly, incredulously. 'On the steps, at the practice yard. She was with Father, watching me. She was there. Could she have – but no, surely not.'

'But why?' asked Padriac angrily. 'Why should she wish to do such a thing? There's no reason to it, it's just a piece of petty trickery. She's marrying him, hasn't she got what she wants already? And Linn is innocent. Would she cause her suffering for nothing?'

Conor's mind was on a different track. 'What did she try to glean from you, Sorcha? What did she want to know?'

'Just – things. About me, and all of you – she asked about each of you. Little things. But it felt bad, not as if she just wanted to get to know us, but –' I shivered. 'I don't know. As if she would store the information and use it somehow. Use it against us.'

Conor turned back to his twin. 'You love this dog,' he said, looking Cormack straight in the eye. 'She is a part of you. She owes her life to you. You would not hurt her.'

'But I did hurt her. No matter who made me, who put the thought into my head, it was my hand that struck the blow.'

'What's done is done,' said Conor. 'You cannot change that. But you can make it better, you know how. *Be* the dog, feel her pain, feel her sense of betrayal. Feel also her simplicity, her forgiving, her love and trust for you. The two of you will heal together.' He dropped my hand and took Cormack's, drawing him into the circle. After a while, Padriac moved in and took his brother's other hand, and we sat quietly again.

'We ask for guidance,' said Finbar. 'We bear our lights within, and sometimes the path is clear. But often they are dim, and we cannot trust even our own. Spirits of the forest, spirits of the water, ghosts of the air, beings of the deep and secret places, help us in our time of need. For ahead is darkness and confusion.'

His words sent a shiver through me. Had he seen something of our future?

'I heard a tale once,' I said, 'of a hero who came to grief, after long journeys and mighty deeds, when he met a monstrous creature with jaws like iron, and the strength of three giants. The hero was torn limb from limb; and when the monster finished with him, the parts that were left were strewn far and wide. So he had a shin bone that lay in a deep cave where water dripped constantly down the walls; and his hair was blown by the east wind till it tangled in a hazel tree in a far off corner of the land. His skull was used as a drinking bowl for a time, then abandoned in a stream, which bore it to the very shores of the western sea. A wild dog carried off his little finger bones to feed its young. And after a time, there seemed to be nothing left of him. Years went by, and tiny pale toadstools grew where his leg bone lay, and the leaves of the hazel grew around his bright hair. On the sea's rim, his skull filled with soil, and in it sprouted and flourished the seeds of wild parsley; and through his finger bones, where the pups had left them white and clean, grew spears of crocus. And they say, if ever a traveller plucks the wild parsley, and takes the bark of the hazel tree, and the secret toadstools, and mixes them with crocus from the patch of forest where the hero's last bones lie, a powerful spell will come to life. The hero will be reborn, not as he was before his destruction, but many times stronger in body and spirit; for he will be filled with the strength of earth, sea and air. I think of the seven of us as the parts of one body. We may be torn asunder, and it may seem as if there is no tomorrow for us. We may each travel our own path, and we may fall and be broken and mend again. But in the end, as surely as the sun and moon make their way across the arch of the heavens, the strength of one is the strength of seven. Don't forget what our mother said, as she lay dying. We must touch the earth, we must look into the sky and feel the wind. Like pools in the same stream, we must meet and part and meet again. We belong to the flow of the lake and to the deep beating heart of the forest.'

The candles were lower now, and we fell into silence. It was a time of year when spirits were very close, for it was less than two moons to midwinter day, and I could almost catch small voices in the shadows around us. Padriac had not spoken again, but he placed his hand on Cormack's shoulder briefly, and Cormack nodded. And Conor said to his twin, very quietly, 'I'll come back over to the barn with you, for a while.'

'Thank you,' said Cormack.

Finbar stayed behind when all the rest had gone. He sat staring into the fire. The mood was sombre. Despite our brave words, we were looking into an abyss.

'What are you thinking, Finbar?'

'Something I cannot share.'

I moved closer to the fire, thrusting my hands into my pockets for warmth. The smooth surface of Simon's carving fitted exactly into my palm.

Tell me. Tell me what you see.

I tried to look into his mind, but there was a barrier there, a dark wall around his thoughts.

I cannot share this. I will not frighten you.

I caught an image of myself as a small child running barefoot through the forest in dappled sunlight.

Are you afraid?

A feeling of intense cold. Water. The whistling of air past the body, the strangest sensation of falling, flight, falling. That much he revealed to me. Then he shut it off abruptly. *I cannot share this with you.*

'You cannot close yourself off from the whole world,' I said aloud, exhausted already from the attempt to break into his mind pictures. 'How can we help one another, if we have secrets?'

'Sharing my last secret didn't help you much,' he said flatly. 'Or the Briton. I wonder now how much my efforts to undo my father's work were worth. You were hurt, and the boy – his fate was little better for my interference. Perhaps I should cease meddling. Perhaps I should accept that our kind are all killers under the skin. If the lady Oonagh wants us as play-things, what's the real difference?' He gave a crooked smile.

'You don't really believe that, Finbar!' I was shocked; could he have changed so quickly? 'Look me in the eye and say it again.' I took his face between my hands quite firmly. And when I met his gaze, his eyes were as clear and far-seeing as ever.

'It's all right, Sorcha,' he said gently. 'I have been thinking hard, that's all. I have not changed my tune so much. But my mind tells me there is a great ill about to befall us; and I wonder if our strength is enough to withstand it. I wish you were safe some-where, not here in the middle of it all. And I need to rely on my brothers; I must be able to trust them, all of them.'

'You can trust them,' I said. 'You heard what they said. We are all of a mind, and we always will be. Whenever one is in trouble, there will be six to help.'

'Their business is torture and death. How can they be of a mind with you, or with Conor, or myself?'

'I can't answer that. Only – only that, if you believe the tales, it's in the nature of our people to go to war and to kill, just as it is to sing and play and tell stories. Perhaps they are two halves of the same whole. I know that we seven are of the one family, and that we only have each other. It has to be enough.'

But there had been one brother missing; and when

I opened the door for Finbar to go, we saw him, down the long hallway, as he slipped silently from a bedchamber that was not his own. She was concealed behind the door where she stood to bid him farewell, but we saw her white arm stretch out, and her fingers move softly down his cheek, and then Diarmid padded barefoot away, his face as dazzled and unseeing as some lad bewitched by faery folk. Finbar looked at me, and I looked at him; but we never said a word.

So they were married, she in her long gown of deepest russet, and my father looking at her as if there was not a soul in the world but the two of them, while all around them the family, the guests, the men of the garrison, the servants and cottagers muttered and exchanged sideways glances. I stood there in my green gown with my hair in ribbons, and by me my six brothers in a line. It did not seem to me a proper ceremony at all. In the tales, such things were done in the open, under a massive oak, and there would be play acting and mock fighting and riddles, and the druids would come out of the forest to perform the ritual of handfasting. There were none of the ancient ones at my father's wedding, and no concession to the old ways. Perhaps the lady Oonagh came from a Christian household, but there was no way of telling, for none of her folk were there. Father Brien spoke the words tranquilly, as was his way, but it seemed to me his face was drawn, and his tone remote. As soon as the formalities were over, he packed his cart and left. A feast followed, with a laden board and flowing ale. And the next day things began to happen.

Eilis was taken ill, something she ate, they

thought, but it went on too long, and I was called to her. Her face had lost its rosy plumpness, and she was purging and bringing up blood. I sent a boy for Father Brien, but he did not come, so I held her head and talked to her, and walked her up and down the room, and when she was done I made up a mixture for her, and sat by her bedside until she dropped into a fitful doze. Liam hovered outside, and so did Eilis' father, muttering under his breath.

I stayed with her through the night, and did what I had to. The next day she was weak but seemed a little brighter. She needed rest, and careful nursing. It was something she ate, sure enough. I recognised the symptoms of monkshood poisoning, and I knew it was no accident. The amount must have been precisely calculated, for a person could survive only the very smallest dose of this lethal substance. The intent was mischief, not murder. I could not tell how the root of this herb had made its way into the wedding banquet, and so specifically onto one person's platter. And I was not about to accuse my new stepmother aloud, though her eyes were on me as Seamus Redbeard took his hasty farewells. A covered litter was made ready, and he bore his daughter away home to Glencarnagh. Liam questioned me intently, with a white rage on his face that I had never seen before; but I cautioned him, reading the lady Oonagh more accurately than he. She knew enough of my skills to realise the source of Eilis' mysterious illness would not be undetected for long. An accusation was just what she expected, for what better to drive a wedge between father and son? Besides, I told Liam, Eilis would be safe now. She was a strong girl, and I had caught the poison early. Better if she were to return home, for a while at least.

Diarmid had a black eye, and Cormack a nasty gash on his cheek. Perhaps a certain piece of information had not been kept entirely secret after all. In this matter I would not interfere, though I saw Diarmid watching her, watching her, and growing a little thinner and paler every day, like a man who has tasted faery fruit but once, and is eaten up by his craving. My father's face bore a shadow of the same look, though he went about his business more or less as usual. Oonagh sat at the table, her smile serene, her eyes commanding. People scurried nervously to obey her. Everywhere you turned, it seemed she was there, watching. The men at arms gave her a wide berth.

Then Padriac's animals began to sicken, and to die. First it was the old donkey, found cold and stiff one morning in her stall. We were sad; but she had lived out her allotted span, more or less, and we accepted her loss with a regretful glance at the empty corner. Next the mother cat disappeared, leaving her nest of kittens behind. Padriac tried to feed them, and I helped, but one by one they pined and weakened and their tiny lives slipped away. I wept as the last one died in my hands, its once bright eyes fading to a filmy grey. Two days later, I found Padriac beating his fist against the barn wall, his knuckles bloody, his eyes swollen with tears. And at his feet, the raven whose damaged leg had almost mended, whose brave plumage had grown glossy and healthy again; but now she lay still, her head twisted back strangely, her eyes fixed sightless on the wide expanse of winter sky. The old barn was empty. Padriac's wordless grief and anger twisted my insides. He was consumed with fury, and we could not comfort him. For me, there was worse to come. I should have been prepared, but I was not.

CHAPTER FOUR

T he lady Oonagh had told me my trips to the village were to stop; it was unsuitable, she said, for the lord Colum's daughter to be out and about the neighbourhood like some tinker's child, getting her feet muddy and mixing with all sorts of riff raff. I must put all that nonsense aside, and start learning to be a lady. Music – now that was appropriate. I spent a morning performing to her on the flute, and, reluctantly, the harp, for she ordered our little instrument brought down to the hall. Fortunately, my father was occupied elsewhere that day. It quickly became plain to her that I had little more to learn. Sewing, then. She asked to see my handiwork, and I was obliged to confess that I had none. Oh, I could mend, and hem a gown or a tunic. But fine work had never been called for in this house of men. Oonagh showed me a veil of thinnest lawn, sprinkled with a myriad tiny birds and flowers. It was indeed beautiful; draped over her shining hair, it gave her the look of a queen. She would show me the techniques I needed for such work. It would take a great deal of time and application, so no more trips to visit the sick with a basket of lotions and draughts. Let someone else do it. 'No one else has the skills,' I said without thinking. It was the simple truth. Oonagh's eyes narrowed and her fine, arched brows tightened with displeasure.

'Unfortunate,' she said. 'Then these people will do whatever they did before you came along, my dear. Be here with your needles and thread straight after breakfast tomorrow. We have a great deal of lost ground to make up.'

I lasted no more than a few days. My fingers, so deft at bandaging and mixing and measuring, were clumsy and awkward with needle and fine silk. Under her scrutiny I broke the thread, and dropped the needle, and stained the delicate fabric with blood from my pricked finger. I longed for one of my brothers to interrupt and rescue me, but they did not. Planning was under way for another journey beyond our borders, and they were consulting maps, or exercising horses, or endlessly polishing and sharpening weapons.

Even my father was preoccupied in the lady Oonagh's presence and she did not like it. Something was troubling him. But I continued to ply my needle, and she watched me. Sometimes she asked questions, and sometimes she sat there in silence, which was worse, for I could feel her mind reaching out towards mine, as if she would know my most secret thoughts. I tried to shield myself from her, the same way Finbar had learned to veil his mind from me. But she was very strong, and if she could not read me direct, she was clever with words, and knew how to trap.

'Your father is busy these days,' she said pleasantly enough one morning, watching me as I stitched laboriously at a long stem in shades of green. 'Planning to ride out again soon, he tells me. I had hoped he would remain longer at home, but men become restless.' She gave a little laugh, shrugging narrow shoulders in her elegant blue gown. 'Wives get used to it eventually, I suppose.'

I hated her efforts to be chatty even more than her hostility. 'It's what they do,' I said, frowning at my needle.

'Still, it is barely a season since the last campaign,' said Oonagh, wandering over to the narrow window that overlooked the yard, where Liam and Diarmid were passing and passing again on horseback, practising slipping sideways out of the saddle and back up again with sword in hand, a nasty trick they used occasionally in close combat, if what they told me was to be believed. It had a surprising effect on your enemy, they said. 'One wonders what calls them away again so soon. More intruders on our borders maybe?'

'I wouldn't know,' I said, unpicking a couple of stitches.

'Or perhaps they are searching for escaped prisoners,' she said lightly. 'My lord informs me he intends to dismiss his master of arms, since it seems there has been some neglect of duties here. Strange. They put so much energy into it all. And yet captives go mysteriously missing in the night. One wonders how such an error could occur.'

I was suddenly chilled to the bone. She knew. She had as much as said it. I remained silent as she turned back towards me, smiling.

'Poor Sorcha, I'm boring you, child. Of what

154

interest could all this be to a little girl, after all? Blood feuds and missing hostages? You have indeed had a strange childhood, growing up in such a household. It's as well I am here now to tend to your education. Now, show me what you have done. Oh dear, this is quite crooked. I'm afraid it must be unpicked yet again.'

Finally I was free to go and I sought out Finbar; for surely Father could not really be intending to get rid of Donal, who had been a part of his garrison for longer than I could remember, who had overseen every part of my brothers' training since they were small, whose grim features and sturdy frame were as much a part of our household as the stone walls themselves. But Finbar was not to be found; instead I was waylaid by a girl from the cottages, come to seek help for her grandmother, whose fever would not go down. How could I tell her I was forbidden to help? These people relied on me. So I fetched my basket, threw on an old cloak and my sturdy boots, and set off.

Once they saw me in the settlement, others came to seek my help. After tending to the woman with the fever I moved on to old Tom's, to reassure him over a boil that had erupted in a very awkward spot. I treated him, and he heaped thanks upon me, and praised my brother Conor, who had given his grandsons work in the stables, and so, said Tom, got the lads out of his daughter's hair and taught them something useful at the same time. Then I was called to a tiny, sickly babe. I left the anxious young mother some herbs to make a tea which would help her milk, and promised to bring fresh vegetables from my garden.

By the time I was finished it was mid afternoon, and I made my way home as quickly as I could. It was a long time since breakfast, and I could almost taste Janis' oatcakes on the crisp winter air. A fine mist was starting to settle around the hawthorn bushes as I headed up the path towards the kitchen garden. I was deep in my own thoughts, and nearly walked into Father and Donal as I turned a corner of the hedge. They were absorbed in conversation and did not see me. I stopped dead in my tracks, then faded back into the concealment of the hedge for the quiet intensity of Donal's voice told me this was a deeply private interchange.

'. . . not my intention to challenge your decision, my lord. But at least hear me out before I leave.' Donal's voice was under the same tight control he exercised over his mounts, and his sword, and his men at arms.

'What can you have to say to me?' returned Father coldly. 'My decision is made. What more is there?'

They had stopped right in front of me, and I could not move without being detected. Father had his back to me. Donal stood erect as ever, but the deep grooves around his mouth and nose betrayed his emotion. 'I accept full responsibility for what happened. There is no excuse for such an error. My men have been duly disciplined, and I have received your chastisement. The past cannot be undone. But this degree of punishment is unwarranted, my lord Colum.'

'A prisoner escaped. Not the first. An important prisoner, this time. How can I sanction such an error? I leave here with the man safe in custody, not just securely guarded but unconscious, scarce able to walk, let alone make his way out of here. The next day I receive a message to say the captive is nowhere to be found. Your men were drugged. There must have been help from inside. As a result of your negligence

156

our position has been much weakened. Who knows what advantage such a hostage might have brought us? I cannot afford another such mistake. If you cannot maintain an adequate level of control amongst your men there is no place for you here. You should count yourself lucky that I allowed you to remain in my service while the matter was investigated. I should have dismissed you the day I returned home.'

'Father.' I had not realised until he spoke that Liam was there, out of my view back along the path. His boots crunched on the stones. 'Hear Donal out, please. Has he not been our guide and tutor these fourteen years and more? All our skills we owe to him and his patience. Surely dismissal is too harsh a penalty for one breach?'

'This is my decision, not yours,' snapped Father. 'You are over young yet to meddle in such affairs. Perhaps you do not appreciate the importance of this particular breach. Because of this piece of ineptitude, and the delay in informing me of what had happened, our British captive may even now be back home spreading his knowledge of our troops, our terrain and our positions amongst his fellows. His group was no ordinary raiding party. We cannot afford to expose ourselves thus again.'

'He was near death, that night,' said Donal. 'He could not have travelled far. Besides, we had already established he had nothing to tell. I believe you misjudge his importance.'

'I misjudge? I?' Father's voice rose. 'You are hardly in a position to question my judgement.'

'Maybe not,' said Donal, 'but there is a question of loyalty. I have served you well, as your son says, these fourteen years. Since your lady's day, when this household was a place of joy. I have turned your sons into fine young warriors well fit to battle beside you for your lost Islands; well trained in all the arts of war, to defend your lands and bring honour to your name. I have taken the time for them which you could not spare. I have seen your daughter grow up in the image of her mother, as sweet and fey a girl as ever these forests gave birth to. I have drilled your men in body and spirit, and their loyalty to you is beyond question. But now – by the lady, Colum, I must speak out, since it seems there is nothing further to lose by honesty!'

'I will not hear this,' said Father grimly, and his cloak swung out as he turned on his heel.

'You will, Father.' Liam laid his hands on Father's shoulders, halting him, and I saw Father's clenched fist rise as if to strike him, and then come down again slowly.

'You find it hard to look at me, and to listen to my words.' Donal spoke with some difficulty. 'Believe me, it is even harder for me to speak to you thus, and I do so only because I must leave this place which has become my home. My lord, I never asked for much, beyond my keep and the chance to do a good job. But I beg you now to listen.'

There was a silence. Eventually my father said 'Well?'

'I'll be plain, my lord. I know you well, better sometimes than you do yourself. In all these years I've never known your judgement to falter. As your men say, you can be hard at times, but you're always fair. That's why they follow you, even to death. That's why you are master of wide lands from the great forest to the marshes, feared and respected throughout the north. You don't make mistakes. Until now. Until –'

'Go on,' said Father in the chill tone he normally reserved for Finbar.

'Until you met my lady Oonagh,' said Donal heavily. 'Since then, your mind has not been your own. Her will is behind every decision you make, and her influence has blinded you –'

'Enough!' My father's fist swept through the air and cracked sharply across Donal's cheek. The master at arms held his ground as an angry red mark bloomed on his face.

'I speak the truth, and in your heart you know it,' he said very quietly. 'You have never struck me in anger before. You do so now because of her. She has poisoned your thoughts, and now you lose your judgement. Take care, my lord, for if your men lose faith in you, your lands will not hold.'

'Be silent!' My father's rage was palpable. 'Do not speak my lady's name, for your words sully that which is spotless. You repay me thus for my trust in you? Get out of my sight!'

'Father, he begs you simply to listen.' Liam's voice shook slightly. 'Donal is not alone in these thoughts. The lady Oonagh has a power which – which affects us all. Your men are uneasy, your household fearful. Eilis and her father were forced away. Your lady seeks to divide brother from brother, father from son, and friend from friend, until each of us is alone. She will destroy this household if you let her.'

There was a long pause this time, and I could hear Father's breathing, and see Liam's white, anxious face. He had taken a great risk. After a while Father said slowly, 'What do you mean, forced away? The girl had a weak stomach, that was all. What can that have to do with my lady?'

'There was poison in the food,' said Liam quietly. 'Very specific poison, and in her dish alone. We tried to tell you. Sorcha knows much of these things, which was fortunate for Eilis, who else might have died. There is no proof who put it there, but rumour runs fast.'

'To blame my lady is as foolish as to blame my daughter herself,' said Father, but his tone had changed, as if he were at last hearing what they were saying. 'Why should she wish to do such a thing?'

To divide father and son, I thought, so that her own child can inherit. Or perhaps her plan is bigger still.

'There was poison before,' said Father. He looked Donal straight in the eye. 'You said your men were given a sleeping draught, the day their captive escaped. But that was before ever the lady Oonagh came here. These theories are nothing but inventions, fantasies to salve your pride, a ruse so I will change my mind and perhaps keep you on here a little longer.'

'Not so,' said Donal, and he picked up the small pack he had by him. I noticed, then, the sword by his side, the bow over his shoulder. 'My heart is here, and my life's work, but I will leave as I am bidden. I ask only that you heed my words, and your son's. Be warned, and be watchful.' He reached out to clasp Liam by the elbow, and there were tears in my big brother's eyes. Then Donal was gone, out of sight down the path. I heard the jingling of harness as he mounted his horse, and the hoofbeats going steadily away into the distance. Father stared after him through narrowed eyes.

'First Eilis and her father, now Donal,' said Liam. 'If you do not wake soon you will lose us all, one by one.'

Father looked at him. 'Perhaps you had better tell me what you mean,' he said. Liam moved closer, putting one hand on Father's shoulder, and began to speak very quietly. A moment later, there was a peal of laughter, and a sound of light footsteps, and there was the lady Oonagh, a vision in silk running down the path on dainty slippers. Her cloud of red hair whirled about her flushed cheeks, and her breasts were barely cupped by the tight bodice of the blue gown. A tracery of fine veins showed on her pearly flesh, and suddenly I knew, perhaps before she did, that she carried his child. Her alabaster skin seemed to glow from within. Behind her my brother Diarmid trotted in pursuit, all dimpled earnestness.

'My lord!' She fanned herself with her hand, feigning exhaustion. 'So solemn, so serious! Here, let me cheer you up! It is too fine a day for such portentous looks!' She stood on tiptoe, both small hands grasping the front of his tunic, and kissed him full on the lips. Liam's moment was lost forever. My father's arm went round his wife possessively, and she clung to him like a vine to its tree as they turned back towards the house. I watched as Diarmid followed them, crestfallen and confused. I watched as Liam scooped up a handful of stones from the path and hurled them, hard, back to the ground. I saw him stride off towards the stables, his frustration written clear on his face. Then, only then, I crept out of my hiding place.

It took a moment or two, after I went through the house and into the stillroom, to realise something was wrong. When a place is so familiar, so much your own, you just take it for granted, scarcely seeing the colours and shapes around you save as an extension of yourself. So, it was a moment or two. I took off my cloak and hung it on the peg. I turned to put my basket on the table. Then I saw. The shelves were bare, the hanging herbs, the plaits of onion and garlic, the

161

drying plants were gone. Every jar and bottle, every knife and bowl was missing. My spices, my ointments and tinctures, my cloths and basins and bundles, all the tools of my trade had been taken away. There was a scattering of dried lavender on the flagstones, and the outside door was ajar. Heart pounding, I walked out into the garden.

Right down the bottom, by the wall, a small fire burned, and its fragrant smoke cast a gentle haze over the devastation before me. On either side of the central path, every bed had been dug up, every plant uprooted, and a confusion of broken stems, pale exposed roots and shattered paving covered the whole area. I stumbled forward in a daze. Lavender, wormwood, tansy and chamomile. Mallow and rosemary. I walked across their tumbled remains, and the sweet smell from their bruised leaves drifted up in farewell. Larger branches were strewn on the ground or piled up for burning. My lilac tree had been cut down. *Never cut live wood,* Conor had said, *unless you must. And never without a warning for the spirit that lives within. Do not destroy her home without good reason.* Still I was silent, shaking, wandering blindly from one victim to the next. The early bulbs whose secret life lay hidden deep within their protective coverings; the crocuses I had bedded down so carefully against the chill of winter. Shredded, crushed, exposed on the ravaged soil. My tender creeper, ripped from the wall and chopped into a thousand pieces; it would never open its tiny white star-flowers to welcome the spring sun again. I walked on. The little oak tree, most cherished of all, barely shoulder-high, gentled and guarded since I was eight years old; I had expected to watch it grow, year by year, to shade and protect my domain. It was snapped off at the base, and would never bud again with new season's life. I fell to my knees, scrabbling wildly in the soil in a vain effort to save something, anything; but I could not cry. This went beyond tears, beyond thought. In my heart, I gave a great wordless scream of anguish.

I did not call my brothers aloud, but two of them heard me. Finbar was there first, putting his arms around me, stroking my hair, swearing under his breath. A moment later, there was Conor, striding up the path with a face like thunder, roaring for the gardeners, turning his fury on two men I had not noticed, who were cowering now by the bonfire, spade and rake in hand, wilting under my brother's ferocious interrogation.

I gripped Finbar's jacket and fought to get my breathing under control. My head was exploding with rage and grief and shock. After a moment or two he stopped talking and sought to calm me with his mind.

Weep, Sorcha. Let go. What's done cannot be undone.

Even my violets! Even my little oak tree! They could have left the oak tree!

You have survived. We are strong. And these things can grow again.

How can they grow, with such evil here? How can anything grow? My herbs, my herbs are gone, all my things — how can I do my work without my things?

Weep, Sorcha. Let go. We are all here for you. Let go, little sister. The earth takes your garden to her heart. She weeps with you.

He was strong, and finally I collapsed in angry sobs, and soaked his shirt front while he held me; and then Conor came.

'This was at my lady's orders,' he said tightly. 'Very specific orders, with no detail omitted. The men cannot be blamed, they had no choice; they know now to check with me first. But it is too late for you, little owl. I'm sorry. I know how you have worked on this haven, and loved its inhabitants. I know what it means to you and those you tend.'

'Just because – just because –' I hiccupped.

'Did you offend her in some way?' asked Conor gently.

'There is no need to offend.' Finbar's voice was as cold as I had ever heard it. He sounded like Father. 'The lady Oonagh needs no provocation to take such action. She will destroy us one by one if she is not stopped.'

'She – she told me not to go to the village,' I managed, blowing my nose on the square of linen Conor produced. 'But they sent for me and I never thought – I only wanted to – and she – and she –'

My brothers exchanged glances.

'Sorcha, take a few deep breaths,' said Conor, leading me over to the stone seat which was the solitary survivor in the wasteland. 'Sit down now. That's better.'

They knelt one on each side of me, and Conor took both my hands in his. 'Good girl.' Down by the fire, the two gardeners were raking up debris, throwing more shattered branches on the pile. They threw nervous looks in our direction.

'Now, Sorcha. I want you to go to my quarters and I want you to remain there for the night. You must not try to see her, or Father, until we have all spoken together and decided what to do. I know you are sad; but Finbar is right. Plants can grow again, and with your skills and your love, they will flourish in the hardest of places. You are safe. That is the most important thing.'

I could not speak. The pain in my heart was still overwhelming, and tears poured unabated down my cheeks. Now I had started crying it didn't seem possible to stop.

'We must talk, all of us,' said Conor. 'I believe you may hold the key to this, Sorcha. But first, you must come inside, and you need time to collect yourself.'

'It's not safe for her here,' said Finbar bluntly. 'This strikes at her very self, and through her at all of us. It was a blow well calculated, and aimed with skill. We cannot stand back and let our sister endure such things. We should send her away, before it is too late.'

'Not now,' said Conor. 'Sorcha must rest. And you, brother, keep yourself in check, for hasty words now can only put us all at more risk. Do not seek to have this out with the lady Oonagh, or with our father. That is not the way.'

'How long? How long must we wait to take action? How long before we make him see what she is, what she can do?'

'Not long,' said Conor, helping me to my feet. His arm around my shoulders was strong, hard and comforting. 'Tomorrow we will act, for like you I believe the time has come. Meanwhile, tell the others what has happened, and bid them to my quarters after dark. But keep your mouth shut, brother, and guard the message of your eyes. The lady Oonagh reads you better than you think.'

As do you, I thought. It had come to me gradually, and was still not clear. But he had come to help me, right behind Finbar, and something he had said confirmed it. I had believed the wordless meeting of minds was for Finbar and me alone. I wondered how long Conor had been able to read our thoughts and feelings, and why he had never let us know. It fitted, somehow, with what Father Brien had explained to us. I supposed, if people looked on you as some sort of spiritual guide, it might mean you had a few powers beyond the usual, perhaps some that nobody knew of.

'Conor –' I said as we went up the back steps, careful not to be noticed.

'It's all right,' said Conor, opening the door for me to slip through. 'Your thoughts are safe with me. I use this skill sparingly, and only when I must. Your pain spills over, sometimes, and so does Finbar's. I am here to help.'

We reached the chamber shared by Conor and Cormack. Not long after us, Cormack came in, grim-faced, and Linn padded in after him, jumping up to settle next to me on the narrow bed. Padriac and Liam followed, the one with a cup of spiced wine which I was persuaded to drink, the other holding my hand, kissing my cheek, then drawing his brothers aside to talk rapidly and in low voices just out of earshot. After a while they all went away but Cormack, who stayed just inside the door with a knife in his hand. Finbar did not reappear. After spreading the news, he had gone about some business of his own, it seemed. I felt bruised and empty, and I lay there a while watching the light fade, and letting the dog lick my fingers. And after a time, the wine worked, and I dropped into a restless sleep.

Later, much later, they were all there, all but Diarmid. I was awake, and they had brought me barley bread with honey, but I could not eat and I fed it to the dog. Perhaps this was what the stories meant when they called somebody heartsick. Your heart and your stomach and your whole insides felt empty and hollow and aching.

'Think about the good times,' said Conor, but I couldn't. Finbar, when he came in, placed a small, damp bundle beside me on the bed. Linn sniffed at it hopefully. I unrolled the strip of sacking. There lay my garden in embryo: slender cuttings of lavender, tansy, rue and wormwood; a sliver of lilac wood that might be grafted; a round white stone from the shattered path; a solitary acorn. I wrapped them carefully up again. Maybe, just maybe I could start again. My brother stood with his back to me. I sensed the love in him, and the rage.

'Now,' said Conor, 'I must ask you, Sorcha, if you will share a secret with your brothers. With all of us.'

'What secret?' I dreaded what he might be about to say. The lady Oonagh had all but stumbled on my most dangerous secret, one that would most surely divide brother from brother. For there were three of them who were warriors, committed to the cause, quick to pursue vengeance in blood; and there were three who would always seek first to arbitrate, to mend, to fight their battles with words, not with blows.

'He means the vision, or spirit, you saw in the forest, Sorcha,' said Finbar from his dark corner. 'Conor believes this may help us. You can tell them.'

'She came to me,' I said. 'The Lady of the Forest. Just like the stories. She – she spoke to me, words about what I must do. That it would be long and difficult, and that I must stay on the path. That was all.'

Not quite all. But I would not tell the rest.

'Would such a vision come to you again if you bid her?' asked Liam. The room was dark, with but a single candle lit, and my brothers seemed tall and grim in the shadows, three of them around the bed, Finbar in the far corner and Padriac taking his turn by the door.

'I cannot call her at will,' I said, remembering how badly I had wanted guidance in my desperate attempts to help Simon. 'She comes only when she sees fit.'

'The lady Oonagh flexes her wings a little more each day,' said Conor. 'Her power grows. I believe we must harness an even greater strength to combat her. You could try. At the right place, at the time of need, with us around you, you could try.'

'Will you do this for us, Sorcha?' Cormack had come late to the knowledge of what we were battling. Linn glanced up at the sound of his voice. Her wound was beginning to mend nicely.

'How?' I asked. 'When?'

They all looked at Conor. Suddenly, he appeared much older than his sixteen years, as if the shadow of another self overhung him.

'Tomorrow,' he said. 'By our mother's tree, at dawn. I will arrange what is needed, and Sorcha will come with me. You, Liam, must make sure Diarmid is there. I don't care how you do it, but bring him. We must all be present. No horses; come on foot. Sorcha, bring a bundle with necessities for a night or two, for you will not return here for a time. You too, Padriac. I won't send Sorcha off alone. After we are finished, the two of you will go on to Father Brien's and he will get you away to a place of safety. I believe her next step will be to kill, perhaps by turning one of us against the others. We are a sorry bunch if we cannot protect our sister from such evil.'

'What is it you are planning, Conor?' asked Cormack, looking closely at his twin.

'Don't ask,' said Conor. 'The less said the better. We must rouse no suspicion. Why do you imagine I bade Sorcha and Finbar be absent from our evening meal? The two of them are like open books, they speak the truth at the risk of their own lives, and when they keep silent their thoughts blaze like a beacon from their eyes. Admirable, but dangerous. It was bad enough with big brother here sitting tight lipped and frowning under my lady's polite questions.'

'She is angry, for all her sweet manners,' said Liam. 'She stopped me this afternoon, before I could talk to Father. But not before he caught my drift; not before a small seed of doubt was sown. She must act soon; I read her intent in her eyes.'

'I, too,' said Conor gravely. 'So, stay out of sight tonight. When the sun dawns over the lake, we'll meet on the shore where our mother's tree grows. I believe a power can be summoned before which even the lady Oonagh must retreat.'

Cormack left his dog with me for company and went off to sleep elsewhere, and it was Conor himself who watched by the door that night with a weapon at his side. I slept in bursts, often waking with a start, as in the long dark nights at Father Brien's; and each time my brother was standing there with his gaze on some far distant vision, chanting softly in some tongue unknown to me. Maybe the half-light was deceiving me, and maybe it wasn't, but I thought he stood with one foot lifted a little from the ground, and one arm bent behind his back; and that one of his eyes was open and the other closed. He was still as a stone. The single candle threw shadows on the wall, and for a moment I saw a white-winged bird gliding, and a great tree. I drifted back into sleep.

Next morning there was a heavy dew, and a clinging mist blanketed the lake shore. We set out before

169

dawn, and the hem of my gown was soon soaked. I clutched the small pack I had brought with me. I had not many treasures. We made our way down the forest paths in total silence, without light. Conor wore white, and I followed him like a small trusting shadow. Behind me Linn trod in my footsteps. Sensing the need for secrecy, she curbed the urge to chase off after every rustle in the grass, and kept her silence.

We were the first to reach our destination. And yet, others had been here before us, for on the sward beside the young birch tree, where we had gathered so often before, objects had been laid out precisely, awaiting our arrival. The first hint of pre-dawn light showed white and yellow daisies strewn on the grass to the east of the tree where the land rose up to the forest. Amidst these lay a knife, unsheathed, with a hilt of bone. On the western side where the bank sloped down to the lake, a shallow earthenware bowl rested by the tree, and like the cup of Isha it was full to the brim with clear water. South and north, a slender wand of birch wood, a mossy stone from the forest's heart. Such were the makings of our ceremony. Who had laid the ritual objects here, I could not tell, nor would I ask Conor, for I felt the need to keep silence, the immense secrecy and importance of the moment. I wondered, though, who had carried them here, since my brother had been with me all that night.

Slowly they came. Cormack, a tall figure looming out of the mist. Close after him, Padriac, bearing a small pack like mine. Conor was standing close by the tree, waiting. One by one we took our places beside him without speaking. Now Finbar was suddenly there next to me, though I had neither seen nor heard him coming. His urgent whisper broke the hush.

'Sorcha. Look at this. Tell me what it is.' A small bottle, glass stoppered. An elegant little vessel, well suited for a lady's perfume. I removed the stopper and sniffed, then shook out a tiny amount of black powder onto my hand. There was enough light now to confirm by eye the conclusion my nose had given me. This was one of the deadliest of poisons. I looked at Finbar, and he read his answer in my eyes.

'It's monkshood,' I whispered back. 'Where did you find it?'

'In her quarters, amongst her things. It proves the case where Eilis is concerned, at least.'

'Hush,' said Conor. 'Wait for the others. It is not yet dawn.'

So we stood there, and I tried to empty my mind of the turbulent thoughts that raged there, and focus on our purpose. The forest was quite still; it was not yet time for the tree dwellers to start their songs to the dawn. It was a moment of truth, and we must make it ours. But we were not yet all assembled. And without the seven, our goal would not be achieved.

It seemed like forever, but was probably not very long, until there was a slight, rhythmic splashing, and a small boat put in to shore. Liam was rowing; Diarmid sat slumped in the prow, a grey cloak wrapped around him like a shawl. Cormack scrambled down the bank to help them ashore; it took him and Liam both to get Diarmid up to the sward. There was a heady reek of strong ale. Diarmid swayed between his brothers, half conscious, red-eyed. Liam did not look much better. It seemed he had matched his captive drink for drink in his effort to lull him into compliance.

'We are assembled, and it lacks but a few minutes to daybreak,' said Conor.

I felt again the presence of others, wiser, stronger, older ones, settling around him like a mantle. Instead of a dark-haired youth in a white robe, it was as if some ancient sage stood there before us, and the clearing seemed in some way to open up around him.

'Soon we will begin. But I warn you all. We stand together, we seven; she who tries to sever the bond between us does so at her peril. This is a great mystery, and may achieve our end. But in all things, we draw from the spirit world only such aid, and such strength, as its dwellers are willing to give us. Beyond that we must rely on our own wit and courage and resolve. Now, we begin our ceremony. And when it is ended, we part for a while. You, Sorcha, and you, Padriac, must go into hiding. Father Brien will shelter you and see you to a place of safety. When all is finished here, we will come for you. And whether what we do this morning brings help or no, the rest of us will act today for better or worse. We have the proof; our father must confront the truth and make his choice.'

We made a formal circle around the small tree as we had done many times before, standing close enough so that, if each had reached out an arm, he could have touched hands with the next. But there was no need to touch. This was our place of ritual, of oneness; the old oaks and beeches here had heard our childish rhymes, our tender secrets, had witnessed our communion with our mother's spirit. Sometimes we had been solemn and serious, and sometimes we had joked and laughed. These trees held in their hearts the tale of our growing years, and now they were to witness a mystery greater than any in our experience.

The first glint of the rising sun lightened the rim of the sky. Conor faced the south, and held the birch wand up before him.

'Creatures of fire, darting salamanders,' said Conor, 'children of the cleansing flame, steadfast of purpose, we salute you!' It seemed there was a stirring of the air, a momentary flickering of light; but the clearing was mist shrouded still.

Liam stood on the western side, and he looked out over the lake waters. Diarmid could not hold his place in the circle, but sagged against Cormack's shoulder, blinking in the growing light. Cormack held his errant brother's arm in a fierce grip. Liam raised the bowl to catch the pale dawn.

'Water spirits, changing and turning, deep-hearted, knowing ones, keepers of mysteries, we salute you,' he said, and lowered the bowl again.

Finbar faced north, where the tumbled boulders made a sort of giant's pathway between the great trees. His long hands held the mossy stone; the wakening light showed its surface etched with tiny marks and symbols.

'Earth dwellers, holders of secrets, truth-tellers, wise and worthy ones, we honour your presence,' he said. He turned inwards and placed the stone carefully on the grass.

'Now, Sorcha,' said Conor quietly. I looked up at the mighty trees, stretching before me into the east. A lark burst into song high overhead, and Padriac, standing next to me, grinned with pure pleasure at the sound. The lightening sky showed dawn was upon us, though the forest masked the exact moment of the sun's rising.

The knife was in my hands, and flowers about my feet. 'Sylphs of the forest,' I whispered. 'Spirits of oak, beech and ash, dryads of rowan and hazel, hear us. You who have guided and guarded our every footstep, you whose canopy has sheltered our growth, we honour you. Lady of the Forest, Lady of the blue cloak, hear me now. Come to us in our time of need, come to us in our time of darkness. Come to us if you will.'

I lowered the knife, turning to complete the circle. Birdsong rippled around the clearing, filling the air with fluting sound. Around our feet, and over the lake surface, the mist began to dissipate with the rising sun. We stood silent, our heads bowed. The circle must not be broken. We waited as the sky turned from grey to blue, and the shine of the lake waters broke through the trailing tendrils of vapour.

And then she came. It was as if she had been with us all the time, a slight hooded figure standing alone just where the rim of the lake touched the sand; and behind her, a low dark boat drawn up next to the other. She had heard me, and she had come. She took a step across the shore towards us, and another. The curling mist clung about her skirts. But something was wrong. Linn gave a growl, deep in her throat. And then, a sudden, silent flash of warning from Finbar, from Conor.

Run, Sorcha, run!

The forest. Now. Run!

I saw the first predatory fingers of mist stretch out and writhe around my brothers' bodies, holding them fast, and then reach out towards me where I stood on the far side of the tree, and then I saw her eyes, dark mulberry under winged brows, and the curl of auburn hair under the deep hood. She raised a white hand to slip back the covering from her head, and triumph was written bold on the lady Oonagh's

174

delicate features. I turned and fled, terror giving wings to my feet, over stone and boulder, scrabbling through mud and gravel, up, up the hill until the forest hid me in its still shadows. Ahead of me ran Linn, tail between her legs.

When I had gone as far as I could, I scrambled up into a great oak tree which cradled me in its massive limbs as I fought to get my breath back and still my pounding heart. Linn cowered in the undergrowth, giving tiny whimpers of unease. I had no need to see the lake shore, for I could see through Finbar's eyes, feeling with my brother, moment by cruel moment, the inevitable unfolding of the story.

Run, Sorcha, run! Our sister turns and flees across the clearing like a little white owl, and some power unknown shelters her into the safety of the trees. But we, we six, are held immobile as the clammy shreds of mist move like some live creature up our bodies with inexorable purpose. Our legs are rooted to the ground, our arms pinioned, our tongues silenced. Only our minds still struggle, powerless, to free themselves.

She slips the hood back, and the morning light dances on her curling hair. She throws her head back in triumphant laughter.

'Oh, if you could see yourselves, little brothers! So comical, so droll!' Her voice darkens. 'Did you think to outwit me with this paltry play-acting, this pathetic attempt at sorcery? Shame on you! You would have better kept to your war toys, and left off dabbling in matters beyond your understanding. Well, you have your just desserts now, my boys; let us see how well you fare when I have dealt with you. For I am afraid you have underestimated me quite badly.'

She paces around the circle where we stand helpless. Before each in turn, she stops and speaks.

'Liam. Protector and leader, isn't that the role your unfortunate mother intended for you? You have done a poor job of it today, first-born. But never mind. Your father can get more sons as he got you. These lands will never be yours. Oh, Colum will mourn your loss, I doubt it not, but only for a while. I will comfort him. And he has already forgotten your warning.'

She moves on to Diarmid where he still leans on his brother's shoulder, barely comprehending. 'Well, my sweet lover, my tender one. Thought you could take your father's place, did you? But you are nothing, nothing.' *She emphasises the insult by snapping her tapering fingers under his nose. Diarmid blinks.* 'Why would I dabble with an infant like you, when I can have a real man in my bed?'

She turns to Cormack. 'Did you enjoy the twist of your knife in living flesh, pretty warrior? You might be interested to know what your sister gets up to, when you are away from home. For you do not all share the same enemy, I fear. You learned your father's lesson well – smite first, ask questions later. Perhaps you should have tried that technique on me.'

I see Conor's eyes, for he stands directly opposite me. They blaze with courage. He summons every scrap of will to resist her. But he is young yet, and it is not enough.

'You have failed, little druid. Failed them all. And there are no second chances for those that cross me. Did you really think her power was greater than mine? How little you know, yet think yourself so wise. We are one and the same.'

She whirls around, and now she faces me. I will not be afraid. It comes to me again, the cold, the strangeness, the great beating of wings. I see the face of death.

'You would have challenged me before your father,' *she*

says. Ice creeps up my spine. 'You would have saved your sister at any cost. But I have your measure, and I see you for what you are, my old enemy. Your sister will never be safe from me; I will find her and she will suffer till she longs for death. And I will send you where there are no brave ideals, no moral heights, no right, no wrong. There is only survival. What price your fine heroics then, I wonder?'

Last, to Padriac, standing slack-jawed in shock. 'You wanted to know it all. The secrets of flight, the turns and twists of everything that moves and has being, the patterns of all living creatures. You shall know what it is to fly, and you shall feel the terror and pain of a wild beast. You shall live it until you beg to return to the human world. You will suffer and you will die thus; and there is no remedy.'

I lay curled in the great tree, my eyes squeezed shut, my hands tight over my ears. The pictures played through my mind for now I could not shut Finbar out if I tried. His anguish overrode any control he might have over his thoughts, and I was one with him as the terrible tale unfolded.

She raises her hands slowly. The dark cape falls back to show her blue gown, her filmy scarf with its delicate tracery of petals and butterflies. Her hands point to the sky, and her dark eyes seem to draw shadows down. She begins to chant, high, eerie, in an unknown tongue, dark with menace. Suddenly, darting light begins to flicker around our bodies as we stand immobile. The light comes from her hands, from the sky, from the earth. The whole clearing is full of sparks and flares. The birds are hushed in fear. The chant reaches its peak, and ceases. And then it happens. The cold, the rushing, the changing. Where there were sturdy leather boots, the webbed feet of a great water bird. Where the cloak shielded muscular young arms, a stretching, arching, white-feathered wing. Last to go, the mind, the spirit. Farewell, Sorcha. Farewell, little owl. The lightness, the morning, the water. We are swans. We are one with the lake. We are . . .

They were gone. My brothers were gone. But her voice went on, ringing in my head. '*I have not forgotten you, Sorcha, little sister. When you are tired and hungry, when the forest no longer shelters you, I will find you. When you least expect it, I will be there. For without your brothers you are nothing. First I will deal with your father; and then I will come for you.*'

My passage through the forest that day to Father Brien's is a blur in my memory. I tore my clothing, and cut my knees, and bruised my body clambering from rock to rock, from tree to tree. Linn kept pace with me, watching me anxiously, waiting for me as I struggled across the river, as I crept my way up the cliff face. My head was a blank, my vision blurred with tears that would not stop flowing, my throat swollen and dry with anguish. I climbed and wept, and wept and climbed again, and at last I came to the hermit's cave.

The sun had stayed out and the day was warm. It was mid-afternoon; my blundering journey had been a quick one, and at some cost, for I was dizzy and breathless and my whole body ached. It was Linn who saw the dark figure first, the figure of a tall woman sitting quietly on the bench under the rowan trees, her black hair flowing down her back. Her long cloak was the blue of distant mountains at dusk. The hound paused, then moved slowly forward, tail wagging hesitantly. The woman stretched out a hand.

'Come forward, daughter of the forest.' Her voice was deep and resonant. I did not move. Linn submitted to the caressing fingers; she too was tired from our headlong flight, and gave the woman's hand a brief lick before heading for the water trough to drink in long, thirsty gulps.

'Come forward, Sorcha. Do you not know me?' She made no move towards me. I sniffed, and raised a hand to wipe my nose. Where was Father Brien?

'Come, child. You called me at your time of need. Now I am here, and I will help you.'

Anger rose in me then, and I moved at last to stand before her and met her deep blue eyes with mine.

'You did not come! We called you, all of us – and now my brothers – my brothers are gone – and she said, she said you were one and the same, it was her we called.' I could not erase the image of each of them in turn, changing, changing from man to swan, and the terrible emptiness as their minds slipped away from me and were lost forever. 'How do I know which of you to believe?'

Her gaze was sharp. 'Her kind will tell you there is no black and white, only shadows. That any way can be wrong or right, that good and evil are two sides of the same coin. Believe her if you will. Perhaps she tells the truth, and I a falsehood. You must decide that, and you must choose your own path. You must choose it now.'

'There is no choice,' I wailed. 'She took them, she changed them, and now they are gone! What can I do but run and hide, and be alone? She said she would come after me, I must not stay here, I must find Father Brien –'

'Stop,' she said, holding up her hand, and I did, snatching air in a shuddering breath. 'He cannot help you this time. Listen.'

I listened, and was suddenly struck by the absence of sound. Even the insects seemed to have stopped chirping. The grove was deeply silent. 'You may wonder why this place is so quiet. It is the stillness of sleep, of farewell. He is here, but he is not here.'

'What do you mean?' I had thought myself unable to feel any more; but her words turned me cold.

'There is little time,' she said, standing up, and now I could sense the power of her presence as once before in this place; it was as if the heart of the great forest were centred here. 'You must listen, and listen well. For indeed you have a choice. You can flee and hide, and wait to be found. You can live out your days in terror, without meaning. Or you can take the harder choice, and you can save them.'

I stared at her. Linn had drunk her fill, and now lay down in the sun, tongue lolling. There was a little silence.

'Save them?' I whispered after a while. 'You mean – this spell can somehow be undone?'

'It can,' said the Lady, 'but it will not be easy. You are the only one that can achieve this, and so you must be extremely careful, for she suspects this and will seek to find you, in order to stop you. Your brothers' warning saved you, but they could not save themselves. Only you can do that.'

'But she told them – she said, *there is no remedy*.' I could hear the words now, like a death knell.

'She wished to leave them without hope, thinking always that they had failed, not just to save themselves but to protect you and to redeem their father. Without hope they will be vulnerable, less able to survive. Or so she believes.'

'That is cruel,' I said. 'Why does she do this?'

'It is her nature,' said the Lady tranquilly. 'According to her whim, she makes mischief of one sort or another; some harmless enough, some petty. This is a grand plan; but she has not learned that there are other patterns older and larger than her own. You can undo her work, this time, if you have the will.'

I felt a small glow of hope within me. 'What must I do?'

'It will be long, and arduous, and painful, Sorcha. Are you strong enough?'

'Yes! Yes! Tell me what I must do.'

Her eyes were compassionate as she moved to seat herself on the bench again. 'Sit here beside me, daughter. That's better. Now listen carefully. You must fashion a shirt for each of your brothers. The thread, the weaving, every stitch of these garments will be your own work.'

'I can do that, I can –'

'Hush. That would be an easy task indeed, even for a wild little thing such as you. But there is more. From the moment you leave this place till the moment of your brothers' final return to humankind, no word must pass your lips, no cry, no song, no whisper must you utter. Nor will you tell your story in pictures, or letters, or in any other way to a living creature. You will be silent, mute as the swans themselves. Break this silence, and the curse remains forever.'

'I understand,' I said quietly. 'And what more? How do I find my brothers, to clothe them in these shirts?'

'Ah, not so fast,' she said, and she took my hand in hers. 'This is still too easy. The shirts will be made not of wool, nor of flax, nor of skins. They will be spun and woven from the fibres of the starwort plant. The barbed stems will cut you, the spines will tear at your flesh. There will be no brother to comfort you and bathe your ruined hands. You will weep in silence, biting your lip not to cry out in pain. Can you do this?'

'Yes,' I whispered. Linn came over to me, thrusting her cold nose into my hand. I buried my fingers in her soft coat. 'Will I see my brothers?'

'You will see them. Next year on midsummer eve, and thereafter twice a year at midsummer and midwinter between dusk and dawn, they will resume their human form, and they will come to you if they can. But remember, you must not make a sound, you must not tell your tale, even to them, or they will be swans forever. The task will be long, Sorcha. You must leave this place and travel to safety as your brothers planned. Take the cart track to the west. Just before the crossroads there is a very old track to the right, that leads back into the forest. Look carefully, or you will miss it, for it is well concealed. Follow that path along the lake shore. It will lead you to a place of safety, where the forest will hide you for a time at least. Take from here what you need. Choose with care.'

I spoke hesitantly. 'Sometimes my brothers – sometimes we talk without words. Through images of the mind. Is even that forbidden?' How could I survive, if that link were broken? I looked up at her. Her features were very severe. I thought she was assessing me, wondering whether I was indeed as strong as I thought. She opened her mouth to speak, then hesitated. I took a deep breath.

182

'I will do as I must do,' I said. 'But my brothers are part of me, and . . .' I could hardly ask her any favours.

The Lady gave a little smile, as if she understood all too well. 'I did not make this spell; I seek only to counteract it. This silent speech will still be safe, I think. The lady Oonagh plays with forces she does not fully understand. The bond between your brothers and yourself is far stronger than she could ever imagine. You will not reach them in this way while they are swans. But you may use it when they return. You take a risk if you do. Remember, you must not tell them your story, for if you do the spell cannot be broken. You must learn to guard your mind, even from them.'

'But what if –'

'Hush, child. It is the way of spells, and charms, to set these tasks for us. You may choose to do as I ask, or not. Remember, when your shirts are sewn you must place them over these swans' necks, all six in the same place, one after the other, and if you have kept silence, then your brothers will be men again.'

There was a rustle as of a sudden wind in the bushes around us, and in the wink of an eye she was gone.

I had seen dead people before. The nature of my craft made this inevitable. But never, till now, someone close to me. Father Brien lay on the cave floor, where he had fallen. There was no time to grieve. Had there been longer, I might have wept over him, and I might have found out the cause of his passing. Perhaps it had been natural, a spasm of the heart or a rush of ill humours in the blood. It could equally have been poison, or a thumb cunningly applied to the neck. I

183

closed his sightless eyes and touched his cheek. Whatever had occurred, his face now showed the tranquillity of deep, abiding acceptance. He was at one with himself and with the great wheel of being. They say the spirit does not leave the body, not fully, until the third morning after death. My old friend had not been gone that long, but his inner self had flown, out into the arching expanse of sky he used to watch from the top of Ogma's Peak, out above the dark tree tops and the wide waters of the lake, and on into the west. I placed the wooden cross between his hands and the words of a Christian prayer were in my mind, but I said nothing. Who knew where his spirit would fly? He had always been open to both ways; in death, many doors would open for him.

I had no wish to abandon his body, even untenanted as it was, without further ceremony. There should have been burning, but to kindle a fire was to ask for discovery. Besides, I must pack and leave while it was still day. There was time only to sprinkle rue and tansy leaves, and a little of his store of monkshood. Linn hovered in the doorway; she would not come in. I did not weep for him. Instead, I felt a cold sense of purpose take hold of me. The grief was still there, and the emptiness. But I was able to focus on what must be done, and I moved swiftly through the necessary tasks.

More than once I blessed the good Father for his practicality. His old horse was there, tied up under the trees. Because of the need for speed and conceal-ment, I would not take the cart, but the animal could carry a load, and so aid me well. For I had no doubt I must live alone, and fend for myself, for quite some time. If I had known then just how long it would be, my courage might have failed me. Six shirts, I thought. That could take at least until midsummer. And I would meet nobody during that time, so I would need food, and seeds, and medicines, and the wherewithal to make fire and to sew and spin and weave. Father Brien had not foreseen that part, but nonetheless he had prepared well, expecting to provision me and my brother for a trip well beyond the forest's boundaries. I had abandoned my own bundle back on the lake shore when I had fled in terror. I would not have my clothes, or my special salves and remedies, or the remnants of my ruined garden which Finbar had gathered so carefully for me. I felt in the pocket of my gown. The small, smooth piece of wood with its carved symbols was still there.

Father Brien kept his stores at the back of the cottage, and I took anything that might be useful. A bag of barley meal, a sack of dried beans, a small crock of honey. The weather was already chill. I helped myself to an old cloak and a homespun tunic. Simon's boots were still there, and I took them. A sharp knife, a sickle, a cooking pot. It was going to be difficult to feed the dog. I trusted she would develop a sudden skill for hunting. Father Brien had no distaff and spindle, no weaving loom. But even a holy Father's garments need mending sometimes, so I found bone needles and a spool of thread, and these I slipped into the small pack. A water bottle, a spade. The horse looked at me a little plaintively, his ears twitching. I placed some rolled-up blankets on top of the load and tied it firmly. The little pack, which contained carefully selected items from Father Brien's stock of herbs and spices, I would carry myself. And his oaken staff I would use to ease my way.

I stood there a moment before I took my farewell. The clearing was full of memories. The coming of

Father Brien, his prayer, and reading, and healing, his solitary life in the forest and his teachings. His young visitors: the solemn Liam and sunny Diarmid, the twins like mirror images, Cormack, bold and fearless, Conor, deep and subtle. Finbar with his passionate integrity. Padriac, eager for knowledge. And their small sister, who was not the seventh son of a seventh son, but who trailed along after them anyway. He had taught us much over the years, and now he was gone. Now my brothers' human selves were indeed just that, just a memory, until I should bring them back. Here was the rowan tree where I had seen the Lady of the Forest that first time. Here the spot where Simon had held his knife to my throat and asked us why we would not end his miserable life. The trees whispered the memories of my stories, and the air still held the trace of his voice; don't leave me, it breathed, don't leave me alone.

I rubbed a hand fiercely across my cheeks, and then snapped my fingers for Linn to come. She would learn fast enough that I could no longer call to her, or praise her with kind words. Then I took up the horse's leading rope, turned my face towards the forest and walked steadily away into the west.

CHAPTER FIVE

The Lady of the Forest had chosen our refuge well. It was close to the northern shore of the lake, at a spot where the curve of a small wooded promontory sheltered a tiny bay from view. Where the land rose above this bay there was a cave which owed as much to artful engineering as to nature. Although it was so near the shore, gnarled rowans and overhanging creepers concealed it completely from view, so it would be invisible from any track or thoroughfare. Some way further up the hill, in a small clearing, a tiny spring welled, and here herbs grew half-wild, where once they had been cultivated by some solitary wanderer such as I. And all along the stream bed, all the way down to the lake, grew the strong stems and feathery leaves of starwort. This plant does not die down in winter, but remains green even in the coldest time. So I could start right away.

The cave itself had been a surprise. Its walls bore marks of careful excavation, and here and there they were engraved with mysterious symbols whose meaning I guessed at only dimly. I thought Conor would have known what warning or protection they gave, what tale they told. There were cavities in the walls, and not all were empty. I found blankets in an oiled wrapping, and several old cloaks, and a couple of knives with decorated bone handles and remarkably well-preserved blades. It seemed others had sheltered here before me, perhaps protected by the Fair Folk. More useful still, there was oatmeal in a crock, and a store of sweet, wrinkled apples.

The blankets were the best discovery, for it was close to midwinter, and I did not feel safe enough to light more than the smallest fire, lest my presence be detected. I was always cold, chill to the bone during the long nights, aching and slow on frosty mornings. I wrapped the blankets around myself and tried not to feel it.

Perhaps I was stupid to believe I could lift the spell. Too many stories, you might say, a head too full of old tales, where it's just a matter of completing the tasks, and then the hero wins his heart's desire. But I was not so foolish, even then. I had once told Simon he could make his tale end any way he liked. But this was not strictly true. I set my path straight ahead; but there were others that influenced its course, that diverted and changed and confused it. And as the Forest Lady had warned me, even at the start it would be very hard. Far harder than I had believed it could be when I had first listened white-faced to her description of my task.

Perhaps you have tried spinning or weaving, with flax maybe, or fine wool. It takes a toll on the hands, as the combing and twisting rubs and blisters the fingers, as the movement of the spindle starts to wear a deep aching into the joints. You can tell a spinner by her hands. As they give beauty to their work, the hands grow gnarled and twisted and old. The noble ladies of the ancient tales, Etain, and Sadb, who became a deer, and Niamh of the golden hair, whose name my mother had shared, they cannot have been spinners and weavers, for their hands are described as white and fair, decorated with silver rings, hands for a brave warrior to kiss when he returns victorious from battle. Hands suited to fine embroidery, or playing the harp. Slender fingers for masking a delicate yawn, or touching a lover's cheek. The ladies in the old tales had never heard of starwort.

I have told of this plant before, how it seems soft like a pigeon's feathers, with its grey-green foliage and delicate, starlike flowers. How it buries its tiny needles deep in the flesh, to burn and burrow and torture like fire. How the flesh swells and reddens and throbs, how the pain remains until every trace of the poison is removed. I barely knew where to start, for there was no way to protect my hands and still do it. I could use a knife to cut the stems, and I could catch them in a cloth. That was one thing. But I could not shred the stems and leaves and twist them into thread with my hands in gauntlets. Besides, I knew enough of magic to recognise there was no cheating allowed. To save my brothers, I would have to suffer as they were suffering. As my father no doubt was suffering in his own way, for even he could scarcely be untouched by the sudden disappearance of all his sons in one cruel stroke. I wondered what explanation the lady Oonagh had given him. No, I was meant to grasp this plant and to make these shirts with my bare, bleeding hands and do it I would, for I knew that only this way could the spell be broken.

I had no tools, and little skill. I had some idea of how it was done for I had watched the women in the settlement as they sat on their high stools drawing out the fibres of wool, feeding them across from distaff to spindle, letting the thread twist and grow while the spindle spun its way slowly down to the ground. Then the length of thread would be wound onto the shaft, and they would set the whorl turning, and the whole thing would start again. There was a rhythm to it, and often they sang at their work. It had looked simple enough. But this was not wool. A fibrous plant like starwort would have to be soaked, and beaten, and dried before I could even think of forming a thread from it. Well, I would have to start somewhere.

I made the spindle first. There were pines further up the hill, and an even length of narrow branch, stripped of its twigs, would furnish me well enough as a spindle shaft. As I used the hatchet I did not forget a silent greeting to the tree spirits. If I were to live out here alone, their good will would be essential. Linn solved the next part of the problem for me, as she snuffled about in the undergrowth, tracking interesting smells. She had learned a game of fetch, and now she brought a green pine cone which had fallen from the tree before it could ripen, and dropped it expectantly at my feet, hoping I would throw it for her. The cone was well shaped, symmetrical, and a good weight. So there was my spindle whorl. I gave Linn a pat and threw another cone for her to bound after. When I returned to my cave, I used my little knife to make a hole in the base of the cone, and into this I wedged the end of the shaft. I cut a notch in the other end, where the thread would be

190

hooked around. So far, so good. Then I took my knife and went to gather starwort.

I will not dwell too long on that process. I cut the stems and caught them in a piece of sacking, and that spared my hands a little, but still the spines lodged themselves in my flesh and my hands hurt more than I could have believed possible. Despite the abundant supply of the plant, the task was slow. When I had a bundle of stems ready, I went down to the lake shore, hunting for a place where they might be soaked. I was lucky. The spring flowed down between large mossy rocks, and here and there little pools had formed. Just above the pebbly shore there was a place where I could move a stone or two so there was only the gentlest flow through one shallow pool. Here I placed my spiny armful. With some plants, ash was used to hasten the preparation for spinning. I knew that from my study of herb lore.

Deciding it could not hurt to try, I waited until my tiny fire had cooled in the morning, then scooped up a handful of the soft ash and took it with me to the water's edge. I sprinkled the ash on to the stems, and used a round stone to pound and break the tough fibres apart, until they had more the look of single threads. I twisted each of these rough hanks around a stick, which could be wedged between the stones in the pool so that the water flowed all around it. Then I waited. Three days' respite, I had, time to pluck the starwort spines from my hands and to apply a soothing salve, time to do an inventory of my meagre stores and to realise that without foraging or stealing I would not last beyond the spring. Long enough to practise boiling oats in water over the fire to make a simple porridge, and to explore my new home a little. I was taken aback to discover that it was not so very far to the top of the western hill, and that from here I could see an area of cleared land, carved out of the forest for grazing. There were small farmhouses there, one or two. They were close enough to provide supplies, maybe. And they were close enough to be a threat to my safety.

On the fourth day I took the starwort from the water, and pounded the fibres again, and hung them up inside the cave until they were almost dry. On the next day I began to spin.

Poor Linn. She was well attuned to my moods, and was simple and faithful as only a good hound can be. It was beyond her understanding why I wept, and why my whole body was tense with pain, and why she could not make it better by licking me and whining and sitting as close by me as she could. Her distress bothered me, and I tried to work while she was away hunting; but the task was slow, so slow, strand by creeping strand of brittle thread that broke and unravelled and would not twist, and try as I might to keep going, the pain would soon be too much to bear and I would drop the spindle and run to plunge my poor hands in the stream to soothe them.

They were dark times, and in the depths of them I would hear an inner voice that said, this task is impossible. Why not give up now? Look, your hands are swollen and ruined, you weep day in and day out, and what have you to show for it? A little spool of ill-spun thread, lumpy and fragile, scarce enough to hem a jacket for a butterfly, let alone a shirt for a man. Surely this task cannot be completed. Besides, how can you be sure the Lady of the Forest did not lie to you? Perhaps this is all some cruel trick, and your labours are for nothing.

It was hard to ignore this voice. More than once I took out the small, smooth piece of wood, and looked at the little tree carved there, and imagined myself talking to Simon, talking and talking through his despair and self-hatred and wretchedness. And I began to tell myself stories, not out aloud, but in my mind; and I practised focusing all my attention on the tale, whether it was of a hero or a giant or three brothers setting off to seek their fortune. If I could not remember a story, I invented one, or elaborated on what I knew.

All day my hands went about their terrible work, and the pain was still there, as was the swelling that made it so hard to control spindle and thread. But my mind went beyond the pain and dwelt with lovely lady or noble warrior or lucky traveller, and with dragon, serpent and magic wish.

When dusk made work impossible, I would put away what I had done, trying hard not to see how meagre the length of thread my long labour had produced. There was no brother to pull the needles of starwort from my flesh, no singer of songs to comfort me, no friend to bind up my hands with healing ointments. The barbs had to stay in the skin, for my swollen, numbed fingers had not the fine control needed to extract them. From time to time the flesh began to weep, and ill humours rose beneath and oozed from the lesions. Then I would grow feverish and dizzy. But I had chosen wisely from Father Brien's store of remedies, and so I had brought a salve of self-heal and comfrey, and I made an infusion of dried willow bark and herb of grace in spring water which I used for both washing and drinking. After a while I would be well enough to begin again, though weaker. Eventually it seemed my body accepted the inevitable, and my hands grew scarred and hard in defence at their ill treatment. The pain still remained, but I could go on.

Winter slipped into spring, and I grew thinner. I could count my ribs and felt the chill at night even though Linn slept beside me. And I was hungry. For a bag of meal lasts only so long, even for one girl, and then unless you can beg or steal, you have to rely on what can be found. I had not eaten flesh or fish since I was a small child, for I had always felt a closeness with other creatures that made my senses revolt at the very idea. Linn had learned to hunt in the forest; and to dispose of her prey neatly and out of sight of her human companion. For me it was harder. There was food to be found now the weather was warmer, a good supply of mushrooms, cresses in the streams, wild onions. It was too early in the season for much more, and I rationed the last of my barley meal, my dwindling supply of beans, against the time when berries and nuts would ripen. Despite my hunger, I grudged every moment wasted in foraging.

The horse had grown gaunt and wild eyed, and I could no longer keep him. One day when the sun was out and the first real warmth of spring was in the air, I took him up through the woods to the place where the land had been cleared for grazing, where you could see green fields and stone walls and a cow or two in the distance and a plume of smoke from a little cottage. I rested my forehead against his neck for a while, trying to let him know that Father Brien would want him to be safe and useful and well-fed. Then I slapped his flank and pointed ahead. He set out cautiously across the field, and I slipped back under the trees and left him. I hope he found kindness and a warm stable.

Early in spring there was a great storm that lashed the forest for a day and a night, whipping tree tops into a frenzied dance, driving needles of icy rain deep inside my shelter, so that every blanket, every piece of clothing, every corner of dry flooring was saturated. My firewood was useless, and I sat and shivered helplessly while the dog did her best to keep me warm. By the second morning, as the storm slowly abated, I was convulsed with shaking, and could think only of the big fireplace in the hall at home with its crackling pine logs, and the little fire in my bedroom which had cast its glow on tapestried owl and unicorn. Half-dreaming, I imagined strong arms wrapping me in a blanket and cradling me safely until I believed I slept warm and secure. To wake from this dream drenched and trembling with cold was cruel indeed. After a while Linn grew tired of me and went out into the morning, while I sat silently weeping, thinking I would give it all up, almost, if only someone would bring me a bowl of Fat Janis' barley broth.

I don't know how long I sat there, but eventually my trance of self pity was interrupted by Linn's barking, and I hobbled outside, cramped limbs protesting all the way, to find one of the great ash trees had fallen in the night, bringing down many smaller sisters in her path, and now lay not far from my doorway. Linn was further up the hill, chasing something in the undergrowth.

The death of this great tree had opened up the dense woodland around my cave, and I could see the glint of the lake between the close-spaced ranks of young elm and willow. I stood by the fallen giant, resting my scarred hands on her smooth grey bark, and spoke inwardly to the spirit that had dwelt there, for the storm had taken her home in one violent gesture. I thanked her for the years of shelter the tree had given to small creatures, the nourishment she had shed for the forest soil, for her deep and abiding peace and understanding. I told her I would use the wood well, to make new tools for my work, and to fuel my fire, and I reassured her that the light which now bathed the hillside in its white, cold after-storm brightness would draw up new life from the soil. In time, another great ash would grow here. I told her this, and the cool smoothness of the bark soothed my injured fingers. I felt the knowledge and mystery of the great tree absorbed into my spirit, so that I knew her oneness, her aloneness, the dignity of her life and of her passing. I would not cut the wood yet. I would wait for the spirit to move on, and then at the right time, I would chop and dry and fashion new distaff and spindle, and I would try my hand at making a weaving frame, for I judged that I might have spun enough thread by now to start on the first shirt. My strength was not such that I could use the massive trunk or major limbs of such a giant, but my small hatchet could tackle the lesser branches. I looked at my damaged hands and flexed my aching fingers. It was going to get harder.

Meanwhile, the great ash would rest where she lay, and mosses would creep over her trunk, and tiny creatures make their homes in her dim hollows. Even in death she was a link in the great chain of the forest's being.

The season moved on. Bees clustered heavy on the sweet florets of lavender and the woods were carpeted with jewel bright flowers. Day and night were in balance, and birds were busy with wisps of straw and twig, readying havens for a new brood.

Venturing to the lake shore early one morning, I saw flocks of waterbirds far out towards the small islands, drifting on the silver expanse of water, rising to the sky in great clouds of beating wings or stooping for fish. I could not tell, at such a distance, if any of them were swans.

The water was warmer and I steeled myself to strip and wash, and to clean my mud-covered garments. In this time I had seen no sign of human life on this shore. It was as if this corner of the wilderness were somehow protected from mortal interference, and indeed perhaps this was true, for a time at least. The forest will hide you, the Lady had said. Who could say how much her influence was at work here?

Time passed, and the forest burst forth with new life. I played out my small domestic round day after day. I would rise at dawn to wash in lake water, and I would blow the embers of my tiny fire back to life, and boil water with maybe a handful of cress and wild onions for a meagre breakfast. After this, Linn would set out along the shore or into the woods, hunting, and I would go out to search for food. As spring moved into summer this task grew easier. Blackberries ripened, gooseberries and red currants were here and there for the taking. Elder trees were crowned with clusters of white. Wild herbs were abundant, parsley and sage, marjoram and figwort. I noted where apples grew, and hazel trees, for these would provide a good harvest later, in the autumn. I knew by now I must live here at least one more winter, for my progress with the task was wretchedly slow. I had barely enough thread for one shirt, and it was already close to summer.

When I returned from my foraging, I would fetch distaff and spindle, and the unforgiving bundle of fibres, and I would spin and spin, and feel the barbs piercing my skin, and I would tell tales in silence with my eyes fixed on nothing. From time to time I would get up to walk out under the trees, and I would rest my aching back and shoulders against a strong oak or sturdy elm. Then my mind would reach out for them, out across the lake, into the sky, anywhere my brothers might be.

Where are you, Finbar?

But there was nothing. For all I knew they might be dead, brought down by some hunter's arrow or prey to wolf or wild boar.

Where are you?

I did not allow myself to do this for long. Linn would come back, licking her lips, and settle by me companionably, and I would spin again. Later in the day I would take the thread I had made in the morning, and add it to my weaving. It was beyond my ability to make a loom such as I had seen the women use at home. But I had found a flat piece of bark, two hand spans in length, a little less in breadth, and I had notched the edges and tied the warp threads around. The weft I wove in by hand, with a needle of bone taken from Father Brien's. Under and over, under and over. The fabric was lumpy and uneven, but it held together. Time enough later to think about how such work might be sewn into a shirt.

Midsummer took me almost by surprise. I was working as steadily as I could, and began to search further afield for starwort, for I had almost exhausted the supply near my cave, and must now leave it to recover. One day I ventured back along the old path where I had taken the horse, up the hill between vines and creepers, ferns and mosses, in the dark green filtered light of ancient forest, until I was close to the place I had left him. There was a strange feeling in me, as if I must make sure the rest of the world had not gone away while I hid solitary in my cave spinning. For what about the tales of lad and lass taken by the Folk under the hill? They might spend but one night with the fair ones, singing and dancing, and come home to find a hundred years had passed and their people all dead and gone. Who was to say the same might not happen to me?

I came as close to the forest's edge as I dared, and then I climbed quietly up into the spreading arms of a walnut tree. Linn guarded my bundle, happy enough to rest amongst the ferns and bracken, for the sun was hot and there was a still heaviness that presaged summer storms. From my vantage point I looked out over a stand of young elder trees, down to a cart track bordered by hawthorn bushes, and beyond this to stone-walled fields, some planted with barley or rye, others left for grazing. There was a cottage or two, far enough away. Here and there the land rose to small conical hills, some crested with pines or oaks. And beyond the farmlands, the forest began again. I sat quiet amid the stillness, scarcely thinking of anything. The sweet smell of hawthorn blossom drifted in the air, and I sensed the movement of small creatures about their business, insects sluggish in summer's heat, rustling of rabbit and squirrel in the undergrowth, and the lesser-seen, mysterious dwellers of the trees, whose voices floated in the air like fragile, whispering music.

Sorcha, hail. Sorcha, our sister. A tinkle of laughter, and the flash of a delicate wing or a cobwebby veil, half seen in the dappled light. Sometimes you would come across a long strand of golden hair, or a slender footprint, where they had passed. *Come and dance with us, sister.* I greeted them silently, knowing they knew I could not follow them. And then in a flurry they were gone; for along the cart track came an all too human band of youths, both boys and girls, laughing, whistling and shouting, with flowers and ribbons in their hair. I watched them quietly, and Linn stayed silent where she was; one sharp gesture from me was enough to command her obedience now. As the band passed between the hawthorn bushes, they paused to wrap coloured streamers on branches still fragrant with late blossom, and sang an old rhyme, asking the great Mother for a bountiful harvest. They sang with shining faces and bright eyes; and when they finished the girls broke into fits of giggles and ran off down the track, and the boys ran after them, and then they started again.

Two of the young men had bundles of sticks on their backs, and the party split up, the girls continuing down the track until every hawthorn bore its summer garland of gold and white and green ribbons. The boys made their way up the nearest small hill, and now I could see a bonfire in readiness on its very top, and realised this must indeed be the final preparation for Meán Samhraidh, the midsummer solstice.

Tonight there would be offerings passed across the fire, and flaming herbs would be carried to stable and barn, to field and cottage, to ask the blessing of Dana, the mother goddess, on every creature that dwelt there.

And so it was time. Time to find out if I could believe what the Lady had told me. Time to learn if it was true I could break the spell. For I remembered well her promise; twice a year, at midsummer and midwinter, they will come to you if they can, and from dusk to daybreak they may resume their human shape. The words themselves were hedged with uncertainty. But I believed my brothers would come, and that I must return to the lake and wait for them.

The girls were still in sight down the track and I dared not move while I could be seen. And now there was another young man coming, more hesitantly, well back from the rest. He was thickset and had the coarse, innocent features of one born not quite right, one who would be always one step behind the others. He hurried along the path as best he could, limping a little, his big hands stretching out to touch a ribbon bow here, a blossom there, his broad smile revealing a prominent set of teeth.

The others had moved on without him, but he didn't seem bothered. Instead, he chose the place just below my tree to sit down by the road and rummage in his pocket. I was eager to be off, but could not move. The boy took out a lump of bread and cheese and began to partake of his meal in a leisurely way. I could hardly begrudge him; after all, he had chosen the same spot as I to enjoy the sights and smells of this glorious summer day. So I waited, watching him take each mouthful. It was a long time since I had tasted bread. After he had finished, the boy seemed to drift off into a half-doze, his hat tilted almost over his eyes, his hands dangling between his knees, apparently scarce taking in his surroundings. I waited a little longer. He showed no signs of moving. I thought of my brothers, and the long walk back to the lake, and I began, very slowly, to climb down from my perch.

There had been a time when we could move through the forest, my brothers and I, with speed and in total silence. Nobody could have seen us, or heard us, or caught us. But now my hands had lost their fine touch. They were swollen and hardened and the joints ached even in summer's warmth. I lost my grip for a moment and grabbed at a branch, and I made a twig crack, just the tiniest noise. He was on his feet in a flash, staring straight at me, and his round brown eyes were full of wonderment.

'Faery!' he exclaimed in a loud, slightly indistinct voice. 'Faery girl!'

His grin was huge and joyous, as if his fondest dream had come true; as if he had seen the most wonderful object of his imaginings. For an instant I stared back at him. Then I slipped away to the ground, grabbed my bundle and fled into the forest, and I made sure my path home was so hard to follow that none could track me there. Poor boy. I wonder how many times he had waited in that spot, hoping for a sight of the Fair Folk. Often it was to just such as him that they chose to appear. I hoped, if he told his tale, that it would be put down to excessive imagination. With luck, they would believe it really was a faery girl that he had seen.

The encounter had shaken me. To risk discovery thus, on the very day of my brothers' return, had been foolish in the extreme. I vowed never to come that way again, however great my need to see humankind, however painful my isolation. No word must make its way back to my village, and thence to the lady Oonagh. For she would come for me if she found me, I was in no doubt of that. Besides, I had wasted precious time. Already midsummer, and the first shirt barely begun. At this rate I would be here for many moons. I hastened home through the forest, eager for nightfall.

To speak truth, I scarcely doubted that first time

that they would return as she had told me. And so I prepared for them, washing myself, dragging a comb through my dishevelled curls, making my simple home as orderly as I could. I left the fire alight, though damped down, and I walked to the lake shore well before sunset. There I performed the ritual alone and in silence. I was careful to leave nothing out. In turn I greeted the spirits of Fire, Air, Water and Earth. I did not ask any favours. Instead I opened my mind to what would come. Told them that I accepted it, whatever it was. Asked them to accept me for my part in the great web of life, and to use me as they would. When I had finished I took up my staff of oak that had been Father Brien's, and I cast the circle on the white sand around me. I sat cross-legged at its very centre and waited, with the wide, empty waters of the lake before me. Gradually the sounds of the forest began to make their way back into my consciousness. Trees rustled, birds called and answered high above. I could do no more.

The sky deepened to rose and violet and a dusky grey. An owl flew overhead unseen, her mournful cry floating in the evening air. Not long. Not long now. Linn had been quiet, crouched in the grass, watching me carefully. Now she crept closer, growling softly. And they were there, out on the water, drifting together, white ghosts on the darkening ripples. My heart leapt, but I sat still and waited. Thunder rolled far away to the west, and the air clung damply to the skin.

The last trace of sunlight was extinguished; night stretched her hand over the forest. As dusk became dark, there was a movement in the water, and they came to shore, one by one. The moment of changing was veiled from me by the night, for the moon had yet to show herself through gathering clouds. I saw dimly the shape of a great wing, the bending of a strong, arching neck. And then they were here, my brothers, my dear ones, on the sand before me, dazed and wet, half-clothed in the self-same garments they had worn before, and then, best balm for the spirit, came the silent greeting of mind to mind, stumbling and incoherent at first, but filling my heart with the deepest joy.

Sorcha. Sorcha, we are here.

I moved forward, touching each one in turn, half-seeing by the light of my small lantern the wildness and confusion in their eyes, hearing their voices halting and hesitant. All was not well with them. If I had expected them delivered to me whole and unchanged, brave and true and laughing as I remembered them, then I had misapprehended the nature of enchantments.

It is not so bad. Conor put his arm around me as I heard his inner voice. *Remember the tale of the four fair children of Lir? Turned into swans they were for nine hundred years, and when at last they came back to human form they were like little old men and women, bent and deformed. We have returned unharmed, in body at least – and somewhat sooner than they.*

This did little to reassure me. Did my brothers know nothing of the spell and counter-spell? Nothing of the length of their enchantment, and the method of undoing it? How would I explain this, without the power of speech, and with the command of silence on my story? And there was something else wrong here.

Where is Finbar? For my mind was able to touch but the one brother, and my hands found but five.

'He comes. Give him time,' said Conor aloud, and I was reassured that he sounded quite like his normal self. And now the others were getting up, groaning slightly as if from excess of ale or a hard beating in the practice yard, and as their human consciousness slowly returned to them they gathered around me, and hugged me, and gripped each other by hand or shoulder as if to be sure that this was not just another vision or trick of sorcery. The dog sidled across to Cormack, still cautious. He bent to fondle her ears and stroke her scarred face with gentle fingers. Then she knew him, and jumped up to plant huge paws on his chest, barking ecstatically. I saw him draw back for just a second, and a look almost like fear passed across his face; and then it was gone as he roughed up her coat, grinning.

I took hold of Conor's jacket, drawing him away from the shore. In my other hand I held the small lantern. My brothers followed me up the hill to the cave, but they were still slow to return to full recognition and were silent for the most part, following my direction without question. We reached the cave, and I rekindled the fire and lit another lamp. It should be safe enough. Tonight all souls would be gathered for midsummer revels, and only the most foolhardy or ignorant mortal would venture deep into the forest at such a time.

My brothers sat around the little fire like lost spirits that had drifted off their chosen path. There was little talk at first; they seemed stunned, though from time to time one would reach out to touch another's hand as if to reassure themselves that they were indeed returned to human form. After a while I became aware that Finbar was there as well, come silently up from the water to join our small circle. It was as I stretched to throw another piece of ash wood on the fire that his hand came out to grasp mine; his eyes had always been sharp.

'Your hands,' he said grimly, 'what's the matter with your hands?' and his long fingers moved gently over mine, feeling the roughness and the swelling and the hardening of the joints. 'Sorcha, what has happened? Why don't you speak to us?'

I was mindful that my story could not be told, not even to my brothers. So, I touched my closed lips with my fingers then placed my hands together and swept them swiftly apart, shaking my head. *I may not speak. Not at all. I may not tell you.* I had a strong shield around my thoughts, but I had reckoned without Conor's intuition.

'She has laid this curse on you,' said Conor, 'that much is plain. With what end? Is there an end?'

I shook my head miserably, showing him again with fingers on lips that I could not tell him.

'You can say nothing at all?' ventured Diarmid, his face a picture of frustration. 'But then how will we know – how will we –'

'Have you no memory of the time away?' Conor asked him cautiously.

'Memory? Not exactly. It's more like . . .'

'Feelings, not thoughts,' put in Padriac who, of them all, seemed most like his old self, if somewhat quieter. 'Hunger, fear, warmth, cold, danger, shelter. That's all a swan knows. It was – different. Very different.' I saw him look down at his arms for a moment, and I suspected he was wishing that, as a man, he could still fly.

'You must understand, Sorcha,' said Conor in his measured way, 'that the mind of a wild creature is unlike that of a man or woman. I believe very little crosses the boundaries with us, when we change. As swans we can see the things that occur to man and woman, but we cannot comprehend them as you do;

and once transformed back to our human shape, we remember the other life only dimly, as through an autumn mist. Padriac summed it up well. A wild creature knows the need to hide, to protect, to flee, to seek food and refuge. But conscience, and justice, and reason – these are outside the span of its mind. Finbar finds this punishment hard, for he values these things above all others. The lady Oonagh might almost have chosen the curse especially for him; it is hard enough for the rest of us.' He looked across the circle of firelight at Finbar, who watched us silently, his face in shadow.

'Sorcha's own punishment has been worse,' said Cormack soberly. 'To be alone in the forest, so far from everything, and unable to speak.' He looked at me closely.

'At least we have returned, and can set things right for you,' said Liam, who was stretching his long legs cautiously as if to check they still worked properly. 'Or is this some vision, to be gone before we have time for thought or action? For how long are we returned to our human form?'

But I could not answer. To tell this was to tell part of the story, and it was forbidden.

'Not long, I suspect, from Sorcha's look of misery,' said Diarmid bitterly.

'I would suspect, as little as one night,' said Conor. 'In the old tales, it is dusk and dawn that are the times of changing. We must be prepared for the worst.'

'One night?' Diarmid was outraged. 'What can be done in one night? I would have vengeance; I would undo the ill I helped create. But we are far from home, too far to return. Why are you here, Sorcha? What about Father Brien who was to have helped you?'

That was another story, and so could be told. I

mimed for them. A Christian cross; coins on the eye-lids. Flight up, up into the distant sky and away to the west. They understood me well enough.

'So our old friend is dead,' said Liam.

'And not from natural causes, I'll be bound,' added Cormack. 'That fellow was like an oak, slight though he was; he'd a strength in him better than many a good fighting man's.'

'The lady Oonagh's hand stretches out,' said Diarmid.

Conor glanced at him. 'There will be vengeance,' he said. 'Full and terrible vengeance. His killers will be scattered in pieces, and crows will pick at their white bones.'

We all stared at him. His tone had not even changed.

'We believe you,' said Diarmid, raising an eyebrow.

'He was a Christian,' put in Padriac. 'Perhaps he would have wished forgiveness, not retribution.'

Conor stared into the fire. 'The forest protects its own,' he said.

'This was a great loss to you, Sorcha,' said Liam. 'Have you now no companions here, save solitude?'

'She cannot tell you,' said Conor. 'But all this is for a purpose, I have no doubt. Sorcha, do you know the length of this enchantment? Is there an end to this? And when may we return here?'

I shook my head, placing both hands over my mouth. Why wouldn't they stop asking questions? I felt a tear trickle down my cheek.

'It will be a long time, I think.' Finbar's voice was very soft. 'A time to be measured in years rather than moons. You must not press Sorcha for answers.'

Not one of them questioned what he had said. When Finbar spoke thus, it was always the truth.

'Years!' exclaimed Liam.

'She cannot be left here alone for so long,' said Diarmid. 'It is not safe, nor seemly.'

'There is no alternative,' Conor said. 'Besides, you know your old stories as well as the rest of us. There must be a purpose to this, but she is forbidden to tell. Right, Sorcha?'

'Tasks,' said Cormack quietly, from where he sat with his arms around the dog. 'There will be tasks to complete before the end.' He saw my nod of agreement. 'What can we do, Sorcha?'

I shook my head, spread my hands wide. *Nothing. Nothing, but stay safe. Stay alive for long enough.*

'It has something to do with her hands,' said Conor slowly, and his voice was dark with some feeling I could not fully understand. 'Not for nothing would you damage yourself thus. There is some evil at work here, I am certain of it.'

I shook my head, for he was only half right.

No. Not evil. This is the way. You must let me do this. I can save you.

'Here,' said Padriac from behind me. I had not noticed him going into the cave, but now he emerged with my spindle in one hand and a length of the tell-tale thread dangling, sharp and brittle. The firelight glowed on its deceptive, delicate strands. There was a general intake of breath, and Padriac sat down amongst the others, the spindle balanced between his capable hands.

'What is this?' asked Liam, outraged, as his fingers touched the fibre. 'This thread is full of fine needles. No wonder her hands are ruined. This thread is –'

'It's starwort,' said Padriac. 'Sorcha has the fibres ready for spinning, and the start of a woven square.'

'Spinning with starwort!' exclaimed Cormack. 'Who ever heard of such a thing?'

209

'You yourself mentioned tasks,' Conor reminded his twin. 'It looks as if you were right.'

'You don't need to sound so surprised,' said Cormack with a trace of his old grin.

'Six brothers.' Finbar had been very quiet, and now his voice was constrained, as if he spoke only because he must. 'Six brothers, six garments, maybe?'

'Garments of starwort? I would not gladly wear such a rough shirt,' commented Diarmid.

Conor's level gaze went around them all, appraising. 'You might be glad to wear it,' he said slowly, 'if it had the power to undo the spell.' It had not taken him long to work it out.

For a moment, as they looked at one another across the fire, it seemed to me that there was some communication between my brothers which needed no words, and that this time I was shut out. I looked around the circle, sensing that they were closer now than they had ever been, and then I met Finbar's eyes where he sat a little aside, watching me. There was a wariness in his expression that I had never seen before, an uncertainty that concerned me, for of them all, he had always been the one surest of his way. I tried to reach him with my mind.

What is it, Finbar?

But it was Conor who replied.

'It is hard to come back, Sorcha, and harder for some than others.'

'We may have little time here,' Liam said, getting to his feet. 'If what Conor suggests is correct, we may have only until dawn. We must do what we can to provide for our sister.'

'Only one night, and stuck out here in the forest,' said Diarmid bitterly. 'Where can we start, when there is so much to be done?'

'Some things can be achieved, ' said Liam, taking control. 'Small things, maybe, but useful. Believe me, Sorcha, it pains and shames each one of us to be forced to leave you here alone. But we can at least ensure a little comfort for you. The cutting of wood, the readying of this place for winter, for I fear we will not return before the snows are deep here; this can be done by lantern light. Have you an axe?'

I nodded.

'To the west there is grazing land, and grain stored,' said Conor.

'How far?' asked Cormack.

'You can get there and back before daybreak,' his twin answered. 'Take Linn. It's dark, and the paths are treacherous. She will lead you. I suspect she would not consent to stay behind, in any case.'

'I'll go with you,' said Padriac. 'Or would do, but these boots are killing me. That's the problem with transformations. You keep on growing, but your clothes stay the same size. Maybe yours would fit me, Finbar.' They fitted him well enough, for my youngest brother was half a head taller than when I had last seen him. His outgrown pair might do for me one day, if I ever grew into them. Then Padriac and Cormack were off under the trees, small lantern in hand and knives in their belts, for they had found those as well. I hoped the weapons would not be needed. I thought they might go unnoticed amidst the midsummer revellers, whatever their errand. Linn followed; it would have been beyond anyone's power to stop her. At least of the three of them she knew the way.

Liam and Diarmid set to with axe and hatchet, lopping branches off the dead ash tree and stacking them under the shelter of an overhang. They worked with a speed and precision that startled me, and stopped for neither food nor drink. They took the second lamp to light their task, leaving the rest of us in semi-darkness by the glowing fire.

'Now,' said Conor, 'I want to see those hands. Have you a supply of salves? Beeswax?'

I showed him my dwindling stocks, stored in a niche of the cave.

'This will not last long,' he said gravely. 'Then what will you do? Is there not some other way this task can be accomplished?'

I shook my head.

'Then at least I can tend to you tonight, and perhaps seek some help for you. You must understand, little owl, that this is the worst thing for us. Not being here with you, having to watch you suffer on our behalf, seeing you sacrifice your life for ours – this cuts us deep. For Finbar it is hardest. He, of us all, needs to follow the path that leads straight ahead, whatever obstacles are in the way. To have that taken from him, on what seems little more than a whim, tears him apart. And now he must hurt what he loves best.'

We moved back to the fire, where Finbar still sat silent. Conor took my small hand in his and began to rub the salve gently into my skin, rolling and kneading my fingers with his own. He stopped talking and instead began to hum softly, a monotonous little tune that had beginning and ending woven into one, so that it went on and on, and seemed to fit well with the strange stillness of the night. Further away the dull thud of axe on wood punctuated the flow of the song. I began to relax. At first I had flinched, for it hurt to have anyone touch my hands; but after a while the song lulled me and I heard owls in the trees around, and the croaking of frogs in the many tiny waterways around the lake. And then Finbar came over to sit by me and took my other hand in his. Conor's hand was warm and full of life; Finbar's was like ice. For a while we sat thus, and I surrendered my damaged fingers to my brothers' ministrations, storing up images and feelings to last me the long, weary time till midwinter. It would have to be enough. Conor was still humming scraps of song under his breath, working his own strength into my hands and through them into myself. At last Finbar spoke.

'I'm sorry, Sorcha. I hardly know what words to choose. One night. It is too short a time to waken our memories of this world. My mind holds so much, and I have seen – I – no, some things are best left unspoken.'

I turned to face him, and this time he met my gaze direct. I saw firelight flicker in his grey eyes, and there was doubt in them.

What is this? You can't give up! You, of all people. What is wrong?

Still he kept his shutters down.

'You can talk to us, Finbar,' said Conor quietly. 'Here, we three are linked hand in hand. We know you. We know your courage. Speak aloud of what troubles you, if you will not open your mind to us.' It was spoken gently enough, but there was an authority in his words that seemed to give Finbar no choice.

'Why Sorcha?' he said. 'Why single her out for such suffering? She is innocent of any wrongdoing, incapable of an evil thought. Why should she make this sacrifice for us?'

'Because she is the strongest,' said Conor simply. 'Because she can bend with the wind, and not break. Sorcha is the thread that binds us all together.

Without her we are leaves in the wind, blown hither and thither at random.'

'We are strong. We are all strong.'

'In our own ways, yes. But each of you would break before this storm. Even you, for there comes a time when the path straight ahead crumbles underfoot, or is washed away by floodwaters, and then if you will not take another way you are lost. Only Sorcha can bring us home.'

'You speak in riddles,' said Finbar impatiently. 'What of yourself? How can you be so calm, so accepting, when you see your sister as thin as a wraith, dressed in rags and her skin weeping with sores? I would rather die, or remain under this curse forever, than let her suffer this way for me. How can you stand back and accept this?'

Conor regarded him gravely. 'Do not misjudge me. I feel Sorcha's hurt deeply, and she knows it. But I have travelled this way before; and I have stood on the threshold between that world and this. Perhaps that makes it easier, for unlike the rest of you, I can carry both within me. For you, the changing will be harder each time. But your doubts do nothing to ease Sorcha's task. She needs our strength, while we are here. She needs to touch us while she can.'

We sat quiet for a while. It occurred to me that Conor had not really answered his brother's question. It was late, and the forest was still save for the axe blows ringing out in the darkness. I recalled another time, when I had seen Finbar's mind-pictures despite his efforts to shut me out; the cold, the falling, the flight . . . was this what he feared, the flashes of sight that told him of things to come? How much did he see? And was the future so ill, that he did not dare to share his visions?

My mind was well shielded, but Finbar spoke as if he knew my thoughts. 'Sorcha,' he said softly. 'Believe me when I tell you that you should not be doing this; it would be better for you to go away, far away and forget us. Leave the forest and seek protection with the holy brothers in the west. You will never be safe here.' He twisted the ends of his hair in restless fingers.

'So we should all perish?' questioned Conor mildly. 'The lady Oonagh would certainly be pleased with that result. You offend your sister with such a suggestion, Finbar. We are her brothers; she loves us as we love her. She could not take such a choice.'

'She must not stay here,' said Finbar. The shutter in his mind was firm; whatever dark knowledge he held there, it was not to be shown us.

'These images of the mind,' said Conor, poking the embers with a long stick, 'they can be riddles in themselves. What you see may be truth, or half-truth, or a nightmare of your own making, born of your fears and wishes. The lady Oonagh's enchantment may even now be at work within you. Perhaps she meddles with your inner voices as she changes your outer form. You cannot trust these visions.'

'What else can I trust?' Finbar replied. 'With no knowledge of the time we were gone, what other map have we to guide our choices? There is scarce time to recall who we are, before it is blanked out again. Our father could be dead or worse.'

'He still lives,' said Conor softly. 'Stricken sorely by the loss of his children, and bound fast by his wife's spell, but not wholly under her domination. He survives, thus far.'

How do you know? His words had shocked us both; we asked the same question together, I inwardly,

Finbar aloud. Our eyes were fixed on Conor intently. Our expression, I think, was the same.

Conor looked down at our linked hands, smiling a little ruefully. 'You are right, of course,' he said. 'One cannot be man, and bird, at the same time. Entering that new state of consciousness, you lose the memory of the old. You are not a man in swan's feathers; it is not so simple. You change entirely; and your vision of the world is a wild creature's: flight, safety, danger, survival. The lake; the sky. There is little more. During that time, you may fly over the lord Colum's stronghold, or swim by the shore where Eilis and her ladies play at ball, but you do not see them, not as a man would. You cannot; *but I can.*'

Finbar drew his breath in sharply. 'I should have known,' he said slowly. 'You are further down the path than I guessed. I am sorry, as well as glad; your burden may be worse than mine, in its way.'

The lady Oonagh. What of her?

'She still rules there, Sorcha. And will bear a child by harvest time. Her influence is strong. She still seeks you, but without success, for the dwellers in the forest protect you.'

'Father. You said he was not entirely under her spell. What did you mean?' asked Finbar tightly. I looked at him in surprise. Perhaps I did not know him as well as I thought. He caught my expression.

'The power of enchantment is great, Sorcha,' he said more calmly. 'The power of loss is strong too. I begin to understand, now, why he has acted as he has. So, it does matter to me that he survives. It matters that she is stopped. But there is a limit to the price I would pay for this. There is a limit to the price any of us should pay.'

'I could tell you about Father,' said Conor. The

ring of axe on wood had ceased; now my two eldest brothers came down the hill, breathing heavily, and squatted down next to us. 'I could tell you much; but sometimes it is better not to know.'

'Not to know what?' asked Liam, settling between me and Conor and putting an arm around my shoulders.

'What passes, what changes in the world, while we are in that other state,' said Conor. Liam glanced at him sharply. 'So you *do* know,' he said, not altogether approving.

'Some things yes, others no. I am not able to be in all places at all times; my bodily shape is the same as yours. I see differently, that's all. Rest assured that your father still lives, and is not altogether lost, though his grief is terrible. He longs most to see his daughter, in whose face is his last memory of her whom he loved and lost. The lady Oonagh hates that,' Conor said.

My jaw dropped in surprise. Me? But he had scarcely noticed me when I was there. 'What tale did she spin, that he could accept her innocence in this?' asked Diarmid with a dreadful bitterness in his tone.

'That I can't tell you,' said Conor. 'Besides, why deepen your own sorrow and frustration? We can do nothing for him, or against her, until the enchantment is broken. So, we must do as Sorcha wishes, and leave her here to complete her task, though it breaks our hearts to do so.'

It was terrible how quickly the remainder of that night passed. We sat by the fire, talking of this and that, trying not to glance skywards too often for the first traces of dawn. Later, much later, the boys and Linn came back from their expedition. They had escaped the worst sadness of the night by filling it with activity. It would be a night long remembered by the local people, a Meán Samhraidh of more than usual activity by the wee folk; several washing lines would be missing items, a few dairies and cellars would have unexpected spaces on their shelves. Padriac passed me a warm woollen gown in a vivid shade of red, several sizes too big, a capacious shawl and some homespun stockings, well mended. They'd be good for winter. Cormack bore a large sack of meal and a bundle of turnips, a round of ripened cheese and a length of stout rope. Both had pockets full of small treasures. Linn was licking her lips.

'I hope you took good care not to be seen,' said Liam, frowning. 'I want no trace of Sorcha's whereabouts spread amongst these people – you know how tongues wag. It takes but one traveller to catch idle gossip, and the tale is away down the road and to the lady Oonagh's ears before you can draw breath.'

'It's all right, big brother,' laughed Cormack. 'We may be unsure if we're man or bird, but we haven't lost all our skills. I guarantee you we left not a trace. Even the hound cooperated, didn't you, Linn?'

She danced around him happily; he was back, and her world was in place again. I could have wept for her, knowing how short his stay.

'We must make it up to these people, when we are ourselves again,' said Diarmid. 'It is wrong to steal; besides, they are poor and can ill afford to spare these things. Still, I believe Sorcha's need is greater, just now.'

'Don't worry,' said Padriac lightly, sensing this lecture was aimed at him. 'We won't forget. Some midsummer eve, in years to come, the little people will leave them a stack of wood, and a jug of ale, and some finery for themselves. We'll be back.'

'Maybe,' said Finbar.

'That's enough!' Liam's voice was sharp. 'To finish her task, Sorcha needs our support, she needs our trust. Haven't you yourself always said we seven must be here for each other, that our strength is in our oneness? Of course Sorcha will complete her work, and of course we will return. I don't doubt this for an instant.'

'As surely as sun follows moon,' said Conor quietly. 'As surely as seven streams become one strong river that flows and swirls over boulder and under towering cliff, never faltering on its journey to the sea.'

'Next time, Sorcha,' said Padriac, 'I'll be able to make you a better weaving frame. There are some good bits of ash, I've put them to dry under the overhang at the back of the cave. They should be ready by midwinter, if you keep the rain out. And save that rope, I'll be needing it.'

I smiled at him; so eager to help, so young yet. He might have outgrown his boots, but in essence he had changed not at all. No, it wasn't my youngest brother I was worried about.

'I ask myself,' said Finbar, with a stubborn note in his voice that we all recognised, 'why this must happen. Why must Sorcha endure what must occur, why sacrifice herself thus when she could be safe and protected, and move on with her own life in peace? Why not leave us as we are? For all we know, by the time the task is done, if indeed it can be done, our father might be dead, or changed forever; why then need we be saved, and thus ruin our sister's life?'

We all stared at him. There was a slight pause. It was Conor who spoke first.

'Because evil must not be allowed to prevail,' he said.

'Because we must reclaim what is ours,' added Liam.

'And save our father, if we can,' said Cormack. 'He's a good man for all his faults, and without his leadership our lands are as good as lost. Briton and Viking and Pict will be swarming over the Islands, and to our very door.'

'Because Sorcha believes it's the right thing,' said Padriac with devastating simplicity.

'I cannot let the lady Oonagh's work go unpunished,' said Diarmid. 'If it weren't for my stupidity, perhaps we could have stopped her. My honour requires me to seek her out, to make an end of it.'

'Listen,' said Padriac. 'It's almost dawn.'

They were silent. A solitary bird had begun to chirrup high in the elms. And the sky was indeed beginning to lighten with the first pale grey of the morning.

We made our way to the shore. Liam went ahead, carrying the lantern. I walked by Finbar, and I tried to let him know how I felt, but could not tell if he heard me.

All will be well. Believe in me. Hold on, and live. For us all. It was like sending thoughts into empty air, to be blown away by a passing breeze.

We waited for the light, clasping hands in our circle, saying nothing, passing strength and love one to the other. Finbar was between Conor and myself; he let us take his hands, but they were still icy cold, as if nothing could ever warm him again. Just before dawn, Conor bid me go back to the cave, for, he said, it was better if I did not watch them go. They hugged me one by one; Conor first, then the others in turn, till only Finbar was left. I thought he would go without a word; but he touched me on the cheek and for a moment he let me in.

Be safe, Sorcha. Till next time. I am still here for you.

The chorus of birdsong swelled. It was like that other morning, the morning the mist had arisen from the lake and taken them from me. It was suddenly too much to bear, and I felt my lips trembling, and tears welling in my eyes.

'Go back inside now, little owl,' said Conor gently, and his voice came to me as if down a long, narrow tunnel.

'Until we return,' said Cormack, or maybe it was someone else, and then it was really dawn, and there was a sound of rushing wind, and swirling waters, and beating wings, and I ran blinded by tears back to my cave and lay there face down weeping, for losing them now was no easier than last time and I did not want to see, or even to imagine, the slipping away of their minds and the transformation of their selves into creatures of the wild.

Outside, Linn began a terrible howling that went on and on, echoing through the woods, and over the water, and up into the wide pink and orange and dazzling blue of the sky as dawn turned to day.

CHAPTER SIX

Living out there for so long, I began to feel as if I were part of the forest itself. It was like an old tale, perhaps the story of a young girl cruelly abandoned by her family, who grew up able to talk with the birds and fishes, with raven and salmon and deer. I'd have liked that; unfortunately the presence of a perpetually hungry Linn meant the wild creatures gave our small dwelling a wide berth. There was a family of hedgehogs who ventured close at dusk once it grew warmer and, whenever I had some morsel of food to spare, I put it out on a smooth stone under the bushes for them, and made Linn stay inside until they crept off again into the undergrowth.

The changing moods of the forest worked their way deep into my being. As nights became longer, as berries ripened on bramble and hawthorn and nuts hung heavy on hazel and chestnut, I too underwent some changes. I was always a small, skinny thing and my diet was frugal at best. Nonetheless, that autumn my body began to change from a child's to a woman's, and I began my bleeding. This should, I supposed, have been cause for some form of celebration, but it felt like no more than an inconvenience, for my whole will and energy was focused on the tasks of gathering starwort, and spinning and weaving my six shirts. Nonetheless, I took time that first night of bleeding to bathe myself by moonlight, and then I drank some rosemary tea for the cramps, and sat under the stars listening to the owls and the stillness. That night I felt that the Lady of the Forest was very close, and I sensed the movement around me of a great and deep magic, but I did not see her.

It became necessary to go further afield in search of starwort, for the supply of brittle, thorny thread was running short. Six squares of the woven fabric had been enough to make one rough shirt, and I had started the second, but had thread enough for a sleeve, maybe, but no more. I went out with a small sack and a sharp knife, looking for the patches of feathery grey that sprang up in forest clearings, where dappled sunlight could penetrate the autumn canopy. This plant liked the damp, and grew closely on the banks of little streams, crowding out the ferns and mosses. It was a plentiful time, and often I was lucky enough to bring back a bundle of hazelnuts and elderberries as well.

I began to understand, exploring the forgotten pathways and dim glades of the forest, where Finbar might have been, those times when he disappeared for days on end and returned with his grey eyes fixed on some distant vision no one else could see. I noticed the Ogham notches on tree trunks and here and there on mossy stone; and knew that the mysterious arts that Conor had begun to learn had their roots here in the ancient growth.

One day, by chance, I discovered one of the most secret places. I was clambering up a stream bed in search of the spiny plant, and Linn was ahead of me splashing enthusiastically about, slurping up mouthfuls of the clear water in passing. We rounded a curve and ducked under a boulder. Then she stopped. I stopped behind her. Across a round pool stood a huge and venerable oak, its roots stretching wide around the bole, knotted deep into the earth. Its canopy spread densely above, so that the light barely penetrated its lower branches. The leaves would fall soon enough though, for they were every shade of red and bronze. Goldenwood hung thick from its topmost limbs. And carved into its bark, looking straight at me across the dim water, was an ancient face, set there by some seeker of truth. It was neither male nor female, neither friendly nor forbidding. It was simply there.

Linn would go no closer, but settled down in the undergrowth to wait for me, ears alert for danger. I felt respect, but not awe. After all, the forest was my own place. So I made my way around the pool for a closer look. Before the face, on the water's edge, lay a great stone, its surface worn gleaming smooth with time and touching.

Then I froze. Others had been here before me, and recently. For on this stone an offering was set out. A hunk of country bread. A wedge of cheese. I glanced back at the dog, motioning her to be still. There was no sound of human activity nearby, only the fluting of birds and the faint rustle of leaves far above us where the crisp autumn breeze stirred the canopy. I held my breath. Whoever had left these simple gifts may be gone, but Linn and I should leave, for these items bore no trace of ant or beetle; they had not been here long. Yet the food held my senses fast. Though it was the fruitful time of year, I had been frugal as a squirrel, storing nuts and drying berries for the winter, so I was hungry. The supplies my brothers had brought were dwindling fast. I was, after all, not yet fourteen years old and I could almost taste the chewy graininess of the barley loaf, the mellow bite of the soft cheese. Linn gave a little whine, and that decided me. I nodded respectfully to the old face in the oak, believing he would not object. Then I slipped the bread and cheese into my pocket, and we were away for home.

Hindsight is a fine thing. At the time, safe back by our little fire, sharing this wonderful, unexpected feast as dusk fell, I basked in the forest's protection, and I never thought such a small act could herald such terrible consequences. Indeed, at the time I believed the windfall might have been meant for us, a bounty that had fallen into my hands through the good will of the forest spirits, or maybe the Lady herself. I did have some common sense, though, and so I did not go that way again for a long time. I was not foolish enough to court discovery.

Time passed, and I spun the thread for the second shirt. The first was a sorry-looking garment, the woven patches cobbled together, the sleeves strangely uneven. But it would serve its purpose. One morning there was crisp frost on the ground and the bushes bore robes of sparkling silver that melted into droplets with the sun's hazy rising in a sky of lavender grey.

Winter was coming and with it my brothers. I worked on as steadily as I could, always thankful for the dry wood heap my brothers had left, for my fingers ached with the chill. I took the risk of making a bigger fire, and roasted stolen turnips in the coals. Once or twice snow came down, gentle flakes escaping the net of bare branches to drift silently to the ground outside my doorway. Here, where the trees grew close by the water, it did not lie deep; and for that I was grateful. I wore my own old dress, and the red woollen one over that, and a blanket around my shoulders, and on my feet Padriac's boots. And still I was cold.

By the time my brothers returned, I was weaving the back of the second shirt. It almost made me laugh, thinking back to the day I had set out from Father Brien's. It seemed such a long time ago. A few moons, from winter to summer maybe, I had believed this task would take. Now here I was, nearly a year later, and I had scarcely begun. I had become a little quicker with practice, but my hands did not always obey me, so misshapen and abused were they from the treatment I gave them. Just as well, I told myself, that I did not care about marriage and all that went with it. What man would look at a girl with knobbled hands like an old crone's? That sort of life, with weddings and banquets, with music and reading and fine embroidery, seemed so far away now that I could not imagine any of us would ever return to it. I never dwelt on what might happen afterwards, when finally I would slip the sixth shirt over my last brother's head and restore them to this world once more. I worked as fast as I could, and let my mind travel ahead only a certain distance, no further.

I do not remember their second visit as well as the first. It was on the eve of the winter solstice, Meán

Geimhridh. It was my fourteenth birthday. Some of it, I suppose, was blotted out by the things that happened afterwards. I remember that Finbar arrived a little later than the others, as on the first visit. I remember the look in his eyes, a hint of wildness that he could not quite keep hidden from me.

There was news. Conor could tell I craved it, but he passed it on with some reluctance.

'The child was born at Samhain,' he said. 'A boy. They have called him Ciarán.'

Liam threw a stick on the fire. 'It's a good strong name,' he said grudgingly.

I held up my hands in the flickering light. It was freezing cold, but still we sat outside, for the small blaze gave a warmth that was cheering to the heart as well as comforting to the bones. Here we could make some semblance of our old circle, pretend some likeness of our old unity.

I held up the five fingers of one hand, and two of the other. My brothers understood; their eyes also spoke their pain at the sight of my twisted hands.

'Yes, Sorcha,' said Conor. 'He is the seventh son of a seventh son. That must be respected.'

'Respected?' spat Diarmid furiously. 'Hardly. He is *her* child, the spawn of pure evil. He should be destroyed, along with the sorceress.'

The others looked at him, and there was a short silence.

'He's our brother,' observed Padriac after a while.

'He is our father's son,' said Liam, agreeing, 'and he is innocent of the ill done to us. Cannot we hope that his birth may change things for the better?'

Nobody answered him. Father had always made it clear that he intended Liam, as his eldest son, to inherit Sevenwaters. Although any man of Colum's line could challenge this decision and make a claim of his own, for that was the law, this had not seemed at all likely. Until now. And who was to say our father might not prefer the son his new wife had borne him?

It seemed Conor had worse news for Liam, for he took his elder brother away from our group. They stood talking earnestly for some time, just out of earshot. After a while Conor came back, but Liam remained staring out into the dark, and the bleak greyness of his expression reminded me of our father.

'What's wrong with him?' asked Cormack not very tactfully.

Conor gave his twin a sidelong glance. 'Woman trouble.'

'You mean Eilis? She's not dead?'

Conor shook his head. 'Oh, no. She recovered well enough from the poisoning, and Seamus has guarded her fiercely since. He has taken care she makes no more visits to Sevenwaters. No need for it, really, since Colum's marriageable sons have conveniently disappeared for parts unknown. No, Eilis is well. Blooming in fact, and ready for marriage. Her father has promised her to Eamonn of the Marshes. If he can't secure his eastern border by wedding her to one of us, then he may as well go for the northern.'

Diarmid drew his breath in sharply. 'That will be a formidable alliance. What if they should turn against Father? I hope he's strengthening our defences up beyond the river. Seamus was ally enough before, but this news makes me uneasy. We should be concentrating our joint forces against Northwoods, and to do that effectively we must be able to trust our neighbours.'

'I know little of his defences,' said Conor wearily. 'There's no sign of a replacement for Donal, and not much activity around the place. But it is winter. Perhaps when the warm weather comes, Father will take heart and rally his men.'

'What about Eilis?' asked Padriac, his hands busy. He worked rapidly and precisely by the dim lantern light, fashioning a new weaving frame from ash wood bound with twine. 'Does it suit her to wed this fellow? Isn't he a bit old for her?'

'It will be against her wishes,' said Conor quietly, glancing over at our eldest brother, who still stood in the shadows, his head bowed. 'But she is a good daughter and will do as she is told. She never understood how Liam could leave and not tell her why. Her heart is still sore for him, but she will be a faithful wife and a loving mother. It is better thus.'

'Better for whom?' asked Diarmid bitterly.

It was a bleak visit. I wanted so much to be able to speak, for I could see their grief, their anger, their guilt, and I could feel how it was tearing them apart, even turning them one against the other, but without words there was little I could do for them. I gave Liam a hug, but could not tell him I knew Eilis loved him, and would have waited for him if she could. I took Diarmid's hands in mine and studied the bitterness in his face; I would have told him that we all forgave him for his indiscretion; that Oonagh could have picked on any of them; it was just his bad luck that she chose him for her plaything. I wanted to tell him not to hate so much. But I could not speak. As for Finbar, he sat alone, his arms around his knees, his long hair unkempt and blowing across his eyes as he stared out towards the dark water of the lake. He did not look at me, and he said nothing at all.

So the night wore on, and Padriac finished the weaving frame. Cormack mended my boots, closely watched by an edgy Linn. These two brothers had not changed so much, I thought. Padriac was always so clearly focused on some task or some problem, perhaps the terrible thing that had happened to them was merely another interesting challenge for him. Certainly, he seemed content enough to spend his one night of freedom building and fixing and throwing the odd word or two into the general conversation. He at least would survive, I thought. In Cormack's case it was probably lack of imagination that helped him cope. This was not kind of me, I suppose; but Cormack tended to see the world in black and white, and in some ways this made life easier for him. His aggression was his point of weakness, as the lady Oonagh had deduced earlier than any of us. By turning that against his dearest and most trusting companion, she had made him doubt his own integrity, and that doubt would always be with him now.

Later, they spoke more of the Islands, and what strategy might be used to win them back; and they drew maps in the sandy soil, replacing man and tree with leaf and twig. I half listened; well enough to hear Conor tell them the Islands would never be taken back by force. Hadn't they heard the tale, he said, that one would come that was neither of Erin nor of Britain, yet both; one that would bear the mark of the raven, and would restore the balance? Only then could the rift between our peoples be bridged.

'That's just a story,' said Cormack dismissively. 'We might wait a hundred years or more for such a one. We might wait for ever. But the sacred trees cannot wait while the blows of the axe ring out across the water.'

'The spirits cannot bide their time while the foreigner's boot defiles the caves of truth,' added Diarmid.

'Besides,' said Liam, 'I'm not sure we're interested in bridging the rift between our peoples. Taking back what is rightfully ours, and driving them from our soil forever, is closer to what we have in mind.'

'These old stories do often turn out to be true,' observed Padriac. 'Sometimes they don't mean precisely what they seem to mean. Maybe Conor's right. Things are changing now; look what happened to us. Our story is as strange as any old tale.'

'Mmm,' said Diarmid doubtfully. 'Faith is one thing. Me, I prefer mine backed up with a sharp sword and a troop of good men.'

'A little forward planning never did any harm,' said Cormack, in agreement with his brother. 'When we return, we must be ready. Father may be in no fit state to command, and our old foe may have used his weakness to make a move. We must make sure our previous gains are not squandered.'

Conor talked sparingly that night. He had been strong; to hold the awareness of both worlds was a burden, and I thought the weight of it showed. But Finbar, his isolation was something else. I went to sit by him, when it was growing close to dawn, for I had waited and waited for him to speak to me, and he had not. I sat down next to him. It was a new moon, and I could barely make out his features in the dim light. But I did not need my eyes to see him, for all my brothers' faces were held in my heart. Long nose, wide mouth, a dusting of freckles on pale skin, a firmly set jaw, and under the dark hair tangling on his brow, eyes like clear water of an unfathomable depth. That was Finbar.

'I'm sorry to shut you out.' He spoke after long silence, startling me. 'I cannot open my mind to you, not any longer.'

231

Why not? Don't you trust me any more?

'Dear Sorcha. I would trust you with my life. Are not all our lives in your hands? But I have seen – I have seen things I would give much to erase from my mind. Terrible things. I find myself hoping beyond hope that Conor was right – that these visions are not the Sight, but some evil planted in my head by our father's wife for her own purposes. Perhaps she thinks to drive me mad. These images are cruel indeed. It is better that I do not share them. Not with you, not with anyone.' His voice told me that, in his heart, he believed them to be true.

Why not? Sharing could lessen the burden.

He shifted slightly, hunching his shoulders, twisting a strand of hair in his fingers.

'Not this burden. Besides, if it is false, why give others pain? What troubles me most is not knowing what to do. If I do see things to come, bad things, I should act to try to prevent them. But even if I had time to do anything, I would scarcely know where to start. Besides, perhaps that is exactly what the lady Oonagh wants. And perhaps, again, these things are intended; there may be no stopping them. Always, before, I knew which way was right. I have lost that certainty.'

You are still the same. Still strong.

'But will I be strong enough? And it grows harder, each time. Each time a little part of me changes, so the man becomes more like the swan; but the swan can never be the man. Oh, Sorcha, I have seen my own end; that is a weight of knowledge no man should bear. I have seen my brothers perish by the sword, and by water, and I have seen one go far, far away beyond the reach of furthest thought. And you – I have seen a great ill for you, and I do not know how

232

to prevent it. If you can go away from here, you should do so, and as soon as you can.'

Tell me what it is. How can I do anything about it, if I don't know?

'No. It may not be true.'

He was adamant, and I could get no more from him on the subject. We sat there quietly together, and after a while he took my hand in his, and for no reason at all I had a terrible feeling that this would be the last time he would ever touch me. The last of our precious time slipped away, and I fought back tears as the sky grew lighter with the approach of dawn. Weeping would not help anyone.

We gathered on the shore to say our farewells, and there Finbar did something that terrified me more than all his words of warning. Reaching up, he took off the amulet from around his neck, the smooth, holed stone with its runic imprint, and placed the cord over my head so that I wore the charm against my heart.

I raised a hand in protest – *no, it is yours, Mother gave it to you* – but he was already turning away and I could not see his face. It had been a gesture of terrible finality. In all my life I had never seen him without our mother's gift around his neck.

Farewell, until next time. Farewell, dear one.

I had told Simon he could end his story any way he wanted. The choice was his, I'd said; there were as many pathways as the threads of a great tapestry, and he was the weaver. Oh, but my story. Why couldn't I do this with my own story? Why must the strands of this tale form a fabric of violence, turn the red of blood and betrayal, take the way of corruption and anguish and parting? With the clear-eyed confidence of an innocent, I had lectured Simon on the need to take control of his destiny, never thinking to find myself helpless before its blows, not two years later.

Finbar always was a seeker after truth, and I was to discover his vision had not played him false. It was later, though, that it happened; so much later that I had dismissed his warning from my mind and was going about my business as usual, enjoying the warm weather, for half a year had passed and it was almost midsummer again. There were two shirts stored away and the third was half-sewn. From my cave, I watched the path of the sun and I saw the gradual ripening of the berries, and I believed my brothers would come any evening now. Perhaps tonight. There were swans on the lake, some with half-grown children; out there somewhere, maybe Conor watched me with human sight as he drifted in his cloak of white. Linn learned to catch fish in the shallows, a rare trick for a dog. Her patience amazed me as she stood stock still in the water, eyes fixed on an unseen quarry, until the silvery prey edged close enough for one fatal snatch. While she practised this new game, I spun and wove and plied my needle, and the shirt was lacking but its right sleeve.

Then in one day, so quickly, everything changed. The sun lured me out of the cave, and I went down to sit on the rocks by the lake, in the afternoon, and took my needlework with me. I dabbled my hot feet in the water, rolling my toes over the fine pebbles. There was a group of swans not far off shore, floating, preening, fishing leisurely. I thought they were waiting. The sleeve was quite tricky to attach, and I bent over my needle, ignoring the barbs in my fingers through long practice, wishing yet again that I had concentrated better when one of the servants had tried to teach me plain sewing.

I had forgotten Linn until I heard her bark, somewhere back along the lakeside. She was headed home from hunting, I thought. It was late for her to be still out. Then the barking started again, and there was a sharp note of warning in it. I got up, shading my eyes as I sought along the shoreline and up between the trees for a sight of her. There was nothing. A moment later I heard a voice cursing, and her barking ended in a horrible, gurgling yelp, and then there was silence. A cold feeling moved up my spine. I started up the path towards the shelter of the trees, treading as softly as I could. My senses were sharpened by fear, but even so, the men were too quick for me. There were three of them, one coming through the bushes behind the cave entrance, slack-lipped smile showing uneven, yellowish teeth. In his hand was a bloodstained knife. Another suddenly behind me as he dropped down from the rocks, grabbing me round the neck, the foul smell of his breath filling my nostrils. And behind them, one more familiar, whose voice rang out loud, uncontrolled, half excited, half distressed.

'Faery girl! Don't hurt faery girl!'

What came next is very hard to tell. Indeed, I have told it but once before, when I needed to, and I will tell it this time only because it forms a strand in the fabric of my story, and it wove itself into what came after. I have tried to blot their words and their actions from my memory, but I cannot. They said and did terrible things. I suppose it did not take much time to be over, but it seemed long, so long; and their words were burned into my head, scars like Simon's that never quite healed.

'So this is your faery girl, eh, Will? Looks like flesh

and blood to me. And a nice ripe little piece at that! Get an eyeful of this!'

He put his hand to my tunic and ripped it open right down the front, exposing my body from neck to ankle. I tried to cover myself, but found my arms pinioned from behind.

'How about that then?' said the other, almost drooling in his excitement. He fumbled with his belt. 'Prize piece of fresh meat! Just the way I like it, young and juicy. Should be very tasty.' He turned to the simpleton, who was whimpering on the edge of the clearing, wringing his hands. 'Leave off, Will! Your turn will come, lad. Big boys first.'

'Don't hurt! Don't hurt faery girl! Don't hurt doggy!'

But they did. 'Shut him up, will you?' said the first one, and the second one gave the boy a clout over the ear that sent him moaning to his knees.

Then, while the one held me down, the other spat on his fingers and shoved them inside me, and I sank my teeth through my lip, holding back my scream, and felt blood and tears wet my face as he pulled down his pants and forced himself into me. It hurt; it hurt so much, and I had no voice to curse him. I tried our old trick, tell a story to block out the pain . . . *her name was Deirdre, Lady of the Forest* . . . I screwed my eyes shut, not to see their red, sweaty, excited faces . . . *if you were very quiet, as quiet as a . . . as a mouse, you might see her* . . . I tried and tried, as it went on and on, and one shuddered and pulled away, and the other took his place. 'See, not a word out of her! She loves it, don't you, little slut? Some faery girl; this one's mortal enough, belongs in the farm yard, she does. Best thing that ever happened to her, I'll be bound.'

236

. . . the willows would rustle, as she went by . . . He was huge inside me, too big; I could not believe how big. The other gripped me around the chest, fingers bruising my flesh, hot breathing into my ear . . . *in her cloak of deepest blue, and on her hair a crown of little stars . . .* he thrust and thrust, until I thought I might split open, until I thought I would faint with the pain . . . *she would . . . she would walk under the tall oaks and she would . . .* The story slipped from my grasp, and there was only the awful, endless pounding, and the ugly voices, and the rising scream that threatened to burst out of me, however hard I clenched my teeth shut.

'You wouldn't want her to handle you,' said the first one. 'Seen the paws on her?'

'She's a faery girl, ain't she?' said the other. 'Maybe her mother was a toad.' Gales of coarse laughter.

At last it was over. He groaned and relaxed and pulled out of me, and the other let go, and I collapsed in a heap on the ground, arms wrapped around my head.

'Come on, half-wit,' said one. 'This is your big chance! Come on then! Bet you've never done it before, eh farm boy?' He gave me a kick in the ribs. 'She's ripe for it, aren't you, toad girl? Never said a word. Just what you wanted, wasn't it? Well, there's plenty more where that came from, don't you worry.'

'Hurry up,' said the other one. 'She's going to pass out. Not much fun then.'

But the simpleton was weeping, and I heard him turn and crash away through the forest in the general direction of home.

'Curse him,' said one. 'He'll blab the whole thing out if he gets back first. Come on, no point in hanging around here. We'd better catch him. She'll keep for another time.'

'Bye, sweetie,' said the other one, disgustingly. He gripped my hair, pulling my head up and leering in my face as he bent over me. 'Sorry to desert you so soon. We'll be back for more, sugar plum. Feel this.' He forced my head between his legs, rubbing himself into my face, and I gagged and choked and struggled to keep silent.

'Oh, by the way, your dog's up the hill there,' said the other one, sniggering. 'Bit the worse for wear.'

'Gave me a nasty bite, he did,' observed the first one, dropping me to the ground again. 'Vicious brute.'

Their voices faded away under the trees, and I lay there, unable now even to weep. Then a strange wind came up, and all the trees began to rustle and thrash about, though on the ground all was still. It was as if a darkness had fallen over the forest.

I don't know how long I lay there. It grew steadily darker, but whether it was the day drawing on to dusk, or part of the strange, foreboding silence that overtook my home that afternoon, I could not say. I was lost in my misery. Above me the trees moved and sighed in the wind, and there were voices in it. *Sorcha, Sorcha*, they whispered. *Oh, little sister*. On the ground, nothing stirred. The birds were silent.

After a while, there was no choice but to move. I was bleeding; and there was Linn. I could not hope that she would return to me, running down between the trees with her joyful tail held like a banner in the breeze; but I must at least find her before nightfall. And I needed water.

Everything was an enemy. Everything was too hard. I did it very slowly. My clothes, torn and filthy. I never wanted to touch them again. I dropped them next to the fire. I was desperate to get clean again, but I was afraid to go down to the lake. There was a bucket of water and a harsh cloth, and I washed their filth from my body, shaking and shaking, though the day was still warm. I washed and washed, and when the water was all gone, I went on rubbing my body with the cloth until the skin was red and sore. There was quite a lot of blood; I felt detached from this, dealt with it as well as I could, then wrapped one of the old cloaks around myself and went on up the hill, my legs unsteady, the trees blurring and dancing before my eyes. *She's going to pass out. Not much fun then*.

I reached the top of the hill, and almost tripped over Linn, who was lying across the path where she had fallen, her jaws still holding a scrap of fabric from the man's tunic. Her teeth were bared in a last grimace of challenge, and her eyes stared blindly up at the sky. Her brave tail lay limp in the dirt. Her hair was drenched with blood from the long, slicing wound across her throat, and small red pools formed amongst the rocks and ferns. I suppose it was a good death for a dog, to lose her life in defence of the one she loved. I only knew my friend was gone, and now I was really alone.

She was a big dog, and I was still quite a small girl. Nonetheless, before dusk I carried her back to the cave mouth, and laid her down on the grass. Then, trembling from head to foot, I crept into the smallest space I could find under the rock wall, and wrapped the cloak all about me, and I tried to make my mind as quiet as a feather in the breeze and as still as a stone. But my body shook and shivered, and my spirit was full of fear and hatred and shame. I thought that I would never be clean again.

At dusk they came. I heard their voices and I did not move. They knew what had happened. I thought later, if it had indeed been my brothers I had seen before, drifting out there on the tranquil waters, how it must have been for Conor, seeing it all as it passed, unable to act until the sun set. They exchanged words in low, furious voices.

'Diarmid? Cormack?' Liam queried.

'No, let Cormack stay here and tend to the dog. I will go. This task is mine.' Finbar's voice was shaking.

Then, peering between my fingers in the half light, I saw the three of them take cloak and knife from the cave, and slip away into the forest with death in their eyes.

Conor knew where I was. I felt his mind reach out to touch mine, but I drew deeper into myself. He did not approach me, not yet. Padriac, blinking back tears of rage and confusion, set about rekindling the fire and lighting the lamps and heating water. Cormack's face was like a carving in stone as he took the spade and began to dig a resting place for the bloodied remains of his dog.

After a while, Conor came over to sit near my bolt-hole. I remember still the feeling of solid rock at my back, how I pressed myself in tight against the wall, curled in on myself as small as I could, biting my knuckles, one arm up over my head in protection. I remember wishing the earth would absorb me, take me in and soak up the hurt and the guilt and the wretchedness. I was full of hate; hate for the men who had done this, hate for the innocent who had led them to me, hate for the lady Oonagh who had driven me to this lonely place. I hated my father for his weakness. I hated my brothers as well, for not being there when I needed them. Besides, they too were men, and so how dared they try to make it better?

But Conor sat there, not too close, and talked to me in his quiet, measured tone, and the fire Padriac had rekindled spread its golden light on tree roots and ferns, and even into this tight rock crevice; and after a while I looked out through the tangle of hair that covered my face, and saw the sorrow and love in their eyes.

'Will you come out, little owl?' Conor said gently. 'We have but a short time in which to help you.'

It was hard, very hard. I could scarcely bear to let them touch me. Padriac had a deft hand, having helped many a sick animal in his short years, and, shuddering, eventually I let him tend to my injuries. Finally, wrapped in blankets despite the night's warmth, I lay by the fire and they spoke in low voices as the fragrant smell of healing herbs rose in the night air.

Cormack's grim task was finished, and he returned to the fire. 'Linn's been dead a while,' he said soberly. 'Whoever did this would be well away and out of the forest by now. Our brothers cannot track them down and return here before daybreak. They would better have stayed and helped us here. Perhaps we could have taken Sorcha to some place of safety.'

Conor glanced at his twin, and away. Cormack seemed calm; but his eyes were red, and his cheeks were smeared with earth where he had dashed away his tears.

'I don't think so,' said Conor. 'Sorcha cannot be moved, not tonight. For better or worse, she must remain here for now. As for the other matter, strange things happen in the forest at night. Especially this forest. People sometimes get lost in the dark, even on a familiar path. It's not unusual for a mist to come up suddenly, and mask the true way, or for mysterious voices to lead a wanderer down a deceptive track. Glades can appear where there were none before, and tangles of branches suddenly fill a clearing. Many have died under these trees, and their bodies never been found.'

His two brothers looked at him, and then at each other.

'Mm,' said Cormack. 'You'd know, I suppose.'

'I do know,' said Conor.

Padriac was boiling a pannikin of water with more herbs in it; the smell told me he was using self-heal, sometimes called heart-of-the-earth, and the spores of wolf's claw, that herb of power which must be gathered with such care. They'd already made me drink, but my stomach rejected even what was good for it. Now I sipped again, but not too much. I had no wish to sleep, for no infusion could promise me a sleep without dreams. I watched the stars, and my brothers talked on in quiet voices. I am a healer; I was then, and I am now. Strange, then, how on that night I felt deep in my spirit that I would never be healed, as if I could never rise out of the well of despair. I had been there to help Simon, and others before him. But who was there to help me? Even my dog was gone. I watched the stars until they seemed to wheel and spin above me, until their images blurred with my tears.

It was stranger still that on that night I did not care

whom I hurt. Conor's face was white and drawn; he bore not just the burden of what had happened to his sister, the guilt of not being there to stop it, for they all felt that, but he knew at first hand my every feeling. He was tuned to my wordless curses and silent screams, my anguished sense of betrayal. *You weren't there. I needed you and you weren't there.* Such was the flood of emotion that there was no holding it back. My mind overflowed with pain and he took it all and never once spoke of it. But it could be read on his face. The worst of it was that I didn't care any more. My brother was a man too. Perhaps it was just that he should share the damage that men had done.

I must have dozed off briefly, for I remember waking with a start as Liam drove a bloodstained dagger into the earth by the fire and wiped his hands on his cloak. The three of them had returned. Diarmid's face was a mask of fury, Liam's tightly controlled. Finbar sat apart, and he held his hands to the sides of his head, as if his thoughts threatened to burst it apart. His hands were dark with blood. At home, the Armsmaster Donal had drilled them with iron discipline. Even I knew a weapon must always be scrupulously cleaned straight after use; cleaned and oiled and put away safely. Tonight it was different. Their three daggers stood in the soil around the fire, and its gentle flicker showed the bright metal encrusted with their quarry's life blood. It had been a hunt, not a battle. A swift, violent meting out of justice. I did not care how many they had killed, two or three. I did not weep for the innocent caught up in something beyond his understanding. It was late, too late. My body ached, and I was scared, and even with my six brothers around me, I was all alone.

'Oonagh will pay for this in blood,' said Diarmid,

his voice thick with fury. His thirst for retribution had not been slaked by the killings. 'I will draw the knife across her throat myself, if no other will do it.'

'She bears responsibility for this, though maybe not directly,' agreed Liam. 'But this is not the time. We have done what we had to. Now we must look to Sorcha. She must go from this place, and straight away. How soon can she be moved, Conor?'

They discussed me as if I were a piece in their game of strategy; a prized one, but still just an object to be manoeuvred to best advantage. I lay there unblinking, silent in the darkness. My body was throbbing with pain, my mind endlessly replaying the thing that had been done to me. I didn't seem to be able to stop this happening, and I almost wished I had taken enough of the herb to blot it out for a time with a drugged sleep, nightmares or not. My mind would not be still; I could not focus my thoughts on a story, or count the stars, or take in properly what my brothers were saying.

Their voices swam in and out of my consciousness, Conor saying I could not be moved tonight, Diarmid furious, Liam trying to make plans. Flashes of pain, memories of other voices. I put my hand up to cover my eyes, its roughness brushing my skin. *Maybe her mother was a toad.* There were other images there too. My broken garden. Father Brien lying on the ground, an empty shell of himself. Simon screaming in the dark. Oonagh combing, combing my hair, and the creatures twisting on her mirror. Pain and fear. Their voices, again and again. *Prize piece of meat, eh? Just how I like it, young and juicy.* How could my brothers talk on, planning, arguing now, as if I weren't there?

'This is impossible! It's out of the question!'

Diarmid was yelling. 'We can't just leave her here! There must be some other way!'

'There is no other way,' said Conor quietly. His face was turned away from me.

'Then, by the Lady, let us end this enchantment once and for all,' said Cormack, and there was a reckless note in his voice. He got to his feet and faced his twin across the fire. 'We cannot abandon her, not now. I say we use what time we have left to take her to the nearest farm, tell our story, throw ourselves on these people's mercy. At least then Sorcha has some chance. Left alone here, she will not last the season out.'

'These people showed little mercy when they raped our sister,' said Diarmid savagely.

'Anyway, we cannot do that and return here by daybreak,' said Padriac. There was an unspoken question in his voice.

'Padriac's right, we cannot do it,' said Liam. 'Tell your story to these cottagers, and the lady Oonagh learns of Sorcha's whereabouts tomorrow or the next day. Be away from the water at dawn, and you may end up on somebody's dinner table tomorrow. You are not fools, I hope.'

'What are you saying?' Diarmid had pulled his dagger up from the earth and was tossing it restlessly from hand to hand.

'I'm saying this plan is impossible. I see no choice but to make Sorcha as safe and comfortable as we can; and leave her. Perhaps next time we can move her; there must be other caves down shore.' Liam did not sound altogether happy with his own suggestion.

'What do you say, druid?' Diarmid's tone stung like a whip. 'No wise pronouncements, no rhetoric to inspire us? What price your mystical craft now? Perhaps it is time we stopped heeding your advice and took matters into our own hands.' He was like a hunting dog straining at the leash.

'That's not fair,' said Cormack, springing to his twin's defence despite his own doubts.

'Nor is it quite accurate.' Liam spoke firmly. 'You cannot have forgotten how we were able to track down our quarry tonight with such speed. Seldom have I seen a mist come down so quickly or so selectively. Or dissipate in a flash as it did when we were done. Nor have I ever before witnessed ferns and mosses creep and spread in moments to cover men's bones and flesh so. There was a magical craft at work there; you can thank your brother for that.'

'Bollocks,' growled Diarmid, but he sat down again, the knife still in his hands. Their words faded out of my consciousness and the evil images returned. I tried again to block them out, but they would not go. I wanted to scream, to shout out, to let go the anger and hurt in my head; but somehow still I clenched my teeth and swallowed the sounds that threatened to break forth, and my tears flowed silently. My brothers meant well. But I almost wished it were dawn, and they were gone again. The voices went on arguing, and after a while Padriac brought me more to drink and I took it, and he went away again. The images passed and passed in my mind. The brand of hot iron on human flesh. Eilis racked with convulsions, her pretty face distorted with retching. The dog with her trusting eyes and the knife wound deep across her throat. The wide smile of the simpleton as he gazed up into the trees. *Don't hurt faery girl! Your turn next, farm boy*. Under the thick cloak, I was shivering.

I'm here, Sorcha.

I would not believe it at first; it had been so long since he had touched my mind in this way.

I'm here. Try to let go, dear one. I know how it hurts. Lean on me; let me take your burden for a while.

I could scarcely see him; he was on the far side of the fire, behind the others and half turned away, with his head still in his hands. It seemed as if he had scarcely moved at all.

How can you? How can you know?

I know. Let me help you.

I felt the strength of his mind flow into mine, and somehow he managed to close off the terrible, the dark and secret things that he had dreaded sharing with me, and fill my head with pictures of all that was good and brave. Myself, a small child dancing joyfully along a forest path, sheltered by the arching branches, lit by dappled sun. This was an old image, stored deep in his consciousness and influencing all that he did. Then, the two of us, lying on the rocks by the spring pools, face down, chins on hands, still as small basking lizards, watching the tiny jewel-like frogs as they hopped and dived and sprang amongst the fronds of watercress. Finbar, patiently extracting the barbs of starwort from my hands as Conor told the story of Deirdre, Lady of the Forest. The seven of us in our circle around the little birch tree, our hands linked.

He gave me no time to think, but flooded my mind, blotting out, for now at least, my wretchedness and fear. It was as if his mind had slipped itself around mine to shelter it from harm. So there was more: he and I again, sitting on the roof slates at home, looking out far, far over forest and lake. A little image of Father Brien, tip of tongue between his lips, as with deft brush strokes he worked on an intricate page of manuscript. Conor in his white robe, reading notches on the trunk of a great rowan. Diarmid and Liam wrestling in the shallows, strength against strength, until one gave way and the contest ended in splashing and hilarity. Padriac splinting an owl's wing, clever hands moving without haste, not to frighten. Cormack and Linn running along the shore, and the west wind whipping up the water to cover their footsteps in the sand.

My tears began to flow again at that, but the hurt was different now.

Weep, dear one. Our love wraps you like a blanket. Our strength is yours, and yours keeps our hope alive.

The forest holds you in its hand. This was another voice, Conor's. *The pathway opens before you.* The rest of them had fallen silent, sensing maybe that dawn was coming, and something was happening that was more vital than any plans they might make.

What – what do you see for me? It took a great effort of will to ask. *What will happen to me, Finbar? This time, show me.*

There was an image, broken up, hard to discern. A girl, myself I supposed, drifting in a little boat. An owl hooting. Or was that here and now, not part of the mind picture? A pair of hands, holding a little knife, carving a tiny block of wood. A fire burning green and purple and orange. The picture faded and was gone. Whether that was all Finbar saw, or whether he closed off the remainder, I did not know. And through all that time, he never spoke one word aloud, but sat there with head in hands, as if in a trance.

Soon enough the first trace of dawn grey touched the sky, and it was almost time for them to go. My breathing was quiet, my body more rested although there was still a deep aching there. My head was filled with brightness, scraps of hero tales, pictures of our childhood, a bastion of loving memories to keep out the shadows. Finbar let no evil thought or ugly image touch me. I lay still in my blanket, and now the lightening sky seemed gentle, and the canopy of trees benign. I heard an owl's voice calling again through the still dawn, and it touched my spirit deep within. My brothers sat silent and grim-faced around the last embers of the fire.

'Sorcha.' Conor spoke aloud this time, so they could all hear. 'There is one choice none of us has spoken of. I want to put it to you.' I found I was able to sit up and nod my understanding. The grip on my mind relaxed just a little; but still Finbar held me safe. I glanced at him across the circle. My brother's face shocked me; he was parchment white, and there were deep purple shadows beneath his eyes. He looked like an old man, or one who has spent a night with the Fair Folk and will never quite be himself again.

It's all right, Sorcha. Listen to Conor. Finbar did not move a muscle.

'We've all thought of it, I have no doubt; but none of us was prepared to say it, though Cormack came close, I think. I want you to decide, Sorcha. You must take your time, and make the choice for yourself, not for us.'

Liam took over. 'Don't talk in riddles, Conor. This must be said in plain words. Sorcha, what he's trying to say is that maybe this is the point where the task should be abandoned. To me at least, the cost now seems too great. Each of us would gladly give up his chance of the future in return for your safety.'

'We would give our lives for you. What is hardest

to bear is the guilt; for you risk yourself daily in struggling to complete this task for us.' Cormack's voice was chillingly matter-of-fact.

'We can't protect you,' said Diarmid bluntly. 'We're worse than useless, we're just a burden to you.' I saw then that he held the small bundle of starwort shirts in his hands, heedless of the barbs, and they were close, so close to the burning coals. 'I say, destroy these magical garments, leave off the task that consumes you, seek shelter with the holy brothers who can protect you from the sorceress. And if we are lost to the human world, what then? It matters little.'

This speech must have cost him dear, for I knew the desire for vengeance burned deep in his heart. I knew how Liam longed to return home and set things right with his father and his lands, before it was too late to salvage anything. And Conor; what of his pathway, his years of preparation, what of the villagers that spoke of him with awe as one of the wise ones? Who would take his place if he never returned to the mortal world?

'We should have made a boat, or raft,' said Padriac suddenly. 'There are few settlements here; you could move a long way down the lake, going softly by dusk or dawn, under the trees close by the bank. I should have thought of it.' The others looked at him. 'Well, it was an idea,' he said.

'Haven't you been listening at all?' snapped Liam, frowning.

Padriac was stirring his pot over the fire again, brewing enough of the herbal tea to last me a day or two.

'Oh, yes,' he said tranquilly. 'Sorcha will choose for all of us. What more is there to add?'

I felt Finbar's grip on my mind relax and slowly

withdraw, leaving me clean and empty. Conor's presence, too, retreated as subtly as it had slipped into my head. They wanted me to make this decision alone. But there was no choice, not for me. I reached out for the bundle of weaving, and Diarmid passed it to me.

'Are you sure, Sorcha?' asked Liam quietly. I nodded. Unlike Finbar, I still knew which path I had to take. It seemed that, whatever happened to me, this much would not change.

'Very well,' said Liam. 'We honour your decision. We will survive, and return again at midwinter.'

'We will not return here,' said Finbar in the faintest of voices, and as we all turned to look at him, he swayed and fell to the ground as if lifeless. Conor reached him first and knelt by him, shielding his face from the others.

'Get him up,' said Diarmid harshly. 'It is nearly dawn.'

'What's wrong with him anyway?' Cormack was only marginally more sympathetic. 'Haven't heard a word out of him all night.'

'Tasted his first blood,' said Diarmid. 'Takes them like that sometimes. Hasn't the stomach for it. Yet he was keen enough at the kill. I've never seen a man hack so deep, nor twist the knife with such relish. Look at his hands.'

Tactfully, Padriac drew me aside to speak of poultices and fomentations, and how he'd had to put in a stitch that I would have to remove myself, which would be tricky but not impossible. I half-listened. He had no need to explain my own craft to me. Liam was slapping Finbar's linen-white cheek; Conor was holding fingers to his neck, feeling the throb of his life-blood beneath the blanched skin, talking in an undertone.

'Hurry up,' said Diarmid. 'By the Lady, what a time to throw a fit of the vapours. The sun already touches the tree tops beyond the lake. Slap his face hard, bring him to his senses quickly. He's becoming a hindrance to us.'

'Hold your tongue!' said Liam, in a voice just like his father's. It was the voice that made grown men suddenly silent.

'You misjudge Finbar,' Conor said, as he and Liam hauled their brother to his feet and began a slow progress towards the lake. For Diarmid was right; it was almost time. Half-conscious, Finbar sagged between them, moving his feet like leaden weights. 'He has given more of himself this night than you could ever imagine. Do not judge too quickly that which you cannot understand.'

'I understand well enough,' growled Diarmid, but he made no further attempt to interfere. And so they reached the shore again, and again bade me farewell. And this time, standing swaying in my big cloak, I did not want any of them to touch me, and they knew it without any word said. So they slipped away, one by one, and I understood in my heart that it would be a long time, longer far than the span of summer to winter, before I would see them again. My love for them had not lessened, but I did not think I could ever again hold them or hug them, although they were my brothers. I could no longer really trust them, because they had not been there when I needed them. That this was none of their doing made no difference. Such was the power of the evil thing done to me. So, as I watched them walk to the water's edge, with Finbar still slumped between his two brothers, and the light from the first sun touching his pale features with gold, I did not call to him with my inner voice. I did not say *thank you* or *goodbye, dear heart.* I turned my back and made my solitary way up under the ash trees, and my mind and my tongue were as silent as death. There was no farewell for my brothers as the waters rose up to take them once more.

Cormack had predicted I would not last long alone in the forest with my injuries. He had not considered the strength of my will, nor my skill as a healer. He did not foresee the intervention of the forest itself, through its most secret inhabitants. Time passed, and the moon waxed and waned, and the warm days of summer turned slowly to the crisp, cool ones of early autumn. It was quiet, so quiet that even the sudden screeching of a bird made me jump. Too quiet. The pile of smooth river stones that marked Linn's final resting place spoke to me daily of the void her passing had left in my little world. My day had been ordered by her patterns as much as my own, my labours at loom or spindle timed for her trips to forage in the woods for rabbits or up the lake shore for fish, my meal taken companionably on her return, and our slumber warmed by the same blanket. Once, earlier, I had found her footmarks still printed neatly in the sand where she had run with the breath of the wind in her stride, and I wept and knew how much I had lost.

My body mended, thanks to Padriac's ministrations and my own knowledge. After a time, I knew I was not with child, and gave wordless thanks for it. But I was still scared, and sometimes even my small daily routine was too much of a burden. The haven which had become my home was a refuge no longer, changed forever by the evil that had happened there. I fancied my herbs dying slowly by degrees, or bringing forth gross, misshapen flowers and shrunken berries. I would not venture out to harvest a new supply of the plant I needed, not even with a sharp knife in my belt.

The slightest sound set my heart thumping. I had dreams, and those I will not recount. I tried to fight them. I did my best to sleep by day, and stay awake during the dark time. But my candles were almost gone, and the dreams came even by sunlight. I resorted to the use of herbs, and for a time they gave a brief respite. But the dosage I needed grew stronger and stronger. After a while I made the decision to stop, knowing the grip such potions can exert over the weak. The demons returned.

I thought of Simon a lot. I thought of his injuries, and how I had made him promise to survive. I decided I was weak and must re-apply myself to my task. But there were days when I simply did not have the will for it, and the thread of starwort remained unwoven while I sat with my back to the ash log and stared at nothing. I felt as if I were waiting, but for what I did not know.

I had not gathered much food, being afraid to go far from home. I had neither the will nor the energy to prepare berries for drying, and my small herb patch grew rank with weeds. There was a little sack of dried peas which I had found some time ago beside the cart track, fallen from a farmer's load. I had been saving these, and now I would boil up a handful in the mornings to make a sort of broth, when I could summon up the strength. Some days, even combing my hair was too much effort. I grew thinner and found myself falling asleep unexpectedly, only to be awoken by evil dreams. As the days grew shorter, my work made little progress. Then, finally, she came. Silent as a deer, she was suddenly there in the shadows amongst the grey trunks of the ash trees, her deep eyes watching me with an expression I could not read. Today she wore no mid-night blue cloak, nor were there jewels in her long dark hair. Instead her garment was plainly cut, flow-ing to her ankles, its fabric a mossy green; and her arms glimmered palely in the filtered light of the trees. The leaves and twigs stirred around her, and I felt the deep throbbing heartbeat of the forest, as if it came alive as she passed. Last time I had vented my anger and fear on her. Now I only felt a hollow emptiness.

You're too late.

Her face was impassive. If there were any expres-sion, it was slight disapproval.

'It's time, Sorcha,' she said. 'Time to move on.'

Move where? I thought dimly. It all seemed too hard, too much effort. Perhaps I would just crawl in under the rock face again and close my eyes.

I'm tired of being strong.

She laughed at me. Laughed, as if I were ridiculous.

'You are what you are,' she said in her low, musi-cal voice. 'Now come on, get up. You are not the first woman of your race to be abused thus by men, nor will you be the last. We saw with sorrow what was done to you; but vengeance was swift and just. Now you must go from here.'

There was a very small core of anger inside me, struggling to get out through the profound weariness that made my head fuzzy and all my limbs heavy and aching. I got up, and the trees seemed to shiver and move around me.

'Good,' she said quietly. 'Now you will leave here. You may take just one pack with you. Choose its con-tents carefully. You will find a small boat moored under the willows not far from the northern end of the bay. It will carry you where you need to go.'

I blinked at her. The trees seemed to be wavering around me in all directions, the late afternoon light flickering between their leaves, grey, green, gold, russet and brown. Her form was already starting to fade.

But what if – but I can't – and where –

She was gone. I stood still, willing my vision to steady. Slowly the world came to rights, more or less. I thought vaguely that perhaps I hadn't eaten since the day before. Maybe that was the problem. I did feel rather strange. But there was nothing much around. Besides, if I could take only one bag with me, it certainly wasn't going to be filled with dried apples or bunches of watercress.

When the Fair Folk gave you an instruction, you followed it, whether it suited you or not. That was just the way it was. Anyway, when you looked at it, I didn't have much choice. I was not prepared for winter, and my brothers had more on their minds than chopping wood or seeking out supplies for me, that last time. So I left my oaken staff, that had been Father Brien's, and I left the winter boots and the warm cloaks, and the three sharp daggers with carven hilts. I left the pile of smooth stones where my good dog lay, and I left the last bunch of dried lavender, which held the summer's warmth in its sweet, faint fragrance, and the dwindling stack of ash wood. I even left the spindle and the little loom my brother had crafted for me. But I took the two shirts of starwort and the third half-sewn, along with the fibres I had not yet spun, and I took my needle and thread, and in the bottom of the bag was Simon's carving. I wore my old dress, and around my neck Finbar's amulet, which had been our mother's. I walked away

256

from the cave without a single backward glance. But I heard faint voices whispering, rustling, and the beat of delicate wings in and out of the tree canopy.

Sorcha, oh Sorcha. Farewell, farewell. The sounds followed me along the shore, as I made my way barefoot between stones and across rough grass, until I found the little flat boat with a pole to push it along. *Sister, oh sister. Where are you going? When will you return?* I dug the pole into the sand and sent the boat out into the current, and the water carried me away.

CHAPTER SEVEN

I f I had any will at that moment, I would have followed Padriac's suggestion and hugged the bank of the lake, travelling close under the draping willows until I should reach some place of relative safety. I thought, fuzzily, that the Lady had intended this and had moved me on for protection while I completed my task. But I had no energy to guide the craft. My mind was hazy with hunger, and I supposed I was ill; the faint rocking of the boat felt strangely erratic, the water was turbulent, and the passing trees tilted and swayed, making me dizzy. I sensed other hands were moving the small vessel on a path not of my choosing.

The forest sylphs faded away behind, and within the ripples and surges of lake water other voices arose, liquid, evasive, murmuring one to the other as their owners bore my little boat swiftly, too swiftly, out on the increasingly choppy water. I blinked and stared, wondering how much was real and how much some feverish vision. There were long pale hands in the water, and faces with wide-set eyes, and hair like fronded weed, grey and green and blue. There were tails with jewel-bright scales. 'Make haste, make haste,' they sang, one to another. 'It's time.'

And so the boat moved faster and faster, as if on a swift river, and in the sky above heavy clouds gathered and hung, and the day grew dark. Fat raindrops began to spatter down around me, and there was a distant rumble of thunder. The small part of me that was still awake registered these things, and that I was alone in the middle of a large expanse of water, barefoot in my old dress, in a boat designed for peaceful shallows. The wind rose, and the little craft bobbed up and down as it went.

Wavelets sloshed in over the sides, soon soaking me to the waist. But it didn't feel cold; instead I was burning hot and I heard their voices calling to me, around, under, behind, and before me in the darkening water. 'It's easy, easy, Sorcha. Slip over, slip over the side and down to us. It's cool here under the water. Slip away down.' And another. 'Come away, come away down. Say farewell to your pain, let the water wash it away. Come, let the water take you. Come and dance with us in the deep.' Their voices were sweetly coaxing. I wanted to feel the cool water on my burning brow, wanted to sleep and forget. It would be so simple to lean over, to slide under the water and away from it all. 'Throw me your bundle! Throw it! Let go your burden!' I saw the long, clutching fingers stretching up, up towards me, and I came awake, and clasped the bag tight to my chest, never mind the barbs that pricked me through the canvas.

No. I will not. Then I heard them laughing, high voices, deep voices, and the splashing of their tails as they moved around the boat. And they were gone, leaving me to the wind and water.

I suppose I did come close to drowning, that evening. But I was ill and tired, and at the time the danger seemed unimportant. After a time the sky blackened, and lightning split the darkness like great white spears flung with tremendous force into the earth. Squally rain passed over, and the boat was half filled with water. I gripped on with both hands to keep my balance, and knew it was only a matter of time before it sank. I knew, too, that I would not last long in the water. The lake had long since narrowed to a swift-flowing river, and the shore was closer now; a flash of lightning illuminated rock walls and low clumps of bushes. We were beyond the edges of the forest, in more open country. Here and there I could see gaps in the rocks and small stretches of bank where one might crawl ashore, if one had the strength. I fumbled for the pole, hoping to guide the craft to safety, for possibly it was shallower here. But my mind didn't seem able to direct my hands, and the pole slipped away from me and over the side, floating rapidly out of reach. I was too weak to swim after it, let alone gain the shore. And if I did not drown, the cold would finish me before morning. I was on fire with the fever, and could not feel the chill, but the healer in me knew how this heat could deceive, and a person freeze to death while in its burning grip.

The storm clouds parted briefly, and the moon appeared. Pale light spread suddenly across the surging water. There was a light on the shore too, and a moment later a man's voice, shouting. 'Hey! What's

that?' And another. 'Out there – look! There's somebody in it! I think it's a girl.' The wind gusted,
blowing my hair across my eyes. The boat was floating away from the shore again. I peered towards the
small light. There were two men, one carrying some
sort of lantern, and the other was stripping off his
shirt and wading into the water, then striking out
towards me, swimming into the storm. 'You're crazy!'
shouted the other after him. He was coming closer.
Despite wind and current, his powerful body, white
in the moonlight, moved in a straight path purpose-
fully towards me. He was a big man, moving with
grim intention. My body tensed with fear, and suddenly the thought of slipping over the side, of sinking
down below the water and out of this world seemed
altogether good, the only sensible thing to do. I
clutched my bag with both hands and stood up
unsteadily. The wind did the rest for me, tipping the
boat over so that it filled and sank. The water closed
over my head.

For long moments the cool was blissful, the wish
for oblivion strong enough to blot out everything.
Then the lungs craved air, and the spirit said *No. Not
yet*. And I came up to the surface, choking, gasping,
shivering and terrified. Came up as he swam the last
few strokes towards me and gripped me round the
chest with a pair of arms like iron. I could not scream,
but I fought him as hard as I could, scratching and
kicking with the last of my strength.

'Stop fighting, you fool,' he snapped, and clamped
a large hand over my mouth, turning me on my back
and pulling me shorewards. I bit him. He swore,
using a word I had heard but once before, for the language he used was that of the Britons. His grip
loosened enough for me to slip beneath the water

again, and I tried to swim away, evade him somehow, but my nostrils filled with water, and I felt it painfully in my chest, and then he grabbed my hair and I felt myself inexorably towed to shore, held in a grip too strong to break. I was weeping and my nose was running, and I was so scared, this time, that I truly wished I had drowned.

We reached the bank, where he slung me over his shoulder unceremoniously, like some prize of the hunt. 'Fool,' remarked his companion. The two of them began walking up amongst the bushes, away from the water. I noticed he was carrying my bag in his hand. Both of them had knives in their belts. I thought I would snatch one when they stopped to put me down. Before I let them do anything to me, I would kill myself. For why else would men like these bother rescuing me, but to make use of my body then throw me aside? What else could they want with a wretched girl, half starved, half drowned? But I would not let them have me, not this time. I would stop them by whatever means there were.

But when we reached shelter under a rock wall, and I saw that there was a third man waiting there for them in the darkness, I had no strength left to protect myself, and I lay there helpless where he dropped me. They had dimmed the lantern, but I could see they were Britons, and dressed for fast and silent travel across country.

'We'll have to light a fire.' This was the voice of my rescuer.

'You're mad,' said the other one, him with the lantern. 'What about Redbeard and his men? They can't be far behind us.'

'You heard him. Light a fire.' That was the third man, who sounded somewhat older than the others. I dared not open my eyes further than a slit. 'A small fire. This storm will keep our pursuers away until dawn. We should be well clear by then.'

I heard someone fiddling with the lantern, and after a while a gentle crackling. A little glow spread out, casting its orange light over their grim faces. They spoke quietly amongst themselves, and after a while I managed to put names to them. The older one was John; the man who had carried the lantern, young, golden-haired, was called Ben. As for the tall man, who had fished me out of the river, his name seemed to be Red, unlikely though that sounded. Now he was going through my bag. I shut my eyes and tried to stop shivering.

'She held onto that tight enough. What's in it, the family jewels?'

There was no answer. After a while I opened my eyes a little. Red was closing the flap of the bag.

'Not much,' he said. His voice sounded strange. He looked strange too, his face went in and out of focus as he bent over me. I clenched my teeth in revulsion.

'I think she's sick. Here, give me your cloak, Ben.'

'Hey, it's cold. What about me?' The reply was plaintive, but his companion handed it over, and I felt its warmth settle around me. The man's hand touched my shoulder, and I flinched away, biting back a scream. For a moment I stared straight up into his eyes, which were blue and bore a puzzled look. He was frowning.

'Easy,' he said. 'Easy there,' as if talking to some nervous horse or half-wild dog. Now, I thought. Now they'll try to grab hold of me and I'll – and I'll – my mind got no further, for there were three of them, all armed, and all far bigger and stronger than

263

those others. These were hardened travellers. I had no chance. But I had sharp teeth and nails, and I would use them until I had no strength left.

'Take your clothes off,' said Red, and my body curled in on itself in terror. I felt myself shaking. My thumping heart measured the silence. How long before they laid their filthy hands on me? How long could I stifle the scream of outrage that welled in my throat?

'What's wrong with you?' his voice was exasperated. 'Here.' He was holding something out to me. Ben spoke.

'She doesn't understand you, Red. After all, she's one of the natives, and a couple of sheaves short of the haystack at that.'

'More likely she's been hurt before,' put in the older man. 'Terrified to let you near her. Give her the clothes, and move back. Not much point in trying to talk to her; I doubt if she has the wit to understand you, let alone the language. You need to show her you mean no harm.'

My rescuer raised his eyebrows and put what he was carrying down on the ground next to me. Then the three of them moved back to the edge of the overhang and, exchanging glances, turned away from me.

'This is stupid,' Ben said, with his back to me. 'Who is this, some princess of the blood? First, she's a barbarian; second, she's about as bright as a lump of wood, and third, Redbeard's men are on our trail, armed to the teeth, and here we are observing the niceties of female modesty. I think this forest waif has turned your heads.'

'Shut up, Ben,' said Red, and his companion did.

I realised I'd been given a rather big shirt of coarse linen, and a belt to keep it on. It smelled of sweat, but it was dry. There was some sort of undershirt as well.

Red glanced back over his shoulder. 'You're supposed to take off your wet clothes, and put those on,' he said, but it was clear he did not expect me to understand. He turned around fully and mimed the action for me as I stared.

Perhaps, I thought, they really didn't intend to hurt me. In any event, there was little to lose. I could feel the fever gripping me, burning. I had enough common sense left to know dry clothes would help. Red turned his back again.

'Why bother talking to her?' enquired Ben. He looked several years younger than his friend, possibly only just old enough for an expedition of this kind, whatever it was. If they were indeed Britons, they were a long way from home. 'You've only got to look at her to tell she's not all there. You may have had your reasons for coming here, but even you must admit it has been a waste of time. And now we're risking our one chance of escape for some half-witted girl. This is the last time you drag me along on some fool's errand.'

'You talk of fools,' said John, 'in the heat of the moment. But when he asks you, next time, you will go with him. Now hold your tongue, lest you make bad worse.'

And while they argued, I managed, heart pounding, to take off my sodden gown and struggle into the dry garments, tying the vast shirt as well as I could around my waist. The belt went round me twice, and was still loose.

The argument, such as it was, drew to a close. The three of them turned back and scrutinised me as I sat, still shivering, by the tiny fire. There was the faintest hint of amusement on the older man's face as he regarded me. I suppose I did look a little odd.

'So far, so good,' said Red, whose own expression gave away nothing at all. 'Put the cloak on, too.' I gave no sign that I understood. He picked it up and dropped it over my shoulders. I flinched as his hands drew close, but its warmth was welcome now, and I drew the folds around me.

'Good,' he said. 'Now rest. Rest.' He pointed to the ground by the fire, and pillowed head on hands. That seemed, suddenly, like quite a sensible idea, and I lay down, still shivering, and soon sank into a feverish half-sleep in the midst of which their low voices came to me in snatches.

'You're mad, Red. We've got less than a day to get down there and meet the boat. What are we supposed to do with her?' That was Ben, who had held a lantern on the shore.

'In any event, not leave her to drown,' said John. 'She'll do well enough here by morning, if we leave her a blanket.'

'I wonder what she was doing out there. Pretty strange weather for fishing,' remarked Ben.

'These are strange people,' said the older man. 'I've heard they sometimes cast their own adrift from the shore, as a punishment. Maybe this girl offended someone.'

'She would have drowned.'

The one they called Red seemed to be a man of few words. He spoke now, more quietly than his companions. 'She has a fever. More than that, she's scared to death.'

'Well, she would be,' said Ben. 'She's one of *them*, isn't she? That makes us the enemy. Maybe she expects the sort of treatment her own kind hand out to people they don't fancy.'

'She hasn't spoken,' observed John. 'Nor made a

sound. Perhaps not so much lacking in her wits as mute, or deaf. She looks half wild. She may well have been abandoned by her people, seeing she has a deficiency, and left to fend for herself. I wouldn't be too concerned about her, Red. You've done your good deed. She'll recover.'

There was silence for a while. They shared a bottle of water and a few strips of dried meat. A ration was left close to me, but I could not touch the salt beef and I drank only a sip or two from the cup. Then Red volunteered to keep watch, and they put out the lantern. The others rolled into blankets and soon slept. They seemed like men who had been on the move for a long time, and knew how to do things neatly and quietly. But my presence there clearly made things far from neat.

Amazingly, I must have slept for some time, to be woken abruptly before dawn, heart pounding, by some nameless dream. Even in my sleep I must hold back speech or sound, but the Briton saw me start and sit up. I suppose my face reflected the demons still lurking on the edges of my consciousness. He sat there quite still by the tiny glow of the remnant fire, watching me. I could see, now, where the name Red came from. His hair was cropped ruthlessly short, but both it and the few days' stubble of beard were lit by the fire's glow to the bright red-gold of autumn sun on oak leaves. His face was formidable though he was young in years, perhaps not much more than Liam's age. The nose was long and straight, the jaw set firm, the mouth wide and thin-lipped. You would not want this man as an enemy. Further away, his two companions still slept, cocooned in blankets. It seemed he had taken more than one watch, to let them rest. The rock overhang had kept us dry; outside the storm had abated and the only sound was the dripping and running of water between the stones.

I wrapped my arms around myself, gripping the cloak with both hands. My head felt clearer and the nightmare was receding. Maybe I had enough strength to run. Maybe, when his back was turned, I could slip away quietly. They'd be glad to be rid of me. It sounded as if speed was of the essence, and from the look of him, this large young man would rather not have me around to slow the expedition down, wherever it was going. No doubt he was already regretting fishing me out of the lake. I was thinking hard, gauging how many steps would take me out into the open and away amongst the bushes. Then he spoke, startling me.

'Better eat something. And drink.'

I stayed quite still. There was wisdom in not making it obvious I understood their language. If they thought me some sort of wild girl of the woods, some village idiot, I would be safer. I would not be much of a trophy, or worth a hostage price. After all, I was my father's daughter.

'Mm.' He scrutinised me as I sat there, huddled in the half-dark. Then he tried again, muting his voice so as not to wake the others. 'You – food? You – water?' It seemed he had learned a few words in our tongue. His accent was laughable. I looked at him, and he held out a traveller's cup. I edged away from him, for however kind his words, he was a man, very tall and broad of shoulder, big enough and strong enough to do whatever he liked to me. My fever had come down, but I didn't seem to be able to stop shaking.

He put the cup on the ground near me, and retreated. When I failed to respond, he tried again.

'You – water,' he repeated. 'Unless,' he went on in his own tongue, 'you feel, like me, that you've swallowed half the lake already. You made a good attempt to drown me, I thought.'

For an instant, a most curious feeling came over me, as if we were replaying a scene already a part of my life from somewhere long back, but subtly changed. Then it was gone, and I picked up the cup, annoyed at the way my hand trembled, and drank.

And he was right, I did feel better.

'Good,' he said, not taking his watchful eyes off me. I drank again, my hand steadier on the cup now. In a minute I would try to get up. See if I could walk. If I could run, just for long enough to get away. For the Britons had their own desperate mission. They would not waste time seeking me, they would more likely be relieved at losing their unexpected burden. Then I would . . . at that point the train of thought reached a blank. I was in unknown territory, without proper clothing, without food or tools or any help. And if I had understood right, a band of armed and dangerous men would be moving swiftly down on us once dawn broke. They'd said Redbeard. Could this be Seamus Redbeard, the father of Eilis? What if I were here, and they found me? There would be men there that would know me, even after nigh on two years. What then? It did not bear thinking of. There would be a swift return to my father's house, and to the lady Oonagh. The thought made my flesh crawl. That way was all darkness and death, for me and my brothers. I was in danger from both the Britons and their pursuers. I had to get away.

'Here. Eat.' The Briton held out a strip of the dried meat, as if to a nervous dog. I shook my head. 'Eat,' he repeated, frowning. His eyes were as blue as ice, as blue as the sky on a frosty winter morning. I was hungry; but not so hungry that I could stomach flesh. Then he was putting the meat back in the bag where it seemed they kept their travellers' rations, and he was looking maybe for something else, and his eyes were turned away just for a moment. I moved fast and silently, using all the skills I had. Up, across, under the overhang, away –

His hand shot out so swiftly I barely saw it. He gripped my arm painfully, jerking me to my knees beside him. I bit back a yelp of frustration and fear.

'I don't think so.' He didn't even raise his voice. The others slept on. His hold did not slacken; he knew how to use the least force to cause the most hurt, that was certain. I was drawn up close to him, too close for comfort, for I smelled his sweat and his anger and I felt his breath on my face and saw the chill in his eyes. His strength and quickness alarmed me – how could I ever have thought I could get away? The fever must indeed have made me stupid. But I was angry too. What game was he playing? Why keep me here now, when they needed to move on swiftly and unencumbered?

He had hardly moved from where he sat, save to imprison my arm and hold me by him. His fingers dug into my flesh. He had very big hands. I could not quite stifle a gasp of pain, and his grip loosened, but not much.

'Damn you,' he said, still in that quiet, level voice. 'Three moons and more I've been in this godforsaken country, searching for answers. Travelled to the strangest places on earth; followed every lead, turned every wretched stone. Put my friends at risk of their lives. And for what? Hunger and cold and a knife in the dark. There is no truth on this island of yours.

Rather, there are as many truths as there are stars in the sky; and every one of them different.'

I gaped at him. Whatever I had expected him to say, it was not this.

'I could swear you understand me,' he said, looking direct into my eyes. 'And yet, how could you?'

What was it Conor had said once, about me and Finbar? *The two of them are like open books ... their thoughts blaze like a beacon from their eyes* ... I hoped this Briton could not read me so well. It was starting to get light; I heard his companions stirring.

'You want to go,' he stated. 'Where, I can't imagine; but I suppose you have some bolthole near here. Perhaps to hide in until your countrymen arrive; maybe you think to watch them hack us to pieces. I did not think you one of our enemy; not when I stopped you from drowning yourself. Perhaps you really are an innocent, as my friends believe; too simple to be dangerous.'

I tried to wrench my arm from his grip. 'No,' he said without emphasis. 'Three moons with no answers, and now, on the last day, the very last, I find the first piece of the puzzle. And who do I get to explain it? A girl who can't talk, or won't. See this?' He was reaching into his pocket, and for the first time there was a note in his voice beyond the quietly conversational. *'Tell me where you got this.'*

And there it was. Simon's little carving, the small oak tree in its protective circle and the wavy lines, which may or may not have been water. Nothing of interest in my bag, he'd said to his friends. Nothing much. That in itself had been strange enough; you'd have thought the starwort shirts were worth a comment. But it was this item that had caught his attention. *'Tell me,'* he said. *'Who gave you this?'*

271

And now he was really frightening me. I willed all expression from my face. Think of nothing. Let him know nothing. It was as well I was bound to silence. I was no liar; but think how the truth would sound. *It came from another of your kind. He was tortured at my father's home, and came close to death by the hot iron. Close to death, and closer to madness. We saved him, and I tried to help him, and he was getting better, and then . . . and then I left him alone when he most needed me. He went out into the forest without the means for survival. Even now, the mosses creep on his white bones, somewhere under the great oaks. Birds pluck his golden hair to line their nests, and his empty eyes gaze up for ever at the stars.* That was the truth.

'Damn you,' said the Briton again, 'why won't you speak? I will have this answer from you before ever I let you go.' And then the others were waking, rising in silence to roll bedding and stow gear, to check weapons and make all in readiness for a swift departure. And I thought, you will have a long wait for your answer. For you must wait until the six shirts of starwort are spun and woven and sewn together; until the day my brothers return, and I slip the shirts over their necks, and the spell is broken. Until that day, you will hear no answers from my lips. And no man has the patience to wait so long.

In the grey light before dawn, I watched them ready themselves, and marvelled at the silent understanding between them that spoke of long days and nights in the field or on the run. I did not know what they were, or where they were going. They were spies perhaps, like those my father had captured and held in his secret chamber; or perhaps they were mercenaries for hire. Their watchful faces, their hard bodies, their light gear and carefully tended weapons told of long experience and serious purpose.

They were soon ready, finding time, even, to allow me a few moments' privacy for the body's essentials. I knew now not to try to run. He would outpace me, wherever I went. He would outwit me, whatever I tried. For now. When I returned from my ablutions, they were talking in low voices.

'. . . no point in arguing. If Red says we're taking her, we're taking her. We'll be slow; best leave now and cover as much ground as we can before full light.'

Ben was enraged; his words came out in a sort of hiss, for they were all muting their tone. I supposed the men who sought them might be close at hand.

'This is complete folly! Forget the girl; she'll do well enough here, and if not, what of it? Her kind are no more than savages, killers every one. How many good men have been lost in those accursed woods, or come home mere shells of their former selves? I don't know what chivalrous impulse has got into you, Red, but I know I'm not risking my hide for her. As for you, John, your brains must be addled to let him get away with this. It's insanity.'

Red took no notice of him, but hefted his pack onto his back and held out a hand to me. 'Come on,' he said, snapping his fingers, and I stared at him. I would not be treated like some hound that would follow her master's every bidding. 'Come,' he said again, and this time he gripped my arm where he'd hurt me before, and I sucked in my breath.

'She's got a few bruises,' remarked John. 'I hope you know what you're doing, Red.'

Red looked at him. 'I do,' he said. 'Now we split up, so my good friend here can't complain about the girl slowing him down. You two will take our original path back down to the cove. You should keep ahead of them if you go now, and the boat should be ready to pick you up before they get there. With luck.'

'What about you?' enquired Ben.

'I'll take the girl, and come round by the bluffs and down the cliff path. More dangerous, perhaps, but more direct. They're more likely to follow you, I think. I'll skirt the river as far as I can. If I'm not there in time for the boat, don't wait. Cross over to safe mooring; I'll meet you at the priory.'

'How?' said John, scratching his head. But there was no reply, and nobody was going to argue. That seemed to be the way it was. Red made the choices, and the others accepted them, even when, as it seemed to me, they were foolish beyond belief. How could a man who acted so unpredictably, who made such erratic decisions, be their leader? If it had been Liam, now, he would have consulted his men and reached a sensible compromise. Here there was no more discussion. Ben and John shouldered packs and disappeared between the bushes, silent-footed, and Red grasped my wrist and pulled me after him, back down towards the river. I resisted, tugging hard enough for him to turn back, exasperated.

'We're not going to get far this way,' he said. 'I –' He saw where I was pointing. My bag, with its cargo of starwort, still lay where he had dropped it under the overhang, near the smothered remnants of our small fire.

'All right,' he said, scooping it up and throwing it to me. 'But you carry it.'

It was a long and desperate morning. I tried to keep up with him, but I knew I was holding him back. The going was not easy, especially once the land rose in scarp and ridge, the meagre track traversing rock and scree and scrubland, climbing high above the winding course of the river. The lake and the forest fell behind us as we moved ever eastwards and a little north. The sun rose steadily in the sky. I had done many a trip with my brothers through the forest, staying out at night, living wild for a day or two. I was swift, and knew how to move in the woods and choose a path. But this was different. To start with, I was far weaker than I had thought, and found I must stop more and more often to draw breath before going on. And I had no shoes. Tough as my feet were, the rocks cut them and they bled. Red made few concessions, beyond grabbing my wrist or arm to haul me up after him, or waiting silently for me to catch up. His expression was sombre. Regretting his decision, I thought, and no wonder. He had water in a skin bottle, and shared it with me. The sun rose higher, promising a warm day. We crossed the river; or rather, he crossed it, wading steadily through the waist deep waters of a ford, and carrying me over his shoulder. When we got to the far bank, he dumped me down on a flat-topped rock.

'So far, so good,' he said, squatting down beside me so that his eyes were on a level with mine. He looked at me closely. The light blue gaze was shrewd.

'They are still far enough behind,' he said. 'But not so very far. They have divided their forces, I think. Can you go further?' I tried not to show I understood him. It was not easy. My feet were hurting and my head was getting that strangely fuzzy feeling again. Yet I knew there was no choice but to go on.

'Men,' he said, trying the language he knew I might understand. 'Bad men. You – me – walk?' He used gestures to convey this message to me and I was taken with an urge to giggle, despite the seriousness of the situation. I set my mouth firmly, determined to show neither weakness nor any other emotion. I considered vaguely what path I had been meant to take when the Forest Lady had sent me down the lake in a little boat away from the forest. Where had I gone wrong? For this, surely, was the wrong way, eastward, ever eastward with pounding head and bleeding feet, and a grim-faced stranger for company. How would my brothers find me, so far from home?

I looked at Red again. He was studying my feet, and then my hands, and his expression was quite odd. Mocking, I thought; but his derision was not turned on me, but inward.

'Strong-minded, aren't you?' he said, slipping the pack off his back and hunting inside it. He took out an old linen garment which he proceeded to tear into strips, holding a corner between strong white teeth. 'But these feet will take no more today. Here.' His hands worked deftly to bind both my feet with strips of cloth, tying them neatly in place. He was good; I could hardly have done a better job myself. I let him do it, thankful for the brief rest. Never mind that these soft bandages would not last the day's walk. I supposed he meant well. After all, if I could not make the distance, neither could he. Unless he left me behind.

'Good,' he said, 'and now you must eat something, and then we finish our journey. There are apples growing here, did you see? It seems they ripen early in these parts. Perhaps they are more to your taste than our rations.' And apples there were; little green ones with a faint blush of pink on the skin. Round and perfect. He picked one and quartered it neatly with a small, lethal knife.

'Here,' he said, offering me a segment. I took it, wondering greatly. They had indeed ripened before their due time, and strangely. There were several trees in this sheltered spot, but only one whose fruit seemed ready for eating. On the others they hung hard and green. There are many stories in our country with apples in them; they are the fruit of the Fair Folk, and used more than once to tempt mortal man or woman to stay in the place under the hill far longer than is good for them. Apples are a token of love, a promise. It was clear that Red had never heard what it meant, for a man to share an apple with a young woman. Perhaps, I thought, it didn't work with Britons anyway. Besides, I was hungry, and there was a long way to go. So I took his gift and ate it, and another piece, and it was the best thing I ever tasted. When we'd finished, I got up to walk on, but Red stopped me.

'No,' he said. 'This will be quicker.' He picked me up in his arms like a small child.

'You'll have to hold on,' he said. 'Don't worry, I don't bite.'

It was a losing race from the outset. Perhaps, if his prediction had been right and the pursuers had gone after his two companions, we would have made our way to safety in time. The Briton pressed on tirelessly, bearing my weight with no apparent difficulty, putting me down to scale a rock wall, pulling me up one-armed as he clung on; or helping me round an overhang or down a crumbling bank. But before long it became evident that they were closing in on us. I did not know how far there was to go. There was a damp, fresh smell in the air that suggested a large expanse of water, and many birds wheeled overhead. We were passing through thickets of rowan and, as we went, our clothes were torn by brambles, and our faces and arms whipped and scratched by twigs and thorns. The pace was fast; I felt the steady thump of the Briton's heart as he began to run soft-footed under the trees. He swore under his breath. And I heard the undeniable sound of many boots crunching on leaves to our right, and to our left, and behind us, and the hiss of an arrow coming over his shoulder to lodge, whirring, in the trunk of a stately berry-laden rowan tree. The Briton whispered an oath and dropped me.

'Run,' he said, drawing his short sword and turning his back to the tree. 'Go on, run!' He made an urgent movement with his arm; he meant me to go on alone, while he fought them off. 'Go, damn you, go!' I found I could not move; and then it was too late. They were all around us, stepping out from cover, men with the field armour my brothers wore, men with the long clever faces and dark curling hair of my own people. Men with hatred and vengeance in their eyes. One was re-loading a longbow; the others had drawn swords. They took their time advancing.

'There's a knife in my left boot,' muttered Red, moving his sword from hand to hand. 'Take it. Use it. And run if you can.' I snatched it and he glanced at me sharply before he stepped forward, thrusting me behind him, and the first of our attackers charged, yelling and wielding his blade in a manoeuvre I recognised well from the practice yard at home. My brothers would have responded by ducking, and slashing at the opponent's knees. Red didn't duck. Instead his boot came up, lightning swift, and he knocked the sword out of his opponent's hand, catching it neatly in his own. In an instant, it seemed, he sent the man reeling away with blood staining his right sleeve.

They gathered in a semicircle, not too close.

Amongst them were men I had seen before, at my father's table. I stayed behind Red, as far as I could.

'He can fight,' said one. 'The bastard can fight. Who's next?'

It was like the tale of Cu Chulainn, when his son comes to do battle. But I had not realised men still played such deadly games. A sort of single combat, where each took his turn with the interloper, until at last he was vanquished, or they had enough and moved in together to finish him off. It could be a slow way to die.

'I'll take him on,' said another, hefting his sword. 'My brother died in the ambush on Ardruan; aye, and many a good friend as well. Let him pay in blood for the blood that was spilt there.' The archer stood back, his bow drawn; it was clear that, while they might choose to have each his turn with the Briton, there could be but one end result. The second man set grimly to the fight; he had more skill than the other, and his tactic was clear – to edge Red out from cover, away from the rowan at his back and into a more vulnerable position. But Red had the advantage of them all in both height and weight; and he was no mean hand with the sword himself. In addition, he was light on his feet for such a big man, and the clashing of blades and sound of laboured breathing went on for some time. The men who were watching kept up a running commentary; derisive of their own when he made an error, and Red's blade drew a delicate scarlet line across his cheek; foul and abusive when they addressed the Briton. They accused him of the vilest things. It was a cruel sort of sport.

Red fought on without a word, apparently tireless. I supposed he understood their meaning, if not their words. His silence, I think, unnerved his opponent, so that for just a moment he took his eyes off the Briton. The moment was enough; the flat of Red's blade whacked down on his forearm, and he dropped his sword, his arm suddenly useless. Probably broken.

'Bastard,' he hissed through gritted teeth. 'You fight dirty, like all your people.' Then the rest of them closed in, and it was suddenly four or five against one, and chaos was all around me. Red had been keeping me behind him; but now he was forced to whirl this way and that, as one man after another came in to the attack. Further away, the archer waited, silent. I held the small knife in my hand, wondering if I would have the will to use it, if I got the chance. Bodies were falling to the ground, there were groans and curses, and I could see at least one man was dead; his head was at a most improbable angle. Red had moved away from the tree, and was wheeling amongst his opponents. I gave him a matter of moments.

'Run!' he shouted without looking at me. 'Run, damn you!' Then one of the men thrust and he parried it, and at the same time another slashed low at his legs, and a third came at him from behind, and he let out his breath with a hiss as his weapon fell to the ground. And I felt a grip on my shoulder, and my hair, and I was turned about to face one of Seamus' men at close quarters.

'I know you,' he said slowly. 'I know you from somewhere, I'm sure of it. What's a good little lass like you doing out here in the wilds with a British freak? Huh? Or perhaps not such a good little girl after all. Selling him secrets along with your body, maybe? We'll see what my lord has to say about that.' He yanked my hair back painfully.

'Hang on,' said one of the others. 'Isn't she – no, it

280

can't be. She died. This two year ago or more. Can't be her.'

'You mean –'

'But it *is* her. Look at the green eyes on her. Like a cat's. It *is* her.'

'Tie her hands. We'll take her back.'

'Make her a prisoner? You could get in big trouble for that. You know whose daughter she is. And you know what Liam's like. Think what her brothers would do to you, if they found out. She's our own kind.'

'Fat chance of them ever coming back. Besides, why's she with *him*? Tie her hands.'

As the man reached for my wrists, rope in hand, I struck upwards with the little knife, and he let out an oath, and released me. Blood was welling from his hand. I dropped the knife. Red was under attack from all sides; he seemed to be having trouble staying upright, as if one leg was giving way. One of the taller men had a knife close to Red's neck; Red gripped the man's wrist and held the knife away, muscles straining. Above the bright blade, his eyes met mine, and their expression at last showed something beyond icy calm. He was going to die, and I would be taken home. Home to the lady Oonagh, and certain death for my brothers.

I called for help. If at any time I needed the Fair Folk to intervene, this was it. Not that they'd been much help thus far. I called out to them, to anyone that might hear, with a silent scream from deep in the heart. *Help him. He should not die, not like this. Help me. For if I perish, so do my brothers.*

The rain came. It came from a clear sky that turned suddenly grey, as the warm day was in an instant as chill as midwinter. A drenching, uncanny, druidic rain that blinded and deafened; that cut off each man from the world. It was like standing under a great waterfall; it was like being in the heart of a storm. I could see nobody, hear no sound but the roaring of the torrent as it thundered down, soaking me in an instant, turning the ground to mud under my bare feet. Then I reached out through the sheets of water, and a large hand took mine, and the two of us were running, stumbling, slipping through the mud, sprinting blind between bushes and brambles, gasping for air, our faces and bodies streaming, our feet making sucking noises in the wet earth. I could hear Red's breathing this time; the laboured, gasping sound of a man with a serious injury, who pushes himself too far. I thought he could not go much further; and then the ground gave way, and we were sliding, falling, down a steep drop, clutching at branches, crashing through foliage, bouncing off rocks that bruised and battered us, until finally we came to rest on hard, dry ground. The sound of our precipitous descent died slowly; small stones still fell from above, dislodged by our passing. Then it was quiet, save for the sound of the rain, and the two of us gasping for air.

'Are you all right?' asked Red eventually in an odd sort of voice. I blinked the water out of my eyes, used both hands to push back the saturated curls that were plastered to my face, tried to wring my hair dry. We were inside a cave; glancing up, I could see the narrow gap through which we'd fortuitously fallen into this sheltered space. The ground was hard rock. Behind us, a narrow passage seemed to lead to some larger cavern, but it bent around, obscuring further vision. I looked out the other way. Light streamed in through a curtain of concealing foliage; the rain, it seemed, had ceased as abruptly as it started. I moved towards the entrance.

'Careful,' said Red, grabbing hold of my shirt tail as I passed him. I wrenched it out of his grasp, but went slowly, for the rocks became slick with water near the cave entrance. I peered out through the network of vines and creepers. And stood stock still in wonder.

'You have never seen the sea before,' observed Red quietly. I had not. Though my brothers had told me of the great expanse of wild water, and the myriad birds, and the light that glittered and changed and played on the shifting surface, nothing could have prepared me. Our cave was high up on a steep slope, that lower down became a sheer cliff, and I looked out over a vast distance, and the whole of the distance was water, water all the way to the horizon. The sky was hot blue; there was no sign of cloud. The rocks around me steamed gently in the sun. All trace of the sudden rain storm would soon be gone. Except maybe later, in stories. And our pursuers would be on the move. I turned back to the Briton.

He sat with his back against the rock wall, and one leg stuck out awkwardly in front of him. There was blood on his clothing, quite a lot of blood. Now that I looked at him properly, he was rather white in the face, with a grim set to his lips. Men can be a bit stupid about injuries they get in battle, as if pretending there's nothing wrong will make it go away, or that people won't notice if you keep quiet about it.

'They'll be after us,' he said. 'And not a dagger nor a bit of scrap metal between us. I'm afraid there's no choice but to stay here until after dark. Maybe then we can slip by them. There's a settlement up the coast a way, and small boats moored there.'

I stared at him, thinking of that vast expanse of water, unwilling to accept the implications of what he said. But from the looks of that leg, he'd be lucky to hobble as far as the cave mouth, let alone down the cliff and off to some village. And what was meant to happen then? I decided his friend Ben had been right. He was crazy. That being said, he needed my help, and I was determined to give it. For I had no doubt he had saved my life, once at least, probably twice. I owed him something, whatever his motives.

I still had my little pack, and he his. A small mercy. He watched me as I crouched by him, examining the wound. So he'd lost his sword, and I his other weapon. That was a problem. But wait. What about the little knife he'd used to cut up an apple so neatly? I rummaged through his pack. He looked on in silence. I found the knife and the remnants of the old shirt he'd used to make bandages for my feet. I looked down ruefully; the wrappings were completely gone and my feet were a mess of blood and dirt.

'Water,' he said helpfully. 'You'll need water. You can understand me, can't you?'

I nodded; it seemed as if the time of pretence was over. He had known, I thought, as soon as he told me to take his small dagger and defend myself, and I did as he bid me. I pointed within the cave; there was the sound of running and dripping, and I knew that I would find fresh water further down. What to do first? His clothing was already torn open; I slit it further, and eased off his damaged boot. This must have caused him great pain, but apart from a sudden intake of breath he did not acknowledge it. There was enough light for me to see the ugly gash that split his calf from knee to ankle; to see the fresh blood still welling out, to see the depth of it and the glint of metal lodged far inside the wound. I glanced up at his face. *Strong minded, aren't you?* The injury would not kill him; not if he had prompt treatment, and a healer skilled with the knife, and the right nursing after. But here, trapped in a cave, with no supplies, and the two of us covered in mud and debris, and the need for quiet on us, that was a different matter entirely.

'Not good, huh?' he said expressionlessly. 'Can you patch it up? Wrap a bit of something around it for me?' I nodded, trying to look capable and reassuring. I don't think I succeeded; I saw one corner of his tight mouth twitch up for a second in what might have been an attempt at a smile. On second thoughts, it was probably an involuntary grimace of pain. A Briton had no sense of humour; how could a people with no magic, with no life of the spirit, ever really know laughter?

I found the skin water flask in Red's pack and made my way deeper into the cave. Further down, it opened up wondrously. It was quite dark, but I caught the shadowy shapes of great rock pillars reaching up, and others stretching down to meet them; I sensed small creatures sleeping, high above me in the gloom. And I found fresh water, dripping down to rest gently in stone-rimmed pools. I filled the flask and returned.

I wished badly for Father Brien, or another of his skill, that day. I did my best. At least it was possible to wash my hands, and then to clean the wound. The fresh flow of blood was good, oozing only, not rushing forth in deadly tide. It would help the ill humours to leave the body. I remembered the man I had slashed with Red's little dagger; he might have lost a

285

lot of blood. I could have told them how to stem the flow; but I had not. Watching them close in on Red, I had forgotten I was a healer.

So far, so good. My dumb show was proving ever more difficult. I tried to indicate to Red that there was something in his leg; something I would have to remove. It would have helped if he'd been a little less stoical, or if there had been some mead, or ale, or a few well chosen herbs for a sleeping draught.

'I'm not sure what you're saying,' he said. 'You need to do something else to it? It's going to hurt? Well, get on with it then.'

I mimed that he would have to stay very still, for I had only the sharp point of the tiny knife with which to dislodge the metal object. He nodded grimly. I wondered why he hadn't told me to stop messing about and leave him alone. He had no reason to trust me.

It took a while. I learned another oath in the British tongue. Apart from that, he kept quiet, although I heard his breathing change, and his face grew clammy with sweat. My hands were not as deft as they had been, but all the same, it had been some time since I had spun or woven starwort, for I had neglected the task in my misery, and the swelling in my fingers had begun to go down. Just as well. It was a tricky job. The small sliver, where dagger or sword had chipped against bone, was deeply lodged, and I had both hands covered in blood above the wrists before I got it out. I cleaned the wound again with fresh water, and dried it as well as I could. There was no chamomile, no sweet lavender nor poultice of juniper berries. There were no skilled hands nor fine thread with which to sew up the wound. I took a few deep breaths, and then I got out a bone needle, the smallest I had, the one I used to bind the necks of the shirts when I had finished them. And in my pack there was one good spool of thread, a thread not made from the starwort plant, but soft and strong, which one of my brothers had thieved for me that midsummer night. I clenched my teeth and set to work, with an ear to his breathing. He was keeping it slow and steady, but with some effort. I did not hurry the job; it was done as neatly and thoroughly as I could manage. He'd have a scar, but the leg would mend. I finished, and bit off the thread, and felt his large hand encircling mine.

'Tell me,' he said levelly, 'why does a girl of good breeding, with skin as white as new milk, have hands like a fishwife's? Who has inflicted such punishment on you? Your crime must have been heinous indeed.'

That was it for my strength, I'm afraid. All at once, hunger and shock and exhaustion got the better of me, and I sank down to the ground, as far away from him as I could get, and put my poor hands over my face as bitter, silent tears coursed down my cheeks. I wasn't angry at him, or at the men who had attacked us, or at anyone in particular. I was wet and miserable and tired, and I wanted my brothers, and I wanted my little garden and my dog, and to be able to tell tales and laugh again. I wept in self pity, and because I knew you could never go back. You chose your path, and that was it. I wept for Father Brien and for Linn, and for what my brothers might have been, and for my own lost innocence. I wept because I had ugly hands. After all, I was but fourteen years old.

'I'm sorry,' he said awkwardly. It didn't help much. I found that now I had started to cry, I couldn't stop. Much like it is for a small child, whose woe often outlasts the injury, as if the weeping itself engenders more tears. I wept until my head ached and I saw stars before my eyes, and finally I lay down on the hard rock and went to sleep, still sniffing. After that, he must have forced himself to move, to lay a cloak over me, and a folded shirt under my head, for that was how it was when I woke, much later. It was dark everywhere, night time outside. For a moment I was quite disoriented, groping around me in a panic. I forced myself to sit still, to breathe slowly. And after a while, pale moonlight was apparent, thin fingers of it creeping through the foliage at the cave mouth, and by its dim light I could see the Briton lying asleep against the far wall, his face white, his eyelids heavy with the slumber of complete exhaustion. His bandage looked clean enough, what I could see of it. No new bleeding. That was good.

I sat there for a while as the light brightened, and small sounds made their way into my consciousness little by little. An owl hooting, near at hand. Far above me, there must be another entrance to the cavern, for I sensed rather than heard a myriad tiny creatures moving in and out, a creaking, rustling sound. And behind this, a more distant, pervasive roaring, a great, hushed, endless movement. The sea. The sea that was so wide it had no margins; the sea that stretched westward to the isles of ancient lore. The sea that made a shining moonlit pathway to the east; to the home of the Britons. I need not gaze out from the cave mouth; its vast wildness was imprinted on my mind, and I feared it even as it captured my spirit. Did not we once cast our own transgressors out beyond the ninth wave, to perish or be washed up on some inhospitable shore as the gods willed? And had not this stranger, who lay sleeping at my feet, come not just from beyond the ninth wave, but from many times beyond? He had spoken of boats, and cursed the land which had given him no answers. He was going home. A chill invaded my body, making the small hairs on my neck stand up. He was going home; and he would keep me by him until I told him what he wanted so badly to know. I understood with a certainty that weighed like a stone in my heart that I too would travel beyond the ninth wave, and leave my brothers behind.

You could leave now, said my inner voice. You could leave while he sleeps, slip away to that village maybe. Help yourself to a few things, go back to the forest and set yourself up again. He will not wake yet awhile; and when he does he will be slow. So I heard myself; and answered myself. I can't leave him. His leg is hurt, his enemies are nearby. I won't leave him.

There were a couple more apples in his bag. I took one and ate it, pips, core and all. I took a sip of water from the bottle; it was cold and sweet. And then I heard the voices. From deep within the cave, soft, compelling, echoing up from the darkness of the vaulted chamber. *Come down. Come down, Sorcha.* And there were lights flickering gold and silver, tantalising lights just around the corner, coaxing me to follow.

I was compelled to walk after them, hands outstretched to touch the rock walls, bare feet light on the hard cave floor. Down and down and down, where the air was cool and damp, and the weight of the earth hung heavy above me. Down where tree roots hung suspended above the vault; where crystal clear water trickled and dripped and pooled in darkness under the pillars of stone. The lights beckoned, torches, lanterns, always just around the next corner. I stumbled, and thought I heard laughter. And music, the faint humming of a harp, the lilt of a fiddle, and a whistle weaving a garland of notes around an old tune. Even so far to the east, even on the farthest shore, then, the Fair Folk had their dwellings. For I did not doubt that this place where we had come by chance was one of those doorways, told of in many old tales, one of those portals between our world and theirs. In such a place were they found often enough, a cave or crevice, an opening in the earth, where the two realms might touch for a brief moment, when the time was right.

I came at length to a chamber, vaster and more grand than any before, where the pillars of living stone reached from smooth floor to arching roof, their stately forms reflected in a long, still pool. They were there, and their laughter and song ceased abruptly as I came forward into the light of their torches. Many eyes were on me. I saw one face I knew, palely beautiful, with dark intense eyes and hair like rippling black silk. She nodded gravely. But around her were many more of her kind, all of them tall beyond mortal span, and clothed in shimmering fabric, in garments of gauze like butterflies' wings, or black and glossy as the plumage of a raven. Their heads were crowned with strange adornments, of feathers and shells and seaweed, of nuts and berries and leaves. Their eyes were strange, deep, knowing, searching; their faces were both wonderful and terrible. They watched me in silence. Then the circle of torches closed in slightly, and the tallest of the men stepped forward.

'Well, well,' he said, looking me up and down. 'You're here at last, I see. Step forward, show yourself.' I stared up at him. A long way up. His face was very bright, brighter far than the torches might make it; some light from within seemed to turn his skin to gold and silver. His hair stood back from his face as if he were crowned with flames, and it was a brilliant red, except where frost touched it at the temples, and on his full beard. His eyes were no colour, and every colour. He wore a plain white robe, but where the light caught it, the cloth sparkled as if with many tiny gems.

My lord. I greeted him silently. I turned to the Lady of the Forest, who stood by his side. *My lady. What do you mean, here at last?* He laughed, throwing his head back, letting the sound reverberate round the great rock chamber. There was a buzz of voices, which died down instantly as he became silent again. The Lady did not laugh, but watched me gravely.

'You didn't imagine you were here by accident, did you?' queried the Bright One. 'You did? I forget how little your kind can understand, how limited your grasp. Your time in the world is brief, your knowledge matches it.'

I did not come here to be insulted. I found my temper was short. They had been precious little help to me so far, apart from the rain storm, which I had to admit had been pretty good. But, Fair Folk or no, I would not let them bully me. *What do you want of me?*

'Of you, nothing, child of the forest.' It was she who spoke now, the Lady, and her voice at least bore a trace of warmth. 'Nothing beyond what you know you must do. Show me your hands, Sorcha.'

I held them out, blinking as a lantern was moved closer to me. My hands were inspected.

'These hands bear no traces of recent work,' frowned he with the head of flames. 'How will your brothers live, if you neglect your task? How will these shirts be made, without spindle or loom?'

I glared up at him. *That's not fair*. And they all laughed again, lords and ladies, their musical voices filling my ears with sweet disdain.

'Fair!' gasped the Bright One, amidst his mirth. 'Fair, she says? What a child it is, to be sure! Are you certain, my lady, that this is the right girl? For it seems to me she is a fool, and lazy with it.'

He moved right up to me and, taking my chin in his hand, tipped my head back to scrutinise me more closely. His eyes were very bright, shifting, changing. It was hard to look into them and not be dazzled.

'You have no need to ask me that,' said the Lady of the Forest. 'You know well enough that this is she. She spits back at your mirth, she holds her head high, after everything. There is no cause to doubt her strength.'

'She neglects her work. Time runs short,' he said, and he was holding my hands now, turning them this way and that. 'Is this vanity, I wonder? Do you weep, that your hands will never again be soft and white?'

'Let her go.'

My head snapped around; the Lord and the Lady and their companions all turned their strange, luminous eyes to the cave entrance through which I had come. The flickering light of their torches showed Red swaying there, his face as pale as chalk, one hand resting on the rock wall for balance. His expression was ferocious.

'I said, let her go.'

The Bright One's hands dropped away from mine and he smiled a small, dangerous smile that was totally lost on the Briton.

'Touch her again and you'll answer to me in blood,' said Red very quietly, and he limped forward to stand at my side. There was a brief silence, and then the attending folk put their hands together in a slow, derisive clapping. Red started to raise his arm, and I put out a hand and stopped him. Clearly, he had not the faintest idea who or what he was dealing with.

The Bright One folded his arms and regarded us with a half smile. Whether he spoke in the Britons' tongue, or some other, I cannot remember, save that we all understood him.

'The Lord Hugh of Harrowfield, I believe that is your name? They say still waters run deep; you bear a weight of anger beneath that mask of control, young man. You are far from home; too far, some might say. What brings you across the sea, and into the forest, and alone in the dark amongst strangers?'

Red looked him in the eye. He was using my shoulder for balance now; it seemed the leg would not take his weight much longer.

'I am not answerable to you,' he said.

'*Nonetheless, you will answer,*' replied the Bright One, and I saw a flash of brilliance like a tiny lightning bolt flare from his eyes and towards the Briton. Red sucked his breath in; whatever it was, it had hurt him.

'*You will answer.*'

The Briton stood silent; he moved me slightly behind him. I saw the Bright One's face tighten, and his eyes take on a reddish tinge. He was eager for a battle of wills, but I knew there could be but one outcome. You did not play games with the Fair Folk and expect to come away unscathed.

Leave him alone. I sent my message to him of the flaming crown, but also to the Lady. *He does not know how to play this game. Let him go.*

'Tell me, Lord Hugh.' It was the Lady who spoke

now. 'Why do you take our girl with you, when you know all she wants is to go home? She does not belong in your world.'

This stung him into response. 'The girl is not yours, or mine, or anyone's. But for now, she travels under my protection, and let him who lays a hand on her answer to me.'

'Fine words,' said the Lady. 'But you have lost sword and dagger. Your leg is laid open to the bone, you are hungry, and lacking sleep, and in hostile territory. Your threats can surely have little substance.'

'I have my two arms, and my will,' said Red, stepping around so that he shielded me from the two of them. 'That's enough. Let him who dares, try me.' His back was solid enough; even on tiptoe I had trouble seeing over his shoulder. Pity about the leg, which would not last a moment if he were put to the test. He was a fool; a brave one, but a fool nonetheless.

'Step aside,' said the Bright One wearily. 'Let the girl show herself. We mean no harm to her; she is one of our own.' And the moment of crisis seemed to be over.

'You chose well, daughter of the forest,' remarked the Lady, looking at Red and then at me.

What do you mean, I chose well? I chose? I did not choose any of this. Would I be here, if there had been a choice?

'Hush, child. There is always a choice; you knew that when you first set foot on this path.'

'You have not answered truly, Lord Hugh of Harrowfield,' said the Bright One. 'You have not answered at all. Why do you take the girl away from her forest? Why does she go across the sea? What is it you want from her?'

'Tell the truth,' said the Lady, and there was a warning in her voice.

'I am not beholden to you, whoever you are,' said Red. 'I will give you no answers.'

'You're a fool.' The Bright One threw up his hands in a pantomime of exasperation. 'I thought you wanted to know what happened to your brother, I really did. But keep silent you will; if you cannot ask the right questions, you can expect no sensible replies.'

The effect of this speech on the Briton was electrifying. He started forward, forgetting his damaged leg, stumbled and half fell; then he forced himself back upright, his face dewed with sweat. Something new had awoken in his pale, cold eyes.

'My brother!' he gasped. 'You know about my brother! Tell me!'

'Ah – ah – ah – not so fast,' said the Bright One, slyly. 'No information comes free, not down here. Besides, it's she who can tell you, not I.' He flicked a long finger in my direction. 'That's why you want her, isn't it? Not because she's alone, and helpless, and needs protection; but for the information she can give you. And give it she can; she saw him, she talked with him, and he gave her the thing you guard so jealously in your pocket there. Ask her, she'll tell you all you want to know about your precious brother; aye, and some you don't want to know besides.'

'The girl cannot talk,' said Red, and I could tell he was fighting to keep his voice under control, 'or will not. You say she spoke with my brother; she does not speak now.'

'Oh, she speaks well enough,' said the Lord lightly. 'We hear her. She asks us to stop tormenting you. She says you're too stupid to be dangerous.'

'But I can hear nothing,' said Red. 'She is silent. She is always silent.'

The Lady looked at him. 'That is because you have not learned how to listen,' she said. 'But she will speak to you one day. Are you good at waiting?'

Red looked wildly from one to the other.

'Just tell me,' he said. 'Does my brother still live? Will I find him?'

But the torches were starting to fade, and the bright folk with them, and the traces of laughter and rustling silk and the faint notes of the harp seemed to dissipate upwards in the cool dampness of the cave, fragile as the perfume of an autumn flower.

The Lady stood before me, when all others had gone.

'Take this to light your way, daughter of the forest,' she said. 'You told me you were tired of being strong. Maybe you will not need to be so strong, now.' She placed a tiny round candle, herb scented, in my open hand. She turned to the Briton.

'You hurt her with your unthinking words,' she said, and her eyes had lost any warmth they had once had. 'Make sure she is not hurt again.' And before he could draw breath, she turned and was gone.

We made our way up to the surface in complete silence, our hands touching so as not to lose one another in a profound darkness, relieved only by the dimly flickering candlelight. I held the tiny light in the palm of my hand; it smelt of rosemary, of meadowsweet and caraway. Like the sharing of an apple, it too was full of hidden meanings. I wondered, not for the first time, just what game the Fair Folk were playing.

Up in the outer cave, it was freezing cold, for a sharp breeze was blowing in from the east. Our clothes were still damp from the rain, and the cloak was not much better. It would be an uncomfortable night. Not that sleep seemed possible anyway. My mind was turning things over and over, and would not let me rest. I lay down on my side of the cave and closed my eyes, but I could not stop shivering. And I thought, his brother! I should have seen it. His brother! No wonder he pursues this quest so single mindedly. And then I thought, Lord Hugh. Lord Hugh of – of somewhere. How did they know his name? He certainly didn't seem like a lord of anywhere, with his cropped hair and his well-worn clothes, and the way his friends spoke to him, as to an equal. On the other hand, though, I considered how my father had warned his men to make sure Simon remained alive that night. He had been a prisoner of some consequence; a person of future value as a bargaining tool, maybe. So perhaps his brother really was Lord Hugh of somewhere or other. I thought Red suited him better. By the Lady, it was cold. I wished dawn would come; but my mind shrank from the problems of the next day. I rolled over, trying to make myself comfortable.

'You're shivering,' said the Briton from the other side of the cave. 'Best come over and lie by me. That cloak will cover us both.' But I shook my head, drawing the wet cloak about me tighter. After what had been done to me, I did not think I would ever be able to lie by a man, not even to sleep, not even with somebody I trusted. And I did not trust him, with his cold eyes and his silences.

'You need not be afraid of me,' he said. 'It would be a lot warmer.' But I shrank in on myself, wrapped my arms around my chest, drew my knees up to my stomach, made myself small under the cloak. I stared at the candle; it still burned, tiny and golden, in the space between us. There was silence for a while.

'Suit yourself,' said Red. He lay on his back, staring up at the vaulted roof of the cave, and the candlelight flickered on his high-bridged nose, and his set jaw, and his grim, tight mouth. I drifted in and out of a fitful sleep, with snatches of half-seen nightmares, with fragments of painful memory and visions of an unimaginable future. And every time I woke, I looked across to see him lying stretched out with his head on his pack, and his face white in the moonlight, and his eyes wide open. But once, waking, I found him sitting up, motionless, and staring towards the cave mouth. When I looked, there on a dark branch that stretched across the opening perched a perfect white owl, preening her feathers fastidiously with a delicate beak, regarding us from time to time with her shining, ancient eyes. I held my breath, watching her, and when at length she spread her great wings and rose to flight I sensed an end to things, a moving on and parting that would not be halted by any burning of magical herbs, by any intervention of human or spirit world. It was as inevitable as death, and I put my hands over my mouth, to keep silent.

'What is it,' said Red in a whisper, 'what is this fire in the head, that will not let me rest?' I glanced across at him; but it was not to me that he was speaking.

Towards dawn, we both fell into an exhausted sleep. It was as well that, when the first rays of sunlight began to spread across the sky, it was one of his own that found us, and not Seamus' men. I came to with a start, and was getting shakily to my feet, and so was he, but more slowly because of his leg; we had both been woken by a rustling in the bushes outside. There was scarcely time for thought. Then we heard the call of a seabird, very close by; and Red amazed

298

me by cupping his hands to his mouth and echoing the same call. It was a signal; and a minute later a figure with flaxen hair, with stained travelling clothes and well-worn boots, appeared in the cave mouth, parting the greenery to step rather breathlessly inside.

'A steep climb,' said Ben, for it was the Briton's companion, bending now to catch his breath, hands on knees. And after him, the other man, John. He looked at me, then at Red, his expression quizzical.

'You've still got her then,' he observed.

Red frowned. 'I told you to go on without me,' he said. 'What of Redbeard and his men? Were you not pursued?'

Ben grinned. 'We were; but we're quick and quiet, and we had a few tricks up our sleeve. There was a small problem in the cove, but nothing we couldn't handle.'

'I told you to go on without us,' repeated Red. It sounded as if he didn't like being disobeyed. Myself, I had never been so pleased to see anyone as I was those two. At least now there was some chance of getting him down the cliff in one piece, even with that leg.

'We stood offshore overnight,' said John, sounding not the least apologetic.

'Rough enough to turn your guts inside out, it was,' added Ben picturesquely. 'So here we are. You may want to kill yourself being a hero, but don't expect us to help you.'

'The boat's waiting under the rocks down below,' said John. 'I'd say we've time enough before full dawn; with luck we can be away before they're stirring. But we need to move now, and quickly. Lucky we found you so soon.' Red said nothing, but fumbled for his pack, and limped forward.

'Wonderful,' said Ben, looking at the makeshift bandage, and at Red's face. 'Just how did you expect to get away without us? You wouldn't have made it half way down this track; it's steep as a church roof and crumbling away.'

'We'd have managed,' said Red. His companions looked at me, and at each other, but no more was said.

As we left the cave, I looked around for the remains of the candle, for its herbal scent still hung lightly on the morning air. But I was too late. It was Red who bent, awkwardly, to lift the small remnant of beeswax from the rock, to hold it in his hand a moment, before slipping it into a pocket.

'Nonsense, of course,' he said to himself. The others were at the cave entrance, Ben keeping a look-out, John clearing away branches to make a safer path. 'Nothing but dreams. And yet, such dreams. A man could lose his mind in this accursed country.'

Then he turned and went out, and I followed him, since that seemed to be the only thing to do.

CHAPTER EIGHT

I wondered, later, why it did not break my heart to go away across the sea, far from the forest, leaving no sign my brothers could read, no map or chart by which they might find me. The boat went east, and perhaps a little south; I supposed that we were heading for Britain. But where? Had I been able to think, had I been myself, that would have been a day almost beyond bearing. But the sea, as well as being wide beyond imagining, was stirred by freakish winds, and before long I was lying across the side of the small sailing boat, retching convulsively, as my body rejected what little food it had in it. Between the spasms, I heard the caustic comments of the two men, Ben and John, and the dour boatman who held the tiller. Red kept himself busy and said nothing. I wondered how much he'd let them get away with, before he decided to inform them that I could understand their jokes and curses. For all this, they took their turns in holding my head, and wiping my face, and shielding me from the wind. The voyage seemed to take forever, and I vowed to myself that when at last I returned home, that would be the one and only time I would ever go by water again. I felt so wretched, I hardly thought beyond my churning gut and my aching head. And so my homeland slipped away, and I scarcely felt the pain of parting.

At last the rocking stopped, and the boat was still. It was dusk, and I could hear gulls calling. The men were keeping their voices down. *Norsemen*, they said, and *lie low*. Then I was plucked out of the boat and carried into the shelter of a shallow cave, little more than a shelf of rock under which the wind was slightly less biting. I lay there wrapped in my cloak, shivering. I had not even the energy to look around me in the last light, to try to work out where we might have landed.

'No fire,' said Red. 'John, you'll take the first watch. Then wake me. We must be off again before dawn; the less attention we attract in these parts the better. The islands provide safe anchorage, but once out in open waters again we are easy prey for Dane or Pict alike.'

My heart sank. Off again by dawn. So there was to be more. This was only some mid-way point, and we must sail on, up and down, up and down . . .

'The girl's not well,' John said bluntly. 'You'd best get some water into her at least, if you expect her to last the journey.'

There was no response to this, but some time later a cup of water was placed beside me, and I took it and drank it, knowing what was good for me. I managed to keep it down, and I began to feel a little better. But I was cold, and my limbs were cramped and aching. I sat up and looked around me.

The pale expanse of sand and the jagged rocks around it were bathed in cool moonlight. We were quite close to the water's edge, for the stretch of shore that sloped up to this half shelter was narrow; and above the gentle whisper of the small waves, as they advanced and retreated, I thought I could hear the deep, hollow voices of strange creatures, far out in the darkness, calling to one another. Along where the rocks ran into the sea, John stood looking out across the water.

'Here.' The other two, Ben and Red, were sitting near me, backs against the rock wall, and they were eating. The boatman seemed to be asleep. Now Ben offered me a strip of the dried meat, and I shuddered in response.

'She eats apples,' said Red. 'Here, try this.'

My stomach was starting to settle, and I realised I was very hungry. He cut the fruit neatly and passed it to me piece by piece, until it was all gone.

'Good,' he said approvingly. 'Now get up and walk to ease the cramps from your legs, for we've another sea voyage tomorrow. But keep quiet. We may be in safe mooring here, but we can't afford to take any chances.'

I walked along the sand and stretched my aching legs, and I looked out over the water, trying to see what lay beyond. But it was night, and I was not sure if I saw land, or if I simply wished it were there in the darkness. Later, cold as I was, I slept, and then it was dawn, and time to set out again.

I heard Red tell the boatman to make straight for the priory. I heard the men talk about horses, and how quickly they might make the ride home, and cheerfully anticipating food and wine and a warm hearth. And then I looked back the way we had come. Looked back at the place where we had sheltered, and realised what it was. The waters were calm, the dawn turning them pearly blue and grey and pink. There was a big island somewhat to the north of us; low, wooded, and dotted with signs of human habitation. But that was not the place we had landed.

'We don't put in there,' said Red, who was watching me. 'Land in one of those coves, and you're as likely to run into an Ostman or a Dane as you are a friend. That's why we use Little Island.'

I had missed it before, when he spoke of it. I had been too tired and sick to think. But there behind us in the shining waters, already vanishing from sight as our small craft made its way east, were three islands. They were not much more than rocks in the wide expanse of sea, places where birds might nest and weeds might take precarious hold on slippery surfaces. They were places a fisherman might pass by, without paying much attention at all, save to take care near the sharp rocks that encircled the tallest one. But even without the name, I recognised what they were. Greater Island, Little Island and the Needle. I had slept on the mystic ground of the Islands, and I had not even known it until I was gone. I looked back until the tall pillar of stone that was the Needle had disappeared from view; and then my stomach heaved and I leaned over the side and it all began again.

It took a good part of another day, sailing east and then a little north, before land came into view again. There were cliffs and breakers, and beyond them a rolling, rising, green hill dotted with groves of oak and beech. There was a long, low building set high, and a tower with a cross. It seemed we were to shelter there overnight before going on.

It was a house of women; holy sisters, dedicated like Father Brien to the Christian faith, but living together communally, unlike my solitary friend. What they thought of our sudden appearance on their doorstep was hard to tell. It seemed they knew Lord Hugh, whom they treated with some respect, almost deference. Quite soon, I was bundled off inside and the men retired to some other area to await refreshment. John had carried me up from the landing; the good sisters took one look at me and ordered him to hand me into their care. As they took me away, I looked around wildly for my bag; it had been on the boat, I knew that, but in my sickness I had forgotten it. There must be no neglect of my task from now on, the Fair Folk had made this plain. Where were my three shirts of starwort? They must be kept safe, that was the only thing that really mattered. Swans could die so easily; the huntsman's arrow, the jaws of the wolf, the bite of winter. How could I have left this so long? As the sisters led me away, I strained to look back over my shoulder. The men were just leaving the building. As he went out the door, Red turned back for a moment. He met my rather wild look, and gestured to where he had my small pack tucked into the top of his own. Then he was gone. Within the cloisters, only women could come. We would see the men later, the sister informed me, at the evening meal. Now I must come with her, for, the twitch of her nose told me, I was in serious need of cleaning up.

I was sick and exhausted. I let them pour warm water over me, and wash me from head to toe, exclaiming at the way my bones stuck through the flesh, at my damaged hands, noting with tight lips my other injuries, not yet fully healed, questioning me kindly but shrewdly about who I was and where I came from. They washed my hair with rosemary oil and rinsed it with lavender. They found me a home-spun gown and a girdle, and they fed me bread and milk while a young novice with a fresh, rosy complexion undertook the long and thankless task of combing out my hair. They were careful not to let me eat too much; I myself knew well the effect this might have on one long starved of proper nourishment. After this I rested, with my newly braided hair down my back, and my clean clothes harsh and uncomfortable against my skin. Gradually the world stopped wheeling and turning around me, and my stomach settled. For a while a tranquil-browed sister sat by me, but when she thought I slept, she left me alone in the tiny whitewashed cell, with a plain cross of ash wood its only ornament. I could not sleep but lay there thinking; and later I got up and went out into the garden which now lay dim and peaceful in twilight. It was well tended, with culinary herbs in neat hedges, with flowers for drying and vegetables for the table keeping harmonious company in its narrow space. I was happier sitting there on the earth amongst the cabbages, my hands around my knees. It had been a long time since I had slept inside.

There was a wholesome smell of new-baked bread, and a savoury soup cooking. Lights showed in the building at the far end of the garden, and dishes clattered. There had been bells, before; maybe the sisters were at prayer. However, I heard voices outside the garden wall.

'. . . would be best to leave her here. She hasn't the strength for further travel. She needs a long rest, proper food and spiritual counselling.'

'That's not possible. We have been away too long already. Your hospitality for tonight is very welcome, but we must move on in the morning.'

The sister's sigh was audible. 'Forgive me, Lord Hugh. I hope you will heed an old woman's advice, and not take my words amiss. This is just a child, and she has been hurt, I think, more than perhaps you know. Leave her with us, and travel on if you must. It will be better for her here, and better for you if you leave her behind.'

There was a pause.

'I can't do that,' he said. 'The girl travels with me.'

'Have you considered how it will be for your family, if you return with her to Harrowfield? Her kind are not welcome here; and you have powerful enemies.'

'You think I cannot protect her?'

'My lord, I have no doubt of your strength, and your integrity. I think, rather, that you do not fully understand what you are taking on here. Perhaps you do not fully appreciate the depth of feeling against these people. You cannot house an orphaned owl amongst your chickens, and expect no worse than ruffled feathers. By insisting on this, not only do you lay the girl open to attack, but you risk your own safety and that of your kin.'

There was no reply to this. I heard their steps on a gravel walkway, which must pass up and down just outside the kitchen garden.

'I must ask you,' added the nun in diffident tones, 'and you should not take this wrongly. I have known you a long time, my lord, and it is in the awareness of this that I speak of such a delicate matter. I said before that the girl had been hurt. She is not much more than a child; tired, hungry and heartsick. But for all that, she is a woman; and some man has used her ill in recent times. I must ask you how well you trust your companions. I will not insult you by suggesting –'

Red swore explosively and I heard the crunch of boots on the stones of the path as if he made a sudden violent movement.

'In the light of this,' went on the sister calmly, 'perhaps you will reconsider the wisdom of taking her back to your household? The silence and contemplation we practise can provide healing for both body and spirit. And she will not be frightened here.'

There was another long pause.

'Thank you for your advice,' he said finally, and his tone distanced her with its formality. 'I will wait another night, maybe, until the girl is rested. Then we move on to Harrowfield.' And with that it appeared the conversation was closed, and they walked away out of earshot.

During the day and two nights I spent in that place, I acquired two things. I walked in the garden, early in the morning, and there behind the neat rows of vegetables, the stakes and strings ready for their creeping blanket of peas or beans, the freshly turned dungheap, I saw a familiar plant growing. It was not so out of place here in this domestic scene, for its leaves give a pleasant yellow dye, if you are prepared to handle the unforgiving stems. There were two sisters working quietly in the garden, and I managed to convey to them in dumb show what it was I wanted. There was serious consultation between them and one of them went off, perhaps to ask the prioress' advice, maybe to ask Red. At any rate, when she returned she held a sack and a knife, and she gave these to me without further question. My delight must have shown on my face, for the sisters smiled back, and went methodically on with their labours as I set to with all my strength. By the end of the morning I had a good sackful of starwort, enough to last me until midwinter, I thought. I tried not to think what would happen, if they would not let me spin and weave and sew, where we were going.

The second thing I acquired was a name. The priory might be a place of quiet contemplation, but the holy sisters were not lacking in good humour, and the evening meal was a chance for relaxed, even spirited, conversation. Some of them, I thought, took great enjoyment from the unexpected presence of three men at their table, and I supposed their elders thought a little mirth not so bad for the soul, after the long days of quiet meditation. As we sat at table on the second evening, one of the sisters brought up the subject.

'Your young lady needs a name,' she said. 'You can't keep calling her "girl" as if she were a dog following your steps. Has she a name?'

'If she has, she can't tell us what it is,' said John. 'But you're right, Sister. Every living thing needs its name.'

'She should be given one before you return home,' said the prioress. 'A good Christian name, Elizabeth perhaps, or Agnes. Agnes would suit well enough.'

One of the young novices spoke up. 'She reminds me of a small bird, perhaps a jenny-wren,' she said, smiling, 'with her fine bones and bright eyes. Jenny would be a good name.' She caught her superior's eye and fell silent, blushing.

'More like some small, fierce bird of prey, something with a sharp bite,' muttered Red, who was seated next to me. 'An owl perhaps, that speaks only when the rest of the world sleeps.' He spoke so that the rest of them could hear this time. 'Jenny will do well enough.'

So Jenny I became, a strange little name quite

unlike my own, but better than being summoned with a snap of the fingers. And on the second morning, there were horses ready for us and we rode off just after dawn, leaving the sisters standing quiet by their gate, and one of them, at least, wearing a frown of deep concern. But it seemed, yet again, that what Red wanted was what happened. And so we rode on to Harrowfield.

Picture, then, a valley folded in green, where gentle swathes of ash and beech are broken here and there by the stronger forms of oaks still clad in their bright autumn raiment. Along the valley floor undulates a shining river, its banks soft with drooping willows. The path follows the line of the river, curving this way and that between well tended fields, past cottage and sheep yard, byre and barn. The farm folk come out to stare as the travellers pass, and their faces beam a bright welcome as they recognise the three men, each of whom now wears a white surcoat over his travel-stained clothing. This garment, fished from the bottom of packs before entering the valley, bears a blue blazon on back and breast. It is a sign of who they are and where they belong; it is that image of an oak tree with noble, spreading branches, enclosed in a circle, and below it wavy lines that might be water. The country folk call out, 'Welcome back, my lord!' 'A good harvest, Lord Hugh! And all the better for your return!' He whom they address does not smile; it seems he seldom smiles. But he acknowledges their greetings with a grave courtesy, slowing his horse once or twice to grasp an extended hand, to touch an infant proffered for his blessing. And when he slows, the people get a better look at the pale young woman seated behind him, with a dark cloak wrapped around her, and her black curls teased by the wind out of their neat plait, and her hands clutching his belt to keep her balance after a long and wearying ride. They will not ask; that is not their place. But they fall silent, and after the riders pass, they mutter amongst themselves, and one or two make a sign with their fingers, unobtrusively, to ward off evil.

This, then, was our arrival at Harrowfield. The valley opened up, and a long, low homestead came in view. There were many buildings, a fine barn, stables, and cottages clustered near the main house. There were neat stone walls and an avenue of tall straight trees. The horsemen paused, and Red looked back over his shoulder.

'All right?' he enquired. I nodded mutely. It was all new, all changing. I wasn't scared, exactly; but I had no idea how it would be, when we reached his home. I had heard and seen enough to expect no great welcome. Was I a prisoner, a hostage? Was I a serving girl? Was I to be guarded until at last I gave him the information he wanted, and could be set free? Or would they try to make me talk by other means, as my family had done with his brother? I didn't think I'd be very good at dealing with that. The Lady of the Forest had ordered him to make sure I wasn't hurt again. But a Briton was not capable of accepting the realm below the surface, and the wonders it contained; Red dismissed that as a dream. He would never understand why I did as I did; it was much easier to dismiss it as some craziness, some strange malady of the wits that caused me to hurt myself, beyond reason. He might love his brother with a fierce intensity; but that could never match what I must do for mine.

Without any visible signal, all three men at once urged their horses to a sharp canter, and I had to hold on tighter than was comfortable. We made our way at speed between the tall, golden poplars, and Ben let out a yell of sheer exuberance, grinning widely as the wind whipped his flaxen hair out behind him like a bright banner. John's eyes were keen with anticipation. And so we clattered into a courtyard as neat and orderly as everything else there, and pulled to a stop before wide stone steps and a massive oaken door, which was set open. They'd been warned, somehow, of our arrival, for a welcoming party stood on the steps awaiting us. Well-trained grooms appeared from nowhere to take bridles and lead the tired horses away, and a small crowd gathered. The first thing Red did, after lifting me down from the horse, was to take his own pack in hand, signalling to the groom to leave it. Then he moved forward, and with his free hand he held my wrist, so I was obliged to follow him.

The woman who stood waiting there did not see me. She had eyes only for Red.

'Mother,' he said quietly.

'Hugh,' she said, and she was exercising the same control I had witnessed in both her sons. I could tell she was resisting the urge to break down and weep, or to give him a big hug, or otherwise behave in an unseemly fashion before all the folk of the household. 'Welcome, back. Welcome, Ben, John. It has been a long time.' There was a desperate question in her eyes, that would remain unspoken till later.

'Welcome back, sir.' 'Welcome, my lord.' There were many folk of the household there to greet the lord Hugh; they clustered around, slapping his shoulder, gripping his hand. He'd put the pack down, but kept hold of me; I was in danger of disappearing in the crush. I glimpsed Ben, still grinning madly, surrounded by a bevy of pretty girls. Further away, I saw John with a small, fair-haired woman some years his junior. She was heavy with child; I judged her to be less than three moons away from her delivery. His wife. She clung to his arm, and he gazed at her as if there were no world for him, save in her. I thought, he too shows that same control. How he must have longed to return home, how this must have twisted his heart, those long moons across the water. And yet, he had followed Red without question. There were loyalties here that were beyond my comprehension.

It was not until we extricated ourselves from this joyful, painful welcome, and retreated inside, that the lady really noticed me. A servant was sent for wine; we moved into a hall within the house, where a great hearth was set with logs of ash and hawthorn, but not yet lit, for the day was mild. She seated herself on a settle near the hearth, and beckoned her son to sit by her. There were others of the household present, but at a discreet distance. Our travelling companions had vanished. Each, I supposed, had his own particular welcome waiting. So Red sat down by his mother, stretching out his injured leg with some care. The long ride had been the last treatment it needed to mend properly. And I was left standing by his chair, feeling quite alone in a circle of curious stares. He still held me by the wrist, so I could not move away. His mother looked me straight in the eyes. Her face was round and soft under the delicate lawn of her veil; there was a network of fine lines around eyes and mouth. Small curls of hair escaped the headdress and showed a faded gold. She had once had hair the

313

colour of her younger son's; and her eyes were the same bright periwinkle blue. I read shock in her expression, and fear, and something like revulsion. She did not speak. Red dropped my wrist.

'I'm sorry,' he said. 'I hoped to bring him home. Even after so long, I believed it possible. As you see, I did not find him. And I have no news for you. I regret that I could not – that I –'

'I've learned not to hope too much,' said his mother, and she was blinking back tears. If there were to be weeping, it would be later, when she was quite alone. 'You are home safe. We must be grateful for that.'

'It was as if he had vanished into thin air,' said Red. 'It is indeed a strange country, and abounds in tales of just such happenings. Nonsense, of course. But we went close, very close to the place where so many of Richard's men perished. That he was once there is beyond doubt. But there was no trace, no sign that Simon had ever been with them. We spoke with whom we could, under cover of darkness. None knew of prisoners taken, nor of fugitive or hostage. I come back empty-handed, Mother. I am sorry, sorry for the trouble my absence has caused you; sorry to bring no answers.'

'I confess, I had hoped for something,' she said. 'Not that he would come home, not now, after so long. But something, some small token to tell me if he lived or died, any answer to end this terrible waiting.'

There was a small pause.

'There was nothing,' said Red. 'Nothing at all.'

I found I had been holding my breath, and let it out in a rush. But I was not safe yet.

'It appears you have not returned entirely empty-handed,' said his mother, and she looked me up and

314

down as if inspecting a cut of meat for the table that was not to her satisfaction. I stared back steadily. I was not ashamed to be Lord Colum's daughter, in spite of everything he had done. My people were old, far older than hers, and I was the daughter of the forest.

'How can you bring one of – one of *them* into your house? How can you bear even to be near her? These folk took your brother; they killed Richard's men in the most barbaric way imaginable, with unthinkable cruelty. Their ways are not just strange; they are lost to all goodness. How can you bring her into my house?' Her voice was quivering with emotion. Here it comes, I thought. Now he tells her I'm the one link with her younger son. Now she demands my information right away, anything to convince her that her boy still lives. And they try to get me to talk, any way they can. How can he deny his own mother? Strangely enough, I understood just how she felt.

Red stood up and moved behind me, and I felt his big hands on my shoulders.

'Her name's Jenny,' he said levelly. 'She's here in my household as my guest, for as long as it suits her. It may be quite a while. And she'll be treated with respect. By everyone.' His mother was staring at him, her mouth slightly open. My expression must have mirrored hers, for I had not expected this. A job in the kitchens, maybe, scouring pans; that was the best I had hoped for. 'I mean no insult, Mother. I'm just telling you how it will be.' He raised his voice, just enough to be sure all those present heard him. 'This young woman is welcome in my house. She will be treated as a member of the household. You will offer her the kindness and hospitality that befits any guest of mine. I'll tell you this once only. Let it be understood.' There was a hint of threat, I thought, in these last words, but he needed to say no more. A deathly hush fell over the room.

The servant appeared with wine. Red made me sit down and take a goblet, but I had only a sip or two. My stomach was still unsettled, and I was very weary. And there were too many people here, too much light, too many sounds. All I wanted was to be alone for a while, and rest. And then I wanted a distaff and a spindle and a loom, and time, lots of time.

'She hasn't much to say for herself,' said Red's mother, sniffing slightly. 'What's she to do here? Can she make herself useful?'

Red's mouth curved in a smile that did not reach his eyes.

'I think you will find Jenny can occupy herself well enough,' he said. 'She's very handy with the needle and thread. But she is not to be employed as a servant here; I expect your women to make her welcome as an equal.'

'I am shocked that you ask this, Hugh. Perhaps I did hope, beyond hope, that you would bring Simon safely back home. Instead you bring the enemy that destroyed him, and ask me to make that enemy a friend.' Under the mask of gentility, she was furious with him.

Red looked at her, and then at me. 'Jenny does not speak,' he said, 'because she cannot. But she makes herself understood very well, you'll find. And she understands everything you say.' With that answer, which was no answer at all, she had to be content, but there was a delicate frown between her arching brows, and I saw the depth of anguish in her eyes.

'You give us no choice,' she said wearily.

I thought about Simon, and the things he'd said about his family. In his tale of two brothers, the younger had never been quite good enough; never been quite the equal of the elder. Why had he thought they did not love him? Why had he seen himself as second best? Even in his absence, he stood between this mother and son as vivid as if he had been there in the flesh.

Their talk moved to safer ground. They spoke of the business of the estate, of crops and livestock, the harvest and the welfare of their folk. Red asked question after question; he seemed eager to take up the reins of his household once more. My mind wandered, reliving those days when Simon was in my care, remembering the long telling of tales, the fevered, demon-filled nights, the slow healing of mind and body. I remembered his knife at my throat; I remembered his tears of furious self-loathing. These mind-pictures were strong; I scarcely saw what was around me. Besides, I was growing drowsy with the wine and the long day, and so I started when I felt something cold and wet against my leg, under the hem of the homespun gown that the sisters had given me. I looked down. Peeping out from under the bench where I sat was a very small, rather elderly grey dog, who gazed up at me with sad, rheumy eyes, wheezing gently. I bent over and offered her a hand to sniff; she quivered and put out a small pink tongue in a lick of greeting. Then, with a sigh, she settled down heavily on my feet as if there for a long stay. I stifled a yawn.

'You're tired,' said Red to me. 'My mother's women will find you somewhere to sleep. It's been a long day.' He got awkwardly to his feet again.

'Your leg,' said his mother, noticing for the first time that he had some sort of injury. 'What happened to your leg?'

'Oh, it's nothing much,' said Red predictably. 'A small cut. Not worth worrying about.' He glanced at me and saw my expression, and I caught, fleetingly, that slight quirk at the corner of his mouth that might, in some other man, have been a well suppressed smile. His mother was watching us both, and her frown deepened.

'Megan!' she called. A young maidservant with a head of unruly brown curls came forward, bobbing a curtsy of sorts.

'Find a suitable chamber for – for – our visitor, Megan,' said the lady of the house, and I felt she had to force the words out. 'Water for washing, something simple to eat. Show her where to find us in the morning.'

'Yes, my lady,' said Megan, bobbing again, and her eyes were demurely downcast. But as we left the hall, I in her wake, and the grey dog trotting after me like a small shadow, her glance was full of a lively curiosity, touched with fear.

'Don't forget this,' said Red as I passed, and he slid my small pack from the top of his own and put it in my hands. I nodded thanks, and left. Behind me, I heard his mother speaking again, and I think I was glad I couldn't hear what she was saying.

I suspect somebody chose for me a bedchamber deemed suitable for a barbarian: small, remote, sparsely furnished, located very close to the servants' quarters and in earshot of the clatter and bustle of the busy kitchens. If they thought to insult me thus, they miscalculated. For I loved, instantly, the tiny, square room with its stone walls and its hard pallet on a wooden frame, with its heavy oak door that opened straight out into a neglected corner of garden full of tangled herb bushes shot to seed. As soon as it was light, I would go out and see if starwort grew there. An old rose clambered up the wall just outside the door, and a tiny, blue-flowered creeper carpeted the stone steps. There was a mossy pathway choked over with weeds. Through the single round window, set high in the wall, the moon would look down on my slumber. There was a wooden chest, and a pitcher and a bowl. Megan brought me warm water, and another girl, furtive-eyed, brought a platter with bread and cheese and dried fruits and then scurried out of the room. I put my bag on the end of the bed, and waited for Megan to go. The dog checked all corners of the room with care, snuffling quietly; at last, satisfied, she gathered her strength and made a heroic, scrambling leap onto the pallet, where she settled, nose on forepaws.

'Where are your bags?' asked Megan awkwardly. 'Your nightrobe, your other things?' I shook my head, indicating my little pack.

'That's all?' She looked quite shocked. I could hear the unspoken questions. Where on earth did he find you? What possessed him to bring you back here, and with nothing but the clothes on your back? Why?

Megan spoke again, surprising me. 'That was Simon's dog,' she said. 'My lord Hugh's brother. Alys, he called her. She's old now; he had her since he was no more than an infant. Never let anyone near her since he went away. Fends for herself, mostly. She'd snap your fingers off, if you went to pet her. Until now.' She reached a tentative hand towards the small hound; it responded with a deep growl, baring its teeth. 'See?' said Megan lightly. 'Vicious little thing. Seems to like you well enough though.'

I managed a smile of sorts, and she grinned back, her natural curiosity overcoming her wariness.

'I'll speak to my lady Anne,' she said. 'Find you a nightrobe and some other things. And I'll come back for you in the morning, show you where to go. We rise early here.'

That night I slept; but bone-weariness and the effects of the wine were not enough to blot out entirely the night terrors that still beset me, and I woke suddenly from a dream that is best left untold, a dream that I had often, the sort of dream that wove its way into my daily thoughts, so that I still shuddered each time a man touched me, the sort of dream that made my whole body cringe, and tremble, and my heart pound in my chest. Alys lay heavily on my feet; she had not woken. A dim light from the waning moon shone into the room. And there were low voices outside.

I got up and went softly to the window. Both doors were barred, although I would have been happier to leave one ajar, to smell the night scents of lavender and woodbine, to feel the cool breeze on my skin. But I had lost the ability to trust; I was no longer protected by the sweet cloak of innocence. So I had bolted my doors. But I stood on tiptoe on the wooden chest, and looked out into the garden. Two shadowy figures were exchanging quiet words; both wore dark clothing, and I saw the glint of weapons in the faint light. One of them went out through a gate in the wall; flaxen-haired, somewhat jaunty in his gait, even in the middle of the night. The other was taller, and walked with a slight limp. He settled by the wall at the far end of the garden, relaxed but alert, one leg stretched out, barely visible in the shadows. It was a long watch till daybreak.

I couldn't tell if I felt better or worse, knowing I was under some sort of guard. Where did they think

I could escape to, here in the middle of their country with never a pair of boots nor a water bottle to my name? Besides, after the reception I'd got so far at Harrowfield it seemed unlikely the local folk would offer me much help if I tried to make it to the coast. And what was I supposed to do then, swim for home? No, I was stuck here whether I liked it or not. So why the guard?

I wondered, for a moment, if these men ever slept. Then I remembered Red lying in the cave, his face white with pain and exhaustion. He was human, I thought; he just didn't like people to know it. And it seemed he set a very high value on the information I could give him; he would make sure it did not slip through his grasp, while he was waiting for me to talk.

They rose early, but not as early as I. Before dawn I was up and about, washing my face in the last of the fresh water, finding the privy, unbolting the outer door and walking out into the neglected garden. Little Alys followed me, but slowly, her joints stiff with age. Someone had planted this garden well, once. But there was no starwort here; later, when I needed more, I must look further afield. I cursed myself for neglecting my task, before I left the forest. There was an old water trough under the wormwood bushes, half full of mud. I could use that to soak the fibres I had brought from the priory. There were still herbs aplenty here; enough, if I tended them, to stock a good set of shelves with salves and ointments, tinctures and essences. I wondered if they would let me have a mortar and pestle, and some knives, and beeswax and oil. Then I thought, there is no time for this. What of Finbar, and Conor, and the others? Time runs short for them, and it is already autumn.

Nonetheless, I could not help myself, and when Megan came to find me I was pulling up weeds, separating out the newly seeded children of the overblown plants, planning how it might be if I pruned, and dug, and planted. I had forgotten, almost, where I was. Of my night-time guardians there had been no sign, save for the print of their boots in the soft earth. They had vanished with the first light.

The attitude of the folk of Harrowfield towards me could best be described as a sort of frozen courtesy. The lady Anne led by example. There was no denying that her son was the head of this household and expected to have his way, and even she would not challenge that. So she spoke to me only when circumstances made it unavoidable. When she looked at me, the hostility in her bright blue eyes was thinly masked. She provided for me, but only so far as basic hospitality demanded. I told myself that this suited me well enough. I had been living wild for the best part of two years now; I had become unused to luxury, if indeed our life at Sevenwaters could be called that, for in our household of men we had lived simply enough. I had no wish for fine gowns, or wheaten bread, or a bolster filled with goose feathers. So I told myself, and it was true enough.

It was the company that was difficult. I had been alone a long time, alone save for those few precious nights when my brothers could take human form, when we might again speak mind to mind, when we might touch and gaze and store up memories for the long, lonely times between. Now I was surrounded by women, women who chattered constantly amongst themselves, who were always there, who broke into my thoughts and made my task harder, and slower, and more painful, because I must work doubly to remember why I was there, and what I must do. And the looks; the looks were sidelong, and bitter, and full of fear. I was the enemy; it did not really matter what the lord Hugh had said, for the long sunny room where we met each morning to sew and spin and weave was the women's place, and I read in the women's faces what they thought of me.

I am the daughter of the forest, I told myself as I drew the long, barbed strands of starwort out of my little bag and began to spin, with borrowed distaff and spindle. *I am the daughter of Lord Colum of Sevenwaters. I have a brother that is a fine leader, and one that is an adept in mysteries more ancient than any your people could imagine. I have a brother that is a fearless warrior, and one the wild creatures know as a friend. I have a brother that – that once had a smile that would charm the birds from the trees, and will again one day.* And as the thread snapped once more, and I joined it yet again, with its fine barbs piercing my skin like strands of hot wire, I told myself, *I have a brother that knows how to heal the spirit, that will give of himself till there is nothing left. What have you, with your smooth hands and your fine embroidery? With every twist of this sharp thread, I cry out to my brothers. With every thorn that stabs my flesh, I call them back home.*

The Britons thought me touched in the head. After the first shock, there was disbelief as they saw my work and realised I was in earnest when I twisted the spines of this plant between my fingers. When they saw me choke back the cry of pain and will my face to calm, they drew away from me, and clustered together, glancing from time to time, furtively, at the corner where I sat alone. I heard their talk, even though their voices were hushed. Because his mother was there, they would not openly question what the lord Hugh had done. But they told tales, terrible tales of how the chieftains of Erin had killed this man, and maimed that one, how the flower of their people had come to grief in the long feud between us. Glancing at me over their shoulders, they told of good men bewitched and betrayed by women of my kind, women with pale skin and hair as dark as night, and a way with words. All of it was meant for my ears. I could have told them our side of the story – my father's story. For Colum was a seventh son, and how often does such a one inherit his father's lands? Only when all his brothers are lost to war, falling one by one in defence of what they hold precious. But I was silent.

Amongst the raised eyebrows, the pursed lips, there was one who dared to be different. She was John's wife. She had been watching me, and hers were the only eyes that made no judgement. On the third day, as I sat on a high stool in my corner wrestling with spindle and distaff and trying to hold back the tears, she moved to sit by me, bringing her work with her. She was hemming a tiny gown; its bodice and sleeves already bore a finely embroidered trail of leaves, with here and there a yellow bee or scarlet flower. I could see her love for her unborn child in every stitch of this small garment. I reached out to touch it with my wretched, swollen hands, and smiled at her.

'Your name's Jenny, isn't it?' she said quietly. 'I'm Margery, John's wife.'

I nodded, picking up my spindle again. There had been a pointed hush amongst the other women; now they resumed their talk.

324

'I'm told you have quite some skill with healing,' she went on, giving me a sideways glance. 'That gash of Red's – of Lord Hugh's – cannot have been easy to treat out there. He owes you much.'

I looked at her, and my surprise must have been obvious. She was amused.

'These men do talk from time to time, my dear,' she said. 'You'd be surprised how much I hear. And though John keeps himself to himself, he is not blind. He's been Red's – Lord Hugh's – friend for a long time, since well before I came to live at Harrowfield. He understands what Hugh does not speak aloud. Your coming has put a stir in this household that will not settle quickly.'

I thought about this. We had seen the men at the evening meal, and all three whom I knew had acknowledged me courteously. Ben had grinned, and tweaked my long plait, almost as Cormack might have done. John had greeted me by my new name, and seated himself by me at table, ignoring the lady Anne's frown. I wondered if the guard were to be continued, in one form or another, even during the day. Of Red, seated at the head of the board as was fitting, I saw the least, but I felt his eyes on me as the meal progressed, and as I endured the noise and the smells and the nearness of so many strangers, and longed for night to come.

John did not talk much, but I noticed he stopped the servants from putting roast meats on my platter, and made sure I did eat something, and when some of the young men grew boisterous with ale and began to aim ribald comments in my direction, he silenced them with a few carefully chosen words. As Red's friend, he had authority. He was, I learned in time, some sort of distant cousin of the family, and had lived at Harrowfield all his life. I was glad enough of his protection, and I noticed again in the days to come, as there was no sign of any mellowing in the household's attitude to me, that there was always someone watching me. While I sat with the ladies, Margery was there, always kind, always ready to step out of the charmed circle and sit by me, happy enough to hold a one-sided conversation, her eyes full of concern as she watched my painful progress with distaff and spindle, never passing a word in judgement. I was sure her motives were kindly, but I also wondered if somebody had asked her to keep an eye on me. The nightly guard continued. One of them would watch from the time I went to my room until midnight, and another from midnight to dawn. Each of them, I supposed, had one good night's sleep in three. I observed them without their knowing it, and noted that this task fell only to Ben, and John, and Red. I wondered if, in all this large and obedient household, there were just two people that Red thought he could really trust.

I noted as well that they were never far away, no matter what the time of day. I could not force myself to spin and weave constantly, though I might wish to, for my hands, part-healed through my neglect of my work, now grew raw and swollen again, and I was forced to take some time away from my task each afternoon, before resuming my slow labours alone by candlelight after the evening meal. I tried to start on the garden, but made slow progress, for my hands would have to harden again before I could wield knife or hoe. But I did a little; the soil was dark and rich and the weeds were not so hard to pull out. When I could manage no more, I went out, with stocky Alys trotting behind, and explored as far as I might, while trying to be as unobtrusive as possible. It was amazing how often one of those three happened to be nearby; Ben, putting a young horse through its paces in the field right by where I chose to walk; John, directing the storage of winter vegetables in the barn just as I went that way. The lord Hugh himself, seated on an old bench in the apple orchard one morning, an ink pot by his side, a small oak board balanced on his knee, with a scrap of parchment laid there. He had a quill in his hand, and was concentrating hard on his work. Alys growled at him.

'She never did think much of me,' he commented, apparently quite unsurprised to see me. 'You're abroad early. I don't want you to go too far alone.'

I felt annoyed, suddenly. He was so sure he was right, so used to having every single person doing what he told them. I thought, it can't be good for him, always to have his own way. Why should I not go out alone? Was he afraid I might slip away forever, and take my information with me?

He read something of this unspoken message in my face, and put down his work carefully. On closer inspection I saw that there were two flat pieces of wood, with strips of leather to hold them together, and between he kept many small pieces of parchment, each marked with a careful tally of some sort, groups of four lines with a fifth across, repeated until fifty were recorded, or twice fifty. Here or there was a tiny image, or hint of an image: a horned sheep, a sheaf of barley, a series of curves and lines that might perhaps indicate the position of the sun. A little tree.

'There are risks. I wish you to stay close to the house. Your safety cannot be guaranteed if you venture further.'

I wanted to say to him, *you took me away from the*

forest. Let me at least walk under your trees, feel your river run over my bare feet, lie in your fields and watch the clouds pass overhead. Let me at least be somewhere quite alone. For in your house I cannot feel the air or sense the fire. I cannot smell the earth or hear the water. I will not run away; I cannot. For without your protection, I will not complete my task.

'This is not easy for you, is it?' he commented. 'You could decide to talk to me, of course. That would be helpful. But I see in your expression that you will not.'

I cannot.

'Tell me something,' he said, regarding me closely. 'If you wished, could you speak to me now? Could you talk to me of my brother, and what became of him?'

I have never been able to lie. I nodded miserably, not wanting him to pursue this.

'Why not tell me?' he said, quite softly. 'I would let you go, you know. Whatever happened to Simon, it cannot have been your doing. You are only a child. I would let you go. But I must know first. If he is dead, then I can tell my mother, and so his shadow is laid to rest, and let that be an end of it. This feud is not mine, and I will not pursue it. I have no wish to meet blood with blood. If he lives, he can be found, and I will find him. Would you not wish to know, if this were your own brother?' I gave a nod and then turned abruptly away, so that he would not see my face. There was a long silence. I did not feel I could walk on; but his words had made me deeply uneasy. I did not understand why he would ask me this, when he had kept what he knew of me to himself, telling neither his mother nor, it seemed, his closest friends. Perhaps, I thought, the Fair Folk really did put a spell on him that night. Perhaps he was called to protect me while I complete my task, and so he acts against his true will. If not for that, surely he would make me give him the information, surely he would force it out. He had no need for kindness, no need for patience. But even if I could have spoken, I had no real answers for him. When I looked back at him, he had closed the book and put away his pen and ink.

'I should keep this leg moving,' he said, getting up. 'Walk up this way, I want to show you something.' He still limped, and so I managed to keep pace, despite his long legs. We followed the path round the lichen-covered orchard wall and up a hill beneath young oaks still bearing the last of their russet leaves. Alys plodded gallantly behind.

'I was five or six years old when my father and I planted these,' he said. 'He had a great respect for trees. When you felled, you planted. An oak takes a lifetime to grow. Like his father before him, he saw a long way ahead.' The path went on upwards, and the trees stretched out on either side in orderly rows. Alys grew weary and lagged behind, and we waited for her to catch up. She was too old to go further, but refused to be carried. In the end, I convinced her by gesture and expression that she was to wait for me, and she settled, grumbling, in the fallen leaves by the path. Her liquid eyes followed us reproachfully as we continued to climb. There was a crisp dawn breeze; looking back, I saw the first curls of smoke from newly kindled fires in house and cottage. The folk were beginning to stir.

We reached the hilltop, where a single great stone stood twined around with wild creepers. There was a wide view; I noted again how tidily kept his lands were, how neat and controlled and – well, how *right*

329

was the only way I could put it. No wonder they had all been surprised when he'd decided to bring me back. That had been no part of this neat pattern. The river wound lazily through the valley; from up here, you could see the vast extent of his domain, the broad fields of stubble with their neat conical stacks of straw, the sweeping pastureland dotted here and there with grazing beasts, the mills and barns and the whitewashed cottages nestled amongst trees. So many trees; and the oaks, I saw, were not only young, but half grown, and full grown, and to the east they were thick and ancient, almost a forest.

'When Simon was still an infant, I was up there with my grandfather, collecting acorns, watching him set a drystone wall, delivering the early lambs. When Simon was throwing sticks for his dog, I was planting trees with my father, and learning to stack straw, and thatch a roof to keep the storms out. When Simon was finding out how to kill a man quietly and leave no trace, I was taking the cottagers wood for their winter fires, and learning the name of every person on the estate. My brother and I passed each other like strangers. Time changes things. My father died early, and it broke my grandfather's heart. Now they are both gone.' He said this quite matter of factly; there was no telling if he cared or not. I thought he must. It is hard to make yourself understood without words, unless what you want to say is very simple. I tried anyway, using hands and eyes. Those trees; so ancient, they surely held the knowledge and wisdom of all that had passed in this valley. They surely held the spirits of the men who had worked their love into the land with the labour of their hands. I tried to show Red this. *Trees – old – young. Men – old – young. Growing. Heart. Valley – heart.*

At least he did not laugh at me, but watched me gravely and gave a nod when my efforts were finished. 'Simon never understood,' he said. 'He was always busy somewhere else, always pushing, challenging, trying something new. What we had never seemed to be enough. And yet we have so much.' He lowered himself to the ground; the leg was clearly still not comfortable. I pointed to it and raised my eyebrows as I sat down beside him, not too close.

'The wound looks all right,' he said. 'Don't worry, I'll call you when it's time to undo your handiwork. Wouldn't let anyone else touch it.' I used my fingers to tell him. Twenty days. My stitching must stay for twenty days undisturbed. Wrap and re-wrap the wound. A poultice. Perhaps I could . . . And then I would undo my work, and it should be well. Red nodded; the message had been easier to convey this time.

We sat in silence for a while, watching the day come up, hearing the faint sounds as household and farm awoke and came to life. It was a good place, near enough to the sky, far enough from man.

'I want to warn you,' said Red, twisting a strand of grass between his fingers. 'For I'm not sure you understand how important it is to do as I say; to stay close to the house, and not go off on your own. It is safe enough here, though I fear not all of my household treat you with kindness. That can be changed. It is not this household that bothers me.' He pointed to the north, to the head of the valley. 'That way lie my uncle Richard's lands,' he said. 'He is my mother's brother, a powerful man, a man of great wealth and influence. It was his battle that my brother ran away to fight; it is his feud that costs so many women their sons, their husbands and lovers. My people are bitter;

it will be hard for them to make you welcome. What they cannot see is that it is this man's quest for power, his lust for blood that keeps the old war alive, that poisons men's minds so that they follow him to death or destruction. My brother was young; too young to pledge himself to such a cause. There was no need for him to hate. But Richard dazzles them, these young men, with his ready words. Maybe you know that. Maybe you have heard this story from my brother's lips.'

I shook my head, amazed that he had chosen to tell me this. *Not this story*. For a man that usually said so little, he had revealed more of himself than he knew.

'You wonder why I tell you this,' said Red, appearing to catch my thoughts. 'I tell you because my mother's brother will learn soon enough that you are here. He has informants everywhere, and a sharp ear for rumour. He will be interested. More than interested. We can expect a visit. You will find it difficult, but there are those of my household that will help you. I wish to ensure that we are prepared for such a visit. That's why I want to know where you are, always. He's a clever man. It would suit him well to run into you, as if by chance, when you're out riding or walking alone, with nothing but that apology for a hound to protect you. I want your promise that you will not allow this to happen.'

It's easy, I said silently, and I mimed it for him. *Why not lock me in my room, and keep the key in your pocket?*

The strangest look crossed his face, as if he were trying not to laugh.

'I don't think so,' he said, getting to his feet. 'The light's not so good in there, for spinning. Besides, how would I keep Ben and John Dury, with nothing to do at night? Idleness is not healthy for them. No, I don't think that would do at all. Now, do I have your promise?'

I nodded. I was sure he expected no less. Didn't everyone always do what he told them?

The conversation seemed to be over. He reached out a hand to help me up, and I took it without thinking, suppressing a yelp of pain as he grasped it firmly with his own. This was not lost on him. The pale blue eyes focused sharply on my hands as he opened them out for inspection. His own hands were big enough to close around mine completely; but he had relaxed his grip to the merest touch, examining the rawness of my flesh, the start of an open wound, the remnant barbs of the starwort plant. My hands were not a pretty sight. I felt uncomfortable, standing so close to him. His face showed little indication of his thoughts.

'I don't like this,' he commented without emphasis. 'Perhaps I should lock you up after all. But I doubt that would stop you. It wouldn't really matter what I did, would it?'

I shook my head. *Don't ask too many questions. There are things I may not tell. Don't come too close.*

'I must have been mad,' he said to himself, and dropped my hands, and we started to walk back down the hill. 'They all think so. Crazy, or bewitched. There are plenty of theories. I don't concern myself with them. We can, at least, do a little better than this.'

The terrier was rested and greeted us with a sharp barking and violent wagging of the tail. She pranced ahead of us back to the house, full of self-importance. There were eyes on us as we walked back together, but no more was said than a 'Fine morning, my lord!' and a 'Looks like fair weather'. I thought, there is a charmed space around him, and while I stay in there I am safe. Venture out, and it will be a different story. This did not comfort me, for I had no wish to be dependent on any man, least of all this sharp-eyed Briton who had given me no choice but to leave my own place. And I did not delude myself that his efforts to protect me were in anyone's interest but his own. In the end he would get what he wanted from me, and that would be it. You suck the juice from a ripe fruit, and then you throw away the husk, and the crows come and peck apart the remnants until the last of the life is gone from it. Still, in the picture of things, that hardly mattered. For never a word would I speak to him, until the shirts were finished. And when they were finished, then – then all would change. When my brothers came. If they came.

I became surer, as time passed and the moon waxed and waned, that there was a small and very effective net of protection around me that was tightly under Red's control, as was all else in his domain. There was Margery, who soon became a friend. That was a novelty for me. I had never had a woman friend, unless you counted Eilis, whom I'd always thought rather boring and silly, although I could not fault her taste in men. Margery was sweet, but she was also strong, in a way that became apparent to me as day followed day, and she parried the other women's comments with firm politeness, and continued with her small kindnesses to me. She was strong as she admonished the girl who said, only half-joking, that Margery had better not let me touch her stomach, where the unborn child now grew large and heavy, lest I put a curse on it and it be born dead or deformed. She was strong as she asked Lady Anne, very courteously, if I might have another change of clothes and a good oil lamp for my room in the evenings. She began to talk to me about other things; about how much she had missed John when he was away, and her baby growing fast in the womb. About how eagerly they awaited this child, for she had once had another that had lived but a few moments in the world, and it was many moons now since they had laid their tiny daughter to rest under the great oaks. About how Red had not wanted John to go with him across the water, for, he said, a man should stay by his woman at such a time, and he'd do well enough with Ben by his side. How John had gone anyway, for he had been dreaming strange dreams, and he had misgivings about the whole idea, and feared for Red's safety. And how John worried now that Red had abandoned the search half done, so his companion could come home in time.

It wasn't as if nobody had tried to find Simon when he first went missing. Lady Anne's brother Richard had instigated a search, and not in vain, for he had discovered twelve of his own men slain. But the younger son of Harrowfield was not amongst them. So, eventually, Red had decided to go and see for himself. And for his mother. Margery told me they had been relieved that the worst that happened to Red was splitting his leg open, and coming back with me. John had said he hoped there would be no more surprises. With Red you didn't usually expect surprises. He was the strong, unchanging centre around which the whole of this small world revolved. I began, gradually, to realise the magnitude of his decision to bring me back home.

The network kept tight around me. I was true to

my promise, and did not venture out alone beyond the close environs of the house. Mornings were spent in the sewing room, and the whispered comments and sly looks of the women continued, but Margery was there, and her calm presence and sweet smile made the hurt easier to bear. In the afternoons, I would take a short time of respite from my task, since my hands were too sore to let me work all day. One day I might be sitting in the garden and Ben would appear out of the blue, spade in hand. It was simple enough to show him what needed doing. He had strong arms, and a wide repertoire of silly jokes. Another day, John might appear as I sat on the stone wall admiring the sheep, pale and pristine after the autumn shearing, and he would walk with me down to the river, talking of nothing much, and sit companionably on the rocks as I dabbled my hands and feet and Alys chased squirrels along the banks. But I did not forget my task, and was painfully aware of how slow my progress was, despite the benefits of good food and shelter, of properly fashioned distaff, spindle and loom. I had finished the third shirt, which was Cormack's, and was spinning the thread for Conor's. There was no hope of finishing before midwinter.

I did not see much of Red, and I wondered if he regretted talking to me as he had. It occurred to me that, because of my silence, because I could neither answer him nor repeat his words, he spoke to me almost as if talking to himself. He did not exactly avoid me; he was often nearby, going about the work of the estate, and he watched me, but he did not speak with me again alone. By night, they kept their watch outside my window.

The lady Anne's brother took his time in coming. It was close to Samhain, with a chill in the air and the last of the leaves falling from oak and beech. Lord Richard came with ceremony, riding down the avenue of bare poplars with his company on well matched horses, and his entourage was dressed to impress in fine silks and furs. We watched them from the windows of the long room, Margery and I, while Lady Anne and the other women put down their work and hastened away. Preparations must be made, and made quickly, for such visitors.

'That's his daughter,' said Margery, and I saw the tall, regal girl riding by the leader's side, her smooth brown hair caught back in a net with jewels on it. 'Her name's Elaine. Elaine of Northwoods. Richard has no sons. When she marries Red, the two estates will be tied together. Whoever controls that, has the better part of the north-western coastline within his grasp.'

I watched the party ride up to the steps. The lady Elaine had a very straight back; she made an elegant figure in her wide riding skirts and her little black boots. It was the master of this house himself that came to help her from her horse. Unprepared for the visit, he still wore his working clothes and doubtless smelt of the stableyard. The morning sun touched his cropped hair to the colour of new-kindled fire.

'A strategic alliance,' observed Margery drily. 'Promised to one another since they were children. Such a marriage, between first cousins, is usually forbidden. But her father has friends in high places. The bishop was persuaded to give his approval. It will happen next summer, I think. It should have been sooner; but Red went away instead. Richard did not like that.'

I watched Richard of Northwoods as he dismounted in one fluid movement, and tossed his reins to the waiting groom. He wore black, and moved with the same effortless elegance as his daughter. I saw him greet Red, gripping him by the arm, and then they moved out of sight.

I did not return to my own quarters that day. Instead, Margery took me to the part of the house where she and John lived, and showed me the wooden cradle carved with acorns and leaves on head and foot, now newly lined with soft linen and wool; and the tiny garments she had made. She kept me there awhile with one thing and another, and I watched her with some concern. She was over busy, I thought, for one so great with child, and there was a puffiness about her face and her ankles that I had seen before on women close to their delivery; this was not a good sign. I wanted to talk to her about this, perhaps ask if I might touch her, to feel how the child lay; but I had not forgotten the woman's words. *Better not let her near your child, lest it be born dead or deformed.* And she had lost one babe already.

She made it easy for me, eventually. 'Jenny,' she said, coming to sit by me, and she had in her hands a box of salve and an implement new to me, which I learned later was used by women for plucking unsightly hairs from their brows, or their chins, or wherever they were not wanted. 'I hope you won't think this amiss,' she said rather shyly. 'But we – I thought, your hands need not suffer quite so badly, with a little help. I wish you would stop this work you do, but I have been told you will not, and that there is no point in asking you. At least let me take out some of the barbs for you, and rub a little of this salve into the skin. That way, I think you will have

338

more movement in the fingers, and the pain may be less.' She began to work on my hands, and I surrendered them to her ministrations, closing my eyes. And I saw Finbar, so many years ago, his tongue between his teeth, using two pointed sticks to pull out the thorns while I wept the loud, unrestrained tears of childhood, and Conor told his tale. *Her name was Deirdre, Lady of the Forest . . .*

'Am I hurting you too much?' asked Margery anxiously, and I started and blinked.

There were tears in my eyes. I shook my head, and managed a smile of sorts.

'It must be so hard for you,' she said, patiently pulling out the fine thorns one by one. 'Not talking, I mean. You must be so lonely. And being so far from home. I suppose you have family of your own, brothers and sisters. You must miss them terribly.'

I nodded. *Don't come too close.*

'I have a sister,' she said. 'But I married John and came up here, and she stayed at home. It's a long way. I haven't seen her these two years, not since . . .' Not since you lost your babe, I thought. Now was the time to ask. But I could not talk without my hands, and she held them captive until the job was done, and the healing mixture of comfrey and dewcup, with beeswax and an aromatic oil, was well massaged into my damaged skin.

'I'll do this every afternoon for you,' she said. 'No need to let them get any worse than they must.' She gave a sudden wide yawn. 'Oh dear. Sorry. I do seem to be getting a little tired these days.'

I gestured as clearly as I could. *You should rest. Child – very big now. Rest, sleep.* Margery chuckled.

'Not much chance of that! I have too many things to do, what with running around for Lady Anne, and keeping John happy. He's a good man; it was hard, when he was away. Now I don't want to waste a single moment.'

I tried again, indicating that I would like to touch her, to feel how it was with the child. She became serious, all in an instant.

'If you like,' she said, and there was a touch of anxiety in her voice. 'You know more of these matters than I do, I expect, even though you're such a little thing. There is a midwife here; she'll do well enough, I suppose, when the time comes.' The babe was still high in the womb, and its head was tight under her breasts. There was time yet for it to turn, but not much time. It kicked and strained, growing too large for its own comfort. I gave Margery my best attempt at a reassuring smile. *The babe is well*. This much was true, for now at least. *But you – you must rest. Rest. Sleep.* It was easy enough to show her this with hands and eyes. Whether she would do it was another matter.

I had my work bag with me, and now I drew out the small bundle of starwort fibres which was all I had left. I tugged at her arm, pointed to what I held, then tried to show her a plant growing, knee high or a little taller. Strong stems spreading. Then I went to the window, gestured out into the valley, turned back with a question in my eyes. *Where? Where does it grow?*

'Oh, Jenny,' she said reproachfully. 'You cannot surely want to go on with this? It hurts you so badly.'

I gripped her shoulders and nodded. *Yes. Oh yes. Help me.*

'I would rather not be the one to tell you this,' she said, and for a moment my heart stopped, for I thought she was going to say it did not grow there at all. 'I'm not happy with what you are doing to yourself, and nor is Red. But this plant, we call it spindlebush, does grow here in abundance. Not near the house; further north up the valley, across the river and up a gully where a stream flows down. There is a bridge. It's quite a long way. If you must have more, you'd be better to send John or Ben to fetch it for you. If you like, I'll ask John.'

But I shook my head, for it must be I alone who cut and harvested the plant. The Lady of the Forest had made that clear. I gave Margery a hug of reassurance and thanks.

Lord Richard had to see me sooner or later. The summons was brought by Megan, who of all the maidservants seemed to be least in fear of me. I was to come to the hall, she said. Myself and Mistress Margery. The lady Anne said we should all be there, as a sign of respect for our visitors. Straight away, the lady Anne said. Margery grimaced, and told Megan the lady Anne would just have to wait. She seemed in no particular hurry. She undid my hair and brushed it, and plaited it up again, muttering to herself. 'I've never seen such an untameable head of hair! No sooner do I put it in order but these little curls come breaking out as if they've got a life of their own. Well, near enough will have to be good enough. Can't keep the lady Anne waiting for ever. She's got a sharp tongue on her, when she wants to use it. Chin up, Jenny, you'll do well enough.'

I followed her along the hallway and down the wide stone steps to the lower floor. Maybe this won't be too bad, I told myself. After all, everyone will be there; we can just slip in the back and make an appearance, to satisfy the lady of the house, and then slip out again. My hands were feeling better; maybe I would go back to my room and spin some more. Surely nobody would notice.

My hopes vanished the moment we came into the hall. For this was a select gathering only. No hope of anonymity here. Lady Anne sat on one side of the hearth, and Elaine on the other. She carried her head like a queen, and her face was as delicate and fine as a gardener's most prized bloom. Her large blue eyes surveyed me tranquilly, without judgement. Beside her I felt every bit the uncouth, feral child that they doubtless thought me.

Red was standing by the window, with his back to the room. Near him was the lord Richard, and I could see on closer inspection a trace of the family resemblance; not much, but it was there in the fair, greying hair with its slight curl, and the shrewd, measuring gaze, the same I had seen in the lady Anne's eyes. He was not a particularly tall man; Red stood a good head taller. But there was an authority, a presence about him, something you sensed instantly. Something that set me on guard. You will find it difficult, Red had said, speaking of his uncle and how it would be when I met him. That was all right. I was the daughter of Lord Colum of Sevenwaters. Why should I be scared of some Briton, even if his name was Northwoods?

'So this is the girl,' observed Lord Richard. His voice was held deliberately soft. Soft, I thought, like a cat's paw when it toys with a mouse. 'Well, come forward. Let me see you, girl.' Margery gave me a gentle push in the back, and retreated to the far end of the room, where her husband stood looking as if he wanted to blend into the tapestry on the wall. Ben was there too, I saw; he gave me a reassuring wink, and Lady Anne frowned. As well, there were two or three men in Richard's household colours, russet with a slash of black, and all of them were looking at me. Red had not turned around. I glanced at Lady Anne. She gave a sort of frozen nod, and I took one step, two steps forward. Held my head high. Looked him straight in the eye. *I am the daughter of the forest. I am not afraid of you.*

'She's younger than I expected,' said Lord Richard, scrutinising me closely. 'Not that it makes much difference. It's bred in them, they imbibe it with their mother's milk. A sort of rage; a blind dedication that breeds killers and fanatics and madmen. I doubt if they'll ever accept that what we took from them was never theirs by rights. A few paltry rocks in the sea, a cave or two, a couple of stunted trees. But they'll kill for it. They'll die for it. Until the very last one falls to the sword. Bred in them. Look at the way she holds herself, and the hatred in those eyes. A lost cause. But she could be useful to us, sister. I hear she's no ill-bred serving wench. She could earn you gold; enough to buy a nice little parcel of land on your southern boundary, or build a strong watchtower. Enough for a goodly purchase of weaponry, or a strong breeding stallion. Who is she? What family let loose their grip long enough to deliver such a choice morsel into your hands? What's your name, girl?'

I kept my gaze on him, unwavering.

'She can't speak,' said Lady Anne. 'The girl has some kind of – of malady. She is a little touched in the wits, I believe, and insists on hurting herself. We don't know who she is.' Her tone was apologetic; I thought she was both embarrassed and fearful. But this was her own brother. Maybe I had mistaken her tone.

'Can't speak?' asked Richard softly, inspecting me from all angles. 'Or won't?' My hands were clasped behind my back; I kept them relaxed, breathing slowly. I ventured a glance at Red. Hadn't he said they would help me? He seemed intensely interested in the view from the window.

'Where did you find her, Hugh? A trophy of some battle?'

'Father.' It was Elaine who spoke, surprising us all, I think. 'You should not speak of the girl thus, as if she cannot understand you. As if she were not here.'

Richard laughed. It was not a pleasant sound.

'Your kindness does you credit, my dear. But you forget, these people are not as you and I. If you had seen the things I have seen, if you had witnessed the atrocities – the Lord willing, you should never be exposed to such horrors. You need not imagine one such as this thinks and feels as you do, the daughter of one of the highest families in Northumbria. She is less than the earth beneath the sole of your boot, my dear. Besides, I can't believe a girl of her years could have much grasp of our language. Her education would be quite rudimentary, if she had any at all. Unless, of course, she has been trained as a spy. That raises more interesting questions. Did you think of that, when you took her into your household?'

Elaine made to speak again, then thought better of it. Richard resumed his pacing.

'She cannot tell us who she is,' he murmured. 'Convenient. Very handy. So you can get no ransom for her. I could guess, maybe. Perhaps the girl has heard of Seamus Redbeard, him whose barbarians murdered good men in the passes above the long lake?' He stared into my eyes, and I was suddenly put in mind of the lady Oonagh, and summoned every effort of will not to show the tiniest flicker of knowledge, to keep my face as still as stone. 'Maybe she knows of Eamonn of the Marshes, son-in-law of Redbeard; his trick is the use of fire, by night. A hot fire that leaves nothing but bone behind.' He circled again. 'Perhaps she knows of Lord Colum of Sevenwaters, the most elusive of all, a thorn in my flesh if ever there was one. Through him the flower of my men perished. Perhaps she knows of these. For every girl is a daughter, or a sister; unless we believe in faery changelings now. Look at me, girl. *Whose daughter are you?*'

Silence. Silence was the only defence. Breathe in; breathe out. Try to think of nothing. Try to hold down the rage that rose in my breast; try to keep the pain from my face. *Your thoughts blaze like a beacon from your eyes; yours and Finbar's.* Keep it back. Calm. Calm like stone.

'You're too soft, Hugh. This would be child's play. But you never did like blood on your hands.'

He turned to the lady Anne. 'What of your younger son, sister? What would you give, to have him home safe? If she could lead you to him, would you not have her speak, by any means you could? She could be made to speak, oh, so easily. But Hugh here, for reasons best known to himself, doesn't seem prepared to do it. That makes me wonder. That presents a whole new set of questions.'

Don't look at the lady Anne. Concentrate on breathing. In. Out.

'She's only a child,' said Red very quietly. I realised suddenly that this whole thing was not about me. It was meant for him. It was part of some game only these two men understood. It was some sort of test. But which of them was being tested?

'She has nothing to tell. She came to my aid when

345

I was in difficulty; I offered her shelter. That's all there is to it.'

There was complete silence in the room. Richard raised his eyebrows quizzically.

'Not such a child, I think,' he said silkily. His back was to his daughter, and to the lady Anne. His hand came up, and one finger touched my cheek delicately, and then ran a slow pathway down my face, and my neck, and my breast above the neckline of my plain gown. I felt the blood drain from my face, and my insides clenched tight with remembered terror, and I caught my breath. I did not see Red move, it was so fast. But there he was, his large hand closing around Richard's arm, rather tightly, and lifting it away.

'Enough,' he said softly. There was no need to raise his voice; the tone had said it all. 'This is my household, uncle. The lady is my guest. Perhaps I did not make that clear.'

'Oh, you make it clear enough, Hugh, my boy, clear as crystal.' He was rubbing his wrist, his expression now comically rueful. He had quite a repertoire. 'I hope it's as clear to your mother, that's all I can say. She may be less enthusiastic about giving houseroom to the – lady.' The little pause before the last word was exquisitely timed. But he had not read his audience as well as he might. Elaine had a small frown on her brow, as if she were thinking hard. Lady Anne was distressed. Nonetheless, she beckoned to me as I stood frozen in the centre of the room, and I summoned up what dignity I had left and went to sit on the embroidered stool at her side. In that one gesture she had said more than many words were worth. She might disapprove of what Red had done; but he was her son, and this was his household, and she would see that his guests were treated correctly, whatever it cost her.

I endured the evening meal. This time I was better protected, for the family sat together, Lady Anne in her habitual place on her son's right, Elaine on his left. Lord Richard was seated by his sister, and if I felt his eyes on me, I did my best not to look at him. Well down the table, I found myself between John and Ben, with Margery opposite. That effectively cut off any need to hear what was being said, or to school my expression. The three of them kept up a lively conversation on a variety of topics, ranging from the winter fair at Elvington, to whether sycamore or walnut was really best for fine furniture, to the merits of Red's new breeding sow. They managed to include me, and a variety of imaginative expressions and gestures came into use, causing a certain amount of merriment amongst our small party. Once or twice, glancing up the table, I caught Red's gaze, neither approving nor disapproving, just noting how things were. He spent much time in quiet conversation with Elaine. They were well suited, I thought. Childhood friends, they knew their place in the world and would work well together to keep what they had. She had impressed me, with her attempt to stand up to her father. Besides, both were tall and well favoured, and they would breed handsome children. But I remembered the expressions on the faces of Liam and Eilis on the night of their betrothal; how they gazed into each other's eyes as if there were no other in the world. I saw no such expression on Red's face, nor on Elaine's. Perhaps it is the way of the Britons, I thought. You do not show what you feel. Instead, you shut it away inside, locked in tight, lest it be seen in the light. But there were exceptions, I thought, watching Margery as she shared a joke with her husband, seeing John's face as he passed her a platter of bread and she took a piece, touching his hand. There were those whose love spilled over into their every gesture, and so was shared by all who knew them. But they were rare folk indeed.

I slept badly; the night demons were strong, clutching at me even in sleep, and it was a relief to wake, finally, cold and clammy with sweat, and see through my round window the first dim traces of dawn light in the sky. I washed in cold water and threw on a cloak over my nightrobe, for the walls were closing in and I was desperate for air. I unbolted the outer door and went softly out into the garden, barefoot on the cold stones of the path. Alys followed with some reluctance, moving stiffly in the early chill. There would be frost within days, I thought. That was good; maybe in spring I would see the earth carpeted with jonquil and crocus. Today would be fair; I could still see stars in the lightening sky, where purple faded to pink and to the first touch of dawn gold.

Alys gave a tiny growl as we neared the foot of the garden. On the bench under the wall, Red lay asleep. It was scarcely large enough to accommodate his long frame; his arms were crossed behind his head, one leg lay stretched out along the bench and the other dangled to the ground. He would have a few aches and pains when he woke. He had his sword, and the small knife in his boot; but right now, any passing stranger could have finished him off. I stood there quietly, as the dawn touched his face with rosy light, and played over the straight nose, and the well defined bones, and the wide, relaxed mouth. *All right for some*, I thought.

He did not take long to wake. When he did, it was in one smooth movement, aches and pains or no, springing to his feet instantly alert, hand ready on sword hilt.

Alys gave a yelp of fright. Then Red saw who it was and sat down again, scratching his head ruefully.

'Sleeping on the job. Not good,' he said, blinking. 'Must have been more tired than I thought. Yesterday was not the best of days.'

I nodded. It was an understatement. Now he was looking at me properly, searchingly.

'You look terrible,' he said.

Thanks. My expression must have told him how I felt.

'And your feet must be freezing. Sit down here.' I sat, tucking my feet under me on the bench, drawing my cloak around me to cover them. It was cold on the stone path, but it was a good cold, that winter chill that sets a sleep on the garden, to dream of spring's new growth.

'You haven't been sleeping,' said Red, and he reached out a hand towards my face. I flinched away, and he dropped it without touching me. 'You have deep shadows under your eyes, and you're white as chalk. I'm sorry about yesterday. They are leaving this morning. I don't want you to be frightened.'

What I wanted to say could not be put into gestures. *You weren't much help. Why didn't you stop him sooner?* I could think of no way to convey this to him. I gave a shrug instead.

'I mean it, Jenny. I will ensure that he does no such thing again. It was not fair to you, nor to my mother.' I studied his face. I thought that he was wrestling with himself, unsure how much to say.

'He – no, let me put this another way. My uncle is kin. I must accept that. I can go just so far, for now at least. I wished to let him talk, in case – no, I need not burden you with this.'

What? Burden me with what? Of that man, with his

349

smooth tongue and his creeping hands, with his ready smile and poisonous words, I could believe anything. Having him as your uncle must be bad enough. I would not have him as father-in-law, if I had the choice. But it seemed that for Red, that choice was already made.

'I know why Simon went away,' said Red in an undertone. I felt, again, that he was really talking to himself, not to me. Setting his thoughts in order. Saying the things one did not say aloud. 'I'm not sure I understand why he did not return. There are ways of conducting a campaign, and Richard knows them well; whatever you might think of his motives, he is a professional with years of experience in the field. This campaign was different. You don't set up camp in the heart of your enemy's territory, not if you know what he's capable of. You don't put all your men together in a vulnerable position, to lose them in a single ambush. When you sleep, you set a watch. And it is not, usually, the newest and rawest recruit that is singled out for special treatment. Why didn't he die with the rest of them?' He ran his hand over his short-cropped hair, frowning. 'Simon had hostage value, I understand that. But there was no demand for ransom, no contact, nothing. And not a word of him, when I went there. Nothing; except –'

Except what I carried, I thought. *And that was precious little good to you.*

'And when Richard himself went to search,' Red went on, and I thought he had almost forgotten I was there, 'what he told us – it did not ring true. John said the same. What he told us, of how they were slain, how the men of Erin came on them by night – it just doesn't happen to men of experience. Not like that. Richard said – implied – that it was Simon's fault, that my brother somehow betrayed them, brought

350

the enemy down on them. But I know my brother. He may be foolish, headstrong, over young for his years. But he is not a traitor.'

I nodded. I knew Simon was no informant. I had had faith in him, even when he had lost faith in himself.

'There is a truth to be found, somewhere in all this,' said Red. 'Amongst the many versions of this tale, one must be right. I hoped, in searching for Simon myself, to find the truth, although after so long, I had little real hope that he would still be alive. But there were no answers there. I came away with no answers, and a head full of questions. In letting my uncle talk yesterday, I hoped for another clue. And so I let him go too far, and I regret that. I used you as a pawn in this game, and you were hurt.'

It was getting lighter. The sky was pale and clear, and the voices of birds spoke in the trees around us. Alys rolled on her back, stretching and scratching. There was something I had to tell him.

You could go back. This could be conveyed by pointing, and the movement of hands. *You could go back there. Look again. Perhaps find him. You could take me back.* And then, I thought, when my brothers come back, I will be there waiting.

Red regarded me seriously. Evidently he had understood me quite well. 'I cannot go yet awhile. There is much to do here; I was away too long, and had to leave others to oversee the harvest, and the culling of stock. The river may flood before midwinter, and –' he broke off, seeing my expression. 'I don't want to go back, not yet,' he said. 'My absence from Harrowfield leaves vulnerable all that I hold dear. This is a time of change, with a new king in the south who is as yet untried. I doubt Ethelwulf has the strength of his father, and that leaves us open to the Danes. My duty lies at home, for now. My brother chose to go. He chose that way. I will not lose all that I have in the quest to bring him back. But I have not forgotten. Nor do I fear spilling blood, whatever my uncle says. If Simon is to be found, I will find him. If I must wait, then I will wait.'

Before he left, he told me to go back inside and bolt the door, and stay there until it was fully light.

'Do as I say, Jenny,' he said. 'There is danger here. You have seen it at work. Perhaps I am wrong; perhaps I misjudge my uncle. I hope I am wrong. He leaves this morning, but I have no doubt he will return, and try again. He has seen you now. I know how his mind works; your strength will be a challenge to him. Remember your promise.'

I did, and, sitting quietly in my room with only Alys for company, I remembered a lot of other things too. In particular, I remembered the Lady of the Forest, as she told him *Make sure she is not hurt again.* And as she told me *You may not have to be so strong, now.* What game were the Fair Folk playing, that they used even Britons as their pawns? That they laid a command on Lord Hugh to protect me, when doing so went against every logical choice he should be making? Well, there was nobody here to ask. Nobody but me and little Alys. I took out needle and sharp thread, and as the morning light came up I began, laboriously, to finish off the woven square I had made, stitch by painful stitch. The first part of Conor's shirt.

After that, things settled down for a while. The weather turned towards winter, with the frosts I had anticipated a mere prelude to days of storm, and a bone-chilling sleet that turned the ground to mud. Farm carts were bogged, and men got filthy shifting them. The river overflowed, and stock were moved to higher ground. In the kitchens, a cauldron of soup simmered constantly on the hob, ready for the next contingent of exhausted men. I noticed without surprise that Lord Hugh and his friends worked side by side with cottager and farmer, clearing fallen trees, shoring up banks, quieting horses crazed with fear when lightning struck the stables. My opinion of Lady Anne rose slightly when I observed her packing baskets with food and, on occasion, venturing out herself to deliver them, accompanied by a maidservant. It went up further when she began to use my name, instead of 'girl', and reprimanded a servant who suggested the accuracy of the lightning strike might have something to do with my presence in the house. There were rows of muddy boots before the fire, and wet cloaks hanging in the kitchens. My room was freezing and I begged an extra blanket.

At least the foul weather meant we had no visitors for a while. The road from Harrowfield to Northwoods was impassable, flooded deep by the swollen river. There was no going in or out, for now. It was the time of year when at home I would have gathered with my brothers to keep away shadows, and to ask a spirit blessing for the dark season to come. There was a Christian feast day, which the household kept, but with no great ceremony. There was no priest here; quiet prayers were spoken for the dead, and candles lit. Nobody spoke the name, Simon. But he was there amongst us; you didn't need to say it to feel it.

In my room, that night, I lit my own candle. I had not undressed, it was too cold. The dog had tugged the blankets into a sort of nest and lay there snoring gently. The light danced over the stone walls, sculpted by the draught into fantastic shadows. Silently I spoke their names. *Liam. Diarmid. Cormack. Conor. Finbar. Padriac.* I saw their faces in my mind, six versions of the same face, but all so different. They swam together, blurred by my tears. It was not long till midwinter. How would I find them? There were still but three shirts in my little bag, and part of the fourth. Soon enough I would have no starwort left. How would I gather it, when the wind outside whipped the bushes to the ground, and water froze hard in the furrows of the bare fields? Finally I fell asleep, still staring into the candle flame, curled up by small Alys for warmth, with my brothers' names sounding over and over in my head, as if by saying them I could keep them alive a little longer, just a little. Just long enough.

CHAPTER NINE

The weather grew fouler and the days shorter. In the mornings the ground was crisp with frost, and the eaves of the barn sparkled with icicles. It had been hard enough in the warmer weather of autumn for my swollen hands to manipulate distaff and spindle, to pass the shuttle through the loom, to thread a needle for the final sewing. Now I felt a dull throbbing in my joints that would not go away, even when I rested. On the worst days, when snow fell soft outside and lanterns lit the room where we worked even at midday, I had to fight hard to keep back tears as I forced myself to go on. Margery had learned by now that I would not accept help from anyone. All she could do was sit by me and talk quietly of one thing and another, and I found her presence reassuring. But my progress was slow, too slow. There was a fire on the hearth, and the women would sit near it to work. But I did not move closer, for I did not like the suspicious glances or the wagging tongues, which were silent only in Lady Anne's presence. I did not like the little signs they made with their fingers, when they thought I was not watching. I worked as steadily as I could, and I watched through the window as midwinter came ever closer, and because I no longer dared to consider how long the whole task might take, I set myself a smaller goal. I would finish Conor's shirt by Meán Geimhridh, the winter solstice.

Cooped up indoors, the men found a new way to occupy themselves. The great hall was cleared of its benches and tables and became a centre for various forms of combat, armed and unarmed. After a day or two and some near misses, Lady Anne ordered the tapestries removed for safe keeping.

I began to see where Red had developed those skills I had observed during our flight from lake to sea. The men practised with swords, and with sword and dagger together, and with staves. They wrestled and used hands and feet as weapons. My brothers could have picked up a new trick or two.

Bored with the morning sewing routine, the girls were often discovered clustered in the doorway, gasping as Ben executed a low dive under John's sword stroke, followed by a flying kick that sent his assailant's dagger sailing through the air perilously close to the viewers' admiring faces. Or exclaiming, as Red demonstrated his method for breaking a head-lock applied by a very determined enemy – an effective manoeuvre, if unethical. And it was not only these three that used their time thus. Red had a small but lethal fighting force, any of whom, I thought, could have given Cormack a good run for his money. And that was saying something. It intrigued me that these cowmen and foresters and millers were able, in a matter of moments, to transform themselves into skilful warriors of deadly purpose. Lord Richard had scorned Red for his reluctance to confront the enemy. But I thought, he will be ready when the time comes. As he was before. If I were his enemy, I would not be making slighting remarks. I would be getting ready for the combat right now. It took me some time to remember that I and my kind were the enemy; I had almost fallen into the trap of thinking I belonged here.

That this was far from the truth was demonstrated to me soon enough. Lady Anne had thawed a little since her brother's visit, but only a little. She shared my concerns, I think, watching her son put his newly mended leg to such energetic use. I had been pleased with my handiwork, for the stitches had come out cleanly, and the wound looked healthy. He would never lose the long scar his assailant's blade had cut into the flesh, but he was demonstrating daily that the leg itself was as good as new. I was somewhat relieved. But this success did not earn me the respect of the household. Instead, there was muttering about how I had done it, and a half-spoken suggestion that one so young and witless could not have achieved this spectacular result without the use of sorcery, or something so close to it that you would not notice the difference.

As it drew ever closer to midwinter eve, I knew I must plan carefully. For I must be ready and waiting, between dusk and dawn, for my brothers' return. No matter that I had crossed the sea and left them behind. No matter under whose roof I now sheltered. I must set aside the knowledge that they had no map, no sign, no light to guide them to me. I had taken this path and they would have to follow. Strange things had happened; stranger still might come to pass. So I kept their names in my mind, as a kind of litany, and I planned my escape. If they came, it must be to water, and so to the river. I could not go far undetected, and had but a small span of time to do it. I could not be there by dusk. It must be between the evening meal and the time when the guard was set outside my door. I would light a candle in my room, and bid Alys be silent. Then I would shut the door and cross the garden stealthily. I could make my way to the river's edge in the dark. I hoped they would wait. Then, in the morning, I would bid them farewell, see them safely on their long way home, and make sure the guard was gone before I slipped back into my room. It should work. It had to work. I tried not to think that they might not come, that there might be a long empty night of waiting.

Midwinter eve dawned clear and cold. With a good fire lit in the long room, and low sunlight slanting through the windows, we managed to coax our chilled fingers into work. In the main hall, a great oak log had been laid on the hearth to be lit that night with ceremony, and boughs of greenery, holly, ivy and goldenwood hung above each doorway. This much was familiar to me from home. But I did not imagine I would see bonfires on the hills, nor find these folk around them drinking midnight toasts to the spirits of field and tree. They would stay safe in their warm beds and lock the doors. That was to my advantage. I should be able to slip out and in by night quite unseen.

The sewing session was short that day; by mid-morning the women repaired to the kitchens, where all hands joined in preparation of the evening's feast. There would be roast meats and cider and plum cakes. The men played their games of combat, or went about the work of the farm. The best stock were housed in barns for the winter, and the cattle must be grain-fed daily. It was a busy day, so busy that nobody had time to notice me, so I stayed where I was, relishing the solitude, and I sewed the second sleeve into the shirt. It was all but finished. As I worked my mind drifted away from the empty room and the dwindling fire. I drew the image of my brother Conor into my thoughts: wise, kind eyes; narrow, fine-boned face, long hair glossy as a ripe chestnut; a strong young man with an old spirit. I saw him in our kitchen counting stores; I saw him by candlelight surrounded by strange shadows. I saw him as he stood on the shore and invoked the spirits of fire. I watched him swim away across the lake, great white wings folded by his side. *Conor. I am here. Where are you?* I sat there a long time, my fingers busy with needle and thread, my mind far away. I reached out with all the power I could summon, to call him. But there was no reply, or none I could hear. They may be flying toward me even now, I told myself. They may be over the great water, or sheltering from the cold in some desolate place between there and here. I will wait; there will come a time when I will call, and he will answer.

Dimly, my ears were picking up an increase in activity outside the room, the sound of raised voices and hastening steps. The light was too poor for working, and my mind was numb and exhausted with my efforts. I went to the door and looked out just as Megan hurried by, her arms full of linen. I caught her sleeve, raising my brows in question.

'It's Mistress Margery,' she said breathlessly. 'Been having her pains all afternoon, very strong they are, but the midwife says there's something wrong. Babe's the wrong way round, she says, and you know what that means. Poor Mistress Margery. Her first babe died, you know. Looks like it might be the same again.'

Her words shocked me back into this world. Margery's child, which was so precious to her. She and John had lost one, they must not lose another. I could help. I had done this before, I knew just what to do. I could not tell them this, but I could show them. I followed the bustling Megan to Margery's quarters, where there were women clustered around the door, and light within. Megan vanished inside with her clean cloths. But my way was barred by one of Lady Anne's waiting women.

'Not you,' she said firmly. I hesitated only a moment, then tried to make my way past her. This was ridiculous. If Margery was in trouble, she needed me. Surely she wanted me. And I knew what to do, at least I thought I did. The woman's arm shot out to block my way.

'You can't go in there,' she said. 'You'll not be allowed to set your curse on a woman in childbirth, nor lay your filthy hands on her unborn babe. Be off with you. Your kind are not welcome here.' I would have slapped her face, if I hadn't known it would only make things worse. I drew a deep breath.

'What's the matter?' came a voice from within the room. It was the lady Anne, who now came to the door, hearing her women's raised voices. 'Jenny. What are you doing here?' She looked tired and sad, and not at all pleased to see me. I used my hands to speak to her. *I can help. I know these things. Let me help. Let me in.*

Lady Anne looked at me wearily. 'I don't think so, Jenny,' she said, and she was already turning away. 'We have our own midwife here. She has skills enough; if she cannot save this babe then I fear nobody can.' And she was gone.

'You heard my lady,' said another woman. 'Be off with you. We don't need your kind. It's a healer that's wanted here, not a killer. Why don't you go back where you came from, witch?'

I left. What was the point? But I could have wept, thinking of Margery who had become my friend, and who now risked losing what she had waited for so lovingly. I went back to my room, made sure my preparations for the night were complete, then paced up and down the garden as Alys sniffed around under the lavender bushes. I felt the chill deepen as the sky grew darker, and nightfall closer. My heart grew heavy with foreboding. Death was very close that day; I felt her in my bones. No warm hearth nor guardian holly branch could keep her out, where she chose to enter. I wished I could don cloak and boots and go to the river now, could be there at the moment when the sun dropped below the horizon and the land grew grey and purple and black. But I knew Red. I must appear at the table or a search would be mounted. There was no escape until full dark. He needed neither lock nor key to keep me prisoner.

It was to have been a festive meal, but there was little joy amongst those of the household that gathered in the hall that evening. It was already dark. I watched the blackness outside the windows, and my spirit called out again. *Conor! Finbar! Where are you? Wait for me.* I pictured my brothers in the cold under the willows, not knowing if I was near or no. Alone, and in the heart of their enemy's lands. Exhausted in the dark. A corner of my mind registered the sight of a distraught John being given a goblet of wine and draining it in one draught, scarcely aware of what he did or where he was. Of Red, with a tight mouth and cold eyes, speaking to his mother in a furious undertone. I thought I could guess why he was angry. He knew I was a healer. He was John's friend, and Margery's. He realised I might be able to help them. But Lady Anne did not want me at Margery's bedside, with my sorceress's hands delivering the babe. She looked uncomfortable in the face of Red's anger, but there was a stubborn set about her soft features. Ben sat by me and said little. Nobody had much appetite.

As early as was polite, I left the table, going straight to my room. Lady Anne and her son were still arguing; I didn't think either of them noticed me. There was still plenty of time. I thrust my feet into my outdoor boots and snatched up the cloak. Alys barely stirred, nestled cosily in the blankets. The candle burned steadily on the wooden chest. *I'm coming. Wait just a little longer.* I raised my hand to unbolt the outer door.

At that moment there was a sharp knocking, and Megan's voice at the other door. 'Jenny! Jenny, are you there?' It was as if a cold hand clenched itself around my heart. No, not now. Don't call me now. But it was for Margery, I knew it, and I had no choice but to open the door and to follow Megan back into the house. It had taken them long enough to realise they could not deliver this child without me. The lady Oonagh herself could not have chosen the moment better.

Lady Anne had spoken to the women; or somebody had. Their eyes still followed me nervously as I moved about the room, and more than one of them made a furtive sign of the cross. But they said not a word. Margery was exhausted. She had great dark circles under her eyes, and her skin was cold and clammy.

'Jenny! You're here!' she said in a faint little voice. 'Why didn't you come? I wanted you. Why wouldn't you come?'

I glanced at Lady Anne, and she looked away, unable to meet my eyes. I think she realised, despite herself, that she had done the unforgivable.

Midwinter is a long night, but this seemed the longest night of my life, as we battled to help this child make its way into the world. Margery tried and tried but grew more and more weak. And yet, it was a night that went fast, too fast as I worked on, and outside, above the tops of the winter trees, the stars brightened and steadied and then began to fade. And as my hands became wet with blood, and my body soaked with sweat, and as I worked to instruct the women and to reassure Margery without benefit of words, a part of my spirit was calling out to my brothers. *Wait for me. Wait just a little longer. Before dawn I will be there.*

It was much too late to turn the child around, for it lay too low now to be moved. So it must be born breech first, if at all. Margery had little strength left. I could not make the women understand what I needed, and so at length I left the room, taking Megan with me, and went to their stillroom to find the ingredients myself. I must get this just right. Something to make her relax first, a short respite to gather her strength. And something to aid that strength, just long enough for one, two, three short pushes. And pray to the goddess that the cord was not around the baby's neck. I had no doubt who would be blamed, if this child never took its first breath. Besides, I did not think I could bear to see Margery's face, or John's, if I could not lay their infant safely in its mother's arms.

Megan held the lamp as I worked. The house was well stocked, but whoever had stored away these herbs so neatly cannot have known their efficacy in aiding childbirth, nor how to mix them precisely. There was still some time until dawn, but not much. *Wait for me.* I scooped the dry mixture I had prepared into a small beaker and headed for the kitchen fires. These herbs must be steeped in hot water. It should be much longer, but time was running short for Margery. The child, too, would be weakening by now, worn out by the struggle. As I crossed to the stairs, I saw the three men grouped in semi-darkness by the hall fire. John had his head in his hands, and Ben was talking softly, a hand on his friend's shoulder. Red stood by the hearth, and he was the only one who saw me. His eyes asked a question. Mine could not lie. *I will save them both, if I can. I will do my best.* I think he understood me, but he said nothing, for John's sake. He gave a nod of acknowledgment, and I went on up the stairs and out of sight, Megan bobbing ahead with the lamp.

The fire was glowing warm in Margery's room. At my bidding, Megan untied the bundle of dried lavender she had brought from downstairs and cast the silvery stems and faded blooms onto the coals, and a sweet healing scent rose in the air. The infusion had cooled enough; I lifted Margery to sit and watched while she drank it obediently. There was thyme and calamint. And brooklime, a herb of last resort. There had been no time to sweeten the mixture, to render it more palatable with honey or spices. But she took it all, her shadowed eyes looking into mine with an expression of such trust that it terrified me. Then for a short time she rested.

As the sky outside turned to violet blue and then to soft grey, the child was finally born. The infusion had given Margery just enough strength for the last wrenching push. My hands, rough as they were, knew their job, and I eased her son out into the world. He was limp and silent.

'What's wrong?' said Margery in a small voice. 'Why is it so quiet?' And the women muttered amongst themselves. Lady Anne was wiping Margery's brow, and she had tears in her eyes. As the light in the room grew ever brighter, I put my mouth over the babe's tiny face, and blew gently into his body. And again. And once more.

The midwife clawed at my arm, trying to stop me, but Lady Anne said, 'No, leave her be.' One more breath. Just one more. And at last the infant gave a gasp, and a small delicate cough, and then he let out a yell of outrage. Then there were many voices exclaiming, and many hands to wrap the babe and lay him on his mother's breast as the joyful tears flowed. There were many helpers to deal with the afterbirth and make up the fire and run to let the men know the good news. Nobody noticed me as I fled soft-footed down the stairs in my bloodstained gown, and slipped the great bolt on the front door, and ran, ran, down the avenue between the tall poplars, past the neat walls and the sheep huddling for shelter, down towards the gleaming curve of the river where the first light of dawn turned the water to liquid silver under the leaning willows. But before I reached the water's edge the sun pierced the canopy of naked trees and burst over the valley and the world was filled with light. Many creatures left their tracks on these soft river banks, ducks and geese, fox and otter. But it was early; the ducks were still asleep. And there were no swans on the rippling water. There were no human footprints save my own. If they had been here, they were here no more.

My heart was cold with grief and rage. *Why didn't you wait for me? I did the best I could. Why didn't you leave me a sign? I cannot tell if you have even come here at all!* I found the tears pouring down my cheeks, all the tears I had not shed before, a flood of weeping that racked my whole body, and I stood with my head against the trunk of a willow and beat my fists against its bark until my hands bled. If I could have screamed my anguish I would have done, until the whole valley echoed with my pain. I stood there a long time. At last I sank to the ground by the great willow and covered my face with my hands. My shoulders were shaking, and my nose was running, and the tears would not stop. If I sat there long enough, perhaps I would become part of this tree, a weeping tree-girl that cried each night by the water. Perhaps I would vanish into the soft earth of the river bank, and in my place reeds would grow, slender and silver-grey, and if a man fashioned a pipe from these reeds, it would sing *too late, too late*.

'These are not tears of one night's making.'

Perhaps, without thinking, I had known he would come. There was the crunch of boots on the frozen grass as he moved closer. Then I felt the warmth of his cloak as he laid it around my shoulders, very carefully so his hands scarcely touched me. It felt good, very good. I had not realised how cold I was, out in the morning frost in my gown and indoor slippers. It was as if the cloak passed the warmth of his body into mine.

'I would know the reason for these tears,' said Red quietly, and he sat down near me, but not too near. 'One day I will know. For now, I bring you John's thanks, and my own, for what you have done. We owe you a great debt. Will you come back home?'

I sniffed, and opened my eyes, but he was not looking at me. His fingers were twisting a length of grass, and he was gazing out over the water. A mallard drake and his mate were swimming by the rushes, leisurely in the first clear light of day. The feathers of his head shone glossy green above his snowy collar. The female moved in his wake, demure in her speckled brown.

The silence stretched out, but it was not an uncomfortable silence. After a while, Red took the little knife from his boot, and an even smaller piece of wood out of his pocket, and began to carve, narrowing his eyes against the sun in intense concentration. I could not see what he was working on. I wondered who had taught them this skill, the lord Hugh and his brother. The day grew ever brighter and the gleaming expanse of water was soon broken by busy duck and goose and moorhen. My thoughts became gradually calmer. Half a year. Two seasons more, before I would see them again. Yesterday had been my fifteenth birthday, and I had not even thought of it until now. Somehow it no longer seemed important. Back home, I might have been married by this time. I wondered who my father would have chosen for me. A strategic alliance, no doubt. But that was a path become so distant now that it seemed like something from a story, the tale of some other girl. Not my story. I was here, and my brothers were not here, and once again but a single choice presented itself. I could go on spinning and weaving and sewing; I could go on waiting. Perhaps, if I worked very hard, if I got quicker, by midsummer my task would be almost complete. Then I would come to the river again, on the eve of Meán Samhraidh. But would they be here? Could they be here? It was such a long flight. How would they know, before the sun dipped below the horizon and they became men again, that they must make this journey? For while they were in that enchanted state, they had no human awareness.

Except for Conor. How strong was Conor's skill? Could it be that, to command the will of wild creatures thus, even a druid's craft was not enough? All might be in vain. Why then should I remain here and toil, and endure the bitter stares of the household, and hear the evil names they called me? Why tear my hands to shreds on the starwort plant, until even I started to believe I was crazy, why spend my days indoors longing for the forest? For deep in my heart I recognised this headlong flight to the river had been for nothing. They had not been here. They would not come, and leave, without a message for me, Ogham signs carved on a willow trunk, a pattern of stones on the river bank, or a white feather. If they had been here I would have heard the inner voices of Conor and of Finbar. *Sorcha, Sorcha, I am here*. It had been a long time. But I was their sister, and the seven of us were of one flesh and one spirit as surely as the seven streams of our childhood flowed and mingled in the great shining heart of the lake. They had not come. And it was a long time, such a long time, until midsummer.

'Do you want to go back so very much?' asked Red quietly, still intent on his work. 'Is it so hard for you here?'

I was surprised. He'd been silent for a long while. Another man would have told me what I should be feeling; that I should be glad Margery and her child had survived. Would have bid me cease weeping and dry my eyes. Another man would have told me to stop sitting on the frosty ground on midwinter's day and go back to the house at once. Would have told me to stop wasting his time. I had no reply to Red's questions. Of course I wanted to go home. My heart yearned for the forest, and my spirit longed to be close to my brothers, whether they could see me or no. But I was not stupid. Common sense told me that staying here was my best chance of finishing the task. I had a roof over my head, good food, and more protection than I wanted or needed. I had the tools of my trade, I even had a couple of people who might be called friends. And I had endured far worse than the sharp tongues and sideways glances of Lady Anne's women. So, the spirit said go. The mind said stay, for now. If your brothers do not come, next time, then go and find them. You would not get far in midwinter. Besides, he would follow you and bring you back. Always.

I got up rather stiffly, and limped down to the river's edge. There I knelt to cup clear water in my hands, first to drink and then to splash my face. As it settled I saw myself reflected on its surface, red-eyed, tear-stained and pallid with exhaustion. The water was freezing.

'I'll make you a promise,' said Red, and when I turned to look at him he had put away his work and was watching me. I wondered why I had thought his eyes were blue. Today they seemed to match the river water, a light, shifting colour between grey and green. 'I promise I will take you back, no matter what happens. I promise I will see you safe home when it's time. As soon as I learn the truth about my brother, I will take you there. I never break my promises, Jenny. I know it's hard for you to trust me. If ever I find the man who did this to you, who made you so frightened, I'll kill him with my bare hands. But you can trust me.'

I stared at him. How could he make such a speech in everyday tones, as if he were telling me how to build a haystack, or describing the best way to dig up a row of turnips? But there was something in his eyes, something hidden so deep that it would be easy to miss it, an intensity that told me he meant every word. I felt a shiver run down my spine. Something had changed; but I couldn't tell what. It was as if the world tilted, and nothing was quite as it had been. Or as if there were the very smallest turning in the pathway, just a tiny deviation, but to take it meant you would end up somewhere quite different. And it was already too late to go back.

My response came without thinking. I made a gesture that said, *I know. I believe you.* And when he held out his hand to help me up the bank, I took it without flinching, as I had done once before in a torrential downpour, when that hand had been my only grip on reality in a flight from death. I trusted him. He was a Briton, and I trusted him. Perhaps he really would keep me safe until I finished the shirts, and then – but that was the point at which my mind reached a blank wall. Red might be all kindness now, with his promises and his protection. But he was still waiting. Waiting for me to tell him Simon's story. Waiting for me to tell him how his brother was burned, and violated, and driven half crazy by my own people. How I had left Simon alone in the forest, alone with his demons, how I let him go out into the dark and

perish from cold and hunger and terror under the
great oaks. What price Lord Hugh's kindness, when
he had heard this tale? How easy would it be to keep
his promise, knowing what we had done to his young
brother? I had seen the strength in that implacable
mouth, the hardness in that uncompromising jaw. I
had seen how cold those eyes could be. And just once,
I had heard the passion in his voice, as the Fair Folk
teased him with their talk of Simon. He would set
little store by my safety, and that of my kin, when he
learned the truth.

So we made our way home, slowly, because I
found I was suddenly terribly tired, so tired my feet
would scarcely take me in a straight path.

'I could carry you,' offered Red. 'It worked quite
well last time.' But I shook my head at that. Trust
went just so far. He was a man, after all. 'Oh, well,' he
said as I walked grimly on, 'I expect you're too heavy
now, anyway. Amazing what a bit of good food can
do.' When I glanced at him I surprised the fleeting
hint of a smile on his face, just for a moment.

I almost made it all the way to the house. There
were people about, despite the cold; a gardener, well
wrapped in woollen hat and mittens, trimming a
hedge; a boy with a long stick of ash wood, herding a
difficult flock of geese. We went in quietly, avoiding
the main door, and managed to escape attention. Just
by the outer entrance to my garden, my legs gave
way from sheer exhaustion and to my extreme
annoyance he did have to carry me those last few
yards. When he opened the door to my chamber and
took me inside, Alys sprang forward, growling and
barking in a protective frenzy. Red deposited me
quickly on the bed and retreated to the doorway. The
small terrier stood her ground between us, her legs

planted square, growling with all the menace she could muster.

'All right, all right,' Red said mildly, brows raised. 'I know where I'm not wanted. I'll send you some help, Jenny. Make sure you sleep. It was a long night.' I looked up at him, thinking he too looked weary. It was easy to believe him tireless, since he seemed to rest little and be none the worse for wear. But that morning there was a pallor about him, a shadow behind the eyes that I had not noticed out there in the sun. I pointed to him, put my hands together, laid my head on them and closed my eyes briefly. *You – too – sleep*.

'There's the work of the day to be done,' he said, and he seemed taken aback at my suggestion. 'And I have a word or two to say to my mother. But –' and here he was overtaken by a huge yawn, 'perhaps you're right. In any event, rest well, Jenny.' He slipped away out the door, and Alys gave a sharp yap or two to see him off.

Shortly after, Megan came with warm water and a clean nightrobe. While I washed and changed, she fetched mulled wine and fine wheaten bread with currants in it. She stood over me until I finished the food and drink, and she took Alys out into the garden and brought her back. She told me Mistress Margery and little Johnny were both just fine, and I had done so well to save their lives, and she didn't know where I had learned such things. Then she tucked me in and left me and I slept till evening, and if I had any dreams, I had forgotten them before I woke.

By the festival of Imbolc, which the Christians call Candlemas, I had finished the fourth shirt. I kept them now in the wooden chest in my room, with dried herbs layered between. *Liam, Diarmid, Cormack,*

Conor. Now there was no starwort left. The sharp-eyed lady Anne had observed I no longer had my own work to do, and she found me a tedious piece of plain sewing to keep me occupied. I worked slowly, for my hands no longer had the fine control such tasks required, if indeed they ever possessed such skill. Putting stitches in human flesh, or easing a child into the world was one thing. Plying a needle so small you could hardly see it, making the tiniest even stitches was a quite different matter. Lady Anne watched, brows raised, as my frustration increased. When we were finished for the day, she drew me aside. I felt that, since the birth of Margery's child, she had cooled towards me still further. This was odd. Something was bothering her, I could see it from the way she watched me under her lids. And yet, I had done nothing to offend her. I almost thought she seemed in some way afraid of me. I could not think why.

'You're finding this hemming difficult,' she observed, picking up my work and dropping it again with a sigh. 'Yet this is a task I would entrust to an eight-year-old. Your education in matters domestic has clearly been quite limited. It seems you lack the skill for even such basic work. And yet, if you are to remain under our roof for so long, you must make yourself useful, Jenny. Perhaps I can find something rather simpler for you.'

It was an opportunity, of sorts. There was still one stem of starwort left in my basket, saved for such a purpose. I swallowed my annoyance and showed her what I wanted. *No, not your work. This. I must do this work. But I need more of the plant. I – go out – gather this plant. Cut – gather.*

Lady Anne's lips tightened. 'I can't help you.

There's no place for such – such deviance in my household. I have tolerated your self-imposed madness because I was given no choice. But I will not assist you to keep on with it. Enough is enough. If you wish for acceptance here, you must strive to be more like us, Jenny. If indeed you are capable of it.'

It did not seem to matter at all, that I had saved Margery's life, and the baby's. I turned to go. I had enough pride left not to beg. Besides, I could see it would be useless.

'And don't go running to Lord Hugh with your problems,' she said to my back, with an edge to her voice that suggested some other message, not put into words. 'He has more than enough to do, without bothering with such as you. Keeping you here is a burden to him.'

Nonetheless, there was nobody else to turn to. Red was busy, I could see that. There was ploughing to do, and preparation for seeding, and in addition, there were disputes to settle, the sorts of quarrels that arise when folk are cooped up too close in winter, and start to dwell on the small injustices of their lives. There was a system for dealing with this. Regularly, about ten days after full moon, a hearing would be held which they called the folkmoot. The aggrieved parties would come to the great hall of Harrowfield, and set out their arguments before Lord Hugh, and he would arbitrate between them.

The folkmoot was well attended by Lord Hugh's tenants, for it promised good entertainment as well as justice. There was the time one cottager's pigs had strayed onto a plot of grass reserved by his neighbour for a future planting of leeks and marrow. Made a right mess of it, they had, and if Ned Thatcher couldn't keep his pigs in, then they should be taken off him and turned into sausages, and he, One-Eyed Bill, would be the first to do it, the moment Ned let them get out again. Had a nice sharp knife ready, he did. Ned chipped in at this point to express a heartfelt wish that Bill would go back to Elvington where he came from, and take his lovely wife and his six children with him. If he didn't know pigs was pigs and had a mind of their own, he didn't know much. Besides, all his porkers had eaten was a few wild oats and an old lump of dried-up porridge Bill's wife had tipped over the wall, slattern that she was.

Red was diplomacy itself. He calmed the two parties with a few well chosen words about their undoubted talents and expertise in their own fields. He pointed out the advantages of a block of land turned over and fertilised in advance, so all you had to do, when the time was right, was pop in your seeds and wait. He then explained that in return for the use of the land for his pigs until planting time, Ned might expect a few fresh carrots, a basket or two of turnips and marrows later in the season. His wife could make an excellent soup from that, flavoured with a ham bone. Of course, the pigs must be off the property by the first warm day of spring. He would send out help to build a stronger wall. All parties retired satisfied.

There were more serious disputes. A fight over a woman, in which one man had received a serious head wound and another a broken arm. A wild brawl after the rapid consumption of a barrel of ale, which left two families shouting abuse whenever they passed. I noted Red's fairness and also his authority. He could be hard enough, when it was warranted. But not once did I see his decisions challenged. I thought, these people are lucky. This was what my brother Finbar wanted, this was what we needed at

Sevenwaters. But my father was caught up in the same bitter feud as Lord Richard. This cause gripped them, body and spirit, and it left no room for anything else. So our cottagers had gone hungry, and their walls had crumbled, and they had feared Lord Colum, not respected him. I wondered how they were faring now. My brothers had begun to take some steps to redress the balance. But my brothers were gone. There was only my father and the lady Oonagh.

I decided, eventually, to take matters into my own hands. Lady Anne had said I was a burden to Red. But I had not asked to be brought here. Nobody told him to set a guard outside my door every night, and keep me close to the house where he could see me. Nobody asked him to sit by me and wait while I wept and bring me safe home. Nobody bade him carry me when I was tired, and make sure I ate properly. Nobody but himself. Unless – well, there was that. *Make sure she is not hurt again. You have chosen well.* And yet, Red was so strong. Could he really be acting under a spell, some sort of command laid on him by the Fair Folk that night, to protect me until I completed my task? Could he bear such a burden without knowing it? The more I thought about this, the more I believed it to be so. It explained much. It explained the most difficult thing, why Red seemed to be prepared to wait for as long as it took, for me to tell him about his brother. He seemed in no hurry for this to occur. Men were not usually very good at waiting. Another man would have beaten the answer out of his prisoner the day he caught her. I had no doubt Lord Richard would have done so. I had seen my father try it. There was no other reason for Red to keep me here so long. I supposed I was a burden. I was still far from welcome. And it was only one step for the household's fear and distrust of me to spill over onto him. To destroy the harmony and trust that was at the core of this small community. Questions asked as to why he brought me here. Why he kept this evil influence in the heart of his land, putting his own people at risk. Probably it was only the love and respect they bore him that had curbed their tongues for so long. The lady Anne believed I had outstayed any welcome I might have had. It was only a matter of time before other voices began to say this out loud.

So, I decided I would not ask Red for help. One morning I took an empty sack and a sharp knife, and I waited until a widely yawning Ben left his guard post in my garden and wandered off to the kitchens in search of an early breakfast. Then I slipped away. The night before, I had told Margery I was unwell and might sleep late. My womanly courses had begun again, and this provided a good excuse for a short indisposition. I chose this day because I knew they were busy, the men, preparing fields for seeding on the far western hillside, some distance along the valley. They would be away all day, and nobody would be looking for me. With any luck I would be back before my absence was noticed.

I followed the line of the river upstream, taking hidden paths under the willows. I wore my home-spun gown and a grey cloak, and used my skills to stay unseen. It was a pity about Alys, who had a tendency to bark at squirrels and make busy rustling noises in the undergrowth. But I had not the heart to leave her behind, so keen was she to be included in the expedition, as doubtless she had been long years before with her young master. So I let her follow me, and slowed my pace to suit her short legs.

The further we went from the house, the more my spirits rose. It was a fine, clear day, with a touch of warmth in the air, not quite spring, but the first faint promise of it. Tattered banners of cloud stretched across the sky. I watched a kestrel hovering, intent of purpose, before her headlong dive to the kill. At length we climbed beyond the river banks and up a gully where a small stream rushed down to meet the greater flow. And finally, there on its margins under a rocky outcrop, I found what I was looking for. It grew in luxuriant swathes on either side of the water, choking out the smaller ferns and cresses. I rested briefly, and Alys flopped down in the shade, panting. Then I set to work.

My technique was well practised. I opened the sack on the ground to one side, and I cut sharply into the base of the plant, one, two and three, and the stems fell towards me. If I did it carefully, I did not hurt my hands too much, and the harvested starwort could be rolled into a neat bundle and carried on my back. I worked fast. The sun was high overhead, and it was a long way back to the house. I took as much as I could carry, enough for a whole shirt, maybe a little more. I should not have to come here again until well into summer. When I judged I had sufficient, I fastened the bundle with cord, and lifted it onto my shoulder. Before I reached home, the spines would work their way through the wrapping, and pierce my clothing and my skin. I was accustomed to this. Did I not carry one brother's life on my back? That was worth any pain.

We set out for home. I was happy, thinking of the four shirts lying ready in the wooden chest, and the fifth I would start on tomorrow. I was happy because I had the sun on my face, and I was out under the open sky, and because Alys was frisking ahead like a young pup. She disappeared under a stand of birches, and I bent to negotiate a step down between rocks.

There was a whirring sound over my head, and a thud, and then a terrible cry, a yelping, piercing sound of sheer terror. I ran forward under the leafless trees, my heart thumping. Not again, please, not again. The little dog was pressed up against the silver-grey bark of a birch trunk, and she was howling and jerking her head from side to side. She was trying to reach something, a flash of bright blue. I was there in an instant, dropping knife and bundle, kneeling by her as she screamed her fear and pain. Blue feathers. An arrow, which had pierced the flesh of her shoulder and pinned her to the tree. The point was lodged deep in the bark.

There was no time to think. With a man or woman, you could have said, keep still, I will help you. You could have explained what you would do. Even without words, you could have done that. With a dog, you just had to get on with it. I untied my bundle, looped the cord around her neck and tied it so it would not strangle her. As my hand passed before her mouth she snapped wildly and sank her teeth into my fingers. But once the cord was tied, I could hold it down with one foot and use it to keep her head to one side, more or less. Then the knife. I stretched for it. If only she would stop howling so. If she would just stop. My fingers clutched at the knife. There, I had it. And now, I must cut the arrow cleanly, close to the trunk, and then I must draw the shaft out from her flesh. I watched her carefully as I set to work. She was a very old dog. Perhaps the dreadful noise was a good sign. At least she had the strength to protest. I began to saw at the arrow shaft, blinking back tears, for with every wrenching movement I sent a wave of agony through her small body. It was an awkward task, and she strained her head around, eyes rolling, teeth snapping.

'Need some help?'

I froze. There was no mistaking the smooth, urbane voice of Red's uncle, Lord Richard. I did not turn, but I felt a chill of fear down my spine.

'Oh dear. That does look tricky. My apologies. It seems one of my huntsmen has a poor aim. He shall be disciplined.'

He walked into view, a picture in immaculate riding gear, gloved and booted in the finest of soft leather, his tunic and leggings a deep midnight blue. His expression, under the curls of faded gold, was a study in rueful apology, with a hint of amusement.

'Let me, my dear. Foolish old dog, isn't she? I always did tell the boy he'd be better off with a deerhound, or even a pointer. Come, my hands are more apt for this.'

I shook my head; I didn't want him anywhere near me, or Alys. But he moved close, very close, and suddenly he had an extremely sharp knife in his hand. I shrank away from him. He lifted his brows with a half-smile.

'Anyone would think you were frightened,' he observed as he severed the arrow shaft with one swift slice. Alys staggered a few steps, and I tightened my grip on the makeshift lead.

'What were you planning to do next?' he asked, stepping away. Ignoring him, I knelt and took hold of the arrow near the blue feathers on its tail. Placed my foot firmly on the rope again so Alys could hardly move. Pulled as hard as I could. The shaft slid clear with a horrible sucking sound and she gave a yelp of terror. It was over.

'Bravo,' said Lord Richard, who had seated himself on a nearby tree stump to watch. 'Now what?'

I shot him a glance of intense dislike. The wound was bleeding; not badly, but it was a long way home. I used my knife to slash the hem of my shift, tearing a strip right around, and then I bound up the wound as neatly as I could. Alys did not try to bite me now. She sat shivering, watching me with trusting eyes. Lord Richard had said his man had a poor aim. What mark was this arrow meant for, I wondered?

He sat there watching me, his bright blue eyes following my every move as I dressed her wound, and untied the rope, and did up my bundle again. I lifted it onto my back, and bent to pick the trembling Alys up in my arms.

'Mm,' he said. 'Very self-contained, aren't we? I'd offer to help, but I expect I'd get bitten. By one of you, at least.'

I could not gesture. I tried to let him know, with a jerk of my head and a scowl, that I wished he would leave me to make my way home alone.

'Oh, no, I don't think so,' he said softly, and I did not like the look in his eyes at all. 'I don't think my nephew would like that. Leave his little protégée all alone in the woods, with so much to carry? Oh no, that won't do. I shall at least escort you safely home. It will be well worth it, to see the look on Hugh's face.' He put two fingers in his mouth and gave a shrill whistle. Within a minute, silent men bearing bows appeared from four different directions. Their clothing was grey and green and brown, the colour of the woodlands.

'I'll go on foot with the young – lady,' said Lord

Richard, and again the pause between the last two words was exquisitely timed. 'Make your way to Harrowfield. Take the horses and go openly by road. Inform Lord Hugh, if you should happen to run into him, that there's been a slight accident to one of his household. Nothing to worry about. I will speak to the man who loosed this arrow later.'

They vanished to carry out his bidding, and I was left with no choice but to head for home in his company. He made no offer to take my bundle, though he eyed it with interest.

It's odd, how some things stay clear in the memory and others fade. I can still remember everything Richard said to me that day, on the long walk home. I can still hear every carefully chosen word, every nuance of his soft voice, every subtle change in the insinuating tone. I can feel the weight of the little dog in my arms, and the blood on my hands, and the spiky bundle of starwort on my back. I shiver to recall the touch of Lord Richard's creeping hands on my arms, or my shoulders, or round my waist as he made pretence of helping me over the rough ground. I loathed him. I despised him. But he was Red's uncle, and Lady Anne's brother. I might wish to spit in his slyly smiling face. But I tightened my mouth and looked straight ahead, and set my feet for home.

'I'm surprised my nephew let you out alone,' he observed as we came down the gully by the stream. 'I thought he would know how to protect his investment a little better than that. And what an investment you've proved to be, my dear. Amazing what a bit of good food can do for a girl's figure.' I glanced at him sharply, and intercepted a look that went up and down my body, up and down, as if imagining what lay beneath the demure, homespun gown. My insides went cold. 'You've filled out nicely, young woman. Very nicely indeed.' I tried not to listen, but there was no way to shut him out. We reached the place where the stream ran into the river.

'Hugh's a foolish man, to let you wander off on your own. Very foolish. Doesn't he realise you could be taken advantage of? Too trusting, our Hugh. That's his problem.' His arm snaked around my shoulders and I jerked away.

'Ah!' he murmured. 'She has a temper! So much the better. The lad must have got a lot more than he bargained for when he brought you back. Two-and-twenty, and still as full of ridiculous ideals as he was ten years ago. I fear for the boy. I really do. When will he grow up? Even young Simon had a better hold on reality. And yet – our Hugh is not really so very high-minded, is he? I saw that glint in his eye, when he showed you off to me. Probably thought all his wildest fancies had come true, when he found you. What man doesn't dream sometimes of having an untamed Irish woman, slippery as an eel and hot as hellfire under that milk white skin, with wicked green eyes and hair that tangles around her body like coils of black silk? An education for him, was it? I did hear he came home with some teeth marks on him. How did my nephew suit you, young Jenny? Perform up to your expectations, did he?'

I could not stop the rush of blood to my face, the shame and outrage his words caused me. Why, oh why had I come out alone? Why must I listen? And please, let none of it be true, what he said. Let it not be so.

'Oh, I see,' he said slowly, eyeing my blushing face closely. 'Still playing the innocent, are we? Or near enough. He's saving you up. But for what? I can't

383

imagine. Our boy may be pure as snow on the surface, but there's a red-blooded man below that cool exterior, my dear. He may not have had you yet, but he will, don't doubt it. Ask some of the village girls, they'll have plenty of tales for you. He'll have you all right. Especially now you have more flesh on your bones. Delicious flesh, if I may take the liberty. And I may. Oh, yes.' He laughed, and the trees seemed to shiver at the sound. Alys hid her face against my breast. My arms ached with her weight.

'A long way home, isn't it?' observed Lord Richard. 'Such a long way, for little feet. Why don't we sit down a while? Get to know one another? Put the dog down, dear. You'd like to get to know me a little better, wouldn't you?' His voice was like honey, like syrup, with a generous dash of nightshade thrown in. I wanted to kick him where it hurt most. If not for Alys, I would have done it, would have spat in his face. But I straightened my back, and held my head high, and walked on, trying to move the dog to a better position. *I am the daughter of the forest.* For such a small thing, she seemed very heavy.

Richard stalked a pace behind me, and now he changed his tune slightly. We came onto the path under the willows. The sun had passed its midpoint, and the light was golden on the bare branches. It was still a beautiful day.

'I suppose that *is* the only reason he brought you here,' he said as if musing to himself. 'I can't think of another. Can you?' He rubbed his well manicured hands together. 'You may think it strange that I am not more shocked. For he is to marry his cousin, you know. My own daughter. But a man has to sow his wild oats, even a buttoned-up idealist like Hugh must have his bit of fun. And it places him in a much better position, when at length he does marry. Gives him an edge, so to speak. How else can he train his new wife in the delicate, the delicious skills of the marriage bed? No, I think our Hugh will be quite well seasoned by summer. I can thank you for that, my dear, amongst others. And I may say, Elaine is ready for it. What a good thing you can't talk, poppet. It makes this whole episode just so much more – titillating. Don't you think?'

How could he speak thus of his own daughter? Had the man no shame? My ears burned to hear him, and I wished I could put Alys down and run. I clenched my teeth. *If my brothers were here, they would make you pay for speaking to me thus. They would show you what it is to be a real man.* And oh, I longed for them to be there.

'Now I wonder,' he went on, 'what other reason he might have, to keep you in his household so long. For it doesn't do him any good, you know, no good at all. Tongues are wagging. Powerful tongues. His mother hates it. I hate it. Stay here long enough, and you'll do him real damage. You know what they say? Want to hear?'

I wished I could not hear. Wished I were deaf as well as dumb.

'They're saying you cast a spell on him,' he said, chuckling. 'That you're a sorceress, and that you cast your net over their likely lad and drew him in, despite himself. Even his best friends are saying it. That he's bound to you, and can deny you nothing. And you a woman of Erin, kin to the folk that killed his own brother. What do you think of that, Jenny? But of course it's not really Jenny, is it? I wonder who chose such an unsuitable name for you. Really you're a Maeve, or a Colleen, or maybe a Deirdre. A wild Irish name. Jenny is no name for a little sorceress

385

from the west. You can cast your net over me any time, young Maeve. I have a few things I could teach you. You should try me some time. I might be helpful to you, you know. A person to turn to, if things ever get – rough.' Then he was taking me by both arms, and moving his face close to mine, so that I was forced to look into his. He had the family eyes, bright periwinkle blue like his sister's. Like Simon's. The tip of his tongue came out and ran over his lips, and I read the desire on his face.

My hands clenched involuntarily and Alys yelped. Then I stamped, hard, on Lord Richard's foot with the heel of my winter boot, and he let go with an oath. I could not run, but we were close to a little bridge that joined this path to the main cart-track, and I strode away as fast as I could, not looking over my shoulder. And then there was a sound of horses coming, and voices down the track and, as I emerged from under the willows, a group of riders came into view, moving at speed. They wheeled and halted, and then several things happened very quickly, with scarce a word spoken. Several men dismounted at once. A grim-faced Red gestured to the others. One took Alys from my arms, swearing mildly as she snapped at his fingers. The bundle was removed from my back and tossed up to Ben, who caught it, wincing. Then I found myself lifted like a sack of veg-etables and deposited on Red's horse, and he vaulted up behind me. I doubt if a man could have counted from one to ten, in the time this took.

'Uncle.' Red's voice was neutral. His hands, though, were so tight on the reins that his knuckles showed white. 'You did not let us know of this visit. I'm afraid we were unable to provide you with an appropriate – welcome.' It seemed he, too, was a master of the meaningful pause. 'Rest assured that such an oversight will never occur again.'

'Hm.' Richard was limping visibly. 'You're rattled, boy. Understandable enough. Thought you'd lost your little friend, didn't you? Dog had a slight mishap. Nothing serious. But you need to watch the girl. Let her wander too far, and you might find information gets to the wrong ears. Can't be too careful.'

'My men will find you a suitable mount,' said Red as if he hadn't heard a word. 'I will ride ahead and bid my mother prepare for your arrival. No doubt she will be pleased to see you.' At that he gave the horse a sharp kick and we were off at a brisk canter. I had no doubt the men would take their time in finding just the right horse for the visitor.

It was a fast ride home. Fast and uncomfortable. Red waited for nobody, urging the horse to a fierce gallop as we neared the poplar avenue. I would have fallen off but for the grip of his arm around my waist, holding me hard against him as he controlled the horse with his knees, his other hand tight on the reins. He rode straight up to the front steps of the house and dismounted immediately, lifting me down beside him. As was usual in this most well ordered of households, a groom appeared from nowhere to lead the horse away. I found myself marched indoors and straight upstairs to Margery's and John's quarters. Red knocked, opened the door and thrust me into the arms of an astonished Margery.

'Stay here,' he said. 'And don't move until I come back. That's an order.' Then I heard him striding back downstairs, calling for Lady Anne.

'What is it? What's happened? John? Is John all right?' A frown of worry appeared on Margery's tranquil brow. I nodded reassurance. John, I supposed, was still up in the west paddock, busy ploughing. Margery led me over to the fire, sat me down, put a cup of mead into my hand. I found I was shaking, and my feelings were so confused I could not rightly have explained them, even if I had words.

Johnny was in his cradle, but awake. I saw his tiny hands flailing in the air and heard his voice trying out small sounds one after another. She bent to pick him up, her hand cupped gently around his bald head. She laid him against her shoulder and sat down opposite me.

'Drink it,' she said. 'I don't know what's going on, but you're white as a sheet, and Red doesn't look much better. I suppose I'll find out soon enough.'

At that point the door slammed open and shut again, and Red took two strides across the room and lifted me out of my chair, his big hands tight on my shoulders. I had never heard him raise his voice since we came to Harrowfield. Now he was shouting.

'How dare you!' He shook me, hard. 'How dare you disobey me thus! You gave me your word! Does it take something like this to show you how stupid you are? What were you thinking of?'

Johnny began to wail, and Margery said to Red, rather severely, 'You're hurting her.'

Red swore, and let go, and turned his back, both hands on the mantel shelf. I touched the places where he had held me. I would have bruises again. I had never seen him so angry. Not even when he argued with his mother the night Johnny was born.

'Sorry,' he said under his breath. 'I'm sorry. But what on earth possessed you to go out alone like that? I thought I explained. I thought you knew the risks. By God, if – did he touch you? Did he hurt you?' He was pacing up and down now, looking back to examine my face, staring searchingly into my eyes.

Today, his own were the blue of shadows on deep ice. I shook my head. I would not cry. I would not think of what Lord Richard had said. *What other reason could he have for keeping you?* I would put it out of my mind. *They say you put a spell on him. He can deny you nothing.* I would forget it. It was nonsense. I would not cry. I blinked and sniffed, and a single treacherous tear escaped and rolled down my cheek. Practical as ever, Red fished around in his pocket and drew out a square of linen. As his hand came close to my face, I could not stop myself flinching back, and my arms came around my body defensively. Red looked as though I had struck him. He turned away, his hand momentarily shielding his eyes as if he did not want me to read his expression. It's true, I thought. I am a burden. I should never have come here. I have made trouble in this family, and created discord in a peaceful household. He should never have brought me here. And he knows it.

'*What did he say to you?*' Red had his back to me, and he spoke so quietly I could hardly hear him. The intensity of his tone scared me, and I could only look at the floor, or the wall, or anywhere but at him. This was one question I would never be able to answer.

'Will somebody please tell me what's going on here?' asked Margery mildly, looking from me to Red and back again. Johnny was quiet now, hiccuping gently against her shoulder. 'What did she do that was so terrible, Red? What could Jenny possibly do to make you manhandle her, and yell at her, and make her cry? I thought we were men and women here, not angry children. I hope you will never behave like this again in my house.' Red was staring at her. It seemed to me that there were lines around his mouth that had not been there before.

'I'm sorry, Margery,' he said bleakly. 'It was unfair of me. If there's any fault here, it's mine. But this is the only place that is safe for her, while my uncle is here. I don't have long; I must be downstairs when he arrives. Now, Jenny,' he said, turning towards me, and I could see he was still angry, very angry, but keeping his voice in check with a strong effort of will. 'I must know why you went off so far by yourself. I need to know why you broke your promise.'

My shoulders were aching. My feet were sore with walking, and my arms numb from carrying Alys for so long. My hand was bleeding where she had bitten me. His uncle was a beast; and right now, I didn't think much of the nephew either. I kept my hands quite still by my sides. Red clenched one fist and smashed it into his other hand, swearing under his breath.

'Damn it, Jenny, tell me!'

'I think I know,' Margery put in, glancing at me anxiously. 'Jenny has been asking for a new supply of the plant she uses, the one we call spindlebush, from which she fashions her weaving. She has exhausted the stocks she brought with her. I'm afraid I refused to help, hoping she would give up her dreadful task. But I know your strong will, Jenny. I suppose you set out in search of this bush yourself.'

Red's eyes narrowed. 'You were told to watch over her,' he said, and the chill in his voice turned Margery pale. 'She must have been gone since early morning. Why didn't you send after her? Why did I receive no message until Richard's men were sighted on the road?'

'I'm sorry,' Margery said. She did not tell him I had lied to her. It was probably the first time I had lied in my life.

'Great God, can I trust no-one?' Red was pacing up and down again.

390

I wished he would go away and leave me to my misery.

'Jenny, why didn't you ask me?' he said finally. 'I know where your plant grows, I know every corner of this valley. I can cut this herb for you any time you like, bring it to your door if that is your wish. There is no need for you to venture out beyond the safety of these walls. And you will not do it in future. You understand? You will not.'

I had to answer this as best I could. *You – cut the plant – no. No good. I. I cut, spin, weave, sew. Only I.*

'Then I will take you there,' he said, his voice back on a more even note again, though he held both hands clenched tight behind his back. 'Take you, and watch you cut the stems, and bring you home again. Don't go out again without me. Now I'm going downstairs. Margery, I want you to keep her here. You will both be excused from supper. My mother owes me a favour.' He made to leave, but turned back in the doorway. 'I've a man tending to the dog,' he said. 'One of my stablehands is skilled at these things. She will be well cared for.' With that he was gone.

'Well,' said Margery. She moved to lay the baby, now sleeping, back in his cradle, and to put a kettle on the fire. 'Stirred him up, didn't you?' And she said no more on the matter, but as the afternoon passed and we brewed peppermint tea, and I helped her wind wool and bake flat cakes on the fire, I often caught her eyes on me, shrewdly appraising, and I wondered what she was thinking.

This time Richard stayed longer than any of us wanted, except perhaps Lady Anne. His presence had a subtle but undeniable influence on the household.

Where servants would treat Red and his mother with a respect that showed itself in a wish to please, a service that was always more than mere duty required, the respect they showed Lord Richard was born out of fear. Not that he ever showed outright anger or put his dissatisfaction into plain words. It was, rather, something in his expression, his raised brow or sly half smile. It was in the way he would take a goblet from a serving girl, and touch her hand with his own in doing so. It was in his tone of voice as he gave a groom an order or dismissed one of his own men with an arrogant gesture. I thought he despised us all; believed himself somehow elevated above us. None was immune from his slighting references, his throw-away insults, not even the inner circle of this household. But, as I have said, he was a subtle man. He knew how to wound in a way that perhaps none but his victim could fully understand.

However, they were strong folk. When Richard quizzed Ben on his reluctance to join an expedition, on his firm wish to remain with Lord Hugh rather than test his skills in a real battle, Ben simply laughed it off. If he thought his manhood insulted, he gave no outward sign of it. Richard's weapon against John was more devious. More than once I heard him trying to provoke a response, trying to engage John in a debate about the management of the estate, and its custodians' responsibilities for the wider defence of the area. Hugh, said Lord Richard, was too intent on the future of his plantations, the purity of his stock, and the maintenance of his walls and fences. What of the western coast as a whole? What of his duty to his neighbours, and, more than that, to his mother? When was he going to do something about the people that killed young Simon? John was a taciturn man by nature. His habit was to get on with what had to be done, and speak only when necessary. He dealt with Richard as I would have expected, stating that he was Hugh's man and he had never had any cause to doubt Hugh's good judgement. Besides, it was the Danes that were the real threat, not the Irish. When Richard went a step further and began to ask how John felt about the security of his wife – such a sweet girl, with a bloom on her like a fine rose – and his newborn son, John simply got up and left the room.

Lady Anne, however, was Richard's sister. During the long days his uncle spent at Harrowfield, Red made more than one attempt to prevent them from speaking much alone together. But he could not do so entirely. He could not be in the house all the time, for the season was growing milder and the work of the estate was in full swing, ploughing, planting, early lambing. So, one afternoon, Lady Anne and her brother walked in the garden for some time, deep in earnest conversation, and I watched them from the window of the long room where I sat alone, and wondered what she was telling him. That night at supper I noticed Richard's gaze, narrow and penetrating, passing between myself and Red and back again, and I wondered how long it would be before the next time he found me alone.

At last, one evening at supper, Richard announced that he and his men would be leaving next day. The sighs of relief were almost audible. He had overstayed any welcome he might have had. The whole household was constantly on edge and I believed not one of us would be sorry to see him go. Even Lady Anne made no protest. However, she did express a wish that we assemble for a cup of hot punch later that evening, to bid him farewell, and this request appeared to include both Margery and myself. A number of imaginative excuses had been found for me on previous occasions, but this time there was no way out, and so, somewhat later, Lady Anne sat in the hall with her brother and her elder son, and I hovered in the shadows, trying to be inconspicuous. Red was seated by the window, his hands busy with knife and wood. John stood behind Margery's chair. A young maidservant had been despatched upstairs to sit with Johnny, but he was a good sleeper and she would have little to do. A map was spread on the long table and around it were two of Richard's men and Ben, disputing the accuracy of some territorial line. The tone was friendly enough.

'What's your opinion, young Benedict?' Richard tossed this remark over his shoulder, casually. He had, for all his off-hand manner, been listening carefully to their discussion. 'Think we can take that watch tower on the northern end of the bay before midsummer? Hold that, and you've got a strong enough footing, and safe landing for your men. That's been one of our problems; that and their tricky sailing. Never quite worked out how they do it. Come up on you out of nowhere, looming out of the mist in their cunning little boats. Never know when to be ready for them.'

'They say it's witchcraft.' This was one of Richard's men, speaking with diffidence. 'That each clan has a sorcerer, a magician, that can conjure up storms, and fogs, and winds, by invoking the power of the devil. They say whole troops of men have vanished in this way. Not that I believe it, of course. But there are stories.'

'Stories put about for the sole purpose of striking fear into your foe,' said Richard with some cynicism.

'A well tested ploy. The same trick as painting your body, or beating drums for the advance. Takes the enemy by surprise, makes him edgy, puts a fear into him. There's no witchcraft. A bit of luck, that's all it is, and a good knowledge of the local weather. These folk are no more magical than you or I.'

'Indeed,' said the other man. 'For there are Christian priests amongst them, who surely would not tolerate such goings on. Besides, who ever heard of hailstones as big as hen's eggs, or a fog you could drown in? Who ever heard of a storm come up out of nowhere, or rain from a clear sky?'

At that moment I looked at Red, and Red looked at me, and I remembered the touch of his hand through a blinding torrent of rain, the hard, warm grip of the only real thing in that violent, druidic downpour. That rain had saved both our lives. I read in his eyes that his thoughts were the same.

'These tales go back a long way,' mused Richard, stretching out his elegant legs towards the fire. 'It's a strange place, with odd people. The more I learn about them, the harder I find them to understand. One day, of course, it will all be ours, and the remnant of these wild folk will simply be lost, through death or decay or interbreeding. They have a limited capacity to resist, with their superstitions and their irrational faith. They fight with such ferocity, it seems they hold their own lives cheap. They have lost their precious islands. That anchorage is ours. I hope to take the next step with my summer campaign.'

'How soon do you plan to return there?' asked John politely.

'Soon enough,' said Richard. 'I hold my men in readiness at all times. I plan to take advantage of the first spell of good weather. So while you're out in the fields, Hugh, playing the peasant, you can think of me and mine as we keep the place safe for you. As we rid our shores of this scourge, so you can run your cattle in peace.'

'Oh, I will,' said Red. 'Rest assured, Uncle, you are never far from my thoughts.'

'Hmph.' Richard seemed to take this in the spirit in which it was intended. 'I'd be glad to persuade young Ben here to come along with me this time. Show him a bit of action. But if he won't, he won't.'

'You surely cannot plan to place an isolated garrison on the far shore, if you succeed in taking this piece of land,' put in John, clearly interested despite himself. 'That's asking for trouble. These local warlords, they have a knowledge of the terrain that far surpasses our own, and their forces are considerable. How could you man such a distant post? How would you supply it? The position would be extremely tenuous. What about the Norsemen? You'd be a sitting target. And what would be your intention in setting up there?'

Richard laughed. 'I suppose it seems small enough, in the scheme of things. My main advantage lies in the islands themselves; you are probably not aware of how great a force may lie concealed for a time there in safe harbour. In fact, I am perfectly positioned to provide support for an outpost on the far shore. That will prick their vanity, these petty lords with the unpronounceable names. That the enemy has a toe-hold on their sacred homeland, that will sting them. That will draw them out. Then we shall see.'

There was a brief silence.

'You cannot hope to establish yourself beyond the coast,' said Red bluntly. 'If you plan this, you underestimate your enemy.'

'*Our* enemy, boy, *our* enemy,' said Richard, rising to face his nephew who still sat at some distance, concentrating on his meticulous work with the little knife. 'No, I may have been called many things, but never a fool. I simply wish not to become complacent. It is the islands that matter. Who holds the islands, keeps his coastline secure. While I have them, I have a grip on my enemy's spirit. He believes them a source of magic, a fountain of power. While I possess them, he is weakened. But it is not enough to sit there and wait to be attacked. We must move first, show them our strength of will, show what stuff we are made of. And remember, I am not alone in this. I have the support of three of our closest neighbours, and a hundred of their best fighting men to prove it. Your own household, Hugh, is the only one in these parts that will not be represented on my expedition.' He threw a glance at Lady Anne. 'This shames me, boy. My own flesh and blood. But there is still time. Time to muster a small fighting force. They'll need to be assembled and ready in six days' time. I would welcome your support.'

Red was still working on his tiny piece of wood. He didn't bother looking up.

'You know my feelings on this issue, Uncle,' he said. 'I have no intention of letting good men throw away their lives for nothing. This feud is yours, not mine. Its origins are all but forgotten, so many years has it raged, so many lives has it wasted. Forgive me if I do not add my own, or those of my people.'

'Holding the islands is one thing,' said Ben, who was still poring over the map. 'But you cannot hope to move beyond here, and here – you see this great tract of forest, that stretches out its arms almost to the sea? We were there. That is the strangest of places;

deep, impenetrable, and fiercely defended. The terrain is steep and treacherous. There's a huge lake beyond these stands of trees, and a stronghold within. Nobody gets closer than a day's journey to that. It's bristling with armed men, and if they don't finish you off, hunger and cold and the sheer weirdness of the place soon will. If you wanted to make any impact, you'd have to go in much further north. Here, for instance.'

Richard's eyes narrowed. 'Spoken like a true campaigner,' he said. 'Sure you don't want to come along with me, boy? Seems like you might be an asset. Can't you spare the lad for a while, nephew?'

Red blew a little sawdust away, and put his work back in his pocket. He wiped the small knife on his tunic and stuck it back in his boot.

'I don't make Ben's decisions for him,' he said mildly.

'Well, boy?'

Ben laughed. 'Not me, thanks. I've work to do here. Besides, fighting these folk is like fighting a tribe of – of ghosts, or spirits. Not that we didn't make an impact once or twice. But – they have a habit of appearing and disappearing, and when they talk to you, it's all in riddles.'

'And what about the weather?' put in John. 'Fine one minute, pouring the next. You find yourself almost believing their tales of magic and sorcery, if you stay there long enough. I'm in no hurry to go back. Give me a flock of ewes and a pair of good shears any day.'

They were teasing him, I thought. But Richard was already off on another track, speaking as if to himself.

'Magic and sorcery. That reminds me.' He went to

stand by the hearth, warming his back, his arms stretched along the mantel. His shadow was long across the room, his body outlined by the flickering flames. 'You mention the lake, and the stronghold in the forest. I heard the strangest story from that quarter, a tale that could change the whole course of my campaign, if there were any truth in it. The lord of those parts is named Colum of Sevenwaters. Stories abound of his lake, and his forest, and his fortress; even more tales of the savagery of his fighting men, amongst whom were numbered his own sons. Those tales are true enough. As you are aware, it was in those parts that Simon was lost, and my own men butchered. I have wondered, often, if . . . but never mind that. Colum's forces are no barbarian rabble. They are strong, well disciplined and well armed, and they fight as if they had no care for tomorrow. As you said, young Ben, one would be a fool to mount an attack on such a man's primary defences. But, I am informed, things changed for Colum a year or two back. Just how, it's hard to tell; there are many versions of what happened. One day he was a man with six grown sons. The next day he had none.'

There was a short pause. If you knew anything about Richard, you knew that he would never tell a story simply to entertain. There must be a barb in it, a hidden message for somebody.

'What happened to them?' asked Lady Anne.

'Well, there were a few theories,' replied Richard. 'One was that they were on the lake shore, and a great water spirit blew up a freak storm that drew them in and drowned them. Another, that they were poisoned by an enemy, someone such as I, seeking to weaken their father's power; poisoned, and their bodies hidden somewhere in that vast expanse of forest. A third, that the boys went out mushrooming early one morning and were taken by the little people. They believe in the little people, in elves and faeries over there, you know. Odd, isn't it, how they can keep a Christian priest in their house, can say Mass of a Sunday, and still have a head full of superstition and fancy? Yes, it was an odd tale. If it's true, Colum will have less of the old fight left, less of the will to resist. Now could be a perfect time to strike.' He illustrated the last word with a sharp movement of his arm, fingers pointed. 'Oh, and I forgot,' he said, and now he was looking at me where I stood in the darkness by the wall.

'There was a daughter as well. Disappeared along with her brothers. Clean sweep. I heard their mother was looking for them. Or was it a stepmother? Sent scouts out everywhere. But no trace. Just vanished into thin air. Like Simon. Maybe the pixies took them all. It was around the same time, or so I'm told.'

This time the silence drew out longer. I shivered. I thought they must all be looking at me, seeing me for what I was and who I belonged to. Had this simply been a stab in the dark, a lucky guess? How could Richard possibly have stumbled onto the truth?

'That would be heartbreak indeed, to lose seven children at one stroke,' said Margery softly. 'A man might turn mad at such a blow.'

'I would not wish that on my worst enemy,' said Lady Anne. 'But it pains me to hear you make light of Simon's fate thus, Richard. I hope you will seek more news of him, when you return there. I cannot believe there was no trace of him at all. But that's what Hugh tells me.'

Richard's face transformed itself into a picture of brotherly solicitude.

'I will seek news, of course,' he said. 'I have an excellent network of informants, which serves me well even when I am far away from those parts. You'd be surprised what I hear. But I think you must realise, sister, that the chieftains of Erin are as brutal as their men. They do not value their prisoners highly once they have – served their purpose. And Simon was very young. I think, after such a long time, you should not expect too much. Now if, as you say, there were some sign, some clue . . .'

He was looking at me again, a half-smile curving his mouth.

'Perhaps I did not quite understand you, Uncle,' said Red quietly. 'Are you suggesting that if my brother were captured and subjected to some form of torture, he would have been unable to withstand it? I'm sorry to speak openly of this, Mother,' he added, 'but this is no time for playing games. Perhaps we might speak alone,' he said to his uncle.

'No need for that, my boy,' said Richard affably. 'We're all friends here, I trust. Apart from the little Jenny, maybe, who occupies such a unique position in your household that I can't for the life of me work out just what it is. And as she can't speak, we need not concern ourselves with what she hears, need we? You certainly don't seem to think so.'

'Simon may have been misguided,' put in John, 'but nobody could ever have accused him of lacking backbone. His strength of will was formidable in one so young.' That was true, I thought, remembering the desperation in those bluest of eyes, the hatred turned in on himself. He could not bear to believe himself a traitor. I was convinced that he was not one.

'He was only sixteen,' said Lady Anne. 'We know what stuff he was made of; I have only to look at you,

401

Hugh, to see him before me again. But he was just a boy, for all that courage and resolve. Perhaps this was more than anyone could take.' Her voice was tight with unshed tears.

'This is mere speculation, surely,' said Ben, a small frown appearing on his brow. 'Besides, no Irish lord worth his salt could afford to lose such a prisoner. What about the hostage price? And they'd have an idea who he was, whether he told them or not. It just doesn't make sense.'

Richard strode gracefully across the room. He took his time to speak, as if weighing his words with great care. 'The undeniable fact is,' he said at last, 'that all my men were slain. Each and every one. Except Simon. Now why would our enemy do that? Clearly, the boy was not preserved for who and what he was, for no ransom was ever demanded. Did he simply desert his mission in fear and vanish of his own accord? Hardly. Such a one does not blend readily into that race of black-locked, whey-faced fanatics. Besides, as you say, whatever his failings, the lad had more than his fair share of courage. And so it is far from speculation to suggest that they forced it out of him, the information that would betray his companions, and lead the enemy down on them by night. But we must not blame him. As you said, sister, he was barely sixteen years old. He wanted to be a man. But when it came to the point, the fibre was too weak.'

I found, suddenly, that I was extremely angry, and before I could stop myself I made a gesture with my hands that said clearly, *No. You speak lies*. And suddenly, every pair of eyes in the room was turned sharply on me.

'I would dearly love to hear you speak, little wild girl,' said Richard, and although his tone was soft, his

402

stare was as hard as cold iron. 'Where do you come from? What could you tell us? And why do you suddenly look so fierce, like a mother wolf defending its young? You know something of this, I am certain of it. So convenient, to be without words. I wonder what your people would give, to have you safe home again.'

There was a short silence. I looked him straight in the eye. *I am not afraid of you. I am not afraid.*

'She's a good girl,' said Margery unexpectedly. 'She comes here with no ill purpose, my lord, of that I am sure.'

'Not only that,' said Ben with a crooked grin. 'She wouldn't have come at all if we'd given her a choice in the matter. Very averse to sea travel, is Jenny. She's here by accident as much as anything.'

'Besides,' said John, 'if you are suggesting some noble family would pay a ransom for her return, you are certainly wrong. This is a child who has fended for herself for some time, I am convinced. She has no family but this one to turn to.'

'Child?' Richard seemed like a hunting creature waiting to pounce. 'The girl is of marriageable years, and comely enough in her wild, unkempt way. What future has she here, if what you say is true?'

'My brother and I had an idea, Hugh.' This was Lady Anne, and I sensed this part of the conversation, at least, had been well prepared. 'He – we thought, since we are lacking in suitable company for her here, that Jenny might go to stay at Northwoods for a while. Richard is headed back there in the morning, and sees no difficulty in her joining his party. Elaine has several young companions, and has said she would welcome another. This would please me, Hugh.'

'Out of the question.' Red's response was immediate and abrupt.

'Not so fast,' said Richard, his eyes narrowing. 'There's Elaine to think of as well, boy. Your betrothed. Don't forget, I'll be away from home again soon, and my daughter asks this as a special favour from you. It's lonely for her up there with her father gone. She'd welcome the novelty.'

My heart quailed. I had little doubt of the true purpose of this request. It was not companionship for his daughter that he wanted. It was the information I could give him. And I sensed his interest in Simon's fate was not simply that of a solicitous uncle. No, there was something more to this, I was becoming sure of it. Red had been right to suspect his uncle's motives. Richard needed to know what I knew, and whether I would tell it to others. And he would be adept at making me talk.

'This could be a good idea, Hugh,' said his mother carefully. 'You cannot be unaware that Jenny's presence here has brought some – unrest – to the household and to the folk of the estate. Since Elaine has been so kind as to extend an invitation, surely it could do no harm to send Jenny to Northwoods for a while. It would relieve the pressure here greatly. Perhaps you have closed your ears to what people are saying about her and about – about your motives in keeping her here. It is a delicate matter. But this would be a wise decision, I think.'

Red's mouth tightened. I thought, how little they know him, his own family. Even I understand him better. He cannot be pushed like this.

'It is my household, and my decision,' he said. 'If Elaine is seeking companionship, let her visit us at Harrowfield. For her, there is always a welcome here.

But the other – I will not consider it. And now, this conversation is finished.' He walked over to Lady Anne and kissed her on the cheek. 'Good night, mother.' He looked at Richard, who was leaning on the mantel again, his eyes hooded by their lids, the quirk of his mouth mischievous, dangerous. 'You'll be making an early start tomorrow, I've no doubt,' said Red. 'We'll provide an escort as far as the bridge.'

Richard lifted his brows. 'Seeing me off? Thank you so much. I'll be sure and let Elaine know you'd like her to pay you a call. Let her see for herself how things are here. Of course, she must take charge of Northwoods in my absence. But I can spare her for a few days. For naturally the wedding will be held here. This will give her a good opportunity to plan the festivities. May Day, Anne and I thought, would be most appropriate. No need to wait until midsummer. This time my campaign will be swift and deadly. I'll be back before you have time to miss me.'

CHAPTER TEN

T hen followed what I looked back on later as the last good time at Harrowfield. Richard was gone, and spring burst on the valley as if celebrating his departure. My little garden bloomed with brave crocus and tiny pale daffodils and fragrant herbs. The sun warmed the stone walls and the old terrier stretched her stiff limbs and ventured out to explore under the blossoming lilacs. I took to rising early and walking forth while the air was crisp and the day new. This way, I could almost imagine I was back home at Sevenwaters, and that everything was all right again. Almost. As often as not, I would walk to the orchard with its lichen-covered walls to find Red already there, cloak over his shoulders against the cold, ink pot on the bench beside him, quill gripped somewhat awkwardly in his large hand. Sometimes I would sit there for a while, and he would give me a grave nod of acknowledgment, and go on with his work.

It was clear to me that what he made with such care was some kind of record of the estate, where purchases and profits were marked down methodically year by year. And yet, I could see it was more, for I glimpsed intricate diagrams that seemed to show the layers beneath the soil, and the different roots of plants, and the way the rain fell and nourished them; and here and there a tiny representation of tree or leaf or flower, done with a delicate control. This was the man whose uncle chided him for playing peasants; whose hands were so big mine were swallowed up by them. I liked sitting there quietly with my back against the smooth stones of the wall, watching him work. It came to me how much easier such a task would be if he knew how to write. I began to realise what a rare gift we had been given, I and my brothers, when Father Brien chose to share his skill with us. For it had become plain that there were none at Harrowfield, save the household scribe, with the ability to set down letters and to decipher them. And the scribe himself seemed to struggle when asked to make out a message of any complexity. Had matters been different, I could have offered to help. That would have raised a few eyebrows.

Some mornings I felt the need to keep moving, and Red would put away his quill and ink, and walk with me up through the fledgling oak forest to the hilltop from which he had first shown me the broad acres of his estate. From river to skyline, from road's end to far horizon, the valley was clothed in its first brave green. They were good times, quiet peaceful times. There was no need for words between us. Slowly, the poison of Richard's tongue slipped away from my mind, and I began to trust again.

Elaine came, and her behaviour was as impeccable as her elegant, plain gowns and her glossy, smoothly-braided hair. She was courteous to Lady Anne, but nonetheless made it clear that she had her own opinions and her own intentions once she became mistress of Harrowfield. She was charming to Margery and brought a toy for the baby, a little creature carved from bone on which he could chew, for Johnny was cutting his first tooth. I could tell she was deeply curious about my role in the household but, unlike her father, she tempered this with a natural reticence and what I believed to be a strong sense of what was right. She sat with Margery and me in the mornings to sew, and watched me working without apparent judgement.

Afterwards, she inspected my hands, first asking if I had any objection.

'You know that some folk call you mad, or touched in the wits,' she said, and her big blue eyes looked directly into mine. 'I don't think I can believe that. I suppose there is a purpose, a very strong purpose, in what you do.' She looked at the shirt sleeve I was weaving, and the basket of thorny fibres. 'How long?' she asked. 'How many?' She was the first person to ask me this so directly. I placed my fingers over my lips, then swept both hands down and outwards. *I cannot say. I must not speak of this.*

'Yes, Red told me,' said Elaine gravely. I thought, her use of this name makes her one of that inner circle, one of those few that he trusts. Why did this surprise me so much? After all, they were to be wed soon enough.

'But this work does not go on forever, does it? It has some end, some goal? Perhaps you can tell me that much.' She was as insistent as her father, in her quiet way. To shake my head could have led to misunderstanding. Besides, I needed no reminder of the words of the Forest Lady. She had made it quite clear that not a word of my story, not a single part of it might be told, if I wished to free my brothers from the spell. Not in speech, or sounds, or pictures. Not in embroidery, or song, or gestures. No matter how kindly the manner of asking. And so I turned away, and would not answer Elaine's questions.

She stayed only a few days. She did spend a lot of time with Red, walking up and down the garden, talking gravely. It seemed Elaine hated to be idle; during the mornings she managed to plan the entire wedding with Lady Anne while completing the neat hemming of a fine lawn veil without apparent effort. I heard her agreeing to May Day with no visible enthusiasm, making decisions rapidly and without a great deal of interest as to which guests should be invited, and what she would wear, and whether six courses or seven made a more appropriate feast. She dealt with it all as if she were transacting the sale of a flock of sheep, or negotiating repairs to a barn, as a piece of necessary business to be done as efficiently as possible. The ceremony itself seemed unimportant to her. This seemed a little sad to me. I thought, she is marrying a good man. She could scarce hope for a better. Perhaps she really does care. But it is the way of these Britons, to lock the passions deep inside where nobody can see. On the surface, calm and controlled. Beneath, who knew what?

On the few occasions when I happened to see Red and Elaine together, walking towards the river or across the grass deep in conversation, I saw little relaxing of that control. His manner was polite, hers earnest. They did not hold hands, or link arms, or touch one another as I had seen my brother Liam do with his Eilis. And as, the goddess forbid, I had seen my father do with Lady Oonagh. I found myself watching them too much, and went back to my work, feeling vaguely unsettled. Outsider as I was in this household, I wanted Red to be happy. After all, I reasoned, the wellbeing of this whole small community depended on him. I was uneasy for him, and for her, sensing that something was wrong. There came a day when she spent the whole morning with Red in the gardens, sitting on a bench under the lilacs, walking around and around the hedges. She was talking and talking, moving her hands from time to time to emphasise a point. He was saying little. And then, in the afternoon, she packed up and left. Some of her household remained behind, because of the wedding. A cook, a groom or two. Compliments of Richard of Northwoods.

Had they quarrelled? Apparently not. Red was uncommunicative, but that was nothing unusual. He was by nature a man of few words. Preparations for the wedding continued. The work of the estate was in full swing, and practice with sword and bow was put aside for more productive activities. The men were away from the house for most of the day, leaving us to our handiwork and to gossip. Not that there was much of that; Lady Anne was quite strict about idle tongues and what they might lead to. Nonetheless, I heard a few things I'd rather not have. For instance, that I was a sorceress who had put a spell on Lord Hugh so that he had to keep me in his household, and that when Elaine asked him to send me away and he refused her, she went off in a huff. Said she wouldn't wed him until that barbarian from across the water was despatched back where she came from. This upset me, though I was disinclined to believe it, for I had seen no ill will in Elaine's manner towards me.

Besides, her feelings were always so well in check I could hardly imagine her being angry with Red or anyone else. As for the spell, I'd heard that one before. If anyone had put a spell on Lord Hugh, it wasn't me. And he had his own reasons for keeping me here, as I had mine for staying. The fifth shirt was well on the way and at last I let myself believe that there might soon be an end to this part of my story.

There was another thing being said, and this I liked even less. This was that the evil enchantment they spoke of was in the work I did, the twisted, tortuous spinning and weaving of spindlebush (for so they called it). It was through this strange activity that I spread my influence over the household, and in particular, over Hugh. They could see it was shirts I was making. I had thought them a people with no tales, but once they came on this idea, it seemed every waiting woman, every cottager had some old story of a garment with evil powers, that burned or poisoned or drove its wearer mad. The idea spread frighteningly fast and after a while people did not bother to lower their voices to a hush, for it seemed they no longer cared if I heard what they said about me. My friends in the household tried to protect me from it, but this became impossible.

Then small wrong things began to happen. I slipped and muddied my gown when out walking. Lady Anne gave it to a servant for cleaning, but there was a mishap, and the gown was returned to me strangely stained. Unwearable. But it was the only one I had. So I wore it until Lady Anne, frowning, found me another, even plainer and more shapeless than the last. I wore that, and held my head high. Then Alys went missing. This drove me frantic, for it put me in mind of the lady Oonagh, and the strange cruel tricks

411

she had played on our household at Sevenwaters, and I spent the best part of a day hunting everywhere and trying not to let my panic show. My mind dwelt on my faithful Linn, who had died in the forest trying to protect me, and when I thought of her I was overwhelmed by images of that terrible day when I had carried her body home through the forest and had waited, weeping and bleeding, for my brothers' return. I schooled my face to calm as best I could, and searched methodically in the house, in the stables, in the barn, under hedges, in the orchard. I felt quite alone that day, for Lady Anne kept Margery indoors and the men were busy about the farm. I might have asked Megan to help me search, for she was still friendly enough, but she was minding Johnny and could not be called.

By late afternoon I was becoming resigned to the fact that I would not find Alys; that something ill had happened to her. I resolved to wait in my garden, and to ask Ben or John for advice when they came home. But it seemed there was no need for this, for as I rounded the corner by the kitchen door, there she was, sitting on the stone steps outside my room with an expectant look, apparently none the worse for wear. I let my breath out in a sigh of relief and exasperation. Where had she been hiding all this time? How dare she worry me so about nothing, the rascal? I wasn't sure if I wanted to laugh or cry.

It was only as I came close that I realised all was not as well, or as simple as I had thought. For Alys bared her teeth and growled at me. This was common enough behaviour; she was famous in the household for her bad temper, one of the privileges of great age. But she never directed it at me. I stood a few paces away, not to alarm her, and studied her carefully. She looked all right. Maybe she had simply been frightened. Whatever was bothering her, it needed careful handling. I crouched down and edged closer. She growled again, drawing back her lip. She was trembling, great shivers coursing through her small body. Terrified. Try as I might, she would let me no closer.

Eventually I retreated to the kitchens for a scrap of lardy cake. Terriers are good eaters and find it hard to resist a treat. Slowly, very slowly, I came closer to her, until I was only a few paces away. Then I sat on the ground, with the cake next to me, and stared into the distance. The growls gradually subsided. After a while she crept over; and I heard the sound of furtive munching. It was safe to look at her again.

She had not been hurt. Simply held captive, and frightened. Perhaps, to discover who had done it, I might look for hands with bite marks. For what they had done had disturbed her greatly. I could see now that in the long wiry hair on her back was shaven a crude but unmistakable sign. It was a symbol I had seen chalked above doors to ward off witches. A sign I had seen made with the fingers, against the works of the devil. A message for me. Sorceress, be gone. For now, they had stopped short of hurting her, perhaps mindful of whose dog she had been.

Perhaps it had only been children. A prank. Maybe it was of little importance. So I said nothing of it at supper, trying to act as if all was well, for I did not wish to add fuel to any rumours. But as Conor had told me more than once, I was not very good at hiding what I felt. Not like some. Margery asked if I was all right, and I nodded, and Ben said I looked tired, and I smiled. John tried to make me eat; they were always trying to make me eat, but my body was long used to denial, and accepted only small quantities of the

413

plainest fare. A little bread, some fruit, a bowl of barley broth. Occasionally cheese. They thought I starved myself, but I did well enough. Besides, it concentrated the mind better, going without. I remember Father Brien saying that once.

Looking up and down the table, and around the members of the household as they ate and drank and chattered amongst themselves, I wondered how many of them really thought me a threat. For they were, for the most part, good folk, hard-working, honest people who valued their simple, orderly life. Red provided well for them, they lived safe and secure, and in return they gave their labour and their loyalty. My presence there was like a small but constant disturbance in a still pond; the ripples spread and spread and upset the balance of things. Someone had cared enough about this to act against me. So far, only small things; but there was a deep unease in me, for small things could lead to larger ones, I had seen this all too well when Lady Oonagh came to Sevenwaters. And I was so close to the end of my task, closer all the time. *Liam, Diarmid, Cormack, Conor.* Finbar, whose starwort shirt was growing fast, for I was working long and hard, shrugging off the pain. Soon there would be but one shirt to make, and then the spell would be broken, and I would go home. As long as I could finish the task. Briefly, I thought of going to Lady Anne, telling her what had happened to the dog, for I knew she would stamp hard on such mischievous behaviour in her household, whatever she might think of me. But telling her was to add fuel to the argument for me to be sent to Northwoods, and that prospect struck a deep fear into me. There was something evil about Red's uncle, a menace in his eyes and in his clever words that turned me cold in his presence. Sooner than go to his home, I would leave this place on my own, I would fend for myself again. I decided not to tell anyone about what had been done to Alys. Pretend I did not care. After all, what could anyone do about it?

I reckoned without Red. That was a mistake. That evening I was sewing in my room by lamplight, and there was a knock on the outer door. I could not call out 'Who's there?' and after everything, I would not open it blindly. Then I heard his voice.

'Open the door, Jenny.'

I went to the door with my work in my hands, and slipped the bolt. What was he doing there anyway? It was supposed to be Ben's night on guard duty.

'Come out,' said Red. 'I want to see your face.' For I had my back to the lamp. Leaving the door open, I stepped out into the garden, where the moon spread a soft, cool light over the blue-grey foliage of lavender and wormwood.

'Now look at me,' he said. 'Look at me properly.'

I met his gaze, thinking he seemed tired; they had been long days in the fields, but the grooves around nose and mouth showed something more than the good weariness of the body after labour, and he looked thinner.

'All right,' he said. 'Now tell me what's wrong.'

I knew him well enough by now to be aware I had no choice but to tell him. As he said, he did not play games. So I showed him *dog – go away*. *Me, looking, searching – worried*. I used my hand to show the passage of sun across sky, *all day*. Then I had to take his sleeve, and lead him indoors, where Alys had reclaimed her spot on the pallet and was nearly asleep, curled in blankets. She growled deeply as we came close, and the shivering started again.

Red looked at the mark on her back and said nothing; but the lines on his face were very clear in the lamplight, and his lips tightened. We went back outside, and he gestured to me to sit on the doorstep, while he leaned his long frame against the wall beside me. We were silent for a while.

'You weren't going to tell me about this,' he observed eventually. 'Why not?'

I shrugged. *Why would I tell you? What could you do?*

Red was frowning as he watched me. He did not speak for a while; by moonlight his eyes looked the clear, pale colour of our first meeting, morning blue, and there were memories in their depths.

'I want to ask you something,' he said at length, and now he was studying his hands as if unwilling to meet my gaze. 'That night – that time in the caves, before we came across the water. It was a strange time. I have wondered – I have thought, perhaps, that I ran a fever that night from damaging my leg. And yet, the memories are –' he broke off, scuffing his boot in the soil, failing miserably to say what he wanted. I could have found the words for him, had I not been schooled to silence. After a while, glancing at me quickly and looking away, he tried again.

'I wake at night sometimes,' he said, 'from a dream so vivid it seems *that* dark world is real, and this one a fantasy. Of late, this has happened many times. It disturbs me, to feel I have so little control of my own mind. Have you ever felt this?' I shook my head. The Fair Folk played with your thoughts, there was no doubt of that. What about that man from our village, Fergal, who lost his wits altogether, after they took him and teased him and spat him out again? But they had never taken over my mind, though I had come close to losing it to my own fears. I signed to Red. *Speak. Tell me the rest.*

'That night –' he said hesitantly. 'That was the most vivid of all. And afterwards, I thought for a moment – but no, that could not be. I suppose those images were the product of a fever, a sickness brought on by shock and exhaustion. I am not usually so weak. But at the time, I thought – tell me, is it possible you shared something of this dream? Is it possible you know what – what was said to me? There was a candle, I still have it. But how could there be a candle? And why do I still hear their voices in my sleep? Am I losing my mind? I have heard that rumoured, amongst other things. Yet I feel saner than ever before in my life.' He sighed. 'Sorry, Jenny. But who else could I speak to of such things? Who else would listen, and not call me a fool?'

That made me smile. Who else but a crazy girl, to understand crazy thoughts? I wondered if I would be able to explain it to him. My hands moved, and he spoke quietly as he tried to interpret my gestures. Two hands, each lightly cupped, separate, one weighed against the other, like the halves of a sea shell.

'Two things. Two worlds?'

I nodded. Brought the hands together. Showed above, below.

'Two worlds, one above, one beneath? One mirrors the other. Two worlds that join, and touch? Then where do you belong? Are you, too, some creature of this other world, the realm of dreams and fantasies? Will you vanish one day, as they did that night, leaving me in the dark?'

I shook my head. Pointed to myself, then to the hand still held higher, cupped downwards. *I am of this world.* Gestured again. *Like you.* The next part was harder. I tried to show that there was a link, a bond between one world and the other. But careful; there were some things I might not tell, even in signs. Red nodded slowly.

'I heard their voices,' he said. 'I understood them, though I could not tell in what tongue they spoke. Who were they, Jenny? And how did they understand you, how could they hear you when you have no voice?'

I showed the lower world again. Two. Two people, very tall. I drew a circle around my head, tried to indicate a crown. This was the nearest I could get to what I was trying to tell him.

'A king and queen of that other realm?' I nodded. It was close enough. I must be getting better at signs, or he at understanding. Then I tried to answer the next question. *Mouth, words – no. Mind, thoughts – ear, hearing. Hearing with no words.*

'Then why can't I hear you?'

I looked at him soberly, then I pointed to him and swept my hand around me, showing the place where he belonged. The place which belonged to him. *You're a Briton.* I gave a shrug. *What do you expect?*

I think I offended him. The mouth tightened just a bit further, if that were possible, and the eyes became a little chillier. Whatever answer he had wanted from me, it was not that one. It was a while before he spoke again. 'If I believe this,' he said, 'everything changes. Everything.' He moved to sit on the bottom step, his back to me, staring at his linked hands. I had to move so that he could see what I was trying to say.

No. It need not. You, here; all around you. Your trees; your people. Everything right. I – go away. Far away, across the water. Gone home. You – forget.

He just looked at me.

'Nothing's that simple,' he said, 'you know it as

418

well as I. How could I forget? I told you, their voices are in my dreams, that world is close, it is part of me, whether I wish it or no. Whether I believe it or no. And you are here.'

I – go away. I pointed to him, crossed my hands over my heart. *You promised. I – over the sea, go home.*

'I haven't forgotten,' said Red softly. 'I don't forget, and I will keep this promise, and any other I make. Tell me about my brother, and I will see you return home safely. Whatever it costs me. But – things will never go back to the way they were before. They cannot. That's the one thing that becomes more certain every day.'

His words disturbed me. I knew already that my being here at Harrowfield had disrupted a household hitherto orderly and content. I regretted that, and wished I could change it. More than that, it disquieted me when I heard the folk speak of sorcery and enchantments that had ensnared their lord. For I supposed they felt much as I did when I watched the lady Oonagh come to Sevenwaters, and cast her net over my father. Only here, I was the witch. But I was driven by the need to complete the task, and to save my brothers. Nothing mattered as much as that did. And to do it, I must remain here under Red's protection. I had thought that when it was over, I would go, and the calm pool would settle again as if I had never been there to ruffle its tranquillity. I had never thought about how Red might feel. Perhaps that was because it was too hard to imagine telling him about his brother, as one day I must if he were ever to let me go.

I moved around to kneel in front of him, so that he had to look at me. Showed him a mirror of his own face. *You – tired. You – sad, worried.* This provoked a sort of mirthless grimace. He did not like the talk to turn to his own feelings.

'Somewhat lacking in sleep, yes. It happens when you wake at night with demons whispering in your ear. But how could you know how that feels?' He threw this remark away, but stopped short when he saw my face change. For a moment, my own particular night demons came back to me and I must have turned suddenly white.

'I'm sorry,' he said in a different voice, so different it might have been another man's. 'I'm sorry. What did I say?' His hand came out, very gently, towards my cheek; but I moved back a little, just out of reach. I shook my head, moved a hand across dismissively. *Nothing. It's nothing.*

'You're still afraid of me,' he said very softly. 'Can't you see that I would never hurt you?'

But you have, I thought. With your hands, and with your words. I crossed my arms over my chest, my hands touching the places where he had bruised me before. When he was so angry, angrier than I had ever seen him.

And then he said, 'I wish you would talk to me.' His voice had gone even quieter, as it did sometimes when he was keeping a tight control. Somehow I had upset him. No doubt you do wish that, I thought. As soon as I talk, you can get rid of me, and get on with your life. One less thing to worry about. Back to normal, whatever you may think now. For you will forget, as men do.

'I want to hear your voice,' he said. 'I want – but what does that matter?' It was as if he took a grip on his words, and channelled them back where he thought they should be. Back onto safe ground. Control. Say not what you feel, but only what must be said. I imagined he would regret, later, speaking so freely tonight. 'Your safety, that's of concern,' he said.

It was Lord Hugh of Harrowfield talking now. 'I can do more, I think. First, I'll speak to my mother. She would frown on such tricks, and can seek out the culprit and ensure there is no repetition. In the longer term – there may be a solution. One course of action is obvious to me, but it would not be to your taste.'

What? What solution? Now he was worrying me. He would not send me to Northwoods? Would he?

'It may not be necessary,' said Red, getting up. 'Let us simply be on our guard. If there's a need to do more, we will. But my uncle is away, and I know of no other who might be a serious threat to you.' He looked at me questioningly. I shrugged. It was too frightening to think the lady Oonagh might search me out, even at Harrowfield. I refused to believe it. 'For now, you should be safe in my house. If I cannot promise this, I am not much of a protector.'

My hands moved quickly. *Don't. Don't swear what you cannot be sure of. Don't make a promise you cannot keep.* I don't know if he understood.

'It's getting cold,' he said. 'You'd better go in. Bolt your door, get some sleep. I'll keep watch tonight.'

It seemed I was dismissed. I got up, went in, reached back to pull the door to.

'Jenny,' he said. He stood at the foot of the steps, and such was the difference in our heights that he looked me straight in the eye. I raised my brows in question.

'Talk to me next time. Tell me right away. Don't keep it to yourself. However small, however trivial, you must tell me.' He might have appeared to dismiss the threat to my safety, but underneath he was worried. Deeply worried.

I gave a nod, and closed the door. But, as it happened, there was no need to tell him, next time. For next time, it was no child's trick, no mischievous prank that my unknown enemy played on me. It was something far worse, and it led to a tragic turn of events that woke a deep terror of the spirit, that brought the force of evil down on the tranquil valley and scarred the household of Harrowfield. And it was I who caused it.

It happened in two stages. The first was hard to bear, for me at least; but it paled in comparison with the second. The first was trickery, cruel trickery. The second was murder.

Spring was advancing, and suddenly May Day was close, and the wedding a reality. Activity hummed around me in the long room, women sewing fine fabrics and chattering of dancing and feasting and of certain other aspects of the impending marriage that I would sooner not have heard discussed. I tried to block out their talk. I wove and sewed my starwort, and fashioned Finbar's shirt. As I worked I imagined my brother perched on the roof slates at Sevenwaters, with the west wind tangling his dark locks, and his clear eyes full of dreams. I pictured the two of us running through the forest on a bright spring day, and Finbar waiting for me to catch up. Then, sitting by him in the fork of an oak, listening in silence as the forest breathed around us. I thought of Finbar as I had last seen him, after he had given me so much of his strength that there was none left over for himself. I sewed my love for my brother into his shirt with every painful stitch. I worked hard, and the shirt grew quickly.

I tried not to hear the women whispering over their work, as they did when Lady Anne was absent.

But I could not shut them out entirely. So I heard a lot of opinions about Lord Hugh, including how all the village girls made cow's eyes at him – him being such a big strong man, and bonny with it – and all in proportion, if you knew what she meant. Besides, you knew what they said about redheads. A shame, really, that he didn't – you know, that he kept himself to himself the way he did. There was talk, at least she had a friend of a friend who had a cousin who'd once – and she said, any girl that spent a night with him would soon know how lucky she was. Once you'd lain with such a man, you'd never want to look at another.

'Hung like an ox, gentle as a lamb,' chuckled one of the older women. 'Every girl's dream. His brother was the same, even at sixteen. Poor lad.'

There were a few sharp glances in my direction, and whispers with them.

'Her?' scoffed one of them. 'Hardly. Why would he look at her, when he could have Elaine? When he could have any girl he wanted for the asking?'

'Who'd want one of *them,* anyway?' said another. 'Besides, she's such a scrawny, washed-out little thing, like a child almost. Nothing a man could get hold of there. Breasts like green apples, hips like a bird's. What would a real man like him want with a little runt like that? And with those great ugly hands on her.'

'Sshh!' Lady Anne was returning, and the talk turned suddenly to the relative merits of honey comfits and crystallised violets. I felt my lips compressing into a thin line, and for a little while my sight blurred, but I did not allow any tears to fall. I hated to hear them talk thus, for the idea of Red and some woman lying together, and doing – doing that, made me feel sick. How could these women talk so of the coupling of man and woman as if – as if it were something joyous, something to be longed for and laughed over? I knew it as brutal, painful, an experience that dirtied and shamed and terrified. Yet, in my heart, I had to recognise that it was more than that, for I had seen John and Margery look at each other, and touch hands, and I had witnessed the same wordless, breathless message passing between my brother Liam and his betrothed. But this was not for me. I would never look into a man's eyes as Eilis had into Liam's, with a shining ardour that brought a blush to the cheek. I could never run my hand softly down a man's neck as Margery did her husband's, when she thought nobody was looking. I was damaged; soiled goods. It occurred to me that if there were a future for me and my brothers, this could prove to be a problem. My father, no doubt, would wish me to marry to advantage, in order to strengthen the strategic position of Sevenwaters. But he'd have a hard time finding any takers. Besides, I would never agree. Instead, it would be as I had once said to Diarmid, so long ago I could scarce remember it. I would become an old woman, muttering and mumbling over her herbs, mixing possets for what ails you. Wasn't that what I had always wanted? Somehow, now, it no longer seemed enough.

My fingers worked on steadily, as the barbs of the plant turned them red and blistered and hard. The women were right. They were very ugly hands. As I worked, I told myself a story about such a pair of hands. In my tale, the girl had to toil in the kitchens of a great house for seven years, to win back her sweetheart. Seven years of scrubbing floors, and scouring pots and pans, made her fingers swollen and her palms callused and rough. At the end of this tale, the faithful girl was at last reunited with her dear one. When he held her close, and lifted her hands to his lips, and his tears fell on them, behold, her fingers were at once slender and small again, and when she reached up to touch his face, it was with palms as white and fine as those of a queen. But her lover looked at her in amazement when she told him her story, how she had toiled at witches' work, and made her hands ugly and horrible. For when he had found her again at last, had gathered her close and pressed his lips to her roughened palms, these had been to him the most beautiful hands in the world.

One afternoon, Margery took me up to her quarters and presented me with a gift. From her and John, she said, for they wished to tell me yet again how grateful they were for the gift of life I had given to her and their child. She had made me a new gown; more fit for the wedding than my shapeless homespun. It was a lovely piece of work, plain enough but fashioned to fit most perfectly, in a soft light wool of a shade somewhere between blue and lavender, like the first dusk on a summer evening. Around the neckline and hem was a fine tracery of vines and leaves and little winged creatures embroidered in a deeper blue. It was a gift of love, and I put my arms around my friend and hugged her. I did not tell her I had no wish to wear such a dress, which would show off my figure and draw the eyes of men. I was more comfortable, safer, in the old homespun, which might as well have been a sack, so ill did it fit. But this was still a precious gift, which must be worn with a smile. So I tried it on for her, and she fussed and took a tuck here, and a stitch there, until she pronounced herself satisfied. Johnny watched us from the rug, round-eyed. He was working hard to roll himself over from his stomach to his back. He had not quite mastered this skill, but judging by his purposeful grunts, it would not be long.

Margery plaited my hair down my back, weaving lavender ribbons into it. This was good practice for the wedding, she explained.

'There,' she said. 'Look in the mirror, Jenny. You do justice to my handiwork, girl. You'll have to stop hiding yourself.'

I had no particular wish to see myself, having been quite put off mirrors by the lady Oonagh. But I looked, thinking to see the pale little runt of the women's talk. Instead, there was a small, slender stranger – or perhaps not quite that, for the person that looked gravely back at me had something of the fey, faraway look of my brother Finbar, and a quirky arch of the brows that I had seen on Diarmid's face, and – well, I was Lord Colum's daughter all right. But changed. They were right, I had grown, and I was a woman now. The soft gown touched the body and clung here and there, and fell in graceful folds to my ankles. Small and slight I would always be, but this gown showed the round swell of my breasts, white above its low neckline. I was no longer the wild little creature that had run free with her brothers in the forest. My face was still too thin, but the wide green eyes and small straight nose and curving lips were not those of a child. I had the pale skin of my people, and already wisps of dark hair escaped the neat plait to curl around brow and temple.

'It suits you,' said Margery, pleased with her handiwork. I smiled again and kissed her on the cheek, and made a convincing pretence of showing how pleased I was. And I was, truly; I valued her gift for its beauty and the love that was in it. I just didn't want to wear it. Not yet. Not for Red's wedding, anyway.

It made matters worse that, before I had time to change back into the homespun, all three men arrived home and came straight upstairs, full of plans for the first day of spring shearing. John came in ahead of the others, and looked at us both; and he greeted his wife with a kiss and scooped his son up into his arms.

'That looks well, Jenny,' he said in his sober way. 'Very well indeed.'

And Ben, who came in next, gave the sort of whistle men give when they fancy a girl they see walking by. I was used to Ben; I knew he meant no harm; and so I was able to smile at him before I looked away. Looked straight into Red's eyes as he stood in the doorway, staring at me. He had been talking, and he had stopped in mid-sentence. Slowly the others, too, fell silent, and there was a tension in the room. Suddenly, I found I did not want to meet Red's gaze any longer, for fear of what I might read in his eyes, and I grabbed my homespun gown and, brushing past him, fled to my own quarters and bolted the door. There I took off the blue dress and put on the old one, and I tore the ribbons from my hair, while the little dog watched me, her round, rheumy eyes full of simple affection. I folded Margery's gift and laid it away in the wooden chest, and the silken ribbons with it, and I closed the lid. Soon I would place the fifth shirt there, and only one would be lacking. This chest held the lives of my family within its simple oaken frame. *Liam, Diarmid, Cormack, Conor, Finbar, Padriac, Sorcha. For you are that woman in the mirror*, I told myself. *You are a child no longer, whatever you might wish. You are a woman with a woman's body, and you do not think or feel as you did back there at Sevenwaters, when you ran wild in the forest and the trees spread their canopy to shelter you. Men will look at you. Come to terms with it,*

Sorcha. You cannot hide forever. They will look at you with desire in their eyes. You were taken against your will, and it damaged you. But life goes on. It sounded logical. But I thought, still, that I would never be able to feel a man's touch without fear. The women's talk made me shudder. Showing my body made me ashamed. I could no longer look into my friend's eyes, for fear of what I might see there.

Later, I went out into the orchard, after first making sure nobody was around. I sat on the grass under an old spreading apple tree, on whose gnarled limbs even now blossom gave way to the first small setting of green fruit. Red and I had shared an apple once. That seemed a long, long time ago, in another world. In another tale. I spoke to the Fair Folk, in my mind. I spoke to the Lady of the Forest. If any of their kind were here at all in this foreign land, if any of them could hear me, it would be in such a place as this, under trees. I wished I could have been in the heart of the oak forest, but I had been forbidden to go there alone. I concentrated my mind on this message, and bent it towards her with all my strength. *Let him go*, I said. *Release him from your spell. You're not playing fair. He never did know the rules.* All was quiet. There was no way of knowing if anyone heard me. No faery laughter, no voices in the rustling of the leaves. *He is a good man. I believe, the best of his kind. He is to be wed soon, and has a duty to his people. What you're doing is wrong, and I won't have it. Let him free. Release him from his obligation to me, and give him back his sleep, and his will.* I waited for a while, and there was no sound but a tiny stirring of wind in the branches, and Alys breathing. *It hurts him, the fire in the head. You hurt him. You have done him an injustice, by making him my protector. Besides, I can look after myself. He risks neglecting*

his own; they need him more than I do. Set him free from
your spell.

After I had finished, I sat there quiet as the day's
light faded, hoping beyond hope to hear some
answer, some acknowledgment that the other world
did still exist, here in this land of sceptics and unbe-
lievers, of practical, down-to-earth folk and – what
was it Richard had called his nephew – buttoned-up
idealists? That had not been fair. Red was a difficult
man to know; but I had heard him speak from the
heart, speak from his uncertainty and confusion. I
knew him capable of anger and ferocity, and of great
courage. He could be hurt, just as I could. His uncle
judged him poorly, and would one day discover this
at great cost.

There were no answers here in the orchard. If the
Fair Folk had heard me, they weren't letting on. Not
today. Not that that meant much, for they were ever
fickle and mischievous in their dealings with our
kind. Well, I had said what I had to, and it would
have to do. For now.

Whether it was a clumsy servant, or a freak of the
wind, or something more sinister, nobody ever found
out. I shut my mind to the thought that the lady
Oonagh might have been behind it, for that was an
idea too terrifying to contemplate. The force of evil is
strong and cannot easily be contained. It was as we
sat at supper that night, I picking at shreds of carrot
and turnip, Margery watching me closely from across
the table, John and Ben arguing amicably about the
wool clip. I can't remember which came first, the
smell of smoke or Megan's raised voice as she ran in
from the hallway.

'Fire! There's a fire up in the long room!'

This was a household as well disciplined as its master. Men left their places quickly and without fuss. Buckets appeared and a chain formed, while Lady Anne shepherded the rest of us outside. John had shot out and up the stairs on the first word, face white as parchment; he reappeared with his squalling son in his arms, much to Margery's relief, for their rooms were close enough to be in danger. Johnny was unimpressed at his abrupt awakening; his father soothed him with small words spoken under the breath, and when he was quiet again, gave him to his mother and ran back in. We waited in the courtyard, watching the dark smoke billowing from the upper windows. Figures passed before the flickering light, and the smoke turned white, and finally nothing was left but an acrid smell in the night air. It had been an efficient exercise. No injuries. Quick and effective. No real damage done.

'You'd better come upstairs,' said Red, appearing beside me, his mouth set grimly. 'You need to see this for yourself. I'm afraid it's not good news.'

'My lord?' One of the servants hovered. 'You want the debris cleared away now?'

'Not yet,' said Red. 'Finish your supper, take a cup of ale. I'll call you.'

I followed him up to the long room, not allowing myself to think yet. For a short time we were alone there. The fire was out. Downstairs, folk were clearing away buckets, returning to the table, their voices animated.

It had been a strange fire. Passing strange. One end of the room was quite untouched. There was Lady Anne's upright chair of fine oak, with the carved back, there her embroidery frame with the intricate work of

430

unicorn and vine stretched on it unharmed. There were the baskets of wool and the spinning tools and the small hand looms. But the air was heavy with smoke and at the end of the room where Margery and I would sit to work, everything was black. The fire had scorched the boards of the floor and the rough-hewn benches along the walls and the rafters above. Spiders hung lifeless in the shreds of their webs. My spindle and distaff were charred sticks, my stool a heap of charcoal. The basket which had contained the last of my gathered starwort was ashes. And there on the ground, just recognisable, was the fragile burned remnant of Finbar's partly-made shirt, which I had left hanging over the basket, ready to start work again in the morning. I walked over as if in a dream, crouched down and put out a hand to touch it. It crumbled away in my fingers. I pictured Finbar as I had last seen him, slumped between his two brothers as if the life had been drained from him. A brittle shell of a man. I saw his eyes, once a deep, clear grey like the winter sky, saw them wild and confused and terrified as he tried to bridge the gap between beast and man. Held the ashes of his shirt in my palm; felt them trickle away through my fingers and disperse to nothingness.

'Jenny, my dear.' I looked up with a start. Lady Anne was as soft-footed as her son, when she wanted to be. Now she stood by him, frowning. 'I regret this. But it must be an accident. A careless tending of the fire; a freak wind. I shall, of course, replace these things for you. We have spindle and distaff enough.' Red said nothing; looked at the hearth, which was at some distance, in the middle of the inner wall; looked at the path of the fire. Looked at me. I would not weep. My teeth were clenched tight together, so that I could not weep.

431

'Hugh,' said Lady Anne. She sounded as she might have done when he and his brother were little boys, and she was calling them to account for staying up too late, or stealing pies from the kitchens. 'After this you must consider sending her away. This sort of thing is intolerable. You have the safety of your household to consider. Why can't you send the girl to Northwoods? Surely even you must realise now that she cannot stay here.'

Red's eyes were chilly. 'I see no such thing,' he said levelly. 'Or cannot you recognise Richard's hand in this?'

'What are you saying?' His mother was shocked. 'My own brother? Why should he seek to burn down the house of his closest kin, why stoop to childish trickery? I know he did not approve of the girl's presence here, but to suggest this is – is preposterous. Besides, he is over the water, and has been long since. Unless you believe he, too, resorts to sorcery to achieve his ends? Really, Hugh, sometimes you astonish me.'

He let her finish.

'If not your brother, then who?' he said. 'What other enemy has she so close at hand? For this blow is not for us, mother. This strikes at Jenny's heart and at her will. The price of this fire is three moons, four moons of silence. Another whole season of waiting.'

I'm afraid, at that, I burst into tears. Silent tears, but hard enough to make my shoulders shake and my nose run. Perhaps they had forgotten me, there where I crouched on the floor by the charred remains of my work. But I had not been able to shut out their voices. I put my hands over my face.

'I must confess, I do feel some sympathy for the girl,' said Lady Anne, fumbling for a handkerchief.

'Here, use this,' she said. Red was quiet, watching me. 'Off you go, Hugh,' his mother said firmly. 'There's no need for you here. I will deal with this.' But he ignored her, and I heard rather than saw him come close and kneel down beside me where I sat weeping on the floor.

'Tomorrow,' he said. 'I cannot take you myself, but John will ride out with you to the place where this plant grows. You can bring back whatever you need. This hurts, I know. But you have been strong before, and you will be now. What is burned can be replaced; what is destroyed can be made again. In time you will win back your voice. In time – in time, you will find your path back home.'

I would not look directly at him, but I lowered my hands from my wet cheeks, and used my fingers to speak to him. My thoughts were muddled with distress, my gestures less than clear. *Long. Long time. I – tired. You – too – tired.* That drew a wry expression from him, a lopsided stretch of the mouth.

'I'm good at waiting. You'd be surprised how good,' he said.

There was one more thing I had to ask him. It wasn't easy to show. *How you know – spin, weave – voice?* He understood all right. A tiny shadow of a smile, soon gone.

'I'm learning to listen,' he said. 'Slowly.'

Over his shoulder, I saw Lady Anne's face, frozen in disapproval as she watched us. Well, I didn't care what she thought. It would take all my strength and all my will to set to again, to make up the work that had been destroyed. I would have no energy for speculation or worry. Tomorrow I would go out, and I would gather enough starwort for two whole shirts. And I would work day and night, night and day until

I finished the task. No enemy was going to stop me. I was the daughter of the forest, and if my feet faltered on the path from time to time, at least they were going straight forward into the dark. And perhaps I was not quite alone.

As they went out onto the landing, she spoke to her son in an undertone. Her words were not meant for my ears, but I heard them, for in my state of distress it did not occur to me to move politely away from where I stood just inside the doorway.

'Tell me one thing. Just one. What place is there for this girl in your household, once you are wed? Do you believe for a moment your wife will tolerate her continuing presence here? With all that people are saying about – about you, and about her?'

'I see no problem,' said Red, and his tone was distant, as if he was hardly paying attention to her words. 'Why should anything change?'

Lady Anne lost her control, momentarily. 'Really, Hugh! Sometimes you exasperate me beyond belief! Can you be so unaware, so blind in this one thing alone? I wish you could take a step away. Look at yourself for just a moment. *For you speak to her as you do to no other. You speak to her as if – as if to another self.* It's time you woke up from this dream. I fear for your safety, for all of us, if this continues. The girl must leave here.'

I hovered inside the long room, wishing she would remember I was there, and stop it. I heard Red's voice, very soft, very remote.

'When have you known me make a bad decision, Mother? When have I ever shown faulty judgement?'

She did not reply for a while, and I thought perhaps they were gone. But when I ventured out, there they still stood, Lady Anne looking at her son, love

434

warring with anger on her face, and Red staring into space, expressionless mask well in place.

'This is different,' was all Lady Anne said. Then she ushered me downstairs, and gave me food and drink, and was kindness itself, for she understood the requirements of duty, though her eyes gave me another message. She was afraid, but of what I did not know.

The next day started well. Although the loss of so much work weighed heavy on me, I was now resolute in my path forwards, and forbade myself to dwell on what might have been. John appeared quite early, with his own tall grey horse and a smaller mare for me to ride. There were two other men in attendance. Perhaps Red had over-reacted to the threat of danger just a little. I was pleased at the chance to ride, rather than be carried before or behind like a sack of grain. The mare was docile but kept up a good pace, and we reached the small stream with its mantle of starwort well before mid-morning.

There was no need to tell John the rules. He sent one man up the hill to watch, the other down to the fringe of the trees. He himself settled on the rocks near me, and let me get on with it. Margery must have spoken with him about my work, for he seemed to understand that I must perform every step of this task myself, though I could see his frustration as he watched my laborious cutting and bundling of the fibrous stems. The sun was warm, and there was much activity of bee and swallow and small creeping insect. I remember clearly the smell of that day, for the air held the sweetness of the first hawthorn blossoms and the heady fragrance of wild roses in early bloom. Near the water, a few wild violets struggled free of the invading starwort, and stretched their tiny

435

brave faces up towards the light. I cut back the stems that choked their growth, so that they might enjoy one season's sunshine.

I grew weary, and John made me stop and drink from a flask he had in his saddle bag, and eat bread and cheese. He called the men in, passed out their rations, sent them off again. Neither had anything to report. He watched me finish the small meal, a wry smile on his face.

'Good,' he said. 'You run yourself too hard, Jenny; the body cannot go on working for ever, if you neglect it. I wish I could help you with this task. You're a small girl to do such labour. How much more?'

I had one bundle complete and tied up neatly further down the gully. I indicated, another the same, then we might go home. John nodded.

'Try holding your knife this way,' he said, showing me. 'Good. It makes a cleaner cut, and that will wear less on your hands. By God, whoever set this task on you has much to answer for.'

This was as vehement a statement as I had ever heard him utter. His kind, worn face was creased with concern. I gave him a reassuring pat on the arm. *It's all right. I can manage.*

I held the knife as he had shown me. It helped a bit. Fresh blisters developed on those parts of my hands that were not already too scarred to damage further. I felt the sweat running down my back and between my breasts and across my brow. But it was easy to put the pain aside. Simply focus the mind on the goal: my brothers, safe, back in this world as men again. The unravelled tapestry mended, the seven streams flowing together, the converging paths again joined as one. I moved further downstream, seeking flatter ground where the plant could be more easily reached.

I sensed it just before it happened, for there was a sudden chill in the air, an instant of wrongness that made the hair stand on end and the spine freeze. But so quick; no time to move, to draw breath, to warn; no time to think, even, of what might be coming. Then the roaring, crashing sound of a great quantity of earth and rock moving with speed; something knocking me off my feet, hurling me to the ground. I struck my head, and for a moment everything went black. Then an awareness of the sound dying away as swiftly as it began; my heart pounding in my chest, a sharp pain in my left ankle. I opened my eyes, blinking and choking, for my face, my whole body was covered with earth and dust, and the air around me was full of small particles lit by the sun to a dazzling gold. Overhead, birds still called and little clouds still scudded in a bright blue sky. Nearby, there was an eerie silence.

I struggled to sit up, but something was holding my ankle down. In front of me, I could see the sack still spread, the starwort stems laid neatly across, the glint of the knife where I had dropped it. The other bundle, carefully rolled ready for collection. Beyond this, the stream bed, the ferns, the small trees still stood. I twisted around. And behind me, everything was gone. Everything. I stared, scarcely able to take it in. Where the gully had cut into the hillside, bisected by the green-fringed stream, there was now a huge expanse of tumbled rocks and soil and bare roots. Up above, a great raw gash scarred the hillside, as if a slice of living rock had been crudely carved out and flung carelessly downwards. Had it come two strides further, I would have been crushed. It had been so quick; so quick.

In that moment of recognition, I came closer to

breaking my silence than at any point so far. For there was no movement, no sound save for the trickle of small pebbles, of pockets of soil as they settled and moved. I sank my teeth into my lower lip, to stop myself screaming, *John! John! Where are you?* Somehow, I managed to wrench my foot free of the rock that pinned it, aware that I had done myself worse damage, but not caring. Somehow, I scrambled up and over the rockfall, seeking the place I thought closest to where he had been, dashing the dust from my eyes, forcing myself to move despite the pain. Behind me, at last, there were sounds. The man posted to watch at the tree line came running back up the hill, his face sheet-white. Of the other, who had guarded the upper margin, there was no sign.

It was a desperate search, with no tools for the task, clawing away at stones, using bare hands to scoop out soil, the two of us gasping for breath, not even knowing if the place where we dug was right or not. There was no way to move the bigger rocks, though we tried; by the time you had what you needed, which was ropes and draught horses and eight or nine strong men, it would be far too late.

We found John, finally. A hand, an arm. After struggling, aching labour, an opening to where he lay, all but crushed by an immense boulder that pinned his body from chest to feet. He still breathed, and was yet conscious, for a narrow triangle between deli- cately balanced stones had left him a tiny pocket of air. There was nothing more we could move; no way we could free him.

I sent the man back for help. There was no sign of the other, no way to tell where he lay beneath these tumbled stones. The horses were tethered lower down, under the trees. It would not take so very long to ride to Harrowfield, to fetch men and ropes and tackle. Not so very long. Still, too long.

I sat very still on the rough stones, for a wrong movement might bring more down around him, might cause the weight to settle more heavily on his body. John's face was grey under the dusting of soil, and a small but steady trickle of blood made a crimson line on his cheek and pooled on the rock beneath his head. I listened to the sound of his breathing, and felt the weight of the rocks in my own chest. I did not weep for this was beyond tears.

'Jen –' he was trying to speak. I gestured, *no, no talk. Breathe. Just breathe.*

'No,' he managed, and his eyes already held the shadow of farewell. 'Say – tell –'

Each word needed a breath. Each breath bore the agony of that crushing load, the earth slowly squeezing the life out of him. 'Red,' he said. 'Right thing . . . right choice . . . right . . . you . . . say yes . . .' For a few moments he closed his eyes, and when he forced them open again, with a shuddering, rattling gasp for air, I saw the film of death clouding their steadfast honesty. He was bleeding from the nose as well now, bright droplets that became a little stream and then a steady flow. He tried to clear his throat, but could not; a terrible sound came out instead, a cruel, heart-breaking sound. I held his hand, stroked his brow, longed for words. It is terrible to be a healer, and to know that there is nothing, nothing at all, that you can do.

'Tell,' he managed. 'Tell her . . .' and then a spasm overtook him, and another, and he died, coughing his life-blood over the tumbled stones. Without finishing what he had to say. But there was no need. I knew that part without being told.

439

It did not take long for help to come. And yet, it took forever, as I felt John's hand growing steadily colder in mine, as his blood dripped on the stones and congealed into little pools. There was no sound around me but the crying of birds and the rustle of a spring breeze in the birches. My voice was silent; but my spirit was screaming for anyone to hear. *Why? Why take him? He was good; people loved him. He was innocent of any part in this. Why take him?*

I had been alone so long, cut off from any knowledge of the spirit world, that I could not tell if the little voice that answered me, in my head, was my own or another's.

That's not the way it works, Sorcha. You knew it would be hard. Now you are finding out just how hard.

But why John? He was happy. Why give him a son and then deny that son a father?

A laugh. Not cruel, just uncomprehending. *Would you rather another had been taken? The child perhaps, or him with the hair like fire, and the cold eyes? Would you wish to rewrite the story?*

I stopped my ears and shut my eyes, but the voice went on inside my head. The fire in the head. It hurt, all right.

How strong are you, Sorcha? How many partings can you bear, before you must weep aloud? Then the laughter. I did not know if I spoke to fair folk or foul, or simply to the confused voice of my own spirit. *I will not listen to you. I will not hear this.* Silently, I recited my brothers' names over and over, a charm to keep out demons. *Liam, Diarmid. Cormack, Conor. Finbar, Padriac. I need you to be here. I need you. I will bring you back. I will.*

Help came. Ashen faced, deathly quiet, Red and Ben supervised the desperate, painstaking removal of rocks and soil, the lifting of their friend's broken body from the rubble. Horses dragged boulders, men set to work grimly with shovel and spade and with their bare hands. But they found no trace of the other man's body. Either he lay buried too deep, under the last great immoveable rock, or . . . but the alternative was unthinkable.

Red's face was like some carven effigy. He ordered me to leave, but I would not go until John was taken up, and wrapped in a cloak, and laid across his horse. And so we all rode home, I in front of Ben, with a makeshift strapping around my ankle, which now burned like hot coals. Dusk was falling, and the men who walked at front and end of the small procession bore torches. Nobody was talking. I wanted somebody to say, it's all right. I wanted somebody to tell me, it's not your fault. But it was my fault. I had come here, and made these people my friends, and now an innocent man had died because he had to protect me. On such a fine spring day, he should have been thatching a roof, or putting cattle out to graze, or playing on the grass with his son. Not guarding some crazy girl while she cut bundles of thorns. He should have been safe. Now he was dead. And I could see that Lord Hugh, riding straight backed, leading the horse that bore its master's broken body, had strapped to his saddle the two rolls of starwort I had harvested, before the rockfall had destroyed the place where it grew. The price of that small harvest was his friend's life. Such was the burden on him, such the weight of the Fair Folk's command, that even after this he was obliged to help me. He did not allow the pain of it to show on his face, for he had erased from it any sign of feeling. In the torchlight it was like a mask of ashes, with blind holes for eyes. Ben wept openly, his grief plain for all to see, and many of the men riding there were red-eyed. Not Lord Hugh. He hid his pain deep inside, as deep as the dark secret place at the bottom of a well.

Perhaps I had forgotten that Margery was a Briton too. I soon remembered, as we rode into the court-yard, and saw her face, still sweet, still calm; but aged suddenly, so you could see the tracery of little lines about eyes and mouth that she would have as an old woman. They bore her man's body inside, and upstairs to be washed and laid out, and she said not a single word. Nobody was looking at me; or rather, everybody seemed to be carefully not looking at me. Ben lifted me down, and I found I could not walk on the ankle, which had swollen up alarmingly. So he carried me indoors, but nobody seemed particularly interested in helping me, so I made my way to my room, leaning on the wall with one hand, hopping on one foot, as the other sent spasms of pain up my leg and through my back and into my bursting head. I bolted both doors and sat on the pallet hugging Alys and staring into the dark. What was this pain, com-pared with Margery's?

I did light a lamp, eventually. I did look at the ankle, force myself to move the foot, wrap it in a length of linen to provide some relief. It was not bro-ken. I fetched water and performed my ablutions, brushed the dust and soil from my hair. Distantly, I heard the household still awake, going about its busi-ness. Surely, now, he would send me away. How could he not send me away?

After a long, long time, there was a knock on the door, and it was Lady Anne.

'Margery wants to see you,' she said curtly. I fol-lowed her past the eyes of what seemed to be every member of the household, as they stood or sat in little, huddled groups, unable to rest, united in their grief and shock. I hobbled, and nobody offered assistance, though Lady Anne did wait for me on the stairs.

He was laid out in their own quarters, though soon he would be moved downstairs, and a vigil would be kept, with candles. It was quiet; so quiet. Didn't these people know how to grieve for a good man? Didn't they know how to weep, and scream with rage, and curse the powers of darkness in their sorrow? Didn't they know how to hold one another, and dry one another's tears, and tell tales of the things he had done, and of what he had been, to see him safe on his way? Where were the great fires, and the toasts in strong ale, and the scent of burning juniper?

John was dressed in a robe of soft grey, and his body was clean, but there was no way to hide the terrible bruises, or the damage to the bones of chest and pelvis. He had fought strongly, to hold on so long.

'Jenny,' said Margery. She had not wept. She looked remote, a shadow of herself. Her eyes were calm and empty. I wanted to put my arms around her, to hug her and cry with her, for she was my friend. But she put a space between us without saying a word. Ben was there, sitting against the wall, and at least he had a tankard of ale in his hands. Red stood in the shadows at the far end of the room. I supposed I was there for a reason. I supposed I was there because I had seen him die, and she wanted to know how it was with him. Without words, this was a daunting task.

John – speak – you. My hands were shaking; I could hardly bear her blank, expressionless stare. She gave no sign of understanding.

John – tells me – you, the baby.

'What is the point in this?' Lady Anne snapped. 'These signs are meaningless, and disrespectful in this place of mourning. You're upsetting Margery, girl. What are you thinking of?'

I looked across John's still body to his wife, and thought maybe her eyes flickered, just for an instant. I tried to reach her. *Please. Please listen.*

'Try again, Jenny.' Red was beside me, watching my hands. 'Perhaps I can help.'

So I went through it once more, and as I moved my hands, he spoke my thoughts aloud.

'John wanted – John had a message for you.' Close eyes, hands to one side, rest cheek on hands. 'He died peacefully. With courage.' I brought my hand from the man lying still before me, to cover my heart, and then towards his wife, who stared at me, impassive.

'He said, tell Margery I love her,' said Red. 'Tell her she is in my heart.' It was hard for me to keep going, but I told myself, compared with what she feels, this is nothing. Nothing. So my hands went on moving, saying the things I knew John wanted to say, would have said if there had been time, and Red's quiet voice made my gestures into words.

'He said, tell her I know she will raise my son to be a good man, strong and wise.' I looked at John one last time; his face calm under the bruises, his clean, white feet not quite covered by the robe. I touched the tips of my fingers to my lips, then moved my hand gently towards her.

'He said, say goodbye to them for me. And – and tell my son my story.' There was a catch in Red's voice. I did not look at him. Margery's face stayed calm a moment longer, as she met my gaze.

'Thank you,' she said in a very small, polite voice.

'I'm glad someone was with him when – and now, if you don't mind, I'd like to be left alone.'

'Are you sure that's wise?' This was Lady Anne, who had maintained her disapproving frown throughout.

'Please.' Margery's voice was wobbling a little, and as I turned to go, I saw her face crumple, and tears start to roll slowly down her cheeks.

Out on the landing, Red took one look at my limping progress and picked me up bodily with never a by your leave.

'You are the most obstinate, pig-headed –' he muttered. 'How on earth did you get upstairs?'

'She walked,' said his mother, one step behind and looking like thunder. 'As she can perfectly well do now.'

Red stopped part way down the stairs, with me in his arms. We were in full view of the household assembled below. I could see Lady Anne's thoughts on her face, clear as if they had been spoken aloud. A man died today, because of her. One of our own. Someone's husband, someone's father. She killed your friend. And yet, you carry her about as if she were some precious flower, some princess too fragile for her feet to touch the ground. What will they think of you? What are you doing to this house? Red was looking at her too, and when he spoke it was very softly.

'This is a girl who puts herself through hell every day, who will walk over rocks barefoot until her feet bleed, who puts her own needs last, always. But she will not be last in my household. If Jenny cannot walk, then there really is something wrong, Mother. And I will deal with it as I please.' Very calm and controlled. Perhaps only I heard the slight unsteadiness in the voice. His mother was furious. But people could see her face, and so she followed us downstairs with quiet dignity, and said no more. Me, I would rather have hopped and hobbled back to my room alone. But nobody asked me. I did not have to look about me to know what every person there was thinking. John is dead. With him dies part of Harrow-field. What will she destroy next? And yet he shelters her still. Witch; murderess. It was not spoken aloud; not in his lordship's hearing. Not yet.

In my room, he placed me on the bed and went back to bolt the door. The outer one was open, and on the top step were the two bundles of starwort stems, and my knife.

'Your ankle,' he said, 'is it – ?'

I signalled, *nothing. It's nothing.*

'I don't believe you,' said Red. 'And I would help, if I could. But I cannot stay here, there are matters to attend to, I –'

He made his way to the outer door, stepped over the bundles, down the steps, and he was moving as if in the dark, as if by touch alone. Yet there was a lantern burning there. I thought him gone, and moved to bolt the door behind him. But when I limped over to the doorway, he was standing silent at the foot of the steps, one hand flat against the wall, his forehead on the cold stones next to it, and his other fist pressed against his mouth so hard the knuckles showed white. His shoulders were shaking.

I suppose, at that moment, I forgot that I was afraid to touch. Perhaps I did not think at all. My hand went up, and I laid it gently on the back of his neck, where the skin showed pale and vulnerable between tunic and severely-cropped hair, where the bones showed under the skin. His reaction was instant and violent. His body went completely still, as if frozen with shock; and then he breathed out explosively, and on that breath were words spoken in a tone I had never heard before, harsh, uncontrolled.

'*I don't want your pity.*'

I snatched my hand away as if stung, and backed up the steps, as fast as my injured ankle would let me. For a moment, before he vanished into the darkness, he turned his face towards me, and I saw what it held, when the mask of composure was stripped away. Anguish, fury, grief; and a bitter self-loathing, the mirror of his brother Simon's face. And under this, something else, something far more elusive that dwelt in the depths of the eyes, guarded by barriers only to be breached by the most daring, or the most foolish.

I did not sleep that night. My spirit was heavy and my heart sick. As I lay watching the shadows move around me, listening to the little snores of Alys, I thought, if I stay here, I will destroy him. I may destroy all of them. And I thought, if I leave, I will not complete the task. For the powers of evil draw their net tight. If I do not stay here, I will lose my brothers. And it will have been for nothing. My mind went from one thought to the other, and back again, and there was an ache in my heart that rivalled the fierce pain of my damaged ankle. He hates me, I thought. They all hate me. And with good reason, for in this household I am nothing but a destroyer. And the little voice in my head spoke up, *What is this? Self-pity? You cannot afford such a luxury, Sorcha. And you cannot have this both ways. Put your foot back on the path. Step forwards. And hurry, for the enemy is close behind.* The little voice could not be ignored. But there was one matter to attend to, first.

So, before dawn broke I rose and went out into the garden, and gathered the things I needed. Ben lay in a heavy slumber on the bench, with an empty ale jug for company. I drew a circle in the soft earth, and placed four candles around it. In the centre I made a tiny fire, with sticks of hawthorn and elder. Somebody had to help John's spirit to go free, and to seek its new path. I could not trust these people to do the right things, even though they loved him. The flames burned small but bright and true. I fixed my mind on his weathered, solemn, steadfast face, and on all the things he had been, and I threw onto my fire handfuls of pine needles, and of thyme leaves, so that before long a sweet, cleansing smell spread across the garden. My mind pictured John as a great, spreading tree, that sheltered and guarded many within and under its wide canopy. I thought of the roots of this tree, holding firm to the earth of the valley, a living part of its deep heart. He was a valley man. Wherever he journeyed, whatever his spirit path, a part of him would always remain here. As dawn broke, I quenched the candles and scrubbed out the circle, and I spread out the last embers of the fire and covered them with sand. It was another day, and there was work to be done.

From that night on, until May Day when everything changed again, I set myself apart from the household, as if in some invisible, protective shell. I applied all my will to my task. For I sensed my enemy all around me, drawing ever nearer as spring blossomed and burgeoned into summer, as berries set on bushes, and young birds tried their wings, and the household of Harrowfield swallowed its grief and put on a brave face, in readiness for a wedding.

Instead of walking out in the early mornings, I sat

in my garden spinning, for Lady Anne had provided me with distaff and spindle as she had promised. If I did venture forth, it was not to the orchard, or the fledgling forest of young oaks. At night, the guard remained outside my door. I did not look to see who it was, and the door stayed closed. I took to working in my room, even at the times when the women would gather upstairs; I did not wish to hear them talk, or endure Lady Anne's frowning distrust or, worst of all, sit by Margery as she went mechanically about her work, blank eyed. She did not ask to see me again, and I would not go where I was not wanted. So I sat alone and told myself tales, and when I had no more energy for that, I repeated my brothers' names over and over to myself in silence. My hands got worse, from long misuse without respite; without the daily treatment Margery had administered, they were sore and wretched. I kept on working. The pain was not important.

I could not isolate myself entirely. Lady Anne required attendance at supper. I attended, and sat silently, and ate what I must. There was no John to coax me into finishing what was set in front of me; though once or twice I found Ben slipping an extra wedge of cheese or slice of fruit onto my plate, with a comment about how there was so little of me left, soon I'd be gone altogether. I looked at him sharply, and he winked. Perhaps not everyone hated me. Gone were the cheeky grin and flood of bad jokes, since we had lost John, but Ben was not capable of malice, and I believed he still felt some kind of responsibility for me, born perhaps of being witness to my undignified rescue from drowning. Born also from his failure to prevent Hugh of Harrowfield from making the one wrong decision of his life.

Once or twice I passed Red in a hallway, for we could not avoid one another completely. I lowered my eyes and went by like a shadow, close to the wall. When he had to speak to me, his manner was polite but distant; of what had passed between us that night, not a word was spoken, not a look exchanged. It might never have been, save for the gulf it had made between us, that neither of us tried to bridge. It was better that way. I had a job to do, and no time for distractions. He had his house to put in order, and quickly, for May Day drew on at an alarming pace.

I learned, at third hand, of his investigations into the rock fall and John's death. That the second man, who had watched from above, was on loan, so to speak, from Northwoods, having accompanied Elaine on her visit and remained at Harrowfield. That he had taken the place of another, on the day it happened, without informing John. That there had been no sight or sound of him since. There was a question over it all, for it could still be that his body lay beneath that great, remaining stone. No accusations were made. But things changed subtly. There were more men about the place, and most of them were armed. Foodstuffs were checked and tasted. Red and Ben talked long in the evenings, and started looking at maps. Other men came from time to time, some of them strangers, and were questioned intensely, and given food and drink, and sent away again. All of this I watched, and failed to understand, but I would not ask. I spun and spun, and counted the days as they sped by.

CHAPTER ELEVEN

It was May Eve, and the weather was perfect. At home, folk would have been up and out in the night, gathering flowers to hang about their doors and windows, to honour the first rising of the sun. Gifts of milk would be left in the hollows of certain stones; fires lit on hilltops. I remembered my brother Conor coming home with a burning brand, which he had carried from deep in the forest, and lighting our hearth fire anew. Here the folk seemed to have little time for such rituals, perhaps not understanding their importance. And yet, to my surprise, I saw ribbons woven in the bushes by the pathway, and heard the girls in the kitchen chattering about a spiral dance, and which of the young men they might like to take into the woods when the dancing was over. Perhaps the old ways were not quite gone from these parts after all.

The house was full of flowers and greenery, and

folk smiled, for a wedding meant renewal, and sta-
bility, and another generation to learn the careful
husbandry of tree and beast, the wise and protective
nurture of the good folk of the valley. At home, you
would never choose Beltaine for a wedding, not if
you wanted the marriage to last. I sat in my garden
sewing by lantern light, and imagined Red showing a
small son how to plant an acorn; showing a tiny
daughter how a sheep's wool could be shorn, and
grow again. Elaine was not in this mind-picture; perhaps, I thought grimly, even when wed she would be
kept occupied by her father, who was over keen to
display an interest in the affairs of Harrowfield.

He had arrived that morning, a few days after his
daughter. I saw little of him, but I heard his expedition had not gone according to plan, and he was in an
ill temper. The supper was festive. The household ate
and drank and laughed, and made the sort of jokes
you would expect, but in good humour. Richard sat
back in his chair and watched me with hooded eyes.
Red and Elaine maintained a quiet, exclusive conversation. Ben seemed unusually withdrawn. He was
drinking sparingly and frowning into his goblet, his
thoughts far away. Margery did not come down.

Lady Anne had done us proud, with course following course on silver platters, roast meats and fresh
poached fish, neither of which I could touch; vegetables carved into cunning shapes, soups and sauces
and sweetmeats. I longed for the quiet and privacy of
my room, but would not offend the family by leaving
early. And then they brought on the prize dish,
stuffed and garnished and glazed to a warm, glisten-
ing gold. A great roast bird, flanked by carrots and
turnips and onions, the savoury smell of it filling the
nostrils and causing a small cheer to go around the

452

festive board. I suppose I was slow to react. I did not think, for long moments. And then I realised what it was, and my stomach heaved and my brow was suddenly dripping with sweat and the whole room reeled and danced before my eyes. I knocked over my chair in a headlong dash for the door, and upset a serving woman with a jug of gravy. At least I did not shame them by spewing the contents of my stomach on the floor of the great hall. I made it outside, just, and stood shaking, shivering and retching till my body had rejected every morsel of food it had in it, and long after. The terrible sight was still before my eyes, the ghastly smell in my nostrils, clinging to my clothing, all around me as their voices came in snatches through the open door.

'What's wrong with her?'

'Somebody slip something nasty in the food? Come on then, who's the culprit? Been tempted myself, sometimes.'

'You'd never get away with it, not now. Everything's checked. Makes you wonder.'

'Tell you what I reckon.'

Voices lowered. '. . . bun in the oven . . . that's what I heard . . . just as well he's . . . keep him out of trouble . . . old married man . . .'

'. . . not the first . . .'

'Wouldn't be his, if she is. More likely one of them travelling men that comes and goes by night. Who else'd look at her?'

I had heard of such things before. A roast swan; inside the swan you put a turkey, and inside that a chicken, and so until the smallest quail. A masterpiece of culinary skill. I would never eat food from that kitchen again, I would never put on this gown that smelled of it, I would never . . .

453

'Feeling any better?' It was Ben, a cup of water in one hand, a clean cloth in the other. 'Got a pretty delicate stomach, haven't you? Good timing, I thought. The wedding jokes were getting weaker by the moment. Come on, drink; your stomach has to have a little bit of something in it. There, that's better. Now, I don't suppose you're keen to rejoin the festive party. How about an escort to bed? Maybe I should rephrase that. I'd be delighted to see madam to her door. Smile, Jenny. It's not that bad.'

He was a kind boy, well meaning. And how could they know? I let him walk me to my room through the garden and we sat on the bench a while looking at the stars. I wondered why he did not leave, go back to the party. Not that I minded his company. Anything was better than thinking of that – that –

'I've been asked to give you a message.' Ben was suddenly serious. 'He said – he said he hoped you'd do as he asked, and not have too many questions.'

What? What message?

'He said, be up early tomorrow. Really early, just before dawn. Put on a cloak and good boots, and be ready to ride out. And leave the dog indoors. That's what he said.'

What? But tomorrow is – ?

'Don't look so worried,' said Ben, a frown creasing his own brow. 'He said, tell her it'll be all right. And it's safe to leave your – your work behind.'

So he was not sending me home. Was not sending me away. He would not send me away, on his wedding day, without my things?

'It'll be all right,' said Ben as if trying to convince himself. 'And now I'd better go. I'll be missed. And I hear our friend of Northwoods has some sort of news for us. Just what, I'm not sure. But I'd better be there when he breaks it. Good night, Jenny. Don't look so worried.'

One of the things the folk of Harrowfield liked and respected about Lord Hugh was how reliable he was. Reliable, stable, predictable. No surprises there. If he said he'd do something, he did it. If he made a promise, he kept it. Solid as an oak, was Lord Hugh. You did not have to live there for long to hear them say so. That was why my arrival had shocked them; for it was a break in the long, unchanging pattern. Well, one aberration was all right, folk said. They could tolerate one mistake. Once he was wed, things would settle down. Fine girl, Elaine of Northwoods. But it did happen again. It was astonishing, considering the sort of person he was, that he acted in the way he did. It could scarcely have been designed to have a more dramatic impact, to offend more people, to distress his family more greatly. Yet that was just how he planned it. And in the long run it seemed that even for this, he had his reasons.

I had no problem waking early, having slept but fitfully. Alys was pleased to have the bed to herself, and made no protest at being left behind. I would not wear the homespun, for I imagined it still smelled of roast meat; so I had to put on the blue dress, and my sturdy outdoor boots. It was early enough to be chill, and I wrapped a cloak around myself and went out, with a very strange feeling in my stomach. Nerves? Foreboding? Maybe it was just the aftermath of retching on an empty gut. It was quiet. The house was still sleeping.

By the gate were three horses, and two men in cloaks, with weapons by their sides. Red put a hand to his lips, to signal quiet; there was hardly a need for this with me. Ben helped me onto the mare, and we rode off in silence, keeping to grass and earth where the horses' feet would make less noise. Before the sun rose, we had travelled over the rim of the valley and into a dense woodland, riding on paths visible only to an experienced woodsman. Harrowfield was far behind us, and the day dawning bright. I was quivering with frustration, bursting with questions I could not ask. They stopped briefly to pass round a flask of water. I seized the opportunity.

Where are we going? What is this? Today – you – wedding! Today – you – home! Where?

There was a ghost of a smile on Red's face, though he looked as if he, too, had gone without sleep.

'So many questions! It's all right, Jenny. We have quite a long ride ahead of us, until mid morning at least. I want to show you something. We'll make sure you get back safe. And I have – arranged – for your work to be well guarded. That fierce hound of yours will assist, no doubt. Now, can you ride further? Not too tired?'

I shook my head, but I was not finished. He had not answered me, not really.

Today – you – wedding? The message was surely clear on my face, if the gestures were not sufficient. *How could you do this? How could you do this to them?*

Red shrugged, not meeting my eyes. 'It's of no concern,' he said. 'It's under control.' That was all. We rode on, and I found that despite my confusion and anxiety, despite my deep shock at his action, I was enjoying the freedom of this ride, the sweet scent of the woodlands, the thud of hooves on a soft carpet of fern and moss, the silent company of the two men. It was almost like – it was almost like the time we had made a journey together before, Red and I, when we had rested under an apple tree and shared its fruit.

When we had sheltered in a cave and seen more than we bargained for. Despite the fear and the uncertainty, there had been a bond between us even then, when I had scarcely known him. Red glanced at me and looked away, and I believed he shared my thoughts.

When I had first come to Harrowfield, the ride from the sea had taken the best part of a day. I realised, now, that the coastline must be deeply indented, or curve back on itself, for the way we took was far shorter, though a more difficult ride. The horses seemed to know the path, but it was clearly little traversed. It was not so very long before we emerged from under trees to see the broad, shining expanse of the sea below us, and to hear the breakers' roar and the screaming of gulls. A track led down, between rocks, towards the water. It was steep, too steep for riding. Wooded headlands projected on either side of us; the place was sheltered, almost secret. The two men dismounted, and after a moment, I did likewise, somewhat awkwardly, for I was unused to riding so long. Nobody spoke, but I saw Red grip Ben's arm, as if in thanks, and Ben gave a nod and then took the reins of all three horses and led them back under the trees.

'This way,' said Red, heading off down the narrow, ill-defined path. I had no choice but to follow. My ankle was still a bit sore, but it held up quite well. There were places where the track was steep and crumbling, and he had to take my hand once or twice, but he let it go as soon as he could. I concentrated on not slipping, and did not look about me. At last we paused on a small flat outcrop of rock, some twenty feet above the beach.

'Look that way,' said Red. The place where we

stood was the midpoint of a sheltered cove, where the sand was white and fine, and an abundance of low plants scrambled over the cliff face behind. At either end, the tall headlands blocked wind and weather, cutting off the bay from the rest of the world. Before us a pile of weathered stones divided the beach into two parts. I followed Red's gaze to the left, and my mouth fell open in amazed delight.

I had heard of such creatures, but only in tales. They were basking in the summer sun, huge, sleek, elegant in repose; they fixed their great, liquid eyes on us as if to say, *this is our place.* The mystery of the ocean was in those eyes. There were perhaps ten or twelve of the creatures there, and as I watched another came out of the water, moving up the beach with a ponderous grace. It shook its long, heavy body from side to side, and a shower of silver droplets made a dazzling halo around it. Then it settled, with a sigh, next to its fellows. I sat down very carefully on the rocks, moving slowly in case I startled them. For this was one of those places where the harmony of natural things is quite untouched; where worlds meet and speak; where man and woman must tread with the utmost care. One of the creatures moved its head, watching me; then laid its head and neck across another's back, eyes closing slowly. I felt a grin of pure delight spread over my face. A long time passed as I watched the creatures, as I sat there under the May sky with seabirds wheeling overhead. I felt the power of that place all around me, soaking into me, soothing my spirit and filling me with joy. It was a feeling not easily told in words; the same feeling that had come to me at times in the deepest, most secret places of the forest, or sitting on the rooftops of Sevenwaters, talking to Finbar without any words.

All is well. All will be well. The wheel turns, and returns.
This was a place of soul healing.

After a while I remembered I was not alone, and turned to look at Red. He was sitting on the rocks behind me, and he had his book, and his quill and ink pot, but he was not working. He was watching me.

'We'll stay here awhile,' he said quietly. Then he opened the book and uncorked the ink bottle. 'Ben returns later; he has business in these parts. You are quite safe here.' At that, the questions came back to me all at once. How could he be so infuriatingly calm? Would he offer me no explanations? How do you use your hands to ask *why? Why did you bring me here?*

'Later,' he said. 'We have all day. Later, we'll talk, and I'll tell you – for now, can you understand that I wished to see those hands at rest, just for a day? That I wished to set my prisoner free, just for a little? Enjoy your day, Jenny. Tomorrow it begins again.'

Why this day? What of Elaine, and your mother, and – But I could not put this into signs. Besides, he knew quite well what I wanted to ask, but he brought out from his pack the leather-bound boards which housed his farm records, and extracted a piece of parchment already half-filled with neat markings. He dipped the quill into the ink and set to work, seated there with the open sky above him, and the wide seas before him, and it seemed he had eyes only for his orderly record of the way things had been, and were, and always would be.

So I took off my boots, and climbed down to the other side of the beach, which lay quite untouched save for the light feet of birds. Here there were no great sea creatures basking, but delicate, intricate shells thrown up by the tide, fragments of bleached

459

wood and complex nets of weed. The sand was good under my bare feet, so good that I picked up my skirts and began to run, sore ankle or no, with the breeze in my hair and, at last, the cold touch of the sea round my feet, and my heart beating with the thrill of freedom. I ran through the small waves, and the hem of the blue dress grew wet and gritty with sand; I ran along the beach and the gulls followed high above, crying one to the other. I ran until I was dizzy and breathless, until I reached the far end of the beach, where the rocky headland rose from the white sand. There I leaned my back against the stones and listened to my heart pounding and drew in breaths of wild sea air. I had not realised, had not known how painful a burden had been laid on me, until now, when for a single day I was free.

I could see Red, a distant figure still seated on the rocks. His hair made the only vibrant note of colour in a landscape of grey and green and white; flame on the water. He had put aside the book, and was sitting quite still, straight backed, watching me. Perhaps he thought I would try to run away. But no; he knew I must go back, for he understood, at least, that I was bound to complete my task, though if he knew the reason for it he would find it hard to believe. Such things were beyond the comprehension of a Briton. Voices in the head, strange dreams, those he could accept, reluctantly. But there was a whole world beyond that, and he had barely touched its margins.

I came back more slowly. Half way along the beach, the sea had cast up a treasure trove of shells, each more beautiful than the last. I sat on the sand and held first one, then another in my hand, marvelling at these tiny, convoluted homes that had each sheltered some small creature of the sea. For I was the daughter of the forest, and for all my growing years had not ventured far from its enveloping arms, had not imagined the wonder, the strangeness of the ocean and its secret life. The shell in my hand had been split open by some great storm; inside, it held chamber on chamber, each lined with a shimmering, pearly coat fit for a queen's adornment. It was truly wondrous. I sat there a long time, looking and dreaming, my thoughts growing distant from that place, my spirit turned inwards. And then – and then – how can I describe the moment? A voice in my head, not the one that tormented me, nor the one that spoke sense and woke me up; a voice not heard for a long time, such a long time.

Sorcha. Sorcha, I am here. I'm here, little owl.

Conor? I scarcely dared think his name, hardly dared call him, in case the moment was lost. I stared into the sky, out over the water. There was a lone bird there, wide wings spread, circling, gliding.

Conor? Is it really you?

Listen carefully. I can speak only a little, then I must be gone.

The others – where are they? Why didn't –

Hush, little owl. Just listen.

I stilled my thoughts, made my mind empty and open.

That's good. Tell me, will I find you here, at midsummer?

No. I pictured the valley of Harrowfield, as closely as I could, trying to show him where it lay, over the hills, down to the south-east. How would a swan fly to Harrowfield? A swan does not go by tracks, and bridges, and paths under trees.

I see this place. Who is he, who guards you? Why have you come here, across the water? It is far, too far for us.

I felt tears coming to my eyes, and my throat ached. I did not answer him.

Are the shirts made? Will you be ready, by midsummer?

The tears began to fall. *No. There is one yet to make, and part of another.*

Don't weep, little sister. I will be there. At Meán Samhraidh wait for me. I will come there.

I felt him withdraw his thoughts, delicately, from my mind. He had ever been the most skilful of us at this. I saw the bird circle once more, and with a powerful beat of its white wings, sail off into the west. I was alone again. But not alone, for they still lived. I would see them again, soon, so soon, for it was already May. I had not recognised, until then, how close I had come to believing the task fruitless.

Thank you, I said silently. Thank you, oh thank you. But to whom I spoke, I could not say. There was a power around me so strong it could almost be touched, a strength in the waves and the rocks and the strange sea creatures with their gentle eyes. I had heard my brother's voice because of this, because of where I was. But I had not forgotten who brought me there.

Later, as the tide reached its lowest ebb, I fashioned a sea woman in the wet sand, with long hair of fronded weed, and grey shell eyes, and a graceful fish's tail. Her breasts were round, her waist narrow, and she had small, delicate hands. She was like the creatures I had heard about in the old tales, who would cry out to the sailors as they passed, with voices so enticing they could drive a man crazy. I got wet and sandy, and I was engrossed in my task, so that I never saw my companion come down the beach until the breeze whipped my hair into my eyes, and I raised my head to flick the tangled locks back over my shoulders. He was sitting not far away, watching me, and I surprised a smile on his face, the first real smile I had ever seen him give, a smile that curved and softened the tight mouth, and warmed the ice-cool eyes; a smile that brought the blood to my face and made my heart turn over.

Something deep within me shouted *danger! This turning in the path you cannot afford to follow.* I looked away from him, for when I saw the sweetness of that smile I felt Simon's hand clutching mine in his terror, as if it were a talisman. When I looked into Red's eyes and saw the deep loneliness there, I heard Simon's voice, like a child's: *don't leave me.* These brothers, with scarce a word spoken, they asked for more than I had to give. I sat with my back to him, and watched the birds over the sea. Gulls, and geese, and others which I could not name, great wide-winged travellers. There were no swans there, not now. But somewhere across this wild expanse of water they waited. That was all that mattered.

'Simon and I used to come here,' said Red, behind me. 'A long time ago. Nobody else knew about it. The seals come here to rest, not for long, they live most of their lives at sea, and are seen only when they choose. We never knew if they'd be here or not. I wanted to show you.'

I nodded, but I would not look at him.

'There's an old story about this place,' he said. 'It is a tale about a mermaid such as the one you have fashioned here. Your people are skilled at the telling of such tales. I have no gift with words. But I think you would like this story.'

Now he had really surprised me. I turned half way round. He sat cross-legged on the sand, still wearing his riding boots. At least he had left his cloak up on the rocks, and his book and quill. I frowned at him and showed him my bare feet, then pointed to his. Scrunched my toes into the sand. *You can at least let go this much.* He narrowed his eyes at me, but he pulled off the boots, got up, and walked down to the water's edge, next to the mermaid. He studied her with a half-smile on his face, as the wavelets lapped around his ankles.

'The folk in these parts live by fishing,' he said. 'A youngster learns how to net a catch, or fillet a cod, before he's half grown. But there was one lad who had no wish to follow that calling. All he would do, day in and day out, was sit on the rocks by the headland playing his whistle. Dances, airs, strange tunes of his own making. His father despaired of him. His mother said he'd be the shame of them, that he couldn't turn his hand to a good day's work in the boats. But Toby, for that was his name, just stared out to sea, and played his tunes, and in time folk came to listen with awe, for his music echoed the joys and longings of their own hearts.'

I sat stunned. I had not believed buttoned-up Hugh of Harrowfield had such words in him.

'The lad became a young man. Sometimes they'd ask him to play at a wedding, and he'd come reluctantly, and go as soon as he could. And then came the strange part of the story. Strange, but true, they say, for a man who was mending nets saw it with his own eyes. There was Toby, at dusk on a summer's day, alone on the dark rocks with the notes of the whistle hanging in the air around him. And there beside him, suddenly, was a lovely young woman with skin pale as moonlight and long dark hair like tangled weed that flowed down to conceal her nakedness; and liquid eyes with a look of the wide ocean in them. She came up out of the water, and for a moment the man thought he saw the flash of a silvery tail, the shimmer of scales in the last rays of the setting sun; but when

464

he looked again, she was sitting demurely on the rocks, listening entranced to the music, and she seemed a woman like any other, save that she was more comely, and wilder, than any lass from those parts.'

Red bent down, a strand of seaweed held carefully in his large hands. He laid it on the mermaid's neck.

'Toby took her back home with him, and his mother, frowning, found her a gown to cover herself, and his father was torn between admiration and foreboding when Toby declared that he would wed her the very next day. But his grandmother said, you'll not keep her long. It's always the same with the sea folk. You think they're yours, and then one day they hear the call of the waves, and they're gone.

'The two of them moved away from the sea, all the way to Elvington, where Toby eked out a living playing at fairs and gatherings. The sea woman kept his house neat and slept in his bed, and in time she bore him two small daughters with dark fronded hair and far-away eyes. And folk hesitated to walk by their cottage at dusk, for sometimes you'd hear the sound of the whistle, lilting high, and other times you'd hear the voice of the wife keening a lament that made your hair stand on end, there was such longing in it.

'Three years passed, and things were not right with them, for Toby's wife grew thin and pale, and her lustrous hair dry and brittle. You'd no longer hear the sweet sounds of the whistle echoing out in the twilight. Folk said the wife was close to death, and the man was beside himself, for she was the woman of his soul, and he could not think of giving her up.

'Then, one morning, they slipped away from Elvington as quietly as they'd come: Toby, and his wan young wife wrapped in a big shawl, and the two small daughters side by side in the back of a donkey cart. Down to the shore they travelled, and every step the donkey took towards the pounding surf and the wild expanse of the ocean, the more the wife's eyes brightened, and the more Toby's face grew pale and old.

'It was another dusk, when at last they stood again on the rocks gazing out to the west. The little girls were splashing in the shallows, heedless of the cold bite of the sea. Nobody knows what Toby said to his woman, or she to him. But they say the two of them stood together hand in hand until the very moment before the last sliver of sun disappeared into the water, and then Toby took out his whistle and began to play a lament. And by the time that tune was over, the sea woman was gone, slipped back into the embrace of the waves. But out in the darkening water, there was a movement of flashing tails; and a sound of strange voices, echoing the music of farewell.'

And? I moved my hands, wanting more. A tale must be properly ended.

'She was a creature of the deep, and there she must return, or perish. Toby understood that, but it hardly helped him. For all he had of her was his memory, where he held every moment, every single moment that she had been his. That was all he had, to keep out the loneliness. His daughters grew up, and were wed, and their descendants still live in these parts. But that is another story.'

Red sat down, his back to me, quite near, but not too near. There was a little space of silence, as the tale settled in our minds. I thought, Toby found treasure, he found the woman of his dreams, though he lost her again. All you fished up was a scrawny girl, with a curse on her that damaged all who came close. You got a bad bargain, Hugh of Harrowfield. Might as

466

well cut your losses and let me go. But where did a Briton learn to tell such a tale? This was indeed the strangest of days.

Red had brought the small bag down onto the sand. He offered me the bottle of water, took out a loaf of oaten bread, which he divided, and a wedge of cheese, which he cut with his small knife. I found, despite everything, I was hungry. He watched me eating, but took little himself. The space between us was heavy with unspoken thoughts. When I had finished, he packed away bottle and cloth, and wrapped his hands around his knees, looking out to the west.

'Today,' he said, 'I finished the last page of this record. It's time to begin another. Each set of bindings holds one year. They go back a long way. Every oak they planted, every barn they built, the breeding lines of sheep and cattle. The battles they waged; the fires and floods they braved. The story of the valley. It was all I ever wanted, to carry out the work they had begun; for my beasts to thrive, for my crops to grow healthy and my people to be safe and content. That, I believed, was what I was born for.'

There was a pause. I glanced at him sideways. His profile was very stern. *But?* my hands signalled.

'But – since Simon went away, since – since I found you, and brought you to Harrowfield, it's as if I have been walking through shadows, and dicing with ghosts. As if I have lost my way. Or – or as if the way I always believed to be mine is changing before my feet. Always, before, it seemed enough, for my life to follow this path, as my father's did and his father's before him. But I have stepped out of the pattern, and there is no going back. I am not afraid, not for myself; but I am uneasy, for the real and the unreal draw ever closer together, tangling and twining so that I cannot tell them apart. I hear two versions of the same story, and do not know the truth from the falsehood. Here I am telling tales, and half believing them. For I think sometimes that you, too, will go back one day, hear the call of the sea and slide away under the water as Toby's mermaid did. Or maybe one night, as I watch outside your window, I will see an owl fly out and vanish into the forest; and when I look for you, all that will be left is one small feather on your pillow.'

My hands were unable to speak for me. Since that night, when I had tried to comfort him and had made him so angry, I had given up hope of his ever speaking to me like this again. Had believed the shutters closed for ever. Why had he chosen, now, to reveal so much of himself? I needed words. I could have told him, it is the spell. The enchantment they laid on you, to keep me safe. To accomplish the task. Now, the task is nearly finished, and my brothers will find me, and then your doom too will be lifted. You can go back to your valley, and the ordered pattern of your life, and I – I will go home.

'You're not saying much,' said Red. I made no effort to respond. I thought, whatever I try to say, or do, it will be wrong, and the mask will come down again. Perhaps if I sit here very still, I can hold this moment, with the sky and the sea and the day's warmth, with my brother's voice in my head and Red sitting by me and talking as if – as if –

'Ask your questions now, if you like,' he said diffidently. 'I owe you an explanation. Several explanations. And I have something to tell you, and something to ask you. There's no hurry. We have the rest of the day.'

This worried me. So my first question was, *sun goes down – ride – home?*

468

'That's of no concern,' he said, frowning a little. 'I said we would make sure you got back safely, and we will. You can trust us on that, at least.'

I mimed exasperation. He was skilled at framing answers that were no answers. I showed him, *you – wedding – today?*

'By now,' he said, glancing up at the sun high in the sky, 'Elaine and her father will be on their way home. There will be no celebration at Harrowfield.'

I conveyed to him that I thought this answer quite inadequate.

'They will waste no time in questions,' he said carefully. 'Elaine was to break the news to Richard this morning, and to my mother. She will not wish to stay any longer than she must. Yes, Jenny, she knew. I am not quite so heartless as you would believe me.'

Elaine – sad, angry?

He gave a grim little smile. 'No. Disappointed and inconvenienced, maybe. But it was never me she wanted. Elaine will do well enough. Her father, now that's another matter.'

He still had not answered the real question, the only one that was important. *Why?* There was no clear gesture for this, but I did not really need one; the question must have been written in my eyes.

'I – I will explain, in time. There are reasons. It's complicated. I –'

You will have to do better than that.

'Why this day? Why not tell them, and be done with it? Will you believe me if I say, because I wished to bring you here, and show you this place, and see you run on the sand? Because I could do this only if I kept this day secret from all but those whom I trust with my life?'

I shook my head.

469

'Nonetheless, that is a good part of the reason, Jenny. Since – since the day John died, I – no, I don't have the right words for this.'

I mimed, *take your time. I'm listening*.

'You have suffered, since that day. I am not blind to it, I – you must understand, on that day, when it happened, when we first came there, I thought – I thought you both – and then, I found I could not – I'm sorry, this is – I have no skill with words, and I can only hope you understand me. I have been unfair to you. I did not protect you as I should. What happened, it was not your fault. Each of us blamed himself. If only I had done this, or had not done that – but it was the fault, only, of him who ordered it done. He was clever, there was no proof. But I think, now, he has set a trap for himself that can be sprung. Only –' he fell silent again.

I waited.

After a while he said, 'It's getting hot. You should not be in the sun too long.'

I followed him up the beach, and we sat again, under the headland, where the shadows were starting to creep across the sand. Out by the water, the tide was lapping at the mermaid's tail, coaxing her back into the sea.

'I must ask you a question,' said Red, turning a small shell over and over in his hands. 'You need not answer, if it is forbidden to you. But answer if you can.'

I nodded. It sounded serious. But I thought, on such a day as this, surely there is little more that can surprise me.

'The thing he made for you, the carving,' said Red, and for a moment I could not think what he meant. 'The carving with the arms of Harrowfield – I want to know, did my brother give this to you? Did he place it in your hands, did you know what he intended?'

I shook my head. No, he left it for me, though I had deserted him when he needed me most, and when I came by it he was long gone. I could not tell that part.

'Can you tell me,' he said, and now he looked me straight in the eye, 'that my brother still lived, at the time I first met you?'

The question had been carefully worded. I shook my head. I believe his bones lie scattered in my forest. But I have not seen them. I would not tell that part.

'Do you know, with certainty, that Simon is dead?' His eyes were very pale, under the summer sun. Pale as tidal pools at first light. Deep as memories not to be spoken.

I shook my head again.

'Then you are not sure,' he said, looking away. 'You wonder, perhaps, why I have chosen this moment to ask you. I must tell you that – that there may be an end to your captivity. That the answer I seek may be found elsewhere. You have noted, I suppose, the return of my messengers? For I have informants spread wide, as does my uncle; but I do not tell of mine.'

By now he had my rapt attention, though I could not tell what was to come. I felt he was more at ease now, setting out a strategy, forming a plan; in safer territory.

'I thought all trace of Simon lost. The trail cold, the clues rubbed out by time. My uncle spoke of seeking him, and I dismissed it as idle words, thrown out to keep my mother happy. Nonetheless, I bade my messengers listen out for word of him. And at last, just now, word came.'

What? What word? How could there be word of Simon, now, so long after?

'My informant heard a tale,' said Red, 'of a young man with golden hair and bright blue eyes, a man as foreign to your land as any might be; he was living in a community of holy brothers, on a small island off the west coast of Erin. It is a very long journey from here. This was a young man who seemed unhurt, who seemed to be in his right mind, and of good spirit. Only – only it was as if his memory had been wiped away, and he knew only the present. Innocent as a new-born babe; but, they said, eighteen or nineteen years of age.'

Whoever it was, it was not Simon, I told myself. Unhurt? In his right mind? This could not be the boy I had nursed, whose spirit was as scarred as his wretched body. But I could not say this.

'I believe it must be my brother,' said Red, watching me. 'And so I must go and find him. Go, and quickly, so I reach that place before any other.'

Now he was scaring me. *Why?*

'Because,' he said, 'that was not the only news I had. After you had retired last night, my uncle called us together, and told us he had proof that Simon was killed, soon after the troop he accompanied was ambushed in the forest. Captured, tortured and killed. His body buried under trees, where the forest growth would soon cover it. He had a first hand account, from one who witnessed it and later turned against his own master.'

Both tales are false, I thought. But as I could not deny the one, so could I not refute the other. Not without telling him the truth of what I knew. And I would not do that. Not until I had words. Even then, it would be hard enough.

'Richard's lying,' Red said bluntly. 'For some reason he does not want my brother found. So I must go alone, and secretly. Even my mother does not know of this, for it would be cruel to raise her hopes until I am certain. Besides, she is still Richard's sister. I have told only Ben and now you. There is a wide expanse of hostile territory to be crossed. Jenny, I have to tell you, I must leave tonight. I will not return to Harrowfield. Not until I have found him.'

I was overwhelmed, instantly, with the most terrible panic. It was all wrong, it could not be his brother, someone was setting a trap for him, and – I thought of my return to Harrowfield, and how it would be if he were not there. I thought that he might not return at all. My hand went out of its own accord, and took hold of a fold of his tunic, over the heart, and I bit my lip to keep back frightened tears. What was wrong with me? Was I not the strongest of seven, she whose feet scarcely faltered on the path?

'Which brings me,' said Red in little more than a whisper, 'to the last part of what I must say. Believe me, I have thought long and hard about this; it has cost me many nights of sleep. I would not willingly leave you alone, for the threat to your safety is real enough. But if my brother lives, I must find him. I – I have guarded you as well as I could. Often, not well enough. I have wished to do more, but you don't always make it easy. This time, I'm leaving Ben behind, somewhat against his will. I go alone; I can pass unseen, I think, through the best part of this journey. Ben will watch over you, and there are others who will stand by you. It may not be so long. Don't look so worried, Jenny.'

I felt a tear trickle down my cheek. *It will be too long.* There was a weight of foreboding in my heart, a

473

powerful sense of bad things to come. *Don't go. Not yet.* But I would not say it.

'I said to you once, there was a solution, to the problem of your safety, that is,' he went on, rather awkwardly now, as if picking his way over broken glass. One false step, and damage was inevitable. 'I have seen the way they treat you, even my mother, how they look at you, and speak behind your back. How they distrust your presence in the household. They cannot accept you as a friend, because they do not understand why – that is, your place in my house is unclear to them. That leaves you vulnerable to their tricks, their unkindness and prejudice. To worse. I can change that, I will do so, if you agree. But I have said, this solution will not be to your liking.'

What?

'Promise me,' he said, 'that you will listen. That you will hear me out, will not run away, or block your mind, until you have heard all I have to say.'

I stared at him. My hand loosed its deathlike grasp on his tunic and fell to my lap. I nodded mutely.

'As my guest,' he said carefully, 'your status is – is subject to the whims of others; your security cannot be guaranteed, if I am not there to watch over you. As my wife, you would be safe.'

My heart lurched, I sprang to my feet, my skirts spraying sand in his face. My answer must have been clear in my eyes as my hands moved convulsively to reject his words.

No. You cannot do this. No.

'You promised you would listen,' he said quietly, and I had. So I sat down again, very slowly, and I found I had wrapped my arms around my body as if for protection.

474

The sunny spring day was suddenly chill, its brightness dimmed.

'You're frightened. I expected no less. Jenny, I know – I understand that – that someone has hurt you, has been cruel to you – I know you still shrink from me, though I hope, despite all, that we are friends. This marriage would be – would be in name only, a marriage of convenience, you might call it. I offer you the protection of my name, so that you may complete your task in safety. No more and no less.'

You cannot do this. It is wrong, all wrong. How can you even think – oh, for words to tell him properly. The threads of this story were tangling, knotting, falling into chaos. It was one thing to break the pattern, another to tear it boldly apart.

'At least consider this,' Red went on, his voice very quiet, very level, as it was when he was exercising the utmost control. Me, I wanted to hit him, slap his face, force him to see reality. Didn't he know this was no answer? Couldn't he see that it was impossible? I imagined myself living at Harrowfield as the lady of the house. I would have found the picture comical, if it didn't hurt so much. 'At least give it some thought. We still have a little time before Ben returns.'

I realised then, with dawning horror, that he meant this to happen straight away; today would indeed be his wedding day. For he was leaving to cross the sea; he would not return; and he intended me to be as well protected as I could be, before then. But –

'Look at me, Jenny,' said Red, and I looked. Looked at the strong planes of the face, the pallor of the skin, the flame of hair cut short as the pelt of a fox. The deep, serious eyes.

'I have never taken a woman against her will,' he said. 'Never. And I'm not about to start now. Especially –' he did not finish this particular thought. 'Do you believe this?'

I nodded. *It's not just that; though that is a part of it.*

'Will it help, if I tell you that others know of this, that your return to Harrowfield has been prepared? You will not have to break this news to my mother. Elaine has done so, before she returned home.'

I had thought I could be shocked no further; I was wrong. *Elaine knew? Who else? Does the whole household know, before ever you ask me?* He gave a grim little smile that did not reach his eyes.

'I spoke only to those whom I could trust. Elaine, yes; she deserved an explanation, and I gave one. She is not only my cousin, Jenny, but an old friend; I have known her since we were children. She bore a burden for us today, in telling them; it is a source of wonder to me that my uncle produced such a daughter. Ben knows too; his part in this is vital. He will take you home, and be your protector while I am gone. And – and I spoke of my intentions to John, long since.'

There was silence. A weighty silence. At length I got up, and walked down to the sea again, and the sand was still good under my bare feet, and the afternoon sun still benign. But everything was changed. At the time, I had not understood John's last words, had dismissed them as the jumbled ravings of a man dying in intense pain. What had he said? *Red, right choice. Say yes.* Something like that, when you put it together. And I had nodded to him, mindlessly hoping to soothe his distress. I had agreed. You did not break a promise to a dying man. Especially when his death was your fault.

I walked along the beach again, as the shadows

476

lengthened and the sea grew dark. Down by the water, the mermaid was almost gone. All that was left of her was a strand of dark, knotted hair and one delicate, reaching hand. I sat and watched as the ocean took her back, down to its secret places. I cleared my mind; sought for answers. But this time no wise inner voice came to my aid. There were only hard, cold facts. My brothers were returning. There was still one shirt to finish, and another yet unmade. Someone had burned my work, someone had killed my friend. Red was going away. And I had promised John. There was but one conclusion. I had to trust that Hugh of Harrowfield had made another of his sensible, calculated decisions. That he was, as they described him, a man who could not make a wrong choice. I had to say yes, though it made my heart cold to think of it.

Nonetheless, as we stood together on the rocks a little later, watching the great sea creatures one last time as they made their slow way down the beach and slipped into the water, transformed instantly into magical, graceful swimmers, there was one more question I had to ask. One he knew well.

You – promise – me, home? Me, across the water, home?

'I will not break my promise, Jenny,' he said. 'When it's time, when you are ready to go, I will see you safe home. When it's time, you must ask me, and –' he did not finish this sentence. But it was enough.

It was getting late. The beach was half in shadow, the sky darkening. I realised there would be no return to Harrowfield that night. He did not press me for my answer; he just stood there, watching the seals, waiting. He had done a lot of waiting. A scrap of parchment lay on the rocks behind him; the rising breeze threatened to snatch it away from the round stone that had held it there while the ink dried. Here he had made his final meticulous markings that morning as he sat there in the sun; that morning that seemed, already, so long ago. But there were no tallies of cattle or crops on this page, only pictures, small delicate pictures in careful pen strokes. I had watched him at this task before, and had marvelled at how he could choose to work, and disregard the wonder of the place that surrounded him. But it seemed he had not needed to look, to know its beauty. For this sheet showed the open sky, and the smooth, shining surfaces of wet stones, and the curling lace of breakers. It showed the great seals with their knowing eyes, and the flight of the gull against tiny scudding clouds. At the foot, very small, was the last image he had made. A young woman running, her hair blown out behind her like a dark, wild cloud, her gown whipped against her body by the breeze, her face alight with joy. Red reached across and picked up the parchment, slipping it out of sight between the boards and away into his pack. I thought, after all this time, I do not know this man. I don't know him at all.

There was a sound from above, beyond the cliff top. The hoot of a bird; one I had heard before. Red put his hands to his mouth and echoed the call back.

'It's time to go,' he said; but he wasn't moving. I drew a deep breath. Never had I wished so strongly that I need not answer. My hands set grimly to work. I indicated myself; pointed to the left hand, third finger. Nodded briefly. Could not help adding a shrug and a frown. I watched him to make sure he understood. There was a quick flare of reaction, deep in the pale eyes, instantly suppressed. He nodded gravely, face devoid of expression.

'Good. I hoped you would agree to this. Come on, then. We don't have a lot of time left.'

It had all been planned, down to the last detail. He had assumed, I thought with some bitterness, that I would say yes. Had known I had no real choice. Ben was waiting; we rode a short distance, stopped in a clearing by a little stone building where another man waited. Tonsured head, homespun habit. A holy father; a solitary hermit like my old friend, Father Brien. It was over quickly, so quickly there was no time to think. He spoke the words of the ceremony, we responded as we must. There was an awkward moment, then it became apparent I must make my vow without words. The shrewd-eyed priest looked at Red, looked at me, and hesitated. But he asked me, kindly enough, if I understood the words; if I knew what I was doing. And I nodded, and nodded again, and before long I had taken Hugh of Harrowfield as my husband, in holy wedlock. Ben stood by as witness, and he said little and kept his hand on his sword hilt. Only in that enchanted cove, it seemed, had we been safe. Only for a single day.

It was growing dark. Ben led the hermit aside, speaking in low tones. What now? I thought. Do we wait here, in the woods, until daybreak?

'I have something for you,' said Red, who still stood beside me. He was fishing in his pocket. 'I want you to wear this, if you will. A bride should not return home with no token of her marriage, though she returns without a husband. Here, take it.'

Something small, light, strung on a strong, fine loop of cord. It was a ring; but, as I held it up in the fading light, I saw that it was a ring such as I had never seen before. This tiny object had been carved from the heart of a great oak. It was thin and delicate, the work of a master craftsman. Its inner surface was smooth as silk, its outer patterned with an intricate design wrought over many long evenings with fine strokes of the knife; a circlet of trailing oak leaves right around, with tiny acorns here and there, and a single, small owl perched solemn-eyed in the foliage. This ring had not been made for Elaine. I slipped the cord over my neck, and the token inside the neckline of my gown, over my heart, where it hung beside another, older talisman which had once been my mother's, and then Finbar's. I looked at Red. His face gave nothing away. I thought, this does not make sense. He was working on this before John died, all winter before the fire, long since. But that meant –

'The boat's waiting for you.' Ben's voice came out of the darkness. 'Boatsman says he can land you before dawn, plenty of time to go to ground. Are you ready?'

'No,' said Red. 'But I must go anyway. Farewell, Jenny. Be safe till I return.'

I was frozen, unable to move. *Don't go. Not yet. It's too soon.* But my hands were still, my tongue, as ever, silent.

'I'll bring you an apple,' he said, and he turned and disappeared into the shadows. 'The first apple of the autumn.' And he was gone. I had not said farewell, and he was gone.

A tale can start in many ways. Thus, it is many tales, and at the same time each of these is but one way of telling the same story. There were once two brothers. This is the tale of the elder brother, a man who had everything. He was good, strong, wise and wealthy. He was a man who always made the right choices. He was a man contented with what he had; more than contented, for he was bound by both love and duty to nurture his inheritance. Until, one day, he realised it was not enough. There were once two brothers. This is the tale of the younger brother, who was clever and skilful and wild, a man with curling hair the colour of summer sun on a barley field. There were people that loved him, but he didn't see this. There was a place for him, but he never felt welcome there. Always, he saw himself as second best. His brother would inherit the estate; he, a little parcel of land nobody wanted. His brother would marry well, to safeguard the estate and consolidate his power; but who would want a younger son, with no future? His brother always got things right. He, on occasion, made mistakes of epic proportions. This is also the tale of a young woman. Who she was, nobody was quite sure, except that she had strange green eyes and hair like midnight, and she came from over the water. In a moment of uncharacteristic folly, the elder brother took her for his wife. Then he disappeared, just as the younger had; and all they left in their place was the witch girl, spinning and weaving and sewing her strange cloth of spindlebush, and not a word out of her, not a single sound. They said she wouldn't speak, not even when the rocks fell right by her, and a man lay dying. They said she was a woman with no human feelings, a sorceress, and that when she snatched Lord Hugh from right under the nose of his betrothed, with never a by-your-leave, she tore the heart right out of the valley. That was what they said.

It had been a difficult homecoming. Red's confidence that Elaine could prepare the household had not been entirely justified. She had done her best; everyone knew the wedding was off, and that instead, Hugh had done the unthinkable and married me. Elaine was gone, and so was Richard, and I owed her a great debt for that. What she hadn't told them, and couldn't, because nobody knew but Ben and me, was that their beloved Hugh was not coming back home with his new bride. It was an uncomfortable homecoming, as Ben explained as well as he could, without saying exactly where Red had gone, and I stood wearily in the hall, encircled by shocked faces and curious eyes. Lady Anne was a strong woman. She recovered first, outwardly at least. Servants were despatched for ale and mead. Ladies were dismissed, hovering men at arms sent on their way. For Lady Anne, duty was paramount. So she gave me a chilly kiss on the brow, and said, 'Welcome, daughter,' in a voice choked with restraint. It was only at that moment I remembered that it was just one day since Richard had told her that Simon was dead. Then she sat me down, and put a cup of mead in my hands; and after a while she called Megan to show me where my new quarters would be. I had not thought so far ahead. But all was prepared, in a spacious chamber upstairs, which I suspected had never been Red's, for it was too comfortable by far. There was a wide bed, blanketed in fine wool, and a small cheerful fire burned on the tiled hearth. There were tapestries on the walls, and candles lit. Garlands of flowers decorated bed and hearth and door frame; these had not been placed there for me, that was certain. But in the corner stood my little wooden chest, and my distaff and spindle, and my basket and bundles of starwort. Alys was at Megan's heels, and did not take long to settle gratefully before the warmth of the fire.

I did not sleep much that night, nor on many nights to follow, as summer advanced and the days grew fewer until before my brothers' return. I would sit at my work all day, going down only when I must, to take my place at the table on Lady Anne's right, and eat my small meal under her watchful eye. I knew there were things she wanted to say, questions she was burning to ask. But that was not her way. Besides, she knew she would get no answers from me. I wondered, sometimes, if she had some idea where her son had gone, for Ben's explanations had sounded thin indeed. An old friend; a territorial dispute. Where, they asked? Ben wasn't sure where. But it wouldn't take long; he'd be home soon. But if it were for that, people asked (as the season advanced), why wasn't he back? And if it were so, why tell nobody his plans? Not even his own mother? Rumours abounded, and I was in all of them. So I kept myself to myself, and when I returned from the table, I worked on in my large, candlelit chamber with only Alys for company. Time was growing very short.

Sleep continued to evade me. I paced the room at night, my head full of visions of Red captured by my father's men, and subdued with hot iron. Of the swans flying over storm-tossed water, the movement of their wings becoming ever more difficult. Of Red sustaining some injury, out in hostile territory with nobody to help. Alone in the forest. There would be no handy girl with needle and thread. I had not even had time to sew a rowan cross into his garments, before he left me. I pictured Finbar as I had last seen him, too weak to walk. Too weak to fly. I imagined Red's face, when he at last found the young man with no past. The man he believed to be his brother. It could not be Simon. If I had been able to tell him that, perhaps he would not have gone away and left me alone. Then my little voice, the sensible one, spoke up. *Make haste, Sorcha. Make haste. There is no time for this. Spin. Weave. Make your shirts. Time is shorter than you think.* Nonetheless, I had less control over my thoughts than I'd have liked. The little ring hung around my neck, under my gown, where nobody could see it. When I was alone, I took it out sometimes, wondering how he had judged the size, with nothing but my swollen, knotted fingers to go by. Wondering if my hands would ever be as they once were, small, white and fine. By the time that happened, if it ever did, I would be long gone from here. I would have left behind both husband and wedding ring. It mattered little whether the size were right or no. Yet, when I thought this, I found my hand closing around the ring as if I did not want to let it go. It's mine, something inside me would say. This feeling troubled me greatly.

In her son's absence, Lady Anne took up the reins of the household as she had obviously done before, with calm competence. But the job was not so easy this time. The days followed their familiar pattern, but without Red it was not the same. Disputes took longer to settle. A man burned another's shed, and a donkey was saved in the nick of time. A stranger, passing through on the road, stopped at one of the settlements for ale and shelter. The next morning he was found dead in the yard, with a neat little dagger wound between his ribs. Some of the men complained about taking orders from Ben. Who did he think he was, anyway? He may have been a foster son of the old man, Lord Hugh's father, but that didn't give him the right to start throwing his weight around when Hugh chose to absent himself. Young fellow was getting too big for his boots. Besides, hadn't Master Benedict been there the day Lord Hugh . . . well, you know. Lady Anne told them to get on with their work and stop wasting Ben's time and hers; the estate did not run itself. They obeyed, grumbling. But we could all feel it. The good times were over. As spring grew into summer and a bright, fruitful warmth bathed the land, distrust and suspicion flourished amongst the people. They became fearful and angry, not just towards me and those who protected me, but towards each other as well.

Matters came to a head a few days before midsummer. The wife of a cottager was assaulted; another cottager was accused, but protested his innocence. Factions formed. It seemed only a matter of time before some enthusiast wielding pitchfork or scythe did someone a nasty injury. Lady Anne called the parties in and did her best to arbitrate. Ben, with the assistance of a handful of loyal men, managed to keep them from each other's throats. But no solution was reached, and the mood turned ugly. There had been no word from Red. So Lady Anne sent for her brother.

If the atmosphere of the house had been tense before, once Richard closed his well manicured hand around us, the place was on a knife edge. His method of solving the immediate problem was very efficient. The accused man was summarily taken away, somewhere exceedingly private. He was accompanied by several rather large men in the russet and black of Northwoods. Later in the day, Richard advised Lady Anne that the man had confessed. Still later, he was strung up from a tree and that was the end of it. They said, when they cut him down, that his body had some injuries that hadn't been put there by a rope around the neck. That was what they said, and it wasn't so hard to believe. Nobody had dared try to save this man, who may or may not have been guilty.

There had been no young Finbar and Sorcha to intervene here, no passionate children brave enough, or foolish enough, to take the law into their own hands as we had with Simon. It was the other things that were said, that would have worried Red more. Things like, at least Lord Richard understands what's what. Takes quick action. Lets folk know what they can get away with, and what they can't. Of course, the other faction disagreed entirely. They muttered things like, a man'd confess to anything, if they did *that* to him; and, what about the idea of a fair hearing, and proper questions asked of both sides? Where was Lord Hugh when they needed him? And who did Richard think he was, to decide anyway? Heard what happened to his men, when he sent them off over the water on a fool's errand?

Me, I stayed in my room, scarce venturing out save for the necessary ablutions. Megan understood, I think, and made my excuses at the evening meal once, twice, three times. A delicate stomach. Could not keep anything down. Before, Lady Anne would have summoned me. But now I was her daughter-in-law, and she must show respect for my wishes. I was, in name at least, the lady of the house. Megan came back and told me there were whispers about the cause of my sudden illness. A bit soon, maybe, but – Lord Hugh had evidently been busy, they said; sampling the wares before he bought them, maybe. I felt a cold fury when I heard these rumours, but I kept a tight rein on my anger. It's not important, I told myself. Nothing is important except your work. Working alone in my room, I finished the fifth shirt and began the last.

CHAPTER TWELVE

I t was just unlucky, I suppose. Unlucky and unfortunate, that my plan to slip out of the house after dark and make my way alone to the river was completely ruined by Lady Anne's last minute decision to take the whole household down to the water for an outdoor supper. A torchlit picnic under the trees, to mark the eve of midsummer. For she recognised the unease, the suspicion and mistrust amongst her people. This was her attempt to jolt them out of themselves, to lift their spirits, to get them talking again. It was a good idea. A great strategy. For me, it spelled disaster. I spent most of the day agonising about whether to go with them, or whether to feign illness again, and try to slip down later, unobserved. I had no idea where my brothers would come, but Conor, I supposed, could see things as they were and might guide them to some place of relative safety. If I were at the river before dusk, if I could get away from the others without attracting notice, perhaps they could fly to where I waited alone, and I could warn them. Perhaps. My spirit shrank to think that Richard would be there, so close. Ben had watched over me like an anxious mother with a delicate babe. Even Margery had given me a wan smile the other day. But still I felt alone, so alone; the path was indeed a hard one, and full of dangers.

If Red had been there, he would have engaged his uncle in some complex debate about boundaries or allegiances. If Red had been there, he would have ensured I was surrounded by those whom he trusted, protected from prying questions and suggestive looks. But Red was gone; and his uncle made himself my close companion as the household walked down the avenue of poplars to a broad green expanse of river bank, that warm summer afternoon. It lacked but a short time until dusk. Not long. Not long enough. Lady Anne had provided me with clothing fit for my new status as her son's wife. I had chosen the plainest and most demure of these gowns, dark green in colour with a high neckline and sleeves to the wrist. But still he made comment, with a sidelong glance and an insinuating lift of the brows. His fair beard was trimmed neat as a privet hedge after the first autumn pruning. His black tunic was immaculate, the neckline finished with a thin line of silver thread.

'Well, my dear.' He looked me up and down, taking his time. 'Quite the lady, I see. You surprised us all. Hugh surprised us. Never thought he was one of those men that think with their loins first and their head later. Not our Hugh. Monumental blunder. Still, it may be short-lived enough.'

I walked on, grimly suppressing the urge to kick

him. Before and behind me, people carried blankets and baskets, chattered and laughed. Lady Anne had sound instincts. Where was Ben? I thought I glimpsed his blond head somewhere in front.

'I hear you've been a little – indisposed, my dear,' said Richard in silky tones. 'Too bad. So pleased you thought fit to show yourself today. Must keep up appearances, you know, now you're one of the family. Wonder how the locals will take to a half-breed brat as the new heir to Harrowfield? Not too well, I'd have thought. Not too well at all. Neither of Britain nor of Erin, but at the same time, both. Heard that one? Tell me, was this part of your original plan? Was that the reason they sent you here?'

He continued in this vein for some time, while I tried to block out his words; it would soon be dusk, and I feared what might happen if I could not escape the group and find a place alone. Any meeting with my brothers must be brief indeed. I would see them, and touch them, and utter a warning; and then they must lie low till dawn, for here they were no more than barbarians strayed deep into the heart of enemy territory.

'What I still can't understand,' said Richard, 'is why he had to wed you. Was he so desperate to have you, that he must sacrifice his future to quench his lust? Any other man would simply have taken what he wanted, and got on with things. Don't get me wrong, my dear. Your charms are quite obvious. You would stir any man's blood. But a wedding ring? That should scarcely have been necessary. It's enough to make one believe what they say, about witches and spells and love potions. Something drove the boy out of his right mind, long enough to put the ring on your finger; and I'll wager my best stallion to a pot of porridge it wasn't your sweet young body alone, delectable though it is. Oh, please forgive the remark about fingers. I see you cannot well wear a ring. Those hands are scarcely apt for it. Not the most attractive part of your anatomy, my dear, if I may say so. Now that's another thing that intrigues me . . .'

We had reached the river bank. It was close to dusk; folk spread their blankets on the grass, and Lady Anne ordered the cask of ale to be broached. Somebody got out a whistle and began to play dance tunes. I saw Ben hovering on the outskirts of the group, as if looking for signs of trouble. Five or six of his men were placed strategically around us. He was doing his job, and doing it well. But this was one evening when I could have wished for a less effective net of protection.

There was no choice but to sit by Richard and his sister. I was family now, whatever anyone might think of me. They ate and drank; I sat on the ground, straight-backed, silently thanking Lady Anne for engaging her brother in conversation about the sale of surplus stock. Around us, the household relaxed enough to enjoy the balmy evening, their sense of wellbeing no doubt assisted by the copious flow of good ale. I saw Margery there with her little son. He was sitting up by himself now, and his brown hair had grown sufficiently to show the hint of a curl. Margery was still pale, but she exchanged a quiet word with this one and that. Ben did not relax. He and his men patrolled the margins of the group, weapons at the ready.

The sun sank below the tree tops, and the sky turned to lavender and violet and deepest grey. Above us the willows sighed and were still. Framed by their weeping branches, the river water slowly darkened to black. Torches were lit, and placed on poles around the grassy expanse where we sat. The whistle was joined by a drum and a fiddle, and some of the young folk got up to dance. Out on the river, there had been no sign of swans.

'Tell me, my dear,' Richard turned his attention to me without warning, 'have you no idea where your husband has gone off to so suddenly? I found the official explanation just a little hard to believe. Stretched credibility just a touch too far, I thought. Young Ben's keeping something back. What about you? Did Hugh let on what he was about, when he abandoned you so quickly? Secrets of the pillow, and all that? I should think you'd be adept at that, got him eating out of your hand, I hear. What did he tell you?'

'Richard,' said Lady Anne reprovingly, not liking his manner at all. Her loyalties here were clearly divided.

'I wouldn't trouble yourself, sister.' Richard gave her a comical look. 'You forget a woman of Erin cannot think and feel as you do. She does well enough at the surface appearance, I grant you that, but scratch that surface and you'll find your enemy under it. A spy. A sorceress, even. I'd put money on it any day. You can't trust them.'

'Jenny is my son's wife,' said Lady Anne tightly.

'Mm,' said Richard. 'So she is, so she is. Now tell me, little niece, for so my sister would have me call you, though it sticks in the throat, where did Hugh go? What was his errand? What could be so urgent, that he abandoned his bride on her wedding day? What could be so secret, that even his mother was not informed?'

Sorcha. Sorcha, where are you?

'What is it, Jenny? What's the matter? Are you ill?' Lady Anne had seen my face change, as my mind caught the silent call of my brother.

491

Wait. Wait. I'm coming. Don't move.

I sprang up, trying to keep my expression blank. Nodded and mimed. *Please excuse me. My stomach . . .*

'Take Megan with you, my dear,' Lady Anne called after me, as I walked as calmly as I could towards the river, towards the shelter of the willows. On pretext of needing privacy to rid my stomach of its contents, perhaps I could – maybe I could –

'Where are you going?' Ben loomed up in front of me, face anxious in the torchlight. 'By God, woman, you have the weakest stomach in history. Here, let me help you. No going off alone, it's against the rules, remember?'

But I gestured, and gestured again. *Please. Just for a minute. I won't go far. Please.* He regarded me, frowning. It was true, there were certain bodily functions that did require due privacy. But he respected his orders. *Please. I'll be safe enough.*

'All right,' he said, 'but don't go far. He'd kill me if he knew I'd let you go out of sight. Take care. If you're gone long I'll come looking.'

Then, a sedate walk across the grass until I was out of sight. Feet moving cautiously, mind reaching with frantic haste. *Where are you? How far upstream from the little bridge? Quickly, I don't have long.*

The bridge is not far to the south. A place where a great willow has fallen. I will come to you.

No! There is danger! Wait there; I'm coming.

At last, a bend in the path, and Ben was gone from view. I ran. Picked up my skirts and ran soft-footed under the willows, to the place where I remembered a huge tree lying by the path, its knotted roots laid bare, its guardian spirit long gone to seek another home. I could not see them.

Where are you?

492

'I'm here, Sorcha.' My brother Conor stepped out from behind the tangle of earth-covered roots, a thin, frail figure in the faint moonlight. I saw the extreme pallor of his face, the long, tangled hair, the ragged shreds of clothing that were all he had left. He looked as insubstantial as a wraith.

Don't speak aloud. There are people close by. Oh, Conor! I felt his arms close around me. He was wasted like a man dying of the flux, and his body was racked by a violent trembling. But it felt good, so good to hold him.

The others. Where are the others?

They cannot come. Not this time.

But – but – Bitter disappointment flooded through me.

It takes great strength, great resolve, to coerce them; to force them to follow when every instinct they have cries out against it. I can bring them only once. When you are ready, call me, and we will come. Don't weep, little owl. This is a very brave thing that you do for us.

At Meán Geimhridh, you did not come. I looked for you, and you did not come. That had indeed been a terrible night. Terrible and yet wonderful, for I had not forgotten the birth of John's son.

We went to the cave, and you were gone. We could not find you. A mind picture of my brothers frantically searching; finding my belongings still scattered around the cave, my little hand loom, my warm cloak and boots; the fireplace blanketed in snow. Diarmid cursing. Finbar standing alone by the lake, silent.

The others – Conor, are they all right? What of Finbar?

They still live. But you should make haste, if you can. As soon as you are ready, you must call me. We can come only once.

He was holding something back; still expert at the

arts of the mind, weakened as he was, my brother
was veiling the full truth in order to protect me.

What is it? Conor, what is it you're not telling me?

*Hush, Sorcha. When you call, we will come. This I
promise you.*

I wept, my head against his chest, my arms
around his waist, his wrapped about my shoulders.
He was my brother. I had to believe him.

It was a measure of my distress, and of his weakness,
that neither of us heard the sounds of men approaching
until it was much too late. Then, very close by, a twig
cracked under a boot heel, and I heard Ben's voice.

'Jenny? Are you all right?'

My head came up with a jerk. There he was,
sword in hand, face almost comical in its shock, with
dropped jaw and staring eyes as he looked across and
saw me in my brother's arms. I opened my mouth
and shut it again.

'Seize that man!' Now there were lights, and the
sound of weapons being drawn, and behind Ben was
Lord Richard of Northwoods, his face a wondrous
blend of gloating excitement and righteous outrage.
'Take the girl too. You see how she repays Lord Hugh
for his trust!'

Still I stood there gaping stupidly, numb with
shock. But Conor possessed skills none of these
people had ever dreamed of, and before ever Lord
Richard's men advanced across the open ground, he
had slipped from my arms like a shadow, and vanished back under the willows in total silence. It was
as if he had never been there.

'After him!' hissed Richard. 'Don't let him escape!'
Three men crashed off into the undergrowth, eager
for the chase. But Richard stayed behind, and I felt his
grip close around my arm like an iron fetter.

'That was exceedingly stupid of you, my dear. Put quite a dampener on the family picnic. What, oh what would our Hugh say? What I wouldn't give, to see his face when he finds out. Less than two moons wed, and already she's off into the woods like a bitch on heat, wrapping herself around another man. And not just any man, either; one of her own kind, somebody that's avid for the information she can give him, and – well, come on, boy. Give me a hand. Let's take the little slut back to my sister, and see what she thinks of her son's new bride now.'

And the cruellest thing, as Richard dragged me along after him, was to look into Ben's face and see the expression of wounded betrayal and shocked incomprehension there. What could he do but believe the evidence of his own eyes? He had come after me, concerned solely for my safety. He had found me out in the darkness, locked in the arms of a young man of my own people. He did not want to believe it, but my guilt was plain to see. I could give no explanation. I walked back with him on one side of me, his distress written plain on every feature, and Richard on the other, his vice-like grip telling me plainly, you thought you could outwit Richard of Northwoods? You made a big miscalculation, little witch girl.

Richard believed in swift justice. That way, you showed your people you were in control. So, you identified the culprit. If there was no hard evidence, you made sure there was a confession. Promptly extracted. Then you carried out the appropriate penalty. For adultery, a whipping might do, or some other form of public humiliation. For the reception of outlaws, it was death. It was almost superfluous to add sorcery to the list. As for the punishment, there were various methods. He would enjoy selecting the most appropriate. However, in my case things were not so simple. It appeared certain members of the household had dug their heels in, holding out for any proceedings to be carried out strictly according to the law, as Lord Hugh would certainly wish. The matter could be heard at the next folkmoot, less than two moons away. Before that assembly of all the tenants of Harrowfield, the lord of the estate could hear the points of view of all parties, make a decision and deliver his judgement, according to the king's law. For there was but one king here now, since Wessex had placed its hand on the north. But this case was a tricky one, involving a close family member of the landholder, and combining three charges. Perhaps the hearing should wait for a shiremoot, run by King Ethelwulf's own alderman. And the next shiremoot was not likely before Lord Hugh's return. Best to wait until then, some people said.

But Richard did not see the need to wait so long. The people were unsettled, unable to apply themselves properly to their work, and things must be put right before Lord Hugh's return, not after. Besides, Richard owned the neighbouring estate. He was, by marriage, as good as master of Harrowfield in Hugh's absence. The decision was rightfully his to make. It seemed that daily he took greater control of the shocked and divided household. Locked in a tiny upstairs room, I heard of this only in snatches, as a man unbolted the door to bring me bread and water, or take away the bucket that furnished the cell, along with a pile of straw and a thin blanket. The room had a single, very small opening to the light, high in its outer wall. Through this I could glimpse a little patch of blue by day; at night, one star shone against the dark. Had I truly possessed the power of transformation, perhaps the small owl might just have managed to squeeze out through this slit in the stones. Out into the dark, over the water, back to the deep embracing arms of her forest. My heart longed to cry out to my brothers. But I bade my inner voice be silent. There could be but one call; one summons, when my work was finished, and they could go free.

At first I was in utter despair, for they cast me into this tiny prison with nothing but the gown I wore; even my boots were taken away. I imagined Richard's men searching my room, throwing distaff and spindle to one side, tossing the contents of chest and basket on the fire. That first night, I sat in the corner with my arms wrapped over my head and my knees against my chest, and let the tears pour down my face. I feared Conor's capture. I feared that I would never save my brothers; and yet, while I lived there was still a chance, and so I might not speak to protest my innocence. But if guilty, I would die, and nobody could save them then. I feared to be put to torture; I had seen what my own folk did to Simon, and knew I could not withstand it as he had. Like some foolish girl whose head is full of fancies, who dreams of a hero on a white charger, I longed for Red to come back and rescue me. And yet, I dreaded his return, for would he not believe, as Ben believed, that I had betrayed them all? I did not want to see that look of pain and shock in his eyes. Better that he did not come back, until . . . Towards dawn, I ceased rocking and weeping, and sat like a hollow shell, blank minded. A bird flew by the window, calling to its mate. A voice within me spoke, at last. *One foot before the other. Straight ahead. This is the path. Straight ahead, Sorcha. You knew it would be hard. It will become harder still. One foot, then the other. And again. Into the dark.*

When the men came again, bringing water and a

lump of dry bread, I heard their talk and knew that Conor had eluded them. For they scoured the river bank all night by torchlight, but never hide nor hair of the wild stranger did they find. Vanished into thin air, he had. Like a ghost. You'd hardly believe he'd been there at all, if you hadn't seen him with your own eyes. Big fierce fellow, he was; one of them Irish chieftains you heard about, wring your neck with a single twist if you gave them the chance. Privately, most of the men were glad they hadn't run into him, out there in the night. But Lord Richard wasn't happy. He wasn't happy at all.

For a long time nobody came to see me. The door would creak open and the empty bucket would be thrown back in, or the used one taken. A meagre meal would be left. That was no problem. I was used to going hungry. Worse was the lack of light, the blank stone walls, unbroken save for the small window high above my head. Worse still, the agony of idle hands. For I had been close, so close to the end of my task. Five shirts finished, and only one to make. To have this snatched from me, to be locked up without the means to complete my work was cruel indeed. Close to despair, I resorted to telling tales, an old, much used device to occupy the mind and keep out what was not wanted. Culhan's quest for the Lady Edan. The four fair children of Lir. No, maybe not that one. Niamh of the golden hair. The cup of Isha. That story had a hero who was extremely good at waiting. Medb, the warrior queen with a penchant for lusty young heroes. Simon had laughed at that one. And the tale of the man Toby and his mermaid. Of all the tales I had ever told, of all the stories I had ever heard, that was the one I loved best. Who would have dreamed that Red could tell such a story?

I had lost count of the days, but many passed and I saw nobody but my guards. Then one morning the door opened and it was Lady Anne, with a couple of women behind her, bearing my distaff and spindle, my basket of starwort, my needles and thread. On top of the basket, somebody had tossed the five completed shirts. I restrained myself from snatching these precious items and clutching them to my breast. Kept my face calm. Lady Anne glanced around the cell, and a slight frown creased her brow. The women eyed me furtively. I must have been quite a sight, filthy, my hair tangled, my eyes blinking in the sudden light from the hallway. Lady Anne dismissed the women and shut the door behind her.

'You realise,' she said quietly, 'that this will break his heart.'

It was as if she had slapped me on the face. I stared at her as she took a step forward, wrinkling her nose. I supposed I did not smell as a lady should.

'My son loved you,' she went on, astonishing me still further. 'Loved you as he has never loved any living being; more than he loves the valley itself. I dismissed it as passing fancy, youthful passion, owing more to the urges of the body than to the feelings of the heart. He proved me wrong by giving you his name, though it went against everything he believed in. How could you do this to him? How could you do this to us? We have sheltered you, we have been kind enough to you, considering what you are. Is the hatred in you so bitter against our people that you must destroy all that we hold dear? Was it for this that you were sent here?'

I shook my head slowly. *I do not hate you. I never did. I seek only to complete my task. And you're wrong*

499

about your son, quite wrong, he – Without words, I could explain nothing.

'Your people killed Simon,' said Lady Anne wearily. 'You have destroyed Hugh. What more do you want?'

How can you say that, when you hold me imprisoned here? It was your son who brought me here. But for him, I would never have come to Harrowfield. This was not of my choosing. I was mute. She gave a sigh.

'Despite all, I find myself bound to act by my son's wishes. In spite of all. He set great faith in this strange task of yours, he bound us all to keep your work safe, and you with it. You did, indeed, cast a net over him from which he cannot escape without harming himself and all that love him. I have brought your things. I have done what I must. Work on, if you have a mind to it.'

I forced a smile, gave a nod. *Thank you.* She did not realise how much she had done for me. Now she seemed to be turning to go. I grasped her sleeve, for I must ask a question. She shrank away from me as if my touch would poison her. *I – door, out – what, when?*

'Your future is not in my hands, Jenny,' she said. 'I would not even have taken this step, to bring your work here, had not Hugh extracted a promise from me that I would allow you to go on with it, whatever happened. I am too close to this, too distressed, to judge you with any fairness. It is for my brother to hear your case, and to decide your fate. In Hugh's absence, he is the head of this family, and must judge as he thinks fit. But he, too, wishes to avoid any suggestion that the proceedings will be less than equitable. So he plans to await Father Stephen of Ravenglass, whose business should bring him here after Lammas. On the matter of sorcery, it is prudent to consult a man of the cloth.' She looked around the cell again. 'It would hurt my son to see you housed here. But not so much as the truth will hurt him.'

What truth? I thought bitterly as the door closed behind her, and I heard the scrape as the bolt slid across. Didn't Red once say, there are as many truths as stars in the sky, and every one of them different? Perhaps that was the only real truth.

The rats were my only companions. They crept out at night and nibbled the straw bedding. It was the one time in my life that I was grateful for the spiny barbs of the starwort plant, for that the rats would not touch. With nothing else to occupy me, with nothing around me but the four stone walls, I worked as long as the light lasted, and tried to sleep when it was dark. Many days passed, each like the last. I found that if I disregarded the way my hands stiffened with the pain, if I forced the fingers to move, I could make reasonable progress. I paid for it at night, for my hands ached fiercely, denying me sleep. The sixth shirt slowly took shape. It was not as well fashioned as the others, for the light was poor and my vision sometimes blurred, but it would do. It must do.

By the changing light through my small window I judged it to be around the time of Lugnasad, close to summer's end, when I began to receive visits from Lord Richard. He had taken his time before he came to gloat over me, but once he started, it became a regular occurrence and one I came to dread. Perhaps foolishly, I had allowed myself to feel hope when Lady Anne had given me back my work. The task was within my grasp, and had she not said they were waiting for Father Stephen so that I might have a fair trial? Then Richard came, and I saw that the truth was quite different.

'Well, my dear.' He could have been greeting me over a sociable goblet of mead. His tone was affable. His gaze went around the tiny room, and back to me. 'Your reign as Lady of Harrowfield was indeed short. I had credited you with more cunning; seems I was wrong. Very silly mistake, my dear, very silly indeed. Played right into my hands.' He gave a delicate sniff. 'Odd sort of smell in here. Reminds me of pigswill.' He fished out a snowy white square of linen, and dabbed at his nose. There was a faint scent of bergamot oil. 'Shouldn't bother you, I suppose. I imagine things at home were quite – rough? I've heard your kind have no aversion to wallowing in their own filth. Scum will find scum.'

I set my teeth and fixed my eyes on my work. *If Red could hear you say that to me, he would kill you. Uncle or no uncle.*

He laughed. 'Oh, I do like that grim expression, the spark in the eye. What is going through that little head of yours, I wonder? Think Hughie boy might come galloping back to the rescue? Don't think so. Not a chance. Wherever he's off to, it's far, far away. You can tell by their expressions. Very anxious, they are, certain individuals – very keen to reach him, I'm told, but seems nobody quite knows where he is. Haven't done him a mischief too, have you?' His eyes narrowed. 'I trust that's not part of the plan. I have a role for Hugh and I intend to see he carries it out according to my wishes. Don't hope for salvation in that quarter, girlie. He's not coming. Not until you're done with, dead and buried, out of my nephew's life and mine for good. My network is extensive. When he's on his way home, I'll know; and he may find himself – delayed. Nothing harmful, mind; just a little diversion to keep him away long enough.'

My hands stopped momentarily, the shuttle between the threads. *One foot after the other*. I breathed again, and pulled the weft tight.

'That stopped you in your tracks, didn't it? Surely you didn't imagine – no, even you couldn't be so stupid. Death is the only possible penalty, my dear. It's only the method that gives cause for reflection. So many to choose from, each more – piquant – than the last. There's carrying a weight of hot iron over a marked distance. Not for you, I think. There's plucking a stone from a vat of boiling water. Seen that one carried out, fellow required a certain amount of – persuasion. There are the quick methods, hanging, drowning, various things with a knife. Less entertaining, those. I rather fancy something with heat. So hard to decide. So I'm waiting for divine assistance. Father Stephen of Ravenglass is the bishop's man, a learned cleric and a very old friend. The Reverend Father is skilled in the driving out of demons, and cleansing, and dealing with the art of sorcery. I rely on his judgement totally. I cannot think of a single occasion when we have found ourselves in disagreement. We are of one mind. His support will give my verdict – respectability. Essential, I think, for when your husband returns.'

A shiver ran through me. I would have trusted my life to Father Brien, and I had seen wisdom and kindness in the face of the man who had blessed my marriage, that night in the woods. But something told me there would be no such understanding in Father Stephen's eyes. I began to believe, finally, that I was going to die. But my fingers kept on with their steady movement, in and out, in and out, as I wove another square for the sixth shirt.

'You know,' observed Richard, 'perhaps you really

are a fool. Perhaps you really don't understand our language as well as Hugh thinks. Aren't you afraid? Wouldn't you like a chance to save yourself? Any other girl would be on her knees pleading by now. And it would be easy. Quite easy.' He was almost purring, like a satisfied cat; but no cat would stoop so low.

'Under the filth, you're still quite a succulent little slut,' he said softly. 'Hasn't it occurred to you that you still have some goods to trade? I'm a man, my dear. I might be bought, as Hugh was. Undo your buttons, let me see the flesh where your clothing hides its whiteness. Or shall I do it for you?'

I spat, accurately, on the toe of his polished boot. He responded with a gust of laughter.

'Oh, dear! She took me seriously! Well done, little whore! Standing on her dignity! You don't really think I'd dirty my hands on you? Smeared with your own filth, and with those great rough paws? Once, I might have done. But I'm not desperate enough to take my nephew's leavings. I have far brighter prospects in sight; that young widow, for instance, what was her name, Molly, Mary? Showing a great deal too much interest in your fate; makes me wonder if she's a proper person to bring up a young boy. Must do something about that. Take steps. Needs a good strong man in her life, straighten her out, teach her a few tricks. Well, my dear. I'll leave you now. Enjoy yourself. It won't be much longer.'

There was no time for hate. No time for fear. After a while, I found that there were some tasks I could do in the dark, and I stopped sleeping. There was no time for rest. I finished the front of the last shirt, and began to weave the back. Outside, the season was well advanced, and early leaves were blown across my tiny patch of sky. I judged that it was close to Meán Fómhair, and that I had been imprisoned here for three moons. In my mind I saw the late roses in full bloom, the berries fat and glossy on bramble and currant bush, bees busy amongst swathes of lavender. I thought, the apples will be ripening. He said . . . but I would not let myself finish the thought, for there was no time for foolish hope. *Spin. Weave. Sew. One foot before the other. And again. On and on into the dark.*

Almost every day, Richard came. Sometimes it was only for a few moments, but more often he was in expansive mood, wanting to talk. Now that he had me, as he thought, in the palm of his hand, he grew less cautious. For after all, I could hardly repeat what I heard, could I, even supposing I had the opportunity, which was unlikely. And so, piece by piece, as if solving a puzzle in small steps, I began to learn another side of the story.

'So, here we are again. Can't say you're looking well, my dear, that would be stretching the imagination just a little far. Feeding you enough, are they? Just enough. I want you kept alive, until the hearing. Justice must be seen to be done, after all. Unfortunate that Father Stephen has been delayed so long. Busy man. But he'll be here, never fear. Mind you, if it's too long, we'll go ahead without him. Hugh's weak. Besotted, that's the word. Can't risk waiting till he gets back. Even after this, even after you run out to satisfy your itch with another man, and sell his secrets under his nose, the boy can't be relied on to do the right thing. No, it must be soon, and public. Decisive. Final. That's what people expect, and that's what I'll give them. Something spectacular with fire, I think. That way, we get rid of the sorceress and her spells in one dizzying, dazzling display of heat and light. Orgasmic. Blissful. I shall so enjoy myself.'

My hands plied their steady trade; I made myself breathe slowly. But something must have showed on my face.

'I was tempted,' he said, leaning back against the wall, the stool tilted on two legs. 'Sorely tempted. This handiwork is very important to you, isn't it? What would you have done for me, to get it back? Would you have . . .' his next remarks I will not repeat here, for they were scarce fit for the lowest of drunken gatherings. 'Might have tried that. But my sister forestalled me. Following her dear Hugh's orders. Unbelievable. After I told her what your people did to Simon. Well, there's a sort of perverse enjoyment in watching you hurt yourself, little whore. Why do you do it? Does it excite you? Do you crave pain, to satisfy you? You married the wrong man, daughter of Erin. He would never have been enough for you. Besides,' and his tone changed, 'he was promised. He chose to forget that, but I do not forget. I know the way it should be. The way it will be, when you are – disposed of. Hugh will wed Elaine. Harrowfield will wed Northwoods, and in one grand gesture the largest and richest estate in Northumbria will be established. Easy, so easy. And think what holding that much power does to a man. At one stroke, he takes all pieces on the board. That satisfies him in a way no woman ever could. Who will his neighbours turn to for protection? Who will they trust to train their fighting men and purchase their arms? Who will they pay, to ensure good will?' He was grinning, stretching his arms expansively behind his head. 'Believe me, girl, a man that scents such power lets nothing stand in his way. Nothing.'

Is this Hugh of Harrowfield we speak of here? I could not prevent my brows rising in scornful disbelief.

'Hugh is malleable. Cares only for his trees and his cattle and his tidy little life. Elaine, she's like me. Must have her own way. Problem was, what she wanted didn't suit my plans, didn't suit at all. Everything was smooth as silk until she started to grow up, thirteen, fourteen, used to getting what she wanted, no need to say no up till then. New pony, deerhound, jewels, finery. But she broke the rules. Fell for the wrong brother.'

Elaine and Simon? That was a possibility I had never thought of. But it explained much. It explained, in particular, her manner towards Red, for I could see now that she had indeed treated him like a brother. Poor Elaine. One of them was dead, and the other had married me. She had not deserved to lose them both.

'Once she set her heart on it, wouldn't let go of the notion,' Richard went on. 'Had to tell her, finally. You can't. No. Simple as that. She didn't like it. But I'm her father. Hugh's a milksop, doesn't have that killer streak, that bit of meanness a man needs in him to survive, to get on. Runs a pretty farm, I'll give him that. But he's weak. Suitable. You'd understand that better than most, slut. Bent him to your own will easily enough, didn't you? If he couldn't withstand that, how well do you think he'd deal with Richard of Northwoods? So, he marries my daughter, and the whole valley is mine. If she'd taken the younger brother, that would have been quite another matter. Hopeless. For one thing, he wouldn't inherit, not unless . . . besides, he was too wild. Unpredictable. Unstable, you could almost say. Not at all a safe option. No, it's better this way. Or was, before you came into the picture . . .'

He sat forward suddenly, the wooden stool thumping down heavily on the stone floor.

'You know, I thought Hugh brought you here for information. That was how it looked. You were holding something he needed. He was waiting for you to talk. Cat and mouse game. I could understand that. But my nephew's never shown the slightest interest in that sort of strategy. Never lifted a finger to help in the campaigns, never made the smallest contribution to the cause. Couldn't care less. So why would he involve himself now, I wondered? Had to be about his brother. Young Simon. Somehow, you were tied up in that. Had something you could tell him. Seemed to me, back then, that you could talk if you chose to. Not much wrong there, I thought. There were times when I saw you, about to speak, opening your little mouth and then choking back the words.'

I wound the thread onto the spindle, feeling the fibres sharp against my fingers, knowing my hands were becoming raw and stinking again, from lack of light, from filth and neglect and abuse.

'But then there was the unfortunate accident. It happens. Rocks fall, people get hurt. Freak of nature. They told me you didn't utter a sound, no call for help, no screams, nothing. Can't believe you wouldn't cry out. No girl has that sort of control. Had to come to the conclusion the malady's real. You genuinely can't talk. Mute. Dumb. Silent as the grave. Adds a certain spice to the current situation. Means I can chat away to my heart's content, bare the secrets of my soul, and you can't tell them a thing. Not a thing. Be a shame, though, not to hear you screaming when the fire licks your ankles, and catches your gown, and turns that soft white flesh into an overcooked slab of meat. I'd have enjoyed hearing that. Oh well, can't have it both ways.'

When he was gone, I allowed myself to cry, just for a little. I allowed myself to stare up at the window, where rain was coming down sideways, and a cool breeze gusted in fitfully, and I let myself think, if he were here, he would kill you. It was just as well he was not here. If he were here, he would face a choice that would break him. Better that he did not return, until after . . . But I was frightened. Frightened to die, frightened of the fire. Terrified that I was working too slowly, that I would not be ready in time . . . I did not weep for long. The little voice was there all the time now. *Spin. Weave. Sew.* I worked on, and the half made shirt, which was the last of six, was stained with blood from my hands, and filth from the room, and it was wet with my tears. He who wore this garment would wear my love, my pain and my terror. These things would set him free.

I can remember one good moment in those dark times. I had become used to my guards. I did not know their names, but there was one older man whom I had seen with Ben earlier. He did not come often, and when he did his distaste for the dirty, lightless cell and the duty he must perform was evident in his expression. There was one day when he brought the bucket, and threw it in the corner as usual, and then he took a little package from his pocket and slipped it furtively into my basket.

'Chin up, lass,' he muttered, and then he was gone, the heavy door slamming to behind him. In the little parcel was fresh, good bread with grains in it, and a small round of cheese, and a handful of blackberries. I made it last, knowing my stomach might reject such fare after so long a time of hunger. I shared

509

the crumbs of bread and cheese with the rats, thinking they might as well have a little enjoyment. After that I did not see this guard again, but his kindness warmed me. And I still remember the wonderful taste of that food, the mellow ripeness of the cheese, the tart juicy berries, the bread with its smell of open fields. Every mouthful.

The shirt grew. It was surprising how much I could get done if I forgot about the pain, if I slept only when utter exhaustion forced it, if I kept going in light and dark. Whether love or fear drove me hardest, I could not say. But the shirt took shape as day followed day, and night followed sleepless night, as the breezes that blew in my little window took on the scents of autumn. Leaves burning. Fruit boiling in the preserving pan. River mists rising in early morning chill. There were sounds, too. Men unloading root crops to be stored in the barn. It was harvest time, and I had been at Harrowfield almost a whole year. Women arguing. Cart wheels on the gravel path. One morning, a lone horseman riding out very early. It mattered little. It seemed, now I was locked away, the household had reverted to its peaceful old routine. As if I had never been. For I had seen nobody, since that one visit from Lady Anne; nobody but my guards and Lord Richard. Perhaps I was forgotten.

The waiting could not last for ever. There came a day when I heard the sound of well-shod hooves in the courtyard, and jingling harnesses, and men's voices. And that afternoon, when Richard came, it was to gloat. The bishop's representative had arrived at last, and it was time for me to account for myself before a formal hearing. That would take place tomorrow, and then . . . Richard was elated, almost beside himself with glee. I thought, why does he hate his nephew so much? That was what it was all about. The feeling of power excited him, that was certain, but there was a particular gleam in his eye, when he spoke Red's name, that I thought bordered on madness. He made a mistake, that day. Carried along on the tide of anticipated victory, he said too much.

'Let's talk about fire.' He watched slit-eyed as I bound the shirt's hemline with awkward, fumbling movements of needle and thread. Sometimes my fingers grew numb and it was hard to make them obey me. 'If you have the right materials, you can do interesting things with fire. You'd be surprised who I learned that from. So would your father, my dear.'

For a moment I froze.

'Ah! Touched a nerve, did I? So we guessed right. She thought it must be you, when I gave a description. Want to hear more?'

I moved the needle under, over, through. Another stitch. And another.

'Won't tell him that, of course. The learned Father. Doesn't need to know, does he? Your guilt is plain; we need add no more fuel to that fire.' He gave a sort of giggle. It was not a pleasant sound. 'Joke in bad taste, sorry. Anyway, as I was saying. Had a very interesting time on my recent trip to your homeland, young woman. Lost a few men; that was unfortunate. Failed to secure the outpost I wanted; that was even more regrettable. But once I have the resources of Harrowfield at my disposal, there'll be no stopping me. Minor setback. That was all. Put it behind me. The information I got, that's a different matter.'

He leaned forward, eyes intent.

'Ways to make a hot fire. Ways to make a very special fire that consumes a body, leaving only bare bones behind. I've seen it employed. He showed me.

One of your own kind; but he's a man after my own heart. Astute. Battle-smart. Decisive. No false ideals about Eamonn. He'll trade in what you want, if it suits him. Men. Arms. Information. If you've got something he wants, he'll give.'

I was hard put to it to go on working, and I did not succeed in keeping my face calm. Eamonn. Eamonn of the Marshes? Doing deals with a Briton? I could scarce believe it. Both my father and Seamus Redbeard had considered Eamonn one of their staunchest allies. Hadn't he been wed to Eilis? Who was playing games now?

'We're not all like Hugh, you know,' went on Richard, studying my expression. 'Full of pompous ideals and half-baked do-goodery. If we were all like that, it wouldn't be just the Islands that would be lost. Your kind would be swarming all over us like vermin, and nothing would be safe; it would be the end of the civilised world. Believe me, it's men like myself that hold the land secure so Hugh can potter about with his chickens and plant his precious oaks.'

I was staring at him now, not even pretending to go on working.

'Made the bargain of my life, this last trip. Told you before about that woman, didn't I, remarkable woman, didn't give her name, but she was a friend of Eamonn's, hand in glove they were, and she'd been particularly interested in you last time we spoke. Told me that story, about the children of Sevenwaters and how they mysteriously disappeared.'

My heart was thumping. Woman? What woman? Surely he could not mean Eilis?

'I made an offer then. Said if you were Colum's daughter, I'd accept payment for your safe return. Payment in land, preferably. A nice little parcel between the forest and the coast. Colum wouldn't like that. But they said he'd gone half crazy, looking for the girl. Maybe he was crazy enough to give me what I wanted. It was worth a try.'

I was finding it difficult to breathe.

'She took the message back to Colum, that first time. Extraordinary woman. Mane of auburn hair, delectable figure, quite enchanting. Eamonn certainly seemed to think so. Wasn't paying much attention to that pasty little wife of his. Anyway, she was kindness itself. Said she'd convey my offer, and gave me a couple of her own men to escort me back to the coast. Still got them. Sound fellows. Silent, and handy with a knife, or their hands. So, I went back this time expecting a pretty good response from Sevenwaters. I was optimistic. Not only would I get you out of my way, I'd gain an advantage I never hoped for. Colum's always been the hardest nut to crack. Not one for negotiation, not even with his allies. Position of strength. Everyone's afraid of him. But this was different, I reasoned. Only daughter, and all that.' I waited while he polished his fingernails and held his hand out, studying them. He was playing with me, savouring every moment.

'Why would a chieftain of Erin sell out to such as me, you wonder? What was in it for Eamonn? He wasn't letting on, not fully. But he had an interest in you, and in your father. Don't forget, it was in his house I first heard the tale of Colum's sons, how they vanished one day with not a trace left behind. Seems I'm not the only one interested in a little – expansion. Colum's lands may be ripe for the picking, in the very near future. And Eamonn has a few tricks I could use in the field. I have men, and with the resources of Harrowfield I can arm them better than any other

513

band of fighters, on either side of the water. What couldn't we achieve, between the two of us?'

You're a fool, I thought. A power-crazed fool. Eamonn is merely playing with you, and so is the lady Oonagh. Once they have what they want, they will discard you like the peel of an onion. In this game, you are the merest beginner. *But what did my father say?*

'Well, this visit really surprised me,' he said expansively. 'I'd left the men to get on with it, and travelled as I usually do, very discreetly, to visit my ally on his own territory. Marshlands. Endless peat bogs. Desolate spot. No wonder he wants to expand southwards. Still, it's easy to defend. Anyway, I got there safely. She was visiting again, the redhead, stunning woman. But Colum had knocked back my offer. Daughter or no daughter, he wouldn't budge. Said if she chose to go and live amongst foreigners, she was no daughter of his. She'd made her bed and could lie on it. And if I thought he'd even consider giving away his hard-won land for such a feeble reason, I must be even more stupid than the rest of my kind. That hurts, doesn't it, witch? Don't put your hand over your face, you can't hide that fetching little tear trickling down your cheek. Yes, it looks as if they don't want you back. Not that I can blame them; you're hardly the most appealing sight right now. Well, I was pretty disappointed, I can tell you, coming back empty-handed. But then the lady made me a counter offer. Asked a lot of questions about you first. Had you any allies here, how were you spending your time, what were you telling folks about yourself. So I let her know about Hughie boy, how he was hot for you, but you weren't playing, not yet; how you'd lost your voice, so you couldn't tell secrets; how you spent your time wrecking your hands with your witch work. I could tell she didn't like my answers, but she believed them all right.

'That was when she made the offer. I'd get information, very special information, about Colum's movements for the autumn and the winter, enough to make taking that bay a certainty. Enough to give me the foothold I needed. In return, all I had to do was remove you from the picture. She even told me how to do it. Oh, she didn't mind me playing with you first. She understood that's part of the fun. An irresistible part. But make sure, she said, that the girl burns and her witch's work burns with her. That's the only way you can destroy a sorceress. Hot fire. Eamonn had the wherewithal to make it, and he showed me himself. First you buy a nice little cargo of blue-stone, ostensibly for dyeing, you understand? Costs more than a few head of your best cattle, that does, but worth it. Well worth it. You grind it down in a mortar, very fine, until you get a powder that looks as harmless as dust. You mix it with an oil of the best quality, fit to anoint a bishop's brow – amusing piece of irony, that. Then you're ready for business. It doesn't take much of your mixture, sprinkled over the faggots, to set up a nice blaze. Colourful, too – the green is especially pretty. It flares. It's hot. It's hungry. But Eamonn, he's not content with that. He prepares his wood in advance, leaves it soaking, eating up the mixture until it's full to bursting. Then he dries it. You should see that, when the flames lick at it. I brought home an interesting load of small ash logs, last time I paid my friend a visit. I plan to use them in the very near future. That was what the woman told me, after all. Do it soon, she said. Destroy this girl soon. You must do it before . . . tell me, my dear, how many of these shirts have you made?'

515

I sat extremely still. I was afraid to breathe.

'Let's have a look, shall we?' He rose in a single fluid movement and laid his hands on my basket. 'Not that I believe in magic, myself. But still, I made a promise. How many have we, four, five?'

I sprang to my feet, and my hands went out, clutching desperately at the basket, but I had grown weaker than I realised and he brushed me aside like some troublesome insect.

'One, two, three, four, five. We have been working hard, haven't we? And most of another. Well done, little sorceress. Still, there's not long now. I shouldn't think I'll have much difficulty complying with the lady's request. Make sure you do it before the girl finishes, she said. Gather them together, the little sorceress and her work. Burn them together. And bring me back a report, she said. I want a full description.' He smiled at me. 'Neat conclusion, isn't it? Tidy for all of us. Hugh would approve. He always liked a tidy life.'

Go away. Go now, before shock and fear and loathing overwhelm me. Go now, before rage makes me try something foolish. Breathe, Sorcha. In, out. In, out.

'Tidy in every particular. Well, almost. The witch girl dies; the valley is saved. Elaine marries Hugh. Richard of Northwoods establishes his outpost on the far shore. Eamonn of the Marshes adds a nice little stretch of forest to his territory. The mysterious red-haired lady gets her wish. We all live happily ever after. Pity about Simon. He's the one piece that doesn't quite fit. There could have been a handy spot for that boy under my command, if he'd been able to learn a little discipline. Good skills in the field. Somebody taught him well. But he got too inquisitive for his own good. Overheard what was best kept silent. Saw something he shouldn't. Couldn't be trusted with what he knew. Interested, aren't you?'

I could not bring myself to pick up my work again, but remained crouched by the basket, my arms stretched over it in protection. *Go away*. His presence contaminated the very air we breathed. And yet, I needed to hear the end of his story. The end of this particular truth.

'Unfortunate, it was. Own nephew, and all that. But I knew the boy; straight back to his brother, it would have been, and out with the information. And even Hugh couldn't have ignored that. For as you know, our kind don't mix with yours. Sworn enemies. Chalk and cheese. But he'd seen me, and heard me, with Eamonn's man. Heard who knew what? So I had to issue an instruction for him to be – removed. Silenced. Eliminated. Fortunately, I have a man who's expert at these things. Problem was, I left it just a little bit too long. Big mistake. The boy up and vanished. Went off on his own, who knew where and why? I expect he thought he'd be some sort of hero. Simon was always like that, acted first, thought afterwards. Of course I went after him, had to be seen doing the right thing, close kin and so on. Besides, with what he knew, every moment he was out there was one too many. Fruitless search; and when I got back, they were all dead. Every one of my men. Severed limbs, shredded flesh. Scattered bones in the mud. Every last one. Take years to build up my special force to that level of skill again.'

His tone was bitter. I thought, this is the measure of the man, that he values his people merely as tools in his quest for power.

'Colum. It had to be Colum and his sons. The elusive, evasive warrior lord, who seemed to be able to sweep his opponent's pieces from the board whenever he chose, and disappear as silently as he attacked. Colum of Sevenwaters. No wonder so many men hate and fear him. I came to the conclusion Simon had been captured, and had squealed. Who else could have revealed my men's position? The boy turned out as weak as his brother, all bravado on the surface, no iron underneath. Handy enough with a sword or a bow, or with their fists; but you can't rely on them when things get tough. Wouldn't you agree? Where's Hugh now, when you need him? Hasn't exactly rushed back to rescue the little wife, has he? Got better things to do. Whatever they are, and I'd dearly love to know what they are. Well, I came home. Reported to my sister, your boy's lost. Nobody knows where. That part was true enough.

'Bit of a worry when Hugh went off looking for him, some time later. As if he didn't believe what I'd told them. I was worried about that small piece of information that might just get out, assuming the boy was still alive somewhere. Thought maybe you knew something about it; why else would my nephew drag an Irish brat home with him? I wanted to make you talk. If you were kin to Sevenwaters, it was important to make you talk, before you blabbed the truth to my nephew. I thought that. But I couldn't get near you, he guarded you like some precious jewel. I watched you. After a while, I began to change my mind. You'll never talk. The boy's fooling himself, if he thinks so. You're a girl; girls scream when they're hurt. They cry when they're upset. Girls don't hold out for days and moons and years with never a squeak out of them. You'll burn without uttering a sound. And I will take immense pleasure in lighting the fire, my dear. A slap in the face for Colum. He may not want to pay for your return; I understand that. But he won't like the tale I send back for his ears only; of how his daughter perished by a very special kind of fire. That tale will keep him awake at night.'

He rubbed his hands together in anticipation. 'Yes, it's turned out very neatly,' he said. 'Only one loose end, really. Not at all like your work, my dear, which looks woefully awry; are you really concentrating on what you're doing there? Still, maybe it doesn't matter. Fire will take you, and your pitiful shirts, in one great satisfying burst of heat. Spindle, distaff, loom and cloth. Gown, hair, skin, nails. At first slowly, and then faster and hotter as the flames flow around you and work their way inwards. By the time your husband returns, there'll be no trace of you left at Harrowfield. You'll be gone. Obliterated. He will pick up the pieces of his life and move on. Men forget. They forget easily. Elaine will soon pull him into line. Capable girl. She'll take charge here, and as for me . . .'

He glanced up at the window.

'It's getting late. Time for a flask of wine, perhaps a cutlet or two, I'm always a little peckish at this time of day.' He got up, stretching. 'Must fly, my dear. So nice chatting to you. Talked longer than I realised. Oh well, tomorrow's another day, as they say. Be ready when they come for you. I've had a word to the Bishop's man about your case; your hearing will likely take the full day, and he wants an early start.'

One night, I thought, my heart pounding. Only one night, and then my fate would be decided. I had to be strong, I must keep my mind away from fire, and from death. I thought about Richard's words. It was as well, I thought, that the man was so self-absorbed. Had he watched me more closely during his astonishing recital, he might have read on my face more than I wished him to know. For the rest of the day and on into the night, my mind turned the things he had told me over and over. Red's uncle in collusion with a chieftain of my own people, one whom my father had considered a friend. I found I could believe that. Power games were what they all did best. This was just another game. Lady Oonagh involved; that must be true, for I had already recognised her hand in John's death, and in the slowly rising tide of fear, suspicion and unhappiness that threatened to overwhelm the valley, taking the family at Harrowfield with it. And it seemed Red had been right about one thing. Richard had lied to them. He had no evidence that Simon was dead. His story had been fabrication, based on surmise. Designed to placate, invented to draw a line at the end of that particular tale. This is finished. You need seek for answers no longer. I was glad Richard had not read my face closely. He had not guessed where Red had gone, and why. He must not know. For in my heart, I knew Richard would stop at nothing to get what he wanted. He enjoyed the game while it lasted. But winning, in the end, was the only thing that mattered. All pieces were disposable. The loss of a whole unit of fighting men was hard, but Richard saw this merely as a setback, able to be remedied with time and a bag or two of silver. Good men could be bought and trained. I had been a particularly awkward and unexpected challenge for him. But I had played into his hands, and he had me now. I had no doubt he would sacrifice, without qualms, anyone who stood in his way. Anyone. If one nephew could be – what word had he used, eliminated? – then why not the other, if he learned the unpalatable truth about his uncle?

And who was poised to take control then? Between my father's men and his uncle, poor Simon had not stood a chance.

It was just as well he had given me plenty to think about. Turning it over and over in my mind, trying to make sense of it, kept back those other thoughts. Images of burning flesh, as the flames licked at bare feet and charred the embroidered hem of a gown. I saw the fire catching a dry willow basket and consuming the five shirts of starwort, and the sixth, which now lay incomplete as I wove its first sleeve. Front and back were finished, held together by a rough stitch or two at the shoulder. It was shoddy work, as Richard had observed; my youngest brother would be short-changed. But tomorrow. Tomorrow they would question me. Did that mean that tomorrow I might die? How could you face your last day in the world, and not be afraid? I thought about the old tales, about the way the hero's spirit would complete its journey in this earthly form, and move on to the next at the allotted time.

A good death. *The wheel turns, and returns.* I thought of Liam's tale of our mother, slipping away from the world, calmly bidding her sons farewell. Serene, orderly, inevitable. I did not feel like that at all. I was angry, I was terrified, my heart thumped and I had trouble breathing. My head hurt. I was not ready to die. Not yet, not now. Not before I held my brothers in my arms again.

I did not sleep at all that night. There must be time to finish. There had to be. Did the Fair Folk set a task, and then make its completion impossible? I could not believe that it would be taken from me, so close to the end. I must finish. I would finish. I did not tell myself stories, as the night raced on towards dawn. Instead, working in the dark, I filled the space around me with mind-pictures, shining images to keep out the shadows, as Finbar had once done for me to his own cost. To keep out the flames. To keep out the cruel news that my father knew where I was, and would not ransom me. So I fixed my mind elsewhere. There was the white beach, and the great solemn seals with their soft eyes. There was Red, watching me with his heart-breaking smile and his bright hair like a beacon against the grey and green and blue of the sea. I saw, for an instant, an image of John lifting his tiny son in his arms, love and pride written bold on his weathered face. Margery, plaiting my hair with deft fingers. *It suits you. You'll have to stop hiding yourself.* Well, it seemed my ending would be public enough. Everyone would be out to see a sorceress burn. No, keep those thoughts away. There was the forest, filtered sunlight between leaves, high, high overhead. There was a child dancing down the path, barefoot on the soft earth, her hair dark and wild on her shoulders. There was her brother watching with eyes like clear water, that saw far, so far. There was a girl running on the sand; there was her image done small and neat in careful pen strokes. The very last image in the book.

My hand came up to clutch the two precious items that still hung around my neck, under my stained gown. Lady Anne had said her son loved me. But it was not love, not if you did what you did only because you must, only because of a command laid on you which you could not understand. He would return, and I would be gone, gone as if I had never been. Perhaps he could still weave together the broken threads of his life. And yet, I wanted him here now. I needed him here. In the darkness, if I sat very still, I could almost feel his presence by me, quite near, but not too near. Didn't I promise to keep you safe, he would say softly. I have never broken a promise. Don't look so worried, Jenny. And yet, he would be careful. Careful not to move too close. Careful not to frighten me. Waiting still. I am your shelter. Don't be afraid.

CHAPTER THIRTEEN

T hen it was morning, and they came for me. It was the first time I had been outside my tiny prison since midsummer, the day I had held Conor in my arms and heard him promise to bring my brothers back, when I was ready. Now it seemed I might never be ready. Blinking in the brightness long denied me, stumbling on legs reluctant to obey me, I was conveyed none too gently down to the hall, which was set up for a formal hearing of the folkmoot. There was a long table across the end of the room, with four oak chairs in place, and here sat Richard of Northwoods, attired all in black, and beside him a rotund man in the plain dark robes of a cleric. This, I supposed, was the bishop's man. There were two record-keepers seated there, one a tonsured youth with a pale, serious face, the other the household scribe of Harrowfield. Ink pots, quills and neat piles of parchment were set on the board before them, with small trays of fine sand to sprinkle on for drying. Lanterns were lit near the doorways, for the sun had not made an appearance between the rain clouds and the room was quite dark. A warm fire burned on the great hearth. Around the other three sides of the hall benches were set, and here sat the tenants of Harrowfield, as required by the law. There were many there that I had seen before, and some that were strangers. There was a fair bit of noise, what with old friends catching up on news, and swift bargains being struck over a few pigs or a fine ewe while the opportunity offered. As they watched me walk to the high stool in the very centre of the hall, all of them went quiet.

Richard rose slowly to his feet.

'This moot commences,' he pronounced. 'In the absence of my nephew, Lord Hugh of Harrowfield, master of these estates, I will be presiding over the hearings. There are various matters to be heard, and all of these bar one I carry over to tomorrow, or the day after. Food and drink will be provided to all, for as long as the business of the moot takes.' A mutter of approval. 'For today, there is a single, deep and weighty matter to be decided. This concerns the young woman known as Jenny, who stands before you accused of several offences, each one of which is punishable by death, should the case against her be proven.' All eyes turned towards me, where I sat on the stool, swaying slightly. I did feel rather strange. Whether it was from lack of sleep or lack of food, or the unaccustomed presence of so many people, so much light and noise, my sight was blurring and my head fuzzy. I must try to concentrate.

'As you are aware, these proceedings have been carried over several times before,' Richard went on, 'since the matter is so grave. It was hoped Father Stephen of Ravenglass might grace us with his presence, so that the opinion of the Church might be obtained, especially on the charge of sorcery.' There was a little gasp of horror from the assembly as this word was spoken. 'I am advised that this will not now be possible, and the matter can be delayed no longer. I welcome Father Dominic of Whitehaven, who has travelled here as the bishop's representative in Father Stephen's place.' Was I imagining things, or did Richard sound just a little out of sorts at this change? 'The proceedings will be as follows,' he went on, and now I was sure of it. There was an edge to his voice, the same tone it took on when he debated a point with Red and came out worse off. Something had rattled him. 'This morning the evidence against the girl will be heard and assessed. Later in the day she will be given the opportunity to make what case she can in her own defence. I will question her, and Father Dominic also may choose to do so. If any member of this moot has a real concern in this matter, he too may speak in turn. I will deliver judgement and pronounce the penalty this same day, and this troublesome case will be settled once and for all.'

'Very well, very well.' Father Dominic was reaching across, helping himself to a sheet of parchment, picking up a quill. Apparently quite used to this behaviour, his scribe edged the ink pot closer. 'What exactly are the charges against this young woman?'

'Firstly, spying, for the purpose of passing on information to her husband's enemies. She has made no denial of her origins amongst those Irish chieftains who battle us for control of the Islands. Second, the reception of an outlaw, one of her own kind with no business in these parts. Thirdly, the use of the

sorcerer's art for purposes of mischief and disturbance of this household. All three offences are part of
the same plot. The penalty for each of these offences
is death.'

'I'm aware of that. And what witnesses are to be
called?'

'Several, Father. I myself am the principal witness
in the case against her.'

I saw Father Dominic nod, his face impassive.
Above the collar of his dark robe, there were rolls of
fat under his chin. His small eyes were very shrewd.

'Very well. You had better proceed.' He turned to
me. 'Listen well, young woman. For in due time you
will be called upon to account for yourself.'

I stared back at him, and his eyes narrowed.

'Can this girl understand our tongue?' He turned
towards Richard with a little frown. 'She seems scarcely
to hear what is said around her. And she looks unwell.
I would hazard a guess that something is amiss with
her. She can hardly be expected to make a case for herself if she cannot comprehend the evidence.'

'She understands well enough,' Richard said
curtly, and this time it was quite obvious he was
annoyed. 'But she does not have the power of speech.
Some malady has afflicted her tongue, I'm told.'

'If this is so, how can she account for herself? How
can a fair hearing take place, if the accused cannot
make her case? Has she someone to assist her?'

'She'll manage well enough.' Richard's tone was
dismissive. 'May I proceed with my statement?'

'I am far from satisfied. But go on by all means.
Let us waste no time.'

It sounded damning, the way he set it all out.
Even to me it sounded convincing. I thought it was a
death sentence. Richard gave a fine performance,

527

striding about the centre of the hall between the packed benches, using the full range of his mellifluous voice from whisper to shout of outrage, telling the tale of how his nephew had brought a girl home from Erin with the best of intentions, how the moment folk saw her they knew she was up to no good, how she had wheedled and cajoled her way into the household and then turned against her husband as everyone would expect of a wild woman from the bogs of Erin. He told of the way I would listen to the talk after supper, the news of landholdings and trade and campaigns, and store it all up for future use. He described how he had caught me once, out on the hills by myself with no excuse. Why else would I run away from the house in secret, if not to meet one of my own kind and pass on information?

'This is conjecture,' said Father Dominic calmly, making a note on his parchment. 'Where is the evidence of fact?'

'I'm coming to that.' Richard's voice was sharp. I thought he suppressed his annoyance with an effort of will, for he must convince the folk of the moot as well as the holy Father, if his judgement were to be accepted. Then he launched into the tale of the midsummer picnic, and how I had given myself away. He reached the climax of his story.

'I saw the girl, Jenny, go down the path by the river. A little later, thinking it might not be safe for her alone, I followed. There was one man ahead of me, my nephew's young companion Benedict, son of William of Greystones. The young man has been fostered in this house. We both saw her; and we both saw the fellow she held fast in her arms. There was no question about what they had been doing. Ahem!' He cleared his throat, glancing at his sister in a show of reticence.

'What do you mean?' demanded Father Dominic. 'Make yourself clear, for this is a most serious charge.'

'Well, they – er – to speak plainly, the fellow had very few clothes on, and the girl was – um – wrapping herself around him in a very – intimate – fashion.'

'You wish to add adultery to the charges?' Father Dominic dipped and wrote. 'And then?' he said.

'We challenged the Irishman, and he fled into the woods. The girl was apprehended. One of the men with me said he had heard them talking, earlier, but had not known who they were. They were speaking of men and arms and fortifications. Of the defences of Harrowfield.'

'We will hear this man in due course. What of this Benedict you spoke of? Is he here to give his story?'

'He has no more to add,' said Richard quickly. 'His tale tallies with mine. My men scoured the forest and did not find the Irishman. He escaped with valuable information. Information this girl passed to him.'

'Let us hear Benedict of Greystones,' said Father Dominic, ignoring him. I heard the men who guarded the door calling out for Ben under this rather grand name. Calling again. Calling a third time, after a pause. Father Dominic's scribe got up and went to consult with the guards. Time passed, and there was a buzz of speculative chatter in the hall. I rubbed a hand across my eyes. I felt so strange, as if the room were dipping and swaying around me. The lamps were moving about like fireflies, and Richard of Northwoods had four eyes. I could remember feeling like this once before, on the day I was carried down the river by the current and nearly drowned. The day I met Red.

'He's not here, Father,' said the young cleric.

'They're looking now. Can't be found, that's what they're saying.' Richard let his breath out audibly. Father Dominic pursed his lips.

'Very well. I will hear from the others who were present that night. Do they corroborate this story?'

He was thorough. Surprisingly thorough, when you considered that he had only been invited to lend respectability to a hearing whose conclusion Richard himself had decided before it even began. We listened to three of Richard's men telling how they found me in a compromising position, and how they sought my companion all night without success. There was still no sign of Ben. I thought perhaps, for Red's sake, he will not speak against me, will not seek to speed my death. But he will not defend me either. He was quick to believe me guilty, as quick as the rest of them.

We heard another man tell how he had overheard me passing secrets to the foreign spy, information I could only have learned from my husband. It concerned weapons and outposts and the movement of men. There was no point in shaking my head, or trying to refute what was a complete fabrication. They would not understand me; few could. Besides, I sensed these proceedings could have but one conclusion.

One by one, people came in and said things and went out again. Father Dominic made notes in black ink, dipping and writing, dipping and writing. He had little deep-set eyes under dark forceful brows. Someone said they had seen me at night, dancing naked around a little fire. Someone said I had forbidden plants in my garden, herbs that no respectable person would allow anywhere near their kitchen; that I had tried to poison Mistress Margery, and it was a miracle her baby had survived. Who knew what the child would grow up to be, when the hands that brought it into this world were those of a sorceress? Someone said that, when I sewed up Lord Hugh's leg, I left a little spell inside that worked its way slowly but surely up to the heart. A spell that bound him to my will for as long as I lived. It hurt to hear that. There were other accusations. They let me get up, once, and gave me a cup of water. I saw Lady Anne at the back of the room, white faced and silent. A guard escorted my accusers in and out. It went on for a long time. I began to feel stranger and stranger, as if my head no longer belonged to my body. Then, for a while, it went black.

When I came to, I was lying on the floor and the hall was almost empty. Lady Anne stood nearby, and Megan was wiping my brow with a wet cloth. I tried to sit up.

'Slowly,' cautioned Lady Anne. I grasped Megan's arm, and found it was possible, just, to get to a sitting position.

'Whew!' said Megan. 'My lady, you don't think . . . ?'

'There's a little time.' It seemed Lady Anne understood the half spoken question. 'They must drink and eat, and they'll want to confer. The folk must be fed. Molly has set out a good spread for them in the kitchens. We can at least manage hot water, and a comb, and a clean gown, I think.' Megan scuttled off, and the two men guarding the door made no attempt to stop her.

'You'd better drink this.' Lady Anne's tone was severe as she placed a cup of water in my hands. But I could not hold it, I was shaking so badly, and she had to place it against my lips.

'You'll be given an opportunity to defend yourself this afternoon,' she said bluntly. 'Not all these accusations are true. Many are based solely on fear and superstition. You know what will happen, if you remain silent.'

I gave a nod. What was the point? I was found guilty, and my penalty chosen, before ever I set foot in that room. None of it mattered. All that mattered was staying alive long enough to finish the last shirt.

Lady Anne frowned. 'I cannot forgive what you have done,' she said. 'If they determine you guilty, there is no doubt you will be put to death. I must accept their decision and defer to their wisdom. At the same time, I cannot allow a prisoner so ill fed, so dirty and unkempt in my household. A certain standard must be kept, or we are indeed no better than your own people. I was advised the arrangements for you were adequate. My informant clearly set somewhat different standards from my own.'

At that moment there was a small commotion at the door and a familiar figure burst in, ignoring the guards, her soft features a picture of angry distress. 'Jenny! Oh, look at you! Oh, my Lady, how –'

'Hush, woman.' Lady Anne grasped Margery's arm firmly, halting her flight across the room. 'See, here is Megan with some things for us. Take Jenny into the anteroom there, and help her change that gown. It's fit only for the midden. Don't try to talk to her. You should not even be here. These are formal proceedings. You must be gone before Father Dominic returns.'

Between them, Megan and Margery changed my gown, and washed my face, and sponged the worst of the filth from my body. There were small creatures crawling in my hair.

'Oh, Jenny,' Margery whispered to me, while Lady Anne stood nearby and pretended not to hear. She slipped the dirty clothes over my head, with never a twitch of the nose to be seen. 'Oh, look at you. You're as thin as a spectre. I'm sorry, I'm so sorry.'

'Shameful,' muttered Megan, dipping a sponge into the bucket and dabbing it over my hands and arms. The water turned brown with blood and grime. 'Disgraceful.'

It was not my crimes she was talking about.

'I should have – I would have –' whispered Margery, trying to pull the comb through my hair, as Megan washed my legs and feet. 'But I miss John so much . . . I thought only of myself, and Johnny. If I had not been so selfish, maybe I could have –' she stopped short, and her hand came out gently to touch the ring that hung on its cord around my neck. A smile curved her mouth as she saw the circlet of oak leaves and acorns and the little owl. Lady Anne was watching.

'He will come for you,' whispered Margery. 'How could he not?'

Megan slipped the clean gown over my head. I could have wept, for it was the blue one, which my friend had made for me with such love. Someone had done a passable job of cleaning it, but the skirt still showed a tide mark, where the sea had written its name. I did not want to burn in this dress.

'Quickly,' said Lady Anne. 'Tidy away those things, and no gossiping, mind.' It came to me suddenly that this might be the last time I saw my friend. Margery had the same thought in her eyes, and her arms came out to embrace me, but Lady Anne stepped between us.

'Don't make this more difficult,' she said, and her own voice was a little shaky. 'The girl is a prisoner; her fate is in the balance. She is no longer of this household. You have done what is required. Now go.'

So they left, but Margery looked back and touched the tips of her fingers to her lips, and then waved her hand towards me; and Megan had tears on her cheeks.

The hearing resumed. Neither of my interrogators made comment on my changed appearance, though Lord Richard raised his brows and Father Dominic gave a sort of grunt, deep in the throat. Outside, the day was growing darker. Had we been here so long?

'Now,' said the cleric, leaning forward and fixing me with his little eyes, 'we have heard all the evidence against you, and it seems quite damning, if not altogether conclusive. The purpose of this hearing is to determine if your guilt is proven, and to set an appropriate penalty. All of your offences come under secular jurisdiction, and as Lord Richard bears authority here on such matters, the final decision rests with him. However, I was invited here to assist him in making his decision, in view of the serious nature of the charges, and the close family links between accuser and accused. There is no need to fear justice, girl. You now have the opportunity to defend yourself. Take your time. I understand you cannot use your voice. But there may be some way you can let us know what you wish to say. Let us know if there is anything you do not follow.'

I stared back at him. His eyebrows met in the middle, and his eyes were cushioned in fat. Nonetheless, they possessed a keen intelligence. My hands remained passive on my lap. The hall was silent.

'Are you sure you are correct in telling me this girl has a good understanding of our tongue?' He looked at Richard, and then at Lady Anne, still seated at the back of the hall.

'Yes, Father.' Lady Anne had masked her expression

in a way that was painfully familiar to me. 'Not only can she understand, but if she wishes, she is able to express herself with gestures in a rudimentary way.'

'I'm finding that very hard to believe,' said Father Dominic, shaking his head. 'Why would she choose not to communicate, why now? Does the girl want to die?'

Richard gave a deprecating laugh. 'Perhaps you have not met many of these people, Father. I know the folk of Erin well. Such defiance is bred in them, and nurtured carefully from birth. Their spies are trained to hold silence till death and beyond. This girl's refusal to talk is just another mark of her guilt.'

Father Dominic glanced at him with dislike written plain on his pasty features. Through my exhaustion and fear, I felt surprise. This man saw Richard of Northwoods for just what he was. The last thing I had expected was a semblance of a fair trial.

'There are many learned men on that shore,' said Father Dominic, 'some, indeed, of my own brethren, skilled in debate and in lore. I would not be so hasty to judge. Besides, this is only a girl. She is young and malleable; should she be prepared to speak in her own defence, to recant and abjure her previous ways, the sentence could be commuted.'

Richard said nothing.

I was aware of more people coming into the room, by the door. I did not look behind me. Outside, rain began to fall, dripping steadily past the windows. The day grew even darker.

'Young woman,' said Father Dominic, 'we find ourselves in difficulty here. I'm told you know our tongue. Look at me, child. Nod if you understand me.'

I managed a tiny hint of a nod. I must not be trapped into answering the wrong questions. I must

535

not tell any of my story. But I was very tired, too tired to think clearly. The rain began to pour down, drumming on the roof tops. I wondered if Red were outdoors somewhere, and if he had a dry place to sleep. I wondered if there were any chance, any chance at all, that I could weave a whole sleeve in one night, and sew it to the last shirt by morning.

'That's good. Now answer me. Are you indeed guilty of these charges?'

I found I could not make myself respond. What was the point? Why agree, or disagree, if Richard was to determine my guilt anyway?

'You will not reply? Not even with a nod or shake of the head? You know this must be taken as an admission of guilt.'

I looked at him in silence. His pale brow wore a frown, and his eyes were troubled.

'What could she say,' asked Richard, 'against such charges? It is clear the girl is both adulteress and informant. She has preyed on this household like some creature of evil that sucks the lifeblood of its victims. She has abused the trust of my sister and my nephew in the vilest way. She –'

'Is the last witness still not to be found?' asked Father Dominic mildly enough. 'This Benedict, the man you spoke of? I would hear his tale, before the final judgement is made.'

'He's gone, sir.' The men at the door shuffled their feet awkwardly. 'We sent out, and all hunted for him, but the stable lads tell me now he's gone away. Been gone some days, they're saying now. Gone home to visit his family, that's what they think.'

I saw Richard's eyes narrow at this news, and he called one of his men to him. After a hasty whispered exchange, the man left the room, rather quickly.

'Indeed.' Father Dominic drew a line across the page of notes. He turned to Richard, and his tone was very cool. 'This was an important witness. He should have been heard. Did you make no attempt to keep him here? Must you rely on your stable boys for accurate information?'

'I was unaware that he was gone, Father.' And that was true, I could see it in Richard's face, where there was an ill-concealed anger.

'Well, it is clear this is one witness that will not be heard. Are there no further statements to be made?' asked Father Dominic, looking about the assembled folk.

'I would – I would ask a question, by your leave.' Lady Anne seemed unusually hesitant. Heads turned as she stood up at the back of the hall.

'Very well, put your question.' The priest sounded weary. It had been a long day. A very long day.

'If Jen – if the girl is guilty, I know the penalty is death. But – but what if she were with child? That is possible, even probable. This child would be the heir to Harrowfield; my son's son. I would not wish –'

I felt myself flush scarlet with shame and humiliation. But at the same time, somewhere deep inside me, I knew just how she felt. Such a child would be mine, half a son of Erin; in her estimation that would make him wild, fanatical and a sworn enemy of all she held dear. But the child would also be Red's; a son whose father, and whose father's fathers had nurtured the very life of the valley. I could have told her there was no child. But I sat there like a stone and willed my face to calm. I did not forget I was the daughter of the forest, not for an instant. And something I had heard once, long ago, slipped into my mind and out again before I had time to grasp it.

Something I had been reminded of recently . . . one who is neither of Britain nor of Erin, but at the same time both . . . what tale did that come from? My mind was hazy, I could not remember.

'Look at me, girl.' Father Dominic was standing now, his gimlet eyes fixed on my face. 'Are you with child? Your husband's child?'

Richard guffawed. 'This is rich! You expect an honest answer to that? The brat could be any man's. This girl's no better than a cheap whore to be had in the market place. Why, she even tried it with me, but a day or two since. Thought she could buy her freedom by spreading her legs. The little slut has no shame.'

'Enough.' At Father Dominic's tone, Richard shut his mouth like a trap. 'Good folk of the moot, this stage of the hearing is concluded. Lord Richard and I will take time now to consider our judgement. We will call you together again after supper, and at that time our verdict will be conveyed to you. If there is to be a punishment, the nature of it will be made known in the morning.' The people began to shuffle out, stiff from long sitting. Father Dominic turned back to Richard. 'You'd better lock the girl up again for now. Make sure she's given something to eat; you risk losing her before any punishment can be carried out. We should perhaps retire to a more private chamber for further discussion on these matters.'

'To me, it looks clear enough.' Richard sounded almost petulant.

I heard no more, as my guards gripped me by the arms and I was taken back to the small cell. Someone brought bread and water, and I ate and drank, and shortly afterwards my stomach rejected even this simple fare, almost as if I really were with child. In the cold, damp cell, in the darkness, I groped for my work and found it. I knew this was the last night. My hands gripped the small loom, felt for shuttle and ball of spun fibre, and began to work.

It was hopeless, of course. There was no way I could finish one sleeve, and make the whole of another, and sew all together in a single night, without even a candle for guide. But still I worked on. *Strong-minded, aren't you?* Maybe I would have a little longer. Richard had described the special mixture given him by Eamonn of the Marshes, which burned so hot it destroyed all but bone. He might wait until dusk, to make a more spectacular sight. Outside the rain still fell. It would be good for the small oak trees. Richard would be hoping for dry weather. You did not get a nice hot fire, in the rain.

Towards morning, as if in preparation for a burning, the rain ceased and a cool breeze came up. I heard an owl cry, calling in the last silence before the dawn. Then she was gone, fled to the deep shelter of the trees. The sun rose, and daytime birds began their sweet chatter. I tried with no great success to keep out the thoughts that threatened to overwhelm me. The last rain. The last owl. The last dawn.

They came early to get me, two big men in the colours of Northwoods. Nobody told me what the verdict had been, and I could not ask. The first sleeve was roughly finished, and held to the other pieces of the shirt by a stitch or two. The second was not even begun. *Let it not be now, straight away*, I begged silently. *Not now, not yet. Please.*

They did not take me down to the hall, to hear my punishment read out before the assembled moot.

Instead, I was led to a private chamber upstairs, and the only person there was Lord Richard of Northwoods. I was numb with fear, almost beyond further feeling, but my face must have registered surprise.

'Change of plan, I'm afraid,' he said smoothly. He stood by the window, an immaculate figure from his fair curls to his polished boots. Today he wore a tunic of soft green, with snowy linen beneath. I stood before him in the middle of the floor, hands by my sides. Obeying some unspoken order, the guards retreated outside the door. 'Our learned friend was unexpectedly called away. Left just after supper last night, in fact. Seems somebody took a knife to the parish priest, across the hill at Elvington. So Father Dominic's gone. Didn't even have time to help me announce the verdict. No great loss, I must admit. Set in his ways. Hard man to convince. Not that he left without giving me his opinion.' He paused for a few moments. It was exquisitely timed.

'Of course, there was never any doubt of your guilt,' Richard said, and he was no longer playing, but deadly serious. 'Guilty of passing secrets to the enemy. Guilty of cheating your husband and breaking your marriage vows. And guilty of sorcery. The weight of evidence against you was overwhelming. Come closer, Jenny.' His use of this name made my flesh crawl. 'You won't? Then I must come to you.' He strolled across to stand before me, eyes alight with anticipation. 'You know the penalty for these crimes. No simple banishment; no sequestration in a convent where you can live out your days in comfort. Oh, no. You have done damage here. Serious damage.' He lowered his voice. 'You have been a thorn in my flesh, and I take great delight in ripping out this thorn once and for all. Your penalty is death. You know the method already.' His finger came out to run up my neck, rather slowly. The last time he had tried that, Red had nearly broken his arm. But Red was not here.

'The nice thing is, we have all day to look forward to it,' he said softly. 'So while I go out and see to the building of a very special fire, I'll allow you to stay here, under guard of course. This room is warmer and more comfortable; and you'll be able to watch me from that window there. We might even arrange a little food and drink; a last meal for the condemned. Well, good-bye, my dear. It's been – interesting – knowing you. At dusk, we'll meet again, all too briefly. I thought dusk would be best. More atmospheric, don't you think? Give folks a real show, something to tell their children about. Goodbye, my dear.'

My heart lurched. *But – but –* I broke my own rules and reached out to him, clutching his sleeve, gesturing wildly. *My things – spin, weave – here? Bring here?* He could not do this to me. He could not. His little smile was a triumph of hatred and satisfaction.

'Oh, no, I don't think so. I must keep my part of the bargain. Too bad if you managed to finish this task. Can't risk that, not if I'm going to get what I've been promised. Besides, you've been working much too hard, my dear. Take the day off. Enjoy yourself for a change.' He swept out the door, and the two guards followed him, locking it behind them.

Of all the days of my long time of silence, there are two that remain in my memory clear in every detail. One is the day I ran along the sea shore in my blue dress, and heard the story of Toby and his mermaid, and got my wedding ring. The other is the day of the burning.

541

For a little, I stood at the window and watched them building it, a neat stack of ash logs that would burn hot without smoke, arranged around an upright central pole. They built it in the courtyard, far enough from the house so the fire would not spread uncontrolled; near enough to allow a fine view of the spectacle from the ground and from the windows above.

It was hard to believe Harrowfield had sunk to this. I could not imagine Lady Anne, or Megan, or Ben, or Margery, relishing such a sight. Most of Red's men would turn their backs on such barbarity. But Red's men were strangely absent. As the day passed, a steady line of Richard's workers came and went, and the pyre took shape and was almost finished. You could see how the condemned one would be bound to the pole, her feet resting on a narrow ledge built there. You could see how the wood might be lit from the bottom, where plenty of dry twigs had been wedged between the great logs, and how the flames would catch, and lick upwards at first slowly, and then more rapidly, and . . . Richard was busy, directing a worker here, adjusting a faggot there; and when it was done to his satisfaction, he had two of his men carry out a small chest, which he unlocked with care. They had built a platform beside the fire, a makeshift structure that would surely be consumed itself once the flames rose to a certain point. Perhaps it was intended to burn, to add to the spectacle. Now Richard climbed the steps to this platform, and had the men set the chest beside him, and he reached in and drew out what appeared to be plain lengths of wood. He stepped neatly across to the pyre and began to place these with some care on the topmost tier, one here, one there, all the way around. He took

his time, stopping frequently to admire his handiwork. They were, I supposed, the logs he had told me
of so gloatingly, logs obtained from Eamonn of the
Marshes, a traitor of our own people. Prepared by
soaking in a carefully calculated mixture of special
components. When those caught alight, then you
would really see something.

It became apparent that I was not going to get my
work back. Not in time. I knew it was to burn with
me at dusk. There was no real choice. Once I was
gone, my brothers had no chance at all. The Lady of
the Forest had been very specific. The six shirts must
be made from start to finish by my own hands. Then,
when all were ready, I must place them over the
necks of the swans myself. All six in the same place,
one after the other. Only then, if I had remained
silent, would the spell be broken. I would not let
them kill me, not without having tried. I must try,
though it seemed hopeless, for this would be my
brothers' very last chance. I could not finish the sixth
shirt. But I must call them anyway. Maybe, just
maybe this would be good enough.

I moved away from the window, sitting on the
floor so I looked straight out into the sky, westwards.
So that I could not see the men, and what they were
building. I made my breathing slow, and cleared my
mind until it was still and calm as a stone in the heart
of the forest. Then I bent my energies on my brother
Conor, somewhere beyond the sea. Every shred of
thought. Every fibre of will. Pictured him in my
mind. Tall, pale, an ancient spirit in a young man's
body. Gaunt-faced, wild-haired, dressed in rags.
Conor. You must come now. It is today, at dusk. A deathly
silence, save for the faint sound of hammering.

Conor. Please hear me. Come to me in the courtyard of

*the great house, where I showed you. You must be here by
dusk. Bring them. Bring them all.* No answer. Perhaps,
after all, it was too far. *Bring them. This is the last
chance. You must bring them.* A little wind stirred outside the window, and a bird called. That was all.
Maybe he could not hear me. But he had said, call,
and we will come.

Men seemed to make a lot of promises. Finbar had
said once, I will always be there for you, and I had
believed him. Red had said, I will come back.

I shivered. What if Richard's men had intercepted
him, what if . . . ? Without Red, Harrowfield would
become cold and lifeless. Already it was changing.

Later in the day they took me out to use the privy,
and brought me back again. On the way I heard
women's voices arguing downstairs. I heard someone
say, Father Dominic, but I could not catch the rest. I
saw nobody. Then they brought me food, but I could
not touch it. Finally, I curled up on the floor in a corner,
half-sleeping, half-waking. Outside, the hammering
had ceased and all was quiet. Soft light slanted in
through the windows, catching particles of dust in a
warm haze.

It might have been a dream, or something else. I
thought my eyes were open. But I saw it clear and
bright as an image painted in some great book. At
first I believed I was remembering a time long ago, a
time when I sat with my brothers on the smooth rocks
by the lake's edge, watching the silver shining bodies
of the fish as they slid by in the water. But these children were not the children of Sevenwaters. There was
a girl, tall and sturdily built, with rosy cheeks and a
fall of bright hair like a sheet of flame. There was a

dark-haired boy who lay flat on the stones and looked up, up into the sky with eyes like clear water, that saw far, so far. 'The swans are coming, Niamh,' he said, not moving. 'They're coming today.' The girl lay down beside him, on her stomach, and trailed her fingers in the icy lake water. 'How can you be so sure?' she said. 'You're always so sure.' It seemed to me there was another child there, on the edge of the picture, but I could not make out this figure clearly. Then the image blurred and was gone. *Your children*, the little voice said. And was silent.

My children, that might have been, I thought, as my hand crept up to hold the ring that hung around my neck, and the pierced stone with its runic markings. My son, my daughter. The little stone was carved with the secret sign Nuin, for ash tree. But it was also N for Niamh, which was my mother's name. Niamh, my daughter, with hair like a bright beacon, flame on the water. Then I could not stop the tears from flowing, and I wept and wept until my face was swollen and my head ached, and the light through the tall windows began to fade and die. The day was almost over.

By the time they came for me, I was empty of tears. And so I walked, blank faced, between guards out to the courtyard, as someone beat slowly on a drum, and one after the other, torches on poles flamed on either side all the way to the pyre. A big crowd had gathered, and I heard snatches of their words as I walked by ... *holds her head high ... not quite human, that's what I heard ... me, I'd be screaming ... wait till the flame catches ... then you'll hear her sing right enough ...*.

Once, I looked back, and saw a man carrying my basket and another bearing distaff, spindle and handloom, and everything else that had been mine. Even my old walking boots were there. It seemed all were to burn. There would be no trace of me left here to poison the household of Harrowfield. *Please*, I begged silently. *Please put the shirts where I can reach them. Please don't bind my hands.* The guards were grim faced. I sensed they took no pleasure in their duties, but were bound to obey. They were good men, I supposed; after the fire, they would go home to their wives, and kiss their children goodnight, and maybe reflect for a moment or two on what they had done. It was a measure of the power Richard wielded, that all would obey his orders without question.

The sky was changing colour; the first purple tint of dusk began to wash across its late afternoon blue. We had reached the pile of ash wood, and the platform with its neat steps. And Richard was there, resplendent in a tunic of fine wool, with silver glittering at his throat. He wore a ring shaped like the head of a kestrel, with gleaming ruby eyes. The drum stopped. The crowd hushed. I saw few familiar faces. There was no Lady Anne, no Ben. I could not see Margery. But Megan was there, her round face white in the torchlight, her freckles standing out against the pallor. She had dark rings under her eyes.

They led me up to the platform where Richard stood. A small torch burned in a bracket at the base of the pyre. I was in no doubt as to its purpose. My heart thumped its own fast rhythm; there was no need of a drumbeat. The sky darkened to lavender grey; out in the west, the setting sun touched the clouds to the colour of a rosy apple.

'You are gathered to witness due and lawful punishment,' announced Richard grandly. The crowd shuffled. 'The case against this girl, known as Jenny, was heard in full yesterday. Witnesses were called, and evidence produced that was damning and irrefutable. You already know the verdict. The girl stands before you guilty of receiving an outlaw, of spying, and of practising the arts of the devil, in addition to her adulterous conduct. The penalty for her offences is death. In this, Father Dominic and I were in complete accord. The girl's refusal to defend herself was a clear admission of guilt. Good people, with this burning we remove the evil canker that has eaten away at the very heart of Harrowfield. With her death, peace and prosperity can return to this household and to the valley. I call on you to witness.' There was a scattering of applause, and somebody yelled, 'Get on with it, then!'

But the crowd seemed uneasy. There was mumbling and muttering, as if, now that they had finally got what everyone had been saying all along should happen, they were not so sure about it. And a familiar voice called out, 'Shame! Shame! Jenny saved my life, and my child's! You cannot do this!' Margery was there, somewhere, and she at least was not afraid to speak up for me. Then someone else shouted, 'What about Lord Hugh, then? What does he think about this?' Richard made a small movement with his hand and all of a sudden there was a line of his men, right around the front of the crowd, holding back the press of bodies. The dissenting voices were drowned out by shouts of 'Burn the sorceress!' 'Death to the filthy spy!' 'Let's see her burn!'

The noise built as I was dragged across the platform and onto the narrow ledge around the central pole. The pyre had been deftly stacked about this point, its top tier lying just below the ledge. Here and there I could see the little logs that Richard had placed with his own hands so carefully. There was an oily sheen to their surface. The guard took out a stout rope and bound me tightly to the pole. Once, twice, three times around the waist, and fastened at the back where I could not reach. But he left my hands free.

Down below, the excitement was growing. Some whistled, and some called foul names, and one threw a soft fruit, which fell short, thudding down between the logs. People were arguing. The guards were struggling to hold the crowd back. I could see Margery now, just behind Megan, her face running with tears. She was shouting, but I could not hear the words. The drum began again, and I thought stupidly, now a whistle, and a fiddle, and dancing. The guards who held my things were standing at the foot of the pyre. One of them threw the spindle, and the distaff, and the small loom onto the pile. I heard the cracking as they landed and splintered. The guard with the basket hesitated, looking at me. It was the same man who had brought me blackberries in my tiny cell, when I had thought myself without a friend in the world.

'Make haste, man,' said Richard testily.

His hands, I thought, are itching to pick up that torch. In the west, the clouds had the faintest rim of pink. A little wind rose, sending leaves scurrying across the courtyard. People started putting on their cloaks.

Please. Please put them in my hands. Oh, please. The guard could not hear me; I tried to speak with my eyes, with my heart. He lifted up the basket. *Just a little closer, I cannot reach. Please, oh please.*

'No need for that,' said Richard sharply. 'Just toss them on the fire with the rest. All must burn.'

But the man stepped up onto the ash logs, and

higher, and lifted the basket onto the ledge beside my feet, and I gripped it with both hands like a lifeline.

'What are you doing, man?' Richard snapped. 'Step down, unless you, too, wish to burn.' The man glanced at him, and at me, and his honest eyes showed both compassion and distaste.

'Last time you catch me doing this job,' he muttered. 'Only a youngster, she is.'

He took his time to climb back down, while Richard's fingers twitched with impatience. The last sliver of sun slipped below the horizon. The wind came in little gusts, making the torches flare and fade, flare and fade. Leaves blew in circles on the ground. Whipped by that wind, the fire would burn hot.

Come now. Come now. Where are you?

I could hear nothing, nothing but the howl of the rising wind, which blew strangely, this way and that. It tugged at the basket in my hands. Richard was making his way down the steps. The wind whipped at his tunic and ruffled his neatly combed hair. The torches blazed.

A sudden hush fell over the crowd. I closed my eyes. *Now. It must be now. Hurry.* The people were waiting, waiting as Richard walked steadily to the foot of the pyre, where the small torch burned in its holder. They were silent. Then, bright, clear and innocent through the dusk, a child's voice rang out. 'Look, mother! Look up there!'

Like ghosts, like great, soaring spirits they moved across the sky, spread out in file behind their leader, long-necked, broad-winged, white as the crest of a wave, their wings beating in solemn rhythm. They circled the courtyard where we stood, and the eyes of the crowd followed their flight. One, two, three, four, five. Finbar had always been the last to come.

Come down. Come down to me. They circled again, and I saw Richard reaching for the torch. Then down they glided to land on the platform close by me. They huddled together, eyes wild with confusion, webbed feet padding up and down on the rough boards.

Now, Sorcha. Do it now.

No time to ask questions. No time to gaze up into the darkening sky for another. I reached into the basket, grasped a shirt, flung it over the arching neck of the first great bird. The crowd muttered and whispered.

Quickly, Sorcha. Where was he, where was Finbar? Out over the water still? Left behind, too weak to fly so far? Where was he? I drew out the next shirt, and the next.

'What evil sorcery is this?' Richard's voice was a snarl, and I heard the torch rasp from its socket as he gripped it in his hand. 'What familiars does she call to her aid? All must burn! All!' And he touched the fire to the bottom-most layer, where twigs of birch and willow twisted between the ash logs. There was a little crackling, and a flare of light. The crowd gasped as one.

The fourth shirt. The fifth. And I held the last shirt in my hands, the very last, which had but one sleeve, and was stained with dirt and blood and tears. *Quickly, Finbar. Quickly.*

The swans shuffled in an awkward group, stretching their long vulnerable necks to the sky. The shirts of starwort hung loosely about their great white bodies. *Now, Finbar!* My eyes went here and there, scanning the sky, scanning the crowd. I would not look down, down beneath my feet where the fire glowed, and spread, running up the length of one twig and another, fanned by the capricious breeze. I felt the heat on my feet and legs, the draught from the fire stirring my skirts. It was not quite pain; not yet. The swans edged away, the flames reflected ever stronger in their frightened eyes. The sky was dark; I could see no birds there. At the back of the crowd, people were jostling and exclaiming. I looked that way. Looked straight into a pair of eyes the colour of shadows on ice; into a face I had seen in my dreams these many nights since. He was haggard with exhaustion, his face wild with terror and fury. He had a long, fresh scar on his left cheek, and bruises around his eye. He was elbowing his way fiercely through the crowd, heedless of whom he thrust aside. Behind him, two other men, one with flaxen hair, and the emblem of Harrowfield on his tunic. The second, young, tall and well built. A man with hair like a field of barley in the summer sun, and eyes of periwinkle blue.

'Lord Hugh,' folk were exclaiming. 'Lord Hugh is returned.' And they were saying, 'Simon. Look, it's Master Simon!' Somewhere, a small dog was yapping hysterically, a sound not of fright or pain, but a canine fanfare of ecstatic welcome. The flames began to lick at the second tier of logs. I tried to lift one foot, then the other, out of their path. Now it was really hurting. Above me, the wind twisted and turned, a strange, meddlesome wind such as I had never seen before. And on its eddies, another swan came flying, slowly, so slowly, as if it barely had the strength to move its great wings. People pointed upwards.

'Let me through!' shouted Red. 'Let me by!' But he was trapped by the surge of bodies, all craning to watch the swan, or to see the fire, and his voice was lost in the hubbub as they chattered and cried out in their excitement. The heat rose from the ash logs; the lone bird drifted downwards, down to where I stood, clutching the last of my shirts of starwort. Beneath my bare feet, the wood was smoking. *Quickly, Finbar, quickly*. Now he was circling as if unsure where to land. *Hurry*. People began to move, to let Red through, perhaps because of the way he was shouting, perhaps because of the small sharp knife that had appeared in his hand. At the foot of the pyre, Richard stood motionless, watching me, blind to all but his moment of victory. The flames grew higher, steadily advancing. They had almost reached the first of the special faggots. Hot fire, that burns and glows and leaves nothing but bones behind.

'Jenny!' shouted Red, pushing aside two of Richard's men. 'Jenny!' His face was ashen white. And I saw something glinting, something reflecting the firelight, high above the heads of the crowd. In a window of the house, overlooking the courtyard, an archer stood poised, bow drawn, finger ready on the string. He was not aiming at me, nor at the sixth swan which now circled low over the heads of the crowd again. He was not aiming at Ben, nor at the golden-haired man who followed his brother through the crowd of gaping, round-eyed folk. He was aiming at Hugh of Harrowfield, he who stood head and shoulders above the people around him, he whose bright hair, like some flag of war, made him a clear and easy target. Richard had told me, as he taunted me in my cell, that he wanted me out of the way before Red's return. He had said he might create a delay. A diversion, Richard had called it. This was something more than a diversion.

Nobody had seen. Nobody but me. I sensed rather than saw the slight movement of hand on bowstring, the tilt, the steady aim. My eyes went back to Red, as he struggled against the sea of bodies packed tight.

My feet were in agony, and the hem of my gown was smouldering. And then a gust of wind came up, out of nowhere, and snatched the sixth shirt of starwort out of my hands and up, up into the air, far from reach. Red was trapped behind two guards, their solid forms blocking him from any movement. The archer went very still.

I screamed. 'Red, look out! Behind you!' My voice came out rasping, and broken, and weak from years of silence. But he heard me, and turned, and the arrow took him in the shoulder with a sickening thud.

The enormity of what I had done was like a blow straight to the heart. After all this time, after everything, I had spoken. I had not been able to stop myself. I had broken the silence. There were flames everywhere; the platform by the pyre was starting to turn black. There were little fizzing, popping sounds from the uppermost layer of wood. I watched blankly as Red reached up behind him and snapped the shaft of the arrow in two, as if breaking a twig; and wrenched the other part out, teeth bared in a grimace of pain. Still he was shoving his way forward. And now, the crowd parted quickly to let him through, and he reached the foot of the pyre. Richard thrust out an arm to stop him, his features suffused with rage, and received in return a blow to the face that sent him reeling back into the crowd. Then Red jumped, jumped through the flames and the heat to the second tier of logs, booted feet agile on the smouldering wood, stepped to the top, slashed once, twice with the little knife at the ropes that bound me there. His face was white as death. The flames were licking at the highest logs. He grabbed me around the waist, slung me over his shoulder like a sack of vegetables and leaped again, awkwardly this time, so that the two of us landed in a heap on the middle of the smouldering wooden platform which stood beside the pyre. An instant later there was a flaring, and a whooshing, and the fire began to take on an eerie green hue, its strange light illuminating the whole courtyard, playing on open mouths and startled eyes, shining on the figure of an archer carefully backing away from an open window, lighting up the staring features of Richard of Northwoods, on which rage now warred with fear.

I felt Red's arm close around me like a shield against the rest of the world. His mouth was against my hair, and his heart thumped violently under my cheek. I shut my eyes, and held onto his shirt with both hands, and wept. Now I had lost them, I had lost them all. How could I? How could I do it? How could I speak, after so long, after all this time, how could I let the words out, before the spell was broken? And yet I knew in my heart that I would not have stayed silent, for in that moment, the only thing that had mattered was for Red to be alive. I had saved him; but I had lost my brothers.

CHAPTER FOURTEEN

The fire burned green and gold, and small explosions popped and crackled. There was a smell of scorched feathers. The crowd gave a great gasp, and another, and broke into a babble of sound. Under my cheek, Red's shirt was wet with blood and tears. 'It's all right,' he said over and over. 'It's all right, Jenny, it's all right.' Neither of us seemed able to move. Then, suddenly, I felt his arm tighten around my shoulders.

'Lay a finger on her,' he said very softly, 'and I'll kill you.'

'I'm her brother, you fool,' said somebody in a tongue Red could not understand. I could not turn around, he held me so hard against him.

'He can't understand you, Diarmid.'

I could not believe it, but Conor's voice went on, translating calmly. 'We are her brothers, and are come to take Sorcha home. We will do no harm, if safe conduct can be granted from your lands. Our sister has no further need of your protection.' For an instant, the arm tightened around me still further; and then he let go. I twisted around to be scooped up into Conor's arms like a child, and soon they were all around me, Liam exclaiming, Diarmid cursing, Cormack and Padriac already armed with short swords deftly removed from a couple of men who now lay groaning at the foot of the steps. Diarmid was scanning the crowd, sizing up the opposition, measuring the distance to cover. I began to be aware that we were very exposed, up here on the platform, and that the boards not far from where we stood were starting to burn.

'Were you planning to bleed to death or wait for the fire?' Ben appeared as if from nowhere, his hair bright gold in the light from the flames. He bent down and hauled Red to his feet, grimacing. 'In case you hadn't noticed, this thing's burning. Here.' He put an arm under Red's good shoulder and began half dragging his friend down the steps. Red looked back, just once. I had not thought it possible for him to turn any paler, but he had; and he had wiped every trace of expression from his features. The left side of his shirt was soaked with blood.

'Come on, Red,' said Ben. 'Your mother is here, and your brother. There's no need for you to stay. Besides, a dead hero's no use to anyone. As for you,' he glanced back over his shoulder in the general direction of my brothers, 'my advice would be to get out of here as soon as possible. Make your way to the house. That should be safe for now. I'd take you there myself, but as you see . . .' And they were gone.

Cormack made his way down the steps, sword in hand, with Conor close behind him carrying me, and the others at the rear.

'Where's Finbar?' I whispered, but nobody heard me. The noise was bedlam. Voices shouting, here and there a clash of swords, the crackling and roaring of the great fire as it consumed ash wood and sawn timber and all it could reach. The flames were monstrous now, towering high, edged with sparks of green and orange. The ledge where I had been standing was long gone, the pole burned through. Around us, the crowd surged forward, and there were men with daggers and swords, and fear in their eyes. There was no way through, no route to the safety of the house. My brothers had formed a tight ring about me, but the crowd was moving in, and the mood was turning ugly. There were those amongst them that had come to see a sorceress burn, and felt cheated. There were those that saw only that, suddenly, their enemy was in their midst, armed and dangerous. And there were Richard's men, who had certain orders to carry out.

'I can't believe we've been saved only to perish at the hands of some British rabble,' growled Cormack, trying with little success to clear a path through the shouting, angry crowd. A man cursed at him, and Cormack raised the sword. Conor's arms tightened around me.

'It's not looking good,' agreed Liam, swinging his arm out and downwards to knock a man to the ground. Behind him, others were toppled by his fall. A group of guards in the colours of Northwoods began to advance on us.

'Good people of Harrowfield!' A voice rang out, sharply authoritative. 'You have witnessed a great wonder this night. A miracle, it could be said.' Slowly the crowd hushed, and turned. Seated on a tall piebald horse, straight-backed in his black robe, Father Dominic of Whitehaven fixed the people with stern gaze. There was a deathly silence. From the safe haven of Conor's arms, I looked up. Why was Father Dominic here? Why had he come back?

'This girl has come close to death. But you have seen the transformation here, how these young men have been brought back to human form by her faith and hope, and the good work of her hands. Surely the devil laid this evil affliction on them, and it is through God's will that they are saved.'

More muttering; heads shaken, heads nodding. I was tired. I was so tired. Where was Finbar? Where was . . . ?

'The hand of the Lord is on this young woman,' Father Dominic went on in measured tones that carried right across the courtyard. 'You should count yourselves blessed that you have seen it. And be thankful that help arrived in time, for there nearly was a gross miscarriage of justice here tonight. The girl was not condemned to death. The charges against her were not proven; besides, who would condemn a child who has not the powers of speech to plead her innocence? I believed it imperative in the interests of justice for the case to be held over until her husband returned, and could speak for her. I conveyed this much to Lord Richard, before I was called away. Why he chose to announce another verdict to the folkmoot, and to enact the penalty so swiftly I intend to discover for myself in due course. Had it not been for the lady Anne, who rode out herself to reach me and question me today, I would have known nothing of this burning until it was too late. And the Lord's mercy would not have been granted to these unfortunate young men.'

I saw, now, that Lady Anne was beside him, seated on the little mare and clad in riding clothes. She looked very tired.

'Where is the man who ordered this done?' asked Father Dominic, and I saw Richard's men melt into the throng of people and disappear. There was a flurry of activity on the edges of the crowd, in the semi-darkness.

'What about him, then?' came a voice from somewhere in the crowd. 'That fellow, the one that's holding her. He's the one from the woods, the fugitive, the Irish bastard we nearly caught that night. You can't tell me he's just here for a quiet visit. What about him?'

Conor looked up and across the sea of bodies, and there was a sudden hush.

'I am her brother,' he said quietly in the tongue they could understand. 'We are all her brothers. Her silence kept the darkness from us. Her labours released us.'

'Good people.' Lady Anne spoke, and there was a desperate weariness in her voice. 'We have indeed seen wonderful and terrible things here at Harrowfield tonight. There are many questions to be asked, and answers given. You see that – that my sons are returned; both of my sons, and my heart is too full of gratitude to see any man hurt, or punished, or offered less than courtesy this night.' She was trying not to weep, her voice tightly controlled. 'These young men are guests in my house, for now. I believe Jenny is innocent of any wrongdoing. The hand of God does not bestow its blessing thus on those that have guilt in their hearts. There will be time enough, in the morning, for explanations and reckonings. Now put away your weapons, go home to your beds, and be glad that no innocent blood was shed here in the heart of the valley. Rejoice with me, that my sons are home again.'

There was a half-hearted cheer, and the people began to disperse, a little reluctantly. Many glanced our way; but the wild, haggard faces of my brothers with their fierce eyes were enough to frighten off anyone. Then men of the household came to escort us indoors, and into Lady Anne's small parlour that she used when guests came. There was a fire, and lamps. Conor put me carefully down on a cushioned bench near the hearth. They were all there, Liam listening, tight-lipped, to Lady Anne, and Conor translating; Padriac turning a half-burnt stick from the pyre over and over in his hands, touching and testing the residue that coated it; Diarmid and Cormack by me, naked swords still in their hands, and their eyes on the doorway. And by the far window, looking out, stood Finbar with his back to us. His right hand, spread flat against the stone wall, was thin and transparent as if sculpted from ice. And now I could see the legacy of that last shirt, the shirt with but one sleeve. For in place of his left arm, my brother still bore the strong shining wing of a great swan. He had been the last to return, and so, for all his life, he would carry this burden, the doom of the incomplete garment made with love and tears and blood. He made no sound; he would not turn towards me where I lay encircled by my brothers. And there were strong shields around his mind.

I tried my voice again. After so long, it was not easy to make it work.

'How did – I thought – ?'

Conor came over to kneel by my side.

'Well. You've done it. Only just in time, it seems.'

He had a crooked little smile on his face, but his eyes were very serious. 'This lady tells me we are safe here; but for how long remains to be seen. For now, you must rest. It's over at last.'

'But – but I spoke, I spoke before the shirts – I did not keep silent! How is it that you are here, and the spell broken?' Still I could not believe that, after all, they had been saved. Are not the dooms of the Fair Folk set out and determined in every cruel detail, so that the least slip, the smallest deviation from the rules brings the whole thing collapsing around the hapless victims? How was it the spell could be undone, when I had cried aloud before ever the last shirt was slipped over Finbar's neck?

'You could not see it,' said Conor gently. 'But these things have a way of working themselves out, when it is time. Have you forgotten the wind, the sudden wind that whipped that last shirt from your hands and up into the air? Who is to say that wind did not let this garment drop over Finbar's neck, an instant before your cry rang out? The spell really is broken, Sorcha; all but . . .'

We both turned to look at Finbar. I thought, this tale will live a long time, and will change over the years as it is told and re-told. But he will always bear the evidence of its truth. He will never come back, not fully. He will always be torn between that world and this, neither completely of the one nor of the other. It will be his curse and his blessing.

'Jenny, how are you? But perhaps I should call you by your real name, Sorcha, is it?' Lady Anne had moved closer. 'I can hardly believe what I have seen; and yet I must believe it. Father Dominic is right; it is a miracle, and we have been blessed to witness it. And now you have your voice back, by God's will.

My dear, you have turned this household upside down today.'

'I – I'm sorry.' I looked up at her. She seemed different; behind her calm words was a barely suppressed excitement, and her eyes were alight with joy.

'It is I who should be sorry, for I misjudged you terribly. I never thought to see such astonishing sights. One might have thought it a trick of the flame and the smoke; the sudden change, as feathers became flesh, and the long necks and wild eyes of those birds transformed themselves into six young men. I have to say, the people of my household have been both frightened and confused by this, and will take time to recover. The sudden appearance of these brothers of yours right in their midst, as fierce a band of Irishmen as you would ever see and with scarce a rag of clothing between them – that shook them badly. One thing we can remedy. I have a man fetching suitable garments, and food and drink. I can scarce come to terms with this myself; for my people, it will be a night long remembered.'

'There's blood on your gown,' said Cormack, frowning. 'Are you injured, Sorcha? Are you hurt?'

I shook my head wearily, looking down at the blue dress. As well as the mark of the sea, it now had scorches on the hemline, and the front of the bodice was stained dark. But it was not my blood.

'I thought he was meant to look after you,' said Conor bluntly, coming across to me. 'Was he not chosen to be your protector?'

I looked at him. *What can you know of that?*

'I saw him watching you as you ran on the sand. I saw him pluck you from the fire. I can guess as well as the next man. Maybe better,' he said. 'Why would

562

such a man choose to stand by you, unless he was under a doom of the Fair Folk? I would wager that when the Lady of the Forest set you on this path, she set him right there next to you.'

'Pretty poor job he did of keeping her safe,' said Diarmid. 'Just about lost her. Who does he think he is, anyway?'

'He's her husband,' Liam growled.

The others turned to stare at him.

'What?'

'The priest said it. Conor told me. Waiting till her husband returned to speak for her. That's him, I'll be bound.'

I was surrounded by disapproving eyes.

'Sorcha?'

'Can this be true? That you are wed to a Briton?'

'Rubbish. She's still a child.' This was Diarmid, his expression outraged.

Even though I had my voice back, it seemed to be very hard to speak. Instead, I clutched the ring that hung around my neck, and put my other arm around my knees, and turned my face away from them. By the window, Finbar still stood with his back to the room, utterly still.

'Ahem.' I think they had forgotten that Lady Anne was there. She had not understood their words, but she recognised my distress. 'Your sister needs rest, and a drink of ale, and some quiet. You're upsetting her.' She put her arm around my shoulders, and held the cup so I could drink. 'There, my dear. Slowly.' Then she looked at Conor again. 'Jen – Sorcha has had a difficult time; tonight's strange events have taken a toll on us all. I will take your sister to bathe and change her clothes. I will arrange also for each of you to receive what you require; warm garments, food and drink. When I return, there will be time for explanations, for questions to be answered. Father Dominic will want to speak with you; and so will my son.'

'Sorcha's not going anywhere on her own,' said Conor bluntly. 'You think, after what we have witnessed here tonight, we intend letting her out of our sight for one instant? Bring what is needed here.' Then he spoke rapidly in an undertone, explaining to the others.

'Tell her,' said Liam grimly, 'no time is to be wasted. Every moment is precious; every delay lengthens our time on these accursed shores. I want Sorcha out of this place and on a boat for home early tomorrow, and us with her.'

Conor relayed this word for word. Lady Anne's eyebrows went up.

'Sorcha,' she appealed to me, 'is it possible to explain – can you –'

I found my voice, with some difficulty.

'It's all right,' I croaked. 'Lady Anne means no harm. And – and I would like, very much, to be clean and warm again. Please.'

'It's not the lady I'm concerned about,' said Conor. 'What guarantee have we of your safety, once you step outside that door? How can you have any trust in these people, after what was done to you tonight?'

'Conor.' I stood up shakily, clutching at Lady Anne's arm. 'I'm tired and dirty, and I promise I will be back soon. I have lived here almost a year; a long time. This is the closest thing I have had to a home since we left Sevenwaters, and I have farewells to say. I know it is hard for you to believe, but these people have been – kind to me, in their way. And as you say, I have had a strong protector, who is still here. I will not be harmed.'

'Then Liam shall go with you, and stand guard.'

'No. These people know me. You must not leave this room; they are still angry and confused. Please, Conor.'

'After what Sorcha has done for us, we are scarcely in a position to say no to anything,' put in Padriac.

So I went with Lady Anne, along a hallway of curious eyes, as far as a square, neat chamber where Megan was already busy with hot water and rosemary oil and clean towels. She was a little shy this time, as if the wonders of the evening had distanced me too far for comfort. She took her time washing my hair, and later, as I tried to comb out the tangles, she held up the blue dress in dismay.

'Oh, dear! I'm afraid this one's beyond repair. You'll never wear this again.' She bundled it up, as if to discard it to a rag heap or even to the midden.

'No!' I whispered. 'No . . .'

Megan turned her head, brown curls bobbing.

'This gown is mine,' I managed. A sweet smile spread over her features.

'You can talk now,' she said in wonderment. 'Your voice is just as I thought it would be. But this gown must at least have a good cleaning. Leave it with me; I'll do what I can, and get it back to you safely.'

'No,' I insisted. 'There's no time.'

'What do you mean?' asked Lady Anne, who had been sorting linen on a side table.

'My brothers,' I said, wincing as my comb caught on another knot.

'Here, let me do that.' Megan took the comb from my hand and began, expertly, to separate the strands of my neglected hair. At least the oil had removed the small crawling things.

'They'll be wanting to leave at first light,' I said. 'I have to be ready. I'll need my boots; and I will take this gown, at least, when I go.' I had not many possessions. I did not care what I left behind, but for the blue gown marked by water, and fire, and blood. Three things were precious: this gown, and Finbar's amulet, and my wedding ring.

Megan's face was a study in confusion.

'But – but what about Lord Hugh?' she said straight out, heedless of Lady Anne. 'The young men, your brothers, I can see why they might want to go, and fast; you've only got to hear what folks are saying round the house. They're best out of here. But you? You can't just leave. What about him?' Then she blushed, and dropped her eyes. 'Not my place, I know. Sorry.'

'Indeed.' You could not tell, from Lady Anne's voice, what she thought on the matter. 'Jenny, I must leave you for a little. My son – my younger son – is returned; I have not spoken with him alone yet. A few moments. I'll come back for you soon. Please wait here for me.'

'Did you see?' asked Megan as the door closed behind her mistress. 'Simon, Lord Hugh's brother – he's here, large as life, when they all swore he was dead, killed by the – well, they did say that, and yet he's back. Lost his memory, apparently; can't recall anything since the time he left here with Richard's men. Lord Hugh found him in some monastery, out of the way place, an island I think they said. Lady Anne was dying to talk to Simon, but couldn't go, not until she attended to you. And what with Lord Hugh's injury, and all . . .'

'Megan . . .' I touched her arm; it was hard to get back into the way of using words. 'How bad is – is he all right? Did they stop the bleeding, did they –'

'Still in one piece,' she said, looking at me sideways. 'But they rode out again straight after, him and Ben and one or two more. Lord Hugh had his arm in a sling, and a strapping on his shoulder. Looking for his uncle. Stayed around just long enough to get patched up, that was all. Master Simon wanted to go with him, eager for it, but Lord Hugh wouldn't let him. Told Simon to take charge here instead. That way his mother could see him before he went rushing off again. Are you really sure you want to go home?'

The question caught me off balance.

'It's best if I go,' I said. 'I am not one of you, and I never can be.' *What if the wound starts to bleed again? What if he finds Richard and . . . Why didn't someone stop him?* 'I have brought nothing but trouble here. Now it's over. It's time to go back to the forest.'

'Did you ask Lord Hugh what he thinks about that?' Megan's glance was sharp as she fastened the wrists of my clean gown.

What if he is too weak to ride, what if his enemies lie in wait? What if he does not return, before it is time for me to go?

'Did you ask him?' She smoothed my hair back and tied it with a ribbon to match the gown, the soft blush pink of an autumn rose. An impractical shade.

'This is what Lord Hugh would want,' I said. 'I don't belong here, and my brothers need me.' *And he will forget. Once the doom is lifted from him; perhaps even now. Perhaps even from the moment he took his arm from where it held me safe, and put the mask over his face again.*

Megan raised her brows at me as she began to clear away bottles and bowls and cloths. 'Perhaps you should ask Lord Hugh when he comes back,' she said. 'I wouldn't be in Richard of Northwoods' shoes tonight, for anything.'

When we returned to the parlour, things had

changed. The best wine and wheaten bread had been provided, with cold roast meats, and Lady Anne herself was cutting wedges of cheese. I looked quickly around the room, but there was no sign of Red, or of Ben. My brothers looked slightly more respectable, though their long tangled hair and fierce eyes sat oddly with the neat plain clothes they now wore. Father Dominic had gathered them around him, by the window, and he spoke with them quietly. Finbar stood at the back of the group, silent. With Conor's translation and a range of gestures, the others seemed to be managing quite well. I saw knives in my brothers' belts. It had been risky, I thought, allowing them weapons. Whose idea could that have been? Perhaps nobody had dared to refuse.

Leaning on the hearth, there was another man; the tall, golden-haired man who could not be Simon, and yet, incredibly, must be Simon, for at his feet Alys stood quivering with joy, her tail wagging so hard it seemed the two halves of her body moved in opposite directions. A dog does not make mistakes, not when she has waited so long for her master's return.

How do you read a person's face, when his past has been wiped away? Simon was older; in the three years since I had last seen him, he had grown from a boy to a man. He had the same straight nose and strong jaw as his brother, but the mouth was more generous, the eyes less guarded. There were no scars on neck, or ear, or well-muscled arm where the shirt was rolled above the elbow. And yet, how could that be? Did he remember nothing? I glanced over at my brothers. Intent on the priest's words, they showed not a flicker of recognition. That was just as well. Simon's bright eyes were as innocent and merry as a child's; his expression quite without guile.

'Simon,' said Lady Anne, 'this is Sorcha, of whom I spoke to you. Sorcha is – is –'

'Red's wife,' said Simon, looking past his mother, and straight into my eyes. I saw his face change. He too had worn a mask, and for the instant that he let it slip, I knew that whatever he had forgotten, he had not forgotten me.

'Sorcha. That name suits you well,' he said quietly. 'I had not thought my brother would wed a woman of Erin.'

'It was not . . . he did not . . .' My heart was thumping. He knew me, I was certain of it. And if he remembered me, he remembered my brothers, and . . . but then how could he stand there, smiling, with them so close? Where was the frantic, damaged boy I had struggled to nurse back to some semblance of sanity? The boy without hope, who clung to my tales for survival through the nightmare of pain and shame? And why did this man bear no scars?

'You did a remarkable thing tonight,' Simon went on. 'It is almost past the understanding of our people, that such a transformation could be possible. For now, they dwell on the wonder of it; by tomorrow, some will dismiss it as a trick of the light, and others tuck it in the back of their memory to be brought out only as a tale for their grandchildren. And there are some, I'm afraid, who may start to think again of sorcery.'

'You need not fear for your brother,' I said with some difficulty. 'I will not remain here to be a burden to him. We had – we had an agreement . . .'

'Interesting,' he said softly. 'What agreement was that?'

I was saved from reply by Father Dominic, who now rose and came over to greet me. Lady Anne,

569

glowing with happiness at her son's return, had barely listened to our words.

'Young woman,' said the priest, 'your brothers have told me something of your strange story. Come, be seated and take some wine. You still look pale; you are not yet recovered from your ordeal.'

I sat; and at once, my brothers closed in around me, so that the protective circle was back in place. Diarmid was watching Simon, and the look on his face said, the only good Briton is a dead one.

'Richard of Northwoods,' said Father Dominic. 'The man did wrong here today – well, I suppose it is yesterday, since we are past midnight. I made it quite clear to him that it would be – unwise – to rule in this young woman's case without hearing all the evidence. And when we spoke in private together he expressed agreement. It was most unfortunate that I was called away before I had time to explain what we intended to the folk of the moot. For Lord Richard to announce a guilty verdict in my name as well as his own was not only a lie, but blatant misuse of the authority vested in him. To enact the penalty so swiftly smacks of something more sinister. He must be called to question for that, at least; and possibly also for other matters.'

'In all the excitement, it appears he slipped through the net,' said Simon, sounding very like his brother. 'But he will not get far. I, too, have matters to discuss with my uncle. Though much of my past seems lost, some things I do recall. He has many questions to answer.'

'My elder son has gone tonight, with his men, to bring my brother back,' said Lady Anne. 'This has been a matter of some distress to me, as you may imagine. I knew, when I rode out to fetch you today, that it might come to this. But I cannot expect my own people to act with integrity and courage if I do not show an example.'

'Well spoken,' said Father Dominic, and his eyes on her were compassionate. 'I will take a keen interest in Richard's answers. Tell Lord Hugh to send for me, when his uncle is found. I was shocked that a man in a position of such authority would act so; such abuses of power deserve a swift and firm response.'

'Indeed,' said Conor. 'We, too, have heard tales, and are learning more. If this man is responsible for the charges against our sister, and the cruel treatment she has received, he has made deadly enemies today. To put it bluntly, his future prospects appear to me both limited and unpleasant.'

'Due process should be followed,' said Father Dominic mildly, looking around the circle of grim-faced, tight-lipped warriors. 'Meanwhile, you should rejoice in your deliverance, and your sister's selflessness.' He turned to me, smiling. 'My dear, your story is one of great courage. Were you not already wed, one so strong in the virtues of patience and faith would have been welcomed into our community of holy sisters. Your example would have shone indeed, a light amongst lights.'

I could think of nothing to say. I took a sip of wine, and tried to ignore the way Simon was looking at me.

'Your brothers are angry,' the priest went on. 'They are bent on revenge for what was done to you. For what was nearly done. But that is not the way. It is best if they leave here, and leave swiftly. There should be no more blood shed, no more hatred in this place.'

I nodded. It was becoming clearer every moment

that again, there would be but one path for me, but one choice.

'You seem sad. You have done a wonderful thing, child. Rejoice, for you are amongst the blessed of the Lord. And rest. Your rest is well earned.' He got up. 'I, too, find myself more than a little weary. Lady Anne, I will avail myself of your good hospitality tonight, if I may. Alas, I am a little too advanced in years, and too generous of girth, to ride so far, so fast without suffering for it. We must all rest, and reflect on the wonders that the Lord bestows. Wonders indeed. In the morning, I will speak to the folk of Harrowfield and tell them something more of this tale of suffering and redemption. There is much to be learned from it.'

It was Simon who escorted the good Father away to rest, with Alys yapping about their ankles. I closed my eyes for a moment as my brothers moved around me, talking in quiet, purposeful voices, planning, preparing. They would not rest tonight; not with so much ahead. So they spoke of horses, and arms, and boats. And they spoke of my father and of the lady Oonagh. They talked of vengeance. It all seemed so unreal; like another world. Perhaps, if I sat here very still, hardly breathing, they would forget about me altogether; and then I would not have to say goodbye.

'Our sister,' said Conor. 'Has she many belongings to be packed and made ready?'

'I will arrange it.' Lady Anne's response was very quiet. 'She has little. My woman will pack her things and bring them here. Sorcha's very tired.' There was a strong note of disapproval there.

'Nonetheless,' said Conor, 'we must depart at dawn, for the sake of this household as well as our own safety. Your good priest intervened just in time,

I fear. As your son said, it would not take long for the mood of your people to turn sour again, and put our lives in danger. Once we are gone, you can, with your sons' help, put all to rights here. These have been strange times for all of us.'

There was a little pause. 'You understand,' said Lady Anne diffidently, 'that your sister is but newly wedded to my son?'

Conor translated this for the others, and there was a flood of angry response. It was fortunate that Lady Anne could not understand the tongue my brothers spoke.

'So it's true,' growled Diarmid.

Padriac was incredulous. 'Why bring it up now? She can't mean –'

'Marriage?' Cormack spat this out. 'What sort of marriage would it be, between a helpless girl and some great brute of a Briton?'

'It seems probable,' said Liam coldly, 'that this marriage was never consummated.' They were talking as if I were not even there, as if these things were to be dealt with in the manner of a campaign strategy. I felt my cheeks grow hot with embarrassment, but at the same time I was angry. They should leave Red out of it. None of this was his fault, none of it. But nobody was asking me for an opinion.

'Our sister is young,' Liam continued, 'and the fellow has been away, in search of a lost brother. Besides, I cannot believe Sorcha would willingly consent to such a thing. It is a bond which can be readily undone, I trust.'

Conor translated for Lady Anne.

'I can't speak for Hugh,' she said tightly. 'You will have to ask him.'

'We will,' said Conor, grim-faced.

After a while Lady Anne, stifling a yawn, made her excuses, and we were left alone, save for the two men who stood outside guarding the door. I let Padriac pour me more wine, and I accepted a piece of bread, though I had no stomach for either. The room felt strange, as if it were floating around me in some dream. I knew if I did not eat or drink, I would be unable to ride out at dawn. Finbar was sitting on the bench by the window, looking out, and I took my small meal over and settled beside him. Outside, the wind had died down completely. You could just see, in the darkness, a faint glow from the ashes of the fire, still smouldering in the courtyard. If they rode back tonight, I would see them from here.

I know how it feels, dear one. As if your heart were torn in two. I feel your pain.

I took a deep breath. Another.

Finbar?

I know how it feels. As if you will never be whole again.

I reached inside my dress, where I wore two cords about my neck. One held my wedding ring; the other, the amulet that had once been my mother's. I left the one, and took off the other. *This is yours. Take it back. Take it back, it was to you she gave it.*

I slipped the cord over his head, and the little carven stone with its ash tree sign lay on his breast. He had grown painfully thin.

Show me the other. The other talisman you wear.

Slowly I took out the carven ring, and lifted it on my palm for my brother to see.

He made this for you? Him with the golden hair, and the eyes that devour?

Not him. Another. Images were strong in my mind; Red with his arm around me like a shield; Red cutting up an apple; Red kicking a sword from a man's hand,

and catching it in his own; Red barefoot on the sand with the sea around his ankles.

You risked much, to give your love to such a one.

I stared at him. *Love?*

Did you not know, until now, when you must say goodbye? Then he let me look into his mind. Pictures, no words. There was a reedy shore, a place of shelter and serenity. There was a tiny white beach, and a stretch of tranquil lake water. On it swam a beautiful swan, her neck proudly arched, her eyes clear and bright. Beside her, two downy young ones but half fledged, dipping and splashing in the water. *I too have said my farewells.* The image faded. My brother's face held nothing but a distant, remote sadness. *I had a little time. More than you have had. But I fear the cold, and the wolf, and the long loneliness. More than I can tell you, I fear for them.*

He, too, had made a terrible choice. A swan mates for life. I reached out and took his hand. In the end, there was no choice. The seven of us were one; and each was a part of the seven. We must always be there, one for another.

Time plays cruel tricks. That night, it seemed to pass very slowly, as I stood watching by the window for his return, with Finbar silent by my side. Once before, he had soothed and comforted me all through an endless night; had exhausted all his strength in doing so. Now he simply kept me company. My mind showed me Red bleeding, injured, exhausted, spurred on by hate; seeking his uncle through woodland and across ford and up and down the dark hills of Harrowfield. More than anything, I longed to see him ride safely back into the courtyard. And so I stood and waited, watching the last embers of the great fire fade and die. And I thought, is Finbar right? Can this be love that twists and tears the heart so? Does love give nothing but the power to hurt each other? Is this what makes the simplest touch blend longing and terror in equal measure? Whatever this is, it feels like a mortal wound. And suddenly it seemed the night was passing quickly, so quickly. For soon it would be dawn, and we would slip away from Harrowfield by secret paths, and home across the water. Soon it would be time to say goodbye. I could not tell which feeling was stronger, the fear that he would not return in time, or the dread that he would.

When they did return at last, it was with little ceremony. There were no blazing torches, no beating drums. Just five men riding out of the dark in single file. The first was Ben, a black hood not quite concealing his flowing blond hair. Then another, clad also in dark clothing to pass unseen in the night. This man led a horse on which a captive rode awkwardly, his hands bound behind him. There was, nonetheless, an arrogant turn of the head, a set of the shoulders that suggested defiance. There were heavy bruises on his face, and blood ran unchecked from a gash above the brow. They had found Lord Richard.

'That man's days are numbered,' said Cormack, as my brothers moved to stand behind me. 'He will be accounted for six times over.'

'And more, I would say,' said Liam, watching the horsemen draw closer. There were lamps hanging by the entry downstairs, and their light fell on the faces of the four men escorting the prisoner. I let my breath out all at once. For there he was, riding last, right hand loose on the reins, left arm across his chest in a sling. His face was as pale as the linen wrapping around his arm and shoulder, his mouth set in a grim line. He was sitting very upright in the saddle. As they passed beneath our window, he looked up, and looked away again. Then they were out of sight.

I felt sick, and as if I would burst into tears at any moment; and yet drained, as if I would never be able to weep again. Confused, and frightened, and – and why was my heart thumping so fast, as if I had run a race? I knew what I must do, and say. I must get it over with, and then go. That was all. That should not be so difficult.

The door opened, and it was Ben, striding in, making his way straight over to me with never a by-your-leave. There was a sharp metallic sound, and suddenly a number of weapons were pointing in his direction.

'All right, all right,' he said, raising his hands in mock submission. 'I'm not staying long.'

'We will not get far this way,' I said crossly. 'He's a friend.' Cormack scowled, but Liam made a sign with his hand, and they moved back slightly.

'Jenny,' said Ben, looking at me closely. 'Are you all right?'

I managed a nod. Why was it so hard to speak? There was a fresh bandage on his wrist, and his jaw was bruised.

'What – ?'

He gave a crooked grin. 'In present company, an explanation might not be wise. Let's just say, it's as well I went off looking for him when I did. Managed to make myself useful in a tight place. Not that he thanked me, of course. Half-killed me for leaving you here alone, that was all the gratitude I got. Sure you're all right?'

'I thought – I thought you –'

'Me, doubt you? Not for an instant. Well, perhaps for an instant. Then I used my head. The way you and Red look at each other, where was there any room for another? Had to be a different explanation. But Richard shut me out, nobody could get near you, the place was bristling with Northwoods men. In the end, I went after Red.'

'Tell us,' said Conor, 'what will be done with this man, Richard of Northwoods?'

Ben glanced at him appraisingly.

'My brother Conor,' I said. 'He is fluent in your language.'

'So I see. Lord Richard is in custody. Alive, and in passable health. I had some difficulty convincing your husband that due process should be followed. The alternative was very tempting, when at last we caught up with his uncle. But there are questions to be asked. Red tells me Simon talked a lot, on the long ride home from the monastery where he was found. He has not forgotten quite all, and he remembers more each day. It seems Richard has had a finger in many pies. In the end, Red was persuaded we must wait, and hear his answers. But I have never before seen him so angry, not even on the day John died; I have never before seen him lose sight of his good judgement.'

'His anger will pass,' I said. 'When I am gone, he will set all to rights here; he can receive answers and dispense judgement, without fear of error.'

'Gone?' said Ben. 'What do you mean, gone?'

'We have requested safe passage to the coast; we leave at dawn,' said Conor. 'You surely can have no wish to see us linger here where our presence threatens to disrupt your household. We are sworn enemies; your people's wonder at our sudden appearance will turn soon enough to resentment and fear. I understood you believed this too and that an escort was to be arranged.'

Ben looked round the circle of angry faces, and then at me. 'Well, yes,' he said. 'That's true. But –'

'He cannot imagine,' growled Diarmid, who had followed the drift of this conversation well enough, 'that we would think of leaving our sister behind?' The room seemed to grow suddenly colder, as Conor passed on this message.

'I – well, it may be stating the obvious,' said Ben, 'but he is her husband, after all.'

'Husband?' Conor's voice cut like a dagger. 'What sort of husband is this, that we have not seen hide nor hair of the man, since Sorcha came close to death by fire? Is he afraid to show himself, having failed utterly to provide our sister with protection? How can such a one claim the title of husband?'

Ben was not easily intimidated. 'He has his reasons,' he said calmly. 'When we first met your sister, she was sick, and starving, and terrified. Lord Hugh saved her life. Jenny was never coerced into coming here.'

'Jenny?'

'When we found your sister, she could not speak. She could not tell us her name. This is the name she was given.'

'And also the name of Harrowfield, it appears. Well, she will keep neither for long,' said Conor. 'Is our escort arranged? Dawn approaches fast.'

'All will be ready,' said Ben. 'We have a boat at a secure mooring, and a man to take you across. The ride is half a morning; more, perhaps, for you. Simon is seeing to it, and he will escort you there.'

'No, I will take them,' a voice interrupted.

All turned to look at the man in the doorway. He was standing upright with difficulty, his face grey with the pallor of extreme exhaustion. There was fresh blood on the bandage, near the shoulder.

'Don't be a fool,' said Ben quite sharply. He strode over and tried to take Red's arm, but was shaken off with some violence. Around me, my brothers shifted. Cormack fingered the blade of a dagger. Liam folded his arms. Diarmid bore a thunderous look.

'With respect, my lord,' said Ben, apparently mindful of the delicacy of the situation. 'You should let your brother handle this. I will go too, if you believe you cannot yet trust him. How can you ride to the coast and back, when you have scarce slept these three days or more?'

'I am her husband. I will take them.'

I could not look at him. The voice was bad enough; distant, formal. It chilled my heart.

'Husband,' said Conor carefully. 'Yes, we heard about that. A less than impressive job you've made of it, for all your belated heroics.'

Red was silent.

'Did you see her,' Conor went on, 'when she was hungry and dirty and cold? Did you watch her as she stood silent before her accusers, as she heard the filth they spoke of her, the lies they told? Did you see her when she wept in the dark, when she waited and watched as your uncle built her funeral pyre? Did you? What kind of husband were you then?'

There was a short pause.

'Are you finished?' asked Red quietly.

'Ask him,' urged Liam in our own tongue, 'ask him the nature of this marriage; if he has laid his filthy barbarian hands on our sister. Ask him!'

580

But Conor was not what he was for nothing. He had not, after all, misjudged his opponent.

'Just tell me,' he said, 'whether my sister is free to go. Do you plan to hold her to any promise, any commitment she has made to you?'

'Do you hold a wild creature once it is healed, and ready to fly home?' asked Red. 'Jenny makes her own choices. She knows that she is free to go. She knows she need only tell me, when it is time.'

Conor spoke to his brothers, quietly, in our own tongue.

'What about our safe conduct?' asked Liam, while Conor translated. 'I want us to be away at dawn, or before. There is little time left.'

Red's response was softer still. I had heard this tone before.

'First I will speak with my wife alone. Then we leave, with all you request. It won't take long.'

Conor passed this on to the others.

'Out of the question!' snapped Diarmid.

'Alone? I think not,' said Liam grimly.

'Who does this man think he is?' demanded Cormack. 'He has no claim on Sorcha, and he knows it. Tell him to bring horses, and we will make our own way. There are no bargains to be struck here.'

'We cannot allow this,' said Conor gravely. 'You understand, after what has happened, our concern for our sister's wellbeing. She will not leave our sight until we quit these shores. It has been three full years since we last had our human form. Three years of silence and suffering for her. Now she is returned to us, we will not part with her, nor risk her safety, even for a moment.'

Red's mouth tightened in an alarmingly familiar way, and I saw Ben's hand hovering by the hilt of his dagger.

'This is my household,' said Red. 'You want to leave in safety, do you not? With horses and a degree of protection? This I will provide; but first I will speak with Jenny alone.'

'Your arrogance astonishes me,' said Conor coldly. 'It was your people who would have put my sister to death; your people who went about their business while she was shut away in the dark, while lice crawled in her hair and rats came out at night to feast on the filth of her cell, while she wept and toiled and waited for the end. How dare you demand anything of us?'

Red was very pale, but he was determined to speak. 'For whom did she work, for whom did she keep her silence these three years, for whom did she choke back her laughter and her tears and her screams of pain? You accepted what she did for you. You are as guilty as I, all of you.' He had taken the support of Ben's arm; gripping it, his hand was white at the knuckles.

It was as if they had forgotten I was there.

'Conor,' I said.

'What!?' snapped my brother in a tone he had never before used to me.

'This is my decision,' I said quietly. 'I will be quite safe. I will not go far; just beyond the door.'

And I walked out, eyes straight ahead. Nobody tried to stop me. Outside the room, two men still stood on guard. The door closed behind me.

'You can go,' said Red to the guards. Ben had remained within; a gesture requiring some courage, under the circumstances.

We were alone. I stayed where I was, by the door. He was quite close, leaning back against the wall. Looking up into his eyes took all my strength. They were wintry cold, his face blank as an empty sheet of parchment.

'It seems I have fulfilled my purpose,' he said. 'Clearly, you have no further need of my protection.'

'It's better this way.' I forced the words out. 'Better for you, and for your household. Better for everyone.' And I thought, if the doom the Fair Folk laid on you is not yet lifted, wait only until I leave these shores. The boat will carry me beyond the ninth wave, and you will begin to forget.

'I told you once,' said Red, 'that I wanted to hear your voice. I did not think the first words I would hear would be these.'

It's true, I thought. We have become adept at hurting each other. In a whole year, after everything, is this all we have learned?

'Those were not the first words,' I whispered, fighting tears. I would not weep.

'No,' he agreed. 'They were not. You saved me; and I you. Perhaps that was what it was for. Perhaps that was the reason. And now that it's over, you wish to return home.' Red's tone was courteous. He might have spoken thus to any departing guest. 'I will see to your safety as far as the coast. I have no doubt your brothers will guard you well for the journey home.'

I swallowed. The light was dim; one lamp burned low in a niche, casting deep shadows. But outside, it was nearly dawn. There was so much to say; and nothing I could say.

'I said that I would tell you about your brother,' I ventured. 'About Simon.'

'Oh, yes. Our agreement. Safe conduct home, in return for information. I had almost forgotten.' He made an attempt at nonchalance, but I could see how his hand was shaking as he reached up to adjust the bandage.

'You're bleeding,' I said. 'Let me.'

'*No.*' Now it was he who shrank from my touch. 'Leave it. It's of no concern. You asked about my brother. Memory is a strange thing. Simon remembers little of this lost time. Of recent events he has a better recall, which returned to him piece by piece on our slow journey home. Enough to incriminate my uncle many times over.'

'I know,' I said. 'When I was – your uncle spoke to me, unguardedly, at some length. He told me many things which he will now regret. He thought . . . he thought I would not tell you, he thought I would never . . .'

I could hear Red's careful breathing, in, out, in, out, as if he could not trust himself to let go.

'My uncle – did he lay a hand on you, when – did he touch you, Jenny? I was prevented from – from – Ben stopped me, but if –'

'It's all right,' I said with difficulty. 'I am not hurt. He said to me, "I don't want my nephew's leavings". I was not harmed.'

'I'll kill him,' said Red softly, turning his face away from me.

'You're a just man, and a fair one,' I said. 'These people depend on you; you are the centre of their world. Let your anger go, and then judge him. They look to you for their example. It will be easier, when I am gone.'

He turned his head towards me; let me see, for an instant, the deep loneliness of the eyes, the shadows and lines drawn stark on the white skin. How could a man who had so much, be so alone?

'My brother,' his tone was bleak, 'has few memories

of those lost years. So he says. But wherever it is that you fit in, he will not hear a word against you. I heard him talking to my mother tonight, when we returned. He spoke of you as if – as if of an angel. He said, *her hands are the gentlest in the world, and she tells such tales, tales you would not believe, and yet, when she speaks, you know every word is true.* He may have forgotten the rest, but you he remembers.'

'I –'

'Ssh,' he said, and he reached out his hand and touched his fingers very gently to my lips to silence my words. 'Don't tell me.' He touched me only for a moment; and yet I fought the urge to put my hand over his, to turn my lips to his palm. I made myself keep very still. Then he took his hand away, and I moved back a step. Unspoken words lay heavy between us. Unspoken words, and unmade gestures. With any other, I would have said farewell with a hug, a kiss, the touch of fingers to cheek, the clasp of hand in hand. With Red, I could do nothing.

'You have a circle,' he said, 'that you draw tight around you; John, Ben, these feral brothers of yours. Simon is as fiercely protective as the rest of them, and yet he has little cause to love your kind. But once you touch us, our hearts are no longer our own.'

My lip quivered, and I sank my teeth into it, wincing with pain. *I will not cry. I have wept enough. I, too, can be strong.* I reached up and slipped the cord over my neck.

'You'll be wanting this back,' I said, blinking rather hard. The ring lay on my open palm, light and warm. It took all my will not to close my fingers around it. I saw Red's hand clench into a white-knuckled fist.

'If it means so little to you,' he said after a

moment, 'put it in the fire, or throw it on the dungheap. I have no use for it.' Then he turned and made his way down the hall, and I was reminded of the night of the rockfall, when he had walked as if blind, although his eyes were open.

The little mare bore me as sweetly as on the day we had journeyed to the bay of the seals. My brothers were quiet, as if the wonder of seeing the daylight world through their own eyes, after so long, was almost too much to bear. Red rode at the head of the column, his hair bright as the oak leaves that drifted down around us, catching the autumn sunlight. Ben was watchful at the rear.

It was hard to keep back the memories of the last time we had come this way, along the hidden track, under the trees, over the hills and away from the valley. I had not expected that Simon would come with us, but it seemed he had argued his case and convinced his brother. He rode close by me, and I told him what Richard had said to me, about Eamonn of the Marshes, and about bargains and deals, and about what had happened that night, when Simon had disappeared from the camp. He listened, and nodded, and let me talk. I did not tell quite all. Some of it was too close to our own story, too close to the part of it Red had waited so long to hear, and then, in the end, had not wanted to hear.

'My uncle took a risk, in telling you this,' said Simon thoughtfully. 'A great risk. Once this becomes known, he will forfeit any influence he had left, and be cut off from his family and from his allies; I cannot think what future he could contemplate. I am concerned for Elaine. He has placed her in a very vulnerable position by his actions. And he has no sons. There will be kinsmen aplenty jostling to take his place at Northwoods.'

Elaine had been a good friend to Red, I thought. Maybe now she would get what she deserved. Maybe now she could choose as her heart prompted her, and not as her father ordered. Simon was a fine young man, and I wished them joy in each other.

'Richard thought I was going to die,' I said. 'He believed that I would never speak again. How could he lose? Such a man loves to gloat, and cannot resist sharing his triumph. Had Red . . . had your brother not returned in time, it would have been as he intended.'

'My brother made sure he was here in time,' he said wryly. 'I have never seen a man ride so, as if driven by demons. Good old reliable Hugh. So calm, so capable. So utterly predictable. But you have changed him.'

There was a smell of salt in the air, and I thought I heard a gull. Padriac's face showed the ghost of a smile, as we headed steadily westward. Steadily homeward. He was young. Of us all, he seemed least hurt. I thought he would be able to make his life again, and make it a good one. For the rest of us, I was not so sure. Liam must face what lay ahead at Sevenwaters; must try to deal with our father, and our father's wife, and mend the shattered pieces of a once strong holding. Diarmid seemed eaten up with bitterness, and Cormack was like some explosion waiting to happen. As for Conor, deep, wise, mysterious Conor, even he had shown me today he could be blinded by his own convictions. For he had not seen Red for what he was. And Finbar, who rode now as one in a dream, scarce seeming aware of what passed right by him, Finbar would live a life far removed from what might have been. I had brought them back; but each had lost a part of himself, in the long time away.

We made good progress, and now rode up between tall trees, our horses separated by the difficult terrain. Simon and I were somewhat apart from the others.

'You're going home,' he said. 'But you still have my brother's ring.'

I was taken aback, and could think of nothing to say.

Then he said, 'Why didn't you wait for me, Sorcha?'

I gazed at him. Then I said carefully, 'I could not stay. I told you that. I did not want to leave you, but my brothers made me go. I was only a child then.'

'I remember a tale you told me,' he said. 'About a magical cup, from which only the pure in heart could drink. There was a man who waited and waited until he was old, and his patience was finally rewarded. I have waited far longer. I was gone a long time, Sorcha. Beyond the span of mortal man or woman. Nine times nine years, in that place you told of in your stories. Longer than my brother could ever imagine.'

Still I stared at him, as we crested the hill and our horses walked together across a clearing and on into the woods. Their feet trod softly on the carpet of fallen leaves. I was unwilling to believe what he was telling me, and yet I knew, as a teller of tales must know, that this was the truth.

'In the story, his sweetheart waited for him,' said Simon, fixing his bright blue eyes on me with a frightening intensity. 'She waited until both of them were old. Years and years. For you, it was only three. *Why did you marry my brother? Why didn't you wait for me?'*

'I – I – how could I know?' I whispered, shocked. 'I didn't know. I never even thought –'

He was silent.

'You were hurt,' I said. 'Burned. What about –'

'There are those that can erase such scars, as if they have never been. There are those that can offer such sweet inducements, that a man might forget this world forever, and when he is cast back up, when they have no more use for him, be destroyed utterly by his longing for what he left behind in the land under the hills. They kept me a long time. I bear no scars, not outwardly. What injuries were done to me by your kind, belonged to another life. Long, long ago. But I am not out of my wits, Sorcha. I kept my mind clear and fixed of purpose, through all those long years. Through all that time of waiting, I thought only of returning to find you again. Prayed only that time would be kind, and pass more slowly in this world. When they cast me out at last, I had few memories of the old life; those that I had were like phantoms, nebulous and fleeting. But one remained bright and true.' He reached up and slipped a cord from around his own neck; passed me the small pouch of supple leather that hung there. 'Open it, look.'

I loosened the fastenings, and felt inside. Something fine and soft, like a strand of silk. The little mare kept up her steady pace, needing no guidance. In front, Cormack and Conor rode together; behind, Padriac had engaged Ben in an animated debate on the principles of flight, and whether one might build a machine that would carry a man through the air. Finbar was there somewhere, silent behind them. I could not see Red, or Liam, or Diarmid. I drew the small thing out of the pouch. There in my hand was a lock of dark hair. The curl he had cut from my head that day long ago, with his sharp little knife. *Don't leave me*. What cruel game had they been playing with all of us? What twisted path had we been following, like blindfold puppets in some wild dance? Had we no will? Had we no choice?

'So the Fair Folk took you,' I breathed. 'Took you from the forest . . .'

'You know their ways,' he said. 'How they cajole, and charm, and delight. How they bully, and play tricks, and terrify. But for this talisman, I would indeed have run mad. Would have lost myself many times over. Would have forgotten all. But I would not let them take it; and at last they gave up and released me, and sent me back. You should have waited, Sorcha. You should have waited just a little longer.'

What could I say? He took the lock of hair from my shaking fingers, and stowed it away again, and put the cord around his neck so that the pouch lay over his heart.

'I told you a story once,' he said. 'Do you remember it?'

I nodded. 'I remember it. A story of two brothers.'

'You said I could make it end in any way I chose. This path or that. I came to believe you. But you were wrong. I have waited, and waited to find you again. But you married my brother. This, too, he has taken from me.'

There was nothing I could say. I stumbled ahead with words anyway. 'I didn't know – how could I know? . . . Do you remember everything? Then why –'

'Who would believe the truth?' he asked, and the blue eyes were for a moment as deep and stark and lonely as his brother's. 'This way is easier. Who would believe, but you?'

We rode on in silence. Ahead of us I could see Red riding alone, leading the way, and behind him four of my brothers, Liam and Diarmid, Cormack and Conor, their horses following his along the track, which had narrowed as the terrain grew steeper. We rode on through the woods, until we reached the place where the trees opened up, and you could see the wide expanse of the sea before you. Across that shining water, in the west, was home. And the forest. My forest.

'We used to come here long ago,' said Simon. 'There are seals, sometimes.'

'I know,' I said.

His gaze sharpened. 'He brought you here?'

'I have seen the cove,' I said, thinking, *I cannot go back there. Don't make me say goodbye there. I may be strong, but I am not strong enough for that.*

'Nobody else knew,' said Simon very quietly. 'We told no one of this place. Even Elaine, we never told.'

I said nothing. A little further along the track, the others waited for us. Behind us, Ben and Padriac emerged from the trees and came up at a crisp canter. I saw a huge grin of delight appear on Padriac's face as he got his first glimpse of the wide, glittering expanse of water which had so astonished me when I had first seen it. As we sat there, looking out to the west, Finbar rode up slowly behind. His eyes showed nothing, and his expression was blank.

'It's just up there to the north,' said Red. 'We keep a boat in the next cove, not far from here. Our man should be ready. You have a good day for it; a fair wind.'

'Have a mind to your sister's stomach,' put in Ben. 'She's not over-keen on sea voyages.'

All too soon, it seemed, we were gathered on the shore, and by the sea a dour boatman I had met once before was readying his small craft. Padriac, whose ventures had hitherto been confined to the calmer waters of the lake, sprang to help him, and was soon busy with ropes and oars. The horses grazed further up the hill, too well disciplined, or too weary, to wander far. Red had walked away from us, and stood alone on the rocks, looking out to sea.

I said goodbye to Ben, as Liam took my pathetically small bundle of belongings down to the boat, and the others stretched cramped limbs and gazed into the west, across the tumbling waves, across the wide water, straining for some glimpse of the land they knew lay there. Ben hugged me, and said, 'Don't forget us,' and I said how could I forget such a fine head of hair, and that I would pass all his jokes on to my brothers. He turned away and made himself suddenly very busy with a troublesome piece of harness.

'Goodbye, Simon,' I said. He had tucked the little pouch under his shirt again, out of sight. Each of us wore our memories of what might have been.

As I turned away he said, 'How can he do this? If you were mine, I would fight to keep you. I would die, before I let you go.' Then Liam called out from down by the water, 'Hurry up, Sorcha! We're almost ready.'

The moment was finally here. Red waited, a still figure on the rocks, his gaze turned on the distant horizon. The gulls screamed overhead. This was a different cove, but the memories still lingered, of that other day. Somehow, I was standing before him, and we looked at each other. Looked at each other, and there might have been no world, save for the two of us. I could find no words. Not a single one. The Fair

Folk had warned me my path would be hard. But nothing could have prepared me for something as hard as this. Red, too, was silent. It had been easier for us to understand one another when I had had no voice. Looking at him, I could see how his face might be, when he grew old. A face marked by grooves and lines, where his tears would have flowed, had he allowed himself to weep. His eyes were empty.

'Come on, Sorcha!' yelled Diarmid.

I can't go. I must go. I blinked back tears, unable to move from where I stood.

'I almost forgot,' said Red. His voice sounded very strange, as if from a long, long distance. He reached into his pocket. 'I have something for you.'

He put it into my hand. A round, shiny, perfect apple, green as new grass with a faint blush of rosy pink. And now his eyes had changed so that I saw what lay there, hidden deep, so deep only the bravest or most foolhardy would seek to find it.

He had always understood me better, without words. So I laid my hand on my heart, held it there for a moment, and then moved it over and touched my palm against his breast. *My heart. Your heart.*

'Come on, Sorcha, we haven't got all day!' Padriac shouted.

I turned away, just before the tears began to well in my eyes and spill down my cheeks, and I ran to the boat and was hauled over the side. They pushed it forward, and the wind and waves took us and began to carry us westwards, westwards over the sea and home to Sevenwaters. And I sat with the apple in my hands, and my eyes fixed on the shore, where he stood like a man carved in stone. Tears blurred my vision, but still I looked back, until all I could see of him was the small bright flame of his hair against the grey and green and white of the shore line. *All that he had of her was his memory, where he held every moment, every single moment that she had been his. That was all he had, to keep out the loneliness.* But Red would forget. Now that I was gone, he could begin to forget. As for my own heart, it had been torn in two, and I did not think even the best healer in the world could mend it.

CHAPTER FIFTEEN

W

e sailed on through the day and into the night, and when we made landfall it was on our home shore and in darkness. Once at sea, it had become quickly clear that it would be Liam who was in charge from now on, and at the end it was he who directed the boatman by means of precise gestures to a wild stretch of coastland apparently peopled only by wind-battered vegetation and scattered stones. Cormack lifted me out of the boat, and Conor took my bag, and there were the seven of us, standing in the cool of the night on the ground of Erin once more. The small boat vanished away into the darkness with a faint splashing.

My brothers had not been sick. They had enjoyed themselves, almost. Between spasms of retching, I had had time to see the glow of excitement on Padriac's face as he was allowed a turn at the tiller, as he took his place with sail or oar. Not that my brothers were unfamiliar with little boats; a family of boys does not live so long close to a great lake and not teach itself some skills in going by water. But this was different. I could see in Padriac's face a vision of far wider seas, a yearning for wild adventure and mysterious lands beyond the reach of maps. I read in his eyes a reflection of what I had seen long ago, when he released the owl from his glove and she spiralled up, up into the endless sky. And I heard Finbar's inner voice. *Soon enough he, too, will fly away.* My brother sat silent in the boat, his dark cloak not quite concealing the sweep of white feathers. *Be glad of Padriac's joy. For this homecoming cannot be a triumph.*

We had been well provisioned by the household of Harrowfield, and once we had reached the shelter of a patch of woodland, my brothers made camp with the quiet efficiency of long practice. A small lantern was lit, and shielded so that its light spread no further than the little grove where we sat.

'No fire,' said Liam. 'Not tonight. And we will not seek horses, though I am eager for home. It is best that we arrive unannounced, and on foot.'

'Sorcha will be tired.' Conor was keeping a close eye on me; watching that I finished every mouthful of the barley bread and bean curd he had given me. 'It is a long way; four or five days' journey, even for us.'

Liam frowned. 'These Britons will pay for what they have done to our sister. But that must wait. We have more pressing business.'

'My hands itch for the sorceress' neck.' Diarmid clenched and unclenched his fists. 'Cannot we ride there openly, and see justice done swiftly? I would tell our tale to all, and make the lady Oonagh pay the penalty where all can witness it.'

'You're too hasty,' said Cormack, breaking off a

piece of his bread and chewing thoughtfully. 'We don't know anything about what's happened at Sevenwaters yet. Liam's right. We can't just rush in with swords raised. That approach tends to lead to slaughter, and not always of your enemy.'

Conor regarded his twin levelly. 'You've learned something, this long time away,' he observed with a little smile. Cormack threw a crust of bread at him, and missed.

Padriac nodded agreement. 'The element of surprise might help us,' he said. 'Best if the lady Oonagh is not forewarned of our arrival.'

We fell silent for a while. The memories hurt, and the fear was not altogether gone.

'Still,' said Diarmid, 'it seems too long to wait.'

However long, it can never be long enough. Long enough to walk through the forest, and to come home. Long enough to be ourselves again.

I had heard Finbar's voice, if the others had not. 'We must do as Liam advises,' I said quietly. 'After such a long journey, we must go home the right way. I can walk the distance. I'm quite strong, really.'

'Hm.' Conor was eyeing me up and down. 'Perhaps we should extract a promise that you will eat five good meals a day until we get there. But she's right, Diarmid. This is the only way.'

So we moved on foot across the land, and my brothers took their pace from me. This was a different way from the one I had taken when I left the forest, when the river had borne me so swiftly away from my home and deposited me into the hands of a passing Briton. This way took us across open ground, moving from one rocky outcrop to the next, taking what cover could be found in isolated groves of storm-bent trees, camping at night and moving off soon after dawn. We avoided the tracks of men, moving like seven silent shadows, our progress witnessed only by cliff and rock and tree. And on the third day we came to the edge of the forest.

We paused on the crest of a rise as sun broke through the clouds, and watched a solitary hawk balance its wings on the air, high above the vista of grey and green and autumn gold that stretched before us as far as the eye could see.

'We're home,' Conor said. I breathed deep, and felt a cloak of stillness settle on my spirit. Then we started to walk, down between moss-covered stones and under the blanket of the trees, and we made our way homewards on tracks that were plain to us without map or guide, though no stranger could have followed them. The trees shivered in the cold autumn wind, and voices followed me. *Sorcha, oh Sorcha. Home. You are home at last.* The wind rose, and leaves fell about us in a bright rain of scarlet and gold. *Little sister, why are you still sad? For you have come home.* If you looked up, you could almost see them. They moved in the cool sunlight, on the wind between the bare bones of birch and ash, always just on the edge of sight. If you turned to look, they were suddenly gone.

'The lookouts are unmanned,' observed Liam, frowning. 'That is folly.' And as we came closer and closer to Sevenwaters, the faces of my brothers grew still and watchful.

Three nights we spent in the forest, and my brothers made sure I had a comfortable bed of bracken, and ate what I was told to. Our pace was slow, for I was not the only one weakened by hunger and lack of sleep, and the journey was not an easy one. Here, we could make a small fire, and brew a kind of tea made from whatever herbs were to hand. This warmed the body if not the spirits. Here in the forest it was quite safe, and my brothers slept well at night. All but Finbar. For him there was no rest. By day he walked as if in a dream. By night he sat cross-legged, looking into the distance with eyes that did not seem to be seeing. He had eaten nothing; had spoken not a word. It was as if he were not really there at all, his body a hollow shell whose spirit inhabited some world the rest of us could not touch. As for me, I lay there open-eyed in the darkness, waiting for sleep to come. I should have been joyful. Was I not back where I belonged, in the place of my spirit, with my brothers all safe around me, ready to start their lives anew? Had I not saved them and achieved the task against all odds? But my heart was shrivelled and cold, my mind unable to see a future that was not one of stark loneliness, of half-being, of dreams unfulfilled.

The further time took me away from that far shore, the more I recognised how much I had given up. I told myself not to be stupid. Not to be selfish. What did I expect, that Red would have begged me to stay? Even in that most unlikely event, I would have been obliged to refuse him. How could I have remained there to drag him down, a burdensome wife, object of hatred and distrust to all his people? I could not have done that to him. What I wanted didn't matter. If I had stayed, I would have destroyed him. So why did I feel so miserable? What was wrong with me? Anyone would have thought . . . *anyone would have thought you were no longer afraid of men.*

That was the small voice of common sense, like a dash of cold water. *I am. I am still afraid,* I said to myself, for I still remembered how those men had hurt and shamed me, the ugly things they had said, in every vivid detail. The memory still turned my body cold with disgust. It would never go away. That was one side of the balance. As for the other side, for there was now another side, I thought I would give almost anything to have that one moment again, the moment when I had felt Red's arm around me like a shield against the world, and his lips against my hair, and his heart drumming under my cheek. In that moment, he had not wanted to let me go. *It's all right. It's all right, Jenny*, he had said. But it was not all right. I lay in the darkness under the trees, and silently cursed the Fair Folk for the way they used and discarded us in their strange games, heedless of the damage they did.

It was the seventh day, and we were coming close to the keep of Sevenwaters. Between the bare branches of the willows the waters of the lake glinted bright, and ducks dabbled in the shallows. It was very quiet.

'There are no scouts,' said Liam grimly. 'No forward posts. Any man could ride in here unchallenged. What can he be thinking of?'

We emerged from the margin of the trees behind the settlement, and my heart lurched in shock. Beyond the walled fields and the cottages, beyond the stone-walled keep, on the hill once clothed in graceful birch, strong ash and noble oak, a great scar lay across the landscape, where a stand of the oldest trees had been felled and burned. Not a scrap of life was left there, no bold holly tree nor branching hawthorn to soften the wound. Behind me, Conor began to chant softly, a lament whose words I could not understand, but whose message went straight to the spirit.

'Wanton destruction,' said Liam. 'An act of sheer

wilfulness, with no intent but harm. They have not even put the wood to use, but burned it where it lay.'

We walked through the village, where the track had become rutted and bogged, and folk had a weary, pinched look about them. But these were our own people, people who knew the thin line between this world and the other. All of them had seen a cousin taken by the folk under the hill, or known of a strange child found under a nettle bush, or spoken to one who had ventured too far into a cave or walked into a ring of mushrooms by moonlight. There were no probing questions, no narrowed eyes or looks of distrust. Instead, they came out with faces wreathed in smiles, and hands outstretched in welcome. Only when they looked at Finbar did they fall silent, and that was a silence of deep respect.

'Master Liam! Master Conor! You've come home!' Niall the miller strode forward to clap Liam on the back

And Paddy the pig man, grinning from ear to ear, gripped one brother's hand after another, exclaiming 'Sure and you've returned at last! Didn't I say they'd be back, Mary, didn't I say it now?'

And before I'd gone three steps up the track, the granddaughter of old Tom was taking me by the arm, and leading me into his cottage to listen to the old man's wheezing chest. I promised an infusion of balsam and peppermint to ease his breathing.

'And a fire,' I added. 'It's freezing in here. You must light a fire.'

But there was no dry wood, and no men from up yonder to help cut and store it. This year the crops had not been good; rot had set in with the heavy autumn rains. Little had been stored for the long cold season ahead. The flock had been stricken with the sheep murrain, and there had been heavy losses.

'What of our father?' asked Conor, his dark brows drawn together in a frown. 'Has he made no provision for your wellbeing these last winters? Is there no factor to oversee the harvest, no steward to send supplies to those that are in hardship?'

They shuffled their feet.

'Well?' demanded Liam, sounding just like our father.

'Lord Colum, he – he's not been himself, not since you went away,' ventured the miller. 'Things changed for all of us.'

'What do you mean?' asked Cormack, frowning.

But nobody was prepared to voice a reply.

So, with assurances of help, with promises of repairs and supplies, we left the village and made our way up the track towards our old home. And there, by the hawthorn hedges, at last there was a challenge.

'Who goes there? Identify yourself and your business!' We could not see the man, but the voice sounded familiar.

'Rest easy,' responded my eldest brother. 'I am Liam of Sevenwaters, returned home with my brothers and my sister.'

'Returned to reclaim what is ours,' put in Diarmid, scowling.

The man stepped out, his sword pointed firmly in our direction. He was clad in a leather jerkin and trousers, and over them a well-worn tunic which bore on its breast the proud symbol of two torcs interlinked; the crest of Sevenwaters. The man's mouth fell open, and the sword dropped.

'Liam!' A broad grin spread across his weathered face.

'Donal!' For it was indeed the old master at arms, who had been banished by our father at his new wife's behest. 'I thought you long gone from these parts! I thought the place quite unguarded. At least there is some sense left here.'

'Precious little,' growled Donal, slapping an arm around Liam's shoulders and shaking his head in wonderment. 'By all that's holy, it's good to see you, boy. Come on, come on, I'll take you up to the house.'

But once we came closer to the courtyard he was not in such a hurry to go in. Instead, we paused on the pathway where once I had heard him take his leave of my father, and Conor explained to him what had happened to us, and where we had been.

'Mm,' mused the old warrior as the strange tale came to a close. 'There were plenty of stories flying around, of course, and folk knew she had a hand in it. One look at her, and you knew she was up to no good. Some said you were gone for good, but I knew the seven of you could look after yourselves. Only a matter of waiting for you to come back.' He glanced at Finbar, and gave a little shake of the head. 'But I see your brother's sadly changed.'

Nobody made comment, and Finbar might not have heard, so little did his expression reveal. Donal shook his head again.

'You'll find things different here,' he warned. 'Very different. It shocked me, I can tell you. Came back not so long ago myself, thinking the past might be forgotten, and he might have a place for me. I'm too old to sell my sword to the highest bidder. Three years of that was more than enough. I began to hear tales, around midsummer, that Colum was in trouble. Those brought me back, and I've stayed. Someone has to keep watch.'

'Trouble? What sort of trouble?' queried Liam.

'They said he was losing his grip. Men deserting

his command in droves, posts unmanned, councils unattended. Autumn culling wasn't done, and the best part of the herd starved last winter. Land cleared for no good purpose. They said he just didn't care any more. She had her hand on him all right, and he couldn't shake it.'

Diarmid was pacing restlessly, brows set in a scowl, hand fingering his sword hilt.

'Where is she?' he asked impatiently. 'Where will we find the lady Oonagh?'

There was a brief pause.

'She's gone,' Donal said.

'What!?' The air seemed to crackle with Diarmid's fury and frustration. 'Gone? How can she be gone?'

'Packed up and left in a hurry, seven or eight days ago it was, around dusk. As if she got a sudden fright. Took the boy, and her own men, and away off with her into the night. And good riddance, if you ask me.'

'She took our brother?' There was a note of deep concern in Conor's question. 'So Ciarán, too, is gone?'

'That was the final blow for your father,' said Donal soberly. 'You'll find him much altered.'

'Your words trouble me,' said Conor, frowning. 'What has become of him, now she is gone from here?'

'Colum's always been strong,' Donal said 'But losing you cut him deep. Some of the old household stayed here, and I've heard how it was from them. He blamed himself for your disappearance, and maybe rightly. As time passed, the guilt began to eat him up. He would have done more, but he couldn't break free of her. Lost his will. His efforts to find you were all thwarted. Now that you're here at last, I can't tell you if you'll be greeted with joy or simply with confusion.'

'You said he tried to find us,' I found myself saying.

'I was told – I was told he was offered my safe return, in exchange for gold or land. And that he refused.'

'What!?' Diarmid's tone was outraged. Cormack swore.

'Ask him yourself,' said Donal grimly. 'I'd say that was impossible. He wished for nothing more fervently than your safe return. I believe he'd have given anything to secure it. Whoever told you that tale must have been lying.'

'We'll see,' said Liam, stony-faced.

If I were telling this tale, and it were not my own, I would give it a neat and satisfying ending. The children would come home, and their father would greet them with open arms, rejoicing. The wicked stepmother would be punished for the evil she had done, and driven forth from their home. The father and his sons would put all to rights, and everyone would live happily ever after. In such stories, there are no loose ends. There are no unravelled edges and crooked threads. Daughters do not give their hearts to the enemy. The wicked do not simply disappear, taking with them the satisfaction of vengeance. Young men do not find themselves divided between two worlds. Fathers know their children.

But this was my own story. And surprisingly, it was I who met our father first, for when my brothers followed Donal indoors, I slipped around the side to my old garden, which Oonagh in her spite had destroyed. I had thought my heart broken, then. How little I had known of sorrow.

My garden was still a mess of tumbled stones and mounded earth, but the seasons had been kind since my departure. Mosses clothed shattered path and weathered stone wall. Creepers rioted over the remains of a trellis; in spring it would be blanketed in blossoms of pure white. There were brave spikes of lavender amongst the weeds, a faint haze of blue-grey, and I could smell the healing scent of thyme. The stillroom door stood ajar. The old bench was almost overgrown with soft feathery fronds of worm-wood and chamomile, and there my father sat, wrapped in a dark cloak, staring in front of him with vacant eyes. His once stern, strong face seemed some-how blurred, as if someone had smudged a wet brush across the features of some painted king. Of his two wolfhounds, who had once shadowed his every foot-step, there was not a sign.

I advanced across the garden, picking my way on the broken paving. He turned his head slowly at the sound, and his deep-set eyes took on an expression of sheer wonderment. I came closer.

'*Niamh?*' he breathed, incredulous.

'No, Father,' I said, swallowing hard. 'It's I, Sorcha, your daughter. I've come home. We are all back, returned to you safe.'

I came up and sat on the bench by his side. There was a long silence. After a while, I reached out and took his hand in both of mine. It was trembling.

I scarcely knew what to say. I had been a child when I left, he a stern, distant figure whom I hardly knew. Now it was as if I were the parent, and he the child.

'Father?' I ventured. 'Do you know me?'

He took a long time to reply.

'My daughter was a little girl,' he said finally.

'It – it's been quite a while.'

'I lost them, you know. All of them. Even the smallest one.'

606

Around us the garden was quiet.

'Father. Perhaps we should go in. My brothers are here, all of them. It's all right now.' But I knew this was untrue.

He sighed. 'I don't think so. Not yet. I will stay here for a while. You go in.' He settled back into silence, and his eyes again lost their focus. At length I got up and walked to the door, my skirts brushing the trailing chamomile and creeping thyme, sending a sweet scent into the cool morning air. As I reached for the door he spoke again, behind me.

'I'm sorry, Niamh,' he said. 'I'm so sorry.'

But when I turned my head, he was not looking at me. You might have thought his gaze was fixed on the stone wall, but I sensed he saw something far, far away, as distant as an ancient memory, but still sweet and strong as the note of a harp, and painful as a sword thrust deep into the vitals. I went indoors to find my brothers.

It would take time. That was what Conor said, as each of us took a share of the tasks that must be done, the decisions that must be made. Time for Father to regain his strength of will, to gather his shattered wits, to come again to the knowledge of where he was, of who he was. Time for Finbar to emerge from his silence, to lose that feral glint of the eye, that ghastly pallor of the skin. Meanwhile, there was work to be done, and those that had the strength and the will must get on with it. It was fortunate that my father had no cousins, or nephews, that might have challenged him for his estates before now, in his sons' absence. But we had powerful neighbours, who would not delay long before they took advantage of Lord Colum's weakness. I heard Liam discussing this with Donal over a quiet cup of mead one night.

'It's a wonder Eamonn has not yet moved in for the kill,' Donal said.

'Seamus Redbeard is still our ally, for all he wed Eilis to that traitor,' said Liam. 'I have Eamonn's measure, and when the time is right I will act.' I had related to my eldest brother, long since, the tale of Eamonn's duplicity and his alliance with Richard of Northwoods. Liam had listened gravely, curbing his anger. We had not passed on to Diarmid any knowledge of the link between these men and Lady Oonagh for, Liam said, it was a situation calling for sensitive handling and exquisite timing. In due course, he and Seamus would deal with it. Diarmid, fairly bursting for revenge, was best out of the way until this was done. 'The idea of swift vengeance is tempting, I know,' Liam went on. 'But I plan to employ subtler methods, for the man has information of value to us, and I will learn it before I make an end of him.'

'Seamus has a grandson now,' observed Donal. 'Don't you fear that alliance? Who's to say the old man will not change his colours?'

Liam gave a little smile that did not quite reach his eyes. 'Eamonn's son will not be raised as an enemy of Sevenwaters,' he said.

Word of our return spread fast, as such news does. So too did the story of what Lady Oonagh had done to us, and of the task I had completed in order to free my brothers from her enchantment. As I have said, our people accepted this with no great wonderment, but in time the story grew and was embellished, and took its place among the grand and heroic tales folk told on cold winter nights after supper, over a jug of ale. There was never much in the story about the Britons and how they had helped me; save for Lord Richard and the burning. Everyone loves a good villain.

Liam stepped into our father's shoes, as he had always known he must some day. There were but few of the household left at the time of our return. Donal, and half a dozen of my father's men, those too loyal to leave him even at such an extreme; those too strong or too stubborn for the lady Oonagh to drive forth. Fat Janis, grown sunken-eyed and lean as a whippet, still toiled in a kitchen bare of all but the remnants of a late and desperate harvest. There were a couple of boys who slept in the stables and tended the beasts. That was all. But before long they began to come back, a huddle of men here, a pair of giggling maid-servants there. All felt the force of Liam's tongue, for their desertion. All then found a place in the house-hold and work for their hands. Visitors from further afield began to appear, and spend evenings in deep discussion with my brother. I believed that one morn-ing Eamonn of the Marshes would wake up and find a net had been drawn very subtly around him, from which there was no escape. I did not ask for details. During the day, Donal's voice rang out from the yard, and the familiar sound of clashing metal and drum-ming hooves could be heard. In the kitchen, Janis barked out orders as wood was chopped and fires stoked, as linen was scrubbed and hung out to dry. The house of Sevenwaters began, slowly, to breathe again.

It seemed right, somehow, to come back to our mother's birch tree on a day when the air was crisp and cool and the bare trees were still around the little sward by the lake. We had not planned it. It just seemed to be that on this particular morning, I took Finbar by the sleeve and led him through the forest after me, and that the others too made their way down to the shore by ones and twos until all seven of us were there. This time there were no ritual objects, and no ceremony. We simply stood in our circle about the silvery trunk of the tree, and drew the silence deep into our spirits. A voice within me said, *You are here. You are home, my daughter, and the wound is healed. Don't leave us again.* But whether it was my mother's voice, or the voice of the forest itself, there was no telling.

I watched my brothers' faces as they stood there quiet. The spell had been undone, and we were home. That much was true. The shattered household, the broken alliances could be put together with hard work. But there was deeper damage here that lay still unmended, and some that might be beyond healing. I sent a silent entreaty to the Fair Folk that my brothers might be themselves again, all of them. And that I might somehow be relieved of the terrible ache in my heart, which never quite seemed to go away.

'It is almost winter,' said Conor quietly. 'Out of winter's darkness comes spring's light. Out of winter's sleep is born spring's new life. We cannot be without hope, not when this truth is shown us year by year.'

But the others said nothing, and after a while each of us touched a hand to the tree's pale bark, and made a quiet way home again.

Not all were happy simply to pick up the pieces and start again. It was too much for Diarmid to bear, that our stepmother had fled the forest unchecked, apparently unscathed, taking her infant with her. She must be punished, must be made to pay for what she had done. Without due vengeance, the tale was not finished, the pattern not completed. Liam and Conor tried to reason with him. What was done could not be undone, Conor said. He must let go his anger, and start to rebuild. It wasn't as if there were no other outlet for his energies. But Diarmid was adamant. She must pay. The sorceress must pay. Why did they not go forth, and seek her out, and exact the price?

He remained on a knife-edge of anger, and took it out on his opponents in the practice yard. He fought with a frightening intensity, apparently heedless of his own safety. Whenever a bout involved Diarmid, you could see Donal hovering close by, watching every move; and that was just as well.

Finbar did not venture out to the settlement often, for folk would follow him and reach out to touch the soft feathers of that great shining wing, as if it were a talisman; and he shrank from any touch, as if something of the wild creature still lived deep within him. I feared for him, and did not know how to help him.

Conor made an inventory of the meagre stores. He cast his eye over the remaining livestock, the state of the home farms, the disrepair of cottages and barns. He rode out to the other settlements to ensure the loyalty of the tenants there, to check the state of herds and flocks, and on Liam's behalf, to arrange the manning of outer guard posts. But he was unusually abstracted, spending much of his time standing at a window looking out over the forest; as if he were waiting for something. Some days he would simply disappear, to return late in the evening without explanation. And he received his own visitors; ancient, robed figures, and young men with old eyes. He spoke to them in private, out of doors, and afterwards he would be very quiet, as if his thoughts were in some distant place far from Sevenwaters.

Meanwhile the villagers began to succumb to a winter ague that went deep to the chest, and caused the breath to rattle and squeak, and the body to grow hot and cold. I extricated Cormack from the practice yard, where he had stepped into the role of Donal's right hand man as if it had always been his own. I found Padriac where he was tending to a lame horse in the stables, the two lads hanging on his every word. I got a cart loaded with firewood, and the three of us, with the two boys, went around the village and made sure every household had a small supply. I brought soup which Janis had contrived from turnips and sorrel and a few scraps from a wiry old chicken. There was no lack of work for my hands. Old Tom was very sick; I knew no amount of balsam and peppermint would cure this cough. The fire helped ease him a little. But there were others that might be saved, given the right care. Back home, I set one of the girls to gathering and preparing what herbs were still growing around house and garden, and we began to stock the stillroom shelves once more. This was my work; this was my place. I was the daughter of the forest, a child that had grown up in the heart of its mystic growth, ever changing, yet ever the same. But I could not keep away the images that rose from deep in my heart. I wanted him so much; wanted him here by me, longed to feel his arms around me, to hear his voice, very quiet, the way it went when he was fighting to control his feelings. *It's all right, Jenny. It's all right*. I went about my day's work, and however hard I tried, every moment I was wondering where he was, and what he was doing. I imagined him in the hall at Harrowfield, settling the disputes of his household, listening gravely, delivering his wise judgement. I thought of the winter mornings, of him and Ben practising their games of combat. Bodies straining one against the other, one flaxen head, one red as flame. The girls clustered in the doorway, admiring. When it was finished, the two men would slap each other on the shoulders, grinning. Ben would tell a silly joke. The next day they might be mending a roof, or building a drystone wall, or breaking ice from water barrels. The cottagers of Harrowfield would not go hungry, or succumb to the ague untended. I had not said farewell to Margery. That was cause for sadness. Perhaps Johnny would be taking his first steps by now. I would not see that. I had to accept that I would never see Red again. I should let go, and move onto a new path. But like Diarmid, I found that I could not let go.

They say time heals the heart, and that such feelings fade with absence. It was not so with me. By day I exhausted myself with work, but his image was always there in my mind. By night I slept little, and when I did, I dreamed of what I had lost. My brothers joked about it, dismissing it as a young girl's calf-love, something I would soon grow out of. Despite all, they still saw me as little more than a child, and they expected me to slip back into my old place at Sevenwaters as if nothing had changed. They could not imagine that I would love a Briton, that I could give my heart to a man in whose house I had so nearly been put to death. There was no point in trying to explain it to them. Only Finbar had understood the depth of my bond with Red.

Father did not talk much. He liked to sit in my little garden, whatever the weather. If gentle rain fell, he spread an old sack over head and shoulders, and let it fall. If the wind was chill, he wrapped himself in a cloak. When I was not busy in the village, I worked close by him, digging, weeding, clearing, while my little helper busied herself in the stillroom.

As often as not I would find Finbar there in the garden too, a pale, silent figure whose face was still gaunt and wasted; whose eyes still held a wild knowledge beyond human understanding. Since that last night at Harrowfield, he had laid a shield on his thoughts to keep them from me, and his inner voice was all but silent. I could not tell how it was with him; but I knew he was speaking to his father, mind to mind.

Perhaps Father answered him in the same way. I remembered what Father Brien had told us long ago. How the ancient ones would have taken Colum, had he been willing to learn their secret crafts and memorise the long lore of their kind, to become in time one of their mystic brotherhood. But Colum had laid eyes on Niamh, with her dark curling hair and her skin like new milk and her wide green eyes, and he had lost his heart. After that there was but one path for him. And so Conor had been chosen in his place. Father Brien had spoken of love, and of our kind. What had he said? *You know not, yet, the sort of love that strikes like a lightning bolt, that clutches hold of you by the heart, as irrevocably as death; that becomes the lodestar by which you steer the rest of your life . . . it is in the nature of your kin, to love this way.*

I knew now, painfully, what it felt like to love thus, as my father had loved my mother. I understood that Finbar sought to help his father back to self-knowledge, back to a place where he could touch this world without being destroyed by his guilt, and regret, and anguish. So they sat there in silence, and I moved around them clipping lavender and rosemary, and failing utterly to quell the longings of my own heart.

The weather grew chill and more chill. The rains ceased, and were overtaken by clear, bright days, and nights of deep frost. The last leaves fell from ash and birch, from the great oaks whose spreading roots were now blanketed in the golden brown remnants of their summer cloaks. The legacy of Lady Oonagh was a long and terrible one. Old Tom died, and then his granddaughter developed a rattling cough and a feverish brightness of the eyes. I tended to children whose bodies were clammy with sweat, who cried out for cold water while snow lay deep outside the cottage doors. I saw strong men grow feeble as infants and clutch at my hand as if frightened of the dark. That winter we lost ten good folk from our village. Had they not been so weakened by neglect, they might have been able to fight back.

I grew weary, and angry, so that I understood when one day Diarmid announced suddenly that he was off to seek the sorceress and bring her to justice, and if nobody was prepared to go with him, that was not his problem. Someone must be bold, and have the courage to do the right thing, he said. He took his sword and his bow, and he rode off alone. A little later Cormack, mouth set tight, saddled up and went after him, for as he said, Diarmid was like an arrow loosed at random, which might find the right target or the wrong one, and he had better make sure no more ill was done than had been already.

'I'll bring him back safe,' said Cormack as his horse fidgeted and stamped, eager to be away. 'There's a child to be found. Our brother. Diarmid forgets that, in his passion. I'll stay by him until he comes to his senses. We'll be home by spring.' Conor reached up from where he stood by the horse, to clasp his twin's hand.

'Go safe on your journey, brother,' he said quietly.

'And you,' Cormack replied with a crooked smile. 'I think it is your journey that will be the longer one.'

Seamus Redbeard came to visit Liam. They spent two days conferring, and reached an agreement to share men and arms and the duty of defending borders. They talked of Eamonn of the Marshes, who had wed Eilis. Their faces were grim and their manner purposeful. Seamus left behind a small troop of his own men, and assurances of help. But before his departure, Seamus sat with Lord Colum all one afternoon, speaking quietly, and I thought there was a glimmer of recognition in my father's eye.

With Diarmid and Cormack gone, the rest of us drew closer together. It was a fierce winter, and it became harder to keep the village supplied and the outposts manned. We worked each day until we were dropping with exhaustion. In the evenings, there was little ceremony. The household would gather, lord, servant and man at arms together, in the kitchens where a fire was kept burning. Janis would provide what she could, usually a soup and loaves of dark bread. We ate together, as we worked together. The hall was deserted, too big to keep warm with our carefully rationed stocks of dry wood. When the simple meal was over, tales would be told by one or another, as Janis passed round mugs of mulled wine, seasoned from what I knew to be her diminishing stocks of spices and dried fruits.

And slowly, as dark, still night followed night, my father's eyes began to lose their dead, frozen expression and wake to the tales of heroic battle or star-crossed lovers. He gave a little smile as I told the tale of the warrior queen with a raging appetite for young men. He nodded gravely as Padriac related the old saga of Culhan's routing of three giants, each bigger than the last. Even Donal, reluctantly, was persuaded one night to join in, telling of the great voyage

616

of Maeldun and the wondrous things he found, such as an island where the ants were as large as horses, or a grove of apple trees that bore fruit all year round, or a fountain that gushed forth fresh milk. Once this story was begun, everyone had a bit to add, and it took many nights before all was told. My father sat close by Finbar, listening to this story, and once or twice he would lean towards his son, making quiet comment, and Finbar would give the smallest of nods. Then there came a day when, instead of making his way to the garden to sit in silence, Father went in search of Liam, where he watched the men schooling their horses. He stayed there through the afternoon, and what they said to each other, I did not ask. But that evening, there was a new warmth in his eyes.

Slowly he began to speak and to respond as if he knew us. Things were not, however, as they had once been. Our father now seemed like a man much older in years. The burden of what he had brought on himself, and on us, was near intolerable for him, and I fancied he sometimes held onto his sanity by the merest thread. Now Finbar watched over him, silent, always there in the shadows to one side, as if his mind held our father's in check, weaving a net of protection about the gradually mending spirit. So father and son came to understand each other, and another wound was healed. But the victory had been hard won. Finbar grew thinner and thinner, eating little, speaking not a word. One could not give so much of oneself, without a terrible cost.

Father did not talk to me much. I told myself, that was nothing new. Before, he had seemed not to know what to make of his small daughter, who looked so much like her mother. Now, I was even more like Niamh, so alike that at first he had mistaken me for her whom he had loved and lost. My brothers had told him my story. He knew that I was wed to a Briton, one of that breed he despised so bitterly. One of those who had taken the Islands that held the most secret of our people's sacred places, and for nothing but a foothold from which to venture forth in anger and greed, to lay waste our lands. They told him that. But, Liam quickly assured him, it had not been a real marriage. The union could be annulled, said Conor, and in time, a suitable husband could be found for me. In time. There was no hurry. My father listened, and said nothing.

CHAPTER SIXTEEN

Midwinter passed, and with it my sixteenth birthday. The weather remained piercingly chill. I went early to the village, taking rye bread that Janis and I had baked, and an infusion made from the root of all-heal for Tom's granddaughter, who was past the worst of her fever. Frost crunched under my boots. I went from one cottage to another, and I finished my errands while the sun was still creeping up behind the winter filigree of the birches. I heard the plaintive call of an owl, deep in the forest, and another answering. Instead of going straight home, I climbed up the hill path beneath the skeleton trees, my breath a vaporous cloud in the crisp air. At the top of the small rise I sat down on a flat rock and looked across the tangle of branches to the still water of the lake. There was a stone in my boot. I stripped off my gloves and reached down to unfasten it. It was only then that I looked at my hands and realised that the swelling was at last completely gone, the fingers small and fine as they had once been, the skin pale and soft. Almost as if they had never held distaff or needle, almost as if they had never heard of starwort. They bore the scrapes and bruises of my work in kitchen and garden, but that was nothing. Perhaps there had been forest magic at work there, for in all my time as a healer I had never seen such damage mend so fast.

Without thinking, I drew the cord from around my neck, and cut it cleanly with the small sharp knife I kept in my bag with my ointments and salves. The little oak ring tumbled onto my palm, warm and smooth from lying next to my heart. I slipped the ring gently onto the third finger of my left hand. It encircled my finger as if made for it; as indeed it had been.

I was overwhelmed by tears, flooding down my cheeks in an unstoppable torrent, and there was nobody sitting quietly by me to offer a clean handkerchief when I needed it. Nobody sitting close, but not too close, letting me weep, but ready to help when I was ready to ask. I covered my face with my hands, thinking I could not bear such sorrow for very much longer. I was only sixteen. Was the rest of my life to be lived thus, half awake, half alive, never fully complete? *What had I done wrong to be thus cursed?*

'Nothing,' said a voice nearby.

I looked up between tear-soaked fingers. She was standing near me, regarding me gravely, her cloak of midnight blue the only vivid patch of colour amid the winter trees. 'You have done well, daughter of the forest. Your work for us is nearly finished. You have been strong. Almost too strong.'

I sniffed. She had taken her time, coming back. 'Nearly finished?' I stammered. 'I thought it was over. My brothers are returned. I completed the task. What more can there be?'

The Lady of the Forest smiled. 'That was all you were asked to do, and you did indeed prove brave and true, Sorcha. There is but one more thing. You will know, when it is time.'

Already she was starting to fade back under the trees.

'Wait!' I said urgently, as if one such as she would heed a mortal's plea. 'Please wait! I need you to tell me – I need you to explain . . .'

'What, child?' She arched her brows as if she found me amusing.

'You hurt him. You hurt both of us. You said – back then, in the cave – you told me I had chosen well. Was that all he was, some sort of guard you bound to me for a time, so that I could complete the task in safety? Was that your only purpose in drawing him close to me? Why cast such a spell over him, and wound us both to the heart? You knew we would have to let go, once the task was completed.'

The Lady frowned a little, puzzled. 'What spell can you mean, daughter?'

'The spell, the enchantment you laid on Lord Hugh, to bind him to me, so that he must guard me, and watch over me, even at the expense of all he held dear. It was a cruel spell. I could have looked after myself, I would rather not have . . .' My fingers were twisting the ring, round and round. She laughed, a high, mirthful laugh like the splashing of a waterfall.

'He needed no encouragement,' she said. 'Believe me, there was no such enchantment laid. Is it so hard for you to comprehend, that such a man could love you, without the aid of the magical arts? Have you looked in your mirror? Have you not seen your own

ƺth of spirit, and your loyalty, and your sweet-
ᴉess? It took him but the space of a heartbeat, to see
these things. If you had not been so strong, perhaps
you would not have let him go. Perhaps your tale
might have had a different ending.'

'But —' I said stupidly. 'But why did he never say
anything? Why didn't he tell me?'

'He tried,' she said. Then she smiled, and shook
her head a little, as if bemused by the folly of
humankind, and she faded away to nothing.

And as I made my way down the hill and homewards, I realised that he had, indeed, tried to tell me;
and that it was I who had not learned to listen. It had
been there in the gentleness of his hands and the elusive sweetness of his smile. It had been there in his
anger, the time I had gone off on my own and
encountered Richard in the woods. It had been there
in the way he had flinched when I touched him, the
night John died. *I don't want your pity*, he had said. It
had been there in the tale he had told me on the
beach. *She was the woman of his soul, and he could not
think of giving her up*. But he had given me up, without a word. I realised, with a feeling like a stone in the
heart, that he had done this because he believed the
only thing I wanted was to return home with my
brothers. How could he know that I loved him, when
I had hardly known it myself? I had tried to give back
his ring, and I had hurt him. So he had kept his
promise, and let me go. And I would never go back.
How could I leave the forest, for like the mermaid, I
would not survive long outside the place of my
spirit? Red had understood that. I walked home,
unseeing, wrapped in my thoughts. Despite everything, despite the heartbreak of it, there was a small
warm glow deep inside me. If I knew that he had

loved me, at least for a while, it made the pain just a little easier to bear.

That same night, when we gathered in the warmth of the kitchen for supper, I wore my blue dress. I had washed it carefully, and the stain across bodice and sleeve was barely discernible on the faded fabric. Such treatment had rendered the gown soft and comfortable, but I had not worn it here before, for it held memories of pain as well as joy. That night I felt compelled to wear it, and the wedding ring on my finger was a badge of pride. My brothers noted both with their eyes, but made no comment, sensitive perhaps to the signs my face bore, of long weeping.

The soup was a good one, with onions and barley, and it did not take long for Janis' vast cauldron to be empty. Then we sat with our cups of wine between our hands, and the glow of the fire on our tired faces, and Liam said, 'Who will tell us a tale for a winter night?' But there was a quietness about the house, and nobody was forthcoming. This midwinter, there had been no branches of holly above the door, no herbs festooned about the window openings, to welcome wandering spirits in. There was no dry wood to be spared for bonfires, and none with the energy or will to celebrate the passing of the seasons. Nonetheless, there was an amity amongst us, a sense of shared purpose that bound us all together. I believed even my father sensed this, as he sat by Liam and looked long at his eldest son, who was already a leader of men. And at Conor, whose serene gaze was abstracted, as if his thoughts were directed far inwards. This son was wise beyond his years; soon it would be time for him to move on, and there was the anticipation of another loss in my father's eyes. Then there was Finbar, standing behind his father's chair, seeing much, saying nothing. This was the son who had once so enraged his father with his steadfast gaze and his outspoken words, with his dogged refusal to play Lord Colum's games. It was this son, now, who had healed his father's wounded spirit. And Padriac, always a favourite. Padriac, who was now no longer a child. He flirted with the maidservants, and grinned at his father, and Colum gave a glimmer of a smile.

We sat awhile, talking of this and that, reluctant to leave the comfort of the kitchen for our chilly sleeping quarters. The fire burned lower, and Donal threw on another of the precious logs. They had cut more wood and stacked it, but it would take a long time to dry, and there were many hearths to warm. The villagers got the first supply, and we took what was left.

Then there were noises outside, and suddenly all of us were alert. The door was rudely pushed open, and Liam was on his feet, reaching for his sword, thrusting me behind him. On my other side, Donal appeared, dagger at the ready. Conor moved to shield his father. In a blast of cold air, two of Liam's guards burst in, a prisoner between them, a prisoner with a blindfold over his eyes, and his hands tied behind him. I had a flash of Simon, dragged into the great hall on the night Liam was betrothed to Eilis, a spitting, ferocious captive. This prisoner was tall and strongly built, and he was not putting up a struggle, but standing still between his captors as if being brought here had been his intention all along. This prisoner had hair cropped ruthlessly short, hair the colour of autumn sunlight on beech leaves, a bright flame in the winter night.

I opened my mouth, and Liam's hand came out and clapped itself across my lips, silencing me. Donal gripped my arm, halting my forward progress. Thus effectively prevented from either movement or speech, I could only watch as they brought Red to stand before the men of my family. The guards let go his arms, and stepped back. The room was silent. This, the household sensed, promised to be far better entertainment than any telling of tales.

'I know this man,' said Liam, frowning at me and taking his hand away, but gesturing that I must remain silent. He motioned me to a seat and, for now, I obeyed him. 'I thought the perimeters well guarded. How is it that he came through so far undetected?'

'Strange, my lord,' said one of the men, who seemed a little out of breath. 'Must be woodcrafty, for he came right up the hill to the north and then down through the ash woods, almost as far as the outer hedge, without our men hearing a thing. Don't know how he did it. Then he comes right out where we can see him, and lets himself be taken. Walks quiet for a big fellow.'

'Can't be quite right in the wits,' offered the other guard.

'I'll talk to you in the morning,' growled Donal savagely, making both his men flinch. 'You let nobody past, you understand me? Nobody.'

'What is your business here, Hugh of Harrowfield?' enquired Conor sternly in the foreign tongue. 'Your kind are far from welcome at Sevenwaters. Have you not done enough damage to my family? I am amazed that you think to set foot in this household.'

Red cleared his throat. 'I'm here to speak with my wife,' he said from behind his blindfold. 'Where is Jenny?'

My heart thumped. Conor translated for the others,

stony-faced. Liam glared at me, placing his finger on his lips, cautioning silence. But I must tell him, I would tell him –

Wait, Sorcha. This is his time to speak.

I glared at Finbar where he stood in the shadows. He had never given orders without good reason. *Why? Why must I hold my tongue?*

If you would hear the words of his heart, wait, and be silent.

'Who is this man?' demanded my father, sounding almost his old self. 'What wife?'

'This is the Briton of whom we spoke,' said Liam, his voice chilly. 'In whose house our sister came close to death. He helped us escape from those shores, but we owe him no favours.'

'I am astounded that such a one thinks to show his face here,' said Donal, fingering his dagger. 'What can he intend?'

The blindfold was tight and strong. Red could see nothing. His face was white below the dark cloth. He had come a long way. He appeared unarmed, though I suspected there would be a small, sharp knife somewhere about his person.

'I wish only to see my wife,' he said again, rather wearily. 'I mean no harm to you. Is she here?'

'You have no wife, Briton,' said Liam, when this was relayed to him. 'Our sister is well protected, and content amongst her own kind. There is no place for you in her life.' Conor's translation was cruelly accurate.

'Then let her tell me so with her own lips,' said Red quietly. 'Let her tell me, and I will go.' I opened my mouth, and closed it again.

Then my father spoke, surprising us all.

'We have been short of entertainment tonight, weary as we are. Perhaps this fellow has a good story for a winter evening. Perhaps he can plead his case through such a tale. Bring the Briton a seat, and give him room. Let him speak, and let us be silent and hear him. Conor will render his words. It will be a fair task. I sense a mystery here beyond what my eyes tell; I would not be hasty to judge.' So they brought out a stool, and Red sat down, long legs crossed before him and the bandage still blinding his vision. They did not untie his hands.

He sat very upright, straight backed, and the fire-light touched his hair to gold and scarlet and copper. I was finding it hard to breathe. Around me, Janis and Donal and the men and women of the household stood or sat with their cups in their hands and expectant looks on their faces. I did not know what to feel. I trembled with delight to have him in my sight once more. I glared at the men of my household, who, it seemed, must always play games; who could accept no stranger without putting him to some test. Ask Red to fight with a sword or a little knife or with bare hands and feet, and he would be more than a match for anyone. I had seen this myself. Ask him to mend a tumbled wall, or a sick beast, or a broken alliance, and he was your man. But he was no teller of tales; not for a gathering of strangers such as this. He was no play actor. He had told me a story once; but that was for an audience of one, and hadn't his own mother said he spoke to me as if to himself? The task my father had set him was the hardest he could have chosen. For such a man, who held his feelings deep within, hard in check, whose cold eyes and tight mouth gave nothing away, whose words failed him most when he let his heart speak, this was a cruel challenge. *You can do this*, I told him silently. *Tell your tale to me. One foot before the other, straight ahead.*

'There was – there was once a man,' he began hesitantly, 'who had everything. Well born, richly endowed, healthy in body and mind, he grew up as the eldest son and heir to a wide estate, whose margins were the sea to the west, and the hills to the east, whose fields were fertile and whose rivers teemed with fish for the taking.'

Conor's voice made a grave counterpoint, rendering the words into our tongue. Finbar sat by the window, eyes fixed on nothing. He understands, I thought. Not just the words, but the meaning behind them. Finbar and I, we are the only ones who know. But Finbar's grave features and unfocused gaze gave nothing away.

'He grew up,' Red went on, 'and his father died, and the estate was his, but for a small part that fell to his younger brother. His life was mapped out, every detail accounted for. He would marry to advantage, he would expand his lands, provide for his family and his good folk, carry on the work of his forefathers. Just so is the path for many good men, and they live their lives to its pattern, glad that they may pass on to their sons a legacy of peace and prosperity.' He shifted slightly. His hands, still bound behind his back, seemed to tighten one on the other.

'Then – then things changed. An evil fell on his family, taking his young brother away and into danger. In time, it became plain that he must go forth and seek him out, dead or alive. But he loved his home, and his acres, and he believed there was no chance his brother had survived. He believed him lost forever. So he waited and waited, until there was no choice but to set out across the sea, and seek what truth he could find.'

There was a pause. Perhaps only I knew how he used it to marshal his thoughts, to force his breathing to be slow and steady, to draw deep on his will so his voice remained confident. For the others, it was still just a tale, like all the tales we told, night by night, tales comical and strange, tales heroic and awe-inspiring, the tales that formed the fabric of our spirits.

'The man journeyed far, and he heard and saw many strange things on his travels. He learned that – that the friend and the enemy are but two faces of the same self. That the path one believes chosen long since, constant and unchangeable, straight and wide, can alter in an instant. Can branch, and twist, and lead the traveller to places far beyond his wildest imaginings. That there are mysteries beyond the minds of mortal man, and that to deny their existence is to spend a life of half-consciousness.'

I saw my father nodding gravely at this point. But Liam and Conor both wore frowns and set jaws, and Donal a fierce scowl.

'One night, everything changed. He – he had cause to save a young woman from drowning; and from the moment he first plucked her from the water, half grown, half starved, half wild as she was, he knew. From that moment on, every step he took, every decision he made, would be different, because of her. She was not much more than a child, lost, hurt and frightened. But strong. Oh, she was the strongest person he had ever met. He had cause to know it, on the difficult journey home, as she stood by him; as she healed him, although he was her enemy. As – as she showed him things that were almost beyond his understanding, so strange and wondrous did they appear. Of that, I will not tell more, for some secrets are best left unsaid.'

He bowed his head a little, took a deep breath.

'In his household she was like a wild creature set suddenly in the farmyard, like a fledgling owl in a chicken coop. With her deep silence, with the strange task she was compelled to do, working in pain and solitude under the uncomprehending eyes of his family, she filled him with a confusion such as he had never known before. He could do little but protect her; it seemed imperative to keep her safe. He did not understand what she did, but he knew, somehow, that he must help her achieve the task, if he were ever to hear her voice, if he were ever to be able to tell her . . . to tell her . . .'

I opened my mouth to speak, then bit back the words. But I must have made some small sound, for Red went very still for an instant, and his head turned. The thick blindfold cut off all sight; but he knew, now, that I was there.

'In his house, she grew and changed, but was still, unmistakably, herself. Strong, sweet and true. Without speech, she spoke to him as no other could, straight to the heart, with her graceful, disfigured hands and her wide green eyes. Though he was often lost for words, she understood him as no other had ever done. He watched her weep over her hands, which were swollen and hardened from her work, and heard others call them ugly. He saw what others could not see, saw the power, the gentleness, and the beauty of those hands, and he lay awake at night and longed for the touch of them on his body. But she had been hurt, and terrified, and she shrank from him. He could not tell her the words of his heart. He dared not risk frightening her away, for if he lost her, he lost everything. Every day, it became clearer to him, going about the business of his house and his estate. Without her, he would have no life.'

There was a marked distaste in Conor's voice as he translated this, but he was bound to be accurate, as there were at least three of us there who understood the tongue of the Britons. Then Conor said, 'I am starting to dislike this tale.' His tone was like a knife thrust. 'If this man possessed such feelings, why did he leave the girl to the mercies of his kinsman, who was both traitor and madman? How could a man guilty of such an error of judgement ever be worthy of a woman such as this peerless creature you describe?'

'With respect,' said Red, and his voice had gone so quiet people hushed each other to hear him, 'my tale is as yet unfinished; you should hear me out. And it is her answer I have come to hear, not yours.'

'Let the man finish,' said my father. 'For a Briton, he has a way with words. Hearing him commits us to no decision.'

'My father says, continue.' Conor's tone was curt as he addressed Red.

'Thank you for your courtesy, my lord,' said Red in my father's general direction. He turned back towards Conor. 'You are right,' he went on. 'This man did indeed make, as you relate, an error of judgement. One that still causes him to wake at night, in terror, at how close he came to losing her to the fire. At how his neglect almost cost the girl her life, and her chance of completing the terrible task that meant so much to her. He thought her secure, protected by his name and his wedding band, safe in the heart of his family. He took the risk of travelling to find his lost brother, who was also in grave danger; he returned only just in time to save her. Never had he experienced such fear as on that night; never had he heard a sound that struck him to the heart so, as her voice crying out his name, to warn him of danger at the very point when she herself was in greatest peril. For a moment, he thought – he allowed himself to think – for just an instant, he held her in his arms, and his heart was whole again. Then he let her go, for she was surrounded by strong men, by fierce protectors who were her own kin. She was safe again, and the reason for the long, cruel time of spinning and weaving was plain at last. She had sacrificed her childhood to save her brothers; she loved her family above all else, and her spirit yearned to return home once more, to the wild forest and the land of mystic tales and ancient spirits from whence he had taken her. That was the place of her heart, and if he loved her, he must let her go.'

The mood in the room was subtly changing. They appreciated a good tale; and this was told with feeling, though somewhat haltingly. Janis had her eye on the teller. I heard her whisper to one of the kitchen-maids, 'That's a man and a half, that is. If she doesn't want him, I'll be the first to offer him a warm bed for the night.'

And then I felt the inner voice of Finbar, whom I had thought scarcely listening, so distant was his expression. *This is a good man, Sorcha.*

I know.

Strong enough to say, in front of us all, that he was wrong. Very strong.

I know.

'He could not find the words to say goodbye. He faltered. He had wounded her, speaking from the pain of his spirit. He had sworn that he would not hurt her, but he had. He would have told her – he would have said, it matters not if you are here, or there, for I see you before me every moment. I see you in the light on the water, in the swaying of the young trees in the spring wind. I see you in the shadows of the great oaks, I hear your voice in the cry of the owl at night. You are the blood in my veins, and the beating of my heart. You are my first waking thought, and my last sigh before sleeping. You are – you are bone of my bone, and breath of my breath.'

His voice had shrunk to a whisper. My face was wet with tears.

'Tell him,' said Liam, 'tell him that if he thinks his fine words of love will win him our sister as his wife, he is sorely deluded. Sorcha will never return to that place; she is the daughter of Sevenwaters, and she belongs here.'

Conor translated this, adding, 'You'd best have left it, back then. Not put yourself to the trouble of coming all this way. Sorcha is barely sixteen years old, and subject to her father's authority. You cannot imagine that even if she were willing, he would allow her to cross the sea and ally herself to a Briton.'

Red took a deep breath. 'Indeed, such a thought was far from my mind. I would not have come, save for – but for – had she not said farewell as she did, I would not have come. But – but she had a way of – that is, I believed, there was the smallest hope, the tiniest seed of a hope, that perhaps she did – that is . . .'

'Is your tale finished?' Conor was unbending. 'Have you more to say? It grows late, and cold.'

'I should make it clear to you,' said Red, his tone firmer. 'I understand your sister cannot return across the sea. I never expected that. It was for this reason that I delayed so long before coming to seek her. Long enough to set right the affairs of Harrowfield, long enough to see my uncle duly punished for his wrongdoing, and to pass over responsibility for my house and my estate to my brother. I will not go back there. Whether Jenny will have me or not, I have said farewell to that life.'

There was complete silence. The magnitude of such a decision was not lost on any of them. Even Conor, after translating these words, had nothing to say. As for me, my mind could hardly credit what Red had said. And yet, I knew it must be the truth. His fair acres, his shining river, his flocks, and his herds, and the good folk that loved him. The valley with its soft cloak of oak and beech, birch and willow. The careful record of generations. My picture had been on the last page of that journal. The last page of the last book. He would never see his young oaks grow to shelter the wild creatures of Harrowfield. All this, he had given up for me.

'You think to stay here,' said Liam incredulously, when at length the silence was broken. 'A Briton, in our household, wed to our sister, whom we cherish more dearly than life itself. You are a misguided fool.'

I turned on my brother, furious.

Wait just a little longer, came Finbar's silent caution, and I held back my angry words.

And then my father rose slowly to his feet.

'Untie his hands, Sorcha,' he said gravely. 'Take off the cloth that binds his eyes. This is your decision, your choice. You are a woman now, and the sacrifice you made for your brothers has earned you the right to determine your own path, though it may not be to our liking.'

Liam made as if to speak, but thought better of it. Lord Colum was, after all, still master of this household. The room was filled with a silence of deep anticipation. Red had not understood any of my father's words.

I walked over to where he sat, and I stood before him and reached around to untie the knot that held the blindfold in place. This I did with my right hand;

but my left, which bore his ring, crept to the back of his neck, where the skin showed white between tunic and close cropped hair, and laid itself there as gently as it could. Red drew in his breath sharply.

'*Untie my hands,*' he said with an intensity that made me tremble. I bent down and took the small knife from him, from where I had known it would be, concealed in the strapping of the left boot, and I moved behind him and slashed once, twice, at the tight cords that bound his hands. He stood and turned, and his arms encircled me, enfolded me as if they would never let go. I felt his lips touch my brow, quite chastely, for even now he was governed by a terrible restraint. Even now, it seemed he was unsure of me. But his eyes were no longer ice-cool, no longer masked with reserve. Instead they blazed blue as a summer sky, and the message in them was plain to read, and simple to answer. I stood on tiptoe, and took his face between my palms, and drew his head down so I could kiss his tight, stubborn, unyielding mouth. I had had no practice at this art, but I managed pretty well; Padriac told me later that I had made Liam blush, which was no mean feat. It was a kiss such as I had not believed myself capable of giving; a kiss that told him straight away what my answer was. For an instant he drew back, and he whispered, 'I am not worthy of such a gift, Jenny.' But I put my fingers to his lips to silence him. 'Dear heart,' I whispered back, 'I would give it to you and no other.' Then his mouth came down on mine, and he showed me the depth of his passion as our lips clung and tasted, and parted as we drew ragged breath, and clung and tasted again. And it was not just my own salt tears that fell as his hands stroked my hair, and drew my body close against his own, so that I knew the strength of his need for me. This was the end of a long and difficult journey for us both, and the sweet excitement that coursed through every fibre of my body told me it was at the same time the beginning of a new path.

'Ahem.' My father cleared his throat, forcing us back to awareness of where we were. We turned to look around us, dazed. The room was almost empty; we had not heard the departure of all the household save Father and the silent Finbar.

'Take your man, daughter,' said my father with a little smile, though his eyes were awake with painful memories. 'Find him a warm place to sleep. Time enough in the morning, for further talk.' Then he gathered his cloak around him and went out, with Finbar behind. My brother paused in the doorway, the white swathe of his single wing turned rosy gold in the candlelight; and this time he spoke aloud.

'The tale is finished at last,' he said, in the tongue that we could all understand. 'Be happy. You have earned one another. The gift of such love is given to but few. You must make each day count.'

Red pressed his lips against my hair. I watched Finbar slip out the door like a shadow. Then I took my husband's hand, and led him to my own sleeping quarters, where somebody had lit a fire in the small grate, and placed candles and wine and goblets, and a bunch of dried lavender on the pillow. I could hear what an effort it was for Red to control his breathing, and indeed I was not much better myself.

'I – I'm afraid I will hurt you,' he said. 'But – but I need you, Jenny, I ache for you, I don't think I can –'

'Ssh,' I said. 'It's all right. It will be all right.'

Real life is not quite as it is in stories. In the old tales, bad things happen, and when the tale has unfolded and come to its triumphant conclusion, it is as if the bad things had never been. Life is not as simple as that, not quite. It would have been good to forget, entirely, the damage done to my body and mind that day in the forest, by men who used me without thought. But such things are never quite forgotten, though they fade with the years. And so, as we lay together that first time, there was one moment when I gasped in remembered fear, and my body froze and trembled. But Red held me, and stroked my hair, and spoke to me softly, little words under the breath, and he waited for me. And, at length, my body opened to his like a flower, and we moved slowly together, and then more quickly, and we sighed and cried out and found release in each other's arms. He showed me that the union between man and woman is, indeed, something to wonder at, and revel in, and laugh over. Until that night, I realised I had never heard him laugh. And as to what the gossips of Harrowfield had delighted in saying about my husband, it was all true, but it scarcely did him justice.

The very first thing Red did, after we rose next morning in a sort of blissful daze, with foolish smiles on our faces and scarce able to keep our hands away from each other, was to come with me to the village, and while I tended to one and to another, he set about learning the names of every man, woman and child there, and how to greet them courteously in their own tongue. At first they eyed him with some unease. But his stumbling efforts to be understood brought smiles and wisecracks, and they saw how it was with the two of us. Me they knew and loved, and if he was my man, then he must be all right, Briton or no. Soon enough he was being stopped to admire a prize sow, or offering grave advice, by means of complicated hand signals, on replacing rotting wood in a byre, or helping to hold a post upright while supports were driven in around it. In time, they were all won over.

At home it was somewhat more difficult. That first day, he was quizzed at some length by Donal and by Liam, for while it was accepted that I had made my choice, that didn't mean they had to like it.

Conor, surprisingly, had little to say. I caught his grave eyes on me, watching with a sort of wry acceptance, and when later I drew him aside alone, he said, 'You thought that unfair, did you? To make a man reveal himself thus before us?'

'You were hard on him,' I said. 'I would have thought you, at least, could see him for what he is, without such a test.'

Conor smiled. 'Without such a test, perhaps he would never have told you how he felt. Myself, I knew the man he was. Knew that it would be thus with the two of you. I cannot see what is to come, as Finbar does; but this meeting of spirits was as inevitable as the path of sun and moon across the sky. I have known it for some time; but it would have been a mistake to make it too easy for him. You had both to learn the power of loss, before you came to your senses. Tell me, did she visit you, that being of the other world who has guided your path? Have you seen her again, since you came home?'

'How do you know so much?' I was astonished, and would have been annoyed, were not the glow of joy so strong in me as to shut out all else.

'I have cause to put what skills I possess to the test, from time to time,' said Conor. 'They are meagre enough; they have been sufficient thus far, but not for much longer. I must soon leave this place, and go on another journey, and it may be long before I see you again. It eases my mind to see you so content after your ordeal. I believe it was ordained thus.'

'You're not saying – you're not saying what I think you're saying? That the whole thing – all of it – that it was all for this end? So that he and I – no, I can't believe that.' His words filled me with confusion. He must be wrong, surely. We were not mere puppets, but men and women making our own choices.

'One thing is certain,' he said. 'You will never hear the answer from the Fair Folk. But it is a long, long game they play, and our stories are the slightest of pieces in its great pattern. You should think about it. Each of you was put through many trials; each of you proved strong, strong enough for their purpose. So strong, indeed, that you came close to thwarting them, for each of you chose to give up what was loved best, in the hope that the other would find happiness. The Fair Folk do not expect such selflessness.'

'But – but it was cruelly done. For us, the ending is a good one, but what about Father? What about Finbar? And there was a man of – of my husband's people, a good man, who died protecting me. What of the child, whom Oonagh took away? Diarmid and Cormack are gone, and you say you are leaving too; soon there will be no family at Sevenwaters. I could almost believe what the lady Oonagh said that day, that she and the Lady of the Forest were one and the same, for the line between light and darkness seems thin indeed. What end could be worth such loss?'

'They care little whom they cast aside,' said Conor. 'But in this game there is, as I said, a far greater goal than we can well comprehend. Perhaps I am wrong.

Time will reveal it. Your part in it, I trust, is over, and your path now straight and true. There will be a family here, and good years. But there is one thing you must remember, if you forget all else. There is no good or evil, save in the way you see the world. There is no dark or light, save in your own vision. All changes in the blink of an eyelid; yet all remains the same. If you wish to know what is to come, you should ask Finbar. Now, enough of such gravity. You had better go and rescue Lord Hugh from Liam's clutches, before he suffers more. Go on, off with you.'

Red had answered them well enough, for now. That he would stay, and watch over me, and make himself useful. That he had skills they might employ, with the husbandry of livestock and the management of crops. He could fight, if that were necessary, but there was one thing he would not do, and that was take up arms against his own kind. It must be understood that he would not do this, on any account. Father nodded, satisfied. Donal growled that it was all very well to talk; a good solid bout in the practice yard and they'd see what he was made of. Red, as I had known he would, took up this challenge immediately. He suggested that perhaps that afternoon might be a good time. Donal's eyes lit up. Liam, tight jawed, was not saying much at all. Then I advanced into the hall where they stood, and a sweet smile curved Red's mouth as he saw me, and a warm light awoke in his eyes, which must have been a reflection of my own. I went to stand by his side, and each of us slipped an arm around the other, for it was not possible to be so close, and not to touch.

'Very well,' said Liam. 'If it suits you, you can show us your skills today. Sure you're up to it?'

'I think so,' Red replied gravely.

It was not, perhaps, in his best interest to retire upstairs with me beforehand, but there was no preventing it, for our bodies spoke to one another in a way that could not be denied. We were, I suppose, making up for lost time. Later, I lay on the bed wrapped only in a sheet and watched him as he dressed somewhat reluctantly.

'Won't you be tired?' I asked, smiling. 'My brothers are adept in the arts of war, and they'll be keen to prove a point. Are you sure you can cope?'

He slipped his tunic over his head. 'Today, I could take on three giants, each bigger and uglier than the last, and think nothing of it,' he said. He was already starting to talk like one of us. 'Stay there, I'll be back before you know it,' and he touched his lips to mine, and drew them away with some difficulty, and went out, buckling on a borrowed sword belt.

I did not stay abed, but went to an upper window from which I could watch them. It was an interesting bout. Liam and Red were, I thought, quite evenly matched; what advantage Liam had in experience was balanced by Red's greater height and heavier build, and by his surprising lightness on his feet. In any event, what started out as a fierce contest developed into a demonstration and then a lesson, first by one and then the other, in the techniques of armed and unarmed combat. Donal became involved, and then a group of others. I saw Red teaching them how to execute the flying kick with left foot extended; then horses were brought out and I saw Liam showing him the trick of slipping low in the saddle to avoid a blow, and then up again in a single fluid movement. Both of them were sustaining a few bruises. I heard the sound of laughter. How Diarmid would have enjoyed showing off his skills with the spear, I thought. And Cormack, he would have been in the midst of it, whirling about with staff in hand. There had been no word from the two of them; their places at the table remained empty. Then I left well alone, and made my way up the stone steps, up and up, to the place where you could sit on the roof slates and look out far over the grey-blue haze of the winter forest. I had known I would find Finbar here. I settled beside him, shivering a little, for the breeze was sharp.

Talk to me, dear one. With such joy in my heart, your loneliness is hard for me to bear.

You will not have to bear it for long.

'What?' I spoke aloud, for his words shook me. 'What do you mean?'

It will not be long. There is no more for me to do here.

Where are you going?

Away. He was being very careful; his mind was shuttered, save for the brief message which was all he was prepared to give me.

Why won't you talk to me any more? What is wrong?

He shifted slightly on the cold slates, and the wing unfurled a little, to balance him.

You ask me that?

We were silent. I could not see what his future might be; I only knew that once, he had burned to set the world to rights, to see justice done and truth revealed. That passionate boy was gone; and I did not know the man who had taken his place.

Was there something you wanted to know?

I shook my head. I had decided I would not ask him what my future held. I hoped it would be good, and happy, and that I would have my husband by my side always.

But I would not ask.

As we sat in silence, a picture made its way into my mind. At first I thought it was one he had shown me before, in which a little Sorcha skipped and ran under great trees, with a dappled light falling around her. But this was different, for this child had copper-red hair that fell straight down her back in a shining curtain, and another ran after her, a dark-haired boy, and he was calling, 'Niamh! Wait for me!' They were the same children I had seen in my mind, on the day of the burning. And somewhere on the edge of sight, there was another child, who looked on hungry-eyed; but this figure I could not see clearly. The girl stretched out her arms and began to spin around, bare feet light on the soft earth, her dress swirling out about her; and the sunlight pierced the canopy of trees and turned her auburn hair to pure gold. Then the light faded, and the picture was gone as my brother drew the shutters firmly closed. *This is all I see.*

It's enough. I shivered again. I had forgotten to put on a cloak.

We will all be gone, one after the other. There will be no sons. It is your children, and his, that will inherit Sevenwaters.

'Don't say that!' I spoke aloud, sharply. 'Don't tempt fate! You cannot know everything.'

Some things I know. He retreated into silence again, his eyes turned far away, beyond the lake, out into the west.

Some time later, men came for Conor. Two very old men, travelling on foot. Their hair was in many small braids, and they wore silver collars around their necks, and robes that moved fluidly about their spare frames. This was the call for which he had been waiting. I found it hard to believe, at first, that he could desert our household so easily, for he had always been there, the voice of balance and reason, the brother who had the power to moderate between the others, the one who had possessed the strength of will to draw his brothers after him to Harrowfield, across the wide sea, to be healed at last. But it was his calling. For he could not learn the ancient lore, the mystic crafts, and at the same time uphold family and túath. He must go forth into the forests and the deep caves, beyond the reach and the knowledge of ordinary folk. There would be years, many years of study and practice, before he became one of the brotherhood.

It seemed to me the eyes of these two old ones looked on my brother with deep respect, novice though he was. Had he not spent the best part of three years as a creature of the wild, and held onto his human consciousness all that time? Did he not, already, possess considerable skills as manipulator of the elements, as instigator of blinding mist, and capricious wind? It was late perhaps, but not too late to begin his years of discipline. He would become strong; one of the strongest of his kind. I honoured him for it, but that did not lessen the pain of losing him.

He said his goodbyes in the hall, embracing first Father, then Liam, clapping Donal on the back, ruffling Padriac's hair. Red he clasped by the shoulder.

'Watch over my sister,' he said. 'Keep her safe.'

But Finbar and I walked with him to the edge of the forest, and stood there to watch him go. The two old men waited quietly. Conor did not touch Finbar, but he spoke to him and I heard his words. *Be strong, brother. You too have scarcely begun your journey.*

Finbar looked him straight in the eye. *Sometimes the way is dark.*

There is a light within. Conor put out a hand and touched his brother on the brow, very lightly. Then he turned and put his arms around me, hugging me so tight I could hardly breathe. *Farewell, little owl.*

I fought back tears, for I knew this was his path and he must follow it. He pulled the hood over his head, and took up his staff of birch wood, and the three of them went down the path into the forest, and in the space of time it took for a tiny cloud to blow across the sun, they were gone.

The men were deep in discussion one evening after supper. Liam had just returned from a visit to Seamus Redbeard. He had brought back a pair of wolfhound pups, and news. Now they were planning some sort of expedition, which they did not bother explaining to me. Even Red had been drawn in, and I half-heard their words as I sat by the fire, yawning over my mead.

'Seamus is no longer young,' Donal said bluntly. 'Has he the will for this, and can he hold on long enough?'

'He won't be without help.' Liam's tone was weighty. 'We'll make sure of that. I will not see Eilis' son raised in a household at enmity with mine.'

'These territories are spread very wide,' Red commented, studying the map unrolled on the table before them. 'Don't you fear that Seamus, given control of the other holding as well as his own, may turn against you in an attempt to claim all for himself?'

'Seamus has always been loyal, and he knows our strength,' Liam replied. 'It is in his best interests to oversee Eamonn's estates until the boy reaches manhood, and to retain Sevenwaters as his ally. He is the child's grandfather; his claim will be hard for others to challenge.'

I was not sure I wanted to hear any more. In particular, I knew I did not want to hear exactly what was planned for Eamonn himself, for there seemed to be no place for him in the picture they painted. So I got up and went to light a candle, thinking to retire to bed, and as I looked over towards the main doorway I caught Finbar's eye just before he slipped away outside. It was very late, and he had no outdoor cloak. And there was that odd, wild look in his eyes. But perhaps he only wanted to be alone, as we all do from time to time. Maybe he would be back soon. I waited, watching the door. Time passed, and the men talked on, and Finbar did not return. At last I could wait no longer. I spoke to Red quietly, not wishing to alarm my father for nothing. The two of us took our cloaks and boots and a lantern, and we set out to follow Finbar's path.

It had been raining but now the air was clear and damp. His footprints were easy to track on the soft soil, all the way to the secret cove on whose upper bank the small birch tree grew. But my brother was nowhere to be found. We moved up and down the shore for a while, searching by lantern light until the moon emerged from her veil of cloud and cast a cool glow over the forest. On the very edge of the lake, where the last footprint marked the margin of white sand and clear water, something caught my eye. Red held the lantern and we bent to look more closely. There was my mother's amulet, with the cord still intact; and a few shreds of woven fibre, that might have been starwort; and a single white feather. But of Finbar we saw not a trace, not that night, nor the next night, nor from Imbolc to Lugnasad. He had vanished

646

as truly as if he had indeed changed again. But you could not go back. I knew that. I did not believe, as many did, that he had simply walked into the lake and drowned. His tale, I sensed, would be the strangest of all. I only hoped that, one day, I would be shown the truth of it.

They were all leaving. It was all changing. There was still no word from Diarmid and Cormack, no news of their quest nor of the lady Oonagh or her child, though I knew Liam had sent messengers and made enquiries from Tara to Tirconnell. In my heart I feared for them, and I thought I saw the same fear reflected on my father's face. And now Padriac was building a boat, down by the lake. We didn't see much of him, or the lads that were helping him. It was a pity, he said, not to be able to fly, not that he really remembered it, not properly, but he now knew there were wider lands, and farther seas to explore, and that was what he would do, when his craft was ready. He looked at maps, and made charts, and studied old books. I remembered what Finbar had said once about this youngest brother. *He will go far. Farther than any of us.* I had not thought this was what he meant. And he was so young; too young, I told him, to think of sailing away and leaving us.

'I'm older than you,' Padriac pointed out. 'And you're having a baby. That makes me an uncle. I must be old enough.'

For I was, indeed, with child. She would be born near the festival of Meán Fómhair, the autumn equinox; and I knew she would have hair the bright copper of the beech leaves. Red was anxious, with a tendency to fuss over me as if I were some delicate plant to be sheltered from all harm. I laughed at him, but I did as he asked. Spring came and the weather grew balmy, and still there was no news. Then one day my father set out on a journey of his own.

'My boys have not returned,' he said. 'It is for me, now, to seek them and to return them safe here, all three. This is my quest,' he added as first one and then another offered to go with him. 'In bringing them home I may undo some of the wrongs I have laid on my family. I leave you in good hands, my daughter,' he said, kissing me on the cheek and clasping Red by the arm in a brief, strong grip. 'My household is well governed, and my people protected. It is time for me to say my farewells.' He touched his cheek to Liam's and grasped his hand, and he embraced Padriac, and then he was gone, vanishing down the track in the plain workman's clothes he had chosen, and I hoped he would not find the trail too cold, where his little son had been taken.

So, one by one, my brothers went away from Sevenwaters. We had always said we would be there one for another, as long as we lived. We had always said that, like the seven streams from which our home took its name, we were all parts of the same whole, and our lives would be interlinked. That nothing would drive us apart, though the greatest distance might separate us. And yet, soon there would be only Liam and me left here. Intense, driven, Liam channelled his energies fiercely into restoring what our father had almost let slip through his fingers. Unsmiling, tireless Liam, working as if possessed, demanded and received an unswerving loyalty from all his people. He had cause to be grateful, grudgingly, for the presence of Lord Hugh in his household now. For it was Red who sorted out the disputes between one settlement and another, while Liam was closeted with Seamus Redbeard discussing the finer points of their strategy. It was Red who saw to the revegetation of the land the lady Oonagh had devastated, explaining to the folk how you must plant before you harvested, and what trees would grow most quickly, to ensure a good supply of usable timber in years to come. It was Red who saw to the cottagers, and brought in new stock, and taught the people how best to mend stone walls and repair thatched roofs. By spring, Liam admitted reluctantly that he didn't know how we'd managed without him.

At Meán Earraigh, when night equals day and the earth comes forth in her spring raiment after the long chill of winter, I took Red out by the lake and up through the woods to a place long unvisited. Here Father Brien the hermit had lived his solitary, ordered life. Here the children of Sevenwaters had learned strange tongues and secret symbols. Here I had first tended to Simon, and the seeds of one part of my story had been sown. I had explained to Red that this was a place I must go before I could be at ease. A place where an old friend had lived, once.

Red frowned on the idea of my riding forth, fearing harm to me or my unborn child, and agreed to go only if he might carry me before him on his own horse, where, he said, he could keep an eye on me. So we rode leisurely up between the great oaks, and he fell silent at their towering strength, and the sheets of gold that hung from their upper branches, where the sacred herb found its home in their shelter. The day was fair and warm, with a fresh breeze that tossed little clouds about the sky. The cave was empty, its shelves bare, and the tiny cottage deserted. If there had once been a scent of illness and fear over this small home, it was gone, and the slanting sunlight invested cave and cell with a warm stillness that suggested both were waiting, only waiting for another to come and take up tranquil, silent residence. We sat on the rocks under the rowan bushes, and shared the water and bread and dried fruits we had carried with us. The horse grazed contentedly on verdant spring grass.

There was no need for words between us. When we had finished eating, Red came and sat behind me, wrapping his legs around mine, and his arms around my waist, so that I could lean back on him, and he laid his large hands very gently on my stomach, where the swelling made by the growing child was still barely discernible.

'This place holds memories for you,' he said at length. 'What happened here touched you deeply.'

I nodded. We had never spoken of Simon, not since I myself had left Harrowfield. But I thought of him often. There was a terrible irony in his story, for I feared the brother who had always wanted the land and the authority for himself, who had always hated being second best, had found, once he was given the unexpected, the wonderful gift of Harrowfield for his own, that what he really wanted was something else entirely. For it was his fate always to desire that which he could not have. But Elaine had seemed a wise, strong girl, and she loved him. Maybe that would be enough.

'Do you want to talk about it?' asked Red.

'Not really,' I said. Some things are best left unspoken, even to those one loves best.

We were silent a little longer, hearing the calling of a lark, high overhead.

'Don't you regret giving it all up?' I asked. 'Don't you long to go back, sometimes?'

His hands moved softly against my belly. I thought, this child will be so loved, surely her path through life must be charmed, wide and straight, and full of light.

'How could I not be content with what I have?' said Red softly. 'For I have so much.' And later, we returned slowly home under the great arching branches of the forest, and beside the ruffled waters of the lake, and up between the hawthorn hedges. The horse walked carefully, as if aware how precious a load it carried; and my husband's arms were strong and gentle, around me and his child. And if the Fair Folk watched us, planning the next chapter in their long tale, we heard from them not a whisper, as we rode home to Sevenwaters.

**Book Two in The Sevenwaters Trilogy
by Juliet Marillier**

Son of the Shadows

Extract from Chapter One

That spring we had visitors. Here in the heart of the great forest, the old ways were strong despite the communities of men and women that now spread over our land, their Christian crosses stark symbols of a new faith. From time to time, travellers would bring tales of great ills done, across the sea, to folk who dared keep the old traditions. There were cruel penalties, even death for those who left an offering, maybe, for the harvest gods, or thought to weave a simple spell for good fortune or use a potion to bring back a faithless sweetheart. The druids were all slain or banished, over there. Perhaps there were solitary survivors, deep in the hills or woods, hugging the last of their mystic craft to themselves, sleeping a trance-like sleep for a hundred years, two hundred, as long as it would take for the people to waken again to the magic of tree and stone, of flame and waterfall. The power of the new faith was great. Backed up with a generous purse and with cold iron, how could it fail?

But here at Sevenwaters, here in this corner of Erin, we were a different breed. The holy fathers, when they came, were mostly quiet, scholarly men who debated an issue with open minds, and listened as much as they spoke. Amongst them, a boy could learn to read in several different languages, and to write in a clear hand, and to mix colours and make intricate patterns on parchment or fine vellum. Amongst the sisters, a girl might learn the healing arts, or how to chant like an angel. In their houses of contemplation there was a place for the poor and dispossessed. They were, at heart, good people. But none from our household was destined to join their number. When my grandfather died and my uncle Liam became lord of Sevenwaters, with all the responsibilities that entailed, it was as if many strands were drawn together to strengthen our household's fabric. Liam rallied the families nearby, built a strong fighting force, became the leader our people had needed so badly. My father, with his talent for good husbandry, made our farms prosperous and our fields plentiful. He, whom the locals called Iubdan, planted oaks where once had been barren soil. As well, he put new heart into folk who had drawn very close to despair. My mother was a symbol of what could be won by faith and strength; a living reminder of that other world below the surface. Through her they breathed in daily the truth about who they were, and where they came from; the healing message of the spirit realm.

And then there was her brother Conor. As the tale tells, there were six brothers. Liam I have told of, and the two who were next to him in age, who died in the first battle for the Islands. The fourth brother was Conor, who was a druid. Even as the old faith faded and grew dim elsewhere, we witnessed its light glowing ever stronger in our forest. It was as if each feast day, each marking of the passing season with song and ritual put back a little more of the unity our people had almost lost. Each time, we drew one step closer to being ready. Ready again to reclaim what was lost, what was stolen from us by the Britons, long generations since. The Islands were the heart of our mystery, the cradle of our belief. Prophecy or no prophecy, the people began to believe that Liam would win them back, or if not him, then my twin brother Sean who would be master of Sevenwaters after him. The day drew closer, and folk were never more aware of it than when the wise ones came out of the forest, to mark the turning of the season. So it was at Imbolc, the year Sean and I were sixteen, a year burned deep in my memory. Conor came, and with him a band of men and women in white, and in gold, and in the plain homespun robes of those still in their training, and they made the ceremony to honour Brighid's festival, deep in the woods of Sevenwaters.

They came in the afternoon, quietly as usual. Several very old men, and one old woman, walking in plain sandals up the path from the forest. Their hair was knotted into many small braids, woven about with coloured thread. There were young folk wearing the homespun, both boys and girls, and men of middle years, of whom my uncle Conor was one. Come late to the learning of the great mysteries, he was now their leader, a pale, grave man of middle height, his long chestnut hair streaked with grey, his eyes deep and serene. He greeted them all with quiet courtesy, my mother, Iubdan, Liam, then the three of us. And our guests, for several households had gathered here for the festivities. Seamus Redbeard, a vigorous old man whose snowy hair belied his name. His new wife, a sweet girl not so much older than myself. Niamh had been shocked to see this match.

'How can she?' she whispered to me behind her hand. 'How can she lie with him? He's old, so old. And fat. And he's got a red nose. Look, she's smiling at him! I'd rather die!'

I glanced at her a little sourly. 'You'd best take Eamonn, then, and be glad of the offer, if what you want is a beautiful young man,' I whispered back. 'You're unlikely to do better. Besides, he's wealthy.'

'Eamonn? Huh!'

This seemed to be the response whenever I made this suggestion. I wondered, not for the first time, what Niamh really did want. There was no way to see inside that girl's head. Not like Sean and me. Perhaps it was being twins, or maybe it was something else, but the two of us never had any problem talking without words. It became necessary, even, to set a guard on your own mind at times, so that the other could not read it. It was both a useful skill and an inconvenient one.

I looked at Eamonn, where he stood now with his sister Aisling, greeting Conor and the rest of the robed procession. I could not really see what Niamh's problem was. Eamonn was the right age, just a year or two older than my sister. He was comely enough, a little serious maybe, but that could be remedied. He was well built, with glossy brown hair and fine dark eyes. He had good teeth. To lie with him would be – well, I had little knowledge of such things, but I imagined it would not be repulsive. And it would be a match well regarded by both families. Eamonn had come very young to his inheritance, a vast domain surrounded by treacherous marshlands, to the east of Seamus Redbeard's land and curving around close by the pass to the north. Eamonn's father, who bore the same name, had been killed in rather mysterious circumstances some years back. My uncle Liam and my father had little enough in common, but they were united in their refusal to discuss this particular topic. Eamonn's mother had died when Aisling was born.

So Eamonn had grown up with immense wealth and power, and an over-abundance of influential advisers. Seamus, who was his grandfather; Liam, who had once been betrothed to his mother; my father, who was somehow tied up in the whole thing. It was perhaps surprising that Eamonn had become very much his own man, and despite his youth kept his own control over his estates and his not inconsiderable private army. That explained, maybe, why he was such a solemn young man. I found that I had been scrutinising him closely, as he finished speaking with one of the younger druids and glanced my way. He gave me a half smile, as if in defiance of my assessment, and I looked away, feeling a blush rise to my cheeks. Niamh was silly, I thought. She was unlikely to do any better, and at seventeen, she needed to make up her mind quickly, before somebody else did it for her. It would be a very strong partnership, and made stronger still by the tie of kinship with Seamus, who owned the lands between. He who controlled all of that could deal a heavy blow to the Britons, when the time came.

The druids made their way to the end of the line, finishing their greetings. The sun was low in the sky. In the field behind our home barn, in neat rows, the ploughs and forks and other implements of our new season's work lay ready. We made our way down paths still slippery from spring rains to take up our places in a great circle around the field, our shadows long in the late afternoon light. I saw Aisling slip away from her brother and reappear slightly later at Sean's side, as if by chance. If she thought her move unnoticed, she thought wrong, for her cloud of auburn hair drew the eye however she might try to tame its exuberance with ribbons. As she reached my brother's side, the rising breeze whisked one long bright curl across her small face, and Sean reached out to tuck it gently behind her ear. I did not need to watch them further to feel her hand slip into his, and my brother's fingers tighten around it possessively. Well, I thought, here's someone who knows how to make up his mind. Perhaps it didn't matter, after all, what Niamh decided. The alliance would be made, one way or another.

The druids formed a semicircle around the rows of tools, and in the gap stood Conor, whose white robe bore an edging of gold. He had thrown back his hood, and you could see now the golden torc he wore around his neck, a sign of his leadership within this mystic brotherhood. He was young yet by their standards, but his face was an ancient face; his serene gaze held more than one lifetime's knowledge in its depths. He had made a long journey, these eighteen years in the forest.

Now Liam stepped forward, as head of the household, and passed to his brother a silver chalice of our best mead, made from the finest honey and brewed with water from one particular spring whose exact location was a very well guarded secret. Conor nodded gravely. Then he began a slow progress between the ploughs and sickles, the hay forks and heavy spades, the shears and shovels, and he sprinkled a few drops of the potent brew on each as he passed.

'A fine calf in the belly of the breeding cow. A river of sweet milk from her teats. A warm coat on the backs of the sheep. A fine harvest from spring rains.'

Conor walked evenly, his white robe shifting and changing around him as if with its own life. He bore the chalice in one hand, his staff of birch in the other. There was a hush over all of us. Even the birds seemed to cease their chatter in the trees around. Behind me, a couple of horses leaned over the fence, their solemn, liquid eyes fixed on the man with the quiet voice.

'Brighid's blessing be on our fields this season. Brighid's hand stretch out over our new growth. May our earth bring forth life; may our seed flourish. This is the life of the heart; this is the heart of the earth.'

So he went on, and over each of the homely implements of toil he reached his hand, and dropped a little of the precious mead. The light grew golden as the sun sank below the tops of the oaks. It was almost finished. Last of all was the eight-ox plough, which the men had made under Iubdan's instruction long years ago. With this, the stoniest of fields had been made soft and fertile. We had wreathed it in garlands of yellow tansy and fragrant heather, and Conor paused before it, raising his staff.

'Let no ill fall on our labours,' he said. 'Let no blight touch our crops, no malady our flocks. Let the work of this plough, and of our hands, make a good harvest and a prosperous season. We give thanks for the earth that is our mother, for the rain that brings forth her life. We honour the wind that shakes the seed from the great oaks; we revere the sun that warms the growing seed. In all things, we honour you, Brighid, who kindles the fires of spring.'

The circle of druids echoed his last sentence, and echoed it again in another, older tongue. Then Conor walked back to his brother, and put the cup into his hands, and Liam made a comment about maybe sharing what was left in it, after supper. The ceremony was almost over.

Conor turned and stepped forward, one, two, three steps. He stretched out his right hand. A tall young initiate with a head of curls the deepest red you ever saw came quickly forward and took his master's staff. He stood to one side, watching Conor with a stare whose intensity sent a shiver down my spine. Conor raised his hands.

'New life! New light! New fire!' he said, and his voice was not quiet now but powerful and clear, ringing through the forest like some solemn bell. 'New fire!'

His hands were above his head, reaching into the sky. There was a shimmering, and a strange humming sound, and suddenly above his hands was light, flame, fire, a brightness that dazzled the eyes and shocked the senses. The druid lowered his arms slowly, and still between his cupped hands flared a fire, a fire so real you watched with awe, expecting to see his skin burn and blister under the intense heat. The young initiate walked up to him, an unlit torch in his hands. As we stared transfixed, Conor reached out and touched this torch with his fingers, and it flamed into rich golden light. And when Conor drew his hands away, they were just the hands of a man, and the mysterious fire was gone from them. The face of the youth was a picture of pride, and wonder, and awe as he bore his precious torch up to the house, where the fires of the hearth would be rekindled. The ceremony was over. Tomorrow, the work of the new season would begin.

I caught fragments of conversation as we made our way back to the house, where feasting would commence at sundown.

'. . . was this wise? There were others, surely, that could be chosen for this task?'

'It was time. He cannot be kept hidden for ever.'

This was Liam, and his brother. Then I saw my mother and my father as they walked up the path together. Her foot slipped in the mud, and she stumbled; he caught her instantly, almost before it happened, he was so quick. His arm went around her shoulders, and she looked up at him. I sensed a shadow over the two of them, and I was suddenly ill at ease. Sean ran past me, grinning, with Aisling not far behind. They were following the tall young man who bore the torch. My brother did not speak, but in my mind I caught his happiness as he passed me. Just for tonight, he was only sixteen years old, and he was in love, and all was right in his world. And I felt that sudden chill again. What was wrong with me? It was as if I were wishing ill on my family, on a fine spring day when everything was bright and strong. I told myself to stop being foolish. But the shadow was still there, on the edge of my thoughts.

You feel it too.

I froze. There was only one person I spoke to this way, without words, and that was Sean. But it was not my brother's inner voice that touched my mind now.

It's all right, Liadan. I will not intrude on your thoughts. If I have learned anything, these long years, it is to discipline this skill. You are unhappy. Uneasy. What happens, will not be your doing. You must remember that. Each of us chooses his own path.

Still I walked towards the house, the crowd around me chattering and laughing, young men holding their scythes over a shoulder, young women helping to carry spade or sickle. Here and there hands met and clasped, and one or two stragglers disappeared quietly into the forest, about their own business. On the path ahead, my uncle walked slowly, the golden border of his robe catching the last rays of setting sun.

I – I don't know what I feel, Uncle. A darkness – something terribly wrong. And yet, it's as if I were wishing it on us, by thinking of it. How can I do this, when everything is so good, when they are all so happy?

It's time. Not by so much as a turning of the head did my uncle show that he spoke with me thus. *You wonder at my ability to read you? You should talk to Sorcha, if you can make her answer. It was she, and Finbar, who excelled in this once. But it may pain her to recall it.*

You said it's time. Time for what?

If there was a way to sigh without making a sound, that was what Conor communicated to me. *Time for their hands to stir the pot. Time for their fingers to weave a little more into the pattern. Time for their voices to take up the song. You need feel no guilt, Liadan. They use us all, and there is not much we can do about it. I discovered that the hard way. And so will you, I fear.*

What do you mean?

You'll find out soon enough. Why not enjoy yourself, and be young, while there is still time?

And that was it. He shut off his mind as if with an iron trapdoor – clang, closed, no more traffic in or out. Ahead, I saw him pause, waiting for my mother and Iubdan to catch up, and the three of them went into the house together. I was left none the wiser for this strange conversation. I wondered why he had bothered to talk to me at all.

DAUGHTER OF THE FOREST

Juliet Marillier was born in Dunedin, New Zealand, a town with strong Scottish roots. She graduated from Otago University with a BA in languages and an honours degree in music, and has had a varied career which includes teaching and lecturing in music history, professional singing, choral conducting, assessing tax returns and administering student allowances. Currently she works part time in a federal government agency, and spends the rest of the time writing.

Juliet Marillier now lives in the Swan Valley area near Perth, Western Australia, where she has tried to grow the nine sacred herbs of the druids, though the climate is not ideal. Two dogs and a cat share her house, and from time to time one or other of her grown-up children.

By Juliet Marillier

DAUGHTER OF THE FOREST
SON OF THE SHADOWS
CHILD OF PROPHECY